**Uthas felt the words like a hammer blow,
her words sealing his future.**

"But we must know of what is happening beyond our borders. Dom-hain cannot remain closed to us. You will lead a company south, learn what you can of Eremon's plans."

"As you command, my Queen," Uthas said.

"Choose who you will, but not too many. Speed will serve you better than strength in numbers. And avoid Rath's notice."

"I will do as you say."

A sharp cry rang out from the chamber behind them. The woman on the bed was sitting upright, sweat-darkened hair clinging to her face, eyes wild and bulging. Balur gripped her hand, murmuring to her.

"Ethlinn, what have you seen?" Nemain asked.

The pale-faced woman took a shuddering breath. "They are coming," she whispered. "The Kadoshim draw ever closer. They *feel* the cauldron. The Black Sun, he is coming to make them flesh. He is coming for the cauldron."

Books by John Gwynne

Malice
Valor

Valor

The Faithful and the Fallen Series
Book 2

JOHN GWYNNE

www.orbitbooks.net

Orbit
Hachette Book Group
237 Park Avenue, New York, NY 10017
HachetteBookGroup.com

First U.S. Edition: July 2014
First published in Great Britain in 2014 by Tor, an imprint of
Pan Macmillan, a division of Macmillan Publishers Limited,
20 New Wharf Road, London N1 9RR

Orbit is an imprint of Hachette Book Group, Inc.
The Orbit name and logo are trademarks of Little, Brown Book Group Limited.

The Hachette Speakers Bureau provides a wide range of authors for speaking events. To find out more, go to www.hachettespeakersbureau.com or call (866) 376-6591.

The publisher is not responsible for websites (or their content) that are not owned by the publisher.

The characters and events in this book are fictitious. Any similarity to real persons, living or dead, is coincidental and not intended by the author.

Library of Congress Control Number: 2014935819
ISBN: 978-0-316-39974-6

10 9 8 7 6 5 4 3 2 1

RRD-C

Printed in the United States of America

For Harriett, the bravest soul I know.

For mum and dad.
I wish you could have seen this. Miss you both.

And for Caroline, of course, just for being you.

Cast of Characters

ARDAN

Anwarth – warrior of Dun Carreg, father of Farrell. Escaped with Edana from the sack of Dun Carreg.

Brenin – murdered King of Ardan.

Brina – healer of Dun Carreg, owner of a cantankerous crow, Craf. Escaped with Edana from the sack of Dun Carreg.

Corban – warrior of Dun Carreg, son of Thannon and Gwenith, brother of Cywen. Escaped with Edana from the sack of Dun Carreg.

Cywen – from Dun Carreg, daughter of Thannon and Gwenith, sister of Corban. Presumed dead in the sack of Dun Carreg.

Dath – fisherman of Dun Carreg, son of Mordwyr and friend of Corban. Escaped with Edana from the sack of Dun Carreg.

Edana – Princess of Ardan, daughter of Brenin. Presumably Queen of Ardan since the death of Brenin, but now a fugitive.

Evnis – counsellor and murderer of King Brenin and father of Vonn. In league with Queen Rhin of Cambren.

Farrell – warrior, son of Anwarth and friend of Corban. Escaped with Edana from the sack of Dun Carreg

Gar – stablemaster. Escaped with Edana from the sack of Dun Carreg

Gwenith – wife of Thannon, mother of Corban and Cywen. Escaped with Edana from the sack of Dun Carreg.

Heb – loremaster of Dun Carreg. Escaped with Edana from the sack of Dun Carreg

Marrock – warrior and huntsman, cousin of Edana. Escaped with Edana from the sack of Dun Carreg.

Mordwyr – fisherman of Dun Carreg, father of Dath and Bethan. Escaped with Edana from the sack of Dun Carreg.

dathran – battlechief of King Brenin. Held prisoner by Evnis in Dun Carreg.

afe – young warrior belonging to Evnis' hold. Childhood rival of Corban.

Thannon – husband of Gwenith, father of Corban and Cywen. Slain by King Nathair of Tenebral in the sack of Dun Carreg.

Vonn – warrior, son of Evnis. Escaped with Edana from the sack of Dun Carreg.

BENOTH

Aric –Benothi giant, companion of Uthas.

Balur One-Eye – Benothi giant.

Eisa – Benothi giantess, companion of Uthas.

Ethlinn – Benothi giantess, daughter of Balur One-Eye, also called the Dreamer.

Fray – Benothi giant, companion of Uthas.

Kai – Benothi giant, companion of Uthas.

Morc – Benothi giant, keeper of the wyrms.

Nemain – Queen of the Benothi giants.

Salach – Benothi giant, shieldman of Uthas.

Sreng – Benothi giantess, shield-maiden of Nemain.

Struan – Benothi giant, companion of Uthas.

Uthas – giant of the Benothi clan, secret ally and conspirator with Queen Rhin of Cambren.

CAMBREN

Braith – warrior. One-time leader of the Darkwood outlaws, now huntsman of Queen Rhin.

Geraint – warrior, battlechief of Queen Rhin.

Morcant – warrior, first-sword of Queen Rhin.

Rhin – Queen of Cambren.

CARNUTAN

Mandros – King of Carnutan, slain by Veradis in the belief that Mandros murdered King Aquilus of Tenebral.

Domhain

Baird – warrior, one of the Degad, Rath's giant-killers.

Conall – warrior, bastard son of King Eremon. Brother of Halion and half-brother of Coralen. Sided with Evnis in the sack of Dun Carreg.

Coralen – warrior, companion of Rath. Bastard daughter of King Eremon, half-sister of Halion and Conall.

Eremon – King of Domhain.

Halion – warrior, first-sword of Edana of Ardan. Bastard son of King Eremon, brother of Conall and half-brother of Coralen.

Lorcan – young Prince of Domhain, son of Eremon and Roisin.

Maeve – bastard daughter of King Eremon, half-sister to Coralen, Halion and Conall.

Nara – mother of Coralen.

Quinn – First-sword of King Eremon.

Rath – Battlechief of Domhain, giant-hunter.

Roisin – Queen of Domhain, wife of Eremon, mother of Lorcan.

Helveth

Braster – King of Helveth, wounded in the battle against the Hunen at Haldis.

Lothar – battlechief of Helveth.

Ventos – a travelling merchant-trader.

Isiltir

Eboric – warrior, Gerda's huntsman.

Gerda – estranged wife of King Romar, lady of Dun Kellen, mother of Haelan.

Gramm – horse-trader and timber merchant, lord of a hold in the north of Isiltir. Father of Orgull and Wulf.

Jael – warrior of Isiltir, nephew of King Romar and cousin of Kastell. Allied to Nathair of Tenebral.

Kastell – warrior of Isiltir and the elite Gadrai. Nephew of King Romar and cousin of Jael.

Maquin – warrior of Isiltir and the elite Gadrai, shieldman of Kastell.
Orgull – warrior of Isiltir, captain of the elite Gadrai. Son of Gramm.
Romar – King of Isiltir, slain in the battle against the Hunen at Haldis.
Tahir – warrior of Isiltir and the elite Gadrai.
Thoris – warrior, battlechief of Gerda at Dun Kellen.
Ulfilas – warrior, shieldman of Jael.
Varick – Lord of Dun Kellen, brother of Gerda and uncle of Haelan.
Wulf – warrior, son of Gramm and brother of Orgull.

NARVON

Camlin – outlaw of the Darkwood. Recently allied to King Brenin and
     Edana of Ardan.
Drust – warrior, shieldman of Owain.
Owain – King of Narvon. Conqueror of Ardan with the aid of Nathair,
     King of Tenebral.
Uthan – Prince of Narvon, Owain's son. Murdered by Evnis on Rhin's
     orders.

TARBESH

Akar – captain of the Jehar holy warrior order travelling with Veradis.
Enkara – warrior of the Jehar holy order. One of the Hundred travelling
     with Tukul.
Javed – slave and pit-fighter of the Vin Thalun.
Sumur – lord of the Jehar holy warrior order.
Tukul – warrior of the Jehar holy order, leader of the Hundred.

TENEBRAL

Aquilus - murdered King of Tenebral.
Armatus – warrior, former first-sword of King Aquilus.
Bos – warrior of the eagle-guard and expert in the shield wall, friend of
     Veradis.
Ektor – son of Lamar of Ripa and brother of Krelis and Veradis.
Fidele – widow of Aquilus, now Queen Regent of Tenebral, mother of
     Nathair.
Krelis – warrior, son of Lamar of Ripa and brother of Ektor and Veradis.

Lamar – Baron of Ripa, father of Krelis, Ektor and Veradis.

Marcellin – Baron of Ultas.

Meical – counsellor to Aquilus, King of Tenebral.

Nathair – King of Tenebral, son of Aquilus and Fidele. In league with Queen Rhin of Cambren.

Orcus – warrior of the eagle-guard, shieldman of Fidele.

Peritus – battlechief of Tenebral.

Rauca – warrior, a captain of the eagle-guard and friend of Veradis. Slain by Gar in the sack of Dun Carreg.

Veradis – first-sword and friend to King Nathair. Son of Lamar of Ripa and brother of Ektor and Krelis.

The Three Islands

Alazon – shipwright.

Calidus – spymaster of Lykos, Lord of the Vin Thalun, and later counsellor to Nathair, King of Tenebral.

Deinon – warrior, shieldman of Lykos and brother of Thaan.

Emad – shieldman of Herak. Guard and trainer of pit-fighters.

Herak – pit-trainer.

Jace – member of Lykos' ship's crew.

Lykos – Lord of the Vin Thalun, the pirate nation that inhabits the Three Islands of Panos, Pelset and Nerin.

Thaan – warrior, shieldman of Lykos and brother of Deinon.

THE

BANISHED

LANDS

THE BONE FELLS

JOTUNHEIM

Kavala mountains

ARCONA

Drassil

FORN FOREST

Haldis

Brihan

Bairg mountains

Halstat

HELVETH

Taur

Ultas

Jerolin

Agullas Mountains

TENEBRAL

Balara

Tethys Sea

Ripa

TARBESH

PELSET

NERIN

Telassar

War eternal between the Faithful and the Fallen,
infinite wrath come to the world of men.
Lightbearer seeking flesh from the cauldron,
to break his chains and wage the war again.
Two born of blood, dust and ashes shall champion
      the Choices,
the Darkness and Light.

Black Sun will drown the earth in bloodshed,
Bright Star with the Treasures must unite.
By their names you shall know them –
Kin-Slayer, Kin-Avenger, Giant-Friend, Draig-Rider,
Dark Power 'gainst Lightbringer.
One shall be the Tide, one the Rock in the swirling sea.

Before one, storm and shield shall stand,
before the other, True-Heart and Black-Heart.
Beside one rides the Beloved, beside the other, the
      Avenging Hand.
Behind one, the Sons of the Mighty, the fair Ben-Elim,
      gathered 'neath the Great Tree.
Behind the other, the Unholy, dread Kadoshim who
      seek to cross the bridge,
force the world to bended knee.

Look for them when the high king calls, when the
      shadow warriors ride forth,
when white-walled Telassar is emptied, when the book
      is found in the north.
When the white wyrms spread from their nest,
when the Firstborn take back what was lost, and the
      Treasures stir from their rest.
Both earth and sky shall cry warning, shall herald this
      War of Sorrows.
Tears of blood spilt from the earth's bones, and at
      Midwinter's height,
bright day shall become full night.

CHAPTER ONE

UTHAS

The Year 1142 of the Age of Exiles, Birth Moon

The cauldron was a hulking mass of black iron, tall and wide, squatting upon a dais in the centre of a cavernous room. Torches of blue flame hung on the walls of the chamber, pockets of light punctuating the darkness. In the shadows, circling its edges, long and sinuous shapes moved.

Uthas of the Benothi giants strode towards the cauldron, his shadow flickering on the walls. He climbed the steps and stopped before it. It was utterly black, appearing to suck the torchlight into it, consuming it, reflecting nothing back. Just for a moment it seemed to shudder, a gentle throb, like a diseased heart.

A muffled request from the chamber's entrance reached him but he did not move, just continued to stare.

'What?' he said eventually.

'Nemain sends for you, Uthas. She says the Dreamer is waking.'

The giant sighed and turned to leave the chamber. He brushed his fingertips against the cauldron's cold belly and froze.

'What is it?' his shieldman Salach called from the chamber's doorway.

Uthas cocked his head to one side, closing his eyes. *Voices, calling to me.* 'Nothing,' he murmured, unsure whether he heard or felt the whisperings from within the cauldron. 'Soon,' he breathed as he pulled his fingers from the cold iron.

A shape slithered from the shadows as he walked towards the exit. It blocked his way, gliding about him. A wyrm, white scales glistening as it raised its flat head and regarded him with cold, soulless eyes. He stood there, still and silent, let it taste his scent, felt an instant of unease as he waited, then the snake slithered away, its huge coils bunching and expanding, back to the shadows to rejoin its brood. He let out a breath.

'Come, then,' he said as he strode past Salach. 'Best not keep Nemain waiting.'

He glanced at the chamber's dour-faced guards, all wrapped in fur and iron, as he marched past them. Salach's footfalls followed him. In silence they passed through the bowels of Murias, the last stronghold of the Benothi. It was nestled deep in the highlands of Benoth, carved into and beneath the grey, mist-shrouded land.

In time they reached a wide staircase that spiralled up into darkness and soon Uthas was muttering under his breath, the old pain in his knee gnawing at him as he climbed higher and higher.

'*Bitseach*,' he swore, thinking of Nemain waiting for him at the top of this high tower. Salach chuckled behind him.

Eventually they were at a doorway. Salach nodded to the warrior standing there, Sreng, Nemain's shield-maiden. She opened the door for them.

The room was sparsely decorated, with little furniture apart from a large, fur-draped bed at its centre. A woman lay upon it, slender, sweat-soaked, her limbs jerking and twitching. A white-haired man sat beside her, his huge bulk crammed into a chair, holding her hand. He looked over as Uthas and Salach entered the room and stared at them, a ruined, scar-latticed hole where one of his eyes should have been.

'One-Eye.' Uthas nodded. 'How is she?'

Balur One-Eye shrugged.

'Where is Nemain?'

'I am here,' a voice said, drawing Uthas' gaze to the far end of the room. A figure stood in an arched doorway, framed by the pale day beyond.

Nemain, Queen of the Benothi. Ravens gathered on the balcony beyond her. One fluttered onto her shoulder.

'My Queen,' Uthas said, dipping his head.

'Welcome back,' she replied, hair the colour of midnight framing her milky, angular face. 'What news?'

'Events are stirring in the south,' Uthas said. 'Narvon wars with Ardan, and the warriors of Cambren are marching east.' He paused, breathing deep, his next words frozen on his lips. He feared the answer he expected. 'Our enemies war amongst themselves. It would be a good time to strike and reclaim what was ours.' *Please, Nemain, give the order. Save me from what I must do if you refuse.*

Nemain smiled, though there was little humour in it. 'Strike south? We are a broken people, Uthas – you know this. Too few to fill this fortress, let alone the south that once was ours. Besides, we are set a different task, now.' She walked out onto the balcony.

He sighed and followed her onto the balcony's edge, where cold air stung his skin. A cliff face sloped steeply down, wreathed far below in mist, a sea of dark granite and snow and wiry heather rolling into the distance. Ravens swirled about the balcony, riding the updraught. One cawed and veered to land besides Nemain. Idly she reached out and scratched its head. It clacked its beak.

'What of the west?' she said. 'What of Domhain?'

Uthas shrugged. 'There we know little. I suspect that Eremon grows older, content to do nothing in his dotage. That *bandraoi* Rath keeps us out,' he spat. 'He does not rest. He hunts our scouts, raids our land, him and his giant-hunters. There have been some casualties.'

'Ach,' Nemain hissed, eyes flashing red. 'I would like nothing more than to march out and take back what we have lost, remind Rath why he hates us.'

'Then let us do it,' Uthas urged, feeling his blood surge, hope flaring.

'We cannot,' Nemain said. 'The cauldron must be guarded. Never again can it be used. It must not fall into the wrong hands.'

Uthas felt the words like a hammer blow, her words sealing his future.

'But we must know of what is happening beyond our borders. Domhain cannot remain closed to us. You will lead a company south, learn what you can of Eremon's plans.'

'As you command, my Queen,' Uthas said.

'Choose who you will, but not too many. Speed will serve you better than strength in numbers. And avoid Rath's notice.'

'I will do as you say.'

A sharp cry rang out from the chamber behind them. The woman on the bed was sitting upright, sweat-darkened hair clinging to her face, eyes wild and bulging. Balur gripped her hand, murmuring to her.

'Ethlinn, what have you seen?' Nemain asked.

The pale-faced woman took a shuddering breath. 'They are coming,' she whispered. 'The Kadoshim draw ever closer. They *feel* the cauldron. The Black Sun, he is coming to make them flesh. He is coming for the cauldron.'

CHAPTER TWO

CYWEN

Cywen woke slowly, like the tide creeping in.

First she felt. A dull throbbing in her head, her shoulder, her hip. She ached everywhere, she realized, but worse in those places. Then she heard. Groaning, low voices, the thud of footfalls, a dragging, scraping sound, and behind it the cry of gulls and the distant murmur of the sea. She tried to open her eyes; one was crusted shut. Daylight felt like a knife jabbing into her head. *Where am I?* She looked about and saw warriors in red cloaks dragging bodies across the stone-paved courtyard, leaving blood-smeared trails across the cobbles, piling them onto a heaped mound of corpses.

Suddenly it all came flooding back, memory upon memory tumbling together: talking on the wall with Marrock, Evnis in the courtyard, the black-clothed warriors within the walls, the gates opening, *Conall . . .*

There was something soft beneath her. She was sprawled upon a body, a female, staring at her with lifeless eyes. Staggering she climbed upright, the world spinning briefly before it settled.

Stonegate was wide open, a trickle of people passing in and out of the fortress, most in the red cloaks of Narvon. Columns of black smoke marked the pale sky, a soft breeze from the sea tugging at them, blurring where smoke ended and sky began.

The battle is lost, then. Dun Carreg is fallen.

Then another thought cut through the fog filling her mind. *My family.*

She looked at the bodies strewn about her, remembered falling with Conall but could not see him amongst the dead. Her mam and da's faces flashed through her mind, Corban, then Gar's. Where was everyone?

She left the courtyard unchallenged and drifted slowly through the streets, following the trail of the dead. They were littered every-where, sometimes in mounds where the fighting had raged fiercer, some still locked together in a macabre embrace. The smell of smoke and fire grew thicker the deeper she walked into the fortress. Her feet took her to the stables. There were more warriors here, red-cloaked men tending wild-eyed horses. She glimpsed Corban's stallion Shield in the paddock, then he was gone, lost amongst the herd gathered there.

Where is Gar?

As if in a dream she walked on, peering at the faces of the dead, searching for her family, relieved every time a lifeless face was not one of them. Her search continued, becoming more frantic until she found herself in the courtyard before the feast-hall.

Another pile of the dead was heaped here, greater even than the one before Stonegate. Warriors were everywhere, wounded, covered in ash and blood. In one corner Cywen saw the grey-cloaks of Ardan, the defeated warriors gathered together, many injured. They were guarded by a cohort of Owain's men.

A great ululation came from the feast-hall. Something – a board, a tabletop – was being carried from the entranceway. As Cywen watched, it was hoisted upright and leaned with a thud against one of the columns that supported the entrance. A body was fixed to the board, covered in blood but still recognizable. Cywen's stomach lurched.

Brenin. His head was lolling, arms twisted, wrists and ankles nailed to the tabletop. A great bloom of blood surrounding the wound in his chest. Cywen spat bile onto the stained cobblestones, motes of ash falling softly about her like black snow.

She wiped her mouth and stumbled towards the hall's doors, eyes fixed on Brenin's corpse.

'Please, Elyon, All-Father,' she prayed, 'let my kin still live.' She stopped before Brenin, stood staring up at him until a warrior bumped into her and told her to get out of the way. She glared at him.

Noise from the feast-hall leaked out into the courtyard, some kind of commotion – men shouting, a deep growling. *Storm?*

Then she was dashing through the open doors, blinking as her eyes adjusted to the gloom. Everything was chaos in here, tables and chairs overturned, timbers blackened and charred with fire, clouds of smoke still clinging to the rafters where the flames had only recently been doused. There were many people gathered in here. She saw Owain talking with Nathair, a cluster of the black-clothed warriors that had stormed the gates gathered about him. Evnis was amongst them, and Conall. Anger flashed in her gut and her hand instinctively reached for her knife-belt. She scowled as she remembered she'd used all the blades last night on the wall.

Then her eyes were drawn back to the commotion that had first caught her attention. A group of warriors were circling something, a snapping, snarling something.

'Just kill it,' she heard one of the warriors say and saw a flash of sharp white teeth, a flat muzzle, brindle fur.

'Buddai,' she whispered and ran forwards, elbowing through the line of warriors.

They were grouped in a half-circle about Buddai, the great hound standing with his head lowered, teeth bared.

Cywen stumbled to a halt and Buddai's big head swung round to face her, teeth snapping. Then, suddenly, he knew her. He whined, his tail wagging hesitantly at seeing someone familiar in this place of death, someone that was *pack*. She threw herself upon him, arms wrapped about his neck, and buried her face in his fur. She stayed like that long moments, tears spilling into Buddai's fur. In time she leaned back, got a lick on the face and looked down.

'That's why you're here,' she mumbled. Her da lay sprawled on the ground, eyes glassy, flat, wounds all over his body, blood crusting black. With a deep sob she knelt beside Thannon's corpse and gently brushed her fingertips across his cheek. *Are they all slain, then?* She laid her head upon Thannon's chest. Buddai snuggled in close to her and nudged Thannon's hand with his muzzle. It flopped on the ground.

'Girl,' a voice said and a spear butt dug into her back.

'What?'

'You need to move,' the man said, an older warrior, silver streaks in his red beard.

'No,' she said, squeezing her da tighter.

'We have to clear the hall, lass, an' that hound won't let us near him.' He prodded Thannon's boot with his spear butt. Buddai growled. 'If you can get that hound to go with you all the better, otherwise we've no choice but t'kill it.'

Kill Buddai. No more death.

'I . . . yes,' Cywen said, wiping her eyes and nose. She knelt before Buddai, running her hands over him. Blood crusted the fur on his front shoulder and he whined when she probed the wound. 'Come with me, Buds,' she whispered, 'else they'll kill you too.' He just cocked his head and stared at her with uncomprehending eyes.

Cywen stood, took a few steps away from the hound and called him. He took a hesitant step towards her, then looked back at his fallen master and whined pitifully.

'Come on, Buds. Come.' Cywen slapped her hand against her leg, and this time he came to her. The red-bearded warrior nodded and continued with his work.

No one was taking any notice of Cywen; she was just another blood-stained survivor of the night's dark work. All of the warriors in the room seemed to be busy clearing the floors, tending to wounded comrades. Owain and Nathair were still deep in conversation, though Cywen saw that the King of Tenebral's shieldman – the black-clad warrior called Sumur – was staring back at her.

'Come on, Buddai,' Cywen said. 'Best be getting out of here.' She turned towards the feast-hall doors and with a thud crashed into someone.

'*Oof*,' the man grunted. 'Watch where you're— *You*.'

Cywen stood frozen, staring at the person she had collided with. It was Rafe.

The huntsman's son glared at her. Buddai growled and Rafe took a step backwards.

His fair hair was dank, ash stained, his eyes red veined with dark hollow rings. He had been crying. There was a gash in one leg of his breeches, just above the knee, and drying blood soaked down to his boots. A ragged bandage was tied tight above the wound.

'Your brother did that to me,' he said, following her gaze to his wounded leg. 'One more thing I owe him for.'

'Ban,' Cywen gasped, her heart twisting at the mention of her brother. 'He lives, then?' She was almost too scared to speak the thought out loud.

'Maybe, but not for long. We'll catch him, catch all of them.'

'*All* of them? Who else? My mam, Gar?'

Rafe just looked at her, then smiled slowly. 'All on your own, little girl? Best be getting used to that.'

She felt a swell of rage, hated Rafe at that moment as much as she'd hated anyone. She reached for her knives again, cursed silently when she remembered they were all gone. 'Traitor,' she hissed at him.

'Depends where you're looking from,' Rafe said, but frowned nevertheless. 'Way I see it, Evnis is my lord. I do as I'm bid. And it seems to me he's on the winning side, at least.'

'For now,' Cywen muttered.

'Things have changed around here.' Rafe wagged a finger at her. 'And if you don't realize that quick, you'll end up sorry. You'd best be minding your manners from now on. All your protectors have left you. Not so special are you, eh? Why'd they leave you?' He grinned. 'Think about that.'

Cywen wanted to hit him. His words were sharp, cutting deep like one of her knives. She clenched her fists, knowing attacking anyone right now was not a good idea.

Rafe looked over her shoulder and she followed his gaze. Evnis was beckoning to the huntsman's son, Conall still beside him. 'I'll be seeing you,' Rafe said. 'And don't worry, we'll find your kin for you.' He grinned, an unpleasant twist of his mouth, and drew a finger slowly across his throat, from ear to ear. Before she knew it, Cywen was stepping forwards, ramming her knee into Rafe's groin.

He crumpled forwards, folding in upon himself and curled up into a ball on the ground, whimpering.

'Best you keep away from me and my kin,' she snarled at him, then heard a chuckling behind her. The red-bearded warrior was watching her, along with a handful of others.

'You'n that hound, you're a good match,' the warrior said. He grinned and she flushed red, biting back angry words, thought she'd best be making herself scarce. Lowering her gaze, she headed for the feast-hall's open doors, Buddai following. She glanced back as she stepped out into the daylight to see Rafe pushing himself up from the ground. Sumur was still staring at her.

Consumed with an urge to go home, she ran through the streets, Buddai limping along beside her.

When she opened the door and stepped into the kitchen she almost expected to see her mam standing there, bustling about by the ovens, her da sitting at the table, eating something. She even called out, hoping to hear someone. She searched every room until she found herself back in the kitchen. Her home was empty, as cold and lifeless as her da's gaze.

Where are they?

'Gone,' she whispered. A sob bubbled out of her and she swayed, steadying herself against the kitchen table.

All gone. And they've left me behind. Rafe's words rang loud in her memory. *How could they just leave me?* She looked at Buddai and the hound stared trustingly back at her. An image of her da flooded her mind, crusted blood all over him, those terrible, empty eyes. She wished her mam was there to hold her, comfort her. And Ban, her brother, her best friend. Why had he abandoned her? Another sob burst out of her and she sank to the floor, wrapped her arms about Buddai and began to cry in great, racking waves. The brindle hound licked Cywen's tear-stained cheek and curled himself protectively about her.

CHAPTER THREE

VERADIS

Veradis drank from a water skin, pouring some over his head and neck. He and his men were spread in a half-circle before the great gates of Haldis, last bastion of the Hunen giants. Only a short while ago Calidus and Alcyon had disappeared inside, with over two hundred warriors at their back.

Survivors of the clash against the giants were trickling into the clearing and Veradis sent half a dozen scouts out to help guide the stragglers in.

'It's thirsty work, eh?' Bos, his comrade-in-arms said, grinning. 'This giant-killing.'

The big warrior was bleeding from a cut to his ear, blood matting his hair. As Veradis stared he realized it was more than a cut; a large chunk of his friend's ear missing.

'Where's your helmet?' he asked.

'Lost it.' Bos shrugged. He touched his ear and looked at his bloodied fingertips. 'Better'n losing my head.'

'That's debatable,' Veradis said as he passed his friend the water skin.

Bos drank deep. 'We have a fine tale to tell Rauca, eh?'

'For sure,' Veradis said. 'If we make it out of here.' He gazed at the surrounding cairns, each one at least twice as tall as a man and grave to a giant. The sounds of battle still drifted on a cold wind, faint and echoing. Beyond the cairns the trees of Forn Forest rose all about. At Veradis' back a sheer cliff face reared, covered in huge carvings; an open gateway at its foot led into darkness.

The blood-rush of battle was slowly fading, replaced now by aching muscles, tiredness and a throbbing in Veradis' face. He reached up and pulled a splinter from his cheek, from where a giant's axe had carved into his shield, chopped through its iron rim and spat splinters of wood into his face.

Many of his five hundred had fallen in the battle amongst the cairns, but those left stood proudly. They knew they had turned this battle, somehow pulled victory from defeat with their shield wall.

Braster and Romar's warbands had been decimated, laid low by giants' magic and giants' iron. Braster himself had fallen amongst the cairns, carried wounded and unconscious from the field. Romar, King of Isiltir, had led a force in chase of the routed Hunen through the black gates. Despite Calidus seeing him as a thorn in their flesh, opposing Nathair and his servants at almost every turn, Veradis didn't envy Romar the close-quarters battle he would encounter in the dark tunnels.

Especially as Calidus had hinted that it was time to take drastic measures against the recalcitrant King. That was Calidus' business. Nathair had made it clear to Veradis that he had no authority over Calidus, that the man could do as he wished. And Calidus had the Jehar to enforce those wishes.

Whatever happens, happens, he thought. Romar meant little to him, but Veradis did have friends in there, inside those tunnels. Kastell and Maquin. They were part of the Gadrai, Romar's elite warriors. He would not like to see them come to harm. But he had warned them, or tried to. What else could he have done?

Even as Veradis looked into the tunnels, noise filtered out of the darkness – the clash of iron, faint screams.

Bos tapped him and nodded towards the mounds. One of the scouts had returned.

'I've found something,' the scout breathed, chest heaving.

'What?'

'A doorway, hidden. I heard voices, and something else. It was strange.'

Veradis gathered a dozen men, left Bos in charge of the rest, then marched after the scout. He led them on a path through the cairns. All was eerily silent.

The barrows ended, replaced by clustered stone buildings, empty and shadow filled. Their progress slowed as Veradis and his men checked there were no giants lurking in the darkness.

'There,' the scout said, pointing at the cliff face.

Vine grew thick across the rock. Veradis stared but could see nothing out of place.

'No, there,' the scout urged, walking forwards. He stopped before the escarpment and scraped the soil at his feet with a boot, revealing a handle. It was attached to a trapdoor.

Veradis knelt, putting his ear to the ground. At first he heard nothing, but then, distinctly, he heard a muffled cry, like a child.

He pointed to the handle, whispered orders until two warriors were gripping it, the rest gathered about the trapdoor, weapons drawn.

'Now,' Veradis ordered, and the door was heaved open.

Wide stone steps led down, sunlight shafting into the hole, revealing faces staring back up at them. Many faces. Giant faces, though something immediately struck Veradis as strange. Different.

Before he had a chance to do anything, there was a roar and a figure hurtled up the steps, swinging a war-hammer. Voices cried out from behind the giant. Veradis leaped to the side, the hammer missing him, smashing into another warrior. Bones crunched, the man crumpled, the giant surging onwards, sending other men flying.

Veradis and his men circled their foe, who snarled curses at them, turning defiantly. Veradis darted forwards, stabbed, retreated. The giant roared and spun around, only for Veradis' warriors to move in, all stabbing. The giant bellowed his rage, charged the circle, smashed one warrior to the ground. Swords slashed. The giant stumbled on a few steps, collapsed, blood staining the grass.

Veradis stood still a moment, breathing hard, then strode forward and nudged the fallen body with his boot. He would not be getting back up.

'Come out,' Veradis spoke into the trapdoor. The only answer was silence. He peered in, saw shadowed figures beyond the sun's reach. 'I'm not fool enough to come down there. If you stay, you will all burn,' he said, louder. Still no answer. He shrugged and turned away.

'They are only bairns,' a voice grated from the darkness. 'We will come up. Please, do not kill them.'

Giant bairns. What a day this is. 'Come up. If it is as you say we

will not shed the first blood.' Veradis stepped back, holding a warning hand up to his men.

A figure emerged from the hole in the ground, a giant, tall and
broad. A female, no drooping moustache, though she was as muscled
as any male. Black strips of leather crisscrossed her breasts and she
held a war-hammer loosely in her hands. Her dark eyes darted from
Veradis to the giant lying face down on the grass. Grief swept her
face.

Veradis ushered her forwards. She took hesitant steps, said something unintelligible and others appeared behind her.

Veradis blinked. There were between twenty and thirty of them.
They were a mixture of heights, ranging from shorter than him to
taller, and many in between. They were muscled, though leaner than
full-grown giants, their limbs longer, almost gangly, like newborn
colts. Tufts of hair grew on some faces, though most were hairless,
appearing softer, somehow, lacking the stark angles of the adult
giants that Veradis had seen. Some held weapons, daggers as long as
a sword to Veradis, one or two – the larger ones – hefting hammers
or axes. All looked terrified, on the edge of fight or flight. Veradis
felt the tension, knew this could turn into a bloodbath at the slightest misstep. Their guardian said something; the ones with hammer
and axe lowered their weapons slightly.

She feels it too.

'They are only bairns,' the giant repeated, pride and pleading
mingling in her voice.

Children. 'Most of them are bigger than me,' Veradis snorted. He
ran a hand through his hair. 'I shall not harm them, or you. As long
as you show no aggression.'

The giant's eyes darted between him and his men. 'The battle is
lost, then,' she said. It was not a question.

'Aye. You will need to lay your weapons down. All of them.' *And
then I can figure out what I am going to do with you all.* Veradis glanced
at the small host gathered at her back, uncomfortably aware that they
outnumbered him and his men.

She snapped something over her shoulder and iron clattered to
the ground. A few hesitated and she spoke more loudly at them, at
the same time dropping her own hammer. As she did so, something
behind Veradis caught her attention, a frown creasing her thick brows.

Alcyon was striding towards them, Calidus and the Jehar behind him, spread like a dark cloak.

'What have we here?' Calidus said.

'They were hiding,' Veradis said. 'And they have surrendered.' He did not like the hard look in Calidus' eyes, the way the man's hand was resting on his sword hilt.

'*Dia duit*,' Alcyon said, stepping forwards. He touched a hand to his forehead.

The giantess eyed him suspiciously, but returned the gesture. She lifted her head, sniffing the air like a hound catching a scent. Her eyes narrowed, focusing on Calidus. '*Cen fath coisir tu racan ar dubh aingeal.*'

Alcyon shrugged. 'I have made my choice,' he rumbled, some emotion sweeping his face.

Is that shame? Veradis thought.

'They cannot live,' Calidus said behind Alcyon.

The giant raised a hand, scowling. 'They are only bairns.'

'They will not be bairns forever. They will seek revenge for their kin. And for what you have taken.'

'Taken what?' the giantess demanded, pronouncing the words slowly, grimacing as if they left a bad taste in her mouth.

'The starstone axe,' Calidus said.

The giantess' eyes whipped to Alcyon, and Veradis saw the axe slung across his back. It was a dull black from blade to hilt. As Veradis stared at it, a sound fluttered in his mind – a faint wind, the whisper of voices – just for a heartbeat, then it was gone. He blinked.

The giantess snarled something, snatched her hammer up and flung herself at Alcyon. He reeled backwards, shrugging the axe into his hands and blocking a strike that would have taken his head from his shoulders.

Behind her a handful of the giant bairns grabbed their discarded weapons and followed their guardian. With a sound like a wave breaking, the Jehar drew their swords.

Veradis stumbled back, sword and shield ready, but something held him from entering the battle. He did not want to shed the blood of these giants. They were only children. *They are your enemy*, a voice said in his head.

And what of mercy, even to an enemy? he thought.

15

Alcyon was blocking the female giant's attack, using his new axe like a staff. There was a flurry of blows, Alcyon retreating before the onslaught. He too seemed reluctant to draw blood. About him the Jehar fought with the adolescents, who threw themselves at the black-clad warriors with more passion than skill. Many were dead already.

Alcyon cracked the butt of his axe into the giantess' head. She reeled back, sank to one knee. About her the battle lulled, the young giants staring.

'Drop your weapon,' Alcyon grated.

Calidus appeared between them. Alcyon yelled at the silver-haired man, but Calidus ignored him. He swept his sword in a looping blow, chopping the giantess' head from her shoulders.

Her charges screamed in grief-stricken rage, some renewing their attack, others breaking away, running amongst the cairns.

Alcyon bowed his head.

The Jehar made short work of the remaining giants, and in moments the conflict was over.

'Well met, Veradis,' Calidus called out, grinning as he strode over. With his cloak he cleaned the blood from his sword. Akar, the dour-faced leader of the Jehar, walked behind him.

Veradis nodded a greeting, his eyes drawn to the giantess' head, the bodies of children strewn about her. 'Did things go well? In the tunnels?' he asked, trying to look away from the faces of the dead.

'Well enough. The Hunen are broken, now. And we found a great prize for Nathair.'

'Prize? What?'

'This.' Alcyon lifted the axe. 'One of the Seven Treasures.' He was still scowling.

Now that he was closer, Veradis saw that the axe haft was dark-veined wood, smooth and shiny from age and use, bound with iron rings all along its length. The double blade was a dull matt black, seeming to suck light into it, casting none back.

He glanced beyond them, saw the Jehar and a handful of other warriors. He recognized Jael amongst them.

'Where is everyone else?' A sick feeling grew in the pit of his gut, his thoughts turning to Kastell and Maquin.

'There were casualties,' Calidus said with a shrug. 'This is a battlefield, Veradis. Men die.'

'Men. What men?'

'Many,' snapped Calidus. 'Romar fell, along with some of his men.'

'All,' Alcyon corrected.

'All,' Calidus repeated coldly. 'A tragedy, but, such is the way of these things.'

Veradis stared at him, Kastell and Maquin's faces hovering in his mind's eye. *I tried to warn them.*

'Come, Alcyon,' Calidus said, turning away. 'Clean up here, Veradis. We will meet later, talk of what happens next.'

Alcyon strode after Calidus, balancing the black axe over his shoulder. Akar remained with Veradis, frowning. He looked as if he was going to say something, wanted to say something, then he turned away and marched after Calidus, his black-clad warriors falling in behind him.

Veradis watched the light and shadow of the crackling fire flicker across Calidus' face as he sat opposite him, deep in conversation with Lothar, battlechief to King Braster of Helveth.

Behind the counsellor, hidden in shadow, was the bulk of Alcyon. A dark mood had been upon him since the killing of the giant children. The black axe lay across his lap. In his hand was a long thin needle, black ink dripping from its tip. Veradis watched with fascination as Alcyon rhythmically stabbed at his forearm, adding more thorns to the swirling vine tattoo that marked the lives the giant had taken in battle. Veradis scowled. *Are Kastell and Maquin marked by one of those thorns?*

Akar sat at the fire with another of the Jehar, a dark-haired, sharp-featured woman. She looked young, as far as Veradis could tell, not much different in age from him. He frowned, still not comfortable with the thought of female warriors, and especially not ones as skilled as the Jehar.

Lothar made his farewells and strode off into the darkness. No one had wanted to camp amongst the silent graves of Haldis, so they had settled on the sloping approach to the burial grounds, not far from where Veradis had viewed the battle that morning. It seemed a long time ago.

Campfires flickered all along the ridge, warming the survivors of the battle. Around four thousand warriors had marched into Haldis. Fewer than a thousand had survived, and half of that number belonged to Veradis' warband and the Jehar. Romar's warband had been almost entirely destroyed, only Jael and a few score others surviving. Braster's warband had fared little better, only the few hundred that had carried his wounded body from the field remained.

'Well?' Veradis said across the flames. 'How is King Braster?'

'His wound was not fatal,' Calidus replied. 'A hammer blow crushed his shoulder. Lothar said their healers are happy with the setting of his bones, so . . .' He shrugged. 'He may not swing a sword again, but he'll live.'

'Good,' Veradis said. He liked Braster. There was a gruff, blunt honesty about Helveth's king. 'So, what is our plan, now?'

'Now it is time to find Nathair. We have been apart from him long enough.'

'Excellent.' Veradis had felt a fierce pride at being given command over this campaign, more so now for bringing his warband successfully through the conflict, even though he knew that Calidus and Alcyon had played a large part in that, counteracting the magic of the Hunen's elementals. Throughout the whole campaign, though, he had felt a nagging worry about Nathair, knowing that his king, his friend, was sailing into the unknown in his search of the cauldron. He was Nathair's first-sword; he should be at his side.

'How will we find him?' he asked. 'He was about to sail for Ardan when we parted, but who knows where he is now?'

'I have received word,' Calidus said, tapping his head. 'Remember, I was spymaster to the Vin Thalun for many years. Nathair is at Dun Carreg in Ardan. We will head there. Nathair needs us, needs his advisers about him. I will make sure that Lykos meets us there.'

'Huh,' Veradis muttered, not sure if he wanted to know how Calidus would manage that. He liked the thought of leaving this forest behind, but part of him still prickled with suspicion at the mention of the Vin Thalun. Some distrust burrowed deep.

'So we leave on the morrow?' Veradis asked.

'At first light. We will travel east with Jael to Isiltir, then carry on to Ardan.'

'Jael?' Veradis said. He had disliked Kastell's cousin the first moment he set eyes on him. He was a very different man from Kastell or Maquin, both of whom Veradis had considered friends and who now lay dead in the tunnels beneath Haldis. By whose hand Veradis did not know, and some part of him did not want to. Another part of him could think of nothing else. *Let it go*, a voice whispered in his head.

'Yes. Jael,' Calidus said. 'Is there any problem with that?'

'No,' said Veradis. He thought of saying more but held his tongue.

'Good. Jael has a strong claim to the throne of Isiltir, now that Romar is gone. And Nathair will support him in that claim.'

'It is strange,' Veradis said, the words spilling out, 'how Romar and all his shieldmen died in the tunnels. Yet Jael survived.' He raised his head and stared hard at Calidus.

The counsellor gave a thin-lipped smile. 'It is war. These things happen.'

Calidus was right, men did fall in battle. Veradis had lost more shield-brothers than he cared to think about in battle, many of them friends, and he knew that in life things were not always clear cut. But this? What had happened in the tunnels felt like *betrayal*. 'Did you see Romar die?' Veradis pressed. 'And the one that slew him?'

'Oh yes,' Calidus said, his face as expressionless as stone. 'A giant slew Romar. Think more on the living than the dead, Veradis. We are all serving Nathair here. What we do is for the greater good, for Nathair's good.' His eyes narrowed. 'I hope that you have the conviction to serve your king fully.'

'Of course I do,' Veradis said. 'Never doubt my loyalty to Nathair.'

'Good.' Calidus gave a faint smile. 'Well, I am for my rest. We have an early start and a long journey ahead of us.'

Alcyon rose and followed Calidus into the darkness, Akar making to do the same.

'Akar. Did you see Romar fall?'

'Aye.'

'And . . .'

'Calidus spoke true,' Akar said. 'A giant did slay Romar.'

'Oh,' said Veradis, both surprised and relieved. He had been so certain that Calidus had been involved.

'A giant wielding a black-bladed battle-axe,' Akar said, then turned and strode into the darkness.

CHAPTER FOUR

MAQUIN

'I'm going to let you go, now. Don't do anything stupid.'

The words filtered into Maquin's mind as if from a great distance. *Where am I?*

He opened his eyes, though at first it seemed to make little difference. It was pitch dark, his face was pressed hard against cold stone and a pain bloomed in his shoulder.

'Careful. They've been gone a while, but sound carries in these tunnels,' the same voice said.

Tunnels? Then it came back, an avalanche of memory. *Haldis, the battle in the tunnels, Romar arguing with Calidus over that axe. Betrayal. Death. Kastell . . .*

'Kas . . .' he breathed.

There was a long silence, then. 'He's dead. They're all dead.'

Kastell.

He had seen Jael stab him, knew instantly that it was a killing blow. He had tried to get to him, but Orgull, captain of the Gadrai, had grabbed him, dragged him into the darkness while battle still raged nearby, though the end had been in no doubt. Romar, King of Isiltir, had been betrayed by Calidus of Tenebral. And by Jael.

And Kastell had been slain.

At first Maquin had fought, trying to break Orgull's grip on him, but the man's strength was immense, and then . . . nothing.

'I can't remember it all. What happened?' he croaked.

'You were fighting like a draig to run off and get yourself killed. Had to crack you one on the head.' Orgull's voice drifted down to him. He felt the big man shrug, a ripple of pain through his back. 'Sorry.'

He became aware of a pressure on him, a great weight pressing down. 'Are you sitting on me?'

'Had to be sure you wouldn't jump up and run off the moment you woke up.'

'No chance of that,' Maquin grunted. 'Get off.'

He felt Orgull's weight shift from his back. Maquin rolled onto one knee, groaning as he stood, a hand reaching instinctively for his sword.

Orgull frowned. 'You thinking straight?'

'Aye.' Maquin scowled. He rolled his shoulders, cramped muscles stretching. And there was a greater pain shouting for his attention. He remembered catching the wrong end of a giant's war-hammer. Waves of pain pulsed from his shoulder. He gritted his teeth and looked about the chamber.

Torches still burned, blue light flickering from some kind of oil held high in iron bowls that marked an aisle to the dead giant-king, his cadaver still sitting in its stone chair upon its dais. Bodies lay strewn before it.

Maquin and Orgull shared a look, without a word walked back to the battle scene, treading carefully amongst the dead.

We're all that's left of the Gadrai, a voice whispered inside his head. *The rest are gone. All dead.* He closed his eyes, saw again Jael's sword punch into Kastell's belly.

Orgull knelt beside Vandil and closed the eyes of their leader's corpse. There was a gaping wound in his chest where the giant Alcyon had struck him with that black axe.

Maquin strode to where he had seen Kastell fall.

He lay face down, a black pool of blood spread about his waist. Maquin knelt and rolled him over, cradling him in his arms.

'Oh, Kas,' he whispered, tears rising up and choking the rest. *So many memories.* He remembered the day Kastell had been born, when he had been a warrior in the hold of Kastell's da, remembered his pride when he had been chosen as Kastell's shieldman, remembered carrying the boy from the flames and wreckage of a Hunen attack, remembered his oath, solemn words to protect unto death.

Tears dripped off his nose, smudging pale tracks in the grime on Kastell's face.

I have failed you. He had loved Kastell as the son that he had never had, and he had let him die by Jael's hand. A cold rage ignited in his belly.

Tenderly, Maquin brushed dirt from Kastell's face, then laid him back down. He found Kastell's sword and placed it on his body, folding stiffening fingers about its hilt. Then he knelt, whispered a prayer, asked for forgiveness and swore a new oath. *And this one I shall not fail, except by death's intervention. Jael shall die by my hand.* He drew a dagger from his belt and cut a red line across his palm, let his blood drip onto Kastell.

Orgull came and stood beside him, head bowed.

'Jael killed him,' Maquin mumbled.

Orgull nodded, torchlight gleaming blue in his eyes. 'Jael seemed overly close to that Calidus. I should have seen it. They have much to answer for.' He tugged thoughtfully at the warrior braid bound in his blond beard. 'This ran deeper than some blood-feud between uncle and nephew. I am thinking that Jael has designs on the throne of Isiltir.'

'The throne?' said Maquin.

'Aye. Romar's boy is, what, ten summers?' Orgull said. 'And Jael is blood-kin to Romar, though distant. He would have a claim, if those closer were removed.'

'Such as Romar,' Maquin said.

'And him,' Orgull added, looking pointedly at Kastell.

Maquin ground his palms into his eyes. 'Jael will pay for this.'

Orgull gave him an appraising look. 'If I am right, the best revenge is to deny Jael the throne of Isiltir.'

'A sword in his heart will do that,' Maquin said.

'And if you fail? We do not know how things lie up there, but likely he has shieldmen about him, and Calidus, along with his giant and the Jehar. Chances are you won't get close to him. Then Jael still gets the throne. Don't call that much of a revenge.'

Maquin glared at Orgull, part of him recognizing the truth of his words, but the greater part of him not caring.

'Word must get back to Isiltir of this – of Jael's treachery. I'll not see all our sword-brothers dead for nothing.'

Orgull bent besides Romar, recovered the dead king's sword and wrapped it in a cloak. 'I did not save you to see you throw your life away the instant we set foot above ground.'

'My life is not yours to decide,' Maquin said. 'I am going to kill Jael.'

Orgull stooped to look Maquin in the eye. 'I need your help. There is more at stake here than one man's vengeance. Please, help me to get word back to Isiltir of this slaughter.' He paused, eyes locked with Maquin, then shook his head. 'I will make a pact with you. Help me to do this, and then I shall help you. We shall bring about Jael's death together, or die trying. I swear it on our fallen brothers.'

Maquin sucked in a deep breath, chewing over Orgull's words. There was sense in them: if he went charging after Jael now he was most likely rushing to a death that accomplished nothing. 'All right,' he whispered, glancing at Kastell's corpse.

They gripped forearms.

'Course, we've got to get out of here first,' Maquin said.

'True. Are you injured?'

'I've been better.' His left arm hung limp at his side, his face was pale, slick with sweat. 'I blocked a hammer blow with my shoulder.'

Orgull stood behind Maquin, his fingers probing the warrior's shoulder and arm. 'Dislocated, not broken. Here, bite on this.' He gave Maquin a strip of leather, then gripped the warrior's shoulder in one large fist, placing his other hand between shoulder blade and spine. Then he pushed, hard.

There was a loud crack, Maquin hissed and slumped.

'Next time, use a shield, not your shoulder,' Orgull said.

'I'll try and remember,' Maquin mumbled, spitting the leather from his mouth. He sank to one knee.

'Take what you need,' Orgull said, reaching down to grab a shield from a fallen warrior. 'We need to find a way out of here.'

With an effort, Maquin walked away from Kastell's body and began searching the ground. First he looked to his water skin, drinking deep, then refilled it from others about him. In short time he found a plain wooden shield, iron-rimmed and bossed. Its face showed signs of the battle, but only shallow scratches. He hefted it, checked its straps, then slung it across his back. He also found a broad-bladed spear. Orgull was holding an axe that had belonged to one of the long-dead giant warriors left guarding their king. As Maquin stared at him, Orgull swung the axe at the stone floor, sparks flying as it chipped a chunk out of the rock. Rust fell from the blade. Orgull ran his thumb along its edge and nodded approvingly.

'You thinking to chop your way out of here?' Maquin asked.

'If I have to. It's still sharp enough.' Orgull smiled humourlessly. 'I'm not taken with the idea of using their front door, though. Can't see that Calidus leaving it open, or unguarded. And if I start chopping at it I'll wake all between here and the forest.'

'Agreed,' Maquin said.

'See those flames?'

Maquin looked up at the blue flames. Some flickered and crackled, touched by a breeze.

'Let's find where that air is coming from and hope it's more than a crack in the ground.'

There was a sudden muffled groan from amongst the bodies around them. Maquin pulled at the corpse of a Jehar warrior, revealing twitching fingers, a moving arm.

It was Tahir, one of their Gadrai sword-brothers. He was a young man, not much older than Kastell. *They had been friends.*

They uncovered him and checked him for wounds but could only find a large, egg-shaped lump on his temple. The stocky, long-armed warrior touched it and winced.

'What happened?' he muttered, his eyes unfocused.

Orgull recounted Jael's treachery.

'Vandil?' Tahir asked, rising unsteadily to his feet, gazing at the dead strewn about him.

'Dead. Slain by Calidus' pet giant,' Orgull said.

Tahir whistled, shook his head and instantly looked as if he regretted doing it. 'What now, then?'

'Find a way out of this hole. One thing at a time.'

Maquin fashioned torches out of axe and spear shafts, wrapping them in strips of cloth torn from tattered cloaks, and dipped them in the oil-filled bowls that lined the walkway. They flickered with the same blue light.

Together they marched to the edge of the chamber and began tracing its edge, searching for a doorway. It was not long before they found an archway draped with thick cobwebs, a slight breeze stirring it. Maquin touched his torch to the web and blue sparks crackled out in a widening circle, consuming the web right back to the stone.

Orgull looked at them both, then strode into the darkness. Tahir followed.

Maquin paused, looking back into the chamber. 'Farewell, Kastell,' he said, and after a few long moments he gritted his teeth and stepped into the tunnel.

The three of them trudged in silence, blue-tinged torchlight flickering on the tunnel's high roof and walls. Other corridors branched off, Maquin eyeing the dense shadows suspiciously. This place was in Forn Forest, after all, or beneath it, and Forn was the dark savage heart of the Banished Lands. Its inhabitants were by and large unpleasant. And predatory.

His thoughts drifted back to those left behind, to Vandil, to his Gadrai sword-brothers, to Romar and most of all to Kastell. Yet again he saw Jael stepping in front of Kastell, stabbing him. He should have stayed closer. His vision blurred with tears and he swiped at his eyes, fist clenching.

A sound drew his attention: a scraping, submerged in the deep shadows of a side tunnel. He stared into the darkness, thought he saw the hint of movement just beyond the torchlight's reach. Something big. There was a faint reflection. He hissed a warning and drew his sword.

'What's wrong?' Tahir said, as Orgull joined them.

'Something's down there,' Maquin muttered.

'What?'

'I don't know. *Something*.'

Maquin walked into the side tunnel, his torch held high. Darkness retreated before the light, revealing nothing but empty space.

'Nothing there now,' Tahir pointed out.

'Come on,' Orgull said. 'Tahir, guard our backs.'

'Aye, chief.'

They walked on, their pace quicker, now, the tunnel rising steeply. *A good sign*, thought Maquin, sweat trickling down his back. *Up is far better than down.* The tunnel was also getting narrower, the roof lower. *Not such a good sign. Will it just end? What then?* Soon after, Orgull called a halt. He raised a hand to the tunnel's roof, fingers tracing a tree root poking through the stone, twisted and knotted.

'Must be near the surface,' Maquin said.

'We must have walked more than a league by now,' Tahir commented.

'Aye. We're out past Haldis, I'd guess, but not much further,' Maquin said.

'Is all well back there, Tahir?' asked Orgull.

'Nothing to see,' the warrior replied.

'Good. Onwards,' their leader said and set off.

It was not long before Orgull stopped again. The tunnel came to an abrupt end, a dozen wide steps leading sharply up to the roof, where it met a round, flat-bottomed stone. Orgull climbed the steps and tapped the stone with his axe. He climbed higher, braced his shoulder against the stone and heaved. With a grating sound the stone shifted, minutely, earth falling from about its rim.

'Help,' grunted Orgull.

The steps were wide enough for two abreast so Maquin climbed up beside Orgull, adding his weight and strength. Together they strained and Maquin felt the stone shift, dirt falling into his face, then there was a wash of fresh air, a glimpse of moonlight.

'Keep pushing,' Orgull muttered. 'Nearly there.'

Then Tahir screamed. Maquin and Orgull dropped the stone back in place and turned.

Something had hold of Tahir: a many-legged, chitinous creature, all bristle, eyes and fangs, as wide as an adult boar, but far longer, its segmented body swallowed by shadow. Tahir was screaming as he hammered futilely at the creature with his spear.

Maquin darted forwards, jabbing his own weapon. It slid off a hard, shiny carapace. He thrust his torch at the beast, but a sharp-spined leg smashed it out of his hand, the blue light sputtering out. He launched forwards with his spear again; the blade scraped along the creature's hard shell, then sank into a gap between segments. It let out a high-pitched squeal, dropped Tahir and reared up, fangs and forelegs waving, almost filling the tunnel. Maquin grabbed Tahir's wrist and dragged him back. The creature scuttled after them, a green, jelly-like substance oozing from the wound in its side. It sank a fang into Tahir's leg, just below the knee. Tahir screamed and thrashed.

Then Orgull was there, bellowing for Maquin to get back, for Tahir to stay down. He swung his new war-axe, smashed it with all of his prodigious strength into the creature's head. There was a sickening crack. The thing's legs jerked, twitching furiously, its mandibles clacking. With a sigh it sank to the floor, spasmed once more and then was still.

'Get it off me,' Tahir hissed, a fang still buried in his leg. Maquin heaved and wrenched the fang out. Tahir gasped with pain, blood running down his leg.

Orgull ripped Tahir's breeches up to the knee, poured water over the wound and tied a strip of the torn breeches above it.

'How is it?' Tahir asked, a touch of panic in his voice.

'As good as it can be down here,' Orgull muttered, 'though I'd like something stronger than water to flush it with. Can you stand?'

'I'll stand to walk out of this place,' Tahir breathed, steadying himself with his spear.

Orgull gripped his axe haft and with a wrench pulled the blade free of the creature. He threw one of their torches back down the tunnel, where it wavered but stayed alight. 'Maquin, best get that stone shifted. Who knows what else we're sharing these tunnels with.'

Maquin ran up the steps and put his shoulder to the stone. Nothing happened. He tried again, grunting and straining.

'What's keeping you?' Orgull called.

'It's heavy,' Maquin muttered. 'Could do with you here, chief.'

'Can't be in two places at once,' Orgull said. 'And you'd best get a move on. Light's fading.'

Even as he spoke, the torch he had thrown back down the tunnel guttered and then winked out. The darkness surged forwards, held in check by Tahir tightly clutching the last torch.

Maquin renewed his efforts, fear of being trapped in the dark giving him an extra strength; the stone shifted, grinding against rock and earth. Maquin dug his spear butt into the gap, levered and shoved as he strained, veins bulging with the effort, and finally the stone lifted clear. Pale moonlight greeted him.

He reached up through the hole, savouring the sensation of air on his face and grass under his fingertips; he grabbed a tree root and pulled himself up. He could hear the sighing of a breeze amongst branches, the distant murmur of voices, faint song, could see the pinpricks of many campfires.

Back in Forn, then. Must be the survivors of the battle. For a moment the thought of Jael filled his mind, sitting beside a campfire, eating, drinking, celebrating. Without realizing, he stood and took a step forwards, hand reaching for his sword hilt.

'Could do with some help down here,' a voice whispered to him. He froze, remembering Orgull's words to him, their pact in the burial chamber. *Soon, Jael.*

The moon slipped behind ragged clouds and all was in darkness.

Maquin set to pulling the others out of the tunnel and, as quietly as hunting wolves, the three warriors slipped into the forest, the last surviving remnant of the Gadrai. Maquin looked back once and then followed his sword-brothers into the trees.

CHAPTER FIVE

CORBAN

Corban gripped the boat's rail as he stared back into the distance. Dun Carreg had long since disappeared and in all directions a grey, foam-flecked sea stretched as far as he could see.

It was late in the day now, well past highsun, and Corban's stomach was rumbling. He had not eaten since the evening before – nor had anyone else on this boat. No one had given food much thought in their desperate bid to escape.

Dun Carreg, he thought, wishing that he could still see the fortress, still see Ardan, still see his home. *Home no more.* Everything had changed so quickly. And Thannon and Cywen were both still in Dun Carreg. His da and sister, both dead, both needing a cairn to be raised over them. It wasn't right. Tears filled his eyes.

His mam lay sleeping upon a heaped pile of nets. She looked older, the lines in her face deeper, dark hollows about her eyes. Gar sat beside her, chin resting on his chest, sleeping too. Most of this band of runaways were in the same state. It had been a long, hard night, in more ways than one.

Footsteps drew Corban's eyes up to Halion, his weapons-master from the Rowan Field, making his way along the fisher-boat towards him. The warrior nodded grimly as he walked to where Mordwyr, Dath's da, stood guiding the boat's steering oar.

'We need to find land. Somewhere to get food and water.'

'Uh,' Mordwyr acknowledged. His eyes were red rimmed, his face lined with grief. He had left Bethan, his daughter, amongst the dead in Dun Carreg.

I was not the only one that lost kin last night, Corban thought.

Mordwyr pointed into the distance, northwards, and Corban saw a dark line on the horizon. Land.

'We'll have to risk it,' Halion said. He patted Mordwyr's shoulder and made his way back along the boat, to where Edana sat with her head bowed.

The Princess of Ardan, now heir to its throne, had said nothing since they had climbed aboard the fisher-boat. The last sound Corban had heard from her was screaming as she witnessed the death of her father.

She's lost both her mam and da, now. At least I still have my mam, someone to share my grief with.

Storm's muzzle touched his hand. Corban tugged on one of her ears, grimacing as the movement sent a ripple of pain through his shoulder. Brina had tended the wound where he had been stabbed during the battle in the feast-hall. Helfach had done it. The man's life-blood still stained the fur around the wolven's protruding canines. Brina had assured him the wound was not deep and was clean, but it still hurt.

He looked for the healer and she caught his eye, beckoning him over. Craf, the healer's unkempt crow, clung to the boat's rail above Brina's head.

'*Cor-ban*,' it squawked as he squatted down before Brina.

'What was that about?' she asked. 'Between Halion and Mordwyr?'

'Time to find some land. For food and water.'

'Ah. Out of the cook-pot and into the flames,' Brina muttered.

'What do you mean?'

She looked over the boat's side at the growing line of land. 'That's not Ardan. Not that Ardan's the safest place to be right now. Still, that's Cambren. Rhin rules there.'

'Oh.' Corban frowned, remembering the kidnapping of Edana's mother, Queen Alona, back in the Darkwood, where Alona and so many others had died. All because of Rhin. 'But what choice do we have?'

'None, I suppose.' Brina sighed, wiping rain from the tip of her pointed nose.

'*Wet*,' muttered Craf.

'Why should you care?' Brina snapped at the bedraggled bird. 'You're a crow.'

'*Cold*,' it grumbled. '*Fire*.'

'I've spoilt you,' Brina said.

The rain was falling heavier now, a cold wind throwing it stinging into Corban's face. In the distance the black smudge of land had grown closer, blurred by rain. The sea was an impenetrable iron grey, the waves about the boat higher, white-flecked with foam, whipped by the wind. Corban grabbed the rail and steadied himself as the fisher-boat rode a huge swell then sped down the other side. The boat's only sail was straining, thick ropes creaking. Corban felt a flutter of panic in his gut, then he saw Dath climbing amidst the ropes and sailcloth. His friend flashed him a weak smile.

He doesn't look so worried, thought Corban.

The sun was sinking, only a diffuse glow behind thick cloud, when they reached the coastline. Mordwyr steered the small skiff into a narrow steep-cliffed cove sheltering a strip of empty beach. Craf exploded into the air with a noisy squawk. Everyone disembarked – Storm needing a little encouragement from Corban – and the skiff was beached safely.

Marrock, Camlin and Dath set off to scout the area and to try and hunt something to eat.

Brina and Heb, King Brenin's old loremaster, led Edana off the narrow beach and settled her in a sheltered dell under a dense stand of rowan and yew, an icy stream bubbling through its middle.

Storm lapped at the stream, then padded off into the deepening gloom.

Halion set two men on watch. The rest of the small band set to chopping wood, clearing space for sleeping, digging out a small pit for a fire. Soon flames were crackling greedily in the dell and the rain-soaked band crowded round for some heat, even the crow.

It was dark when Marrock and the others returned, Dath carrying two hares over his shoulder. In short time the animals were skinned, gutted and boned, chopped into little pieces and dropped into a pot of boiling water.

Craf made disgusting noises as he helped himself to the hare's entrails.

That bird makes me feel sick.

It didn't stop Corban eating, though. The stew tasted like the finest meal to him, even as his mind told him it was watery, the meat stringy.

Two men were sent to relieve those on watch, Vonn being one of them. Dath glowered at his back as Vonn trudged into the gloom.

'His da betrayed us all. Can he be trusted to guard us?' he muttered to Corban.

'None of that,' Halion said, overhearing. 'He's suffered, lost people, same as the rest of us.'

'She was *my* sister,' Dath grumbled.

'And *my* daughter,' Mordwyr said. 'He loved her. Leave him be.'

Dath's mouth became a hard line but he said nothing more.

The small group sat around the fire, full dark settling about them, the trees sheltering them from the worst of the rain. Grief hovered amongst them like a heavy mist. Corban sat in silence, just listening, feeling exhausted, numb. His da and sister's faces danced in his memory every time he closed his eyes.

'So, Halion. Tell us of this plan to take Edana to Domhain.' It was Marrock who spoke. All other conversation stopped as everyone waited Halion's answer. 'Domhain is a long, dangerous journey,' Marrock continued. 'We could still sail from here to Dun Crin and the marshlands in the south of Ardan.'

'We could,' Halion said, glancing at Edana. She sat staring at the fire, giving no sign of interest in the conversation.

Edana should be leading us, but she can't. Marrock is her kin, so has the right, but Halion is her guardian, was given the task to protect her with Brenin's dying words, as most of us here heard.

'Eremon rules in Domhain, and he is distant kin to Edana. I know him, and he will not turn her away, or betray her.'

'He turned you away,' Marrock said.

Halion stared at Marrock a long, silent moment.

Heb spoke up now. 'Tell us of your father. Will he give aid against Owain?'

Halion grimaced. 'My father is old, beyond his seventieth year now. When I last saw him he was still sharp of mind. I am his bastard son, you understand, not his heir, but he always treated me well enough.'

'Then why did you leave Domhain?' Marrock asked.

Halion looked about them all, then took a deep breath. 'Conall, my brother, he has, *had* . . .' He paused a moment. 'He had a temper, and a lot of pride. It got him into trouble more than once. Growing up, we were fine; my mam was looked after by my da – she was his mistress, one of many. But in his old age he took a wife because he had no heir. Roisin. She was young, beautiful, and she treated us and my mam well enough, when we saw her, which was rare. Then she fell with child, birthed a boy – Lorcan. Things changed then. She became jealous, fearful that Conall and I had eyes for the throne of Domhain. And not just us – we were not Eremon's only bastards. Accidents began to happen; people died. My mam was one.' He threw a twig on the fire. 'Of course, Conall didn't take that well: he thought that our mam had been murdered. He confronted Roisin, said things he shouldn't have. Soon after that my da came to see us, told us he would arrange sanctuary with King Brenin of Ardan.' He shrugged. 'We left.'

'So how can you take us there, when your own life is at risk? Surely your enemies will become Edana's enemies,' Marrock said.

'There is no safe place, now,' Halion said. 'But my father will give Edana sanctuary, of that I am certain. He thought well of Brenin. Maybe he will give other aid. I cannot promise men, but at least it will be a safer place than most, and far from Owain's reach.'

Marrock frowned, thinking over Halion's words. 'I see the sense of it. But I'd rather be doing something, fighting rather than running away. And I know we've all lost people, but there are still others that we've left behind in Dun Carreg, others that still live. More warriors to join our cause, and others. Defenceless others, like my Fion . . .'

He dropped his gaze, staring into the fire.

Fion, his wife, Corban thought. *That must be hard on him.*

'My troubles are my own,' Marrock said, lifting his head, 'and my duty is to protect Edana, but still, running away, allowing Owain to just hunt down and kill any that would stand against him in Edana's name; it does not sit well with me. And the thought of Owain sitting in Brenin's feast-hall . . .' His lip curled in a snarl and others around the fire muttered their agreement.

Corban looked between Halion and Marrock, could see the sense in both arguments. He leaned towards Halion; he knew from hard lessons in the Rowan Field that Halion had a strategic mind, and patience. *He believes there is more chance of success if we retreat now, plan to fight another day.* Marrock's argument stirred his passion, though. Part of him did not want to run.

'It angers me too,' another voice said, Edana's finally. She was still staring at the flames. There were scars on her cheeks where she had clawed them in her grief at Alona's death. They gave her a feral, inhuman quality. 'And I will take it back from him. But for now Halion's plan is a good one. I need time.' She looked at Halion and nodded curtly to him. Slowly a silence draped itself over them all.

Twigs snapped and there was a scuffling sound in the darkness beyond the firelight's reach, a hulking figure taking shape out of the shadows. It was Storm, the carcass of a deer hanging from her jaws.

She padded through the group and dropped the deer at Corban's feet, nudged it towards him and waited.

'Seems you're pack leader,' Halion said.

'She thinks so.' Corban placed a hand on the deer, accepting Storm's gift. He drew his knife and began to skin the carcass.

Not long after, Corban was licking hot fat off his fingers and wiping it from his chin. Storm was curled at his feet, cracking one of the leg bones between her teeth, gnawing at the marrow.

Gwenith leaned over and squeezed Corban's hand. 'It is time to talk,' she said quietly. Without looking at him, she stood and walked away, to the edge of the firelight. Gar rose with Corban and followed.

When he reached her, Gwenith took Corban's hand and led him beyond the firelight. She sat down beside a smooth-barked rowan, patting the grass in front of her.

Hesitantly he sat, feeling anxious. It was not as dark here as it appeared from beside the fire. Moonlight silvered his mam's hair and played on her face. Much was still in shadow, but he could see enough to know that she was troubled. She chewed her bottom lip. Gar sat next to her, watching Corban with an intensity that was unsettling.

'There is much to tell you, Ban,' his mam said, a tremor in her voice. 'Almost too much. Now that we are here, I hardly know where to start . . .' she trailed off.

'Whatever it is, can't it wait?' Corban said. 'We are all half-blind with grief and exhaustion?'

'I know,' his mam said, 'but—'

'It cannot wait,' Gar interrupted. 'With each day we are travelling further from our true destination.'

'I don't understand.'

'First,' his mam said fiercely, 'remember this. I love you. We love you. And know that whatever we have done, and will do, it has come from trying to do right. To protect you, and to serve Elyon.'

'Elyon?' said Corban.

His mam nodded.

Elyon, the All-Father, had always seemed just a distant name to Corban, someone or something that he knew about but that never directly affected him. He remembered Brina telling him about the All-Father, how he had given authority to mankind over all creation, and that after the War of Treasures and the Scourging Elyon had turned from mankind, forsaken all he had made. He remembered too what she had said about Asroth, dark angel of the Otherworld: how he yearned to become flesh so as to destroy all Elyon had created.

He shivered. 'But Elyon has abandoned us. Why serve him?'

'Why?' Gar blinked, looking shocked at the question. 'Because he is our creator. Because he will return. Because it is *right*.'

Corban shrugged. 'Why are we sitting in the dark talking about this now? What's all this got to do with me?'

His mam took a deep breath. 'You know that things are happening. Strange things – day turned to night on Midwinter, white wyrms roaming the dark places.'

'I know that,' Corban said, remembering the wyrm that had attacked them in the tunnels beneath Dun Carreg.

'They are signs that something is coming. The God-War.'

Corban's skin prickled, the hairs on his arms standing up. *The God-War.* He had heard rumours, talk, mostly from Edana, spying on King Brenin after his return from the council in Tenebral. It had made him feel strange, even then, but now, in the dark, leagues from home . . .

'You are a special child, Corban,' his mam continued. 'And I do not mean that in the way that all mothers think of their children. You are different. Chosen.'

She paused, looking deep into his face, searching for something. He just felt confused.

'Chosen? Mam, what's this all about? By who? For what?'

'By Elyon. You have a part to play in the God-War. Because of this you have also been hunted, since the day you were born.'

'Hunted? Who by?'

Gwenith looked about, as if to check that no one was creeping up on them. 'Asroth,' she whispered.

'Chosen, hunted?' A smile died on Corban's lips as he saw her expression. *She really believes this. Grief and exhaustion have confused her*, he thought.

His mam shook her head. 'It should be Thannon doing the telling. I do not know how to say this,' she muttered, eyes flickering to Gar. A tear rolled down her cheek.

The warrior frowned, eyebrows bunching. 'Your mother speaks the truth. The important thing for you to know, Ban, is that you are part of this. Part of the God-War. What happened at Dun Carreg is only the beginning. The Banished Lands are falling into chaos.'

Questions were erupting in Corban's mind, one after another. One fought clear of the rest. 'How do you know this?'

Gar waved a hand. 'There is a lot to tell you, too much for now, for here. But I will answer all your questions during our journey, if I can.'

'Journey? You mean to Domhain?'

'No, Ban. We must go to Drassil.'

'What? Drassil?' *The fabled city in the heart of Forn Forest?* Corban shook his head. None of this was making sense. He remembered overhearing his mam and Gar talking, back in Dun Carreg. About the arrival of Nathair and his guard, Sumur. They had mentioned leaving then, spoken of Drassil. But it had felt different. Everything had felt different. Cywen and his da had been alive, then.

'Yes, the giant stronghold. It is vital that you – we – go to Drassil.' Something flashed across Gar's face. *Longing?* 'You will be safe there.'

'But . . . what about the others?' He looked over his shoulder, saw the flicker of their campfire, dark figures around it.

'We must leave them.'

Corban rocked back, recoiling as if slapped. *Leave them.* The thought seemed ridiculous to him, unimaginable. This group was all that was left of Dun Carreg, all that was left of *home*. And his mam and Gar were asking him just to walk away from them. Abandon them, abandon Edana. Suddenly he could see the Rowan Field, smell the sea air. A crowd was gathered about him as he took his warrior trials. He glanced at the palm of his hand, the scar where he had sworn his blood-oath in the Field a silver line. He had pledged his life to king and kin. His king was dead, but Edana was Brenin's heir. Walking away would make him an oathbreaker.

'No,' he heard himself say.

'Ban,' his mam said.

'We must,' Gar said.

'*No*. Everything, *everyone* has been broken, killed, destroyed.' He kneaded his temples. 'Da, Cywen . . .' He looked up and locked eyes with his mam. Tears streaked her cheeks. 'They are all that's left of home,' he said, waving his arm towards the campfire. 'They are our family now.'

'Ban, this is beyond all kin, beyond all friendship,' Gar said, an inflection in his voice hinting at some hidden emotion, a lake of it, buried deep beneath the surface. 'This is about doing what is right, doing what must be done, despite the cost. Please, trust us. We must leave.'

'I have sworn an oath to Edana. I'll not become an oathbreaker.' He stood, feeling dizzy, not wanting to hear any more, not another word; not this madness about Elyon and Asroth, not about Forn, and Drassil, and not about *leaving*. He felt as if he was a dam full to bursting. His mam reached for his hand, but he snatched it away and stumbled into the darkness.

CHAPTER SIX

MAQUIN

Maquin followed Tahir into the forest, almost colliding with the young warrior when he stopped abruptly behind Orgull.

'What's wrong?' Maquin hissed, looking about for any hint of danger.

Orgull was muttering unintelligibly, only the odd curse recognizable. He was looking back at the campfires that flickered distantly behind them.

'What's wrong, chief?' Tahir said.

'Can't go yet,' the big man said, looking as if he'd rather not be saying the words.

'Why not?' the other two chimed.

Orgull grimaced. 'I have to speak to King Braster.'

'Why?' Tahir asked. 'We don't even know if he's still alive.'

Orgull sucked in a deep breath. 'I have been part of the Gadrai near half my life, but I am also bound to another brotherhood.' He gave them a long, measuring look. 'Braster is part of that brotherhood. If there is a chance he still lives, I must tell him what has happened. We all know there are no guarantees that we're going to make it out of Forn. Got a long walk ahead of us with enemies right behind, most likely. If we don't get word back to Isiltir and Romar's kin, that'll be the end of it. Jael will have won. Don't know about you, but that doesn't sit too well with me.'

Maquin agreed; the thought of Jael getting away with his betrayal filled him with a white anger.

'What *brotherhood*?' Tahir asked.

'It is more a cause,' Orgull said. 'The God-War is coming, and we'll all be sucked into it, whether we want to or not. We already have been, if I'm right. There's more to this than dealing with Hunen raiders. That black axe . . .'

Maquin thought of Veradis, of his talk of the prophecy, of Nathair, of the Bright Star and Black Sun . . .

Orgull rubbed a hand over his eyes. 'I met a man, a long time ago. He told me of what was coming, of what is happening now. Said he would need my help one day, to fight Asroth's avatar. I pledged myself to him, to his cause.'

'What, just like that?' Tahir said.

'No, not just like that,' Orgull snapped. 'There was a lot more to it, but I'm not inclined to repeat it word for word right now. Just believe me when I say I was convinced, and I'm not an easy man to convince. So I must find Braster and tell him, or know for certain that he is dead. I'll understand if you'd rather keep walking. I feel like a mad man listening to myself say it.'

'I'll come with you,' Maquin said. 'Watch your back, if I can. Tahir, you wait in the forest for us – you'd not stand much of a chance if we needed to leave with speed, not with that hole in your leg. And if we don't come back, at least you've still got a chance of getting back to Isiltir, telling what's happened here.'

Orgull stared at Maquin, then nodded. 'Appreciate it,' he said grimly. 'Let's be getting on with it, then.' He marched off towards the campfires.

They made their way to where the forest thinned and they could see the survivors of the battle spread along the slopes before Haldis. The campfires were clustered in groups, the biggest lower down the slope. Maquin saw a glimpse of men with swords jutting from their backs ranged about it.

The Jehar.

'Must be Veradis' lot,' Orgull whispered.

'There,' Maquin said, pointing along the slope, closer to the forest. There was a large tent, surrounded by a handful of fires. Slowly they crept closer, until the tent and fires lay between them and the camp guarded by Jehar. Two warriors stood before the tent's opening. The orange glow of firelight flickered across their shields, the symbol of the black hammer clear upon them.

'That's them,' Tahir whispered. 'Helveth's hammer.'

'All right then,' Orgull said, rubbing a hand across his bald head, skin rasping on bristle, 'let's do this.' He passed something to Tahir; Romar's sword, Maquin realized, then stood straight and walked out of the forest, hands raised high. Maquin hurried after him, afraid the guards would mistake Orgull for one of the Hunen, especially with that giant's axe slung across his back.

The guards called them over, and after a few tense moments of explanation they were brought before Lothar, Braster's battlechief. He listened to them, frowned at them a while, then turned on his heel and led them to the large tent. A guard opened the canopy for them and Lothar took them inside.

'You must leave your weapons here,' Lothar said, a tall, shrewd-looking man with a pointed nose and heavy-lidded eyes. He gestured to a warrior standing just within the tent. Begrudgingly Maquin drew his sword and set it down, alongside Orgull's broadsword and giant's axe. Then Lothar led them deeper into the tent. A man lay on a cot, propped upright with pillows. He was big, both muscled and fat. Red hair lay damp with sweat across his brow. His right arm was strapped in a sling. Braster, King of Helveth.

Another man was stood beside Braster, offering a cup to the wounded king. Braster took it, sniffed the contents and pulled a face.

'You must drink,' the man before him said, 'it will ease your pain and speed your recovery.'

Braster sipped tentatively.

'You must drink it all,' the man said, then bowed and left.

'Idiot,' Braster muttered at the healer's back.

Lothar ushered Orgull and Maquin forward. 'We found these men on our camp's fringe, my King,' Lothar said. 'They are the Gadrai of Isiltir, and they claim to have important news, fit only for your ears.'

Orgull stepped forward and bowed, clumsily.

Braster grinned in recognition, made to rise and grimaced in pain. He sank back into his pillows, pale-faced.

'Look at me,' Braster said, 'my shoulder crushed by some giant's hammer and now I'm fit for nothing.' He scowled.

'You should drink your medicine,' Orgull said.

'It tastes like urine,' Braster muttered. 'I am glad you live,' he said. 'I'd heard you were dead, along with the rest of the Gadrai.'

'We were betrayed.' Orgull's smile disappeared. 'Romar was murdered.'

Orgull explained, beginning with the death of King Romar and then the Gadrai's battle against the Jehar and Jael's shieldmen. Braster cursed throughout. Lothar stood silently beside Maquin, who swayed on his feet, feeling utterly exhausted. He tried to remember when he had last slept. It felt like days. He blinked, trying to focus on Orgull's words.

'Calidus and his pet giant, eh?' Braster said when Orgull fell silent. 'I knew Romar was winning no friends from Tenebral, but I never dreamed they would go this far.'

'There is more at play here,' Orgull said. 'The axe that they fought over, I think it was one of the Treasures.'

'What. Where is it now?'

'Calidus' giant has it, or did, last I saw.'

Braster scowled. 'Word of this must reach Meical.'

'As I thought. That is why I have come here,' Orgull said. 'I will be leaving soon and there are no guarantees that I will make it through the forest . . .'

'You have done well, bringing this news to me.' Braster winced as he shifted his weight. 'And you are sure that Jael was involved?'

'I saw Jael strike down Kastell, Romar's nephew,' Maquin said.

'Jael. I never did like that snivelling runt,' Braster muttered.

There was a whisper of feet as Lothar stepped away, behind Maquin.

'The question is why,' Braster said. 'Why do this, risk so much? I think you are right, Orgull. This is part of bigger events. And, if so, Nathair is behind this. He is ruthless, as he showed with Mandros.' He shook his head. 'We have uncovered the Black Sun. What to do? I would march to their camp now and take Calidus' head, but I fear he'd take mine instead. My warband is decimated – only a few hundred left. And me, I can't even wipe my arse, let alone swing a sword.' He drummed the fat fingers of his good hand on his cot side. 'I must pretend ignorance, Orgull, until I am out of this damn forest and back amongst my own people. And you two, you must not be seen. What say you, Lothar?'

There was a thud behind Maquin. He turned, saw the guard minding their weapons slumped on the ground. Lothar had a sword in his hand, blood on it. He swept past Maquin, strode right up to Braster and drove the sword into his King's chest.

Braster shivered, a look of confusion on his face, then blood welled in his mouth and he slumped back onto the pillows.

Lothar stepped back, leaving the sword in Braster's corpse. Maquin's sword, he realized in a wave of growing horror.

'Why?' Orgull asked Lothar.

The battlechief tore his focus away from Braster's face. 'Because Nathair is the future. That was not lightly done – I loved my King. But you had to tell of what happened in Haldis' tombs. Braster would have gone to war with Tenebral, and that just cannot happen.' Lothar drew his own blade and yelled for guardsmen.

Almost instantly, two warriors stepped into the tent. They saw the dead guardsman, then Braster. They drew swords and advanced slowly on Maquin and Orgull. Booted feet could be heard outside.

Orgull shrugged his shield to his arm and charged the two men. Maquin did the same with his own shield, hesitated an instant, then gripped the sword protruding from Braster's chest – his sword – and pulled. With a sucking sound it came free.

He glanced at Lothar, but the battlechief was backing away. He took a step after him, but then Orgull crashed into the two advancing warriors, shield held before him like a ram. One of the men bounced away, collided with a post and sank to the ground. Orgull and the other guard fell to the floor in a tangle of limbs.

More men were pouring into the tent, two at a time – four, six, more behind. One took a swing at Orgull as he wrestled on the ground. Maquin leaped forwards, catching the warrior's blade on his own in a spray of sparks. He kicked the man in the gut, sending him staggering into others who were trying to cram through the tent's entrance. A blade came at Maquin from above. He blocked it with his shield, swung his own sword at the man trying to crack his skull. His blade bit into something, accompanied by a crunch, breaking bones, probably ribs. Maquin wrenched his blade free, swung and blocked furiously as men began to circle him, attacks coming from different angles. He glanced at Orgull and saw the big man was on his feet, the warrior he had been wrestling with lying motionless on the floor. Orgull had his axe in his hands.

'Down,' Orgull yelled.

Maquin dropped to the floor, felt air from the axe as it swung over him. There was screaming, more than one voice. Blood sprayed, splashing hot in Maquin's face.

'Stay down,' Orgull ordered, and the axe was swinging again. This time it crunched into, through, a post, and then tent canvas was draped about Maquin, men shouting, grunting. Heat flared nearby, torches igniting material. The screaming went up in pitch. Something grabbed Maquin's arm and yanked him backwards.

'This way,' Orgull said, striding past Braster's slumped form, towards the back of the tent. He swung at tent posts as he passed them, bringing more canvas down, torches crackling and flaring. Maquin glimpsed Lothar briefly, then there was smoke and canvas between them. Orgull swung at the rear of the tent, cut a great rent in it and stepped out into the night. Maquin followed and then they were running for the treeline.

They were still on clear ground when voices rose behind them; Maquin heared the sound of thudding feet. His heart drummed in his head, louder than anything else. Any moment he expected to feel a spear in his back.

His lungs were burning. The feet sounded closer behind him, almost on top of him, then there was a hiss, a thud, brief motion at the edge of his vision. He risked a glance back, saw a form lying on the ground, a spear shaft sticking from it.

Then they were through the treeline, darkness enveloping them.

'This way,' a voice hissed, and Tahir was there ahead of them, beckoning through the trees.

CHAPTER SEVEN

LYKOS

Lykos' eyes snapped open, his breath ragged. For a moment he did not know where he was; his hands clutched at the arms of the chair he was sleeping in. He blinked, trying to scatter the lingering shadow of a dream – yellow eyes, staring through him – and looked about. The creak and swell of his ship's cabin brought him back. He poured himself a cup of wine with shaky hands, spilling some, and drank deep.

He walked unsteadily to the cabin window. A shaft of sunlight cut through the gloom. The black walls of Jerolin filled his view, rising over the lake where his ship was anchored. Fidele had offered him rooms inside those black walls but, being lord of the Vin Thalun, he would rather sleep on a ship's deck, more home to him than any town or building. Besides, he didn't trust these people, knew that his privileged position in Tenebral was purely because Nathair made it so.

He drank more wine, slung his scabbarded sword and belt over his shoulder, opened the door and strode through, with his shield-man Deinon silently falling in behind him. Together they climbed onto the deck, the bright sunshine making Lykos squint. He nodded to some of his crew, most of them men who had served with him for many years, fought for him, and his father before him.

'Is my boat ready?' he asked.

'Aye, chief,' Deinon said, his voice raspy, distinct. Losing half of your nose in the pits did that.

'Good,' Lykos said and strode to the gunwale. He swung over and climbed agilely down a rope ladder, dropping into a rowing-boat large enough for a dozen men. Thaan, Deinon's brother, was waiting for him.

His two shieldmen manned the oars and started pulling steadily for the shore. They skirted the trading and fishing port on the lake shore, instead heading straight for Jerolin. The boat grounded on a strip of silt and reeds, Lykos jumped into the shallows and splashed the rest of the way to dry land. He stopped there and paused to admire the ships lined along the shore. Twelve shallow-draughted war-galleys, all sleek lines and stinking of tar. They had been the first finished, at the end of the Crow's Moon last year, just before winter had set in. All winter they had sat in their thick-painted coats of moss and tar, and now they were ready for open water. New building had begun with spring, and already five skeletons stood further along the shoreline, the first oak strakes lining ribs of spruce.

Nathair wanted a Vin Thalun fleet and that was what he was going to get.

He raised a hand in greeting to old Alazon, his master shipwright, sitting on a half-built keel with a mallet in his fist and nails in his mouth. Reluctantly, Lykos began striding towards the fortress, resisting the urge to go and inspect the shipyard, speak with his men. There were things that needed doing, and meeting with Fidele was high on that list. He had begun this walk sixteen years ago, the night he had first met with Calidus and sealed his future, so he would not falter now.

The three men reached the road that led to Jerolin's gates. The meadow about them was wider than it used to be; trees from the nearby forest had been harvested for the shipbuilding. Men were gathered on the plain, hundreds of them, warriors training in Nathair's shield wall. It looked a fearsome thing, on land, but Lykos sneered as he passed. *Little use on a ship's deck*, he thought, knowing even as he did so that he was being illogical. *The Banished Lands will not be conquered on the ocean.* Beyond Tenebral's warriors was a cluster of tents, before which at least two thousand of the Jehar were at their training, this *sword dance* that Lykos had watched with a sense of dread. Here were warriors that would take some beating. Good thing that they fought on the same side. *For now.*

He looked back at the war-galleys on the lake shore, at the warriors in the meadow, men of Tenebral and the Jehar of Telassar. This was a land mustering for war, and he was at the heart of it, had been preparing for it for nearly two decades.

45

He swept through the fortress' gates uncontested and passed quickly through the streets of Jerolin, people moving out of his way. A man stood at the stableblock, arms folded across his chest, scowling at them. *A man with a grudge, if ever I saw one,* Lykos thought, making a mental note of the man's features. Wouldn't do for the hard work of a lifetime to be done away with by a knife in the ribs.

The doors to the keep were open and he strode in, continuing through the feast-hall, and climbed the spiral tower that led to the royal chambers. Here half a dozen eagle-guard stood in their black-polished breastplates and silver helms – Tenebral's elite. The royal guard had been increased since Aquilus' assassination.

Fidele was seated behind a wide desk, dark hair framing her pale, beautiful face. Lykos did not allow himself the luxury of staring at her loveliness, close to perfection in his opinion, even if there were creases around her eyes and her lips, a streak of silver in her otherwise jet hair. *Never allow another to know they have any kind of hold over you,* his father had told him. Wise words.

Fidele was not alone. Another of the eagle-guard stood behind her. Orcus was wiry and as knotted as an old tree, dark eyes set in a face with a nose that had been broken more than once. Fidele gestured and he poured three cups of dark red wine, offering one to Lykos.

'My thanks,' the Vin Thalun murmured as he sipped the wine, resisting the urge to gulp it.

'I have had no word from my son in some time. Have you heard from him?' Fidele asked with measured calm, but Lykos could sense something else beneath the surface, something brittle.

'Not since he reached Dun Carreg,' Lykos said. *Though I would hear long before you, with your outdated methods,* he thought. Lykos tried to repress a shudder as his thoughts flickered towards his dreams, the alien presence in his mind, in his soul. 'Calidus has an intricate network of messengers.'

'I am sure,' Fidele said, failing to hide a sour twist of her lips. 'My husband and I had dealings with Calidus a long time ago. He proved . . . *wanting*. And, besides, Calidus is somewhere in Forn Forest, fighting giants, while Nathair is in Ardan.'

'Calidus is very well connected with both his information and his informers, my lady. I am sure that he is in close contact with Nathair, no matter where he is. If I receive any kind of word regarding your son I shall of course forward it on to you. Immediately.'

'My thanks. And how goes the task my son has set you?'

'The shipbuilding proceeds well. Twelve galleys are ready on your lake shore. The other shipyard on the coast does better still. Fifteen war-galleys, and seven deeper-draughted ships for transport. Progress could be even better, though, if the supply of wood was less sporadic.'

'Surely there is enough wood here for your purposes.'

'Oak and elm is in plenty here, and on the coast, you are right. But I need a supply of spruce and cedar as well. That is less readily found.' He paused and sipped some more wine. 'May I speak plainly?'

'Of course.'

'Your barons controlling that supply are not cooperating as well as they might. I speak specifically of Marcellin in the north and Lamar in the south.'

'There is trouble in the north that may be affecting your supply lines,' Fidele said. 'The Kurgan giants are raiding from their mountain strongholds. I have sent Peritus to deal with it.'

'That still would not explain the lack of cooperation in the south,' Lykos said. 'And, allow me to speak frankly – I believe Marcellin and Lamar are being obstructive because I am Vin Thalun.'

Fidele sat back, considering him coldly. 'Yes, I believe you are right.'

Lykos raised an eyebrow. 'We have signed a treaty, formed an alliance.'

'Yes, we have. As we are speaking frankly, let me say this. The situation between our two peoples is new, and old ways of thinking are hard to change in a day, or a moon, or a season, or even a year.'

'Our treaty was signed nearly two years ago, my lady,' Lykos said.

'Yes. But there were decades of enmity before that.'

'Not under my reign,' Lykos snapped, suddenly fierce, feeling his temper flare. 'And the men that ruled then, well . . .' He paused, tugging at an iron ring woven into his beard, a timeworn method of controlling his anger. 'They have either bowed the knee or had their heads separated from their shoulders.'

'Nevertheless,' Fidele said with a dismissive wave of her hand, 'there is a history between our peoples. Lamar particularly has been a bulwark for Tenebral against your past raids. He has seen much bloodshed and does not forgive so easily.'

'True. Lamar I can understand. Marcellin, though. He rules in the Agullas, about as far as any man in Tenebral can get from the Tethys Sea. But he is close to Peritus, I believe . . .' Lykos left the rest unsaid. He knew that Peritus, Aquilus' battlechief, was not a friend of the Vin Thalun, had even spoken openly against them, if only after Nathair had sailed west. It was good to let Fidele see that he was no fool, that he understood something of the politics and people of this land.

'I will speak to them,' Fidele said. 'But I have heard things about your people, practices that hinder any understanding between us, and I believe Lamar and Marcellin will have heard the same reports that I have.'

Lykos sighed; he had a feeling he knew what was coming.

'I speak of your fighting pits,' Fidele said, her mouth twisting with disgust. 'In your own land your customs are yours to do as you see fit, but here in Tenebral, forcing captives, slaves, to fight for your entertainment is unacceptable.'

The fighting pits were part of Vin Thalun tradition, had been part of the three islands for as long as Lykos knew. Men could end up there by many roads – taken on a raid, owing a blood debt, even from a very bad night with dice and a throw-board. There was only one road out, though, and that was to fight your way out, tooth and nail if you had to. With the end of war between the islands and Lykos proclaimed Lord of the Vin Thalun, if anything the pits had grown in their popularity. His people were not made for peace and if his crews were no longer fighting or raiding regularly, they needed something to prevent them turning on one another. The pits acted as both an entertainment and a distraction. He had tried to curtail the use of them while his men were abroad in Tenebral, understanding that the locals would probably object. But the rising tensions amongst his warriors had become a pain in the arse, so he had allowed the pits to happen. Discreetly, he thought.

He shrugged, not wanting to commit to an outright lie that could later incriminate him. 'I'll look into these rumours.'

'We both know that they are not rumours,' Fidele snapped, leaning forward in her chair. 'You attended one of these events only a ten-night gone. This barbaric custom *will not* happen within the boundaries of Tenebral. I expect you to put an end to it.'

'I thought Nathair ruled here,' he said before he could check himself.

'Nathair is not here, and I rule in his place,' Fidele said.

'Of course,' Lykos muttered, pouring himself another cup of wine. *For now.* 'I will make sure the pits stay on the Islands.'

Fidele inclined her head. 'And I will see that your supply of wood is unhindered.'

'How did it go, chief?' Deinon asked him.

Lykos scowled at his shieldman. They were out on the meadow road, walking back to the lake shore. It was hard enough taking orders from Nathair, someone young enough to be his son, though he knew he had no choice with that, at least for now. But Nathair's *mother, a woman* . . . no matter how much he enjoyed looking at her . . .

'She knows about the pits,' he muttered.

'Is that a problem?' Thaan asked.

'Course it's a problem. These landwalkers are soft. She wants the pits closed.'

'The lads won't like it.'

'No, they won't.' *And neither would I.* 'Which is why the pits'll stay open. Just have to be a bit clever about it, that's all. Not so close to Jerolin, not so regular; just for a while.'

'Good,' Deinon said, the air whistling through his ruined nose as he talked. 'Didn't think you'd let a woman tell you what's what, no matter how fine she is to look at.'

'Watch your tongue,' Lykos said, giving Deinon a sour look. There was a lot more to this than he had originally imagined. Conquering the Islands had been so much easier than this politicking – bloodier, aye, but simpler, at least. He glanced up, saw the day was well past highsun.

'You all right, chief?' Thaan asked him.

Soon it would be night again. Why did each day pass so quickly, each night last so long? He felt a knot of fear twist in his gut at the thought of the nightmares he knew would come, and that made his anger return. How could he tell his shieldman that he was afraid of the dark?

He spent the rest of the day at the shipyard, first inspecting the finished galleys, then losing himself in the rhythm of manual work on the new ships. As the sun set, sinking behind distant mountains, he took a turn beside Deinon at an oar, pulling for his ship anchored on the lake. The ache in his back muscles was almost pleasant.

'How long are we here, chief?' Deinon asked.

'Another week, maybe. Make sure Alazon has all the materials he needs, then it's back to the coast to check on the other shipyard.'

'Have mercy,' Thaan muttered behind them.

Mercy's for fools, thought Lykos, almost hearing his dead father whisper the words in his ear. 'This easy life not to your taste?' he asked.

'I'd rather be cracking heads and betting on the pits than this,' Thaan grumbled.

'Not much I can do about the pits, for now,' Lykos said. 'But the head cracking . . .' Something Fidele had said during their meeting had been bothering him all day, that's why he had spent the day with a mallet in his hand – it helped him think. They reached their ship, tied off the rowing boat and clambered up the ladder onto the deck. Most of the crew had been sleeping ashore, with strict orders not to spend time in Jerolin's inns. A few hands were still about though – there was always work that needed doing. Lykos looked about, studying each face. Then he saw who he was looking for.

'One of you fetch Jace, bring him down to my cabin,' he said with a nod, then turned and walked below decks without a look back.

It was not long before there was a knock at his cabin door and Deinon entered, Jace behind him. Thaan stayed in the hall and closed the door.

'Have a drink,' Lykos said, thrusting a cup of wine at Jace.

Jace took it, his smile all teeth and gums, and drank, though only a little. He had not been aboard long, only a ten-night, having earned his place at the oars at the last pit-fight Lykos had attended. Lykos liked him, liked his style – a focused, contained fury when he fought. He was lean, yet well-muscled. Scars latticed his arms and shoulders.

Probably only eighteen years old, maybe nineteen. He looked older, but that was usual for any that made it out of the pits.

'I wanted to share a drink with you, welcome you aboard. I do it with all the new lads.'

Jace relaxed slightly, just a suggestion in the set of his shoulders, his feet.

'Sit down,' Lykos said, more order than request. Jace's eyes flitted to the door and back. He sat, slowly, legs coiled beneath him. *Still wary, then.*

'How're you finding your new life?' Lykos asked.

'It's good, chief. Better'n the pits, for sure.'

Deinon moved out of Jace's view, stepping behind him.

'Aye. Life with the Vin Thalun is not the easiest – some might say the hardest – but the rewards . . .' He grinned, emptied his own cup of wine and placed it carefully on a table beside Jace. 'Stay alive long enough and who knows what you'll earn – silver, your own war-galley, women. Lots of women. Isn't that right, Deinon, even for someone as ugly as you, eh?'

'True enough, chief,' Deinon said with a wide grin.

Lykos stood before Jace, feeling his temper stir, flaring hot.

'All I ask is *loyalty.*'

With no warning, Jace erupted from his chair, headbutting Lykos in the gut. Lykos had been expecting it, but still the lad caught him. *Gods, but the pits make you fast,* he thought, even as he doubled over, fighting to draw a breath.

Jace was trying to step away, reaching for a knife at his belt, when Deinon's hand clutched his hair, yanked him backwards, the shield-man's other fist crashing into the boy's head, just above the ear. Jace staggered, though still managed to stay on his feet. Lykos headbutted him full in the face, felt cartilage break, crunching as blood spurted. Jace collapsed back into the chair, head lolling.

'Loyalty,' Lykos snarled, Jace's blood dripping from his face. 'I gave you a new life, but that wasn't good enough for you. Had to run to Fidele. Why?'

'I didn't do nothing,' Jace bubbled through his ruined face. 'Don't understand.'

'Don't lie to me,' Lykos hissed. 'Deinon.'

The shieldman grabbed one of Jace's wrists and clamped his hand to the table. In a blur Lykos drew his knife and slammed it into Jace's palm, pinning it to the wood beneath. Jace screamed, pain and terror mingled, eyes bulging.

'Why?' Lykos repeated, bending to stare into Jace's eyes. 'Speak the truth and the pain'll end.'

Jace just stared at him.

'All right then,' Lykos said, 'looks like you need a little more persuasion.' With a sigh he drew another knife from his boot, this one small, thin and sharp. He held it hovering over Jace's pinned hand and with a jerk cut one of the man's fingers off.

Jace screamed, shaking his head wildly. Deinon held him clamped in place.

'I can keep going like this all night,' Lykos said. 'There's more than fingers I could be cutting.'

'When I was taken,' Jace whispered, 'my family – mother, father, sister – all murdered, by you.'

'How old were you, boy?'

'F-fifteen.'

Lykos sighed, tutted. 'Shame you didn't learn your lesson.'

'Wha . . .?' Jace said, his face contorted with pain.

'That I control life and death for you.' Lykos nodded to Deinon, who still had a fist twisted in Jace's hair. He pulled the lad's head back and cut his throat.

'Take him out in the lake and sink him with something heavy,' Lykos said, stepping away from the blood pooling at his feet. He poured himself a cup of wine.

'Don't you want to let his body be found, show Fidele what happens to squealers?'

'No, wouldn't put it past that bitch to put me on trial for murder,' Lykos said.

Deinon chuckled, stooped and slung Jace's corpse over his shoulder, heading for the door.

Lykos sat in his chair and started drinking. It was full night now; the exhilaration of the conflict with Jace drained away. He was feeling weary – no, exhausted. Sleep would follow soon. He gulped more wine down, afraid.

'Father, who and what have I become?' he muttered, cocking his head to hear an answer. When no response came he shrugged and continued drinking. Eventually he dozed off, still sitting in his chair.

He woke screaming, eyes bulging. Thaan poked his head through the door.

'You all right, chief?'

'Wha . . . ? I. Yes,' Lykos mumbled, digging the heels of his palms into his eyes. *Making deals with a devil was sure to have a down side.* He reached automatically for his jug of wine. Only a few dregs were left but he slurped them back. 'Good news for you,' he said. 'There's a change of plan. We need to round up the Jehar and take them to Ardan, and – even better for you – after that we'll get to crack some heads. A lot of heads.'

'Ardan?' Thaan said.

'Aye, Thaan. Ardan. We've been summoned.'

CHAPTER EIGHT

EVNIS

Evnis absently plucked at the petal of a rose, let it drift onto the stones at his feet. 'Everything is turning to ash, Fain,' he whispered.

He was standing before a stone cairn, weak sunlight streaming across the walls of Dun Carreg into the courtyard. The sounds of his hold waking stirred about him. Dogs were barking in the kennels, children teasing them with scraps from the tower kitchen. The smell of baking bread and ham frying wafted about on the breeze. The sun had not risen long enough to burn the chill of night away and Evnis shivered, pulling his cloak tighter about him. He took a deep breath, an attempt to steady himself for the coming day, but no matter how he tried to calm himself, to focus on what he must do, all his swirling thoughts returned to one thing.

Vonn.

Where was his *son*?

They had argued, in the keep before the fortress fell, after he had told Vonn something of his plans. All Vonn had wanted to talk about was the girl from Havan, Bethan the drunkard's daughter. Evnis had told Vonn to put her out of his mind, to focus on what was important, but that had only made Vonn worse. He had stormed out into the night. And now he was gone, disappeared in the chaos of Dun Carreg's fall, before Evnis could talk to him and put things right.

Please, Fallen One, do not let him be dead. Evnis had spent most of a day searching, checking every corpse that had been piled in the streets, questioning survivors. Some had spoken of seeing Vonn with Edana and her handful of protectors.

He blew out a long breath. His son with Edana, with Brenin's daughter. In other circumstances the irony of it would have made him smile.

It was two nights since Dun Carreg had fallen, since Owain's boar of Narvon had replaced Brenin's wolf. He remembered little of his fight with Brenin: it had been a red haze, over a year's worth of pent-up rage and grief spilling out in a few moments. Until his knife had pierced Brenin's chest, anyway. He remembered that clearly enough, could never forget it; the brief resistance of cloth, skin and bone, then the hot pulse of blood, Brenin's strength fading so quickly, like a bird taking flight. There was a flutter of something in his gut. *Shame? Perhaps.* Certainly Fain, his gentle-hearted wife, would not have approved. But she was not here now, her corpse rotting beneath the cairn he was standing before. Brenin's choices had sealed her death. If Brenin had allowed him to leave Dun Carreg, to take Fain away, to the cauldron, things would have been different. Fain had deserved a blood-price. There was some kind of justice in the way things had turned out – Brenin dying by his hand.

'My lord.' A voice pierced his thoughts. Conall was limping towards him, a few of his warriors following.

'It is time,' Conall said.

Evnis nodded curtly, crushed the rose in his hand and scattered it over the cairn. He stalked through the grounds of his hold, past the kennels where Helfach's boy was feeding the hounds, through the wide gates. Conall and the other warriors settled about him, a tension amongst them all. They knew the stakes as well as he. The fortress may have fallen but it was far from safe, with many on both sides who would like Evnis dead. He glanced at the buildings either side, searching the shadows for assassins. *I have rolled the dice,* he thought. *No going back now.*

He glanced at Conall, who still walked with a limp. The warrior had fallen from the wall above Stonegate and had only survived because the crush of those fighting about the gates had broken his fall.

The warrior was all confidence and swagger, quick to laugh and quick to anger. Beyond the arrogance there was a keen intelligence. Conall saw much. It had been a wise choice, winning him over, though he had needed a little help. He was learning the power of the earth, extracting secrets from the book he had discovered in the tunnels beneath the fortress. There were ways to influence a man, even control him. He felt like a novice, struggling in the dark, but he had learned enough to add an edge of power, of persuasion to his voice, especially when the target's will was wavering. And so he had won Conall's loyalty.

'You have no regrets leaving your brother, Halion, opposing him?'

Conall looked surprised and his mouth twisted, a haunted look sweeping his face. 'No. I am glad to be out from under his shadow. He was turning from me, in deeds if not in words. It was clear he'd chosen Brenin and flattery over me.' He grimaced. 'We all live with the consequences of our choices, eh?'

'That we do,' Evnis muttered, glancing at an old scar on the palm of his hand, a reminder of a glade in the Darkwood, of a pact made years ago to Asroth, his master, to whom he had pledged his life, his soul. And Asroth had told him to aid Nathair, of that he was certain. So aid the young King of Tenebral he would. And if somehow that turned out to his benefit, then all the better.

Figures burst from an alleyway and Conall half drew his sword, but they were only children, running and laughing as they goaded a skinny hound with a bone.

'Jumping at shadows,' Evnis said.

'Well, you're not the most popular man in the fortress right now. Most of Dun Carreg must want you dead,' Conall said, glaring at the children.

'I'm more concerned over the quality of my enemies than their quantity,' Evnis murmured, thinking of Owain.

'I've heard something similar, though usually from the ladies.'

Evnis snorted, almost smiled. Laughter rippled through the warriors behind him.

'Enemies in high places. I've had that problem myself,' Conall said.

'Really? And what did you do?'

'I ran away.'

'I see.' He regarded Conall silently, wondering about his new shieldman's hidden past. 'Perhaps I have a less drastic remedy.' *Friends in high places. Or in this case friend. Nathair.* The young King had come to him asking questions about the Benothi, Dun Carreg's ancient giant masters and their treasures, and that was a subject that

Evnis knew much about, possibly even more than old Heb or Brina. Evnis had hinted at his knowledge, given snippets of information, whispered promises of more, and it was those promises that he hoped would keep him alive until Rhin arrived. Nathair would protect him, at least while it was in his interest to do so. Or so Evnis hoped. Owain was unpredictable. It had been a gamble, helping the King of Narvon gain entrance to the fortress, but Nathair had asked him for help, and so he had given it. The act of opening Stonegate had won much favour with Owain, but Evnis was not sure how much the act of slaying a king had compromised that favour. Nobody liked that, especially not another king.

'Time will be the judge,' he muttered.

'Aye. It usually is,' Conall replied.

The rest of their journey passed in silence. Evnis hardly spared a glance at the charred pile of ash that marked all that was left of Dun Carreg's fallen defenders, the stench of their burning still lingering in the air. He swept into the keep and marched through it into the corridors beyond until he reached Nathair's chambers.

One of the black-clad warriors that he had spirited into the fortress to such devastating effect was standing guard. The man ushered him into the chamber but blocked Conall as he made to follow.

'Only you,' the man said to Evnis.

Evnis nodded to Conall and those behind him as the guard closed the door.

Nathair sat within, sipping a cup of wine. His bodyguard, Sumur, was standing beside an unshuttered window, sword hilt jutting over his shoulder. A handful of Nathair's eagle-guard were lounging at a table in the far end of the chamber, gathered about a half-eaten round of cheese and a leg of pork. They eyed Evnis suspiciously, then went back to their food. Evnis stared at them, remembering their comrades in the keep the night Dun Carreg fell, arrayed about him and Brenin and Nathair in a wall of shields. They were all dead now, most of them cut down by Gar, the crippled stablemaster. That night had left more than one mystery in his mind that begged to be solved.

'Welcome, Evnis,' the King of Tenebral said, standing and gripping Evnis' wrist. 'Thank you for coming so promptly. Are you hungry? Thirsty?' He gestured to the food and wine.

'I have already broken my fast. Though perhaps some wine.'

'Of course.' Nathair filled a cup for him. 'I was hoping that you might help me.'

'If I may be of service, my lord.'

'I am certain that you can. When I came here it was as part of a bigger journey: I planned to travel north. I still do. The issue is when to leave. Much has happened here that I think has bearing on my alliance, on the future, but the situation here is fluid, prone to change. Dramatically. Would you agree?'

'Your summary is quite correct, to my mind,' Evnis said.

'I am torn, Evnis. My errand in the north is pressing, but I feel that perhaps I should linger here a while longer, as these events play out. To ensure that the results are favourable to me and my alliance.'

'Most prudent, my lord.' *This is a man who thinks before he speaks. Where is he leading this conversation?*

'You are probably wondering why I am telling you this.'

Evnis smiled and dipped his head in acknowledgement.

'I believe that you are pivotal to this situation. And certain that you know more than you have told me.'

'Do any of us tell all that we know, my lord?' Evnis replied. 'After all, knowledge is power.' *This is dangerous.*

'Wise words,' Nathair said with a smile, 'and words that I have heard before. But let me be frank with you. We are both in a position to help each other. I am in a strange land, surrounded by war, a history guiding it that is unfamiliar to me. I need to make decisions, but I lack the knowledge to be confident that I am choosing the right course. You are familiar with the politics of this realm, this conflict, well placed to see much. I need that knowledge. But you are surrounded by enemies – Owain, the man that took your own brother's head, rules here, so you need a friend, someone in power who has some influence. You need me.' Nathair took a deep breath, fixing Evnis with intense blue eyes. 'Tell me, Evnis, what is your heart's desire?'

Evnis blinked, thrown by the question, the sudden change of direction. 'I . . .' *What is happening here? Be careful.* Nathair's eyes pinned him, became the whole world. *Is he bewitching me? Using the earth power?*

'To find my son,' he heard himself say, surprised to hear the tremor in his voice.

'Yes. Escaped with Edana, or so rumours are saying.' Nathair waved a hand. 'I am not completely without information, even here. I could help you find him. I look after those that serve me.'

'Serve you?'

'Yes. I am looking for men: powerful men, brave enough to take risks, brave enough to follow me into a new order, a new world. I think that you are such a man. Follow me and you will gain more than you can imagine. But in return I must have your loyalty. Unquestioning, unfailing.'

I serve you already, Evnis thought. He opened his mouth to speak but then froze, pinned by Nathair's unblinking stare. There was something in Nathair's words that stirred his blood, that would have made him want to follow this man, to believe in a cause again, even if Asroth had not already commanded it. *Your only cause is yourself*, a voice whispered in his mind. 'I will serve you, if I can,' he said.

'Good. That is very good.' Nathair grinned, refilled their cups of wine and together they drank.

'Now, tell me,' Nathair said. 'Does Rhin play a part in this business between Owain and Brenin?'

'Yes. She manipulated this war,' Evnis said. *How much to tell? That is the question. Rhin will not look kindly on me if she thinks I have betrayed her.* He returned Nathair's unflinching gaze and made a decision. 'Rhin tricked Owain into marching against Brenin, her design was that they would weaken one another. She will move against Owain soon. She is the real power now in the west – Brenin was her greatest rival, but now that he is gone Owain cannot match her – he does not have the strength of will nor the wit to outmanoeuvre her. Brenin was the only one who stood that chance. And King Eremon of Domhain is too old, uninterested in affairs beyond his borders. Before long she will rule all the realms of the west.'

'She was always the one to watch,' Nathair murmured. 'A sharp tongue, a sharper mind.'

'Indeed.'

'And what is your relationship with her, Evnis?'

Lovers, once. Conspirators, always. 'We have communicated, in the past, helped one another in small matters.'

'I see.' Nathair paced to the open window, sharing a look with Sumur. 'I would like to communicate with her, too. Can you arrange that?'

'I think so.'

'Excellent.'

Sumur whispered something, too low for Evnis to hear.

'There is another matter that I am interested in. The night Dun Carreg fell, there was a boy in the keep. With a wolven . . .'

'Yes. Corban.'

'You know him, then?'

'Not really. I have had some dealings with him. An insolent, disobedient child.'

'His kin?'

'Thannon, his da, was slain in the great hall. His mother cannot be found, is thought to have escaped along with him and Edana. His sister, though, she is still here.'

'What of Gar,' Sumur interrupted, his voice guttural, coarse. 'What is his relationship to the boy?'

Evnis remembered Sumur and Gar fighting in the keep, swords a blur, with such skill as he had never seen before. Hadn't Gar used a blade similar to the one Sumur had strapped across his back. *This mystery deepens.*

'Gar was Brenin's stablemaster. He has always been close to the boy and his family. I am not sure why – they were living here long before I came to Dun Carreg. I will see what I can find out about them.'

'Yes, do. His sister,' Nathair said, 'I would speak with her. Soon.'

'I will arrange it.'

'Good.' Nathair poured himself some more wine, tugging at something on a chain about his neck – was it a huge *tooth*? 'One last thing, for now. The errand in the north that I mentioned. It is to find something. You recall I have spoken of the Benothi giants.'

'Yes.'

'It is my belief that they have something in their possession that I need. A cauldron, I have been told. One of the Seven Treasures.'

Evnis felt the blood drain from his face and coughed to hide his surprise. The cauldron – how he had longed to see it for himself, to take Fain to it, while she still had time, to call on its powers. To save her.

'I have heard of it,' he said.

'Really?' Nathair stared at him, eyes hard now, all warmth stripped from them. 'What, exactly, have you heard?'

Roll the dice, Evnis thought. 'That it is an artefact of great power.' He paused, swallowed. 'I know where it is.'

'Where?'

'To the north, in Benoth. In the fortress of Murias.'

Nathair slammed a fist into his palm. 'Calidus was right,' he said, then focused back on Evnis. 'How do you know this?'

'I have had dealings with the Benothi, on occasion.' *Well, one of them.*

Nathair's expression changed, became thoughtful. 'You are of more value than I guessed.' He patted Evnis' shoulder.

There was a knock at the door, the Jehar guard peered in. 'Owain has sent a messenger. He is in the great hall and would speak with you.'

'Of course,' Nathair said. 'We shall speak more, and soon, Evnis. For now, though, accompany me.'

Nathair and his entourage passed through high-roofed corridors, Evnis and his shieldmen following behind. Their numbers grew as more of the Jehar appeared, silently joining them from side corridors as they moved towards the great hall.

Owain was standing by one of the fire-pits, a dark-haired, sharp-featured man. He looked haggard, drawn. *You have grasped beyond your reach*, Evnis thought. Owain was in deep conversation with a mud-splattered warrior, a handful of red-cloaked shieldmen hovering about them.

'Greetings, Nathair,' the King of Narvon said, his eyes taking in Nathair's followers. He frowned when he saw Evnis.

'Well met.' Nathair smiled broadly. 'How goes your campaign?'

'It goes well,' Owain said. 'I have just received news of Dun Maen. Its strength was broken here when Dalgar fell and his war-band was scattered. Dun Maen's walls were filled with little more than old men, women and their bairns.'

'So Ardan is yours,' Nathair said.

'It would seem so.' Owain sighed. 'There are still skirmishes between here and the western marshes, but of little consequence, I think.'

'You have succeeded in your task, then.'

'Aye, but there is little joy in it. Uthan is still dead.' He grimaced. 'All that was best in me seemed to live in him, and now he is gone.'

'But at least your son is avenged.'

'Not quite. Edana still lives.' Owain looked up, his mouth a straight line. 'I will not rest while she draws breath. Brenin's stain will be wiped from the earth.'

'Is there any sign of her, any clue as to where she has fled?'

Owain shrugged. 'No, none. I cannot even discover how she escaped the fortress. She could still be here, in hiding.'

'I doubt that,' Evnis said. 'I have searched Dun Carreg stone by stone for them.'

Owain considered Evnis. 'There must be other ways out of this fortress, other than Stonegate. How did you sneak these warriors in?' He gestured to the Jehar spread about Nathair.

Of course, the tunnels. The thought hit Evnis like a blacksmith's hammer. *They must have escaped by the tunnels. Maybe even still be down there.* 'There are many unguarded portions of the wall, especially on the north side,' he said to Owain, concentrating on keeping his face calm, blank. 'Brenin was too sure of his defences, but a strong rope and strong arms were all that was needed. Maybe Edana left by the same means.' Nathair looked at him, but said nothing.

'Perhaps,' Owain muttered, 'though I find the word of someone who would betray his own king hard to accept.'

'Evnis has given us great aid,' Nathair said, taking a step closer to Evnis. 'Without him you would still be camped beyond Stonegate.'

'Even so . . .' Owain scowled at Evnis.

He looked down at the flagstone floor. *Is my Vonn hiding in the tunnels beneath my feet . . .*

He shook his head, with an effort concentrated on Owain's words.

'On your own head be it if you choose to favour him,' the King of Narvon was saying, 'but keep a close eye on him. Once a betrayer . . .'

Evnis felt a surge of anger, with effort pushed it down and painted a smile on his face. *Owain is not long for this earth*, he told himself. *The trick is to outlive him – that will be revenge enough. Rhin is coming, and then his head shall be parted from his shoulders.*

'And what of your plans, Nathair?' Owain asked. 'Will you be staying or going?'

'I will stay a little while longer. I have summoned men to me here, my counsellors. I must speak with them before I depart.'

'As you wish.'

'I have a request, though. An unusual one.'

'If it is in my power.'

'I have something on my ship in the bay, something rare, special to me.'

'What is it? Treasure that needs guarding?'

'In a way. It is a draig, not yet full grown. It needs to come ashore, to be stabled, fed.'

'A draig. Why . . . ?' Owain trailed off.

'It is an experiment of mine –' Nathair smiled – 'and I would be grateful of your assistance, your cooperation.'

'Of course.' Owain frowned, then tried to smile. 'You have helped me more than I can repay. Stables shall be prepared, an auroch slaughtered.'

'My thanks.'

The clatter of hooves on stone drifted in from the courtyard, there was the scuff of booted feet running, and a man burst into the hall. He hurried to Owain and fell to one knee before him.

'Rise, man,' Owain said. 'What news? Is Edana caught?'

'No, my lord.' The man gulped a deep lung-full of air. 'Dire news from Narvon. Rhin has invaded. It is overrun, Uthandun is fallen.'

CHAPTER NINE

CORBAN

Corban shifted uncomfortably; a tree root was digging into his back. He'd slept little, if at all, and now a raindrop dripped onto his nose.

'Wonderful,' he muttered, pulling his cloak over his head. He just wanted to sleep, it was preferable to getting up, having to face people, having to face his mam and Gar.

Their words from the night before were still spinning around his head. They had shaken him, stirred both anger and guilt. The things they had told him; *madness, surely, born out of grief and exhaustion. And they have asked me to leave.* Nothing else could have felt so wrong – to leave this small band of survivors. And so he had said no. Never had he said *no* to his mam or Gar – many times in his head, or muttered quietly after a reprimand – but never to their faces. And then had come the guilt. This was the worst moment in the world to have a conflict with his mam, when they were both grieving the loss of his da and Cywen. But what they asked was so unreasonable. And then anger had followed.

How can they put me in such a position? He wished their conversation had never happened. And so his night had passed, racked with anger or guilt, along with a measure of self-pity. Now, though, with the coming of dawn, he just felt alone. No one was who he thought they were. His mam and Gar felt like strangers.

Something tapped his shoulder.

He poked his head out from beneath his cloak, squinting up at a dark form silhouetted by the grey light of dawn. It was Gar.

'Come, lad,' the stablemaster whispered, prodding him with something.

'Come where?'

'Training.'

'Wha . . . ?' Corban said. 'Are you joking?'

'You still have much to learn,' Gar said with a shrug. 'Come on, there is not much time before we have to get back on that boat.'

He climbed upright, winced at the stiffness in his limbs and grimaced at the stablemaster. 'I don't want to do this,' he muttered. 'You and mam . . .' He could not find the words to express how he felt, did not know where to start.

'This way,' Gar said, walking away. With a scowl, Corban followed; Storm uncurled and padded after them.

Marrock was standing guard, the shadow of his body merging with the tree he was leaning against. He looked inquisitively at Gar and Corban.

Gar stopped beside the stream. 'Give me your sword,' he said, then wrapped Corban's blade with cloth, tied it tight and passed it back.

Without a word, Gar slid into the sword dance, his curved sword wrapped like Corban's.

Sullenly Corban watched him, a host of questions and accusations swirling in his mind. There were so many things that he wanted to ask Gar about, but they were all linked to last night's conversation, and he had set his will to avoiding that subject at all costs. Gar paused, staring at him. 'Don't think; do. Questions, talking later, but this will help.' He resumed his fluid movements.

Corban sighed and raised his sword, stepping into *stooping falcon*, the first position of the sword dance. Skin and muscles around the wound on his back stretched and pulled, but he held the pose, then moved smoothly into the next stance. Gar was right, soon Corban felt his mind calming, his thoughts draining away as he became lost in the rhythm of the dance.

Sunlight was dappling the ground and sparkling on the stream when he finished. Sweat dripped from his nose and the wound on his back pulsed dully. Gar faced him and raised his sword. Corban shrugged and they began to spar, and slowly Corban became aware of movement around him. A quick glance showed him half a dozen figures from the camp watching them, but also earned him a crack to the ribs from Gar.

'Enough,' the stablemaster declared.

Gar stripped the cloth from his and Corban's swords, then began walking back to the camp, ignoring their audience. In no mood for conversation, Corban followed him, purposely avoiding Brina's stare.

Halion drew level with them and grasped Gar's arm, halting him. 'I need to talk to you,' he said to Gar. The stablemaster stopped, drawing a deep breath.

'You fight differently,' Halion said. 'I have travelled much of the west and seen nothing like your style.'

Gar just stared at Halion, expressionless.

'Until the night Dun Carreg fell. The man you fought, Sumur. Marrock tells me there were many like him in the battle, that they opened Stonegate for Owain. You fought like this Sumur, spoke with him. You knew him?'

Gar's gaze flicked to Corban and back. 'Yes.'

'Tell me of him, of yourself. Who are you, where are you from?'

'I have heard others ask the same questions of you, yet you have held your silence. My past is my own,' Gar said.

'True enough, my business is my own, and not a subject for gossip. But things are different now, and so I have spoken of my past. Because it was necessary. Now you know who I am, where I am from, who my father is. It is necessary to hear these things from you. Do you know this Sumur?'

Gar closed his eyes and blew out a long breath. 'I knew him, many years ago. Corban will tell you more, soon.'

Corban raised an eyebrow at that.

'That is not good enough. I am Edana's sword and shield, and you know more about her enemies than anyone else here – seemed almost to be one of them – I must understand all that goes on, for Edana's sake. Are you a danger to her?'

Gar sighed. 'No, I am no danger to the princess. You saw that I fought Sumur – that must answer your fears. I would tell you more, but Corban should hear these things first, and until he has I will speak no more of it, with you or any other.'

Halion still gripped Gar's arm. He held the stablemaster's gaze for long moments then let his hand drop. 'I will wait, but we will have this conversation again. Soon.'

Gar nodded and strode away.

'What's this all about, Corban?' Halion asked.

Corban shrugged.

'Well, whatever he has to say to you, let him say it.'

With a grunt Corban followed Gar back to the camp, where everyone was making ready to leave. Amidst it all Edana sat huddled against a tree. Brina returned and set to helping Gwenith prepare some food – cold venison that still tasted good.

Corban's mam tried to catch his eye but he looked away, immediately experiencing a rush of guilt. *She's lost her husband. My da . . .*

But somehow his feet would not take him over to her.

In no time they were all clambering back onto the boat. Mordwyr and Dath set the sail to catch the wind, guiding them out of the cove they had sheltered in, and soon they were scudding along the coast. The sky was a clear, sharp blue, wave tips glistening in the sun. Corban burrowed into the pile of nets towards the rear of the boat, Storm curling beside him, her nose twitching at the scent of fish.

Days passed like this, the boat hugging the coast, moving ever further from Dun Carreg, from home. Nights were spent huddled around small fires, when they dared, eating whatever Marrock and Camlin could provide. Storm was usually more successful in the hunting. Corban maintained his silence with his mam and Gar, though his mam tried more than once to pull him away from the small company. He always refused, though he was starting to hate himself for it. But no matter how he thought of things, as soon as the suggestion of leaving their small band of friends rose in his mind, he felt an instant surge of anger. Everything else had been taken from him. He would cling to this last remnant of home like a drowning man in a stormy sea.

Every morning Gar would prod him awake and work through the sword dance with him, but the stablemaster did not try to drag him into conversation. His look was enough. It said, *We will talk, whether sooner or later*, as patient as a hovering hawk.

On the fifth day after Dun Carreg's fall Corban was sitting in his customary position on the fisher-boat, Storm beside him. Dath was a half-visible figure climbing on the mast up above. Farrell walked unsteadily towards him, swaying as the boat rose and fell.

'Thank your wolven for me,' Farrell said as he settled into the nets beside Corban.

'For what?'

'Food to break our fast with this morning, and dinner last night. I don't like being hungry. Makes me angry.'

'Well we wouldn't want that. Not while you've got that hammer strapped to your back, anyway.'

Farrell chuckled, patting Thannon's hammer-head which poked over his shoulder.

Corban thought of his da, lying in the keep at Dun Carreg, Buddai curled beside him. He felt a stab of guilt, that he could be making jests so soon after his da's death. He shook his head. 'How'd you get so big, anyway?' he asked, glancing at Anwarth, Farrell's da. He was a short man, the absolute opposite of Farrell, although they shared something in their features, the angle of their jaws, eyes set beneath heavy brows.

'You haven't seen my mam, then,' Farrell said. 'She always said I got my big bones from her. Da must like big women . . .'

Corban smiled, feeling some of the tension in his shoulders begin to lift. It was good, somehow, just to sit and talk with a friend.

'Hope she's all right,' Farrell muttered, his face creasing. 'Mind you, she can look after herself. Me and da can vouch for that.' He tried to smile, but wasn't completely successful. 'Saw you training, this morning.'

Corban nodded.

'It was quite something. Never seen anything like it.'

'Gar's been training me a while now. About two years.'

'Explains why you're so good with a sword, then. I couldn't believe it when you beat Rafe.'

Corban shrugged. 'I don't know where Gar learned all that stuff, though. Always thought it was from Helveth . . .' He trailed off. As it turned out Gar wasn't from Helveth, after all. Turned out most of what he thought about his past was wrong, lies piled on top of one another.

Time passed, the boat rising and falling rhythmically. Corban felt exhausted, worn out by his churning emotions as much as the events of the last few days. Gwenith and Gar sat together. His mam's eyes were red rimmed and sunken, her face pale and drawn. Storm nuzzled his palm and he absently stroked her head. The things his mam had said about him swirled in his mind like flotsam in a whirlpool, different parts bobbing to the surface. Like what she had said about him being hunted – by *Asroth* – how could that be? He had never given much thought to Asroth or Elyon before, was not even sure if he believed them to be real, and so far had not particularly cared. Elyon, the maker of all, and Asroth, his great enemy, leading his host of the Fallen. Corban knew the tales well enough, of Asroth's corruption of the first giants and men, the War of Treasures that followed, and then the Scourging. Until now he'd thought they were little more than faery stories told to keep children in their cots at night. He looked about, at his companions littered around the boat. Beyond the railings he caught a glimpse of the coastline, a dark smudge of dense trees and cliffs. Lifting his hand in front of his face, he stared at his fingers, saw black dirt making patterns in the creases of his skin, the swirling design of his fingerprints. *Someone or something must have made all of this, I suppose*, he thought. *But Asroth, hunting me . . . ?*

He shook his head.

Brina sat down beside him. Farrell glanced at the healer, then looked away. No matter how the recent events had affected everyone, Brina still had a reputation. Corban weathered her silent stare as long as he could.

'Where's Craf?' he asked, more to break the silence than anything else.

'There,' she said with a nod.

Craf was sitting on the prow of the ship, staring straight ahead like some tattered figurehead.

'I wanted to ask you something,' Corban muttered.

'There's a surprise,' Brina snorted. 'All right then, but this time I will be asking a few questions of you, too. Perhaps we can do a trade.'

'What could I possibly know that would interest you?'

'A trade – yes or no?'

'Perhaps.' Corban eyed her suspiciously. 'Let's hear each other's questions first, then decide.'

Brina scowled. 'Well?' she prompted.

'The night we fled Dun Carreg, on the way to the tunnels. You and Heb . . .' He cleared his throat. 'That mist. Did you . . . ?'

'Ah, a good question.' She almost smiled at him. 'My question, then: Gar.'

Corban sighed. He knew it would have to be about the stable-master. 'Go on.'

'He came to Dun Carreg when you and Cywen were bairns?'

Hearing Cywen's name made something twist in his stomach. He nodded.

'I'd like to know where he came by that curved sword of his, and where he learned how to use it. I'd like to know how he was on speaking terms with the King of Tenebral's first-sword. And most of all, I'd like to know why he's so interested in *you*.' She jabbed his chest with a finger.

'That's a lot of questions. I only asked you one,' Corban pointed out.

'Mine are linked,' Brina retorted.

Corban held a hand up. 'Believe me, they are all questions that I'd like to hear the answers to, myself.'

'You don't know, then?'

'No, though I wish I did.'

'Well, go and ask him,' she said. 'Then you can come back and tell me.'

'No,' he snapped, more harshly than he'd intended. 'It's complicated . . .'

She stared at him, then rose with a grunt. 'When you've uncomplicated it, come and talk to me. I'll tell you about the mist.' She walked away.

Highsun had come and gone. Corban was standing by the rail, staring at nothing. He could just make out the coast: a blur of tree and rock, here and there lines of smoke climbing into the sky, marking villages and homesteads. Mordwyr and Dath had taken the boat as far out to sea as possible to avoid being seen from land, and so far Corban had only spied one other vessel on the water, not much more than a black dot in the distance.

There was a cry from the front. Marrock was pointing at something ahead. Halion made his way forward, others following. He spoke briefly with Marrock and then called for Mordwyr. The fisherman set Dath on the steering oar and made his way to the prow.

He doesn't look too good, thought Corban as Mordwyr passed him. The man was pale, a sheen of sweat on his face. Corban followed him, leaning over the rail to look ahead when he could go no further. In the distance, directly in front of them, was a cluster of black dots. Boats. They trailed off to a thin line that led almost back to the coast.

'What is that?' he heard Halion ask Mordwyr.

Mordwyr stared silently, squinting into the distance. 'Boats,' he muttered. 'Lots of them.'

'I can see that,' Halion snapped. 'I mean, what are they doing? Why are they there?'

Even as the two men spoke, Corban could make out the sight more easily as they sped forwards. The boats were of different shapes and sizes, but most appeared to be fisher-boats similar to the one they were on. Corban counted at least thirty. They were heading out into open sea, their line stretching back to the coast, where a fair-sized village lay nestled along the shore.

'I don't know,' Mordwyr murmured, 'but they look to be heading to Ardan. More of Owain's handiwork?'

'This is Cambren,' Marrock said. 'Rhin rules here.'

'Whatever is going on, we need to find the coast. Now. And pray to Elyon that we have not already been spotted,' Mordwyr said, bursting into motion. Nimbly he scrambled back down the boat, yelling instructions to Dath.

Mordwyr took over the steering oar and Dath leaped to the sail, baffling Corban with the speed that he pulled on ropes, the sail abruptly sagging, emptying of wind. Slowly, the fisher-boat turned, losing the rhythm it had maintained. The sea suddenly felt more powerful beneath them, more dangerous. Corban grabbed onto the rail as they all lurched upwards, caught in the swell of a wave. Spray burst over the side.

Then Dath was pulling at the ropes again, darting around the base of the mast, and the sail began to fill. Within moments it was billowing, straining, and soon the boat was cutting towards the coast, a wake of white foam spreading behind them.

Mordwyr guided them onto a shingle beach flanked by a grassy ridge, hidden from sight from the village ahead by a curve in the land. Quickly they disembarked. Corban's heart pounded as they scrambled up the beach, the crunch of shingle sounding deafening under their feet. They passed under a treeline, entering a wood of ash and sycamore. 'We'll have to stay here for now,' Halion said. 'Set up camp in these woods and wait until our path is clear. No fires,' he added. He set a guard on the ridge to watch over the boat and check that no vessels came searching for them. 'Camlin, take some hands with you and make sure we're not too close to any unfriendly eyes or ears,' Halion said with a wave at the thick woodland.

'Aye, chief,' the woodsman said. 'Dath, bring your bow. And Corban, might need your wolven's nose.'

They set off into the woods. Corban saw Dath glance at his da. The fisherman was sitting against a tree, his head in his hands. His shoulders were trembling. Dath hovered, then Vonn sat down beside Mordwyr. Dath shook his head and made after Camlin.

As they made their way into denser woodland Corban heard footsteps following and turned to see Gar behind him. 'What're you doing?' he said.

'Watching your back.'

'I don't want you to. I'm not a *bairn*.'

'Ban, don't waste your breath. I'm coming, whether you're happy about it or not. You'd have to be bind me hand and foot to stop me.'

Camlin looked at Gar and shrugged. 'I'm not complaining,' the woodsman said. 'I saw you the other night; you an' that sword would be handy if we walk into any bother.'

Corban said nothing more and followed Camlin into the woods.

They made their way in silence, Storm shadowing them, rustling through the undergrowth. The woodland was dense with flowering bluebell and ramsons, the strong scent of the white flowers filling the air as they passed through it. Before long the woodland changed, opening into deep-shaded beech, and soon after they were standing on the edge of a rolling meadow, steep hills in the distance. The village that the fleet of fisher-boats had set sail from was visible, smokehouses lining the coast, buildings of thatch further back, spread along the banks of a river. Clustered beyond them the land was filled with tents, paddocks and lots of men. A road stretched into the distance, skirting the river. It was dotted with more men on horseback.

Camlin sucked his teeth and spat.

'What's going on?' Dath whispered.

'Unless I'm mistaken, that looks like a warband,' Camlin muttered. 'What it's doing here, though . . .'

As they stood there staring, the drum of hooves reached their ears. Horsemen crested a rise in the meadow before them, five or six, spread in a line, heading their way. Sunlight glinted on coats of mail and spear-tips. Camlin swore.

'Back into the trees,' he snapped. 'And, Dath, best you string your bow.'

CHAPTER TEN

TUKUL

Tukul blinked sweat from his eyes, gritted his teeth as he held his pose in the sword dance and focused on keeping the tip of his practice sword perfectly still. His thighs and shoulders were burning, trembling with the effort.

When did this start getting harder? he wondered. *Fifty-eight summers is not so old.* He concentrated on keeping his breathing even and smooth. Then, as if responding to some unheard bell, he relaxed. He rolled his shoulders and looked about at the others with whom he stood in rank – about three score men and women – all sheened with sweat. *We are all older now*, he grimaced, *though not too old, I hope.* 'Soon,' he whispered, both a promise and a prayer.

They were gathered in a courtyard built between the roots of a great tree that towered high above them, its branches arcing, blotting out the sun, its trunk wider that any keep he had ever seen.

Drassil.

The fabled city of Forn Forest, built by giants about and beneath the roots of the Great Tree: lost, hidden for countless generations until he had come here with his band of warriors. Five score they had numbered. They were fewer now, some taken by sickness, others by Forn's predators. One they had parted with during their travels. And patiently they had waited.

Tukul swatted sweat from his nose. 'Or maybe not so patiently,' he muttered with a scowl.

People were beginning to spar now, the *clack-clack* of their practice blades growing about him. He looked for someone to try himself against, then heard running footsteps.

A figure burst into the courtyard – Enkara, black hair streaked with silver and tied at her nape, her sword hilt arching over one shoulder. She searched the courtyard, eyes fixing on him.

'Someone comes,' she called, a tremor in her voice.

Everyone froze.

Without a word, Tukul left the courtyard, stooping to collect his curved sword. Slinging its harness over his shoulder, he strode purposefully towards the outer wall.

They had been here over fourteen years, and in that time they had made Drassil habitable. More than that, they had made it defendable again, shearing vines from walls, repairing stonework, mapping the labyrinthine catacombs that burrowed for leagues beneath his feet. He grimaced as he passed a handful of cairns, eyes drawn to where his Daria was buried.

All those who had been in the courtyard followed silently behind him, Enkara half running to keep up with his long strides. He leaped up the steps on the outer wall two at a time, stood above the gateway and looked out into Forn.

A strip of land a hundred paces deep had been cleared beyond the wall, to keep the encroaching forest at bay. Into this clearing strode a figure, cloaked and hooded, a sword at its hip.

The figure stopped, pushed his hood back and looked up at the walls.

Tukul squinted, then smiled. 'Open the gates,' he cried as he made his way through the crowd gathered behind him and ran through the gates. He reached the figure, gripped his wrist and pulled him into an embrace.

'It is good to see you, Meical,' he whispered, looking up at the dark-haired man.

'And you, old friend.'

Soon they stood inside the walls of Drassil, every last man and woman gathered about them.

'You have worked hard here,' Meical said, looking about. 'Accomplished much.'

'I should hope so.' Tukul snorted. 'We have had long enough.' He stared at Meical, realizing that the man looked no different from the last time he had seen him – his hair still jet black, only the faintest of lines around his eyes. He still looked as if he had been through a war, though, and was marked by his battles. *Wounded inside as much as out.* Silver scars raked one side of Meical's face.

'Why are you here?' Tukul asked.

'I have grim tidings. Aquilus is dead.'

'What? No.' *Aquilus was important, had a part to play.* 'What of the child?' Tukul gasped.

'He is a child no longer,' Meical said, his scars creasing as he smiled. 'He is well. Very well, the last I saw him.'

'You have *seen* him? How long ago?'

'Almost a year, now. I left him and came in search of you. This place is not the easiest to find.'

'Hah,' Tukul barked a laugh. 'That I know. And . . . my son? You have seen my son?'

'Yes. He has grown into a fine man. He has served you well, brought you honour.'

Tukul grinned and blinked away tears.

'There is more that I have come to tell,' Meical said. He drew in a deep breath, blew it out slowly. 'Things are changing, moving quicker, in different ways from how I ever imagined. There is war to the south, rumours of war in the west. Asroth is moving. I think there should be a change of plan.'

Tukul felt a fist clench in his gut, a sharp bolt of excitement after so many years of waiting, preparing.

'Tell me, how many men would be enough to keep the spear safe?'

Tukul smiled.

'Ten.'

Meical nodded to himself, as if coming to a silent decision. 'Leave ten men here, then, but the rest of you – you should not stay. Instead of waiting for the Seren Disglair to come to you, you should go to him. He is in danger. He needs you.'

'Go to him,' Tukul repeated, feeling his blood surge in his veins. A grin spread across his face. 'Hah, did you hear?' he cried, turning a full circle to take in all those about him.

'What think you, old friend?' Meical said. 'Do you agree?'

'*Agree?* Yes, we agree,' he shouted, as all around him his people drew their swords and brandished their curved blades at the sky with ululations. 'Make ready,' he cried, 'for on the morrow we march to the Seren Disglair.'

CHAPTER ELEVEN

CYWEN

Cywen took aim, the tip of her knife blade tickling her back, then threw. With a satisfying thud the knife sank into her target, a battered post in the garden. Without taking her eyes from it, she drew another blade from the belt at her waist, aimed and threw. Then she did it again. And again.

When her belt was empty she strode to the post and started pulling the knives free, sliding them back into the pockets in her belt. Twenty in total. After the night Dun Carreg had fallen she'd vowed to never run out of knives again. These she had found in a barrel by the kitchen door, rusted and notched, part of her da's to-do pile. All the best knives, usually kept in a drawer in her mam's room, were gone. Taken by her mam, she supposed.

Her mam. She still could not even think of her mam without feeling her guts twist. She was not dead, of that she was certain, she'd searched the fortress from one end to another, made herself look at the face of every corpse piled within the walls. Her mam, Corban, Gar – they were not there. Rumours swept the fortress about Edana: she was in hiding, had fled west, south, north. One thing was certain. She had not died in the battle, and people had whispered of Corban being seen with her during the conflict.

They are alive, and together, I am sure of it. She leaned her head against the knife post, felt splinters of wood scratch her nose. Buddai whined, curled in the shade beneath an apple tree. She felt a tear run down her cheek, tasted salt as it reached her lips.

Four nights had passed since she had woken in the courtyard before Stonegate, each one a blur of tears and loneliness, of restless, dream-filled misery. The first night she had tried sleeping in her bed, but had woken up cuddling tight to Buddai in front of the kitchen fire. After that she had just settled there with the hound every night. Somehow it helped, just a little. *Why did they leave me? They had no choice*, she thought instantly, *probably thought me dead*. But it still hurt, the sense of abandonment lurking beneath all else, always there. Then into her pain had come a ray of hope. Yesterday she had finished scouring every hand-span of the fortress, her path taking her past the well shaft. In a rush she had remembered the tunnels – what if her kin were hiding in them, waiting for her. The thought had caused a stab of longing so intense that she physically stumbled. It could be true – there was no explanation of how so many had escaped, and Corban knew of the tunnels. Perhaps they were down there now, waiting. Just the thought had almost set her feet running, but there were red-cloaks everywhere, most with the same goal in mind as hers – finding the escapees. She had to wait for a better time to go searching for them.

Buddai growled.

She turned, saw a form standing in the doorway to her house, a deeper shadow in the gloom of the kitchen.

'Don't stop on my account,' a voice said, the figure stepping out into the sunshine. Conall.

She snarled, instinctively reaching for a knife.

'There's no need for that, now,' Conall said, holding a hand up. 'The battle's long finished.' He smiled. 'Besides, it did you no good last time you tried to stick me with one of your pins – won't be any different this time.' He rested a hand on the hilt of his sword, lightly, but Cywen had no doubt that he could have it drawn in the blink of an eye. She'd seen how fast he was.

'How'd you get in here?' she asked.

'Your door was open.'

'No, it wasn't.'

'I mean it wasn't locked – same thing.' He shrugged. 'So, are you going to try some more target practice on me?'

'You tried to *kill* me.'

'True. In my defence, you also tried to kill me. I'm prepared to let that go.' He brushed his cheek, where a huge bruise was fading green. 'Me, I'm quick to forgive.'

'Quick to anger is what I've heard,' Cywen muttered.

'Aye, that as well.' He grinned.

I've heard people say the same about me, she thought.

'What do you want?' she said.

'Someone wants to speak to you.'

'Who?'

'Someone important. Come and see.'

She thought about it. 'No.' She wiggled another knife free from the post and slid it into her belt.

Conall sighed. 'See, this reminds me of something my mam used to say to me every time she wanted me to take a bath. Goes something like this: we can do this one of two ways – the easy way or the hard way – either way it's still going to happen. Your choice.' He took a few steps into the garden. Buddai growled and padded closer to Cywen.

Conall scowled at the hound, his grip closing around his sword hilt. 'I'm starting to get bored with this, lass. And if that dog tries to put his teeth in me it'll be the last thing he does. Come along now.'

'Who wants to see me? Evnis?'

'He'll be there, but it's not him as asked for you. That would be Nathair. A king, no less. You should be honoured. Now come on – I'll not be asking again.'

Nathair. What does he want? Against her better judgement Cywen was curious. 'All right,' she muttered. 'I can always kill you another time.'

'Very kind of you,' said Conall.

'It's only because I'm too tired to bury your corpse,' she said as she strode up to him.

He took a step back and placed a hand protectively over his groin. 'Not too close,' he said. 'I saw what you did to Helfach's boy in the hall the other day. Me, I'm very fond of my stones.'

She hid a grin of her own as she walked through the kitchen and out of her front door, Buddai at her heels.

The cobbled streets were mostly in shadow as she walked through the fortress, the sun setting low, a pink glow reflecting off high clouds. As she passed the stables she scanned the paddocks, quickly finding Shield, Corban's skewbald stallion; he whinnied at her. Over the last few days she had frequently found herself back at the stables, had immersed herself in her old chores, for a small time burying the pain of the present in unthinking habit. No one had stopped her or complained, despite the red-cloaks that now ran the stables. Workers were in high demand. And while she was there she overheard conversations, news of the outside world. She picked apart every word that she heard, desperate for some clue to her family's whereabouts.

The gossip on everyone's lips was that Rhin had apparently invaded Narvon, sacked Uthandun and was even now camped on the far side of the Darkwood. Preparing to invade Ardan, no doubt. *Good,* Cywen had thought. *I hope she takes Owain's head.* Although, to be honest, she hated Rhin as much as Owain. More, if possible. Rhin had been behind all of this, had been the hand pulling the strings, guiding others towards all of this tragedy. She had a memory of the Darkwood, of Ronan slipping through her arms, of trying to stop the blood pumping from the wound in his throat, literally trying to stop his life from leaking out of him. She blinked, her eyes hot, her vision blurred.

Owain was mustering his forces against Rhin. At the moment they were spread throughout Ardan, combating a scattered resistance across the land – remnants of Dalgar's warband that had been routed on the plains about Dun Carreg. *If there is any justice in this world, Owain and Rhin will kill each other.* She snorted to herself, knowing the only justice she would get would be the one she made. With a sharp knife.

They reached the courtyard before the great hall. The mound of corpses had been reduced to a charred heap of twisted bone and ash. Nearby was a dark pile of dung, much bigger than any horse could leave. Cywen had seen the creature that had deposited it, a draig, led through the streets of Dun Carreg by Nathair. She shivered at the thought of it, not even fully grown, but still the most terrifying thing she had ever seen. Lizard-like, its torso had been low to the ground, carried on four bowed legs with curved, raking claws. A broad, flat skull and a square jaw with protruding, razored teeth, a thick tongue flickering. But it was the eyes that chilled her – no liquid, warm intelligence there, like her beloved horses. Its eyes had been small, dull, black. Merciless, a killer's eyes. Conall picked up his pace and strode past her, entering the great hall first. He ignored the red-cloaked guards that stared at them both.

As they passed deeper into the keep, Cywen began to notice more of the same black-cloaked warriors that had stormed Stonegate. At first they appeared as shadows, merging with the walls, but as her eyes adjusted to the gloom she saw more and more of them, spread about the hallways. She could feel their eyes on her.

'Here we are,' Conall said to her, stopping before a door that had two more warriors standing before it. He looked down at Buddai. 'That hound can't come in.'

'He'll howl if he doesn't. He's no danger to anyone, unless they're a danger to me. I'm not in danger, am I?' She smiled sweetly.

'No. All right then, but I will have your belt, please.'

Cywen just looked at him.

'I've seen how you handle a knife,' Conall said. 'There is no way that you are going to take them in there.'

'What do you think I am? Suicidal?' Cywen snapped, eyes drawn to the silent warriors staring at her.

'Maybe.' Conall shrugged. 'I've never understood women. The belt.'

Grumbling, Cywen undid it and held it out.

'Any more? I'll search you if I have to.'

Cywen scowled, bent over and pulled a knife from each boot, and another strapped to her arm.

'Thank you,' Conall said with a smile. Passing the knives to one of the guards, he entered the room. Cywen followed.

Three men stood inside: Nathair, Sumur his guard and Evnis. Cywen concentrated on Nathair, ignoring the other two. He was lean, muscular, with a strength about him, in his gaze. He still wore the two swords at his belt that she had seen on his arrival, one long, one short.

'Welcome, Cywen. My thanks for coming,' Nathair said, smiling at her. He poured her a cup of something from a jug. She refused it.

'What do you want?' she said.

Sumur stiffened.

'Be polite,' Conall muttered.

'I want to talk to you. About your family, about you.' Nathair's smile lingered.

'Why?'

Conall sighed.

'As I told you,' Evnis said, 'she has no manners, is not fit to speak to such as you.'

Nathair waved a hand. 'She has been through much tragedy, much heartache.'

At Nathair's words Cywen felt a sudden pressure build behind her eyes, a burning sensation. Angrily she willed the blooming tears to fade. *Don't be an idiot*, she scolded herself.

'How old are you?' Nathair asked.

'I've seen eighteen namedays.'

'And I understand you have a brother. Corban, I am told.'

'Aye,' Cywen said, feeling uncomfortable. 'What of it?'

Nathair's face hardened. 'I saw him in your great hall, on the night the fortress fell. He interested me.'

'Why?'

'I will ask the questions, and you will answer. The stablemaster, Gar. I am told he is close to your family.'

'Sounds like you've been told a lot,' Cywen muttered, flickering a scowl at Evnis.

'Answer the question. You are addressing a king,' Evnis said. 'Gar is close to your family, yes?'

'Yes.' Cywen glared at Evnis; the act made her feel better.

'There were no others with him, with Gar?' Sumur said, taking a step towards her. 'Men like him?'

'No. What do you mean, like him?'

Sumur didn't answer, just stared at her until she looked away.

'This Gar, tell me about him,' Nathair said, glancing at Sumur.

'What's to tell?' Cywen shrugged. 'He is, was, stablemaster here. He's always been part of my family, like kin, really.'

Nathair's fingers tapped the rim of his cup. He was staring intently at her. 'What else. Where is he from?'

'Helveth, I think.'

'This is a long way from Helveth. What brought him here?'

'I don't know.' Cywen shrugged. 'He never really spoke of his past. Something bad happened, I think, and Brenin gave him Sanctuary. He was a *good* king, renowned for his wisdom and kindness.' She scowled at all of them now, knowing they had all played a part in Brenin's death.

Nathair's lips twitched in a smile, which made her angrier. Was he laughing at her?

'So why was he so involved with your family?'

Cywen shrugged again. 'I don't know – he and my da were good friends . . .' A rush of memories almost overwhelmed her, her voice cracking. She paused. She didn't like this, but it was clear that there must be some kind of reasoning behind this questioning, and if she played along, within reason, perhaps she could discern what was going on here.

'Your brother, he had a wolven with him,' Sumur said, his accent thick. 'How did that happen.'

'Storm? Corban saved her, as a cub.'

'What did you say?' Nathair whispered, a frown creasing his forehead.

'Storm – that is the wolven's name. He could tell you more; he was there when it happened.' Cywen nodded at Evnis.

'During a hunt we stumbled upon a pack of wolven. We killed them, though at some loss,' Evnis said, pausing. 'Vonn, my son, nearly died . . .'

'And?' Sumur prompted.

'There was a litter of cubs. I killed them all, except one – Corban took it, claimed King's Justice when ordered to relinquish it. Brenin was not here – he was at your father's council, I believe – so his wife, Alona, gave judgement. She allowed the boy to keep the wolven. Foolish of her.'

'No, it wasn't,' snapped Cywen. She closed her eyes, could almost see Storm, smell her. And with her, Corban.

'That wolven nearly ripped Rafe's arm off, and it killed Helfach,' Evnis hissed. 'It should have been put to death.'

Anger swelled in Cywen. 'You're the one that should be put to death,' she snarled at Evnis. 'You're the traitor that let Owain in. None of this would have happened if not for you. Corban, my mam, Gar would still be here, my da would still be alive . . .' Suddenly the anger was a white, consuming rage. She snatched for a knife, actually growled as she realized nothing was there and without thinking launched herself at Evnis, fingers clutching for his throat.

Evnis threw himself backwards, eyes wide with shock, but Sumur and Conall were quicker, each grabbing one of Cywen's arms. Buddai snarled at them both, teeth snapping, not sure whom to bite first. Sumur reached for his sword hilt.

'Easy, girl,' Conall hissed in her ear. 'Your hound's about to die on your account.'

Instantly she went limp, the anger draining, consumed by concern for Buddai.

'No, Buddai,' she commanded. The hound paused, looking at her.

'Let me go,' she said. 'I'll not do anything. Evnis' life is not worth trading for Buddai's.'

Conall released her, nodding to Sumur. The black-clad warrior held her gaze a few heartbeats, then let go.

'I can't stay here,' Cywen said, 'the smell is making me sick.' She gave Evnis a withering look, then turned for the door. Conall held it shut.

'Let her go,' Nathair said, 'though I may ask for you to return.'

'Make sure he's not here, then,' she said, and left.

CHAPTER TWELVE

EVNIS

Evnis glared at the closed door, wishing Cywen dead. *Who does she think she is, the little brat?*

'I like her,' Nathair said absently. He looked distracted.

'So do I,' said Conall, 'even if she did try to kill me.'

'Really . . . ?' Nathair raised an eyebrow, focusing on Conall.

'Aye, on Stonegate, the night of the battle. She threw a knife at me, then, when that didn't work, she pushed me off the wall. That's how I got this.' He touched his bruised cheek. 'Course, I did pull her over with me. Thought if I was finished she should be as well.'

'I like her even more, now.'

Evnis snorted and brushed himself down. 'Was she useful, my lord?'

'Yes, very.' Nathair shared a look with Sumur, something passing between them. 'Have her watched,' he said to Evnis. 'I would not have her disappearing in search of her kin. I have a feeling she will be useful. Some of the things she said, they stir memories.' He drank from his cup, then winced. 'What *is* this mead? It really is quite disgusting. What I'd give for a good jug of wine.'

'Unfortunately we have more bees than grapes in Ardan,' Evnis said.

'So. What news of Rhin?' Nathair asked.

'I am told she is camped on the banks of the Rhenus, at the northern fringe of the Darkwood.'

'And what will she do next?'

'I would imagine she'll strike south, push through the forest and into Ardan before Owain can muster a force large enough to hold

85

her there. Once she is loose in Ardan there will be no stopping her. That is what I would advise, at least.'

'I agree,' Nathair said, sipping at his mead. He frowned absently into the cup. 'I need to see her. Without Owain's knowledge.'

'That will be difficult,' Evnis said.

'Yes, I know. But nevertheless, it is what must happen.'

'Of course,' said Evnis. 'I will do what I can, my lord.'

It was late but he could not sleep. Did not want to sleep. Dreams were the last thing he wanted, and he knew they would come. He swirled his cup of usque and sipped it slowly, savouring the liquor's oily warmth as it slipped down his throat, heat spreading from his gut into his chest.

He was tired, exhausted, trying to keep track of the plots and threads that he had become involved in.

Nathair's patronage kept him safe, for now. With luck, long enough for Rhin to arrive and separate Owain's head from his shoulders. But then how would she react to this most recent turn of events, his obeisance to Nathair? *Not too well*, was his gut reaction. *Rhin is famed for her jealousy*. And this situation with Nathair was perplexing, and intriguing – there was so much more going on than he could see, situations he could sense, caught from veiled glances between Nathair and his guard, Sumur.

'What is the link between Sumur and Gar?' he breathed. Clearly they were of the same people – he had seen them duel, saw the similarities of style and weapons. *But how? Sumur is from Tarbesh, more than a thousand leagues away. How is it that Gar is – was – here. And, more importantly, why was he here?*

And now he is gone. Escaped with Edana, and Vonn . . .

He was surprised by a wave of emotion, a constricting within his chest. He closed his eyes and felt a tear roll down his cheek. Almost immediately his anger stirred. *You fool, tears will not help. Use your wits. They have kept you alive this long*. His thoughts drifted to the tunnels beneath the fortress. *That must have been how they escaped. They may be in them still*. He would lead an expedition, but he would need enough warriors with him in case they were there. It would be dangerous.

He smiled to himself. He had warriors of his own, but more than that, he had the book. Found buried in the tunnels dug by the Benothi, the ancient giant clan, builders of Dun Carreg. A book of learning, a book of power. With it he had begun to learn the secrets of the earth power, *magic*, the ignorant called it. Even as he thought of it he felt drawn to the book. That had been happening more and more of late, as if the knowledge it held was some unseen drug, pulling him back with invisible cords.

Without even realizing, he stood and padded towards the secret door concealed within an oak-panelled wall. With a click it swung open, revealing a small space, room enough only for a small table and one chair. Only Fain and Vonn knew of its existence. He had shown it to them as a place to hide in the eventuality of Owain's attack, something they had both scoffed at, but he had known Rhin's plans would bear fruit one day.

He lifted the torch from the sconce, held it high, and gasped.

The book was gone.

CHAPTER THIRTEEN

CAMLIN

Camlin swore quietly.

He was crouching behind a thick-trunked beech, peering through scrub and hawthorn at the line of riders, steadily growing larger. He counted seven.

'What are we going to do?' Dath whispered, one eye on the riders, the other on the bowstring he was fumbling.

'Not sure yet,' Camlin muttered. He glanced at Gar, but there was no help there – the warrior's face was a blank wall. 'Depends on why they're riding into these woods.' He stared at the approaching riders, all grim-faced and wrapped in leather and mail. 'Doesn't look like they've come dressed for flower picking.' *Looks more like they've come for blood.*

Fight or flight? He hawked and spat, looking at the woods about them. They were hidden in the first growth of trees, a track of sorts passing by them. Only a little deeper and the track was over-shadowed, pressed by looming beech and chestnut. If the riders took the track they would have to ride single file. He sighed, his decision made.

'Corban, Gar – you two stay hidden here. Me an' Dath, we're going to move a little deeper into the trees, try and even the odds a little. Don't do anything till the arrows stop coming. And don't let any of them get back onto that meadow.'

'Why are we doing this?' Dath stammered. 'They might just be passing through.'

'Don't think so,' Camlin said. 'The only place this track leads to is the beach. My guess is that our boat was seen, and these lads have been sent to see what's what. No time to get back and warn the others, so best be getting on with what needs doing.' He glanced at Gar again, and this time the warrior nodded.

Corban and Gar slipped into deeper cover, the wolven following, almost invisible in the gloom, the stripes in her coat blending with the shadows.

'Dath – with me,' Camlin snapped, not looking to see if the lad followed him. He could tell the boy's courage was wavering, and from experience he knew that soft words would not help. They hurried deeper, stopping where banks rose either side of the track. 'Here's a good spot,' Camlin said. He pulled a handful of arrows from his quiver, stuck them in a line into the black loam earth and motioned for Dath to do the same. The boy's hands were shaking.

Camlin gripped Dath's wrist. 'Take a deep breath, lad. And do the same before each shot. Pick targets in the centre of their column. Aim for chests, or their horses. Bring them down.'

Dath jerked a nod, his eyes wide.

Camlin felt a wave of pity; he remembered watching his brother as he was cut down by raiders, remembered the incapacitating fear and the shame that followed. 'They're going to feel a whole lot worse than you once the arrows start flying, stuck in the open, not knowing where we are. And that's before they come face to face with your friend's wolven.'

Dath managed a small laugh.

The drum of hooves grew louder.

What am I doing here? The thought was so sudden that Camlin felt as if it had been whispered in his ear. *Not much talent at choosing the winning side. Perhaps I should have stayed with Braith. I followed him for long enough in the Darkwood, and like as not he's more than lord of a strip of woods now, with Rhin's rise in power. I could leave now, walk away and not look back. This lot would never know, and what if they did? Who are they to me?* He glanced at Dath. *He trusts me to bring him through this.*

Camlin peered back down the track, saw the riders had moved smoothly into single file. Branches arched above them, sunlight and shadow dappling the track. He nocked an arrow, held it loosely, saw Dath mimic him. The riders were close enough to make out individual features now. The leader had a thick beard, his warrior braid poking from beneath an iron helm. He gripped a couched spear, shield bouncing where it was strapped to the saddle.

Camlin flexed his shoulders and drew his arrow back.

Walk away, the voice whispered in his mind.

Not today. Then he released his arrow.

It struck the first rider in the throat, a spray of blood marking it. The man clutched at the shaft, choking, toppling from his saddle. He heard Dath's arrow, saw it sink into the shoulder of a piebald stallion. The animal reared and threw its rider. He grabbed another arrow, nocked it, let fly. It skittered off a hastily raised shield.

The riders were seasoned warriors; that was clear. There was fear in their faces, but they did not panic. One of them barked an order and two warriors spurred their horses on, tried to get past the fallen horse, its rider's leg trapped beneath it.

Camlin and Dath drew bows together, releasing only a heartbeat apart. One arrow buried into the meat of a warrior's arm, the other thrumming in a raised shield. Camlin drew again, put an arrow in a horse's flank. It screamed, but its rider yanked on his reins, stopped it from rearing. The warrior looked their way, scanning the bank for them.

Three of the warriors at the rear of the column had turned their horses, were kicking their mounts into a retreat. As Camlin glanced back he saw Corban step into the track, sword drawn and shield raised.

What are you doing, boy? They'll ride you down.

Corban set his feet before the oncoming horsemen. Then Gar appeared, ran before Corban, his long curved sword raised high against the onrushing riders.

There was an explosion of leaves as a great shape burst onto the track, slamming into the first rider.

Storm.

Her long canines ripped into the horse's neck, the wolven's weight flipping both animal and rider to the ground. Camlin heard bones breaking, then screaming. The horsemen behind milled on the path, unable to pass the mass of horse and rider and wolven.

'Move!' a voice screamed in Camlin's ear, then Dath was shoving him to the side. There was a shuddering in the ground, the wild neigh of a horse as a warrior drove his mount up the bank at them. Dath leaped for cover, tripping on a root as the horse's head and chest burst through the thin foliage they had been hiding behind.

The warrior blinked as his eyes adjusted to the gloom, then snarled when he saw Dath sprawled on the ground. He raised his sword.

Camlin clutched for an arrow, drew and fired at the looming figure, so close he could almost touch the horse. His arrow hit the man in the face, snapping his head back. Teeth, blood and gore showered Camlin as the warrior hurtled backwards, one foot catching in a stirrup. His corpse hung limp as the horse lurched forwards, dragging the dead warrior through the undergrowth.

'Are you hurt?' Camlin asked Dath. The lad shook his head, took Camlin's arm and staggered upright.

'Time to finish this,' Camlin said, slinging his bow across his shoulder, drawing his sword and stepping out of the trees. There was one warrior left here, dismounted, trying to help a comrade trapped beneath a fallen horse. Camlin slithered down loose earth on the ridge, heard Dath following. He glanced down the track and saw Storm, who had moved from the horse to its rider, her teeth clamped about his throat. The two other horsemen drove their mounts past the wolven, kicking them at Gar and Corban.

Gar moved faster than Camlin's eyes could follow. There was the flash of iron in sunlight and then a horse was screaming, front legs collapsing as it ploughed head and chest into the ground.

Then Camlin was at the foot of the ridge, fixing his eyes on the warrior before him. The man had been unable to free his comrade from the dead horse he was trapped beneath, and by the look of it the pinned man would not be going far anyway, his leg twisted at an unnatural angle.

Camlin circled left, signalled for Dath to go right, then, in the instant that the warrior was sizing them up, Camlin surged forwards. He struck fast and hard at the warrior's head. His first two blows were hastily blocked, the warrior retreating. Then he stumbled and Camlin hacked his blade between the man's neck and shoulder. Bone crunched and blood spurted. He wrenched his sword free and the man slumped to the ground.

Camlin swung around, marched to the warrior trapped by his dead horse and slammed his sword into his chest. He looked up, saw Dath staring at him, wide-eyed.

'Strike first,' he said, 'else you might not get a chance to strike at all. That's a Darkwood education.'

Dath gulped.

Down the track a horse neighed.

One rider was still mounted, swinging a sword at Corban, who was ducking, trying to pull him from his mount. Gar was on the far side, moving in. Storm was circling the horse, crouched low, about to leap. The rider saw his doom approaching, kicked frantically at his mount. The horse leaped forwards, Corban diving out of the way, and then it was galloping down the track.

Camlin broke into a run, unslinging his bow. He reached the horse that Storm had fallen upon, rested a foot on its flank and drew an arrow, its feathers touching his ear. For a moment he tracked the escaping horseman, pulled in a deep breath, held it, then released the arrow. It arced high, dipped, and the rider stiffened, toppling backwards onto the soft ground. The horse ran on a dozen paces, then slowed, began cropping grass.

'That shot was amazing,' Dath breathed.

'I was aiming for the horse,' Camlin said with a rueful grin.

We've taken too long, Camlin thought. They were almost back to their makeshift camp.

They had dragged the corpses of the slain warriors into the trees, Camlin setting Dath to retrieving as many of their arrows as he could find.

'Do we need to?' Dath had asked.

'Once you've made arrows of your own you'll never leave one behind that you didn't have to. And we may be on this road a long time – what happens if we run out?'

Dath had thought about that and nodded. Then they had rounded up the horses and hobbled them a good distance from the track. That had taken the most time, but if they hadn't done it one of the animals at least would have wandered back to the encampment, rousing suspicion and an angry pursuit far quicker than if the horses were hidden. Without Gar it would not have happened at all; he had a way with horses.

After that they had all but run back to their camp. They needed to get back on their boat and put some distance between them and the bristling warband that would certainly be sent after them. It was just a matter of time.

Marrock stepped out from behind a tree. 'What's happened?' he asked, frowning as he looked at their faces.

'We ran into . . . some . . . company,' Camlin breathed. 'We need to leave.'

'How far behind you?' Marrock said, scanning the trees.

'They won't be following anyone, but can't say how long it'll be before they're missed.'

Marrock raised an eyebrow, turned and led them back to camp.

Camlin gave a hasty account of the ambush; Halion and the other travellers huddled round close to listen. Dath interjected comments, most to do with Camlin's prowess, his skill with a bow, a sword, and his strategic brilliance. Camlin felt himself frowning at the boy.

'So what now?' Brina said, hands on hips.

'Back to the boat, get as far away from here as possible, as quickly as possible,' Marrock said. He looked to Halion, who nodded.

'But what if those ships are still out there?' Edana said. Her voice was hoarse, dry.

'We'll have to cross one bridge at a time, my lady,' Halion said. 'And staying where we are is no option.'

Brina tutted, bent over and whispered in her crow's ear. That thing still made Camlin uncomfortable. There was far too much intelligence in its beady eyes. With a squawk of protest it unfurled its wings and flapped into the air, disappearing over the trees.

'Craf is a good scout,' Brina said. 'Don't want any surprises, do we.'

The group broke up, checked packs, filled water skins, then Vonn and Farrell burst upon them, running hard from the beach.

'A boat has just beached next to ours,' Vonn blurted as he skidded to a stop, 'full of warriors.'

CHAPTER FOURTEEN

FIDELE

Fidele gazed out of her tower window. In the distance the snow-capped Agullas glistened in the summer sun, before them rich meadows rolling all the way down to the lake shore, where countless ships bobbed on the swell, cold and deep from the mountains' snowmelt. And on those ships: fishermen, traders, all manner of people. Her people. She felt a rush of passion, a fierce pride in the people of this realm. *I love this land.*

Her gaze drifted southward, to the river that carved its way to the sea. The black ships of the Vin Thalun had long since sailed that route, disappeared into the distance; the only sign of their presence here at Jerolin was the shipbuilding yard that had risen up on the lake shore. Even that was deserted now. Lykos had told her that the ship-building would continue to the south, near Ripa, but he needed too many hands on his fleet as it sailed to Nathair and Ardan to keep the two shipyards going.

And good riddance. She understood the logic that underpinned Nathair's treaty with the Vin Thalun, knew their skills would be of great value in the coming war, but the reality of keeping the peace between them and her subjects had been difficult. *Too many hard years between us to wash over in a few moons.* She left her chambers, Orcus her shieldman falling in at her side. Fidele marched a quick rhythm through corridors and down the great tower of Jerolin until she was breathing fresh air. Her feet took her to the north, where the city grew quieter, to the cairn ground.

'I miss you,' she breathed, barely a whisper on the air. She was stood before her husband's cairn; Aquilus, King of Tenebral, High King of the Banished Lands, slain in his own chambers, stabbed by

a traitor king. *I wish we had had more time.* She touched one of the
great stones of the cairn, already moss-covered, with lichen growing
in yellows and reds. Aquilus had been so focused, so strong, always
somehow knowing the right path and having the strength to take it,
to see it through. *I wish you had shared more of your certainties with me.
Shared more of your plans.* The knowledge of the God-War and the
coming of the avatars had been a great burden, but Aquilus had borne
it, though not without cost. And, because he had chosen to shoulder
most of it alone, things felt so unsure now. She was scared, scared
of what the future held, scared of the threat to her son. Her poor
Nathair, striving, struggling to do his best, to earn his father's notice.
And now, to live up to his father's legacy, not only to lead a nation,
but to save the Banished Lands, or die in the trying. Fathers and sons
– why did it have to be so complicated.

She sighed. 'I will not let you down. I will not let Nathair down.'

Footsteps crunched on stone behind her and stopped, a respectful silence, then the scuff of an impatient foot. A cough.

'Yes,' Fidele said, turning, wiping all emotion from her face.
It was Peritus, her husband's battlechief. Small, wiry, unassuming,
deadly.

'There is something you must see,' Peritus said, his expression
grim.

'Where did you find him?' Fidele asked.

'Was fishing about a league to the north,' the fisherman said.
'Pulling in our crab baskets and he was tangled in one of them.'

They were standing on the deck of a mid-sized fisher-boat, half
a dozen crewmen gathered around her. Despite the sun the wind was
cold, carrying with it a hint of ice from the mountains. Fidele pulled
her cloak tighter. To one side, huge baskets were stacked on top of
one another, crabs imprisoned within, clacking their great-claws.
There was a body slumped on the deck, mottled blue, the flesh
bloated and peeling, green weed clinging to the limbs, trailing like
extended fingers.

'Course, the crabs have had a nibble at him,' the fisherman
said.

Peritus bent down and rolled the body over. It was decomposing, chunks of flesh missing, but Fidele still recognized the nervous-looking youth that had been led into her chambers only a ten-night ago and told her of the Vin Thalun fighting pits.

Jace. His throat had been cut, the flesh frayed like rotted string.

Peritus spat on the floor. 'So this is how Lykos obeys your commands.'

CHAPTER FIFTEEN

VERADIS

The army marched through the twilight of Forn, Alcyon's bulk marking the column's head. Veradis felt sluggish and ill-tempered after sleeping poorly, disturbed by bad dreams. In them he'd been riding across an endless meadow, the head of King Mandros held aloft on his spear-point. *Murderer,* Mandros' head had whispered to him, over and over. Something had been bouncing against his leg. When he'd looked down he found Kastell's head tied to his saddle. *Betrayer,* his friend had accused him.

He shook his head, banishing the nightmare, then saw Calidus drop back down the column towards him.

'There you are,' the silver-haired man said as he fell in beside Veradis. There was a new energy about the man since he had emerged from the catacombs beneath Haldis, a fierce determination in his expression.

'We are making good progress,' Calidus said. The hard pace had been set from the first day out from Haldis, four days ago. Veradis had woken the day after the battle to the news that King Braster of Helveth had been murdered in his tent by survivors of the Gadrai, Isiltir's elite warriors. That had made no sense to Veradis – the realms of Isiltir and Helveth had been on good terms, but Lothar, Braster's battlechief, had witnessed the deed and told Calidus personally. This news had troubled Calidus and he had ordered all haste in breaking camp and leaving Haldis. *We must speed Jael to claim Isiltir's crown,* he had said.

'I have been talking to Jael,' Calidus said. 'He is not as strong willed as I would like in an ally, but he is all we have, and we need Isiltir's support.'

Veradis frowned at Calidus, suspicious of where this was leading.

'Isiltir will be rocked by the news of Romar's death. There will be others who will try to take advantage of the situation, try to claim the throne for themselves. Not least Romar's estranged wife.'

'What of Romar's son?' Veradis asked.

'He is ten years old. Jael will rule with the boy as his ward, until he comes of age.'

'Unless the boy's mother has anything to say about it.'

'Exactly. And she has the boy in her care, which gives her the advantage. Especially if those survivors of the Gadrai reach Isiltir ahead of us and warn her of all that has happened here,' Calidus said. 'Jael could do with some leverage, in the form of a warband, I am thinking.'

'He has men,' Veradis said, gesturing up the column, where Jael marched with his shieldmen about him.

'Some – a few score here, some others at Mikil, but not enough to be convincing. We need Isiltir; Nathair needs Isiltir. It would be better if we could show our support . . .'

'No,' Veradis said. 'I am Nathair's first-sword, and I am going straight to him.'

Calidus raised an eyebrow and seemed to consider pressing the point, then shrugged. 'As you say. And you are probably not best suited to the task. Lykos and his Vin Thalun, however – they would be perfect.'

'That would take too long – by the time you sent word back to Tenebral, and then the time it took Lykos to reach Isiltir.'

'Yes, unless Lykos had already left Tenebral and was sailing to meet us at Ardan,' Calidus said, a smile twitching his beard.

'But how?'

Calidus winked at Veradis. 'I may look like a withered old man, but sometimes appearances can be deceiving. And where there is a will . . .'

There was a commotion up ahead, Alcyon calling a halt. The column rippled to a stop.

'With me,' Calidus said as he marched forward.

One of their scouts had returned, was talking to Alcyon, gesturing into the trees.

'What is it?' Calidus demanded.

'Tracks in the forest, signs of a camp,' the scout said.

'How many?' Calidus frowned.

'Two, maybe three. The fire was burned out, but still warm.'

'It is the Gadrai,' Jael said. He had sidled up behind Calidus and Veradis.

'Perhaps,' Calidus murmured.

'Take me to this camp,' Veradis said to the scout.

Away from the path, the forest closed about them like a malignant wound, dark and treacherous. The scout led them through thick foliage and hanging vine. Dense webs draped the branches, in one of them hung the husk of something, a bat perhaps.

The ground turned spongier and soon they splashed across a shallow stream, the scout stopping on the far bank. He pointed to a pile of ash inside a ring of loose stones. Veradis bent and sifted the ash, rubbing his fingers together. There was a touch of warmth left, faint as the daylight in this forest.

Alcyon scanned the ground, Jael and a dozen of his shieldmen fanning out. The giant bent and scooped something up, a tattered piece of cloth. He sniffed it. 'Smells of blood. One of them is injured,' he said.

'Which way?' Jael said. 'If one is injured we can catch them.'

The scout pointed into the gloom and Jael marched into the forest. 'Stay close to me; they are the Gadrai – giant-killers, and they know this forest better than any.'

Veradis thought there was an edge of panic in Jael's voice. He shared a look with Alcyon. *Shall we follow?*

'Calidus will be unhappy if we return without him,' the giant said.

Veradis shrugged and followed Jael, Alcyon close behind him.

They laboured through the forest; the going was slow as they searched for signs of their quarry's passing. Soon they spread out into a line that grew more ragged as time passed. All except Alcyon were murky shadows amongst the trees. The axe strapped across his back drew Veradis' eye, dark blades fanning out above the giant's shoulders like wings.

'Is that really one of the Seven Treasures?' Veradis asked.

'Yes,' Alcyon said.

'How old is it?'

Alcyon shrugged. 'Two, three thousand years. And it is still sharp.'

'I know, I saw you fight with it at Haldis.'

A frown crossed Alcyon's face. Was he thinking of the giant children, of their guardian whom Calidus had slain.

'I did not know . . .' Veradis started, trailing off. 'About giant's children.'

Alcyon looked at him. 'We have children. Just not as many as you men. That is why they are precious to us.' Something swept his face, a fleeting raw emotion, then it was gone. 'At Haldis, so many of them killed.' He shook his head.

'Yes,' Veradis agreed. 'These are difficult times.'

'We are at war,' Alcyon said. 'A war begun thousands of years ago.'

Veradis looked about – the others were a distance away, only shadows amongst the trees – and lowered his voice. 'I am thankful that one of the Ben-Elim stands with us. It makes the difficult things easier, somehow.'

A silence grew between them, man and giant focusing on their path through the forest. Veradis could not shake from his mind the look that he had seen sweep Alcyon's face as they had talked of giant children. A look of naked misery.

Time passed, and Veradis was thinking of calling a halt and turning back when he saw something: a snapped stalk amongst foliage that draped a massive trunk. It could have been caused by Alcyon as he passed. Veradis stopped; Alcyon was fading into the gloom ahead. He looked intently at the broken stalk, then his gaze swept the surrounding area. There was a mark on the bark of the trunk – a scuff? Then something dripped onto his shoulder, something dark. He touched it, raised a finger to his tongue. His head snapped up as he reached for his sword. It was blood.

From branches above a dirt-stained face was peering down at him. He drew his sword, sucked in a breath to call Alcyon, then in front of him a figure stepped out from behind the tree, at the same time foliage rustling behind him. His call for help died in his throat as he gazed at the man standing before him.

Maquin.

The grey-haired warrior held a hand up, signalling to the unseen man behind him, and Veradis knew his life hung in the balance, as did theirs. One call from him and Alcyon, Jael and a dozen warriors would be on them. Carefully, slowly, he lowered his sword, holding Maquin's gaze.

'It is good to see you,' he said.

Maquin grimaced, eyes flickering to the figure behind Veradis. He shook his head. Veradis resisted the urge to turn, kept his eyes fixed on Maquin. 'Kastell?' he asked.

Grief twisted Maquin's face. 'Jael killed him.'

Veradis hung his head. 'Was it you that murdered Braster?'

'No. That was Lothar,' a voice grated behind him. Maquin nodded confirmation.

Lothar? But, he has been in close council with Calidus.

A voice called from the gloom. 'Veradis, where are you?' Alcyon. There was a sound of approaching feet.

He made his decision in an instant. 'You are being hunted,' Veradis hissed. 'Get back into the trees. I will lead them away from you.'

'Do we trust him?' the voice behind Veradis said. Maquin looked at Veradis, then nodded.

'I am sorry,' Veradis whispered, 'about Kastell.'

Maquin stepped back into the foliage, pausing before the gloom took him. 'Before the battle you warned us about what side we were choosing.'

'Yes,' Veradis said. 'I did.'

'I would give *you* the same advice,' Maquin said, then disappeared into the forest.

CHAPTER SIXTEEN

EVNIS

Evnis stood frozen in the doorway to his secret room. The book was gone. He searched frantically. The casket he had originally found it in was there, the necklace still within it, pulsing with its sickly light, but the book was nowhere to be seen. He stared at the necklace, his gaze sucked into the darkness of the single black stone, the size of his fist, wrapped in twists of silver. Ever since he had laid eyes upon it a suspicion had nagged him. Could it be Nemain's necklace, one of the Seven Treasures? An ancient relic from when the world was young, if half the tales were true.

He took a deep breath, trying to calm himself, to think. The last time he had used it he had not put the book back in the casket; he had left it sitting on top. He was sure of this, could picture in his mind reading from it, speaking aloud the words of power, then placing the book on to the casket's lid. That had been days ago – the day Dun Carreg had fallen.

Who could have done this?

Vonn.

But why would he have taken the book? Curiosity? To spite him? They had been arguing over the fisherman's daughter, Bethan. Maybe he thought to use the book as leverage, a trade – the girl for the book? He almost liked that idea, the thought that Vonn was at last growing up, seeing the world as it really was and being prepared to do what was necessary, regardless of its perceived morality. If it had been anything else that Vonn had taken, he would have been prepared to let it go. But he had taken the book, his access to a world of power. He felt a sudden rage boil inside him and took a shuddering breath. He *must* get it back.

The tunnels. He suspected that Vonn and his companions had escaped through the secret tunnels beneath the fortress; Evnis had been planning to begin searching them on the morrow. *To hell with the morrow*, he thought, whirling on his feet and grabbing his sheathed sword and belt as he strode from his tower room.

He called warriors to him as he descended the stairs, sent word for more to be summoned as he made his way to the basement where the boarded-up doorway to the tunnels stood. By the time he had strapped his sword-belt on, ordered the boards torn down from the doorway and lit a torch, almost a score of men had gathered about him, many bleary-eyed, rubbing sleep from their eyes. *It is late*, Evnis remembered, all thought of time having flown his mind, replaced only by his need to find the book. He looked about, searching for Conall, then remembered he had set him to watch over Cywen, as Nathair had asked of him.

A muffled whimper drifted from a door in the cellar, reminding Evnis of his prisoner. He ignored the sound.

'With me,' he said and led his men into the tunnels.

The sun was rising when he at last stepped out of the tunnels, back into his tower; a faint light was seeping down the cellar steps through gaps in the floorboards above. He was dirt stained, weary, and his mood was grim.

Vonn was gone, and with him the book. Of that he was sure.

They had searched long and hard, wary of attack both from Edana's supporters and wyrms. The headless body of the wyrm that had hatched when he'd found the book was still there, its flesh all but gone, rags of tattered skin draped over its skeleton. He had given it hardly a passing look, though it set his warriors to muttering.

Eventually their search had led them to the lowest cavern, where the sea swelled in a channel. Here Evnis knew was the exit to the beach, though none of his men realized, as there was a glamour hiding the way. There was the body of another wyrm here, this one much bigger than the one in the tunnels above. It had been killed only recently, its body in the first stages of decay – skin bloated and swollen, blood and other fluids leaking from it, pooled and congealed around its coiled body. Its skull had been crushed by a heavy blow, and there were various wounds about its body. If this was not evidence enough of Edana's passing, they found the corpse of a warrior nearby, his neck and chest torn open. He had been one of Pendathran's warriors, Evnis was sure.

So, now they were gone, most likely leagues from Dun Carreg by now, and with them the book.

And his son. With a growl he dismissed his trailing warriors and trod wearily up the steps of his tower to his room. There was a message awaiting him – a reminder of Nathair's request to meet with Rhin. *How am I going to do this – Rhin in the Darkwood, Nathair here, Owain and his warbands in between?* Evnis reached for the half-filled jug of usque and took a large gulp, slumping into a chair. Almost impossible, but there must be a way. *Think.* Slowly the glimmer of an idea came to him, but his mind felt slow, could not quite focus on it. *I must sleep.* A ripple of dread coursed through him. Sleep, and with it the dreams. He chuckled to himself and drank another cup of usque. What did he expect, after selling his soul to Asroth, Lord of the Fallen . . . ?

A knock at his door. Evnis looked about the room, checking that all was ready: a cauldron hung over the fire-pit, water bubbling, a cup of dark liquid standing on a table beside it. He checked his cloak, reassured himself that the letter was still there, then he opened the door.

Nathair was there, the dark shadow of his guardian, Sumur, hovering behind him.

'My lord, please,' Evnis said, ushering Nathair in. He held a hand up to Sumur. 'Only Nathair may enter.'

'That is not acceptable,' Sumur said.

'It is fine, Sumur, I am sure Evnis has good reason. And I am sure I shall be safe. Only a door stands between us.'

Sumur peered into the room, weighing the situation. He nodded. 'I consider you responsible for my lord's life, while this door remains shut,' he said to Evnis.

'Of course,' said Evnis and closed the door.

Nathair looked about the room, eyes settling upon the cauldron. He unclasped his sable cloak and draped it across the table.

'Your message was ambiguous,' he said, 'but I am intrigued . . .'

'Thank you for coming, my lord. I have made arrangements for you to speak with Queen Rhin.'

Nathair raised an eyebrow.

Evnis tried to keep his face calm, to disguise the anxiety he felt. *You can do this*, he told himself. He had seen it in the book, was confident that he could remember the pages, the incantation, word for word. He licked his lips and strode to the cauldron, lifting the cup from the table.

'*Fuil glacad anios ag namhaid tor oscail an bealach*,' he said, filling the words with as much power as he could summon, and poured the cup of blood into the cauldron. *Blood taken from a foe, to open the way.* His prisoner, still shackled in a room beneath his feet, hadn't given up his blood easily and his screams had brought a brief relief from these stressful times. The prisoner could scream as long and as loud as he liked – no one would hear him down there. Evnis had not even bothered placing a guard on his door; there was no point. He could not escape, and even if he did, there was nowhere for him to go.

Evnis reached inside his cloak and pulled out a crumpled piece of parchment, the letter Rhin had sent to him, delivered by Braith's outlaw so long ago, written in her spidery hand. He drew his knife, cut his hand and gripped the letter, soaking it in his blood. Then he dropped it into the cauldron.

'*Croi ar an comchor tor stiur an ruthag.*'

The water bubbled pink and a vapour hissed out of the pot, swirled upwards, glistening, thick and shiny, like cords of mucus. A shape took form in it, silver-haired, a pale, deeply lined face. Rhin.

'What is this?' she said, her likeness turning in the vapour, the voice sounding submerged, muted. Then her sharp eyes focused on Evnis. 'Oh, it is you. I see you have found the book—'

'My Queen, I have someone with me who wishes to speak to you, urgently,' Evnis cut in.

'I'm sure you do,' Rhin said, a smile ghosting her lips. 'Who, exactly?'

'Let me introduce you to Nathair, King of Tenebral.'

Rhin clapped her hands. 'Excellent. No need for introductions – we have met before. A charming young man. Well, step forward, Nathair, I imagine we have much to talk about.'

CHAPTER SEVENTEEN

CORBAN

Corban listened as Vonn and Farrell told of the ship they had seen land on the beach.

'They are looking for us,' Vonn said. 'A dozen men, all well-armed.'

'What of my boat?' Mordwyr interrupted.

'They were climbing aboard it,' Farrell said. 'We did not wait to see what they would do – thought you needed to know.'

'You did right,' Marrock said.

'We need to get Edana out of sight,' Halion said.

'Agreed. Camlin – with me. The rest of you get back into the trees. We'll see you there soon.'

With that, Corban was running back towards the treeline, his feet heavy in the sand and shingle. Halion drew them up within sight of the beach. Marrock and Camlin were dark shadows, crawling through a patch of spindly grass.

'What are we going to do?' Dath whispered. Corban just shook his head. His pulse was still racing from their ambush of the riders on the path. Dath was as pale as a corpse.

'We need to get back on my boat,' Mordwyr said to Halion, who nodded agreement. He was standing protectively beside Edana.

'Agreed,' Brina snapped. 'It's the how that is the problem.'

'They're coming,' Gar said.

Marrock and Camlin sprinted across the beach. Halion stepped into view to guide them back to the group.

'Fifteen warriors at least,' Marrock panted. 'They've torched our boat.' Even as he said the words a thick plume of smoke broke above the ridge.

'No!' Mordwyr exclaimed and started back for the beach. Vonn grabbed his arm, stopping him.

'What are we going to do?' Dath said.

Marrock looked at Edana.

'We'll take their boat,' Halion said.

Corban shifted the weight of his shield on his arm and gripped his sword hilt, trying to still the tremor in his hand. He peered over the ridge, eyes drawn immediately to their boat. It was a burned-out skeleton, flames still licking at the charred ribs. Thick smoke spread along the coast, snatched by a strong wind from the sea. Mordwyr let out a strangled cry, but the sound of the surf was loud, muffling his grief.

A handful of warriors was grouped a little further down the beach, standing beside a half-beached shallow-draughted fisher-boat. Figures moved on its deck – two at least that Corban could see.

Marrock slipped down the ridge and they all huddled close to him.

'Any ideas?' he asked, looking at Camlin.

'There's no chance of sneaking up on them, and the wind's too strong to be accurate with a bow from here. Our best bet is to get from here to there quick as we can, 'fore they have a chance to push off and sail away. An' keep the charge quiet, no point announcing ourselves.' With that, Camlin was scrambling over the ridge, Marrock close behind him. Corban took a deep breath, trying to control his rising fear, and followed.

They were spotted almost immediately as they charged, the warriors about the boat crying out, drawing swords, levelling spears. They were closely matched in numbers, but these were all warriors, no strangers to battle by the look of them. Still, judging from the expressions on their faces, something about the sight of Corban and his companions must have been unnerving. Corban glanced at Storm, the grey streaks in her white fur a blur as she gathered speed, spittle spraying from her bared fangs. He felt the urge to laugh; a full-grown wolven hurtling towards you would unsettle anyone.

Halion yelled a war cry, high pitched and keening; somewhere close Farrell bellowed, then the bands were upon each other, a bone-shaking collision.

Corban turned a warrior's spear-point with his shield, slammed into the man, sending both of them crashing to the ground. They rolled together, the warrior somehow on top of Corban, grabbing his throat. Corban thrashed, felt a flood of panic as he tried to draw breath and couldn't, then there was the sound of snarling, a ripping, tearing noise, high-pitched screaming, then a crunch, and the grip on Corban's throat was gone. He staggered to his feet, Storm still shaking the dead warrior by his broken neck.

Corban snatched his sword from the ground, looked about him. Gar tugged his sword from a warrior's chest. Farrell was standing knee-deep in the surf, swinging his war-hammer at a warrior who had slipped to one knee. There was an explosion of gore as the hammer smashed into the man's head. Halion blocked an overhead blow, swept his sword round and chopped into the man's ribs, kicked him back into the surf. Edana stood close behind him, holding her sword two-handed. She was staring at the man Halion had just slain. Vonn was trading furious blows nearby, Marrock running past, hamstringing Vonn's opponent as he waded into the sea, making for the boat. Corban realized it was moving away, two men pushing desperately on the half-floating hull. An arrow sprouted in the back of one, sending him face down into the foaming sea, but the other carried on, another arrow skittering off the hull, then the boat was floating, hands reaching down to pull the man over the side. Before he was over, someone was grabbing him from behind, swinging a sword into the man's ribs, clutching onto his ankle as the boat gained momentum. Mordwyr.

Spears stabbed down, one piercing Mordwyr between shoulder and neck. He gave a strangled cry and fell into the sea.

Behind Corban there was a scream: Dath. He dropped his bow and ran into the surf, slipped, fell, staggered on. He reached his da and began heaving him back towards the beach.

Along the shoreline the battle was over, but they had failed; the boat they needed so badly was slipping out to sea, the water too deep now for them to chase after it. Then something punched into the boat's mast. A flaming arrow. Before Corban registered what was happening, flames caught in the sail, leaping up, consuming the cloth. Another fire-arrow slammed into the mast, heartbeats later another onto the deck. Men were yelling, running about, throwing buckets of water. Corban looked back and saw a figure standing knee-deep in the surf beside Mordwyr's burned-out fisher boat. Camlin – he was tying strips of cloth to arrows, igniting them in the flames that still flickered on the fisher-boat, firing them in a steady stream at the retreating boat. Marrock joined him and soon a dozen flaming arrows were burning on the enemy ship. Flames were roaring now, smoke swirling thick and black. The shapes of two men appeared near the rail. A flaming arrow pierced one's neck, sending him crashing back into the smoke. The other leaped from the rail and began swimming for shore.

Corban splashed into the surf, wading out to Dath. His friend was staggering under the weight of his da, his mouth moving, but Corban couldn't hear him over the churning sea. He put his arm under Mordwyr's arm, the water foaming pink around the fisherman. His mam joined them and together they pulled Mordwyr to the shore.

Dath fell upon his da, calling to him, shaking him, tears blurring his eyes, strings of snot hanging from his nose; one look was clear to Corban. Mordwyr was gone, his eyes empty, the muscles in his face loose, like melted wax. He put a hand upon his friend's shoulder.

It is over, and I'm still alive. Relief washed through him, slowly replacing the rush of fear and desperation that had consumed him during the short battle. He searched for his mam's face and saw her standing with her bloodstained spear. Tears streaked her cheeks. Bodies lay limp and twisted about them, blood pooling in the sand, the sea frothing pink. *So much death. Is it ever going to end?* He felt a wave of nausea, fought to keep the contents of his stomach from rising.

Vonn, Farrell and Anwarth had waded into the sea. They were moving towards the man swimming from the boat, all of them with weapons raised.

'Wait!' Marrock yelled, splashing out to them. 'Don't kill him.'

Anwarth heard and lowered his blade, Farrell and Vonn obeying more reluctantly. The three of them grabbed the man and dragged him out of the waves, throwing him to the sand close to where Corban stood with Dath.

'We saw a host of boats sailing; there is a warband camped beyond these woods. What is happening here?' Marrock asked, but the warrior just stared defiantly at him. His eyes were drawn to Storm, stood in the surf beside Corban.

In a burst of speed, Camlin had the man's hair in his fist. 'We don't have time for this,' the woodsman said, and slashed the prisoner across the back of one leg.

The man screamed, tried to pull away, but Camlin held tight to him, then brought his knife-tip to the warrior's throat. He was abruptly still, silent except for his laboured breathing.

'Now answer the question.'

'Queen Rhin has conquered Narvon. We are sailing to invade Ardan.'

'How many of you are there?'

'Over a thousand. Most have sailed.'

'Why not all of you?'

'Not enough boats. We've got to wait for those that left today to unload in Ardan, then come back for us.'

'How many still here?'

A shrug. 'Two, three hundred.'

Marrock nodded grimly. 'And who leads you?'

'Morcant.'

Corban stiffened. He knew that name. Rhin's first-sword, the man who had duelled and lost to Tull, back in Badun on Midwinter's Eve. The man who had led the ambush where Queen Alona had died. The man who had killed his friend, Ronan.

'Is he in the village?' Edana asked. She also knew who Morcant was. They all did.

'No, he has sailed already.'

Marrock looked out to sea. 'And why have you come after us?'

'Thought you were spies of Owain. He cannot know about us.' The man shrugged, causing Camlin's knife to draw a drop of blood.

Marrock sighed and rubbed a hand over his face.

'I have told you all I know,' the man begged. 'Please, let me go. I will say nothing about you, tell them I was knocked unconscious in the battle. Anything you want me to say.'

Marrock frowned at him. 'What's your name?'

'Haf,' the warrior said, his eyes pleading.

Marrock opened his mouth to speak, then Camlin cut the prisoner's throat.

Dark blood spurted, the warrior gurgled and sank slowly to the ground, his blood soaking into the sand.

'He could not live,' Camlin said, facing Marrock's glare, wiping his blade clean in the sand. 'He has seen us, knows our numbers, our strengths. He saw the wolven.' He nodded at Storm. 'She's a surprise that has helped save our necks more than once today.'

Marrock was pale, stiff with anger. 'Right or wrong, it was not your decision,' he said. 'We are no cut-throat rabble. You will wait for a command, is that clear?'

Camlin held Marrock's gaze, then nodded. 'Aye, chief,' he said.

'What do we do now?' Anwarth asked, voicing Corban's own question. 'We have no boat to escape with.'

'It's either steal one or cut inland and walk to Domhain,' Halion said.

They discussed the options back and forth: Marrock wanting to steal a boat from the village, Halion advocating fleeing inland.

'Fleeing to Domhain does not seem to have been the safest choice,' Marrock said.

No one knows what to do, Corban thought. *All of us exhausted, scared.*

'For what it's worth,' Camlin said into the silence, 'I think there's more chance of staying alive if we cut across land. I'm not saying we'll make it to Domhain, but I think we'll stay alive longer that way.'

'But we would move too slowly,' Marrock said. 'We do not have enough horses, even if those that you hobbled are still there. We will be chased, and those doing the chasing will be mounted. We would be run down within a day.'

'Aye, there is that. But let me have a few hands and I think I could steal us a few extra horses – there were paddocks along the river – my vote is that horses are easier to steal than boats.'

They discussed it a little longer, until Heb finished the conversation. 'Talk can accomplish much, but all it will accomplish here is our deaths,' he said. 'It will not be long before the men sent to find us are missed.'

'Heb is right,' Edana said.

'For once,' muttered Brina.

CHAPTER EIGHTEEN

CYWEN

Cywen was on her hands and knees collecting eggs in the garden. Buddai thought it was an invitation to play and was swatting at her with a paw. Absently she told him to *shoo*.

Days had begun to pass in a kind of haze for Cywen. Two nights had passed since she had been questioned by Nathair. She had filled most of her time since then with routine chores – cleaning the house, tending the garden, working at the stables. She was worried about Shield, Corban's stallion. He was such a fine mount, too fine, and there was more than one of Owain's men with an eye on him. It would be a grief too far if one of them were to take Shield from Dun Carreg. She must keep him here, safe for Corban's return. Somehow that was important to her.

In her mind she had spent almost every waking moment going over the questions Nathair had asked her – about Gar, about Ban. Nathair and Sumur were linked to her family, somehow. And it was obvious that Sumur knew Gar, though that should have been almost impossible.

And behind all of this was the thought, the possibility, the *hope*, that Corban and Gar and her mam were hiding in the tunnels beneath Dun Carreg. It was a vision that she clung to, that helped her to rise from sleep every day and put strength in her limbs. All she wanted to do was get a torch and go searching for them, but on the morning after her meeting with Nathair she had noticed a shadow following her as she'd made her way to the stables. *Conall*. That night someone else had stood in the shadow of a doorway opposite her house. All night. She was being watched and she could not lead people – *the enemy* – to the hidden tunnels where Edana might be hiding.

But she could not wait forever; her need to know was a physical sensation in the pit of her stomach. And with that, suddenly, she was done waiting, a plan forming in her mind.

She took the eggs indoors, the last of the day melting into dusk. Quickly she gathered all she needed: a bundle of rush torches, flint and tinder, a bag to put it all in, and buckled her belt of knives across her shoulder. She gave Buddai a thick marrow bone she'd traded for with the butcher earlier. Then, as the shadows were dissolving into night, she stepped into her back garden and agilely scaled the rose wall at the garden's far end, slipping almost invisibly through her neighbour's courtyard and into the street beyond.

Cywen stood staring at the beach. Something was wrong, different.

She had entered the tunnels through the hidden doorway in the fortress high above, made her way slowly through them, and now she was standing in a cave that looked out on the beach and bay. It was still night, dawn a long way off, although she had spent long hours searching the tunnels for her kin. Only at the end had she found evidence that they had been in the tunnels at all – the dead wyrm and warrior nearby, lying in the cavern at the end of this cave. But they were not here now. She felt drained, defeated.

They were gone.

Had they escaped into Havan, then made their way to the marshes in the west that everyone was saying were where Ardan's survivors were fleeing?

A full moon silvered the bay and beach, shimmering on wave-tops and shingle alike. The only shape in the bay was Nathair's ship, bobbing on the swell of the tide, huge compared to the fishing vessels on the beach. The fisher-boats were lined along the shore, none out at sea, as all able-bodied men had been taken to the fortress and forced into labouring at defences for Owain as he prepared for the coming of Queen Rhin. *I hope she rips his heart out*, she thought. *Or the other way round. Either way it is one less that'll need killing.*

Then she realized what was different. A boat was missing, the only boat she'd ever had cause to look for.

Dath's boat.

She checked again, studying the outline of each boat slumped in the shingle. It was definitely not there. So they had sailed away – her mam, Corban, Gar, Edana and the rest. But where to? The thought of following reared first in her mind, but follow them where? Perhaps they'd sailed west to the marshes, but perhaps they hadn't. There was no obvious course, and they would have been scared, maybe injured among them, the need just to get away driving them.

She sighed, long and deep, then turned and made her way back into the cave, striking sparks into a fresh torch once she had turned a corner on the narrow path, hiding her from anyone looking from the beach.

She slipped once on the sea-soaked path that snaked into the cave, then pushed through the glamour and found herself inside the great cavern where the dead wyrm and warrior lay. She gave them hardly a glance as she strode through the room, eager to be back home. Ever up she climbed, the tunnels high and wide, built by giants. Shadows flickered and water dripped, echoing. In time, Cywen found herself in the other cavern, where the skeleton of another wyrm lay, the one she had found with Ban when they had first discovered these hidden tunnels that bored into the cliffs beneath Dun Carreg. As she passed through the tunnel, something caught her eye – a reflection on the far wall. She paused, thoughts of her warm fire and curling up next to Buddai calling to her, but her inquisitiveness won and she walked away from the exit, raising her torch high, looking at the wall.

She blinked, eyes widening. There was the outline of a great creature on the rock. At first she thought that it had been painted on, but as she held her torch closer she saw that she was wrong. They were bones, embedded, fossilized into the rock. The creature had a mouth full of sharp teeth, wings that spread as wide as a fisher-boat. Her da had told tales of creatures, whole species that had existed before the Scourging, great monsters that had been wiped out in Elyon's day of wrath, caught in either flood or fire. She reached up, her fingertips tracing long talons.

Nearby there was a darker shadow in the rock wall – she moved closer and saw that it was an entrance to another tunnel, disguised somehow by a curve in the rock. She peered back at her route home, then looked into the new tunnel.

She took a deep breath and stepped into this new tunnel, driven by curiosity.

It was much the same as those she had already searched, high walled, smooth and damp. It turned more, giving the sense of spiralling, somehow, though it was hard to tell. In time she noticed a change ahead of her – it sounded different, the drip of water louder, a deeper echo. She stepped into an opening, a black hole spreading before her. A chain hung through its middle, disappearing above and below into darkness.

This is the keep's well, she thought, peering up, the darkness a solid thing, consuming her torchlight. The path she was on hugged the well, narrower, twisting upwards. She followed it as the tunnel bored back into the rock, leaving the gaping hole that was the well behind. She breathed a sigh of relief.

It was not long before she stepped into another cavern. At first she thought it was a dead end, but then saw lines of faint light flickering on the far wall. She moved closer, then with a hiss of exhaled breath stubbed her torch out.

It was a door.

She approached it slowly and upon closer examination realized that it was a door frame, with wide planks of wood nailed across it. She peered through one of the gaps, seeing a room beyond, filled with barrels, crates, bottles. Some kind of storage room – a cellar? A torch burned in a sconce on a wall. So this room led into the fortress; it was inhabited. And whoever it was knew of the tunnels, had access to them.

The board she was leaning against gave way; with a creak its nails pulled out of the frame. She fell forward with it and found herself leaning half in, half out of the room.

She froze, too scared to move, too scared to breathe.

To her relief, no one came running. It was as she thought, a cellar of some kind. At the far end of the room steps rose up and disappeared into the ceiling.

A sound caused her to go rigid again. It came from behind a closed door in the room. She was about to bolt when she heard it again. A voice, weak, little more than a whisper.

'Water, please,' the voice said.

Before she could think about what she was doing, she had squirmed through the gap in the doorway, spilling onto a flagstone floor. She hurried over to the closed door, saw it was locked.

'I know you're there,' the voice rasped. 'I can see the shadow of your feet.'

She stepped away.

'Please, just some water.'

Cywen pulled the door, a chain rattling around an iron ring, then drew one of her knives and worried at the lock's hinge, which was bolted to the door frame. It seemed to be the weakest part, but there was no give in it.

She chewed her lip, then ran over to the staircase. It rose up into shadow. She climbed a few steps, then saw a trapdoor above her. Making a decision, she ran back, grabbing one of the axes that were leaning beside the boarded door frame that led into the tunnels.

With a crack and a shower of sparks she hacked through the chain and swung the door open.

A horrible smell leaked out, urine and faeces, a figure inside sprawled upon dirty rushes.

He was thin, haggard, dirty, his beard grown unkempt, a grimed bandage tied about his neck, but she still recognized him.

It was Pendathran.

CHAPTER NINETEEN

MAQUIN

Maquin smiled wearily as he set foot on the moss-grown bridge spanning a black-flowing river. The Rhenus, marking the western edge of Forn Forest and also officially the eastern border of Isiltir.

On the far side of the river the bridge led straight to a gateway set in a high stone wall, crumbling and vine choked. Beyond the wall rose a grey tower: Brikan, home of the Gadrai. At least it had been, when there had been enough Gadrai alive to fill it. Now the Gadrai was just the three of them.

Fifteen nights it had taken to walk from Haldis; ten since they had encountered Veradis. The young warrior had been true to his word, had led the giant and those searching for them away. Maquin owed Veradis his life. It saddened him to think that they were on different sides; he hoped they would not meet again.

He stood in the courtyard, looking around at the silent walls. Orgull climbed the steps that led to the tower, Tahir limping behind him, and together the two warriors disappeared into the shadows of Brikan's keep. Maquin did not follow just yet. He was remembering. The day he and Kastell had first come to the Gadrai: this courtyard full of people, noises, life, being welcomed by Vandil and Orgull as sword-brothers, the long hours spent training in this courtyard, the nights standing watch on the wall, all with Kastell. He felt a lump rise in his throat and pushed it down. *I shall grieve for you soon*, he promised. *When Jael is dead.*

The three of them sat around a crackling fire that kept the encroaching darkness at bay, passing a skin of ale between them. A few stores had been found, skins of ale, a few amphorae of wine, a round of cheese still good enough to eat, some salted pork in the cold room. To Maquin it tasted like the finest meal.

Tahir rubbed his leg. His wound had healed surprisingly well – Maquin had seen many die from infection and fever that came from injuries far less severe.

'We'll be on a boat from the morrow,' Maquin said. 'No more walking for you for a while.'

'Thank Elyon,' Tahir said. He was young, not much older than Kastell, with long, thick-muscled arms that made him look out of proportion.

'Won't be a pleasure trip,' Orgull said. 'A lot of leagues to row between here and Dun Kellen.'

'I'd rather row it than walk it,' Tahir replied, drinking from the ale skin.

Their plan had been to make it to Brikan, where they knew a number of boats were moored, and then take the river north to Dun Kellen, where King Romar's estranged wife, Gerda, dwelt. She had borne Romar a child before she had left him. Haelan, the lad's name was. He was ten years old and now heir to the realm of Isiltir.

'Why is Gerda not queen?' Tahir asked.

'She's an obstinate woman,' Maquin said. He had lived many years in Mikil, had served there when Romar had married Gerda, and seen her ride away from Mikil with her son, Haelan, as well.

'Obstinate?' Tahir asked. 'What do you mean?'

'Pig-headed,' Orgull said.

'She was not given to taking orders, even from Romar,' Maquin elaborated.

'Oh. And we're taking word to her,' Tahir said. 'Not sure I like the sound of that.'

'She's well suited to stand against Jael. She'll not give up her son's throne without a fight.'

'Do you think Jael has a chance of claiming the throne?' Tahir asked.

'He thinks he has,' Orgull said. 'He has Romar's blood in his veins, and he has the stones to try and take it. And he has a powerful supporter in Nathair. It'll come down to a fight, I should think, and that'll be decided by who can field the most warriors. The sooner we get word to Gerda, the more chance she'll have to save her son's neck.'

'Most of Isiltir's warriors are food for crows at Haldis,' Maquin said. 'Even Jael can't have that many men about him.'

'True enough. At Mikil he'll have more men who will most likely support him, but not a war-host. But, as I said, he has strong support. Nathair is on the rise, and with men in his camp like that Calidus and his Jehar warriors . . .' He trailed off, all of them remembering the deadly skill and speed that the black-clad Jehar had demonstrated at Haldis.

Maquin drank from the ale skin, watching Orgull across the flames. He was a big man, bald headed and bull necked. Maquin had always thought that Orgull was the brawn to Vandil's brain, the first and second captains of the Gadrai. But their flight back through Forn had shown there was a lot more to Orgull than muscle.

And those things he had said, about King Braster, about a secret brotherhood, about the starstone axe and the God-War and a Black Sun . . .

He took another swig of ale. On the flight from Haldis there had never seemed a time to talk about these things, fleeing from one danger to the next, evading human hunters and Forn's predators both. But now they were in Brikan with a measure of safety about them, at least for tonight.

'What is this brotherhood that you spoke of, the reason you spoke to Braster?' Maquin asked across the flames.

Orgull stared at Maquin; Tahir glanced from one to the other.

'You have a right to know,' Orgull said at length. 'And if I cannot trust the two of you, my sword-brothers, then who in this world can I trust? It is as I said. When I was young, younger even than you –' he nodded at Tahir – 'I met a man. He came to my da's hold – he was a warrior, strong and skilled, and I looked up to him because of that, but also he seemed wise. When he spoke, it felt as if the whole world should listen . . .' He paused, clearly remembering.

'One night he came to my father and me, told us of things. Strange, otherworldly things, of a war that has raged for thousands of years, which is still being fought. *All will fight in this war*, he said, *all will choose a side, the darkness or the light.* At the time I was young, you understand. I was caught up in the heroism of it, so when he told us that he was seeking out men – a brotherhood, he called it – to help in this coming war, when he asked for our aid, our oaths, I gave mine willingly, and so did my da. My da lives still in the north, with my brothers and other kin. Giant-killers all of us, living so close to Forn and the north, but I felt the call of the Gadrai more than they did. I left.' He paused, stared silently into the flames for long moments. 'I almost forgot about the man, the oath, and just lived my life. But then I saw him again, and he told me of others that had sworn the same oath. Men like Braster. He reminded me of the things he had told me – things that I am hearing whispered about now – of the God-War, of how these Banished Lands will become the battleground of angels and demons, of the Seven Treasures, of the avatars of Elyon and Asroth.' He looked at his palm, tracing an old scar. 'And my oath still stands.'

Veradis had spoken about those things too, on the journey through the Bairg Mountains to Forn, when Kastell had been alive. At the time Maquin had laughed. Angels and demons were hard to believe in when the sun was shining bright and laughter was on the air. But now, in the cold heart of a giant tower in Forn, after the battle at Haldis and all he had seen, it was easier to believe. He shook his head. He had always trusted what he could see, touch, feel. The rest of it mattered little to him. And now, even if it was true, it still didn't matter that much. 'All sounds like faery tales to me,' Maquin muttered. 'Only thing that matters is putting Jael in the ground.'

Tahir looked at him. 'A man with revenge in his heart should dig two graves, my old mam used to say to me.'

'As long as Jael's in one of them, I'll be content,' Maquin said. But still, he could not stop Orgull's words rattling around his head – *all will fight, all will choose a side.*

Whose side am I on?

'The man who told you of these things,' he said to Orgull. 'What was his name?'

'Meical.'

The next day they set out early, dawn a mere hint beyond the trees. The Rhenus was liquid black. Maquin dipped his oar; Orgull sat across from him and they rowed away from the small quay that jutted from Brikan's walls.

On the second day they saw a large barge moored on the eastern bank of the river. No one answered their calls so they approached cautiously. Orgull was the first to recognize it.

'It is the one we were guarding that was attacked by the Hunen and their white wyrms,' he said.

Maquin peered closely, seeing corpses strewn across the deck and other bodies littering the wide track of the east bank; a booted foot, a hand, the shaft of a giant war-hammer, a horse's skull, all lying where they had fallen in battle, clothes rotted, flesh picked clean by Forn's inhabitants.

In silence they pushed away from the barge and moved on up the river.

By highsun on the fifth day the trees began to thin, great shafts of the sun beaming down upon the travellers. Soon the river swept them from the forest into rolling meadows, the riverbank thick with wildflowers; it was as if they had rowed into spring.

'How far to Dun Kellen?' Tahir asked, scratching his leg. He had been complaining of a sore arse, stiff arms and blisters on his palms for two days solid.

'Ten to twelve days, if nothing slows us,' Orgull said. Tahir groaned, looking at his palms.

'We could always put you ashore, let you walk,' Orgull suggested. Tahir did not reply, except to grip his oar and continue rowing.

Early on the seventh day since leaving Forn they were breaking camp where they had pulled ashore for the night. A mist hung heavy over the river, clinging to thick beds of reed. Orgull was shaving his head with a sharp knife.

'Why do you do that? Tahir asked. 'Why not just let it grow?'

'I used to have fine long hair,' Orgull said, 'or so the ladies told me. When I first joined the Gadrai, on one of my first patrols we came upon a party of Hunen. One of them grabbed a fist full of my hair and threw me about like a rag doll. He bashed me into a tree. I didn't wake up till I was back in Brikan – my sword-brothers had carried me there.' He smiled, half a grimace. 'I've shaved my head clean ever since.'

'Do you hear that?' Maquin said, head cocked to one side.

They all listened. The river was silent, muted by the mist. A moorhen cried out, long and mournful. Then Maquin heard it again: horses' hooves, lots of them, the jingle of harness and chainmail.

'Quickly,' Orgull hissed, and as quietly as they could, they climbed back into their boat and pushed away from the shore. As time passed the mist evaporated, giving a good view of the land about them. It was flatter now they were further north, broken up with ragged stands of trees. There was no sign of the riders they had heard.

Late in the day they saw shapes ahead: a stone bridge spanning the river, a tower on the western bank, a sprawling village of timber and thatch behind it. Figures moved on the bridge and amongst the buildings.

Orgull hissed a warning and they rowed to the bank, pulling the boat ashore, then crept slowly through the rushes.

A banner hung from the tower, snapping in the wind. Upon it was a jagged lightning bolt in a black sky. It was Romar's mark, the crest of Isiltir, taken from the name the giants had used – the stormlands. But as Maquin looked at it he saw something else on the banner, something intertwined with the jagged lightning, coiling about it. A white serpent.

'I don't like the look of that,' Maquin said quietly.

'Me neither,' Orgull said. 'Whose banner is it?'

'If you don't ask you won't know, my mam used to say,' murmured Tahir.

'Your mam was a wise woman,' Orgull said. 'Let's go and ask someone.'

Maquin crept through the reeds, wincing at every rustle. He and Tahir were close to the bridge now, though it had taken them a long time to get this close.

A handful of houses were clustered about a squat tower. Maquin could smell horse dung, and hear the gentle neigh of a horse off in the darkness. Torches burned around the tower, small patches of light in the night, and further away larger fires burned. Men stood at the doors to the tower, grim-looking and dressed for war. This was a warband, no doubt, though it was hard to tell their numbers in the darkness – two, three hundred, maybe more. The banner hung limp on the tower, but Maquin remembered Isiltir's lightning bolt and the serpent wrapped around it.

'We'll sit tight a while, see what we see,' he whispered to Tahir.

They lay there waiting a long time before the tower door swung open and a handful of men strode out. At their head was Jael.

Without thinking, Maquin reached for his sword, then felt Tahir's grip on his arm.

'Don't,' the lad hissed.

'It's Jael,' he whispered back.

'I know, but there's too many – you'll get yourself killed, and worse, get me killed.'

Maquin wrestled with the compulsion, then released his sword hilt.

They crept back along the riverbank to Orgull and told him all they had seen, then waited until deep of night, when most would be sleeping, and pushed the boat back into the river, letting the current take them downstream. When they were convinced they were far enough away that sound would not carry, they rowed like their lives depended on it.

By the time the sun rose behind them Maquin was slick with sweat, his back throbbing, muscles burning. They had come leagues since the bridge, giving them a good head start on Jael. Their guess was that he was moving on Gerda and Haelan, Romar's son. Striking quickly, before news could spread and any resistance could rally. So their task was to reach Dun Kellen ahead of Jael.

'Keep pulling,' Orgull said behind them. Maquin wanted to say something but could not find the breath to do it.

Dun Kellen rose out of a river mist, the sun sinking behind it. Built upon a hill, the town around it was a disorderly mass that flowed down the hill's slopes. A mass of quays edged the river; the three men steered towards one of them and made fast the boat.

'What now?' said Tahir. He sniffed and pulled a face as fishermen and traders began to take notice of them. 'And what's that smell?' he muttered.

Orgull strode away, eyes fixed on the fortress on the hill.

'Civilization,' Maquin said, following Orgull.

At the gates to the fortress a handful of guards stood with spears in their hands. Maquin noticed the shoddy state of the fortress' defences. A whole section of the wall had collapsed, timber frame and cladding filling the gap. As he looked along the walls he saw there were a number of similar sections.

Not the best place to endure a siege.

'You – big man,' a guard called, pointing at Orgull with his spear. 'What's your business in Dun Kellen?' He looked at Maquin and Tahir, at their leather war gear and their swords. 'Sellswords?' He sneered. 'We don't need your sort round here.'

'We are the last survivors of the Gadrai,' Orgull said, frowning down at the man. He reached inside his cloak and the guards around him drew back, levelling spears and reaching for swords. Maquin and Tahir spread to either side of Orgull, hands on their own weapons. Bloodshed was only an instant away.

Orgull pulled out a long cloth bundle and slowly unwrapped it, revealing a sheathed sword. He held it over his head.

'This is King Romar's sword. He lies slain in the heart of Forn Forest, betrayed by his own kin. His murderer is two days behind us, at best, and he would add your heads to the pile he has already gathered.'

'That got their attention,' Tahir whispered to Maquin.

Maquin remembered the Lady Gerda as tall, strong-boned and athletic. He had last seen her three years ago, riding away from Mikil with her son Haelan and her shieldmen. Now her tall frame was layered in fat, folds of skin rippling down her bare arms. She was sitting on a chair beside Varick, her elder brother. He was thick boned like his sister, with streaks of grey at his temples and a plain, open face. In his hands he held Romar's sword. It gave a metallic hiss as he drew it and held it up.

'That's Romar's sword,' Gerda said, 'or I'm a fisherman's wife. The question,' Gerda said to Orgull, 'is do we believe you?'

'Why else would we come here?' Tahir blurted. 'Speeding like Asroth were on our heels to give you warning.' He looked at his hands, raw and blistered from rowing.

'Yes, why else would you come here?' Gerda mused.

'Do you want a reward for this?' Varick asked, still staring at the sword.

'Kill Jael, that'll be reward enough,' Maquin snarled.

Gerda looked at him. 'Is this some blood-feud between you and Jael? And you would have us do your work for you?'

'He has cause for blood-feud with Jael,' Orgull said. 'As do you. As do I. I am Orgull, captain of the Gadrai, and I have come to you out of loyalty to Isiltir, out of a desire to see justice done. And to stop Isiltir being used as a pawn in the coming war that will overrun the Banished Lands. If we are deceiving you, or wrong, then nothing will happen. If we are right, Jael will be at your gates soon, probably demanding that Haelan become his ward until the boy is of age. Jael means to rule Isiltir, and he will commit betrayal and murder to do it. He already has.' Orgull shrugged. 'Do not believe us – that is your choice – but in Elyon's name, choose to be wise. Send out scouts to see if a warband approaches from the south. Gather your warriors about you, make ready. Just in case.'

'Better to stay safe than sorry, my mam used to say,' muttered Tahir.

'Wise words,' said Orgull.

Maquin stepped forward. 'Jael can pour honey on his words, but make no mistake: once he has Haelan in his power, he will kill him.' Maquin looked down. 'I have seen what he is prepared to do.'

'No one will harm a hair on my son's head,' Gerda said fiercely. 'I will die first.'

You may get a chance to prove that.

'I'll send out scouts,' Varick said, 'and make sure my warriors are sober and ready.' He looked at his sister. 'It will do no harm.'

'My lord, call in from your lands all warriors sworn to you that you can. The fate of Isiltir could be decided in the next few days,' Orgull urged.

'So you say. Perhaps I will do as you suggest. And if you are speaking the truth, then you will have my thanks.'

Gerda rose and strode to them, standing and looking deep into each one's face. Her expression hardened. 'Fetch Haelan,' she said over her shoulder to a shieldman who had been standing in the shadows of her chair. 'I believe them.'

'There they are,' Tahir said, pointing one of his long arms. Maquin followed and saw a shadow in the distance.

'They have crossed the river already,' Maquin observed.

It was just a day later and they were standing on Dun Kellen's battlements, close to the gate, warriors lined along the wall either side of them. Varick's messengers had been sent out to the holds but they knew it would take time for the men to muster. Time they didn't have. Nearby, the stone wall and battlements were replaced by wooden planks to fill the crumbling gaps of the fortress.

The warband quickly grew larger, a cloud of dust kicked up by the horses. Maquin could see Jael at the front, beside his banner-man, his pennant snapping in their wake. Varick had ordered that the streets of Dun Kellen be evacuated but there were still people to be seen. As the sound of the approaching warband filled the air a sudden sense of panic seemed to spread, people hurrying, running for shelter.

The warband reached the outskirts of Dun Kellen. Riders from the flanks peeled away and began circling the town, filtering into side streets whilst the bulk of the warband rode up the main avenue leading to Dun Kellen's gates.

'I remember wiping the snot from his nose,' Gerda said as she watched Jael approach. 'I wonder what terms he will offer for the head of my son.' Maquin looked at her but said nothing, remembering Jael and Kastell fighting in the cavern beneath Haldis. Seeing Jael plunge his sword into Kastell's stomach. His fingers twitched and he reached for his sword.

'Be ready,' Orgull said as the riders appeared. Screams were rising from the town, people were scattering in the wide avenue before Jael and his shieldmen as they thundered into view. Someone slipped in the road and disappeared under the flood of horses, screams quickly cut short, then in a spray of mud Jael pulled his warriors up, about a hundred paces before the gate.

'Let's hear his terms,' Varick said, stepping forward to stand on the arch above the gateway. Jael clicked his horse on, a spear held loosely in his hand. Only his banner-man accompanied him.

'Greetings, Jael, and welcome to Dun Kellen, kinsman. What brings you here?' Varick called down.

Jael's eyes were fixed on Varick. He turned his horse in a tight circle. As he came back round out of the turn he hurled his spear. It flew straight, striking Varick in the throat and throwing him backwards in a spray of blood. Jael wheeled his horse and galloped back to his cheering men.

On the wall men were yelling in shock and horror, warriors letting spears fly at the retreating Jael. They all missed. Maquin looked at the form of Varick, blood splattered about his corpse; Gerda and a huddle of others were staring at him, wide-eyed. Then Maquin looked back to Jael punching the air as he reached his gathered warriors, men jumping from horses now, chopping with axes at the timber frames of houses.

Jael did not come to offer terms.

CHAPTER TWENTY

CYWEN

Cywen could not believe her eyes. Pendathran, King Brenin's battlechief, was staring back at her. But he was dead, had fallen in the feast-hall the night Dun Carreg fell. Or so she had been told. What was Evnis doing with him locked in his cellar?

'What the hell are you doing here?' Pendathran said, his voice hoarse.

'Don't know,' Cywen said automatically.

'Water?' he asked.

She looked about, but could see no jug or water barrel. She shook her head.

'Quick, girl, help me up.'

Cywen took his hand and pulled him upright. There were deep cuts on his exposed forearm, part-scabbed and weeping blood. He towered above her, taking long, ragged breaths. The bandage around his neck was crusted black with blood.

'Put your arm round me,' Cywen said and steered him out of the cell. They weaved through the cellar to the boarded doorway. Cywen propped Pendathran against a wall and set to levering boards from the door frame. She was acutely aware of the noise she was making, and kept taking furtive glances at the shadowed staircase.

'Looking won't make you any quieter, or quicker,' Pendathran croaked. He picked up a discarded axe leaning against the wall and tried to help her.

Cywen shot him a scowl and set to the last board. With a creak it pulled free.

Cywen pulled a fresh torch from her bag and sparked it with

tinder and flint. 'Come on,' she said and led Pendathran into the darkness of the tunnels.

When they finally emerged from the cave onto the beach Pendathran sank to the sand. It was still dark but the moon was fading, pale and wan as dawn greyed the land.

Cywen could not believe they had made it this far. Pendathran had staggered through the tunnels, at times semi-conscious. When alert he asked for news, information about what was happening in Dun Carreg. In return she discovered that it was Evnis who had imprisoned him. Evnis who knew about the tunnels, had access to them.

The worst of their passage through the tunnels had been when they'd come upon the well, where the path spiralled around the deep hole. Cywen still did not know how Pendathran had managed to avoid toppling into the dark emptiness. But somehow he had. The rest of the journey had passed into terror-filled nightmare, Cywen constantly pausing to listen for the pursuit she expected at any moment: the baying of Evnis' hounds catching her scent, the sound of running feet, the shouts of her trackers as they saw her. But it had not happened, and now they were here, on the beach of Havan, just before the sun rose and betrayed them to the world.

Frantically she looked around. She had given little thought to what they would do if they made it this far. She scanned the shore, eyes drawn again to where Dath's boat was usually beached. Then an idea sparked. 'We cannot rest here,' she said, looping an arm under Pendathran's. He groaned but struggled to his feet.

They splashed through shallow pools, crabs scuttling out of their way, then along the path to the village, past the smokehouses, until Cywen saw a small house.

Dath's house.

The door was open. The smell that greeted them was stale and musty. The place had been ransacked: tables and chairs overturned, cupboards open, emptied. *Probably Owain's men when they occupied the town during the siege, before they moved into Dun Carreg.*

There was a barrel with cold fresh rainwater by the back door. Cywen fetched some for Pendathran, who had collapsed onto a sagging cot. He drank and drank, water spilling over his face, soaking his beard. Cywen had to pull the jug from his lips, worrying that he would vomit.

'I will bring you food when I can,' she said to Pendathran. 'I will try tonight, though Evnis has had me watched.'

'Why, girl?' Pendathran mumbled.

'I'm not sure – maybe he thinks I can lead him to Corban, and Edana.' She shrugged. 'You must stay out of sight. Stay here until I return.'

'No chance of me going far,' Pendathran said.

Cywen stood there, worrying, then turned on her heel and sped to the door.

'Girl,' Pendathran called after her. She stopped and looked back. 'Thank you,' he said.

She flashed him a quick smile and ran.

After a brief hesitation she turned towards the village. With every passing moment it was more likely that Evnis would discover Pendathran had escaped. Surely he would have men search the tunnels for him.

As the sun rose she mingled with labourers from the village who were making their way up to the fortress. She pulled her hood up and slipped across the bridge and through Stonegate unnoticed. Once back in Dun Carreg she ran through the stone-paved back-streets, skirting her house to climb alley walls and slip in through her garden. Buddai greeted her with a wagging tail as she strode across the kitchen and peered out of her window. A shadow still occupied a doorway across the street, though now it was slumped on the floor, sleeping. She felt exhausted, but knew that if she lay down she would probably sleep half the day. That she must not do. *Give the spy no reason to report to Evnis, nothing to raise his suspicions.* So she broke her fast with some bacon and honey-cakes, half of which she fed to a drooling Buddai, and then set about her usual daily tasks. She made her way to the stables, where she harnessed up selected horses for warriors to train with in the Rowan Field. One of the horses was Shield. She took her time with him, gave him an extra apple and scowled at the man that climbed into his saddle. It was Drust, the red-haired warrior from Narvon, the one in the feast-hall who had told her to take Buddai, the day after Dun Carreg had fallen.

As the day wore on she felt a tension growing in her gut. There was something she must do.

Evnis must surely know Pendathran had escaped by now. He would scour the tunnels searching for him, but he would not risk baying hounds during the day – Pendathran was clearly a closely guarded secret, one that King Owain knew nothing about, and Evnis was not fool enough to draw attention with a full hunt in broad daylight. He would not risk his hounds beyond the tunnels until nightfall, surely. That meant Cywen had some time to do what was necessary. She steeled herself, then set about the task.

The sun was sinking towards the ocean when she left her home, her bag slung over her back. She resisted the urge to look over her shoulder, knowing that someone would be shadowing her, and made her way to the stables.

Once there she slipped inside an empty stall. Quickly, she tied her hair back tight to her head, stuffed straw inside her tunic until it was near bursting, then drew a cloak from her bag, pulling the hood up. She emptied the contents of her bag into a saddlebag. Finally she shouldered a saddle and tack as well as the saddlebag. Taking a deep breath, she stepped from the stables and walked purposefully across the yard. She noticed Conall leaning beside a water barrel, eyes fixed on the stable door. She smiled as she walked away from him into the streets of the fortress.

As soon as she was out of sight she dumped the saddle and tack, heading with speed towards her quarry: Evnis' tower. She paused, stepped into deep shadows caused by the sinking sun, then made her way furtively along Evnis' wall. When she judged she was in the right place she stopped, testing the mortar between the wall's stones with a finger. It was soft and crumbling, succumbing to years of salt in the air. She looked about once more, the street empty, silent, then drew two of her knives, stabbed them into gaps in the stone and began hauling herself up the wall. Dath had taught her how to do this – if he couldn't climb a wall, then it couldn't be climbed, though she'd never tell him that.

When she reached the top she wriggled forwards, hooked one arm over the wall, and smiled grimly to herself. A low-roofed building stretched before her. Evnis' kennels. She unslung her saddlebag, undoing the buckle with her teeth and spare hand.

A hound walked out of the kennel, tall and scar-eared. It stretched and sniffed, its head snapping round, catching her scent. Then it saw her and let out a great, baying howl. Other dogs flowed from the kennel, began barking and jumping at the wall. Panicking now, she emptied the contents of the saddlebag, lumps of meat showering the area. The dogs immediately began to wolf them down, snapping and snarling at one another.

A voice called out; a blond-haired figure appeared – Rafe.

Cywen ducked from view, half slid, half fell from the wall, then sprinted into the shadows. She wiped tears from her eyes. Evnis' hounds would not be hunting Pendathran tonight.

Cywen led the stallion through the tree-lined path into the Rowan Field. She had tried not to bring him, had used every excuse besides actually making him lame, but Drust had stepped in, examined Shield himself and declared him fit for use. He had looked at Cywen suspiciously, so she had ceased any more protests, knowing that Drust could stop her working in the stables if he wished.

He was waiting for her, in the Field. He strode over, smiling at Shield.

'He's a fine animal,' he said, his eyes fixed on Shield. He ran a hand down a foreleg, lifted it to examine the hoof. 'See, I told you, girl, there's nothing wrong with him.'

'I was mistaken,' Cywen muttered, handing him the reins.

'That you were,' Drust said, swinging into the saddle. 'Best not get too attached to this one,' he said, pulling Shield in a tight circle, 'he's a warhorse, if ever I saw one. Was made for battle.' He kicked his heels and Shield leaped away with a spray of turf.

Cywen watched as Drust urged Shield into a gallop, charging at the straw targets at the far end of the Field. With a battle-cry he left his spear quivering in one of them.

She skirted the edge of the Field, making for the outer wall that ringed the whole fortress. It was early but the sun was already hot, spring sliding steadily into summer. As she passed the weapons court she caught a glimpse of Rafe sparring. He was fighting an older, heavier man and seemed to be holding his own. Even as she watched, he swung a hard blow that whistled through his opponent's defence, cracking him on the shoulder.

She felt a pang of guilt at seeing Rafe, her thoughts turning instantly to the hounds that she had poisoned. Most had died, only a couple surviving, though they were still weak and emaciated two ten-nights later. Cywen was surprised any had lived – she had mixed a concoction that her da used to give his whelping bitches, both as a painkiller and a sedative, though she had made it ten times as potent as her da had.

Rafe was walking towards her from the weapons court. He had a slight limp, a reminder of the wound her brother had given him on the night Dun Carreg had fallen.

'No girls on the Field,' Rafe said to her as he drew near.

She ignored him and strode on, passing a huge pen on her path to the wall. A horrible smell came from it – rotting flesh and something worse. It was where Nathair kept his pet draig. Wide stone steps were hewn into the wall, made for giant strides. She looked back into the draig's pen as she climbed higher, caught a glimpse of it spilling from the burrow it had dug in the ground. She was sweating when she reached the top of the wall; the breeze up here was fresh and welcome. She leaned on the battlements and looked out beyond the fortress. It felt as if she could see the whole world. To the west the sea was a bright shimmering blanket in the summer sun, the sky and horizon so clear she could almost see the coast of Cambren, a smudge at the edge of her vision. She turned west and south, the river Tarin a bright line twisting through the landscape, through the dark of Baglun Forest. *I hope Pendathran still lives*, she thought.

King Brenin's old battlechief had stayed just one night in Dath's abandoned cottage; Cywen had brought him food and water the night she had poisoned the hounds. He had stayed there the next day, sleeping, then set out the following night. Cywen had told him all that she knew, of Queen Rhin's invasion of Narvon, the imminent battle looming between her and Owain. Of how rumour said that a resistance against Owain was growing in Ardan, based around the swamps and marshes in the west. That had been enough for Pendathran – he hadn't told her where he was going, but the look in his eyes had been enough.

'Come with me,' he had said. 'There's nothing for you here now.'

She had been tempted, but something held her back. Dun Carreg was her home. Buddai would be able to come with her, but not Shield. Who would look after him? *I could steal Shield, take him with me.* But she'd be followed. She was already being watched by Conall. If her kin were hiding in the west she could end up leading Evnis straight to them. *No. Not yet. Best let Pendathran find safety, and maybe I'll follow.*

'If you see my mam and brother, tell them . . .' she had said, then fell silent. She did not know what to tell them. That she missed them, that she wanted them to come back, what?

'I will, lass,' Pendathran had said, cupping her hand in his. 'And I will not forget what you have done for me.'

Then he had left, slipping into the night. As far as she knew, Evnis had not mounted any large search for him. How could he, under Owain's nose? He must be raging. She smiled at that thought.

Something caught her eye, a movement to the west, out on the sea. As she watched, it became clearer. Ships, lots of them, sleek and black-sailed, like the one already anchored in the bay. Closer and closer they came, horn blasts rising along the walls of Dun Carreg as they were spotted. Cywen counted ten, twenty ships, more – all sailing into the bay. Banners snapped from the mast of the first ship – a white eagle on a black field. Nathair's fleet had come.

CHAPTER TWENTY-ONE

CAMLIN

Camlin led them through the woods to where the horses were hob-bled.

They were still there, four of them.

Quickly, Marrock split the group. Edana and Halion mounted one horse, Heb and Brina another, though the old lady complained about having to hold on to Heb.

'You can squeeze me as tight as you like,' Heb said, 'only admit that you like it.' Brina slapped him across the back of the head.

Camlin chose Vonn, Anwarth and Dath to help him; the first two because they had fought well, and they were quick, looked as if they could move fast if they needed to. He chose Dath because the boy could do with a job to do. He felt sorry for the lad, knew what it was like to lose kin. He looked as if he was falling deeper into a pit that could be hard to climb out of.

'I'll help,' Corban volunteered.

'Don't think the smell of your wolven will help us sneak up on a herd of horses,' Camlin said. 'Could do with you, though, Gar. You've a way with horses.'

'I'll be going where Corban goes,' Gar said, and Camlin could see there was no negotiation in that. He shrugged.

'I'll come with you,' Marrock said. 'I could do with a lesson in sneaking about.' He grinned.

Camlin smiled back. 'All right then.'

'We'll ride to where the two hills meet, wait for you there,' Halion said, pointing across undulating meadows into the distance.

'If we have not joined you by sunrise, go on without us,' Marrock said.

With that the two groups split. Camlin watched Halion and Edana lead the riders off, heading along the wood's fringe, away from the village to avoid any watching eyes.

There was a new tension in the air between Marrock and Halion. The turn of events had hardened Marrock's opinion that they should have sailed back to Ardan. *Can't turn back time, though. A good leader should know that.* Camlin liked Marrock, thought of him as a friend. *But Halion's the natural leader, here. He's led men before, given orders.*

It's Edana that should be leading us, but instead she follows where anyone brave enough to speak up points. Edana had a haunted look about her; she had been silent since the battle on the beach. Truth was Edana didn't look fit to lead a pony, let alone a desperate band of runaways through enemy land. *Is she even worth saving? Worth going through all this for?* The thought of leaving, of just slinking away, entered Camlin's head again. But Edana wasn't the reason he was here, anyway. It was a combination of circumstance and a sense of loyalty to the friends he had made. Marrock, Dath, Corban. *Loyalty? What's happening to me?* He had felt a sense of camaraderie with Braith and his outlaws in the Darkwood, but he had always known that any one of them would cut his throat in his sleep if the circumstances called for it. Being here was different. The friends he'd made were not like that. He'd finally found a sense of belonging, of doing something right. *It probably won't last*, he thought, but while it did, he would not be leaving. *Not today.*

Brina and Heb's grumbling faded as they shrank into the distance. Gwenith and Farrell rode the other two horses, Corban and Gar jogging behind them. The wolven looped out wider, became a white blur in the long grass and meadow flowers. There was a noise from amongst the trees, high up, and Craf emerged from the canopy. The crow trailed the riders, soon becoming just a dark smudge in the sky.

'Better get on with it,' Marrock said.

'Aye, chief.'

The sun was low in the sky, sending long shadows behind them as they approached the paddocks. The ground was undulating, with long grass sighing in the breeze, allowing them for the most part to remain hidden from the village strung along the coast and river.

It took them a long time to reach the edge of the first paddocks; Camlin paused behind a post-and-rail fence. The warband's camp was mostly on the far side of the river, and fires were lit as dusk settled, the sound of singing drifting across to them.

At least fifty horses were penned before them, cropping grass, herded together, most in the centre of the paddock. On the far side a smokehouse stood before the river. A warrior was standing at its open doors, silhouetted by light from within. It looked as if the building had been commandeered as an impromptu stable and tack room.

He felt a presence at his shoulder, saw Marrock creep up close.

'So how do you want to do this, chief?' Camlin asked.

'I was about to ask you the same question. You're a bit more practised at this, so I thought I'd learn from you,' Marrock said. 'One thing I do know: if we're going to ride those horses away from here we're going to need saddles and tack.'

'Just what I was thinking,' Camlin said, nodding towards the smokehouse. 'I'll take Vonn and Dath, see what we can do. Wait for my signal, then start catching some horses.'

'Will do.'

Camlin circled the paddocks and smokehouse, making his way almost to the river, where the grass became tall sedge and reed, the ground spongy. He waited for Vonn and Dath to follow, then gave his orders. Vonn looked at him determinedly, but Dath appeared nervous, distracted. When Camlin had finished talking he sent Vonn off to his point, but held on to Dath's arm. The boy looked at him.

'I know you're hurting, lad, but I need to know you're gonna do this right.'

'I . . . I'll try,' Dath mumbled.

'I'm looking for better than try,' Camlin said, holding Dath's face in his hands, locking eyes with him. He could feel him shaking. 'Your da's dead; it's a sad truth. But we're not. And we need you. Do you understand? We are each other's kin, now. You, me, Marrock, Halion, your friend Corban, all of us. We are bound together. Let's see if we can keep each other alive, an' live long enough to avenge our dead.'

Dath sucked in a deep breath, the trembling in his limbs settling.

'I've given you a job to do. A man's job. Because I know you can do it. I've seen you today; you've fought well. And you have skill with that bow of yours.'

Dath looked down. 'I'm afraid.'

Camlin chuckled. 'Aren't we all? You'd have to be dead to be feeling no fear right now. Use it, lad. Let it keep you sharp, alert. Don't let it beat you.'

Something firmer entered Dath's eyes then, a decision made. He nodded.

'Good lad. Now, get on, and do your part.'

The sun was just a glow on the horizon; darkness was pulling in tight around the light from the smokehouse. Camlin watched Dath fade into the grass, giving him more time than he should need to reach the smokehouse and sneak around to its far side. Then he stood and walked tall through the grass, ducked under the paddock rail and made for the building. A warrior still stood at its doors.

'Evening,' Camlin called as he drew near, holding a hand up and smiling. 'How goes it?'

The warrior shrugged, peering at Camlin. 'Well enough. What can we do for you?'

'Just came to check on my horse, an' stretch my legs. Can only do so much sitting and drinking.'

Another figure appeared at the doorway, taller than the first. 'Can never do enough drinking,' he said. 'Don't happen to have a drop, do you?'

'No,' Camlin said, close enough to touch them, now.

'Pity.' The new figure shrugged and stepped back inside.

'All quiet, then?' Camlin asked, glancing through the doorway after the disappearing figure. The smell of fish drifted out. A pot was warming over a fire, saddles and rugs stacked along one wall, bridles, reins, girth straps all hanging on another. There was only one man in there.

'Aye,' the first man said.

'No sign of Haf an' his lads?'

'Haf?'

'He led a few of our boys into those woods over there,' Camlin said, pointing into the distance. 'Someone saw a boat land out that way, thought it might be spies of Owain.'

'I hadn't heard,' the warrior said, stepping forward, peering at the woods. They were just a deeper shadow in the gloom of dusk.

'I'll go check on my horse,' Camlin said, stepping out of the door-way's light.

'There are a lot of horses out there,' the warrior said.

''S all right,' Camlin said. 'I can see her from here – over there – big piebald mare.' He pointed to a cluster of horses.

'Did you see that?' the guard said, taking a few steps into the field. 'Where?' Camlin said.

'Near your horse – I thought I saw . . .' He took another step into the field, further from the light, hand going to his sword hilt.

There was a whistling sound, a wet thud and the guard staggered. In a second Camlin was behind him, one hand across his mouth, the other stabbing into his back, the blade slipping through ribs, puncturing a lung. The man sighed and sank to the ground, Camlin lowering him.

Quickly he turned and strode back to the smokehouse, sheathing his knife. Vonn crept out of the gloom, and he heard Dath's feet behind him.

Camlin held a finger up to Vonn, pointed at the smokehouse and then stepped through the open door.

The man inside was bent over stirring some kind of stew. Camlin's knife took him in the gut as he turned. He struggled, gripping Camlin's wrist, then the strength went out of him and he fell across the pot, spilling it. Flames scattered and Camlin stamped them out.

He looked up to see Vonn staring at him.

'That wasn't very honourable,' Vonn said.

'No,' said Camlin amicably, 'it wasn't. He's dead, though, an' I'm alive. An' you're still breathing too, for that matter.' He pushed past Vonn and stood in the light of the doorway, raised an arm and waved. Dath was standing beside the shadow of the dead warrior in the grass, pulling his arrow from the man's chest. 'You did good,' Camlin called to him. 'Now, both of you, help me get some saddles and tack together before Marrock arrives.'

It had taken over half the night for Camlin and Marrock to catch up with Halion and his companions.

Still, they were all alive, and everyone was mounted on a strong horse. Things could be a lot worse.

Marrock and Halion moved apart, Halion riding to the front of their small column.

'Domhain is north-west of here,' he said, turning in his saddle, 'so that is the direction we will ride, and fast, to put some distance between us and our trackers. I have travelled through Cambren before, but not this far south. I know there is a good pass through the mountains to Domhain, but it is much further north, so that is where we are headed.'

Good. Now let's just get on with it, instead of talking about it, Camlin thought, looking back over his shoulder for the signs of pursuit – a cloud of dust from horses' hooves, the startled flight of birds, anything, but so far the land looked quiet and clean behind them.

They stopped beside a stream at highsun and Camlin dismounted, drinking deeply and splashing some water on his neck. He heard a cracking noise, looked up and jumped; only a pace away Brina's crow was sitting on a dark granite rock, gleefully smashing a large snail to pieces. It speared the soft body within and slurped it down.

'I hate that crow,' a voice whispered beside him. Dath. Camlin nodded, not really wanting to say it out loud, in case the crow heard him.

'Mount up,' Marrock called out.

As Camlin climbed into his saddle he noticed the wolven standing perfectly still, looking behind them. Its hackles were up.

He paused, staring hard into the distance, along the path they had travelled. 'Chief,' he called.

Marrock rode over to him.

'What is it?'

Camlin pointed. In the distance, almost beyond eyesight, something was moving, like a line of ants.

'Best pick up the pace,' Camlin said. 'We've got company.'

CHAPTER TWENTY-TWO

VERADIS

Veradis reined in his horse as Dun Carreg came into view.

Calidus pulled up alongside him, the warband slowing to a halt behind.

'Nathair is there?' Veradis asked, staring at the fortress in the distance.

'Yes, he is there, as is Lykos,' Calidus said.

They spurred their mounts on, the warband rippling into motion behind.

The Jehar had split into two groups, riding on their flanks like two black wings stretching across the green countryside. Further to the south, dense forest rolled away into the distance, carpeting the land as far as Veradis could see and reminding him of Forn. Since finding Maquin, Veradis had been troubled. He'd kept his word, led Alcyon, Jael and the rest of the hunting party away from Maquin and his companions, given them a chance at life, though they still had to survive Forn. He felt he owed it to Maquin, maybe as a blood-price for Kastell. Alcyon had looked at him strangely that day, and Veradis wondered if the giant knew, somehow, what he'd done. But that was not what troubled him. It was the last words Maquin had spoken to him. *Be careful of what side you choose.* He had been careful, had made the right choices. *Haven't I?* Nathair was his friend, but more than that, he was the Bright Star that prophecy spoke of, and Calidus was one of the Ben-Elim, a warrior-angel, come to help them, to guide them through the dark times ahead: the war against Asroth and his Black Sun. Yet if he had chosen right, why did he feel wrong, some-how, somewhere deep down, and why, when he closed his eyes at night, did he see Kastell's face, his dead eyes accusing him.

We are at war, a voice whispered in his mind. *Hard choices must be made, hard deeds undertaken.* Yes, that was true. He was just glad that Calidus was with them, to guide them, and help them make the difficult choices. *For the greater good*, the voice in his head said.

'Yes. For the greater good,' he echoed.

'What was that?' someone said nearby. It was Bos, cantering close beside him.

'Nothing,' Veradis said, shaking his head.

'It's the first sign of madness, you know. Talking to yourself.'

'Is that so? Then I must have lost my mind a long time ago.'

'I could have told you that,' Bos said with a smile.

Dun Carreg was much closer now, a small village spread at the foot of the hill it sat upon.

'Blow that horn of yours, Bos. Let them know we're coming.'

Veradis was ushered by Jehar warriors into a room, Nathair's chambers. A table stood at one end with seven chairs around it. The Vin Thalun, Lykos, already occupied one. Veradis had seen a fleet anchored in the bay below Dun Carreg, sleek-hulled Vin Thalun war-galleys and fat-bellied transporters. Lykos had a cup in his hand, a smile on his face at the sight of Veradis.

'Have a drink,' the pirate said, pouring something and handing it to Veradis.

Veradis smiled as he took it. It was good even to see this pirate – at least Lykos was someone that he associated with home. He took a sip of the drink and winced. 'What is this?'

'Mead. It gets better the more you drink of it,' Lykos said, grinning.

'I would hope so.' Veradis grimaced. 'Have you seen Rauca?' he asked, looking at the empty chairs. It had been such a whirlwind since he had ridden up to Dun Carreg that he had not had a chance to seek out his friend. Nathair had met him before the gates of the fortress, pulling Veradis from his knees into an embrace.

'I have missed you, my friend,' Nathair had said.

'And I you,' Veradis had responded, feeling an immense sense of relief – that Nathair was alive and well, and that he was at his King's side to protect him again. But there had been no time for talking. A man had stridden across the bridge to them, tall and thin-featured, wearing a gold torc about his neck.

'Owain, King of Narvon and Ardan,' Nathair had introduced him. Veradis did not think he looked very kingly – more like a man weighed by great pressures, a man bent almost to snapping by those pressures. He was grey skinned, eyes sunken. He hardly acknowledged Veradis and looked past him, down at Veradis' warband, who were making camp in the meadow beyond the fishing village, then out into the bay, at the fleet of black-sailed ships.

'So many men,' he had said to Nathair. 'You look like a man making ready for war.'

'That is exactly what I am doing,' Nathair had replied calmly. 'War against Asroth and his Black Sun. As you know, I will be travelling north soon, into Benoth, which is ruled by giants. I would be a fool to march into their realm with only a handful of warriors about me.'

Owain had looked at him. 'We must talk soon, but first I must find out where Rhin is, what she plans . . .' he had said briefly before heading down to the village.

'We cannot talk here,' Nathair had said to Veradis' questioning look. 'I fear Owain does not trust me. At the moment he trusts no one: a lesson he has learned a little too late, I think. Come, you will be shown to your chambers, where you can refresh yourself.' He sniffed. 'And wash. I will send for you and we will talk later.'

Veradis had soaked in a hot bath, eaten a good meal and changed into a soft cotton tunic and leather kilt, though he still wore his two swords on his belt. His iron sandals had echoed in the stone corridors as he followed Nathair's messenger back to the King's chambers, and now here he was, drinking something disgusting with a Vin Thalun pirate. He never failed to marvel at the surprises the last few years had thrown at him.

The door opened and in marched Nathair, followed closely by Sumur and Calidus. Alcyon came last.

Nathair ushered them to chairs.

'We must wait for one more before we begin,' Nathair said.

There was a knock at the door. A man walked in whom Veradis did not recognize. He was fair haired, dressed in tunic and breeches.

His beard was neat and trimmed; there was an economy in his movement as he approached the table.

'This is Evnis,' Nathair said, 'until recently the counsellor of King Brenin. He has entered my service, and has already proved his loyalty and his value. You can all speak freely in front of him.'

Evnis smiled, showing creases about his eyes, and sat at the table.

'I am glad that you are all here,' Nathair told them. 'It is no small thing that we are gathered together, hundreds of leagues from Tenebral.'

'A miraculous sign of Elyon's approval of our purposes, if ever we needed one,' Lykos said, raising his cup and drinking deep.

'And also testament of Calidus' talents,' Nathair said.

Calidus waved a hand, frowning at Lykos.

'Lykos, let us begin with you. I am eager for news of my home.'

Home. I miss Tenebral, and so does Nathair, judging by his look.

'Your mother sends her greetings,' Lykos said.

Nathair smiled, warm and genuine. 'Is she well?'

'Her health is good, from what I can tell. And she tries to govern Tenebral well, for her part.'

'Tries?' said Nathair, frowning.

'There is unrest in Tenebral, my King. Your barons seek to take advantage of your absence and your mother's grief.'

What barons? thought Veradis. *My own father is Baron of Ripa.*

'What do you mean? Mother has not sent me word.'

'She has sent a letter for you,' Lykos said and reached inside his tunic. 'Here.'

Nathair looked at its seal closely, then broke it and read the parchment in silence.

'I doubt she would wish to talk much of Tenebral's internal problems,' Lykos said. 'She seeks to reduce your burden, not increase it.'

Nathair looked at him. 'She says that you, the Vin Thalun, have been causing many of the problems.'

'You have enemies that seek any advantage they can.' Lykos shrugged.

'Tell me,' Nathair commanded.

'I had many difficulties building your fleet – some of your barons obstructed the building greatly. Especially Marcellin in the north –' he glanced at Veradis – 'and Lamar in the south.'

My father.

'They limited the supplies, particularly timber.'

I would not put it past him. He hates the Vin Thalun, as does my brother Krelis.

'When I spoke to your mother of this she intervened. But because of their interference I thought it might be helpful to learn more about these people.'

'You mean you spied on them,' Nathair said.

My father would not take kindly to that if he knew.

'Yes. And I learned that there is complaining amongst your barons, of how you have ruled Tenebral, of your embracing corsairs.' Lykos smiled grimly. 'You would expect no different in any realm – there are always those that seek more power. But the things Marcellin and Lamar are saying of you, spreading rumours. It could become more than just words of discontent.'

'I don't believe it,' Veradis said. 'My father may be many things, but he would not speak ill of you, Nathair. You are his king.'

'Perhaps,' said Nathair. 'But I remember our last meeting, as you must. It did not go well. And I recall him being disrespectful, even then.'

Aye, he was. Veradis had almost come to blows with his father over the disrespect he had shown Nathair. Just the memory of it stirred his anger.

'What are they saying?' Nathair asked Lykos.

'They talk of how you have abandoned your country, your people, to pursue your ambitions.'

A look of anger contorted Nathair's face. 'All that I do I do for Tenebral's good.' He slammed a clenched fist on the table.

'I know that, my King, but it seems that Marcellin and Lamar do not. And there is more. Peritus has been seen with Marcellin.'

'Peritus?'

'Aye.'

Peritus had been battlechief to Aquilus, Nathair's father. He had been openly disapproving of Nathair's shield wall and new strategies for battle. Partly because of this he had found his standing in Tenebral shifting as Nathair set about acquiring his own circle of trusted supporters. Peritus was not one of them, though up until now Nathair had not doubted his loyalty to the crown.

'I worry about the affairs in Tenebral,' Lykos said. 'Sometimes these situations require a firm hand, and I suspect your mother is not in the right frame of mind to deal with unruly barons resolutely. Since your father died, she has not been the same, I hear.'

'I know.' Nathair bowed his head. 'I had hoped that leaving her as regent in my absence would help, pull her out of her grief, her introspection.' He crushed the letter in his hand. 'I will not have men take advantage of her kind nature. Or challenge me.'

'The Jehar would willingly cut any rot from your kingdom,' Sumur said. 'We are not afraid to do what must be done.'

'I do not doubt it,' Nathair said, 'but I have only just called the Jehar here – I would have you and your warriors about me.' He looked at Veradis. 'I will think on this. Hard decisions may need to be made.'

Hard decisions about my father? My brothers? A seed of worry took root in Veradis' heart.

'Calidus has told me much of what has occurred in Forn,' Nathair said, clearly wanting to change the subject. 'Much good has happened, not least the discovery of the starstone axe.'

All eyes turned to Alcyon, who had unslung the axe from his back and leaned it against the table.

'It is an extraordinary blessing,' Calidus said. 'With it our position is strengthened. It gives us greater security once we have the cauldron.'

'What do you mean?' Nathair asked.

'This axe is one of the Seven Treasures, its blade forged from the same fabric as the cauldron, the same as the other Treasures. It is alien, powerful; when the Treasures are in close proximity, their power is increased. The cauldron's power will be enhanced by the presence of the axe.'

'This cauldron has been a part of my dreams for so long,' Nathair mused. 'I do not doubt its importance, but I have wondered. What power does it hold? Why is it so important in the war against Asroth and his Black Sun?'

Calidus looked at Nathair, the silence growing. Then he spoke. 'The Seven Treasures are not of this world,' he said. 'They all are linked to the Otherworld, the cauldron most of all. It holds the power to bridge this world of flesh and the Otherworld.'

Veradis thought about that. The hairs on his arm goose-bumped. 'For what purpose?'

'To bring my kin across the veil. To bring the Ben-Elim to this world of flesh. With their help we will be invincible; we will crush the Dark Sun and establish Elyon's kingdom forever.'

A silence fell upon the room.

'That is what I have hoped for, strived for,' Nathair said, his expression one of ecstasy. 'Is that not so, brother?' he said, clapping Veradis across the shoulder. 'To put the world right, to see our labour and hard choices justified.'

'Aye, Nathair,' Veradis said.

'There is something else that I have discovered, which you should know,' Calidus resumed. 'The cauldron can be destroyed, but only if all the Treasures are gathered together. So, possessing the axe is a double surety for us. While we have it the cauldron cannot be harmed.'

'That is good to know,' Nathair said.

'So our task to find the cauldron can proceed.'

'Evnis has confirmed that it is in Murias,' Nathair said.

'That is rare and useful knowledge.' Calidus looked at Evnis with renewed interest.

'I have had cause to study the Benothi giants,' Evnis said. 'And I have had small dealings with the Benothi in the past. They have confirmed to me that the cauldron is kept in Murias.'

Calidus nodded. 'Then we must hasten there.'

'Not yet,' Nathair said. 'I am as eager as you, Calidus, to fulfil this task that Elyon has set us. But there is work to be done here, first. Great gains for the alliance can be made.'

When you say alliance, I think you mean empire, Veradis thought, remembering Aquilus' council and the following argument between Aquilus and Nathair. After witnessing first-hand the discord between the kings of the Banished Lands, Veradis knew Nathair's dream to build an empire made perfect sense. An empire was simpler in concept. One ruler, less diplomacy and politicking, and that appealed to Veradis. But the reality was never as simple: to see an empire would mean kings bowing to Nathair, and that was about as likely as the Black Sun walking into their meeting and surrendering. So the only other option was war – death and slaughter on a unimaginable scale. Now that thought did not appeal. But what else could be done?

Asroth would destroy every soul that drew breath in the Banished Lands: men, women, children. In that light warriors fighting and dying seemed more bearable. *It is for the greater good.*

Veradis' head was starting to ache with the enormity of all that was happening, as if they were walking a narrow bridge across a great chasm, and one misstep could send them hurtling to their doom. He shook his head.

I'll leave the politicking and the decision-making to Nathair.

'Let me explain the situation as I understand it,' Nathair said. 'Evnis, please correct me if I make any mistakes. There are, or were, five kingdoms here in the west of the Banished Lands: Cambren, Ardan, Narvon, Domhain and Benoth in the north, where giants still rule. Ardan was ruled by Brenin, but he is now dead and Ardan has been conquered by Owain, King of Narvon. More recently Rhin, Queen of Cambren, has invaded Narvon and is now pushing into Ardan. She means to take both Narvon and Ardan from Owain.'

'That will make her powerful,' Calidus said.

'Yes, it will. And she is ambitious. I do not think she will stop there. There are two more kingdoms in the west – Domhain and Benoth. I suspect she will turn her attentions towards them if she is successful here.'

'I like the sound of her,' Lykos said. 'She reminds me of me.'

'Will that not make her too powerful?' Veradis said. 'I remember her from your father's council, and I do not trust her.'

'I don't trust anyone beyond this room,' Nathair answered. 'And, yes, it would make her powerful. But I would rather deal with one person that I know the measure of than four petty kings in her place.' Nathair shrugged. 'In the east, Carnutan is ruled by Gundul, who relies on my support. Isiltir is likely to have Jael as its new king, though Calidus tells me he may need some help in claiming his throne.' Nathair looked at Lykos. 'I think you may be of some help there, Lykos. It would give you an opportunity to do more than sail your ships.'

'He needs something to do, before he drinks himself to death,' Calidus murmured.

'I must confess, since I conquered the Three Islands, life has become quieter. Boring, even. I could do with some action in my life.' Lykos grinned and held his cup up.

'If it's action you want, I have just the task for you,' Nathair said. 'We shall speak more on that later. So then Isiltir would be in Jael's control, and Helveth looks soon to be ruled by Lothar, another man in my debt. If the west came under the dominion of Rhin, and she answered to me, then most of the Banished Lands would be under our control.'

'And my Three Islands are yours,' Lykos added.

'Yes,' Nathair answered. 'So Asroth's Black Sun is running out of possible realms to support him.'

'And what of Owain? Is he not already indebted to you? Would he not make a more suitable ally than Rhin, at least a less ambitious one?' Veradis pressed.

'Less ambitious, definitely. But he is small minded, stiff necked and weak – a bad combination. He does not have the strength to weather the coming storm. And in his heart he does not embrace me or the alliance. I am sure of that.'

'Then we should support Rhin,' Calidus said.

'Yes,' Nathair said. 'How to do that is what we must decide while we are gathered here.'

They discussed long into the night, making plans, Evnis proving every bit as useful and knowledgeable as Nathair had said. Also to Veradis' pleasure he discovered that over five hundred eagle-warriors of Tenebral were stationed on ships only a handful of leagues away, part of the new wave of shield wall trained men that had been implemented in Tenebral only the year before. They were to be put under his command, to bolster his depleted warband.

The eagle-guard put him in mind of home, and a thought leaped into his head.

'Where is Rauca?' he asked.

All looked at him.

Nathair shook his head. 'Rauca is dead. He was slain on the night the fortress was taken by Owain.'

'What . . . ?'

Nathair continued to speak, but Veradis did not hear the words. He felt as if he had been plunged into murky water, everything about him becoming vague, unfocused. Rauca, dead. He knew it could happen, but somehow he had never considered it a possibility for his friend. Veradis looked up, saw Nathair's lips were still moving.

'Who?' he asked, the word snapping the world back into sharp focus for him. 'Who killed him?'

Nathair looked at Sumur.

'His name was Gar,' Sumur said with a shrug.

'The same man killed near all of my eagle-guard, single handed,' Nathair added grimly. 'Sumur, tell Veradis of this Gar.'

Sumur looked down at his lap and took a deep breath. It was as much emotion as Veradis had seen pass across his face since the day Calidus had revealed himself as one of the Ben-Elim.

'He is Jehar,' Sumur began.

'What?' said Calidus, leaning forward.

'He is Jehar,' Sumur repeated. 'Do you remember when you first came to Telassar that I told you another had come, that some of my sword-brothers had been deceived by this man and had left Telassar on some fool's errand.'

Veradis nodded.

'Gar was one of them. He was young then, only just become a man, a warrior, but his father led the deceived, and Gar would cross a world on fire to stay close to him.'

'His father? Then where is he now? How many Jehar were there with him?'

'One hundred men and women left Telassar. Where they are now I know not, only that they went in search of the Seren Disglair.'

'They did not find me,' Nathair said.

'Of course not. That I know. They must be dead, their quest long since failed. I cannot imagine Gar leaving his father for any other reason.'

This Gar – I will see him dead, vowed Veradis, only half listening to the other talk, his mind too full of Rauca's memory. He felt a frustrated rage welling up, the desire to draw his sword and strike something.

'Was this Gar with anyone?' Calidus spoke now, his voice quiet, but his tone caused Veradis to focus again. There was something, an underlying emotion, that he had never heard in the old man before.

'It was a battle,' Sumur said. 'All was chaos, but he looked to a boy, with a wolven.'

'I have thought along the same lines as you,' Nathair said to Calidus. 'Evnis has told me something of the boy – this Gar was friendly with his family.'

'A wolven?' asked Calidus.

'Yes,' Evnis said. 'The boy had a pet wolven, though it was far from tame. Storm, he called it.'

'Storm,' echoed Calidus. He closed his eyes. *'Before one, storm and shield shall stand . . .'* he intoned. Nathair drew in a sharp breath.

'What is that? What do you speak of?' Evnis asked.

'Calidus is reciting a line from Halvor's prophecy,' Nathair whispered. 'It speaks of Asroth's champion, the Black Sun.'

CHAPTER TWENTY-THREE

UTHAS

Uthas strode through the heather, starlight silvering the moorland that stretched for leagues ahead of him. He was close to the southern border of Benoth now, would soon be moving into the realm of Domhain. The pain in his knee was a dull throb. He paused, resting his weight on his spear, and looked back. The fortress of Murias was long faded from view, the cauldron within it still drawing his mind, as dead meat draws a crow.

Salach, his shieldman, loomed large behind him, the other giants accompanying them mere shadows strung out into the night. Five he had chosen at Queen Nemain's bidding, five warriors to journey into Domhain, to spy on their enemy, Eremon, upstart king of an upstart race that had driven him and his clan from their homeland. He felt a wave of sadness, looking back at the kin he had chosen. They were young by giant standards, and he had hard choices to force upon them. *But we must have our vengeance, and no path is easy in this grim life. If the Benothi are to return to the south once again, then hard choices must be made. I will make it worth their while.*

If they live long enough, another voice whispered in his mind. He felt the hairs on his neck stand up.

'What is it?' Salach said as he drew near.

'Nothing. Just thinking.'

'You've had years for that. It is time for doing now,' Salach said.

There was a fluttering from above; a dark shape swooped out of the night. A bird landed on a boulder close by, dark eyes glinting in the moonlight. Nemain had sent the raven with them to act as scout, but Uthas new that when they returned to Murias the bird would report back to Nemain on every word and deed.

More spy than scout.

'What news, Fech?' Uthas asked.

'*Men,*' the raven croaked. '*Fire, horses, sharp iron.*'

The border between Benoth and Domhain was mostly a natural one made of black-sloped mountains. There was a strip of land between the mountains, though, thirty or forty leagues wide, which provided much easier passage between the two realms. That was the route Uthas had taken them. While it was always patrolled by the warriors of Domhain, Uthas had hoped that the cover of night would cloak them, and they could avoid any patrols.

'Warriors, then,' Fray said as he loomed out of the dark, the shadow of his axe-blade across his back looking as if another bird was perched on his shoulder. 'How many?'

'*Eight,*' the raven said.

'Eight?' Struan echoed as he reached them. 'A good number to whet our weapons on, eh? And to earn our thorns. Where are they?'

'Wait,' Uthas said. 'Nemain has sent us to spy, not to kill.'

'I cannot walk the length of Domhain just to sneak a look at those maggots lording it in our lands,' Fray said. 'What do you say?' the giant asked as their other companions drew close – Aric, Kai and Eisa.

Uthas smiled to himself, though the darkness hid it from the others. *As I hoped.* Raised on tales of war and glory, but having played no part in those tales themselves, they wanted to make their own stories. *Killing will bind them tighter to me. Blood offers many qualities.*

He could almost see the bloodlust come upon them, the desire to ink the first thorn of their *sgeul* into their flesh. He glanced at the thorns and vine tattooed upon his own arm, most from the war with the Exiles. That was no small thing, to take a life. To see existence snuffed out before your eyes. It had humbled him the first time, sending another's spirit across the bridge of swords. It also gave him pride, whenever he glanced at it, and much honour amongst his Benothi kin. Among those who had been birthed after the wars, anyway. There were those in the clan who had survived the Sundering and the Scourging. Their *sgeuls* were a sight to behold.

'We should attack, teach them who this land belongs to,' Eisa said, her fingers stroking the bone hilt of her knife as she spoke. Her eyes searched out Uthas, pleading. Others grunted agreement.

'I command here,' Uthas said. 'And we are here to discover, not to slay.'

'Why can we not do both?' Kai asked.

'If we did, we would discover first, and slay on the return journey,' Uthas said. 'That is wisdom. But Nemain has bid us to be swift and secret, to leave no sign of our passing. To gather information. We will not kill *tonight*.' He said the last sentence louder, looking straight at Nemain's raven. *If you would report something to Nemain, report that.*

There was some muted grumbling, but Salach snapped a curse at them and rested his hand on his axe hilt, and the complaints faded.

'We will take a closer look,' Uthas said, 'and see what there is to see.'

'And if it is Rath?' Fray said, the challenge still sitting behind his eyes.

'If it is Rath we will kill him,' Uthas said. 'I know Nemain would forgive us that.'

Rath had been Eremon's battlechief. Decades ago a warband of the Benothi had raided into Domhain and razed Rath's hold to the ground. He had not been there, but his wife and bairns had been. Ever since then the warrior had hated the Benothi. Rath had gathered about himself a band of warriors and together they had mercilessly tracked and hunted any Benothi giants that dared enter Domhain's borders.

'Fech, lead us,' Uthas said, and turned, using his spear as a staff, following the raven's shadow.

Soon they saw the light, a fire's orange glow, and Uthas caught the scent of meat cooking. He held his spear up and the warriors behind him fanned out, spreading like a cloak tugged by the wind. Slowly he moved forwards.

Fech had been right – they were warriors. A handful were grouped around a guttering fire, huddled against the wind. Two more stood guard a little further out; one to the east, one looking north, into Benoth. This one was the only danger, though it was unlikely he would see anything on this moonless night. Aric was closest to the northerly guard, crouched low to the heather, moving like a slow mist. The guard saw nothing.

I must change that.

Uthas dug his fingers into the ground, felt the moist earth flow about him, under his fingernails, then he began to whisper, hardly more than a breath on his lips. He knew that Salach would hear him; that was fine, he trusted Salach with his life. But no one else would hear. Fech was nowhere to be seen. A slight tremor ran through the earth about Uthas' hand, rippling away towards Aric.

Uthas heard the sound, a popping, as a patch of ground burst close to Aric, sounding much like a wet branch breaking. Uthas could not tell who was more surprised: Aric or the guard. Certainly the guard heard it.

'Who's there?' the warrior called, half drawing his sword, taking a step towards the sound. The men around the fire stirred, one of them standing. Aric froze for a heartbeat, then exploded forward, swinging his hammer as he did. It smashed into the guard's chest, sending him hurtling through the air. He rolled and fell still.

There was a moment's silence, then the men about the fire were rushing Aric. Giants burst from the darkness about them. Blood sprayed black in the starlight.

Salach made to join the battle but Uthas put a restraining hand on his shoulder.

'Let them earn their thorns.'

The fight was almost done, anyway, the men surprised and out-matched by Uthas' company. Even as Uthas watched, Fray sent a man's head spinning through the night. It fell into the fire, sending up an explosion of sparks.

Uthas strode over, surveying the battleground. Fray was looking around, axe held across his chest, looking for someone else to kill. The battle-madness slowly faded from his eyes. Eisa was bloodied, a hand clasped over her shoulder, blood welling black between her fingers. She grinned at Uthas.

Aric was down. He still lived, but he was clutching his gut, trying to staunch the blood that was pulsing from a deep wound.

Not good, Uthas thought. *Gut wounds are never good.*

'I-I am sorry,' Aric said as Uthas crouched beside him. 'I do not know –' he paused, a wave of pain snatching his speech – 'I do not know what happened.'

I am sorry, Aric. Uthas felt a wave of guilt, knowing his actions had brought this about. *It was necessary*, he told himself.

'Easy,' he said gently. 'It is done now.' Reaching to his belt, he unfastened a skin, pulling the stopper. A smell came out, earthy and he wrinkled his nose. *Brot, the food of giants. Three thousand years, and this is the best we can come up with.* Just a mouthful would sustain any giant for a day's hard running, though, and they could cross twenty leagues in a day. 'Drink some,' Uthas said, holding it to Aric's lips.

He took a sip and swallowed.

'Stay with him,' Uthas said to Salach as he rose and walked away. The others had checked the dead: eight men, warriors of Domhain by the look of them. Fech was perched atop a body, an eyeball dangling from his beak. He gulped it down.

'*Nemain will be angry,*' the bird croaked.

Uthas shrugged. 'They attacked us.'

He strode past it, to the paddocks behind, where eight horses were penned. They were white eyed, gathered at the far end of the paddock.

'We'll eat well tonight,' Uthas said to Kai and Struan. 'Slaughter one.'

Some of the horses panicked and bolted, breaking the paddock rope. They caught one, though, its scream cut short with the crunch of Struan's hammer.

They lit a fire and spitted a hindquarter. Uthas stared into the flames, remembering another fire, felt a twinge on his back, as if his burn scars had a memory, too. It had been many years ago, decades, when he and Salach had been captured whilst scouting south, in Cambren. They had ventured too close to the walls of Dun Vaner, been hunted and caught, thrown in chains into a damp, dark cell. The memory of it blurred, even now causing a twist of fear in his gut. They had been tortured, their screams ringing out for days. He remembered begging for death and weeping when it had been withheld from him. Then Rhin had come to them and the torture had stopped. She had shown them mercy – kindness, even – tending their wounds, silently washing them, applying poultices and bandages. Part of him had known that it was a ploy, but he had been so filled with gratitude, so overwhelmed, that it had not seemed to matter. She had lit another fire then, causing him to writhe in renewed fear, but no tools of torture had been heated. Instead Rhin had whispered and a face had appeared in the flames.

Asroth.

He had spoken – of his betrayal by his angelic brotherhood, of his fall from grace, of his war with Elyon. He spoke of dreams and ambitions, of a new order in the Banished Lands, of the gifts he would give to those who served him. And Uthas and Salach had listened.

Uthas shook his head, banishing the memories. *It's been long enough.* He walked back to Aric, who was lying where Uthas had left him; Salach and some of the others were sitting silently about the wounded giant. He was groaning, eyes clenched shut. They flickered open as Uthas crouched beside him. It took a moment before there was recognition in Aric's eyes. *The pain will do that.*

'You are strong, brother,' Uthas said.

'I have earned my first thorn, begun my *sgeul*,' Aric said.

'That you have,' Uthas said. 'Salach will make the mark for you.'

He touched his fingers to Aric's wound, the slowly pulsing dark blood, then raised his fingers to his lips and pressed them to his tongue.

Brot. The brot he had given Aric earlier was seeping from the wound, mixed with the blood. There was no doubt now. *Aric will die of this wound.* He sat back and watched Salach prepare the paste for Aric's tattoo, grinding the leaves with his stone pestle and mortar, his bone needle lying on a piece of cloth beside him. Eisa and Kai gripped Aric's arm and Salach set quietly to work, dipping the needle, carefully piercing Aric's flesh – dip, stab, stab, stab, dip, stab, stab, stab, countless times – then it was done.

Aric smiled at the thorn on his arm.

'Your wound – it is a brot wound,' Uthas said.

'I know,' Aric whispered.

It is for the best, Uthas thought. *If he had lived I would have had to punish him for disobeying my orders. This way he keeps his honour.*

'Help me kneel,' Aric said, and Salach and Fray lifted him, one at either arm. Aric grimaced, a groan escaping his lips, then he looked up at Uthas. 'I am ready now.'

Uthas signalled to Salach as Aric dipped his head. Salach's axe was sharp; Aric probably did not feel a thing.

CHAPTER TWENTY-FOUR

CORBAN

Corban shifted in his saddle, his backside aching and his shoulder itching from where he had been wounded in the fall of Dun Carreg. Eight days they had been riding since Camlin had spotted their pursuers, and he was exhausted. How was it that sitting in a saddle all day long could be so tiring? And so painful? Halion was leading them swiftly north, through a rolling landscape, much of it coated in dense woodland. Each night they had dismounted and walked extra leagues in an attempt to widen the gap between them and their followers. And each morning, before dawn, Gar would wake him to perform the sword dance and to spar. Others were starting to join them: Farrell and his da, Vonn, Halion and Marrock. Even Edana, claiming that if she were to be a true leader then she would need to learn how to swing a sword. Marrock had grudgingly agreed. And just this morning his mam had joined them: Halion had taken her through some forms with the spear that she now carried permanently. She had done well, her determination and athleticism reminding Corban of Cywen.

Cywen. Just the thought of his sister brought a pain all of its own, a dull ache in his gut. Sometimes he forgot that she was dead and then would be reminded of her by some inconsequential thing – a scent, a phrase, a mannerism in someone – then the weight of it would come flooding back. He shook his head, scattering the memories like gathering flies.

He was riding midway down their small column, along a narrow track which was winding through light woodland. Sunlight dappled the ground, moving as a breeze swayed the branches above. Storm was a flicker of white movement deeper in the woods. Without her they would all be close to starving by now.

He saw his mam and Gar in quiet conversation ahead of him, and scowled. He had hardly spoken to either of them since the night they had taken him into the dark and asked him to leave, spouted all that madness about Elyon and Asroth, about going to Drassil. Though he had not talked to them about it, once they had begun their ride through Cambren he had thought of little else. He did not like things this way between them. He was grieving, and he knew his mam was too, when they should be comforting each other. He felt there was a wall between them instead, something invisible but solid that he could not break through.

Corban stood straight and approached his mam and Gar, who were tending their horses. It was almost full dark and further away the others were making camp. He stopped before the two of them and they looked at him expectantly.

'Can I talk to you?' he mumbled.

'Of course,' his mam said quickly. Gar just looked at him.

'I will not leave our friends,' he said. Gar took a deep breath to say something but Corban held a hand up. 'Please, hear me out. I have words I need to say. I am oath-bound to Edana, and even if I weren't, I could not leave these people. They are my friends, our friends, and all that is left of home. I have thought about it long and hard, thought about nothing else for days, and, even if what you have said is true . . .' He paused, thinking again of Elyon and Asroth, the tales he had heard of the Otherworld, the Ben-Elim and Kadoshim. *How could it be true?* 'Even if it were true, I would not leave my friends. If it *is* true, then Elyon can tell me, not just you two. And until that happens I am not going to change my mind. You can say what you like, but I will not change my mind.' He looked down at the ground. 'I hope that we can be . . .' And suddenly the words dried up. *The same as before,* he wanted to say. *Before they had taken him into the dark and said those mad things.* He looked up at his mam, eyes pleading. The silence lengthened.

She nodded.

'You are a man now, a warrior who has sat your Long Night, and proven in battle,' she said. 'We will respect your decision. And we will wait until Elyon, or his Ben-Elim,' she added with a quick flicker of her eyes to Gar, 'changes your mind.'

With her words he felt his tension drain, evaporating like smoke in the breeze, and he saw the same happen in her face. He reached out and hugged her tight. She felt small in his arms, fragile. When they separated, Gar was busying himself rubbing his horse down, checking its hooves. He avoided Corban's gaze.

Corban sat with Dath and Farrell close to the fire. They had all dined on dried meat and cold water, all that was left of a doe that Storm had carried into the camp four nights earlier, though none complained.

Right now Storm was curled behind Corban, half hidden in the shadows of a tree.

'A fine meal,' Farrell said as he swallowed his last mouthful. 'Even if it was as tough as the leather on my boots.'

Corban chuckled, while Dath sat gazing into the fire. Corban watched his friend. He had been like this since his da had been killed on the beach. Corban wanted to help, to do something, but he understood: there was nothing that he could do, nothing that would make things better. *You can't bring back the dead.* All he could do was let Dath know he wasn't alone.

Storm growled behind Corban. She was half crouched in the darkness, staring into the trees, ears pricked forward. She sniffed, then visibly relaxed and sank back to the ground. Corban looked where she'd been staring. He thought he saw movement, then a figure solidified in the gloom, treading softly into the firelight.

Camlin.

He walked purposefully to Marrock and Halion, who were sat with Edana. They rose when they saw him and fell into deep conversation. Corban watched them intently. Eventually Marrock nodded decisively and stepped away, closer to the fire. 'Our followers are close. Camlin has scouted back along our path.'

'They have gained on us,' Camlin told them. 'They are no more than two leagues behind us.'

'How many?' Anwarth asked.

'Two score, at least.'

Corban looked around his companions' faces, could see fear wrapping its fingers about them.

Halion walked to the edge of the glade. 'Corban – with me,' he said. 'And bring your wolven.'

'Why?' Gwenith said, her hand reaching out towards Corban.

'We are going to teach them to fear us,' Halion said.

'Will she attack on your command?' Halion asked Corban as they picked their way through dark woods.

Camlin was leading the way, Gar and Vonn following closely behind Corban. He had not even tried to dissuade the stablemaster when he had followed Corban silently from their camp; he knew there was no point.

'Yes,' Corban answered. 'You remember? Friend and foe?'

Halion looked at him, then chuckled, clearly remembering a time in the Rowan Field when a wolven pup had attacked his leg. 'That seems so long ago,' he murmured.

Camlin stopped in front, looking up, then changed their direction, leading them down a slope.

'What exactly are we doing?' Corban asked.

'We are going to even the odds a little, and spread some fear amongst them. They will have seen the dead back at the beach and in the woods, will see that some of them have not been killed by a blade.' He looked at Storm, loping almost silently beside Corban. 'They will not know that we have a wolven with us – how would you react upon seeing warriors ripped, torn apart?'

Corban thought about that. 'I'd be scared,' he said.

'Aye,' Halion said, 'and the dark breeds fear.'

Corban crouched in the undergrowth, one hand wrapped in the thick fur around Storm's neck. Gar was close by, a darker shadow in the gloom. Both of them were staring into the darkness.

Camlin had led them in a great loop, so that they could approach downwind of the camp. 'They have hounds,' Camlin had whispered.

Halion and Camlin had whispered the plan to Corban, Gar and Vonn, then drawn their knives, rubbed dark earth over the iron and disappeared amongst the trees, Vonn following them.

'Why did they do that?' Corban whispered to Gar. 'Wipe dirt on their blades.'

'So they will not reflect light – firelight, moonlight,' Gar said.

'Oh,' said Corban, thinking of his companions creeping closer to their enemies' camp. There would be guards standing in the woods, men on watch, warriors sent to catch them, to kill them. With every moment Corban expected to hear voices, horns, the baying of hounds catching their scent, but none of it happened. For long heartbeats there was only silence, just his and Storm's breathing, branches scratching in a slight breeze, in the distance the call of a fox.

Then he felt Storm tense, a vibration deep in her belly, the beginnings of a growl.

'Be ready,' Gar's voice whispered from the darkness.

It was Vonn. He lurched towards them, then snagged his foot on something and staggered forwards, something falling from his cloak and hitting the ground with a thud. Vonn dropped to the floor, hands scrabbling to retrieve the object as behind him the sound of pursuit grew louder, a figure appearing, moving furtively through the undergrowth.

The plan had worked, then. Halion and Camlin were to kill the camp's guards, all except one, who was to be lured into the woods by Vonn. Lured to this point. To Storm.

The figure moved up behind Vonn, stood over him, sword raised.

Get out of the way! Corban's mind yelled, one hand clasping Storm's fur tight. She was growling low and deep, her body quivering.

Vonn picked up the thing he had dropped and shoved it back inside his cloak – *some kind of box, or book?* – and leaped forwards, running past Corban. The warrior made to follow, then Storm materialized before him, lips pulled back in a snarl, showing her long teeth. The warrior froze, eyes growing wide.

Corban stared at the warrior before him. His enemy, yet he felt a surge of sympathy for the man, and guilt at what he was about to do.

He is hunting me, would kill me, kill my kin, my friends. Still he hesitated.

The warrior opened his mouth, sucked in a great breath, about to scream, to call for help, or perhaps beg for mercy, Corban did not know.

'Foe,' Corban whispered in Storm's ear and in a blur of fur and muscle she leaped at the startled man.

He had an instant to raise his weapon, a half-formed cry escaping his lips as she smashed into him, then they were on the ground, his arms and legs flailing. Storm lunged forward, her weight pinning him to the ground. There was crunching, bones breaking, and the warrior's scream rose in pitch, then was cut short as black blood and gore splattered trees and foliage.

'I'm glad she's on our side,' muttered Camlin.

In the distance they heard the first sounds of the camp stirring, a dog barking, a voice calling.

Storm was standing with one paw on her kill, her muzzle dripping. She raised her head and howled.

CHAPTER TWENTY-FIVE

CORALEN

Coralen sat at her mam's table, picking dirt from her nails with her hunting knife.

'How long are you back for?' her mam asked.

'I don't know, Mam. A day, a few days. Rath didn't say.'

'I don't know what you get out of riding around the countryside with those savages,' her mam said.

Coralen bit back the immediate response on her lips. *Because I don't want to end up like you.* She felt a rush of guilt at that. Her mam was sitting close to a window, studying herself in a polished bronze mirror, daubing her face with rouge and kohl.

She had been beautiful once and a shadow of that lingered still, though her hair had thinned and lost its copper lustre, and her figure had expanded. It was more than that, though, something deeper than the simple passage of time. Coralen noticed it so clearly because she was rarely home. *Home? This is not my home. Just timber and thatch in the empty northlands of Domhain.* There was a pervasive weariness about her mam that leaked into everything she did, every word or glance.

'You should try some,' her mam said, offering her the pot of rouge.

'No thanks.'

'You need to be making more of an effort; you won't have your looks forever.' Her mam looked at her, and frowned. 'Look at you, in your prime, and all wrapped in leather and iron. You've more sharp edges on you than the knives in my kitchen.'

Coralen smiled at that. 'Mam, I'm eighteen summers. And all of that –' she waved at the pot of rouge, as if it summed up an entire way of life – 'it doesn't matter to me. I'm happy riding around with a bunch of savages.'

Happy? Well, that's probably an exaggeration. But it's better than the alternative.

Her mam sighed and shook her head as if to say, *You poor, deluded child.*

There was a knock at the door; a figure pushed in, not waiting to be invited. It was a big man, tall, a belly folding over his belt. He smelled of earth and sweat.

'Hearne,' Coralen's mam said, brightening, something of her old aura fluttering into life.

'Nara,' the big man said, his eyes settling on Coralen. He nodded to her. He had small eyes, pinpricks in a large face.

'Take yourself off for a walk,' Coralen's mam said to her as she rose and walked away, crossing into the shadows of another room.

Coralen stood, her chair scraping on the floor.

'No need to leave on my account,' Hearne said. 'You could wait for me, or join us, if you like.' He reached out a big hand, touching Coralen's hip.

Without thinking, she burst into movement, sliding around him, twisting his arm behind his back. In heartbeats he was pressed against the wall, Coralen's knife resting just below his eye.

'I don't think so, you fat, stinking pig,' she hissed. A bead of sweat rolled down Hearne's forehead, around his eye, onto the tip of Coralen's knife.

Hooves drummed outside, stopping close by.

'Cora, get out here. Rath says we're leaving.'

'Be nice to my mam,' Coralen said as she stepped away, sheathing her knife.

Hearne hurried away, following her mam.

Coralen took a deep breath, felt her racing pulse begin to slow. As she left she placed a bag of coins on the table.

'What happened here?' Rath said. He was old, his hair white, streaked with iron, but he was as strong and sharp witted as anyone Coralen had ever met. She loved him fiercely, this old man before her, uncle, protector, friend. *Not that I've ever told him.* That was beyond imagination in this group of hard men.

She had become one of them slowly, something within her rebelling against the life that had surrounded her mam. So she had taken to following Rath and her half-brothers about. Six years old, never speaking, just following, watching. Rath had ignored her at first, then told her to get back to her mam's skirts, then scolded her, eventually clumping her. None of it had made any difference; she had just continued to sneak out, following him whenever he was there. Soon she had become his shadow, accepted, almost invisible, and so she had watched him training with his men, sparring, eating, drinking. She had a vivid memory: eight years old, lifting a practice sword from a wicker basket in the weapons court, of men laughing – all except Rath. He had measured her with his serious eyes, told her to hit him. She'd tried, but ended up on her arse quickly enough. Rath had told her to get up and try again. She smiled at the thought.

It had been Baird who had fetched her from her mam's house; he was a warrior who had served with Rath for more years than Coralen had drawn breath. He had lost both his family and an eye to the giants of Benoth. Rath's score or so of warriors had been gathered swiftly. Once they were all together, Rath told them why. Word had come back that a patrol was overdue.

Now they knew the reason.

Bodies littered the ground, spread around a burned-out fire, twisted and ungainly in death. Their heads had been hacked from their bodies. Nearby a cairn had been raised, stones piled high. Around its base were the heads of the warriors, placed like some decoration. Coralen shared a look with Baird. He slipped from his saddle and began pulling rocks from the cairn. Coralen and a few others joined him. It was not long before a huge body was revealed, laid flat with a war-hammer resting upon its chest. Baird lifted the giant's severed head by its hair.

'The Benothi are loose in Domhain,' Rath said. 'Think we'd better do something about that.'

CHAPTER TWENTY-SIX

CYWEN

Cywen woke suddenly, her heart pounding as loud as war-drums in her head. She was curled in a chair in the kitchen, embers in the fire burned down to a red glow. *What woke me?* Had she dreamed? Then she heard Buddai growling.

She sat up quickly, reaching for a knife. It was dark, but she could tell there were people on the other side of the door; she could hear them whispering. Then the door handle turned.

'Don't go throwing anything sharp at me,' someone said. Cywen's memory fumbled to put a face to the familiar voice. Conall.

'Get out,' Cywen replied. Buddai was snarling now, only her hand in his fur stopping him from leaping at the intruder.

'You've got visitors, girl,' Conall said. 'They were all for putting a sack over your head and carrying you to the keep, but I told them you'd wake all of Dun Carreg, and most likely every demon in the Otherworld as well. So I told them if we asked you polite you'd see sense and be reasonable.'

'What time is it?' Cywen asked, blinking as someone behind Conall lit a torch. 'What visitors?'

'It's nighttime,' Conall said with a shrug, stepping into the kitchen, his gaze flitting between the knife in Cywen's hand and Buddai's bared teeth. 'Got anything to drink?' he asked.

Figures crowded the door behind him, spilling into the room. The first Cywen recognized: Nathair, King of Tenebral, and his shadow, Sumur. Behind them was an old man, silver-haired but somehow youthful; he was looking at her intently.

Buddai whined, tail tucking between his legs, ears going flat to his head, and the old man frowned, then something huge followed behind him, a man's shape, though taller and wider, small black eyes peering out from beneath a thick jutting brow. A giant, a black axe slung across his back.

Conall stepped before her, seeing her knife hand move. 'Be calm, lass. Don't do it, they've just come to talk.'

Cywen froze, fear making her pulse race. *I must still be asleep. Please let me still be asleep.* Her instinct was to throw first and talk later. Then another figure entered the room wearing a black cuirass, the silver eagle of Tenebral embossed upon it, two swords at his hip, one long, one short; a young man, stern faced, with serious, searching eyes. He looked at her and smiled apologetically.

She lowered her knife.

Behind this serious warrior one last man came, shutting the door behind him. Metal rings were woven into his braided beard, clinking as he moved.

'How about that drink?' Conall asked.

'There's mead in the cold room,' Cywen said, waving her hand, and Conall fetched a skin, unstoppered it and took a swig. Nathair shook his head when Conall offered him the skin.

'I'll have some,' the man with rings in his beard said.

'Why are you all here?' Cywen said.

The silver-haired man dragged a chair over and sat before Cywen. 'I need to talk to you about your brother.'

The sky was a searing blue, wisps of cloud doing little to block the heat of the sun as Cywen rode to the paddocks beyond Havan. Over two thousand horses were roaming here, more than she had ever seen in her life – the war mounts of Owain's warband mixing with Brenin's herds. She was on Shield, could feel his barely controlled energy, his yearning to gallop reflected in how he lifted his hooves, how he held his tail straight and proud.

She was in the company of a dozen other stablehands, all ordered by the warrior Drust to bring back mounts from Brenin's herd considered suitable for training in the Rowan Field. She rounded up half a dozen, Gar's piebald stallion, Hammer, amongst them, and roped them in a line behind Shield. As she was leaving, a memory tugged at her and she changed direction, rode to a small copse of alders and followed a track, now overgrown.

She pulled up before Brina's cottage, or what was left of it. It had been burned out, the charred framework still standing, the open doorway leading to a pile of rubble and ash. Brina would have a lot to say to the man that had put fire to her home. Even the herb garden was overgrown, a mass of weeds and grass gone to seed. Then she was remembering the night that Corban had sneaked into this cottage and stolen a comb, to prove his courage. She felt her breath catch in her chest. A tear rolled down her cheek and she brushed it away. *Strange, how a memory from the past can sneak up so quietly.*

Corban.

Last night had been so strange, woken in the dead of night by the strangest bunch of companions she had ever witnessed – *a giant, a living, breathing giant walking around Dun Carreg* – and questioned. Questioned about Corban.

She had been scared at first – who wouldn't be with a giant standing in your kitchen? – but then the silver-haired man had started talking to her. His voice had been so calm. She had not said much, little more than she had told Nathair during their previous meeting, though some of it she found hard to remember. There had been so many questions from the old man with the strange yellow eyes.

He had asked about Meical, she remembered that, and she had thought instantly of seeing him sitting in the kitchen, talking to her mam and da, and to Gar. *They* had spoken about Corban as well. And finally Calidus had asked her for something that had belonged to Corban – an item of clothing, a knife, anything. She had given him Corban's old forge apron, scarred and pitted by heat and flame, sweat-stained on the inside. She had found it in her da's forge when she had been searching for her throwing knives, and for some unexplained reason had brought the apron home with her.

Calidus had held it, run his fingertips over its entirety, then closed his eyes and started singing, so quietly that it had been little more than a whisper. When he opened his eyes he had pronounced Corban gone from Ardan, said that he was across the sea, to the north-west. That had scared her more than anything else, even more than the giant staring at her. Calidus was an Elemental. She shivered at the memory. An Elemental, searching for Corban.

Corban. To her he was just her baby brother. Why were these people so interested in him?

Her thoughts stayed fixed on her brother as she rode Shield away from Brina's cottage, leading the other horses back to Dun Carreg. The fortress and surrounding land was buzzing with activity. Owain's warband was spread between Dun Carreg and the plains south of the giantsway, more of them arriving every day. North of the giantsway Nathair's forces camped, swollen first by the arrival of his fleet and then the warband that had ridden in from the east only yesterday. Rows of tents filled all the land between the giantsway and the beach. She scowled as she saw black-clad figures in Havan, more of the Jehar that had stormed Stonegate the night Dun Carreg had fallen.

The warriors everywhere grew smaller and smaller as she steadily climbed the path to the fortress. Out in the bay a great cluster of ships with Tenebral's eagle upon them were rowing for open sea, their sails billowing and filling as they left the bay's shelter. As she watched, they turned east, becoming specks as they dwindled into the distance, and she wondered where they were heading. Eventually she clattered over the bridge and through Dun Carreg's stone-paved streets until she reached the Rowan Field. Drust inspected the mounts she had brought in, grunting approvingly. He gave particular attention to Hammer, Gar's stallion, who was also the sire of Shield.

'You've done well, girl,' the red-haired warrior said. 'You've a good eye for horses.'

'Thank you,' she replied without smiling.

He took the reins from her and led the horses away, towards a pile of saddles and tack. 'Help me with them,' he called over his shoulder.

She looked around as she worked. The Field was busy, warriors everywhere. She spotted Rafe on the weapons court, sparring with a man bearing the bull of Narvon. Even though he still limped, Rafe used his height and long reach to good effect, and in short time he had scored a hit to his opponent's chest. He caught Cywen's eye as he hobbled from the court and strolled over to her, grinning.

'Enjoy watching men sweat?' he said. 'Or is it my skills that draw your eye?'

'I was wondering what you looked like against my brother, when you challenged him to the Court of Swords.' She had heard about Rafe's challenge in Dun Carreg's feast-hall, how the confrontation had lasted little more than a few heartbeats, Rafe defeated, his blood on Corban's sword. 'Apparently it was quite the sight.'

Emotions swept Rafe's face – too many, too complex to read. 'I wasn't ready,' he said, looking away.

Cheering drifted over from the weapons court and they both turned to look.

Conall was stepping onto the court, a practice sword in his hand. From the far side a figure appeared, flanked by a bald, thick-necked warrior. Cywen recognized the young warrior; he was one of those who had woken her in the night. He still wore the silver and black of Tenebral.

'Who is that?' she asked.

'He's Nathair's first-sword, rode in with a warband yesterday,' Rafe said. 'Name's Veradis, I think. And it looks as if he's about to get a hiding from Conall.'

Quickly the court cleared for the two warriors, Cywen and Rafe hurrying over to watch. Conall was smiling, waiting for Veradis as he chose a practice sword from a wicker basket. He did not rush, testing the weight of a few until he found one that he was happy with. He returned Conall's smile as he walked to him, then set his feet.

In a burst of speed Conall was on him, rushing forward, striking high and low in a blur of motion.

'That's your brother's trick,' Rafe whispered in Cywen's ear, 'catching people off-guard.'

Cywen heard rather than saw the exchange, the staccato *clack* of wood striking wood. When her eyes caught up, Veradis had retreated a few steps, but Conall had not broken his guard. Conall attacked again, feinting high then spinning around Veradis and chopping at the man's ribs. Veradis spun on his heel, sweeping Conall's attack away and striking at Conall's head and chest with two short, solid blows. Conall blocked one and stepped away from the second. They continued like this, neither gaining the upper hand, Conall like a storm-whipped sea, swirling fluidly around Veradis' wall of stone, solid, impenetrable. Then, from nowhere, Conall's blade-tip was at Veradis' throat, Conall grinning wolfishly. Cywen scowled, wishing for some reason that Conall had lost. *He needs some of his swagger chopped away.*

Veradis returned the smile, nodding down. Conall looked and saw Veradis' weapon pressing against Conall's groin.

Cywen smiled; that was one of the kill points that Corban had taught her.

Conall scowled then laughed, one emotion chasing the other as quick as a blink. Veradis stepped away and dipped his head to Conall.

'Well, that was something to see,' Rafe breathed. 'I've never seen anyone except Conall's brother touch wood to him while sparring.'

'What's going on today?' Cywen asked him. 'It feels different, somehow. Tense.'

'Have you not heard?' Rafe said. 'Queen Rhin has broken out of the Darkwood into Ardan. She is marching on Owain. She is marching here.'

CHAPTER TWENTY-SEVEN

CORBAN

Dawn's light was seeping through the trees. Corban's eyes were fixed on Vonn's back in front of him as they sped through the woods. He was sweating, tunic clinging to his back. It felt as if they had been running half the night, Camlin and Halion leading them in a twisting route back to their camp. The two warriors did not think their hunters would attempt to try and track them until the sun had risen, almost certainly not after they had found the torn body of Storm's victim, *but you could not be too careful*, as Camlin had said. As exhaustion threatened to claim Corban, his world shrinking to Vonn's back, to each step, each single drag of air into his lungs, one thought persisted in revolving around his mind. *What had Vonn dropped in the woods, and risked his life to find?*

Gwenith greeted him with anxious eyes as they staggered into their camp; she didn't look as if she'd slept any more than Corban had. Everyone was awake, horses saddled, the fire kicked out. His mam handed him and Gar a skin of water. Corban drank thirstily, and soon he was sitting in a saddle, his horse picking its way along a narrow track through thinning woods.

They stopped at highsun beneath the last shade of the woods they had been passing through, an open meadow rolling away before them. Corban chewed on some cold meat as he told Dath and Farrell of what had happened in the night, of what Storm had done. His thoughts returned to Vonn and he stood and strode to the young warrior sitting close to Halion and Edana.

'What did you drop?' Corban asked him.

Vonn looked up at him, appearing confused.

'Last night in the woods, you dropped something. When you were being chased. What was it?'

Vonn's expression changed and momentarily his hand twitched up to his cloak. He didn't respond.

'It must be important to you, or you'd have left it. That warrior was right behind you.'

Vonn glanced about, saw Halion and Edana looking at him, others as well.

'It's a book,' he said quietly.

'Why is it so important?'

Vonn said nothing, but looked cornered, somehow, a child with his hand caught in the honey jar.

'What're you hiding?' Dath said loudly.

'Nothing. It's no one's business but mine,' Vonn snapped, sitting straighter now, his hand resting defensively on something inside his cloak.

'What is it, Vonn?' Halion asked now.

Vonn looked at him, then about at the other companions. All attention was on him. He sighed. 'It is my father's book. I took it the night Dun Carreg fell. I stole it to spite him – we'd argued about Bethan.' His eyes darted to Dath. 'I was angry with him. It was childish, but I knew he treasured it, so I just took it.'

'What is this book?' Brina said.

'He kept it in a secret room, along with other things he treasured.'

'I didn't ask you *where*, I asked you *what*,' Brina snapped.

'*WHAT*,' Craf squawked from the branches above. Dath jumped.

'I'm not sure,' Vonn said, 'I think it's old, ancient. I think my da found it in the tunnels beneath Dun Carreg.'

'Show me,' Heb said, stepping forwards.

Vonn clutched a hand to his chest, making no move to hand over the book.

'Go on, Vonn, do as Heb asks,' said Edana.

All eyes turned to the Princess. *Or is it Queen, now? I suppose it is, as Brenin is dead.* She was speaking more often now, certainly much more than in those first days when they had sailed away from Dun Carreg.

Slowly, seemingly reluctant, Vonn reached into his cloak, fumbled about and then pulled out a thick, leather-bound book.

Heb took it gingerly, Brina peering over his shoulder. He opened the cover.

'By Asroth's teeth,' Brina said, eyes growing wide.

'What is it?' Marrock asked.

'It's a book,' Brina said. 'When we've read it we'll tell you what's in it, which is what I think you meant to ask.'

'Aye, it is,' Marrock said, looking abashed.

'We will inspect it, see what we can make of it,' Heb said more politely. 'No need to be so rude,' he said to Brina.

'Oh, shut up and give me the book. I need a closer look.'

'You'll have to do it as we ride,' Halion said. 'We'd best move on.'

They rode hard all afternoon and into the evening, an increased sense of tension about them all. They were travelling through open meadows, and more than once had had to change their course to avoid small hamlets and cultivated fields. Once they had seen people poling coracles on a wide, glistening lake. Corban was not sure if those on the lake had seen them, but it was likely.

As the sun was sinking, Brina and Heb cantered up either side of him.

'Heb and I want to talk to you now about the book,' Brina said.

'The book?'

'Yes. The book that we took from Vonn, that he brought with him from Dun Carreg.'

'Ah. That book.'

'It is very old, ancient,' said Heb. 'Written by the Benothi giants that built Dun Carreg.'

Corban raised an eyebrow at that, his interest rising. 'And you can read it? You can read giantish?'

'Of course,' said Heb, as if Corban had just insulted him.

'It's amazing,' Brina said, unable to keep the excitement from her voice. She leaned closer. 'It teaches the earth power.'

Corban blinked at her. 'Teaches the earth power?'

'Yes,' she snapped, appearing irritated. 'The question you asked me, about how we summoned that mist, the night we left Dun

Carreg. Heb and I know something of the earth power – very little, you understand, but enough to do small things.'

Corban looked at them both, wide-eyed, almost falling off his horse.

'Heb and I have spoken,' Brina continued, 'and we'd like to teach you.'

'Teach me?'

'Corban, if you repeat what I say one more time, I swear I will use the earth power on you.'

'Sorry.'

'So, would you like to learn how to use the earth power?'

'Would I li—' He stopped himself. 'Yes, I would.' *Why me?*

'Now that is more like it,' Brina said.

Halion called out from up ahead, halting them to make camp.

'We'll talk again. Soon,' said Brina.

Not long after they had stopped and made camp, Corban sat with his mam and Gar, sipping hot flavoursome stew as the small company sat in a ring around a small fire. Halion joined them.

'Will we take Storm back again tonight,' Corban asked him, 'back to our hunters.'

'Maybe,' Halion said. 'We'll see what Camlin tells us when he returns. I suspect they will not be as close behind us. Last night would have taught them to move cautiously.' He glanced at Storm, who was spread at Corban's feet, making short work of the bones and leftovers from the game that had gone into the stew. Craf was sat on a branch nearby, still as stone, eyeing Storm jealously.

'Besides, they will be on their guard tonight. It would be best to spread our attacks out, give them no pattern to plan against.'

Gar grunted approvingly.

'And you must be tired; I know I am. Best to sleep tonight, restore our strength.'

Most of them were asleep when Camlin returned, though Marrock was quick to rise and greet the woodsman. Corban, though exhausted, had found sleep elusive. He sat up and nodded a greeting to Camlin.

'What news?' Marrock asked.

'They are a long way behind, looks like the wolven's put some fear in their bones,' Camlin said, teeth glinting in the firelight. 'No need to go after them again tonight, an' if we did, I don't think we'd make it to their camp and back before dawn.'

'You've done well, Cam,' Marrock said. 'Get some sleep.'

Corban laid his head down and this time found sleep quickly.

Something prodded Corban. 'Wake up,' a voice whispered in his ear.

He wanted to tell Gar to leave him alone, but he knew the stablemaster would just prod him harder. Grumbling, he sat up, rubbing sleep from his eyes.

Dawn was a suggestion in the air, a grey light invading, pushing back the darkness. Others were stirring: his mam, holding the spear Halion had given to him on his warrior trial, Marrock and Halion, Farrell and his da, Anwarth. Corban stretched and followed Gar to a space on the dew-soaked grass. The others began sparring, Halion talked to Gwenith about different grips for the spear and Corban and Gar began the sword dance. Soon they were sparring too, others rising from their beds to join in – Dath, Camlin and Vonn. Even Edana was there, setting her feet, practising drawing a sword at her hip, making the move smooth. Most times it stuck in the scabbard. Brina and Heb were lighting a fire, preparing some food for them all to break their fasts with.

Corban was sweating when Gar stepped away, signalling the end of their sparring.

Halion was waiting for them, Marrock with him.

'It's time we talked,' Halion said to Gar. 'About who you are. We've waited long enough.'

The bustle around the camp paused as Gar stood before Halion and Marrock.

'Know that you are trusted, Gar,' said Marrock. 'We do not doubt your loyalty. But you have knowledge of our enemies – of Edana's enemies. That is clear, and it is not right that you keep it from us. Someday soon Edana's life, and ours, may depend on that knowledge.'

Gar looked to Corban.

The consequences of this conversation played through Corban's mind. Refuse to talk and Gar would earn a measure of anger and distrust, probably from everyone in their small group. Or answer Halion and Marrock's questions. Corban was as intrigued as any to find out more about Gar's background but, sure as day followed night, Gar would repeat some of what he had told Corban, about Asroth and Elyon, about him being *chosen*. The thought of everyone knowing – his friends – made him cringe. He looked between his mam and Gar, pleadingly, and realized that Gar was waiting for him. The stablemaster would not say a word without Corban's agreement; he would suffer the anger and suspicion of their companions and friends, all on Corban's decision. Emotions swept him, love and respect for this man who had guarded him his whole life. Even if he was a mad man. He gritted his teeth and nodded.

'I will answer your questions,' Gar said to Halion and Marrock.

'Good,' Marrock said.

'How do you know Sumur?' asked Halion.

'How do you fight the way you do?' Marrock asked.

Others called out more questions. Gar held a hand up. 'I'll tell you who I am, something of myself and where I am from, then you can ask the questions I haven't answered.' He looked around, and no one disagreed, so he continued. 'My name is Garisan ben Tukul, and I come from Telassar, a city in the land of Tarbesh, far to the east. Sumur, who served Nathair, is also from there. We are a warrior caste, a holy order, called the Jehar.'

A silence filled the glade. Corban looked around at the faces of his companions, all processing the information Gar had just given them. Brina stepped forward.

'Then why are you here? A member of a holy order, so far from your home?' she asked.

Trust her to ask that question, Corban thought.

Gar looked at him, waiting for his permission, and Brina gave Corban a sharp look. Corban nodded.

'You have all heard something of Brenin's journey to Tenebral, of the council he attended?'

There were murmurs of assent. Corban noticed Edana stand straighter, looking as intent, as focused as he had seen her since they had left Dun Carreg.

'And you all know something of the subject of that council, the God-War?'

More murmurs, coupled with frowns this time.

'What's that got to do with anything?' Dath muttered.

'Some here know more than others about these things,' Heb said, moving to stand beside Brina. 'Why don't you tell what you think is necessary for all to know, to understand what you are saying.'

'All right,' said Gar. 'There was a prophecy spoken of at the council, discovered in the city of Drassil, the heart of Forn Forest. It was written by Haldor, a giant from the time of the Scourging.'

Now everyone in the camp was silent, fixed on Gar.

'The prophecy spoke of the God-War, spoke of signs of its coming: the giant-stones weeping blood, white wyrms roaming the land, the awakening of the Seven Treasures, of Midwinter's Day, when day became night. Those portents have all occurred. It said that the gods Asroth and Elyon, and their angels and demons, would make the Banished Lands their battleground, and that each god would be championed by a chosen avatar: the Black Sun and the Bright Star.' Gar took a deep breath, shoulders straightening. 'I am Garisan ben Tukul of the Jehar, and my life from the moment I first drew breath until now has been dedicated to Elyon. I have been given a great honour, chosen to protect the Bright Star, to defend him with my life.'

'I don't understand,' Dath whispered to Farrell.

'Shut up and listen,' Farrell hissed, jabbing Dath with his elbow.

'So, again,' Brina said, eyes narrowed to slits now. 'Why are you here?'

'Because Corban is the Bright Star, the Seren Disglair, avatar of Elyon.'

There was a long silence, then Dath laughed.

CHAPTER TWENTY-EIGHT

FIDELE

Fidele rode through the wooden gates of Ripa, Peritus at her side, two score of her eagle-guard behind them. Things had escalated since the discovery of the body in the lake. *The discovery of Jace – give the dead a name.* He had obviously been murdered for his part in informing her about the Vin Thalun fighting pits. Peritus had had a fire lit in his bones, then, and had set about rooting out every scrap of information in Tenebral about the Vin Thalun. Word had reached them from Lamar, Baron of Ripa, that had been worth investigating in person.

It was late in the day, the sun low but still warm. The smell of salt filled Fidele's lungs, the calling of gulls and the murmur of the sea underpinning all else.

They were met by a group of mounted men, Krelis ben Lamar at their head.

'My lady,' he said to her. 'You would be best served by staying here. There may be hard words and bloodshed ahead of us. My father is looking forward to the pleasure of your company.'

'Well, he will have to wait a little longer for it. I did not ride over a hundred leagues to sit in a tower and wait for others to tell me of events,' she said, less politely than she intended.

'But—' Krelis began.

'No. I am coming. There will be no discussion on it. I have my guards.'

Krelis frowned but said no more.

Not as brainless as he looks, Fidele thought.

He led them out of the fortress, turning north once they had left all buildings behind. They skirted Sarva, last great forest of the south, travelling steadily north as the sun sank into an ocean of green boughs. Fidele saw the outline of a fortress on a hill, ringed by trees. Its towers and walls were jagged in their ruin, framed by the dying sun.

Balara, once-great fortress of the Kurgan giants.

They rode up the hill, shadows stretching far behind them, through a thin scattering of trees and up to the walls of Balara.

'The gates have been cleared,' Krelis said to her and Peritus, pointing to where fallen rubble was piled high to either side of a wide stone archway.

'You see,' Peritus said to her, 'the reports are true.'

'Let's go and see why they have gone to all this hard work,' Fidele said. As they rode forward a horn call rang out, high and ululating.

'They've seen us,' Krelis called, spurring his horse to greater speed.

He clattered onto the stone, Fidele and their mingled warriors close behind. They passed through a wide stone street, then Fidele saw faces, saw figures running in all directions, others standing, just staring. As she sped closer she could see the iron in their beards.

Vin Thalun.

Some realized what was happening and drew their weapons. Krelis' broadsword swept out of its scabbard; Peritus drew his own blade. Krelis sent a head spinning through the air with the first swing of his sword, Peritus trampled another with his horse, and then Fidele's warriors were sweeping past her as she pulled on her reins, watching in silent horror.

A handful of the Vin Thalun resisted, pulling men from horses and hacking at them, but they were overwhelmed in moments, both by numbers and the ferocity of her men's attack. *Are we so very different from the Vin Thalun?*

It was over soon, the Vin Thalun breaking and scattering, deeper shadows in the gloom disappearing amongst the rubble. Fidele dismounted and tethered her horse, Orcus her shieldman walking protectively beside her.

Peritus and Krelis had rounded up a handful of survivors. One of them barged forwards, hands bound.

'What do you think you're doing, you stupid bitch?' he yelled. 'Lykos won't stand for this.'

Orcus clubbed the man across the jaw and he dropped to the ground, tried to rise and Orcus kicked him.

'Enough,' Fidele said. She looked to Peritus and Krelis. 'Is it true, then?'

'Aye, my Queen,' Peritus said.

'Show me.'

They marched across a rubble-strewn street, a ruined tower looming before them.

'Careful,' Krelis warned as they entered through a fallen arch-way.

Inside, the ground had subsided, revealing stone basements beneath – cellars originally, most likely. They had been dug out, a ring cleared around the edges where Fidele and her companions stood. She looked down into the cleared space and at first did not understand what she saw.

Bodies, the dead piled in a corner, blood pooling, flowing in rivulets. Cells had been erected, built from wood, like tiny stables, and in them stood men, some staring back at her. Some were young, not much more than boys, others older, all battered, battle scarred, all with a feral look in their eyes.

So it was true. They had discovered a Vin Thalun fighting pit.

CHAPTER TWENTY-NINE

VERADIS

Veradis sat in Dun Carreg's feast-hall. Bos sat beside him, the big man devouring his way through a trencher piled high with meat and gravy. The room bore the marks of conflict – charred beams above, smoke-blackened patches on the walls, the dark residue of stains on the stone floor that had been scrubbed at but not removed. Could not be removed. *Blood leaves a stain*, he thought, one finger tracing the scar on the palm of his right hand, mark of his blood-oath to Nathair. *We are brothers now*, Nathair had said to him that night, long ago in Tenebral. Nathair had been only a prince then, Aquilus still alive. He remembered how he had felt – excited, coursing with *life*, the future a grand destiny he had only to claim. And now here he was, a thousand leagues from home, claiming that destiny. There was just too much politicking going on for his liking. That's why he'd enjoyed his morning in the Rowan Field so much, just to be able to face an opponent with a sword in his hand, even if it was only made of wood, not iron.

Just then figures walked through the hall's doors: Evnis and a handful of his shieldmen – no one here seemed to move without a guard – Conall, the warrior he had sparred with earlier, was close to him.

'He was lucky,' Bos said, nodding at Conall. 'You should've beaten him.'

'He was fast,' Veradis said. 'And I'm not so used to fighting like that now; spent too much time in the shield wall.'

'Excuses,' Bos chuckled.

'Not excuses, he fought well. Just the truth.' It *was* the truth, Veradis having felt vulnerable and slow from the first strike of their practice swords. He would have to make sure his training was more balanced from now on – make time for both shield wall and individual sparring. He had already done that today, after his bout with Conall moving on to train in the Field with Nathair's eagle-guard, then travelling out of the fortress, down to the meadows beyond to check on his warband and oversee their training.

He had enjoyed the day. But now he was back, summoned to a meeting with Nathair and Owain, the King of Narvon. *Back to the politicking. I'd rather leave that to Nathair and Calidus.* Lykos had already left, the Vin Thalun sailing with the dawn tide, taking his ships and his Vin Thalun warriors with him. That had been Calidus' idea, and a sensible one – Lykos had looked set to drink Dun Carreg dry if something had not been found for him to do. He had taken half the fleet, only the shallow-draughted attack galleys. The troop carriers would not be able to travel where Lykos was going.

As if Veradis' thoughts had summoned them, Calidus and Alcyon walked through the hall's doors. Dark looks and murmurs spread about them, suspicious eyes watching Alcyon as he passed. Veradis felt a stab of anger at these people, at their ignorance, but understood their distrust. Once upon a time he would have felt the same, but Alcyon had saved his life once and – more than that – Veradis had glimpsed his humanity. And it came as a surprise to him that he liked Alcyon, had almost come to consider him a friend.

Calidus saw Veradis and beckoned him to follow. The three of them marched through the keep's high-arched corridors to Nathair's chambers. Veradis noticed more of the Jehar warriors spread about the keep, standing unobtrusively in alcoves and shadows; more of them materialized the closer they came to Nathair. It gave him a sense of security. *No one will come close to Nathair without their permission, and if anyone is more fanatical about Nathair's safety than me, it is these men.*

Nathair barely acknowledged them as they entered; he had been withdrawn for some time, since they had questioned the girl in the dead of night. Veradis had felt uncomfortable about that, so many of them breaking into her house, probably terrifying her half to death. The conversation with her had clearly affected Nathair, and not only him. Calidus had been uncharacteristically short tempered. *You should not have let the boy escape*, he had said. It was the closest Veradis had heard anyone come to reprimanding Nathair.

'Sit down,' Nathair said, waving a hand. 'Owain has asked me to meet with him soon; things are gathering pace here. A confrontation with Rhin is not far away.'

'Owain will want to know where your allegiances lie,' Calidus said. 'You have a lot of men about you. Enough men to decide a battle.'

'I do. More than enough, when over two thousand are Jehar warriors and a thousand of my eagle-guard are trained in the shield wall,' Nathair said. He smiled grimly at Veradis.

'We must still be cautious,' said Calidus. 'You may be guarded by the Jehar, but even their skill can be overwhelmed by weight of numbers, and you sleep in the heart of Owain's lair. Things are balanced on a knife-edge here. Dun Carreg, Ardan, the west – it is volatile and likely to change at any given time. The maps are being rewritten.'

'I know.' Nathair grinned. 'It is exciting. The new age we have heard so much about, spoken about, it is being formed around us. Right now.'

'Yes, it is,' Calidus said. 'And you are certain of your path?'

'Yes, and so I must play my part here, to make that happen.'

'What of Evnis?' Veradis asked. 'You have given him an important part in all of this. Can he be trusted?'

'Yes,' Calidus said emphatically.

Veradis looked at him but the silver-haired counsellor said no more.

'Do not worry about Evnis,' Nathair said. 'I have his measure. And, besides, even if he were to disappoint me, it wouldn't be disastrous. Not with you watching him.'

'Me?'

'Yes. I want you to watch Evnis, keep him alive. I think he will prove to be useful. And, as you will be watching him closely, you will soon know if he means to betray me.'

'Aye.' Veradis frowned. 'But I am not best suited to that kind of task.'

'There is one other that must be watched,' Calidus said, ignoring his protest. 'The girl, Cywen. Her brother may return for her. We must find that boy.'

'I know,' Nathair said, scowling into his cup. 'I should not have let him escape.'

'What's done is done,' said Calidus. 'And there was much happening, at the time. But we must do all in our power to right the mistake.'

'What is it about the girl's brother?' Veradis asked.

Nathair looked at him, his gaze dark. 'Calidus thinks we have uncovered Asroth's Black Sun.'

'You giants made good roads,' Veradis said to Alcyon.

'All the better to speed us to our enemies,' Alcyon said. 'That is the giant clans – always rushing to their deaths.'

They were marching along the giantsway, Dun Carreg a faint shadow on the horizon behind them. Warriors in their thousands marched before them, the bull of Narvon on banners everywhere. Owain had decided that marching out to meet Rhin in open battle was the best thing to do.

'I will not cower behind stone walls,' Owain had said when he had summoned Nathair to his chambers. 'I have had reports of her numbers, and know that I have more men than she. And she will not expect us to ride out and meet her on the open field.'

Nathair had questioned the wisdom of such a move, but Owain's will was set.

'I will make an end to this, once and for all. And Ardan is mine. I have conquered it, slain Brenin; it is mine by right of conquest, and I will not have that old spider hemming me into a fortress and lording it around the land while watching me starve to death.'

Nathair had said little during the meeting, listening far more than he spoke. Owain had been rambling – a man weighed by a thousand burdens. All that he said came down to one thing: 'Will you fight for me?' he had asked. 'You have a sizeable warband here, and I have seen what a hundred of your Jehar can do.'

'I am reluctant to shed my people's blood over your and Rhin's affairs,' Nathair had replied. 'I will have my own battles to fight soon enough.'

'Fight for me and I shall join your alliance,' Owain had countered, almost pleading.

'I have already given you great aid, opened the gates of Dun

Carreg to you, stopped Brenin from forming a resistance while you stormed his fortress. I would think that such acts would have been enough for you to join with me,' Nathair had retorted.

'I will not be able to join you and your alliance if Rhin has my head on a spike, and you would surely rather have me as an ally than her. You cannot trust her, the scheming bitch.'

'Do you think that Brenin was right about her – that she manipulated your war against Brenin, and then struck when Brenin was dead and you weakened?'

Such a look had passed Owain's face then – doubt, shame, fear. 'How can that be possible? Marrock was seen leaving my Uthan's chamber after he had been murdered. No, I think she is greedy, opportunistic and she saw two realms ripe for the taking. But I am not dead yet. She has underestimated me . . .'

Owain had ranted on, seeming almost to forget that anyone else was there. In the end Nathair had not committed himself, had told Owain that he would talk with his counsellors and speak more on the morrow. That had been two days ago. Veradis had not been present at the final meeting between Nathair and Owain, but Nathair had clearly committed to some level of aid, as their marching with Owain's warband testified.

Nathair rode some way ahead of Veradis. He was sitting upon his draig, the great beast almost filling the width of the giantsway. Horses gave it a wide berth, especially as it looked at them as if it wanted to eat them. Nathair had told Veradis that that had been one of the hardest things in his training of the draig back in Jerolin – to teach it not to chase and kill any horse that trotted past it. Nathair was surrounded by a sea of the Jehar, all clad in dark chainmail, curved swords jutting from their backs. Beyond them the red of Narvon flowed along the giantsway, disappearing into the distance. Veradis had a thousand eagle-guard with him. The survivors of his warband from Forn were all mounted, whilst the recruits that Lykos had brought from Tenebral marched in orderly ranks; the sound of their iron-shod sandals cracking on the stone of the giantsway filled the air. Just in front of Veradis' column rode Evnis, two or three score of his shieldmen about him, Conall amongst them. Beside Conall rode the girl, Cywen, a brindle hound padding at her horse's hooves. She had spent most of her time scowling at Evnis. Veradis grinned to watch it, though if she were as good with a knife as Conall had said, then he worried for Evnis' safety, particularly as Nathair had charged Veradis himself with keeping the man alive.

'There'll be no giants to kill at the end of this march, though,' Alcyon said, unusually talkative. 'It will be men that we are killing at this journey's end. How does that sit with you, king's man?'

'If they are Nathair's enemies it does not matter what shape they take; man or giant, I will slay them if I can.'

'Well said,' called Calidus, riding his horse back down the line from Nathair. He pulled in beside Veradis and spoke more quietly. 'Be on your guard, and keep a particular eye on Owain's rearguard. The King of Narvon is unpredictable at present and likely to behave impulsively.'

Veradis looked over his shoulder. Beyond his own warriors more of Owain's men brought up the rear, at least half a thousand mounted men.

'I will.'

Calidus spurred his horse back to Nathair. *Has he really uncovered the identity of Asroth's Black Sun?* Veradis had always expected it to be some king or man of power, but from what he had been told, this boy – Corban – was a blacksmith's son, no one of consequence. *Maybe Calidus is right. It is a cunning way to grow in secret, a deception from the very beginning, which would be fitting as Asroth's champion. Calidus knows best, and he has guided us well so far. I hope the boy is the Black Sun, for then I will stand a chance of meeting him, and his companion, this Gar. I will see Rauca avenged.*

Nathair had told him how Rauca had died – defending Nathair from this Corban's father, and that afterwards Gar had attacked silently, taken Rauca by surprise. Rauca had deserved better. But time could not be reversed, and nor could the dead be brought back to life.

But they can be avenged.

Five days out from Dun Carreg, well before highsun, Veradis heard horns blowing further ahead. Word slowly filtered back down the column that Rhin's forces had been sighted. It was half a day before Veradis' warband saw them.

Owain's forces had drawn up on the slopes of a gentle hill, spilling in a disorderly crush either side of the giantsway. All seemed to be chaos, with horns blowing, men shouting, oxen bellowing as they were led from the giantsway, pulling wains to a makeshift camp on the hill's crown. To the north-west marshland stretched to the sea, shimmering in the summer sun. Rhin's warband was spread on a plain below them, tents in the distance; a mass of men on foot dominated the centre, whilst mounted warriors were loosely grouped on both flanks. Veradis stood and stared at them a while, the sounds around him fading as he focused.

'How many?' Bos said beside him.

'Six, six and a half thousand men.'

'And us?'

'Between us and the Jehar Nathair has three thousand swords. Owain commands at least nine thousand warriors.'

'She will lose, then.'

Veradis looked at his friend, shielding his eyes from the sun. 'Time will be the judge of that, but I have heard that she is cunning. I think she may have more planned than what we can see.'

'Best keep our wits about us, then,' said Bos.

'Aye. And our swords sharp.'

CHAPTER THIRTY

UTHAS

Uthas crawled through the long grass and wildflowers, up an incline. He stopped when he reached the top, gazing in silence.

Dun Taras stood in the distance, its smooth walls reflecting the morning sun. It had been one of the giants' great fortresses once, alongside Dun Carreg and Dun Vaner, before the hordes of men had come to Benoth. Now Eremon sat upon its throne, ruling all he could see from its high tower. Uthas felt his blood stir, yearning for a lost time. He blinked tears, saw a memory superimposed on the landscape, of his kin gathered on green meadows, celebrating the Birth Moon. Bairns playing in the river, diving and plunging after salmon, the men gathering in contests of strength, throwing tree trunks or the hammer. He walked amongst them, laughing, smiling . . .

The vision faded, shifting into something else: columns of the Benothi marching through empty fields, the landscape behind them black and charred, the walls of Dun Taras fading in the distance. They had walked away from Dun Taras, fled before the tide of mankind.

It will be ours again. A new order is coming. And I will do what needs to be done to make it so.

He glanced over his shoulder, saw Eisa and Struan crawling up the slope, the others standing still, almost invisible amongst the rocks and trees far below. Eisa and Struan settled either side of him.

After gazing for a long while on Dun Taras, Struan whispered, 'What now?'

Uthas rolled onto his back and searched the sky. It was cloudy, the air humid, heavy. Rain was coming. Amongst the clouds a black dot moved. Uthas beckoned and the dot spiralled lower until Fech landed beside him.

'We can go no closer,' Uthas said. 'Can you fly to Dun Taras, seek out Eremon, listen to his plans.'

'*Fech is good at listening and seeing,*' the bird said and flew away, winging towards Dun Taras.

Was that a threat? Uthas thought. *What will he tell Nemain when we return to Murias?* He watched Fech fade and disappear, then he made his way down the slope to his companions. A hundred and fifty leagues they had travelled since they had left Murias in the cold north. Over a moon had passed since they had raised a cairn over Aric's body and placed the heads of their enemies about it. *That will give Rath cause to fear us again, or whoever else discovers it. Too long we have been timid, fearful.* They moved silently through the boulders and stunted trees that blanketed this rolling land of hill and vale. In time they came to a stream and followed it deeper into woodland until they eventually came to a great boulder, part of a cliff face that rose before them. Uthas found the cave entrance and passed through the glamour that had hidden it for over a hundred years. Fray struck a light with his flint and soon they had a small fire burning. Then they settled in for the wait. Fech would know where to come.

Eisa passed him a skin, more brot. He pulled a face but took it and drank some. It had kept them alive, fuelled their journey south, into the heartland of their enemy. Twice they had come close to being discovered, but Fech had given them good warning both times, and Uthas had been more interested in speed than battle. He had already blooded his followers, bound them closer to him through that act. They were more his than Nemain's now.

Nemain.

The thought of her made him sad. Once great Queen of the Benothi, but fallen so far, her fear binding her, disabling her.

She should have fought for our lands, used the cauldron. She should have bargained with Asroth and ensured the survival of our clan. Instead she had done nothing, claiming the Benothi's sole purpose now was to keep the cauldron from being used, thinking to avoid another war.

But war is coming, no matter what she does to evade it.

Ever since he had met with Asroth, in Rhin's cell deep within the walls of Dun Vaner, he had felt like a blind man gifted with sight, as if scales had fallen from his eyes. *The way forward is so clear, but Nemain refuses to see it.*

He had tried to reason with her, to advocate a more active, aggressive policy, but she had refused to see sense. He still clung to the hope that she would change her stance before it was too late, but until then he would pay her lip service and continue to work with Rhin towards their greater purpose. At least he had managed to sway others within the Benothi, and he hoped more would side with him, before the end.

He was glad Nemain had sent him on this mission, scouting into Domhain to learn Eremon's plans. He had counted on it, even, for it kept him within Nemain's good graces whilst allowing him to further Rhin's plans. The journey south had told him that Eremon was paying little attention to the events in the east, to Rhin's attacks on Narvon and Ardan. No warriors were mustering, no crops were being stored. Eremon sat idly by and sank deeper into his dotage. Rhin would be pleased. *She will be here soon. Rhin.* He felt a smile twitch his features at the thought of seeing her. His captor, his saviour. They had a bond he could not deny, complex and deep, its waters murky. *But our goal is clear, and I will see it through or die in the trying; we are united in that. Soon the Black Sun will appear, will come for the cauldron. And I will help him claim it.*

The next part in that task would be to grab Eremon's attention and direct it north. Uthas would slaughter and burn on his way home, make such a noise as Domhain had never heard. He would lead Domhain's strength in warriors north, fix Eremon's attention on Benoth, then when Rhin had finished with Narvon and Ardan and finally came west she would find Domhain open and unprepared.

He rolled up his cloak and laid his head upon it. Looking at Dun Taras had stirred a melancholy within him as deep as bones. He searched for sleep to erase the ache. Besides, Fech would not be back today.

Uthas woke with a start. Salach was sitting with his back to the cold rock, running a whetstone along his axe-blade.

'You were dreaming,' his shieldman said.

Uthas touched his brow, his fingers coming away damp with sweat.

'How long have I slept?'

'A day. They are amazed at you,' Salach said, glancing at the other giants in the cave. Some were standing, restless, others huddled in conversation.

'How can you sleep now?' Fray asked him. 'When we are here, amongst our enemy, in the heart of our homeland.'

'I've been here before,' Uthas said, 'and besides, when you have lived as long as I, sitting in a cave, no matter where it is, is not very exciting.'

Salach chuckled.

'How long have you lived?' Eisa asked then.

'I forget. It has been a long time. I was a bairn, not yet grown my whiskers when the Scourging changed our world.' He tugged at the white hair on his face, bound with thin strips of leather.

'It is true, then. You drank from the cup.' Kai this time.

'I did,' Uthas said. Since the slaying of Skald, the first king, immortality had been stripped from giants and men. But then the cup had been forged from the starstone. The cup was one of the Seven Treasures, and drinking from it gave health and long life. Not immortality, but close enough.

'How long will the cup sustain you?' Struan asked. They had all gathered about Uthas now, regarding him with a new emotion in their eyes. Awe.

'I do not know,' Uthas shrugged. 'Nemain drank from it before I, and she is still here.' *Though she squanders her time, choosing to sit on the cauldron like some skeletal chicken.*

The Benothi giants had emerged from the War of Treasures the clear victors, possessing three of the Seven Treasures. The cauldron, Nemain's necklace and the cup. Two had been lost now, which went some way to explaining Nemain's obsessive protection of the cauldron. The necklace had been hidden in Dun Carreg as the walls had been breached and overrun, the giants holding the stronghold had been slaughtered to the last warrior. The cup had been lost in Domhain. *Somewhere out there.*

Uthas hung his head in shame. He had lost the cup, or at least had been in charge of the column in possession of the cup as it had been evacuating from Dun Taras. They had been ambushed in the marshlands further north; the wain the cup had been kept in sank into the swamp. He had returned so many times, his shame driving him, sending him hunting for the lost Treasure, but never with any success.

A flapping echoed about the cave and Fech appeared through the glamour that sealed the entrance. The bird searched out Uthas and alighted before him. It walked in a small circle, then ran its beak through the feathers of one wing, regarding Uthas with its shiny eyes.

'Well?' Uthas said.

'*Eremon is old, he is scared of change.*'

'So what are his plans?'

'*He did not say. He is idle. He did little more than watch women.*'

'Good news, then,' Uthas said.

'*Not all good. Rath is coming.*'

'What do you mean, coming?'

'*He found the dead, in the north. He is on your trail. He is hunting you.*'

CHAPTER THIRTY-ONE

CORBAN

It was still dark when Gar shook Corban awake. Without speaking, the two of them slipped into the sword dance. Dawn crept over them soon after, picking out Vonn standing on watch, the others rising and setting about the ritual of breaking camp.

Others were sparring about them with cloth-covered weapons as Corban finished the dance.

'Where are Halion and Marrock?' Corban asked, noticing their absence.

'They left in the dead of night with Camlin,' Vonn answered his question. The young warrior had been withdrawn and silent since the book had been taken from him. 'My guess is another visit to our pursuers. Maybe just scouting, though I guess at more.'

Gar grunted an agreement.

Corban didn't know how to feel about that. He had hated the last night attack, especially the killing from shadows. Even though he knew it was an act driven by survival, it had still felt like cowardice. But there had been a sense of camaraderie that had grown amongst them because of it, of risks taken, danger shared. Part of him felt disappointed at being left out this time.

'Do not look so disappointed,' Vonn said with a bitter twist to his lips. 'I offered to go with them but they refused me. Perhaps they do not trust me.'

Being Evnis' son will not help you, and keeping the book a secret did you no favours, either.

'Trust has to be earned,' Gar said.

'Aye. As does honour,' Vonn replied, then walked away.

Corban shared a look with Gar.

'Corban,' Brina called him, hovering close by with Heb.

'It's time we started,' Brina said.

He saw she had the book they had taken from Vonn in her hands.

'Learning to be an Elemental, you mean.'

'Yes, Ban.'

He felt scared suddenly, as if he were standing at the opening of a dark tunnel. 'Why do you want to teach me?' he asked suspiciously.

'Because you're expendable,' Brina snapped. 'If something goes wrong and you end up melted it won't matter too much.' She strode away.

Heb sighed. 'It's a compliment, Corban,' he said.

'Is this something to do with what Gar said – about me being *chosen*.' There had been a number of silent stares at Corban since Gar's shocking confession. He'd even caught Dath and Farrell looking at him oddly. 'You should pay it no mind, you know. Gar's clearly confused . . .' he trailed off, knowing that Gar did not seem the type to be confused about anything.

Heb regarded him silently. 'Not for Brina's part.'

'Then why me?'

'Brina likes you, Corban.' Heb smiled, Corban snorted. 'You must understand: there is a gateway to great power contained in that book, something that must be guarded. In the wrong hands untold damage could be done. Brina trusts you. Do you think she would want to teach just anyone – Dath, for example, or Farrell?'

'I don't know,' Corban said.

'Not even Edana or Marrock. You are the only one she will consider teaching. Brina trusts you.'

He felt strangely pleased at that thought. Honoured, even. 'All right, then,' he said to Heb. Together they followed Brina into the cover of the trees.

'I'll take the risk of being melted,' Corban said to her, 'though my mam may have something to say about that.'

Brina's lips twitched.

'We'll start with a lesson,' Heb said.

'Of course you will,' Brina muttered.

'Once all were Elementals,' Heb continued, ignoring her. 'It was part of the All-Father's design; giants and men were the overseers or guardians of creation, and so they were gifted a certain authority over that creation – specifically the elements of fire, water, earth and air.'

'That is how we summoned the mist, during our escape from Dun Carreg,' Brina interjected.

Corban nodded thoughtfully. 'How did you learn these powers? Were you born with them?'

'It is not something that just happens, like clicking your fingers,' Brina said. 'A bairn is not just able to wield a sword.'

'No,' Corban said, 'but some take to it better than others.'

'There may be something in what you say,' Heb conceded, frowning. 'This book talks of two paths to power. One is the way that Brina and I know a little of. The other . . .'

'The other we shall not speak of,' Brina said.

Heb regarded her a moment, then shrugged. 'Suffice to say that blood seems to be important. There are suggestions that some bloodlines are stronger; perhaps a purer lineage from the first men. And then there is the use of *actual* blood; from a living body—'

'I said we will not speak of that,' Brina snapped.

'As you wish. You must understand, Corban, that this is not set out plain. Brina and I have spent years putting scraps of knowledge together.'

'We studied and learned,' Brina said. 'There is value in reading, as I have always told you, though it took us years, decades, to discover even a small portion of what is contained in this book.'

'So how do I make mist rise from the ground?' He liked the thought of that, remembering the escape from Dun Carreg – a thick mist enveloping them, hiding them from their attackers. *That could be a handy trick to know.* He felt a glimmer of excitement.

'In essence, the act of elemental control can be broken down to two parts,' Heb said in his loremaster's voice. 'You have to believe it, and then you have to speak it.'

'So if I tell mist to rise from the ground, then it will? It cannot be that simple.'

'Well, yes and no,' Heb said with a faint smile. 'Your words show you are defeated already – you do not believe it will happen. I do not mean that you think it might happen, and so give it a try. You have to believe it, absolutely, as you believe a chair will support your weight before you sit upon it, or that an apple will fall to the ground when you drop it.'

'And there is common sense,' Brina added.

'Yes, you must be aware of your surroundings. For example, you could not command a mist to arise from a desert. Mist is moisture, water. In Dun Carreg Brina and I commanded the moisture in the ground to rise up. If it had not been there to begin with, then nothing would have happened. You understand?'

'Yes.' Corban nodded. It did make sense to him. *This is becoming interesting.*

'So, then, I have to believe whatever it is that I want to happen, and then I just speak it.'

'Yes,' Heb said.

'Though it's still not quite that simple,' Brina said.

Of course it isn't.

'You have to speak it in this language,' Heb said, taking the book from Brina and opening it. It was full of runes, a script that Corban recognized from the inscription carved into the archway of Stonegate, back in Dun Carreg.

'Is that giantish?' he asked.

'Yes,' Brina said.

'It is much more than that,' Heb said. 'It is the first language. The tongue of angels, giants, men. It is the language of Elyon, the Maker.'

'So I have to learn giantish.' Inwardly, Corban groaned.

'Yes,' Brina said. She smiled.

There was a rustling in the undergrowth and Storm appeared. She nudged him, making him stagger, and then she growled, looking through the trees.

'What is it?' Corban said, then saw three figures appearing from the underbrush. He recognized Halion. Immediately Corban knew something was wrong – the figure in the middle was being supported, half carried.

Marrock.

He was waxen pale, one arm hanging limp, blood dripping from it.

'What happened?' Corban called as he ran to them, to help carry the injured man into their camp.

'Wounded during our raid,' Halion breathed. 'Think he was mauled by one of their hounds.'

'It's not that bad,' Marrock said.

'I'll be the judge of that,' Brina snapped. She sent Corban running for her pack as she examined Marrock's arm.

'Everyone be ready to ride,' Camlin called out, marching through the camp. 'We need t'move. Think we've been tracked.'

All the mounts were saddled and ready.

When Corban returned to Brina she was pouring water from a skin over the wound. Corban caught a sight of frayed flesh and white bone amidst the blood. Brina took her pack from Corban, rummaged inside it a moment, then unstoppered a jug of something, muttered, 'This is going to sting,' and poured it over the wound. Marrock drew in a sharp breath and Brina bandaged his forearm, placing leaves over the bite-marks.

A horn call rang out behind them, answered by the baying of hounds, much louder than Corban would have liked.

'We must leave,' Halion said.

'Dath, string your bow and follow me,' Camlin said, mounting a saddled horse. Dath looked about nervously, then followed the woodsman.

'Can you ride?' Brina asked Marrock, who was drenched in sweat. He nodded and was hastily assisted into a saddle, then they were all riding hard away from the sound of their pursuers.

They rode through broken woodland all day, the land changing from meadows and wide valleys to rolling hills, the trees turning to pine as they rose steadily higher. In the distance, to the north-west, Corban could see a dark smudge on the horizon: mountains. Corban kept checking over his shoulder, hoping for Dath and Camlin's return.

At highsun they stopped briefly to rest their mounts, then set off again. The afternoon passed. As the sun dipped into the horizon they were strung in a line behind Halion, who was keeping the horses cantering, making the most of the soft pine-needles that covered the ground, allowing a good speed.

We've made good time, covered a lot of ground. Surely we've widened the gap between us, Corban thought. *But where are Camlin and Dath?*

Then Marrock fell from his saddle, sliding like a sack of grain onto the pine-covered ground.

CHAPTER THIRTY-TWO

MAQUIN

As the sun rose, Maquin stared down into the streets of Dun Kellen. Bodies buzzing with flies littered the ground.

The night had been long and hard fought, Jael's warband assaulting Dun Kellen's walls with growing desperation. There had been a dozen moments when Maquin expected to hear horns call the retreat to the keep, but somehow they still held the outer wall. Orgull had played no little part in that. Jael's assaults had focused on the parts of the wall that had been rebuilt, a patchwork of timber and stone. Wherever the fighting was fiercest Orgull was there, dealing death with his giant's axe, and Maquin had been glad to follow, his hatred of Jael fuelling his body well beyond its limits. As he snatched some rest now he felt muscles and tendons complaining, his shoulder throbbing, blood and sweat stinging his eyes. *Not dead yet.* His thoughts drifted to Kastell and he felt his stomach knot, his eyes drifting to the streets, searching for Jael.

Warriors were busy at work amongst the streets, chopping timber from houses, constructing makeshift ladders and battering rams. More than one of those lay discarded at the fortress' gates, surrounded by corpses. Even as Maquin scoured the enemy lines a knot of men stepped forward, Jael emerging from amongst them. He stopped a distance from the gates, mindful of spear throws, and cupped his hands to his mouth.

'Is there any of a rank left to speak with me?' he called.

Muttering swept the battlements and Gerda came forward, dressed now in an ill-fitting cuirass, a short sword in her hand. Maquin smiled. She had grown in his estimation during the night, refusing to leave the wall, fierce in her exhortations to her warriors, terrifying in her cursing of Jael and his men. She had even charged forwards and swung blows at one point, when men had threatened to breach the wall. Warriors flanked her now, holding their shields ready as she approached the wall, no doubt remembering Varick's fate.

Maquin felt a presence at his shoulder – Tahir, moving up to view the street. He had a cut on his cheek, a gash in his chainmail, but he seemed free of serious injury. He smiled at Maquin. 'Still standing, then.'

'Just,' Maquin said, looking back to Jael.

'What do you want?' Gerda shouted down.

'Are you all that Dun Kellen has left?' Jael said, laughing. 'No lord, no battlechief, just a fat old woman?'

'Who are you calling a woman?' Gerda yelled back, her warriors laughing at that. 'Not too old or too fat to teach you a few lessons in warfare, you snot-nosed brat.'

Even Maquin laughed at that. He saw Jael scowl as laughter rippled along the battlements, even some from behind Jael, within his own ranks.

'If there is anyone up there with rank to treat with me, I will gladly do so,' Jael yelled. 'If there is only a woman left to lead you, then Dun Kellen has fallen far already. Let me make this clear to any with intelligence enough to hear. Gerda and her son Haelan are the walking dead. This is only the van of my warband – more are coming. You cannot win, and I will have their heads on spikes before the next moon rises. Hand Gerda and her brat over and I will let you live, even welcome you into my own warband. Fight on and I will kill every last one of you. Not just you: your wives, your women, your children too. There will be no captives – no surrender.'

'He talks a good talk,' Orgull muttered, moving up beside Maquin and Tahir.

Maquin glanced along the battlements, saw fear amongst the warriors there.

'Hard words break no bones, as my old mam used to say,' Tahir shouted down.

'Well said,' Gerda laughed.

'I'll break bones soon enough,' Jael said, then turned, raising his arm as he did so. Warriors swept forwards from the shadows and ran towards the fortress' wall. At a horn blast they stopped and hurled a mass of spears, Maquin and his comrades ducking low. A man close to Tahir moved too slowly and a spear buried itself in his chest, hurling him back over the battlements' edge. Maquin peered over the wall into the street, saw more of Jael's warriors hurrying from the town's side streets carrying ladders, others holding shields high over men that dragged a thick battering ram between them.

Warning shouts ran amongst the defenders; spears and rocks were hurled onto those below. A ladder slammed into place close to Maquin. He leaned out and stabbed down at a man climbing; his sword-tip glanced off an iron helm, burying itself in the man's shoulder. The man screamed and fell backwards, replaced by another who swung at Maquin's exposed arm. Orgull dragged Maquin back, then swung his axe at the enemy as he appeared at the top of the wall. In a spray of blood his head spun through the air, Orgull using his axe to push the ladder away, the headless corpse still draped over the top rung. The ladder wobbled in space, then crashed back to the street below, men screaming as they fell or were crushed.

More ladders appeared along the battlements and Maquin lost himself in the fight. A booming thud marked time to their violence as the ram crashed ceaselessly against the gates, fading to a blur in Maquin's mind as he slashed and stabbed and snarled at the legion of faces that appeared before him. Always Orgull and Tahir were close by, his Gadrai sword-brothers, beating back the tide wherever they stood. When Maquin paused, his limbs heavy and weak, his lungs burning, he saw Gerda standing on the wall above the gates, yelling defiance, encouraging her warriors, even lifting rocks and heaving them over the battlements at Jael's men below. As Maquin watched, jars of liquid – oil, he guessed – were thrown from above the gates, burning torches cast after them. There was the sound of flames igniting, then a terrible screaming. Maquin leaned over the wall and saw the ram and those holding it ablaze, some running yelling through the street, many rolling on the ground. The smell of charred meat hit his throat and he ducked back behind the wall.

Children moved along the top of the wall, taking skins of water to the defenders. Maquin beckoned one over and gulped from the skin. A shadow fell over them as Orgull reached for the water. The young lad's eyes wide as he stared at Orgull's axe dripping with blood and gore.

'Thirsty work,' Orgull muttered between gulps.

The battle lulled again and Gerda walked along the walls. She reached them and paused. 'You know Jael well?' she asked Maquin.

'He was cousin to my lord.' He shrugged. 'We lived in Mikil together, but Jael and Kastell, my lord, they were never friends.'

'His claim that more men are coming – do you think he tells the truth?'

'He is a snake, would lie to his own mother. He betrayed his uncle and murdered his cousin in the caverns below Haldis. I would not trust anything he says. Most likely he was trying to spread fear amongst your men, hoping one would take your head and accomplish his goal for him. And he must know that you have many more men mustering in your outlying lands. He will be scared, knowing that time is against him.'

'That is what I thought, too,' Gerda said. She raised her voice. 'Jael is a liar, he has no more men coming to aid him. We must just resist, hold them off until our banner-men from the outlying holds arrive.' A ragged cheer rippled along the battlements and Gerda strode away.

Someone shouted a warning as ladders slammed against the wall.

'Back to it,' Orgull said, patting his axe.

They fought on, time losing all meaning to Maquin. Again and again Jael's men assaulted the wall, and every time they were thrown back. As the sun dipped into the horizon, reflecting blood red against low clouds, a cry went up and Jael's men finally broke onto the battlements, first one man gaining a foothold, then another, then a handful.

Maquin was fighting over the gates, guarding Orgull's flank as the big man swung his axe into a warrior who had just leaped from a ladder-top onto the wall. The man was off balance and Orgull's axe smashed into his chest, cutting through chainmail, leather, flesh and bone in an explosion of gore. Maquin heard a change in the battle-cries behind him, turned and saw Jael's men forcing their way onto the wall. Without thinking, he ran at them, shouting to Orgull and Tahir but unaware if they heard him or not.

He smashed into a man, feeling his teeth rattle with the force of the collision, and slammed the man over the wall with not even enough time to scream. Maquin set his feet and swung his sword two-handed, chopping into a man's ribs, then bringing his blade up and down onto the man's head as he crumpled. He stepped over the corpse, chopping, stabbing. His blade was parried, sending shivers along his arm, his wrist numbing. A hand grabbed him, dragging him forwards, and he stumbled over a fallen warrior and dropped to one knee. A man appeared before him, sword raised, Maquin's death in his eyes. With a snarl, Maquin drew a knife from his belt, launched himself forwards, punching the knife beneath the line of his enemy's cuirass, sinking to the hilt. He gave a wrench, saw fear fill the man's face, the strength draining from him. Then he was shoving the dying man away and cutting at the man behind with sword and dagger.

He heard a battle-cry behind him, two voices shouting, 'Gadrai,' and he grinned, knowing his sword-brothers were with him. The battle-joy took him then, which he'd heard others call a madness but to him it was a fierce, pure ecstasy, new strength flooding his limbs, his lips drawn back in a half-grin, half-snarl. Soon the tide had turned, Jael's men dying or fleeing before the three of them: Maquin, Orgull and Tahir.

As Jael's men were killed or cast back over the wall, horn blasts called out from the streets beyond the fortress. The attack ended. Men withdrew quickly. All along the battlements the survivors sagged with exhaustion. Maquin gripped Tahir's shoulder and smiled at him, too weary to speak.

There was a lull in the battle, all on the wall taking the opportunity to drink, eat something, some even leaning against the wall and sleeping. The sun sank into the rim of the world, night creeping up behind. Just before full dark Orgull stared out over the wall, frowning.

Men were running from the side streets, some carrying timber beams between them, others with arms full of straw and thatch. They ran to the gates and the sections of the wall that had long been repaired with wood instead of stone. Soon there were high piles spread along the wall's base.

'Don't like the look of that,' Tahir muttered to Maquin when he saw great jars of oil being carried to the piles of timber and thatch. Warriors on the wall began throwing spears and rocks, and screams told that some found their mark, but almost immediately sparks were being struck and flames were curling up.

'They're going to burn their way in,' Maquin said.

He watched as Gerda and her captains organized the fetching of water from wells within Dun Kellen's wall, but by the time the first buckets of water had arrived the fires were burning bright, the thrown water hissing into steam. They managed to put one fire out, but a dozen others raged against different sections of the wall, the wood used to repair it charring and crackling, smoke billowing over the ramparts.

The boy that had given them water earlier in the day hurried along the wall, scurrying over when he saw Maquin and his companions.

'The lady wants to see you,' he said to Orgull, who nodded and followed the lad into a cloud of smoke. Soon he returned.

'Gerda's calling a retreat to the keep,' he said, but quietly. 'She's leaving a handful of warriors up here to watch the back of those leaving, and to give Jael the impression we mean to fight on.'

'A suicide watch, you mean,' Tahir said.

'No. Her orders were that whoever remains must leave as soon as the first ladders hit the wall.'

'They'd better be quick about it – those walls won't be standing all night,' Maquin said, and as if to prove his point timbers nearby creaked, part of the palisaded walkway collapsing with a crash.

'I suppose you volunteered us for the rearguard,' Maquin said. Orgull grinned.

'Best show our faces, then. Give Jael and his lads something to be scared of,' Maquin said, walking into view on the wall.

'Just make sure we keep our feet on stone,' Tahir added, stepping close to Maquin.

The retreat of Dun Kellen's warriors to the keep did not take long. Soon Maquin, Orgull and Tahir stood with a handful of others left to guard the wall.

It was not long after that the first wooden section of wall collapsed, flames and smoke roaring up in its aftermath. Jael's warriors rushed forwards, but the fire flared in their faces, burning fiercer as it was fed by the timber. In their eagerness, Jael's men lifted ladders to the stone walls, done with waiting.

'Best be out of here,' Tahir said, looking over his shoulder at the dark shadow of the keep behind them. Orgull barked an order at the other warriors ranged about them, only a dozen or so, and they began filing down a wide stairwell.

Maquin put a spear to the ladder that appeared nearby, pushed with all his strength, but the weight of the warriors climbing it held it pinned to the wall. Orgull saw and added his axe, bracing the head against the ladder and leaning into it. Nothing happened, then an iron-capped head appeared on the ladder.

'Come on,' Tahir yelled.

Maquin and Orgull gave a last effort and the ladder swayed away from the wall, teetering for a moment before it hurtled backwards into the darkness. Maquin smiled at the screams that drifted up to them. Then the three of them were running, leaping down the stairwell and sprinting for the keep. A warrior stood guard, keeping the doors open. They slammed shut behind them and were barred with iron and oak.

CHAPTER THIRTY-THREE

CAMLIN

Camlin drew an arrow back to his ear, held his breath, and released it as the arrow sped from his bowstring. Beside him he heard the *thrum* of Dath's arrow, then a succession of screams and the two of them slid back down the ridge.

'Must've hit something,' he muttered to Dath, who grinned back at him. Then they were slipping through the undergrowth. Camlin grunted approvingly as he noted how Dath moved lightly, quick on his feet, looking ahead to avoid snagging branches. *He'll make a good woodsman.* Hounds barked behind them, close, from the ridge they had just left. *If he lives long enough.*

They ran through the woods, Camlin leading the way back to their horses, always twisting and turning, his path never straight. They mounted quickly and set off, both of them too winded to speak.

Leaving the cover of trees, they had to ride across open meadows for at least a league. Camlin glanced up, saw it was well past highsun. They had been at their deadly cat-and-mouse game in the woods since mid-morning, striking at their pursuers four times – *enough to make them think there's more'n two of us lurking in the shadows.* Camlin was under no illusions, knew that they could not stop their trackers, only hope to slow them a while. They had just slipped under the shadow of a stand of pines when Camlin heard the baying of hounds rising faint on the wind.

'They've found our trail,' he called to Dath, who looked nervously back.

They spurred their horses on.

They rode all day, not stopping to rest, periodically allowing the horses to walk instead of canter. As the sun was sinking behind the mountains on the western horizon Camlin spied their companions. They were gathered in an open space of green and purple heather.

'Why aren't they riding?' Dath called to him. Camlin just shook his head, wondering the same question. *They should be riding on until nightfall, making the most of every daylight moment.*

Close by a fire had been lit, flames crackling hungrily as the cold wind snatched at it. Camlin scowled. *They are out in the open. As the dark settles, that fire will draw our trackers like flies to dung.* Then he reached them and saw a figure on the ground.

Marrock.

Halion and Anwarth moved out to meet them as they slid from their saddles.

'Marrock has a fever; he collapsed from his saddle. Brina says his wounds are rotting.'

Camlin felt a twist in his gut, like a knife turning. Did everyone he came to think something of have to die?

'What is Brina going to do?' Dath asked.

'She says there is nothing left, except to take his hand. If the rot has not spread to his blood he may live.'

Camlin strode to where Edana knelt by Marrock, wiping his feverish face with a damp cloth.

They are kin, cousins, he remembered.

Brina stood by the fire, holding a knife blade in the flames. Corban hovered close to her, stirring a pot. Frequently Brina snapped orders at him, the young warrior rummaging through a large pack, pulling out stoppered jars, a roll of linen, a handful of small tools.

Is that a filing iron?

'I don't have the strength to do the cutting,' Brina said. 'Not here, without all my tools. Who will do it for me? It needs a strong arm, a sharp blade and a good aim.'

'I'll do it,' Heb said. Brina looked him up and down and snorted. 'You don't have the strength, and if you did your eyes are so bad you'd probably take his head off, not his hand.'

Heb scowled at her.

'I will do it,' a voice said. Gar stepped forwards, drawing the sword from his back.

Brina strode up to him, her knife glowing red in her hand. She nodded to Farrell, who pulled taut Marrock's arm with a leather cord. Gar swung his sword once and Marrock screamed, his body jerking, blood spraying from his wrist. Brina stepped close.

'Hold him,' the healer ordered. Camlin and Halion gripped the thrashing man, then Brina was holding the knife blade to Marrock's wrist, the flesh sizzling, the stench of cooking meat filing Camlin's nose. He held his breath, felt Marrock tense and then go limp.

'He's fainted,' Halion said.

'Best thing for him,' Brina said as she held Marrock's arm up, examining his wound. She looked at Gar. 'A fine cut.'

She barked an order to Corban, who passed her the tool that resembled a filing iron, then she began rasping it across Marrock's wrist bone.

'What's she doing to him,' Dath said beside Camlin, looking as if he was about to vomit.

'She's taking the bone down, getting rid of any sharp edges, so the skin can be stitched over it.'

'I don't like that noise,' Dath said.

When Brina had finished, Corban passed her another tool, long and thin. This time she picked around in the flesh of the wound. Blood began to seep from it.

'She's digging out dirt and bits of bone,' Camlin whispered to Dath.

Dath swallowed.

After that Brina poured a skin of water over the wound and stuck her reheated knife against it, sizzling again.

'Finish off for me,' she said to Corban.

Corban smeared a salve over Marrock's wound, with Brina watching over his shoulder. Then he unbound a cloth from Brina's pack, took out what looked like a leaf, placed it over the stump of Marrock's wrist and then bound it with linen. His hands moved deftly, his face taut with concentration.

Brina grunted with something like approval. 'Time will be the judge, now,' she said.

'We need to get off this open ground,' Camlin said, kicking the fire out. 'Or we won't have much time left to any of us.'

The sky was a deep blue, the last glow of the sun lingering there. Quickly they mounted up, with Marrock hoisted in front of Halion.

They rode as long as they could, found a straggly stand of pines to shelter them and made camp for the night.

'No fire,' Camlin ordered, knowing their pursuers were gaining, and the beacon of firelight would most likely bring enemies down on them before sunrise. He set about cutting branches and making a litter to carry Marrock in the morning. *If he has lived through the night.*

The next morning was cold and damp, a mist veiling the sun. Marrock was shivering. Brina knelt beside him, checking his pulse at throat and wrist, listening to the breath in his chest. Then she unwound the bandage on his wrist and sniffed.

'Clean and bind it,' she said to Corban.

'He's not safe yet; the fever still has him. Beating that is his first battle.' She shrugged. 'His flesh does not smell of rot, and he's still alive, which is a good sign.'

When Corban was done they strapped Marrock tight to the litter, one end of it harnessed to his horse, and set off into the mist.

It was slow going at first, Camlin riding as rearguard, constantly looking over his shoulder, ears straining for any warning. The mist limited his vision and muffled all sound. Anwarth rode next to him.

'Back at Dun Carreg Dath and my boy Farrell were friends,' Anwarth said, nodding forward to Dath, who was riding with Corban and Farrell. 'He's a good lad – had it hard, I heard, when his mam died. His da took to the usque jug, was quick with his fists.'

'Was he, now?' Camlin asked, remembering Dath's father, seeing his hands trembling for no obvious reason. 'Maybe Dath's better off without him, then.'

Anwarth shrugged. 'Don't know if he'd agree with that. But I've seen the way you've looked out for him. Just wanted you to know, I'm grateful.'

Before Camlin could answer, the gangly warrior had kicked his horse on and ridden further up the column.

They climbed higher, the mist slowly burning off as the day approached highsun. Camlin reined in, staring back into the distance. They were following a shallow valley through a region of rolling foothills blanketed in swathes of red and purple heather. Camlin could see no sign of their pursuers, but the valley they were in had twisted and turned, so the distance he could see was limited. *Safe for now. But not for much longer if we can't change this pace.*

He heard a horse approaching, looked around to see Brina, her black crow perched on her saddle pommel.

'You look worried,' she said.

'I'd be happier if I could see further.'

'Maybe I can help you there,' she said, one finger scratching the neck of her crow.

'*Tired*,' the bird squawked.

'Get on with you,' Brina snapped, lifting the crow and hoisting it into the air. 'Try and earn some of the food I keep giving you.' The bird circled once over their heads and then flapped back along the way they had travelled.

'My thanks,' Camlin said.

'A bit of exercise will do him good,' Brina replied as she rode back to the column. She settled alongside Corban and his wolven, the great beast keeping pace easily. *The company I keep these days. Braith would laugh t'see it.* Brina and the other old one, Heb, had spent much of the night with Corban. Camlin had seen them move a little way from the rest of the group and sit huddled in deep conversation long into the night. They were an odd company indeed, and that Gar was one of the strangest. Camlin had thought over what the grim-faced warrior had said the other morning, about Corban being *chosen*.

Extraordinary things had been happening, of late, but there was no doubt that would be the strangest of all. Still, he'd learned not to judge. He was happier to sit back and watch, and that is what he would do with this Corban. There was something about him . . .

Camlin stayed where he was a while longer, watching the crow fade to a pinprick. Then he spurred his horse to the head of the column, pulling close to Halion.

'Any sign?' the first-sword asked.

'No, but I can only see about a league behind us. Wanted to ask you – what's the ground like ahead of us.'

'Much like this until we reach the mountains. The pass into Domhain is two, three days' ride. There's a road the giants built cutting through them.'

'Is the pass guarded?'

'It used to be – only a token guard – although there are more villages and holds all about the giants' road.' Halion shrugged. 'I'm hoping Rhin has taken most of her fighting men with her to Ardan. We've travelled through the wild, but I still would have expected to see more people than we have.'

'We've been lucky,' Camlin said.

'I don't trust to luck.'

There was a squawking up above and Camlin looked up, saw Brina's crow. It swooped in and circled low over their heads, landing on Brina's outstretched arm.

'*Hunters,*' the bird croaked. '*Close, close, close.*'

Faintly on the breeze the sound of hounds baying drifted up to them.

'So much for luck,' Camlin muttered.

CHAPTER THIRTY-FOUR

CYWEN

Cywen sat in her saddle looking out over the battlefield, Buddai sitting at her horse's feet. Why she was here she did not know. Obviously it was to do with Corban, somehow. He was why everyone seemed so interested in her – Evnis, Nathair, his counsellor, Calidus – all their questions coming back to the constant that was her brother. *What is it about Corban?* And now she was about to view a battle. Her main pleasure was that she considered virtually everyone who would be fighting here as her enemy, at one level or another, so, whoever died, there would be some degree of satisfaction.

She was situated amongst Evnis' warriors, about three score of them mounted around their lord. Conall was close to her, his attention rarely leaving her for more than a few moments. She swore under her breath. 'Don't you have anything better to do than babysit me?' she asked him.

'Shut up,' he said, glancing at her irritably. He'd searched her before they'd left and removed four knives that she had secreted in various parts of her clothing. She resisted a smile; he had missed two, and with them she planned to kill Evnis.

'Weren't you Edana's babysitter, too? You're going down in the world.'

He glared at her, but did not answer, his eyes scanning the battleground before them.

The giantsway ran through the centre of it all, through a wide, flat-bottomed vale where Rhin's warband was spread to meet them. Her banners rippled everywhere – Cambren's broken branch on a black field – a host of black and gold, thousands of them. Yet it was obvious, even to Cywen's untrained eye, that Owain had more men – significantly more.

There was a tension in the air, so strong that she could almost see it, like a heavy mist, and it was contagious. Horses neighed, her own mount dancing skittishly. She searched for Shield again. She had tried to take him as her own mount, but the red-haired warrior Drust had been having none of that and had taken Shield as his warhorse.

She muttered a prayer to Elyon under her breath, begging for the horse to survive the coming battle. *Not that you've ever listened to me before.*

She nudged her horse closer to Conall.

'Why is Rhin down in the valley?' she asked him. 'She was here first, but she's given Owain the high ground.'

'I was wondering that myself,' Conall said.

Twisting in her saddle, she looked behind and saw Nathair on his great draig. She wrinkled her nose, smelling it from here. It smelt of death, of rotting things, and its dung – its smell got into your skin, so badly you could almost taste it. Nathair's Jehar warriors were spread in a thick line behind him, near the hill's ridge. Further along were more of Nathair's warriors, these all on foot in orderly lines, holding great round shields. She recognized at their forefront the man who had sparred with Conall: Veradis. Behind them all was Owain's rearguard, men held in reserve for the coming battle, she presumed.

Cywen saw a handful of riders canter out from the rearguard ranks, Owain at their head. Nathair's warriors parted for him and he rode to the King of Tenebral, spoke to him a while. Then Owain led his shieldmen towards Evnis and his warriors. Cywen's heart jumped as she recognized Shield, Drust upon his back. He must be shield-man to Owain.

Owain rode to Evnis, speaking loud enough for Cywen to hear.

'I have chosen to give you great honour, as reward for your service at Dun Carreg,' Owain said. 'You will lead my warriors into the battle.'

'Sneaky piece of dung,' Conall muttered.

Evnis was silent a moment, then bowed his head. 'As you wish.' He looked about, his eyes finding Conall, and signalled for Cywen to be taken to Nathair.

As they rode up the hill, Buddai following her, Calidus raised a hand, beckoning Conall.

'Keep a close eye on her,' Calidus said. Conall nodded curtly. They settled to the rear of the Jehar warriors, Cywen marvelling at the black-clothed warriors' mounts. They were beautiful to the last one, all fine boned and sleekly muscled.

They watched as Evnis and his warriors rode down the slope towards the main host of Owain's warband, the ranks parting to allow Evnis and his men passage.

'Not going to do much fighting back here,' Cywen said to Conall, watching him keenly. At the very least she could see how far she could push his famous temper.

'You never know,' he replied.

'At least you won't get to die as quickly as Evnis and your other friends, standing here at the back.'

'This is a battle; death can come swift enough wherever we stand. And they're not my friends.'

Then horns blasted out, causing Cywen to snap her head around. Rhin's warband was moving.

First the front lines, then all those behind, appearing to ripple like a great beast rousing from sleep. Slowly at first, they moved across the flat plain of the valley, then gathering speed. The bulk of the host was on foot; Cywen could spy lines of mounted warriors gathered at the rear of the field, thickest around a great banner that was planted in the ground. *Rhin must be there.*

Owain raised a hand and horns blew out. His war-host moved to meet Rhin.

Evnis led the charge. The front ranks of Rhin's warband picked up their own speed, many running now, yelling battle-cries, the thud of feet setting the earth to trembling.

Cywen held her breath as Evnis hurtled towards Rhin's front lines, knew that she was about to watch him die. She grinned fiercely.

CHAPTER THIRTY-FIVE

EVNIS

Evnis yelled wordlessly as the first ranks of Rhin's warband loomed closer. Everywhere he could see faces twisted with battle-cries, weapons glinting, hear feet pounding, the drumming of his own horse's hooves, the riders behind him. He risked a glance over his shoulder, saw a large gap growing between his men and Owain's charging warriors. *Owain is cunning, thinking to remove me and slay a fair number of Rhin's warband along the way. Except that Rhin could give lessons in cunning to a fox. Time for her first surprise.*

He sheathed his sword, reached down to his saddle and drew out a rolled banner. Rhin's sigil of black and gold unfurled above him, snapping in the wake of his gallop. He yanked on his reins, saw the warriors before him parting as his shieldmen slowed behind him, drawing into a double column, and like that they cantered through the ranks of Rhin's warband, shouting greetings to Rhin's warriors as they passed them.

Unluckily for Owain, Rhin and I have ways of communicating that he would not dream of. She had foreseen him attempting something like this, and they had plotted against every conceivable eventuality.

His warriors filtered through Rhin's warband, moving to the eastern edges. They regrouped around him. For an instant he focused on Rafe, the son of Helfach, his dead huntsman, and his thoughts drifted to Vonn, who had been a friend to Rafe. *Where is my son? Is he still in Ardan?* Then Rhin and Owain's charging warriors met, the sound like a concussive crack of thunder.

The warbands poured into one another, and almost instantly battle-cries were joined by death cries. The battle fell into a thousand individual duels, no strategy, no tactics, just kill the man in front, then move on to the next one.

Evnis surveyed the battleground, saw Owain still mounted with his shieldmen about him; further up the slope Nathair and his warriors were spread near the ridge. For a moment he thought he glimpsed Conall. *Could have done with his sword beside me.* Too late to change his mind now, though. He had judged that Cywen was important to Nathair and did not want to be excluded from any developments there, so Conall was her guardian.

I'll see them both when this is done, anyway.

He dropped Rhin's banner and drew his sword. 'This is it,' he called out above the din of battle. 'The future of Ardan will be decided this day. Ride with me now, fight with me now, and your place in it will be assured.' A cheer went up from the men as they drew their swords, hefted spears and shields. 'And a hundred gold pieces to whoever brings me Owain's head.' There was a louder cheer at that.

Then he was spurring his horse on, picking up speed as he looped out from the fringe of the battleground. There was an explosion of bodies; his horse reared as he slashed from side to side, his sword hacking, cutting, breaking bones, denting helms, great fountains of blood spraying in his wake. His warriors crashed into the battle behind him, spreading like the cutting edges of an arrowhead. He burst clear into the open. The battle was raging. The marshes to the west stopped the combatants spreading that way, and Evnis was on the east side, a wide stretch of open valley. Owain's warriors were using their great numbers here to curve around the edges of Rhin's warband, flanking them. Evnis had seen Owain use the same tactic at Dun Carreg. If Owain's men were allowed to continue with this strategy again the battle would soon be over.

'With me,' Evnis yelled and kicked his horse on. This time he and his warriors raked the edges of Owain's men, striking fast, killing and then veering away before they could be ensnared in the crush of bodies. They did this time and time again, defending Rhin's flank.

Then there was a thundering in his ears, overwhelming the din of battle. Riders were pouring down the slope, charging straight at him and his shieldmen. He recognized the man at their fore.

Owain.

Desperately he dragged on his horse's reins, ordering his men to pull clear or Owain and his warriors would catch them in the flank. Snarling, Evnis realized he was not going to pull free in time. He hefted his shield and screamed his frustration. Then Owain's horsemen were crashing into his shieldmen.

Horses neighed and screamed, warriors yelled, swords clanged, a multitude of impacts set Evnis' ears ringing. He felt fear churning in his gut, slithering like a restless snake, slowing his limbs, as if he were moving through water.

I will not die here, not now. See it through, see it through, see it through.

Something whispered, in his ear or in his mind, he could not tell. *You are mine, and I have work for you to do. Kill Owain.* He felt the fear drain away, his limbs loosen, and he gritted his teeth, raised his sword and spurred his mount at Owain.

Many of his shieldmen were down, horses spitted on spears, caught by Owain's charge. But others were rallying, Rafe's face appearing amongst them, following Evnis as he struck at Owain's men. He crushed a skull with an overhand blow, backhanded another across the face, stabbed another in the armpit, turned a blade on his shield, punched the wielder with the hilt of his sword, teeth spraying. Then he could see Owain, sitting tall in his saddle, hacking at one of Evnis' shieldmen.

Owain's sword chopped into the warrior, almost severing the man's head. Evnis watched as Owain pulled his sword free, looked about, eyes searching. Then they saw him and narrowed to slits. 'Traitor!' Owain yelled and kicked his horse on.

There was a great noise from the hill behind them, a frantic blowing of horns from the ridge. Men were milling at the hill's crest, turning to stare at something hidden by a dip in the land. A cloud of dust hovered in the distance.

Evnis smiled. *Rhin's second surprise.*

CHAPTER THIRTY-SIX

VERADIS

Veradis stared into the distance, shading his eyes with one hand. Behind Owain's rearguard a thick column of warriors was marching towards them.

'How many?' Bos asked beside him.

'About a thousand. They are Rhin's.'

'I guessed that,' his big companion said.

Owain's rearguard, mostly mounted, were milling around, some turning to face the newcomers, others still facing towards the battle in the vale. Many amongst them were blowing horns in warning. A rider cantered out towards the warband hurrying along the giantsway. He hefted a spear and pointed it at the approaching enemy, began trotting towards them. Ranks behind him followed, raggedly at first; slowly, the whole of Owain's rearguard followed his lead.

They have a good captain, Veradis thought. *That is what I would do. Strike quickly, though the odds are still against them. They are too few.*

'Keep your sword loose in its scabbard; things are about to get bloody.'

'It looks bloody enough already, down there,' Bos said, pointing into the valley where Owain's and Rhin's warbands were engaged in battle.

'That is only the beginning,' Veradis said, pulling his helmet on.

'Owain's going to want to reinforce his rearguard,' Bos said to Veradis. 'To help them before Rhin's men scatter them.'

'I know,' Veradis said. 'And it is our job to stop him. Best get to it.' He held a fist high and his own messenger blew a horn, his warband spreading along the ridge, forming the shield wall. Two hundred warriors long it stretched, five rows deep, an impenetrable barrier as the shields came up. The thunder of hooves drew his attention as a large force of the Jehar rode past the shield wall. Akar, the warrior who had commanded the Jehar throughout the campaign to Haldis was leading them. They pulled up on the far side of his shield wall, blocking any passage for Owain between the hill and the first fringes of woodland down in the valley. For Owain, the only way to his rearguard now was through Nathair's warriors. Veradis watched as Owain began drawing troops out from the rear of his warband, men that were not fully committed to combat; soon he had a few hundred gathered about him, more joining.

Behind them, Rhin's reinforcements and Owain's rearguard clashed on the giantsway. Veradis saw that Rhin's men were huddled tight, shields and spears bristling as Owain's horsemen tried to split them apart. Men were falling on both sides, screams drifting on the breeze.

'Here they come,' Bos said.

'Remember, we will not attack, only defend ourselves.' Those had been Nathair's orders. They would aid Rhin indirectly, by thwarting Owain's movement on the field, by keeping his forces separated. Veradis drew his short sword and braced his feet.

Owain's men were coming up the hill, a little hesitantly. The shield wall had never been seen by these warriors before, and it was not the traditional method of battle. Veradis saw Owain and his mounted shieldmen behind them. The King of Ardan was grim faced. *He is no fool – can see he has been betrayed. Defeat is a knife-edge away for him now.* Veradis felt a moment of sympathy for the man, a flash of guilt for the part he was playing here. He buried it.

Owain called out behind his men, urging them on. The bulk of them ran at the shield wall, clearly preferring that to the mounted Jehar who stood calmly waiting to either side of Veradis' warband.

The first ranks slammed into the shield wall, the impact shivering through Veradis' whole body. A series of jolts and thuds followed as Owain's warriors piled into one another, the weight quickly becoming immense. Veradis bent his legs, pressed his shoulder into the curve of his shield and held on. Screams rang out along the line. *My men are striking back.* It was inevitable, he knew. They could not just stand here – eventually shields would be pulled down and his own men would start dying. He raised his sword, slid it into the gap between shields and thrust. He felt resistance, then his blade was cutting into flesh; someone screamed. He pulled his blade back, stabbed again. And again, kept on stabbing until the muscles in his arm burned. Fingers grasped the rim of his shield and he headbutted them, his iron helmet breaking bones. A sword swiped at his ankles, sliding underneath his shield, but he saw the blow coming, managed to block it, trod on the blade with his iron-shod sandals.

A horn blast filtered through the din of battle, a high, keening sound that he recognized. The Jehar. He risked a glance over his shield rim, saw the Jehar joining the battle, their longswords slashing from horseback, cutting great swathes through Owain's men. In heartbeats the assault on the shield wall was over, Owain's men breaking away, running for their lives. They only had one way to go. The battle in the vale was continuing. Rhin seemed to be gaining the upper hand as Owain's men started to try to escape the combat, panic spreading from the disaster on the hill like a disease. Rhin's main host blocked the way through the vale, the marshland denied any flight westwards and Nathair's forces were an immovable object along the ridge of the hill, removing any hope of a retreat to the south. The only way left was west, into the broken woodland that fringed the vale, and that is where Owain's men ran.

Screams rang out behind Veradis and he turned to see the Jehar joining the battle about the giantsway, too. Owain's rearguard was now caught between Rhin's reinforcements and a group of the Jehar. Even Alcyon was striding into the fray, swinging his axe and taking lives like the angel of death. Owain's men broke apart, most of them on horseback, scattering in countless directions. The Jehar rode them down.

So many dead. Just warriors obeying their lords. He shook his head, surveying the corpses sprawled all about them. *All for the ambitions of kings and queens.* He looked along the ridge, eyes searching for Nathair, and spotted him sitting tall on his draig. Relief swept him that his King had survived the battle – indeed, their entire force seemed to have sustained few casualties. And the battle was won, Nathair's plans furthered. *Warfare is strategy*, Nathair had said to him, and strategy had certainly won this battle. It just did not feel very honourable.

It is for the greater good, he reminded himself.

'What now?' Bos asked him.

'We'll hold our position until Nathair orders differently,' Veradis answered.

The battle in the vale was chaos now, most of Owain's warband realizing that the fight was lost. Owain himself was on the slope, a few dozen of his mounted shieldmen about him, others on foot still rallying to him. The King of Narvon pulled his horse in a circle, surveying the chaos about him, then spurred his horse west, towards the woodland. He did not gallop or leave in wild panic; his passage was orderly, controlled, and he still gathered men to him as he passed, his presence bringing an edge of calm. He rode into the shadow of the woods.

CHAPTER THIRTY-SEVEN

CYWEN

Cywen could not believe what she was seeing, almost did not know where to look, so much was happening at once.

The battle in the vale had been a terrible, vicious thing. She had seen death before – the ambush in the Darkwood, the night Dun Carreg fell – but nothing on this scale. Its savagery and cruelty took her breath away, made her feel sick. The shield wall was like nothing she had ever seen before. It had dealt out death with a cold efficiency that seemed to go against all she had learned of the warrior's code.

Evnis' treachery had shocked her at first. *Though I should expect little else*, she thought. Conall had remained calm throughout, seeming composed as he watched the events unfold. *He must have known*, Cywen realized. His mood did appear black, though – *probably at being denied his part in the conflict.*

Her eyes focused on Owain, saw him sitting tall on his horse, moving away, along the ridge of the hill towards the woodland that stretched into the distance. There was a shieldman clutching a banner beside him, the red bull of Narvon serving as a rallying point for Owain's routed host. She recognized the warrior holding the banner, red hair spilling from his iron helm. Drust, and he was riding Shield. Her heart clenched in her chest. Shield still lived.

No, Shield will be lost forever.

Without thinking, Cywen bent in her saddle and slid free the knife that she had hidden in the leather sole of her boot. She whispered to Buddai, the hound sitting close by. Conall was still focused on the battle, his eyes twitching, fists constantly clenching. She reached over silently and sliced the girth of his saddle, then kicked her horse into motion. The animal leaped away – a dun mare that she had helped Gar break.

Behind her she heard Conall shout her name, glanced back to see him yanking on his reins, urging his horse to give chase, then he was sliding, and falling. Cywen grinned as she heard him swearing.

Her mount was small framed and she was fast. Cywen bent low in the saddle, spurring her to a gallop along the ridge towards the woodland, behind the shield wall, heedless of Owain's scattered troops. Buddai barked behind her as he tried to keep up. Owain and his followers had already disappeared amongst the trees. To her left Cywen saw warriors from Rhin's warband following the stragglers of Owain's routed forces, cutting them down as they ran. Deeper into the vale a knot of mounted warriors was gathered before the treeline. Cywen saw Evnis at their head. Even as she watched they rode into the shadows of the woods.

I still may get to see him die today.

Conall was nowhere to be seen, though she knew he would be after her soon. Some of the Jehar were gathered, one of them pointing towards the woods. *Planning to hunt Owain down.* And then she saw Veradis. He was high on the hill, talking to Nathair, Calidus and the giant close by. They all looked towards the woods, and just for a heartbeat Cywen was sure that Veradis stared straight at her. Then he was moving, picking his way through warriors, heading steadily her way.

'Come on, Buddai,' she said, feeling anxious. 'Let's find Shield.' *And then I'm leaving, heading south to find Pendathran. I should have taken Shield and left with him a long time ago.*

The drum of feet and hooves echoed dull and muted amongst the trees. She followed them, the trail of their passing easy to see. Then, abruptly, there was a loud screaming. She gripped her knife tightly as the sound of skirmishing grew, then she saw the first of the dead littering the ground. Owain's men, red-cloaked for Narvon. All with arrows sprouting from their bodies. She moved on, saw figures moving amongst the trees, saw the sparks of blades clashing, heard the thrum of arrows. All was chaos, horses rearing, men fighting in close combat. She looked about wildly, searching for Shield. Sounds from the canopy drew her attention and she looked up to see figures in the trees, firing arrows into a knot of Owain's warriors, Owain amongst them. Her eyes fell upon their leader and she froze. It was Braith, the outlaw woodsman who had been part of the kidnapping of Queen Alona, when her sweetheart Ronan had died.

Owain and his warriors charged at Braith's line, breaking it and moving deeper into the woods, fighting as they went; Braith's men kept pace, harrying them. Then they had moved on and Cywen was left standing amongst the dead. She heard the crunch of forest litter, turned and saw a horse amongst the trees, a form slumped on its back.

It was Shield.

Cywen slipped from her saddle and ran to him, knew instantly that something was wrong. He was trembling, eyes rolling white. Then she saw the arrow buried in his flank. He whickered as she reached him, nuzzled his head against her, his coat drenched with sweat, salt-stained. She waved flies from his wound, touched the arrow shaft and he shuddered.

'This'll have to come out, boy,' she murmured, stroking his flank, trying to soothe him. Drust was draped upon the horse's back, an arrow sticking from his side too; he had one foot still stuck in a stirrup. She heaved him off and he groaned as he hit the ground. *Still alive, then.*

He looked at her, lips moving but only a whisper coming out. She stared back at him sullenly. *You are Owain's man; you helped to storm Dun Carreg.* Buddai sniffed the fallen warrior and whined. Cywen remembered how the warrior had saved Buddai so she took a water skin from Shield's saddle and, kneeling beside Drust, trickled some water into his mouth.

'Thank you,' Drust said, his red hair plastered dark to his face, and for an instant he reminded her of Ronan, red-haired, freckled – or Ronan as he might have been, if he had lived longer. She pursed her lips, making a decision.

'Take my horse,' Cywen said. 'Owain is finished, will be hunted down before the day is out, so do not follow him. Ride south if you want to join the resistance against Rhin.'

'You are forgetting: I am from Narvon; I fought for Owain against Ardan.'

Cywen snorted. 'Owain is as good as dead. Rhin is the enemy now, and the enemy of my enemy is my friend. Pendathran will be leading the resistance – you'll find him in the marshes about Dun Crin. If you get that far tell him my name. If he doesn't kill you straight away you'll be all right.'

Drust coughed, held his arm to his side.

'If not, you must ride north, back to Narvon, but Rhin rules there now, so I don't know what you'll find.'

'You should come with me, girl. There's nothing for you here, now.'

'I'm heading south,' she said, 'but Shield's not fit to travel. I need to deal with this arrow.'

'I'll help you.'

'You've an arrow in your side. And, besides, won't be long before these woods are crawling with Rhin's men. Me, I'm nobody. They'll kill you as quick as breathing.'

He frowned, wavering.

'Maybe I'll catch you up, if you do choose to go south.'

He nodded to her and she fetched her mare. Drust had the water skin between his teeth, both hands gripping the arrow shaft in his side. With a grunt he tensed, snapping the shaft, and half collapsed back onto the ground.

Cywen heard the sound of riders, quickly growing louder. She ducked behind a tree, with Drust lying hidden from view beside her. Warriors rode into the glade and she saw them through the foliage and tensed. It was Evnis. Her hand reached for the knife stuffed in her belt. She had a clear view of him, only twenty paces away. She knew she could make the throw, bury her knife to the hilt in his back. Her fingers twitched. *He betrayed us all. Caused the death of my da, Brenin, the loss of mam, Corban, Gar. All that has happened is because of him.* Silently she pulled the knife free, rolled her thumb over it, readying for the throw.

Drust groaned, eyes flickering.

If I kill Evnis they'll find us – kill me, kill Drust, probably leave Shield with an arrow in his flank that'll fester and kill him.

Buddai pressed close against her legs, his hackles a ridge on his back.

And you, they'll kill you, too. I don't care if I die, as long as Evnis goes first. But . . . She stared at them, horse, hound and warrior, realizing that she did not want their deaths on her hands. With a wrench of will she shoved the knife back in her belt and watched as Evnis and his men disappeared after Owain and his surviving warband.

She waited a while after they had disappeared from sight, then bent to Drust, roused him and helped him into the saddle of her dun mare.

'I should take Shield,' he said.

'That'd be taking my kindness too far,' she replied. 'Shield stays with me.'

He shrugged, bent in the saddle with pain, then turned the mare and rode into the shadows. Southwards.

Cywen set to cleaning Shield's wound, frowning as she realized how deep the arrow had bitten. *How am I going to get this out?*

She didn't notice Buddai growling, so intent was she, but then the growl turned to a snarl and she turned to see Conall running through the trees towards her. Buddai leaped at him, connecting with a thud, his teeth snapping. Conall grunted and fell, man and hound rolling on the ground. Conall managed to roll and throw Buddai off, climbing to his feet and drawing his sword.

Cywen screamed and threw her knife. It flew straight at Conall's chest, but he was so fast, he managed to twist, clubbing the leaping dog with his sword hilt while Cywen's knife flew wide of her mark, sinking into the meat of Conall's arm. He yelled, his sword spinning out of his grip, and ran at her while Cywen reached frantically for her second knife, hidden in the heel of her other boot.

With a snarl, Conall ploughed into her, sending them both hurtling through the air. Cywen was biting, kicking, punching to get free as Conall grabbed her wrist and knocked the knife from her grasp. Panting, she brought her knee up hard between his legs, felt his whole body go limp and scrambled out of his grip.

With a groan he staggered upright, grabbing for her again. She punched him and he backhanded her across the face; blood filled her mouth as she staggered and fell. Conall pulled a knife from his belt.

Get up. I must get up.

'That's the last time you try to kill me, girl,' he spat, and Cywen felt a wave of real fear pulse through her, sharpening her senses. 'You're more trouble than you're worth,' Conall said, putting the knife to her throat.

'I don't think so,' a voice said, a hand gripping Conall's wrist and pulling him away.

Cywen blinked, her vision clearing. It was Veradis, with the giant towering at his shoulder.

'Let me go,' Conall snarled.

'That depends on what you intend to do with that knife,' Veradis said.

Conall tensed and looked as if he was about to attack Veradis, but caught sight of the giant as he shrugged his axe from his shoulders and patted one of the blades with a huge hand. Conall relaxed and let his knife drop to the ground.

Veradis kicked the knife away and released Conall, never taking his eyes from the man.

'You're lucky I arrived when I did,' he said. 'She is worth more than your life to my King.' He took a step away from Conall, looked closely at Cywen, who had blood trickling from her nose and mouth. He frowned. 'Are you all right?'

'Gave as good as I got,' she mumbled.

The giant laughed.

CHAPTER THIRTY-EIGHT

CORBAN

'Just believe it, Corban,' Heb said.

That's easier said than done.

Corban was sitting with Heb and Brina in a copse of trees, the murmur of voices from their camp filtering through to them.

'Just a spark, Ban,' Brina said. 'See it in your mind, how you want it to be, then speak it.'

He was holding a stick, staring at it. In his mind he saw a wisp of smoke curl from it, a spark, then a flame.

'*Lasair,*' he said, the word feeling alien on his tongue. He held his breath. Just for a moment he thought he caught the faint smell of woodsmoke, then it was gone. He waited.

'Nothing's happened,' he said eventually.

'You have a talent for stating the obvious,' Brina said.

'*Nothing,*' Craf agreed from a branch above them.

'It's early days,' Heb said, patting Corban's shoulder. 'This is only your first attempt.'

It was the fourth night since Marrock had had his hand amputated, every night following the same routine. Make camp. Tend Marrock's wound, then retreat somewhere with Brina and Heb. For the first three nights Corban had been given some rudimentary lessons in giantish. Just a handful of words, but the important ones, Brina had said. The elements that he would seek to command – fire, water, earth and air. Each day he had silently recited them in time to the pounding of his horse's hooves. And now tonight he had attempted to make something happen.

Nothing. Is it really possible, or just another mad faery tale, like Gar imagining me to be Elyon's chosen one.

229

Heb took the stick from his hand.

'*Lasair*,' the old man said. There was a popping sound, a wisp of smoke and then a flame flickered into life.

'*Fire*,' Craf squawked.

'That's amazing,' Corban whispered.

Heb smiled and dropped the stick, stamping the flame out.

'You just have to believe. But,' he added, 'I could attempt the same thing another time and, if I had a seed of doubt, I would fail. It is all about believing, utterly, at that moment.'

'Drink this,' Brina said, handing Marrock a skin of something.

'What's in it?' Marrock asked.

'Something to dull the pain. This is going to hurt. Go on, Corban.'

Marrock frowned but took a long gulp.

It was the sixth night now since Marrock's hand had been removed. He had been gripped by a fever for the first two days and part of the third, then awoke before highsun, weak but complaining he was starving hungry. Brina had said that was a good sign. Corban had tended to his wound, under Brina's constant supervision.

'Stitch over an infection and we'll kill him, sure as a blade through his heart,' Brina had said, so while the skin and flesh was red and inflamed the wound had been left open, allowing for any pus to drain, a compress of leaves and clean bandages bound about it twice a day. Now, though, the redness had gone, and it had stopped smelling bad, so Brina had ordered the wound stitched closed.

'Just start, Ban,' she said.

'Have you done this before?' Marrock asked, his words slurred from the poppy milk Brina had given him.

'Not exactly,' Corban said, holding a bone needle close to the stump that was Marrock's wrist.

'It's no different from darning a sock,' Brina said.

'My arm's no sock,' Marrock blurted.

'Shut up and drink your milk,' Brina ordered.

Corban pressed hard, piercing the skin with a pop, then proceeded methodically.

'This bit will feel strange,' Corban warned, then pulled the thread tight, stretching Marrock's skin across the open wound, closing it off. He tied a knot in the thread and Brina cut it with a knife.

'It will feel uncomfortable, and it will itch,' Brina said. 'Any pain – tell me immediately.'

Marrock inspected Corban's stitching and nodded at him.

'You're doing well,' Brina said to Marrock as Corban applied a salve to the skin and bandaged it off. 'You haven't died, which I expected a few days ago.'

'No, but I'll not be drawing a bow again.'

'There's more to life than shooting pointy things into people,' Brina said.

Marrock snorted. 'What use is a huntsman who can't draw a bow?' He looked straight at Corban, bitterness twisting his features.

'There's plenty of other new and exciting ways to get yourself killed,' Brina said. 'No doubt you'll discover some of them soon enough.' She walked away.

'I can still feel it, you know. My hand, my fingers,' Marrock said. 'I would still have it if we'd sailed to the marshes and Dun Crin.' He glanced at Halion, who was at the edge of their camp, looking back the way they'd travelled.

There's been a tension between them since we fled Dun Carreg, and now Marrock blames Halion for the loss of his hand. This bothered Corban, particularly as he had great respect for both men. Halion he knew better, though, from the countless days of toil and hard work in the Rowan Field. He knew that, whatever Halion did, whatever choices he made, he was not acting out of self-interest.

'He chose what he thought was best for Edana,' Corban said quietly, gathering his tools.

'Did he? Maybe he just wants to go home.'

'I've never known him to choose something he thought to be wrong. Even his own brother.'

Marrock stared at him, the hardness fading from his eyes. 'Aye, lad. Don't listen to me, I'm just . . .' he trailed off, his gaze dropping back to the stump where his hand used to be.

Corban squeezed his arm and followed after Brina.

'What's wrong with you?' Brina asked him. 'Your face looks like its been squashed.'

'That was harsh, what you said to Marrock.'

'Sympathy will feed his self-pity,' Brina said, a softness edging her voice, 'and he has some dark days ahead.'

Corban lay on his belly, staring down a steep slope into a valley. A river wound through it, marking the border of Cambren. A stone bridge arched across the fast-flowing water, houses clustered upon either bank. The road on the far side climbed upwards, twisting into the mountains. They were in a no-man's-land between the two realms of Cambren and Domhain.

On the far side of those mountains is Domhain and safety.

That was the hope, anyway. Halion had said that when he had travelled the other way, coming from Domhain into Cambren, there had only been a handful of guards, a token force.

Not now, though.

Warriors were everywhere: standing guard on the bridge, walking the few streets, their tents spilling onto a coarse stretch of grass alongside the river. Corban had tried counting and lost track when he reached ninety.

'Rhin is no fool,' Camlin whispered beside him.

'Unfortunately for us,' said Halion.

The rest of their group were a few hundred paces behind them, huddled about a stand of gorse. The land had turned bleaker, more barren the higher they had climbed. They had broken camp before sunrise and set out as soon as dawn had lit their way. The sun had been up a while now, though it was still well before highsun. The sky was full of thick low cloud, the air humid.

Corban felt his eyelids drooping. They had been travelling hard, but still their pursuers had drawn closer each day, until now they were almost constantly within sight.

'We can't stay here,' Camlin said, echoing Corban's thoughts.

'No, but there's no way across that bridge. We couldn't fight our way through; there's too many of them.' Halion glanced over his shoulder back along the track. 'We'll have to try another way.'

They all looked up at the mountains, grim and forbidding. In the distance a wolven howled; Storm tensed, ears twitching.

'Best be moving,' Camlin said. 'P'raps we can shadow the giants' road, join up to it once we're deeper into the mountains, and away from Rhin's eyes an' ears.'

'That's a plan I like,' Halion said.

They scrambled back down the slope to their companions, shared the bad news and set off into the mountains. Camlin rode ahead, scouting their path.

Craf fluttered down out of the cloudy sky to land on Brina's saddle. The crow had been keeping track of their hunters.

'*Fast,*' the crow squawked.

'Faster than us?' Brina asked.

The crow bobbed its head.

'Something will have to be done, soon,' said Heb, who was riding close by. He and Brina shared a look.

They're talking about the earth power, Corban thought.

Dogs barked somewhere behind and Corban twisted in his saddle. Dark shapes were visible in the distance, near to where they had stopped to view the pass into the mountains. Shapes broke away from the main party and disappeared down the slope as they moved towards the river ford. *And towards the warriors camped there. Will probably get them hunting for us, too. Things are not looking good.*

They travelled as fast as they could, dismounting at sunset and leading their horses, for fear of twisted or broken legs. A cold night was followed by a grey morning. They were back in the saddle before the sun had risen, winding ever deeper into the mountains.

The path they were following was little more than a fox's trail running more or less parallel to the giants' road. A sheer rock face rose up ahead and the path veered around it, moving deeper into the mountain wilderness. Corban hoped that at some point it would veer back, but it didn't look likely.

Just before highsun Camlin came cantering back from scouting ahead. He was frowning. He rode to Edana and Halion, pulling up before them, but spoke loud enough for all to hear.

'The path dips ahead, follows a stream and broadens out. It's good land to travel on for a while, but then it rises an' turns narrow right quick. Won't be easy going.'

'Easier than turning back,' said Halion.

'Aye, true enough. There's something else: I think we're heading into a wolven pack's territory. Found some spoor and a carcass of something – looks like a horse.'

'We have a wolven of our own,' Edana said.

'Aye. One. This is a pack. In my experience that means anywhere between four and ten of them and they won't like us in their territory. We'll need t'be careful.'

Brina spoke quietly to Craf. Corban thought he heard the word *wolven*, then the bird was flapping away, this time ahead of them.

Brina and Corban checked on Marrock as they let their horses drink and refilled water skins.

'I'm fine,' he said to them, though his eyes were pinched with pain. They reached the end of the vale that Camlin had told them of as the sun was hovering above the mountain tops. The valley sides had narrowed, with great black boulders dotting the land. A narrow ravine closed in, leading sharply up, causing them to ride in single file. Corban looked back over his shoulder and saw tiny figures spill into the valley behind them. *No way back now.*

The terrain changed as they climbed higher, the ground turning stony, patches of shingle appearing underfoot. It became too dangerous to ride so they dismounted and led their horses. Corban saw a nimble-footed goat standing on a narrow rim above them, watching their passage.

Dusk was closing in when they stumbled into a rocky bowl rimmed by pine trees, their scent thick in the air. Corban was sweating from the climb, though there was a cold wind biting at him. He drank thirstily from his water skin. Halion had gone to look back down the way they had travelled and Corban joined him.

To his horror he could see a long line of figures climbing the ravine, not more than half a league behind them.

'They'll not be stopping to make camp tonight,' Halion said. 'They know they can't miss our trail in the dark, because there's nowhere to go except straight ahead. They'll just keep coming.'

'Then we must move on, and not stop either.'

'Aye.'

Footsteps crunched behind them – Camlin returning from scouting ahead.

'How is the path?' Edana asked.

'We're going t'have to leave the horses. Gets too steep; they'll not make it.'

They all looked at him and he shrugged.

'How far behind are they?' Camlin asked Halion.

'Not far. Less than half a league, and they're moving faster than us.'

Best be moving, then,' Camlin said.

Marrock stepped forward. 'I'll stay, hold them back a little, buy you some time.' He looked around at the shocked faces. 'My life's over now. Might as well do something of worth before the end. I know I can't shoot a bow.' He raised his left arm, the wrist bandaged tight. 'But I can still swing a sword. And one of you can strap my shield tight to my arm.'

'I'll do better than strap your shield tight,' Anwarth said. 'I'll be your shield. Two will hold them longer than one.'

'And three longer than two,' Farrell said, stepping close to his da.

'Someone that can shoot a bow would hold them longer,' Camlin said, reaching for his bowstring.

'I . . . I'll stay with you,' Dath said, looking at Camlin.

Heb stood up from where he had been sitting by a boulder. 'I think I might be of some help. I will stay too.'

'What?' Brina said. 'Don't be an idiot, you ridiculous man.' Corban was unsure if she was angry or worried. *Probably both.*

'Stop,' a voice rang out. Edana strode forward, shaking her head. 'We'll either all stay, or all go. I'll not lose you so that I can run a little longer.' A tremor shook her voice. 'And I would be proud to stand with you all – more loyal and brave than I deserve.' She took a deep breath, steadying herself, then looked to Camlin. 'Is this a good spot to face them?'

'Depends if you want to hold them back, or try an' kill them all,' he said. 'If you want to hold them off it would be better up ahead, where the trail narrows. If we're going t'have a crack at sending every last one o' them across the bridge of swords, then this is better. Me an' Dath can pick the first ones off with our bows as they come out of the ravine. Once they're in this bowl you'll have room t'swing a sword.' He looked about. 'This is a good spot.'

To make a last stand, Corban finished for him.

Corban crouched behind a boulder, holding his shield tight, Storm pressed close against him. The sun was just a glow silhouetting the mountain peaks now. Gar was close to him and his mam, her face pale, her knuckles white where they gripped her spear. Dath was just a shadow higher up, amongst a handful of pine. None of the others was visible. He kept his eyes on Dath, knew that when he started firing his bow then the battle was upon them.

Corban heard the arrows before he saw them. The *thrum* of bow-strings as they were released was followed closely by a scream and a high-pitched whine. Corban risked a glance around the boulder, saw figures strewn at the entrance to the bowl, a hound pawing the ground, but no others. *They must have pulled back.*

Then there were battle-cries and men were spilling out of the narrow ravine, climbing over the dead. Two arrows struck the first man and he was hurled back, knocking another off his feet, but others rushed past them, quickly spreading out.

'Now!' yelled Camlin.

Corban drew his sword as he rushed forwards, Storm and Gar a heartbeat behind him. He saw Halion swinging his sword, then a head was spinning through the air, a dark spurt of blood. Storm leaped forwards, smashing a man from his feet. Corban followed her, took a blow on his shield, pushed it away, parried with his own sword, chopping an arm. He wrenched his blade free, swung again, silencing his screaming opponent. Someone else took the warrior's place, came rushing at him. He stepped in quickly to meet the man, felt all the years of drill and practice with Gar and Halion take hold of him, his body moving before he had time to think, falling into the rhythms and responses of the sword dance. Before he realized what he was doing, his opponent was falling back, blood jetting from his throat, and he was facing someone else. He blocked a combination of blows, twisted his wrist and slid to the side, chopped neatly at an exposed neck, then he was moving on to another opponent. A calm filled him as he let his body move, not thinking, just doing, and his enemy kept falling before him.

At his side his mam was desperately defending herself, her spear only just holding off a flurry of blows. Corban swung his sword, severed a hand from his mam's opponent, his mam took the opening and buried her spear-point in the man's throat.

He heard Storm snarl, turned to see hounds circling her. One stepped too close and she knocked it aside, claws opening red streaks on the dog's body, but another leaped, landed on her back, jaws snapping, seeking Storm's spine. She writhed beneath him, rolled over and then the other hounds were jumping in, biting at her exposed belly. Storm regained her feet, shook the hound from her back and snapped the spine of another of her attackers. The rest of the pack cowered back, whining.

It was close to dark now; shapes were blurring, merging as they clashed. He saw Gar, recognizing him by the way he moved, spinning and slashing, in constant motion. Figures fell away in the wake of his passing. Corban backed away as the fighting grew closer, turning to make sure that Heb, Brina and Edana were still safe.

He heard a flapping, saw Craf circling the bowl, squawking frantically. The crow landed on a boulder, close to Brina. It hopped from foot to foot, still squawking. Corban ran to them.

'Who's winning?' Brina said, squinting at him in the dark.

'It's too dark to tell.'

'Let's see if we can do something about that,' Heb said. He held a branch in his hand, splintered from one of the pine trees close by. He spoke strange words under his breath.

Craf squawked again.

'I think Craf wants your attention,' Corban said.

'He will have to wait, impatient bird,' Brina snapped, adding her voice to Heb's.

At first nothing happened. Then Corban felt a pressure on his ears, the air seeming to push in at him, like when a storm is about to burst, but more extreme. Then he saw a wisp of smoke curl up from the branch, quickly followed by a tiny flame.

Craf jumped onto his shoulder and pecked his head.

'Get off,' Corban cried, trying to wave the bird away. Then he finally heard what the crow was saying.

'*Wolven, wolven, wolven, wolven,*' the bird was repeating. '*WOLVEN.*'

The branch burst into flame and Heb dropped it. The fire flared bright, illuminating the bowl, showing figures locked in combat all about, but Corban's eyes were drawn higher up, to the ring of pine trees that circled them. Suddenly eyes glowed green in the firelight. Lots of eyes.

Then the first wolven leaped at them.

CHAPTER THIRTY-NINE

FIDELE

Fidele sipped from a cup of wine. She was in Lamar's chambers at the top of his tower in Ripa. There was a wide window dominating the wall opposite, giving an extensive view of the bay, and her eyes kept being drawn to the sea, the hypnotic swell and roll of waves.

Others were sitting at the table with her: Lamar, Baron of Ripa, and his two sons, Krelis and Ektor. Two more disparate brothers she could not imagine: Krelis larger than life in every way, physically almost a giant, but with a great warmth to him. She imagined that he could love and hate with equal passion. And Ektor, quiet, introverted, pale skinned, almost withered looking, yet with a fierce intellect. Her thoughts drifted to Lamar's third son, and first-sword to her own son, Nathair – the loyal Veradis. *He is somewhere in between these two: physical, a warrior, like Krelis, but quiet, reserved, like Ektor.* She was glad Veradis served her son. His loyalty was beyond doubt, something solid to cling to in these turbulent times.

Peritus sat beside her, fingers drumming on the table, and Orcus her loyal shadow stood behind her.

'So what will we do about the Vin Thalun?' Peritus said.

Always it comes back to this, no matter where the conversation leads.

'I have told you. The men involved have been punished. There is little more to do now, except wait for Lykos to return. Then I shall speak with him.'

'Like you spoke to him before?'

She felt a flare of anger but suppressed it. Peritus was struggling with so much change. Struggling with the death of Aquilus, with Vin Thalun wandering Tenebral, with Nathair's new ways, especially his new techniques of fighting. The shield wall was a particular thorn in

Peritus' flesh. But change had come to them, whether they liked it or not. It was swim or be drowned. She looked hard at Peritus. *He looks like a drowning man.* Nevertheless, an insult was an insult. If Peritus had spoken to her so in private she would have overlooked it, for friendship's sake. But not in front of Lamar and his children.

'If you dare speak to me in such a way again I will have you sent back to the ranks,' she said, coldly. Peritus looked away, blushing, mumbling an apology.

'The Vin Thalun have learned a lesson from you,' Lamar said in his deep voice. 'Learned that you are not to be disobeyed.'

'Or learned to hide their disobedience better,' Ektor added.

It is time to change the subject. 'How go your preparations for the coming war?' Fidele asked.

'Well enough,' Lamar said. 'My warband is ready, and I have gathered every able-bodied man to me.'

'And your warband's training? I am asking of Nathair's new methods. He sent men to aid you in learning the shield wall.'

'Aye, he did,' Krelis said. 'I'll speak plainly, as I know no other way.'

'Please do,' Fidele said.

'My men are learning it, but most of them don't like it. The older ones especially. It goes against our ways, against generations of learning. It feels dishonourable.'

Fidele sighed. All over she had heard the same complaints. But it was Nathair's order, and he was king. And, besides, by all accounts it was devastatingly effective.

'It works,' Fidele said. 'Peritus saw the shield wall first-hand, led by Veradis. Tell them.'

Peritus sat up straighter. 'Veradis led the van against Mandros in Carnutan. We were ambushed whilst fording a river. He and his warband formed the shield wall, knee-deep in the river, and carved a way through two thousand men, almost to Mandros himself.'

Fidele watched their faces as Peritus spoke. Lamar tensed, a tightening around his eyes and lips. *Why? Is there some grievance between Lamar and Veradis? If so I have not heard of it.* Krelis beamed with pride. Ektor showed nothing, whether through self-control or lack of interest, she could not tell.

'And you followed with your warband, did you not?' Fidele said.

'I did.'

'And how many men of yours died in the battle?'

'Around five hundred.'

'And from Veradis' shield wall?'

'Fewer than thirty.'

Lamar raised an eyebrow; Krelis blew out a long breath.

'Peritus is a skilled warrior, wise in the art of war, in tactics and strategy,' Fidele said.

'I know it,' Krelis murmured. He had spent over a year riding with Peritus and his warband, learning from the battlechief, much like Veradis had done with Nathair. Although Veradis had stayed, while Krelis had returned home to Ripa and his father.

'That is why he was my husband's battlechief. I am not highlighting the difference in casualties during the campaign in Carnutan to shame him, because I know that he is truly great at what he does, and the best that Tenebral has to offer. But my son is a strategist, with a craftsman's heart. The fact is that a war to end all wars is coming. The God-War will claim many lives, maybe even our own. My son's logic is faultless – the shield wall stops our men from dying. And it kills the enemy with an efficiency that has not been seen before; is that not right, Peritus?'

'Just so,' the battlechief said.

'You will train your men in the shield wall, and after your first battle remind yourself of this conversation. And your warriors' wives and mothers shall thank you, honour be damned.'

'Of course Krelis will do as you say,' Lamar said, giving his son a stern look.

'The God-War,' Ektor said, animated all of a sudden. 'Nathair and Veradis talked of it when they visited after Aquilus' council. Nathair spoke of a book, a giant book and a prophecy.'

'Yes, the writings of Halvor.'

'I would dearly love to see it.'

'That's impossible, I'm afraid. I do not have it.'

'Why, where is it?' Ektor looked devastated.

'Meical had it. As far as I know, he has it still.'

'I have heard that name before – Aquilus' counsellor, yes?' Lamar asked.

Fidele nodded.

'And where is this Meical?' Lamar said.

I have asked that question more times than you can imagine. Fidele had liked Meical, even though there had been something frightening about him – an intensity thinly veiled.

'He has not been seen since my husband was murdered,' Fidele said.

'What do you know of him?' Lamar asked. 'What realm is he from? Does he have kin that he could be tracked to?'

'I do not know,' Fidele said, feeling foolish before the words were out of her mouth. Meical had come to Tenebral a long time ago, before Nathair was born, and spent a long night in council with Aquilus. When day had dawned, Aquilus had brought Meical to her, and that had been the first time she had heard the God-War mentioned. Meical had soon been declared Aquilus' counsellor, and almost immediately had left – travelling to Forn in search of Drassil, the hidden fortress. Aquilus had trusted him utterly, and so had she. *But, who are you, Meical?*

'Well, he must be found. I need to see that book,' Ektor said.

'Really, why?' Fidele asked.

'My son is a scholar,' Lamar said. 'The past is his passion. We have an extensive library here, at Ripa. Left by the giants.'

'Aquilus spoke of it to me,' Fidele said.

'I need to see that book,' Ektor repeated, almost to himself.

'Why?'

He looked up then, held her gaze with bright, sharp eyes. 'Because I think I know who, or what, Meical is.'

CHAPTER FORTY

CORALEN

'I see them,' Coralen said, turning in her saddle and gesturing to Rath.

'Where?' asked Rath, squinting into the distance.

'There,' Coralen said, pointing. 'Not on the giants' road. To the south, moving into the foothills before the mountains.'

They were riding through grassland, skirting the giants' road. Up ahead loomed the range of mountains that separated Domhain from Cambren, the giants' road cutting a deep gully through them.

'Damn my old eyes,' Rath said, then was silent a while. 'I see them,' he said finally. 'Well done, Cora; you're the best tracker I've known, and I've known a few.'

Coralen snapped a glance at him, surprised. 'You going soft in your old age?' she said.

'Maybe I am. How long till we catch them?'

'Depends. One day, if things stay as they are.'

'Good. My arse is sore – too much riding. I must be getting old – I'd rather be having a drink back in Dun Taras.'

Coralen snorted.

'Still don't like visiting your home?'

'Dun Taras? That's not my home. Here's my home.' She slapped her saddle. 'Anywhere you are is my home.'

'Now who's going soft?'

Coralen smiled at that. Truth be told, she'd rather be just about anywhere than back in Dun Taras.

They had tracked the giants all the way from the border of Benoth, pausing briefly at Dun Taras for Rath to warn King Eremon that giants were loose in Domhain and – worse than that – they had been within half a day's travel from Dun Taras.

She didn't like the fortress, it held too many bad memories, too many reminders, so she was much happier to be back in her saddle, even if it did mean a sore backside. Better that than all the bubbling emotions that rose up every time she was in sight of Dun Taras. It made her think too much, made her head ache. And she always just ended up feeling angry, usually fighting someone.

'Let's keep moving. Soon enough it'll be time to spill some giant blood,' Rath said, kicking his horse on.

That'll do, Coralen thought. They rode hard for a while, a score of warriors in a long column. It was cold and the clouds were low and bloated. As the sun was sinking, Coralen caught glimpses of individual figures ahead, flitting through patches of woodland on the hills.

They're heading for the pass. I know exactly where they're going. She grinned to herself, then looked up and saw a bird high above, circling them; it looked like a solitary crow.

Baird rode up beside her. 'Strange behaviour for a bird,' the warrior said, staring up at it.

'That's what I was thinking.' She reined in her horse and reached for her bow, pulling it from its case, laying it across her saddle. Then she opened a pouch on her belt and pulled out a bowstring. Deftly she strung the bow and nocked an arrow.

'Too late,' Baird said as she raised the bow.

The bird was winging its way into the foothills, squawking, flying in a straight line now.

'Think you scared it,' Baird said with a grin, the scars on his face creasing. 'Don't look so disappointed; there'll be plenty more killing soon enough.'

That there will.

She unstrung her bow and led them into the foothills.

CHAPTER FORTY-ONE

UTHAS

Uthas ran, his legs taking long, ground-eating strides. The old pain in his knee throbbed but he ignored it, concentrating on his breathing. He could hear Salach behind him, the dull thud of his boots on turf, behind that the others: Fray, Struan, Kai and Eisa. Far above, Nemain's raven Fech flew in a jagged line. Up ahead he could see mountains rearing behind the pine-coated foothills they were running through. *And beyond them is Cambren, Rhin's land. We will be safe there.*

He risked a glance behind, his pace slowing a little. There was no sign of pursuit at first, then he saw it, a thin line in the distance, moving, following them.

Rath.

Fech had been right, back at Dun Taras. Rath had picked up their trail in the north and was tracking them south. Panic and anger had rippled through his group at Rath's name, the reputation of the man and his band of giant-killers overriding rational thought. Fray and Eisa had wanted to fight Rath, to march out and meet him and his warriors, but Uthas had known it would be suicide. You did not fight Rath on his own ground, on his own terms. He had been too long and efficient at giant-killing. No, escape was the priority; fulfil the plans. So they had fled east, towards Cambren. Rath had gained on them, somehow, and for the last five nights their pursuers had been almost constantly within sight. He looked forwards and fixed his eyes on the mountains. Five leagues, at least. *We will make it. It will be close, but we will make it. And he will not dare to follow us into Cambren.*

The giants' road was a shadowed line far below them. Uthas paused and looked back; he could see that Rath and his men were closer.

Damn them.

He muttered a curse and led his group quickly into the trees, a growing sense of alarm settling upon him. For the first time he began to consider the possibility of being caught by Rath, of being forced to battle. Of dying. As the thought grew, so did a sense of panic. By sunset he knew he had to do something.

He called a halt. They were still in the foothills, under the cover of dense pines, but further ahead he could see that the trees thinned and the path led into the mountains proper. He set Fray and Kai on watch while he scouted ahead and found a place far enough distant that he would not be disturbed. After making a small fire, he drew a knife and opened a small pouch, from which he pulled out a lock of brittle silver hair. Rhin's hair. This was giant magic, earth magic – he cut his palm, rolled the lock of hair in his blood and dropped it into the fire. The flames swirled as a shape grew within them: a face, old and lined. Rhin. 'What?' Rhin said. Her eyes focused on Uthas. 'This is not a good time.'

'I must talk to you, now,' Uthas hissed. Then he heard a bough creak above and looked up to see a dark shape, feathers. Fech. He froze and the bird flapped its wings, rising into the air.

Nemain cannot know.

He fumbled for his knife, found it, aimed and threw. There was a muted squawk as he found his target, then Fech was gone.

Uthas looked back to the fire, but Rhin's face had disappeared. He stood, hurriedly stamped the fire out and left. He was on his own.

CHAPTER FORTY-TWO

MAQUIN

'Something's different,' Maquin said as he looked up.

'They've stopped banging on the doors,' Orgull said.

'Aye.'

'Not that it seemed to bother you,' Tahir added. 'You've managed to sleep through most of their hammering.'

'I was just resting my eyes,' Maquin said.

'Wish you'd have rested my ears – your snoring's been loud enough to wake the dead.'

'Watch your cheek,' Maquin said as he stood, his back protesting. 'I'm getting old.'

They were settled at the rear of Dun Kellen's feast-hall, a large portion of the surviving warriors scattered about the room. The stone walls were solid and thick; the only wood that they could attempt to burn was the hall's great doors, but the flames had achieved little success.

A warrior strode through a doorway at the back of the hall and approached them.

'The Lady Gerda would speak with you,' the warrior addressed all three of them.

Gerda was sitting in a wide chair when they were ushered in to see her; a warrior in chainmail and a bearskin cloak was before her. A child, the young boy Maquin had seen with Gerda before, sat in flickering shadows at the back of the room, whittling at a piece of wood with a small knife. *Haelan.*

Gerda smiled.

'I am expecting my reinforcements to arrive soon,' she said. 'Possibly today. When they reach Dun Kellen we will rally, take the battle to Jael from within. He will not be able to stand an attack on two fronts, and the reinforcements should outnumber him. I think he will flee.'

'Probably,' Orgull said. 'He does not strike me as one for a brave last stand.'

'No, indeed. He'd rather run and save his scrawny neck, the snot-nosed slimy little piece of dung,' Gerda said with venom.

The boy looked up, appearing to be holding back laughter.

Gerda took a shuddering breath. 'But the Jael I know is unpredictable. He is capable of many things. This is Thoris, my battlechief,' she said with a wave of her hand. The man nodded to them, his warrior braid woven thick in his fair hair. 'We are discussing eventualities.'

Where is she going with this?

'If the unlikely happens, and Jael is victorious, then I would ask one last thing of you all. I would ask you to protect Haelan, my son, and take him somewhere safe.' She looked at them pleadingly. 'I do not expect this to happen, and I pray to Elyon that it will not, but it is better to be safe than sorry.'

'That's what my mam used to say,' Tahir whispered to Maquin.

'I have seen your valour, your strength in combat, seen how you value an oath given. That is why I ask this of you. My other warriors are sworn to me, but also to Dun Kellen, and to avenge Varick. They have too many oaths to serve. You three are different. If you gave your word you would see it happen, or die in the trying. You have served me well, served Isiltir well, and if we survive this, your reward will be great.'

A silence filled the room. Maquin was shocked. Throughout the battle and days of siege he had thought of little except his revenge. Jael dead by his hand. He had given his word back in Haldis to help Orgull escape, to bring word of Jael's treason here to Isiltir. He had done that, fulfilled that promise. And now here was Gerda asking him to take another oath, to place more shackles upon him. He did not want to do it, wanted only to seek out Jael in the coming battle and see his life's blood spilt.

And he had sworn an oath of protection before, to Kastell and his da. A blood-oath. He looked at his palm and traced the old scar, white and faded. Looking up, he saw the young lad staring at him.

Ten years old, fair hair streaked with copper, freckles scattered across his nose and cheeks. He even looked like Kastell. That should not be a surprise; they shared blood, distantly.

'Will you do this for me?' Gerda said.

'Yes,' Maquin heard himself say. *You old fool, Maquin.*

The wind pulled at Maquin's hair. He was standing on a flat tower roof looking over Dun Kellen, from where he could see Jael's men – some camped in the keep's courtyard while others moved among the streets. *He has gathered quite a warband. Where did he come by these numbers, when so many of Isiltir's warriors died in Forn Forest?*

A noise drifted on the wind, coming from the north. Horns. He squinted, looking across the plains, then saw them. A dark stain on the horizon, inching its way closer. *Gerda's reinforcements have come.* He smiled grimly. Jael's reckoning was close.

'Are you ready?' Orgull asked him.

'Aye.'

'And you remember the plan?'

'We stick together, find Jael; kill him.' Maquin grinned at Orgull and Tahir, no humour in the expression.

They were standing close to the barred gates of the feast-hall with Gerda's warriors, all armed and ready for battle. As soon as the signal was given they planned to burst from the tower and join the banner-men, so that Jael would be fighting on two fronts.

'Yes, that's the plan,' Orgull said. 'Or part of it. If things go bad we head back here, to Haelan, take the boy and flee.'

'Aye,' Maquin said. He had taken the oath, said the words, but the weight of them sat in his gut now like a lead ball. *Why did I do it?* He didn't need to ask himself that question. He knew why. For Kastell. For himself – a chance to prove he could fulfil his oath, keep a child alive. A chance to not fail.

A wild clanging rang down from the tower, filling the hall. The gates were heaved open and then they were charging, pouring into the courtyard, blinking in the daylight.

They slammed into a line of warriors, the combat quickly disintegrating into individual battles. Maquin ducked behind his shield and felt a heavy blow shiver through the wood and up his arm. He chopped low and heard a crack as he broke his enemy's ankle. Another man jabbed a spear at his ribs but he swept it away with his sword, stepped in close and smashed his shield into the man's face, sending him staggering back.

Orgull was up ahead, his axe a blur swirling around his head, tracing an arc of blood. Tahir fought beside him, and Maquin stepped in next to his sword-brothers. Together they carved their way forwards, Jael's warriors giving before them.

Surrounded by Dun Kellen's defenders, they fought through the courtyard, out into a wide street, and then finally the fortress' gates were visible ahead. There was only the stone arch still standing, the wooden gates twisted and charred.

Maquin could hear the frantic blowing of horns in the distance, the sound of hooves on stone streets, men screaming, the clash of arms. All about them was a swirling mass of combat, the blood and stench of men dying. Maquin blinked sweat from his eyes, a sword hilt punched into his face and he felt a tooth go. He spat it out, along with a mouthful of blood, grinned wildly and ploughed on.

Gerda's reinforcements were slowly reclaiming the town; Jael's men were breaking, retreating through the streets towards the river. Maquin saw Gerda and her guards pursuing them.

'Come on,' Maquin said to Orgull and Tahir, 'or else she'll find Jael before us and have his head.'

'Think you're right,' Orgull said, watching Gerda disappearing through the gates. 'Where is Jael most likely to be?'

'Now? Preparing to run. Maybe their paddocks?'

'Worth a look,' said Orgull. Some sections of the town were almost empty now, other than the many corpses littering the ground, elsewhere the streets were packed with fighting men. Maquin and his companions cut themselves a way through; there were not many standing to give the three of them any real resistance. They were Gadrai, sword-brothers who had come through the battle of Haldis, had faced giants, fought the Jehar, survived Forn Forest, and together they were death on wings.

The paddocks were in chaos; Jael's routed warriors were scrambling into saddles, desperately seeking a way of retreat. 'There.' Maquin pointed as he saw Jael's banner, then Jael himself, the white horsehair plume of his helmet marking him out. 'Quick, he intends to flee,' Maquin yelled.

The three of them charged across the plain, Maquin leading the way, slipping on the treacherous ground and chopping or battering anyone in his way with sword and shield. A thin line of defenders was soon scattered by Orgull's terrifying axe. Maquin strode through the paddock, slapping horses' flanks with the flat of his sword, making his way closer to Jael, who was surrounded by a handful of his shield-men. Reaching them, Maquin swung his sword overhead, crushing a man's skull before he was even seen, then Jael's shieldmen realized the threat in their midst and were coming at him. It was impossible in the confined space to swing a blade properly, so he drew a knife, pushed in close to his next opponent and stabbed quickly into the man's neck and chest, shoved him out of the way, deflected a weak blow on his shield from another attacker, then moved inside his guard and slit the warrior's belly. And there, finally, he came face to face with his quarry. Jael was mounted, his horse rearing and kicking its hooves at Maquin. Before he got any closer, Jael turned the beast and was riding away. Maquin swore, determined not to let him go this time. He lunged at a man with his foot in a stirrup, dragged him off his horse, climbed into the saddle and kicked his mount into a gallop.

Jael was heading south, towards the bridge that crossed the river.

The warriors of Dun Kellen, under the command of Thoris and Gerda, were moving across the plain, routing out any enemies who had taken shelter in any of the smokehouses and tanners' yards that lined the river.

Orgull and Tahir had found mounts and caught up with Maquin as he reined his horse in at the bottleneck of warriors massed at one side of the bridge. Jael's men had gathered at the far side, had turned and were battling fiercely. Maquin saw Jael amongst them, his white plume snapping in the wind.

'Need to catch him here, or he'll be gone,' Orgull said.

'Aye. It's just getting to him that's a problem,' Maquin replied. The bridge was thick with fighting men.

'Soonest started, soonest finished, as my mam used to say,' Tahir said.

The three of them shared a look and kicked their mounts forwards into the battle on the bridge. They passed Gerda, a handful of shieldmen about her and her sword stained red as she harried the fleeing warriors attempting to regroup with their comrades on the other side. Orgull spurred his horse forwards, swinging his axe in great sweeps to either side. Men screamed, trying to get away from him. Maquin and Tahir guided their mounts to fill the gaps, stabbing and hacking, and they slowly carved their way across the bridge.

Jael's men blocked the end of the bridge, four or five ranks deep. They fought with a desperate ferocity. *They know that if they break here they're dead*, Maquin thought. Jael was screaming exhortations, his shieldmen gathered close about him. Maquin recognized one of them – Ulfilas – he had fought beside the man against bandits on the journey back from Aquilus' council. Ulfilas saw Maquin and stared at him, squinting. He called to Jael, gesturing towards Maquin. Jael gaped, recognition dawning in his eyes and a look of fear sweeping his face.

Maquin pointed his sword at Jael and gave him a bloody-mouthed snarl. *He was so close!* He felt fresh energy fill his limbs and renewed his efforts to break Jael's lines. *Soon, Kastell. Soon we will have our vengeance.*

Then suddenly voices filtered through the sounds of battle. There was shouting spreading through the ranks on the bridge. Jael looked back towards Maquin with triumph in his eyes and spat on the ground.

Around a bend in the river, ships had appeared, lots of them, long, shallow-draughted, painted with black tar. The sails were black, a silver eagle upon them.

CHAPTER FORTY-THREE

LYKOS

'Prepare to land!' Lykos yelled. In response, the drummer beating time increased his rhythm, the rowers put a last spurt of fire in their limbs and men clashed weapons on shields. Lykos felt his spirits soar. He was looking forward to this. No more ferrying other men to battle, watching them disembark for greater deeds. Time to do something that would be remembered in this era when the world was changed. In a hundred years songs would be sung about these days, about this battle. *If there is anyone left to sing them.*

Time to win a nation for Nathair. He gave the runner beside him fresh orders, a young lad, not more than twelve summers, but quick and wiry, who climbed like a monkey. He scurried away and soon Lykos heard the horn blasts, felt his ship steer for the north bank. He looked back and saw the thirty sleek-bottomed war-galleys he had brought with him from Dun Carreg do the same, deadly as hunting wolves. It had been a back-breaking trip, most of it up the river Afren, through the Darkwood that split Ardan and Narvon, through the stinking marshes beyond and then into Isiltir. There had come a point where the river Afren shrank to little more than a stream in the marshlands as it neared its source. There was a wide stretch across the marshland to the banks of the river Rhenus in Isiltir where there had been no choice but to travel by portage, taking the masts down, dragging the ships onto land and rolling them over the masts for a league or more. Then it had been back to the rowing. His back still ached. He might be lord of his cut-throat nation of pirates, but he would not sit back and grow soft, let some other man hungry for power take what he had spent years in the making.

He looked along the riverbank. There were scores of quays and jetties lined along it. *Most helpful*, Lykos thought, pushing his way to the front ranks gathered on the ship's deck. Further ahead was a wide stone bridge, looking to be the focal point of the battle, and there he could see the banner that had been described to him raised at the southern end, a lightning bolt with a white wyrm coiled about it. *My allies*. They didn't look to be doing so well. *Looks as if we've arrived just in time. Perhaps we've had divine help.* He snorted at that, liking his own joke. If divine meant nightmares, sleepless nights and yellow eyes boring into you every time you closed your own eyes, then he was blessed beyond all men. *Nothing is ever as you imagine it; even consorting with a god.*

Oars were drawn in as the boats drew alongside a quay, timbers scraping. Ropes were cast, secured tight, and then he was leaping the rail, boots thudding on the boards of the quay. His shieldmen Deinon and Thaan were close behind, scores of others behind them, roaring as they charged, over a thousand warriors along the riverbank doing the same.

The men on the bridge had finally realized what they were seeing and were trying to turn and face this new enemy screaming towards them. But they had no time to form any kind of cohesive line before Lykos and his Vin Thalun corsairs hit them. Instantly all became a churning chaos as the Vin Thalun carved their way onto the road, only a few hundred paces from the bridge. At the same time Jael and his men at the far end renewed their attack. Lykos could feel the panic spreading, see it in the eyes of the men he faced. Fifteen hundred warriors screaming blood and murder could unman even the most experienced veterans, given the right circumstances. Lykos grinned, ducked a half-hearted sword blow and gutted the man as he surged by.

On the road he stopped and blinked. He saw a fat woman brandishing a sword and hacking one of his warriors into the dirt. She was flanked by a handful of hard-looking men who were stopping his charging men in their tracks.

That won't do. He snarled and ran at them, seeing Deinon and Thaan fall in on either side of him. They hit the warriors like a hammer, cutting men down and forging close to the fat woman. Then he felt the ground trembling, heard hooves and turned in time to see three mounted warriors bearing down on him, one looking more like a giant than a man, swinging a great two-bladed axe over his head. He had just enough time to duck, yell a half-formed warning, then the axe was whistling through air where his head had been, the blade carrying on, burying itself into Thaan's shoulder and back. Deinon gave a bellow as he saw his brother slump to the ground. Lykos snarled and darted towards the big man on the horse, only to be smashed from his feet by another horse's chest and shoulder as it surged forwards. The collision sent him flying through the air. He hit the ground hard, then was rolling and tumbling down the riverbank, coming to a stop in tall reeds and mud.

He climbed to his feet, head ringing, and scaled the bank again. When he reached the top the scene had changed. The giant on the horse and his two companions were disappearing amongst the barns and smokehouses that rose up before the town and the fat woman was nowhere to be seen. Someone with some sense was clearly commanding the enemy, as a rearguard had been formed and was holding back the tide of Vin Thalun and Jael's warriors, allowing others to fall back to the town and fortress.

I don't want a long siege, Lykos thought, scowling. He saw his shieldman Deinon kneeling beside Thaan and strode over. He took one look at his fallen shieldman. *He's not going to be getting back up.*

'Come, Deinon, he's dead. Avenge Thaan now, mourn him later.'

Deinon looked up at him, eyes red, tears washing gullies through the blood and grime on his face. Slowly he stood. 'Don't kill the bald one; he's mine. I want to take my time on him.'

A hand gripped Lykos' shoulder and he spun around, sword readied for attack. It was Jael, grinning as if it was his nameday, his shieldmen about him. 'I must say, I am impressed with your timing,' he said.

Lykos lowered his sword. 'Nathair sends his greetings,' he said, gripping Jael's arm. *What kind of king will you make, who needs the help of corsairs to win your first victory?* He looked up at the town and fortress. 'Getting here in time was only half the job. Best we finish this lot before they dig themselves in too deep.'

'Their walls and gates are thick,' Jael said. 'We may have to starve them out.'

'There are other ways to scale a wall,' Lykos said, signalling to

Deinon. 'We Vin Thalun are not cut out for siege making. I hate waiting.'

One of Dun Kellen's warriors was kneeling on the ground, begging for mercy. The warrior standing above him looked to Jael, who shook his head.

'I need prisoners,' Lykos said. 'The more the better to row me back to Tenebral when we are done here.' *And they'll make good sport in the pits when we're back there.*

Jael was silent, then he nodded. 'You can have all those who surrender, but you look after them. I don't have the men, or the inclination to care for them.'

'Good enough,' Lykos said. He looked to Deinon. 'Let's teach these landwalkers how to scale a wall.'

CHAPTER FORTY-FOUR

MAQUIN

Maquin slid from his horse and stood by the gates to the keep, sword drawn, waiting as Dun Kellen's warriors retreated inside the feast-hall. Orgull and Tahir were still with him, blood splattered and weary.

Maquin had been so close to Jael, just a sword-length away from reaching him, and then the ships had arrived, emptying their deadly cargo. And now instead of victory they were staring death in the face again. They were heavily outnumbered: most of Dun Kellen's warriors had been killed during the battle on the bridge or cut down as they tried to retreat. If it had not been for Gerda and her battlechief, Thoris, organizing the rearguard, Maquin doubted that any would have made it back to the keep alive.

And who were these new warriors? Not men of Isiltir. They were dressed strangely, in leather kilts, tunics and sandals rather than breeches and boots, with iron rings in their beards and hair. And the ships – sleek and fast, looking as if they were built more for the sea than river.

'They are allies of Nathair, is my guess,' Orgull said. 'Remember what I have told you: there is more to this than the throne of Isiltir. The God-War is being waged here. Right now.'

Maquin shook his head. *Why did it have to be so complicated? Revenge used to be simple.*

A knot of warriors entered the courtyard, Thoris at their head, Gerda in their centre. She was sweating, short of breath, her sword bloodied and notched.

'Quickly,' Thoris shouted, 'a few have chosen to stay behind, to give us time to get inside and bar the gates. Inside, now.'

With that they were all piling into the feast-hall, heaving the doors shut, slamming the thick bars into place. Then Gerda was marching through the hall, Thoris summoning him, Orgull and Tahir to follow. They ended up with Gerda in her chambers, her son Haelan standing beside her.

'You must take Haelan now,' Gerda said, 'before they gather and strike. Their numbers are too great; they will storm the keep some-where and we do not have the men to keep them out.'

'But how can we take him?' Tahir said. 'We are besieged – there is no way out.'

'There is a way. A secret tunnel the giants built. It burrows under-ground, comes out on the plain half a league to the north.'

Orgull looked at Maquin and Tahir. 'We swore an oath. Let's keep it,' he said.

Noises boomed in the corridor behind them, voices shouting, screaming, the clash of arms.

Thoris ran to the door and stuck his head out. 'Quickly,' he said, 'the assault has begun. You must leave now.'

'Eboric here will take you to the tunnel and guide you through it.' Gerda gestured to a man standing beside the boy, a huntsman by the look of him, dressed in worn leathers, an archer's bracer on his wrist. 'He knows the land beyond well, and Haelan knows his face.' Her voice wavered. She grasped her son by his shoulders. 'You must be strong now, and do as Eboric and these men say – they will keep you safe.'

'Yes, Mother,' the boy said, looking up seriously into Gerda's eyes. She cupped his face in her hands, kissed him, then ushered them out of the door.

Eboric led the way, Orgull and the boy next, Tahir and Maquin at the rear.

They met warriors further along the corridor, running towards the tower stairs. Eboric grabbed one of them, pulling him to a stop.

'What is happening?'

'Jael assaults the feast-hall gates, but they are holding for now. The danger is these new men from the river – they are throwing ropes with claws that snag on stone, and are using them to scale the towers.'

'Are they inside the keep?' Eboric asked.

The sound of swords clashing rang down the tower stairwell, giving his answer. He let go of the warrior and the man ran up the stairs. Eboric looked grimly at them all and led them down the steps.

They spiralled downwards, reached ground level where the sound of the hall gates being rammed was deafening, but continued on down. Eboric grabbed a burning torch from a wall sconce. They hit level ground and left the stairwell. Maquin heard the slap of feet somewhere above, the echo in the spiral of the tower playing games with his ears. Those feet could be ten paces away, or a hundred.

'Is this the only way down to this level?' Maquin called to Eboric.

'No, other towers also lead down to the cellars.'

Not the answer I was hoping for, Maquin thought.

They twisted and turned through high corridors, sometimes in silence – apart from their breathing, the drum of their feet – at other times the sound of combat was close by, the sound of men moving in numbers.

Then abruptly they were at a dead end. Eboric stuck his hand into a hole in the wall, twisted something that gave a click, and there was a hissing sound. Something like steam or mist poured from the wall as the outline of a door appeared and swung open. Darkness lay within.

'This is the giants' tunnel,' Eboric said.

Maquin peered in, remembering the tunnels beneath Haldis and Forn Forest, and the thing that lived in it that had put a hole in Tahir's leg. 'Don't like the look of it in there,' he muttered.

The sound of people, men shouting, echoed along the corridor.

'Come on,' Orgull said, taking a step towards the tunnel entrance. Then booted feet were clattering in the corridor, tall shadows flickering on the wall. Figures appeared, one flinging a spear. It whistled past Maquin and buried itself in Eboric's shoulder. He was thrown back into the wall with the impact, his head making a cracking sound. He slumped down the wall, lay motionless.

Haelan screamed.

Orgull swore and hefted his axe, moving to meet the newcomers. 'Take the boy!' he yelled without looking back.

Maquin looked at the scene, between Orgull and the crying boy who was shaking Eboric, the huntsman's head lolling.

'What do we do?' Tahir asked.

We swore to protect the boy, but we swore an oath to each other, as well, as Gadrai. He looked at Orgull, swinging his axe, then punching the iron-capped butt into someone's face. Men were crammed in the corridor, for the moment holding back in the face of Orgull's ferocity, but the corridor was high and wide, built by giants. Even the bulk of Orgull could not fill it. Once his attackers gained their courage he would be flanked and overwhelmed. *He won't be able to hold them long enough.*

'Tahir, take the boy, get the hell out of here. We'll buy you some time.' He gripped Tahir's arm, saw the indecision in the young man's eyes. 'One of us must live,' he hissed. 'We are the last of the Gadrai. And we swore to protect the boy. Stay and you make us oathbreakers.' Tahir stood a heartbeat longer, then nodded curtly, tears filling his eyes.

'I'll see you again, on this side or the other,' he said.

'I'm not dead yet,' Maquin said. Tahir took the boy and ran; Maquin slammed the door shut. He turned and yelled as he swung his sword, stepping into line beside Orgull. 'You're not supposed to be here,' breathed Orgull, glancing at Maquin as he swung his axe, severing an extended arm just below the elbow.

'I'm too old for all this running,' Maquin said. He lifted his shield high and stabbed a warrior in the gut, one of Jael's from the way he was dressed. *I'm going to die here*, Maquin thought as he blocked and stabbed. The thought did not scare him. The thought of failing Kastell hurt far more. *At least Tahir has taken Gerda's boy. That is one oath I have kept, unto death.* He smiled grimly. *Come then, Death, take me across your bridge of swords, but know this: I won't be coming alone.*

CHAPTER FORTY-FIVE

LYKOS

'Gerda, where is your son?'

Gerda was tied to a chair, rope burns on her wrists and ankles where she had struggled. Blood speckled her face and one eye was mottled and bruised. It appeared that Jael was not one to spare the rod during questioning. Lykos looked on approvingly.

They were in the feast-hall, corpses strewn about and the stink of death thick in the air. Lykos and his Vin Thalun had used grapple-hooks to scale a high unguarded tower in the fortress. What little resistance they'd met had been surprised and cut down without even slowing them. They had swept into the great hall as Jael had been assaulting the gates, the following slaughter quick and fierce. Gerda had been discovered leading a counter-attack in the corridors. When Lykos arrived the fighting had been furious, her shieldmen savage in their defence of her. And she had not been shy with her blade, either. He might have admired her as a warrior, but for the fact she was a woman. Still, they had been outnumbered, attacked from two sides. It had not taken long.

'Where is he?' Jael demanded.

'Far from your reach,' Gerda said through swelling lips.

'Where?' Jael repeated.

'I don't know.' Gerda's head lolled, her eyes flickering. Jael slapped her hard with the back of his hand.

'You'll not leave us yet,' he said, then nodded to a man at his side. 'This is Dag. He is my huntsman, a skilled tracker. He also has other skills, such as how to skin an animal. Usually this skill is reserved for the dead, for good reason. Apparently the pain is unbearable, like nothing else this side of death. He is going to skin you. Going to peel the skin from your fat body, piece by bloated piece, until I have an answer. It will take some time, I should imagine.' Laughter rippled the room.

Dag stepped forward, a tiny knife in his hand. A warrior clamped Gerda's wrist, her eyes bulging with fear.

'First the nails have to come off,' Dag said as he bent over Gerda. Lykos felt the urge to look away, but resisted. Gerda screamed, a trail of sobs and spluttered half-words between each crescendo of pain.

'Then the skin is cut, just a little,' Dag said over Gerda's ragged breaths.

Footsteps from beyond the feast-hall clattered, and a warrior hurried to Jael's side.

'We have encountered strong resistance, my lord,' the warrior said as he bowed.

Jael waved a hand. 'Take more men and crush it.'

'It, it is not so easy,' the man said, looking uncomfortable.

'How many,' Jael snapped, eyes still on Gerda.

'Two, my lord.' That got his attention. 'They have barricaded the corridor.'

'With what?'

'Our dead. It is hard to explain, but I do not think it will be easy to finish them.'

'Where are they?'

'In the cellars, my lord.'

Gerda's head snapped up at that, noticed by Lykos as well as Jael.

'Let's have a look at this resistance, then,' Jael said, striding to the tower. 'And bring Gerda,' he called over his shoulder.

Lykos walked beside Jael, warriors behind them, and further back a handful of men carrying Gerda still strapped to her chair.

The corridor was high and wide, with flickering torches breaking up the darkness. Ahead of Lykos stood a dozen or so men, all with weapons held ready. They parted for Lykos and Jael.

The floor was slippery, covered in blood, gore, bodies, severed limbs. It was thick with them. Two men stood further up the passage; Lykos recognized them instantly. The bald giant and his companion from the bridge. The ones who had slain Thaan. Deinon knew them as well; Lykos heard his shieldman draw in a sharp breath and felt his weight as he made to push past.

'Wait,' Lykos barked at Deinon, holding a restraining arm out.

Jael recognized them too, by the look on his face.

'Ironic. The last time I saw you, Maquin, we were underground,' Jael said.

The smaller man took a step forwards, a look of such hatred sweeping his face that Jael took an involuntary step back.

'Question is, what are you fighting so hard to keep us from?'

'Why don't you come and take a look?' Maquin invited. Grey streaked his hair, where it wasn't gore splattered, but judging by the corpses piled high about him he was not too old to use a blade.

Jael raised an arm, summoning Gerda's chair-bearers forward. They placed her before the two warriors. Lykos studied her face, saw a question bleeding out through her pain. The big man gave an almost invisible nod and she sagged back in her chair.

'You know where her boy is, then,' Jael said. It wasn't a question. 'Spears,' he called over his shoulder.

'They cannot kill him,' Deinon whispered to Lykos. 'The bald one – he is mine, for Thaan . . .'

Lykos stepped forward, uncurling the grapple rope that was wrapped about his waist. He swung it once over his head, flicked his wrist and then its end was snaking forwards, wrapped around Maquin's sword wrist. Before the warrior realized what was happening Lykos tugged hard, dragging the man forwards, and Deinon was surging towards him, knocking the sword from the man's hand and placing his own blade at the warrior's throat.

The big man took a step.

'No, Orgull,' Maquin snapped.

'Deinon,' Lykos said, and Deinon had a knife in his other hand, had sliced quicker than Lykos' eyes could follow. Blood spurted and then Deinon was holding up a scrap of flesh.

Maquin's ear.

Orgull took another step forwards.

'My man can keep cutting chunks out of him all day,' Lykos said. 'Want him to stop – you drop that axe.'

CHAPTER FORTY-SIX

CORBAN

Corban shouted a warning, seeing wolven everywhere, leaping into the hollow. Instantly all was madness. The wolven were not on a side, did not care who was from Ardan or Cambren; they were here to feast, and they were taking meat where they found it. Horses screamed from where they had been hobbled, wild and terror stricken, the sound echoing around the rock walls. Craf exploded upwards in a burst of feathers and squawks as a wolven snapped at him. Corban saw men wrenched from battle, mauled in slavering jaws, saw hounds scattered like flotsam and two wolven rolling in savage battle. One dark, one white. *Storm.* He felt a rush of fear, the thought of Storm dying launching him into movement. The two wolven were a mass of fur and teeth and claws. For a moment they separated. Corban saw blood on Storm's white fur. He lunged at the other wolven, burying his sword in its belly. It yelped and writhed, a claw slicing his shoulder. He pushed harder, deeper, his sword-point piercing the creature's heart. It sagged, its heart's blood a hot flood.

Storm limped up, her side matted with blood, claw marks raking one side of her muzzle. Corban buried his fingers in her fur and she stepped closer to him, pressing her head against his chest. 'Good girl,' he said quietly, felt an echo of the fear that had consumed him, that she would be slain. *So loyal, fighting for us, for me, even to death. And it's not over yet.*

Where's Mam and Gar? He scanned the dell desperately, but could make little of the nightmare visions set against the flickering light of the burning branch that Heb and Brina had just ignited.

There was a snarl behind him and he twisted on his heel to see another wolven, muscles bunching, about to spring. Then his mam was beside him, thrusting her spear. Gar spun past them, sword flashing and suddenly the wolven was whining, scrabbling away from the double attack.

Everywhere, forms were silhouetted by flames. Corban saw two figures side by side, firing arrow after arrow into a mass of wolven and warriors. Camlin and Dath. A wolven jumped at the two archers and they scattered, leaping different ways. Dath rolled on the ground, tangled in his bow as the wolven surged towards him. Then Anwarth dashed between them, screaming at the wolven, trying to distract it from Dath. It worked. The creature sprang, all teeth and muscle, as Anwarth tried to block it with his battered shield. But the wolven knocked aside the shield as if it were a child's plaything and, jaws clamping about Anwarth's waist, heaved him from the ground. Corban heard the sound of ribs snapping.

Farrell screamed and charged the beast; Dath loosed arrow after arrow into the wolven as it shook Anwarth. Corban ran forwards, sword raised high. Arrows pin-cushioned the beast as Camlin joined Dath. The wolven dropped Anwarth, took an unsteady step, then Corban and Farrell were there, sword and hammer a series of flashes in the firelight. The wolven stumbled and fell.

There was still chaos everywhere, figures fighting, running, screaming, wolven snarling, leaping, tearing at anything that moved. Farrell cradled Anwarth's head in his lap. The warrior coughed blood, his breathing shallow.

Then Brina and Heb were beside them, Heb blood-soaked, his arm hanging limp. They joined hands and shouted into the chaos, their voices a thunderclap. There was a cracking sound; the trees that ringed the bowl about them swayed, rippling, although there was no wind. Then there were sparks everywhere, wood splintering and the trees were bursting into flame. Instantly the dell was transformed, as bright as highsun, a wave of heat searing Corban's face, flames arching high from the treetops, the smell of scorched sap and woodsmoke thick in the air.

The wolven scattered in all directions, whining, howling as they went. Only Storm stayed, pushing in close to Corban, snarling at the flaming trees and the retreating wolven.

People stood about the glade, panting, confused. The surviving attackers scrambled back down the mountain path; only a handful of them were left. Craf came fluttering out of the dark, perched on the shoulder of a dead wolven and started pecking at its eye.

'Where is Edana?' Marrock called, blood soaking the bandages that bound his wrist.

'I am here,' a voice said.

'We must leave, now,' Camlin ordered.

'The dead?' Corban asked.

'They must stay where they lie. Those wolven won't be gone for long.'

'But the fire?' Edana said.

'It will go out. We move. Now,' Camlin grabbed Edana by the wrist and strode away.

The others stood a moment, frozen, then Halion was shoving them on.

Corban touched Farrell on the shoulder, his friend still sitting with Anwarth's head on his lap. The warrior's eyes stared sightlessly, his body still.

'Come, Farrell. He's gone,' Corban said.

Farrell looked up at him. 'He saved my life.'

'Aye. Don't throw it away now.'

'Corban's right,' Halion said. 'Come on, lad.'

Farrell stood and lifted his da into his arms.

'Lay him down, lad,' Halion said gently. 'You'll break an ankle soon enough.'

'No,' Farrell snarled. The look on his face silenced any response. With that they hurried from the dell, picking their way through the bodies that littered the ground, men and wolven and horses. Corban felt sick at the sight and smell of it. *Will death follow us wherever we go?*

Camlin was already some way ahead. He had lit a branch from a smouldering tree and Halion did the same. The path narrowed and steepened immediately, the ground quickly becoming treacherous. Soon they had caught up with their companions.

They trudged on, ever upward, stumbling, supporting one another. Corban's lungs were burning, his eyes stinging from sweat when Camlin dropped back to them. He shared some whispered words with Halion, who sped up and took the lead.

*

Camlin's eyes roamed the steep ridges about them, searching the shadows.

'Do you think the wolven will attack again?' Corban asked him, his voice a croak.

'Probably. It's not as if we'd be hard to find. And we're still in their territory. Judging by their behaviour in the dell they're none too happy about that.' He stopped, looking up high as a stone rattled down the cliff side. Corban froze as well, then saw the shadow of a mountain goat, leaping nimbly between ledges. They started walking again.

'Craf should know if they come back – he tried to warn us last time,' Corban said.

'Did he? Well, that's good t'know. Though he probably can't see as well in the dark. And those wolven could sniff us out with their eyes closed.'

That's comforting.

Camlin was limping, using his bow as a staff. His face was grime streaked, blood caking a cut on his scalp. Corban remembered the first time he'd seen him in Dun Carreg, King Brenin's prisoner. Then again in the Darkwood, an outlaw working for Braith, part of the attempt on Queen Alona's life. But something had made Camlin turn then, and Corban had seen him protecting Cywen, standing against Morcant, Rhin's own champion. *So much has changed since then.* They would have been dead a dozen times over if not for Camlin, probably more.

'Thank you,' Corban said, not realizing he'd spoken out loud.

'What?' Camlin said.

'I was just thinking,' Corban stuttered. 'You've saved my life, our lives. Much more than once. We wouldn't be here if not for you.'

Camlin looked at him a few moments, looking as if he thought Corban was mocking him. 'This isn't the best place to be, y'know.'

'I mean we wouldn't have made it this far.'

Camlin's face softened. He smiled. 'You're welcome, lad. Though I think I may have used all my luck up, now.'

'That doesn't matter. I don't believe in luck,' Corban said.

'Do you not? What do you believe in, lad.'

Corban thought about that. 'This.' He touched the hilt of his sword. 'Him,' pointing to Dath. 'Her,' a hand ruffling Storm's fur. 'Us,' a gesture taking them all in.

'Good answer,' Camlin said.

CHAPTER FORTY-SEVEN

VERADIS

Veradis walked along the hill, the sinking sun sending a long shadow stretching far behind. He was checking the line of bodies that lay before him. Twelve of his men, slain in the battle. It was a good number by any standard, but still it upset him. They had been good men, brave and loyal. Three he recognized from having been with him since the beginning – from the battle in distant Tarbesh against giants who rode draigs. He did not doubt that somewhere on their bodies they would have a draig's tooth. He stroked the one Nathair had presented to him, embedded now in his sword hilt. And something else gnawed at him. Their wounds. All of them had injuries on their lower legs – cuts and gashes on ankles and shins. Not killing wounds, obviously, but nevertheless, it bothered him. Any chain was only as strong as its weakest link, and if this weak link was getting his men killed, then he needed to do something about it. He looked down at his own feet, bound in leather sandals, the soles iron shod, cords of leather wrapped about his calves. An idea began to form in his mind.

Owain had not been found yet, but the battle was over. The defeated dead had been stripped of their precious things – weapons and armour, torcs and rings, any silver or gold – and been piled high and soon their bodies would be burned. The victorious dead were laid out separately, ready to have a cairn raised over them. Rhin had set up a tent at the top of the hill, and was sitting on a huge wooden chair draped with furs, celebrating. Veradis turned and looked over the woodland to the west, rolling away in shades of green into the twilight as night crept upon them. He strained his ears, listening, and thought he heard something on the breeze – shouting? *Perhaps they've found Owain.* Woodland was not a place he would choose for battle – he had had enough of trees in Forn. Just stepping into these woods earlier had brought those memories flooding back. He hadn't been in these woods long, though. Just long enough to find the girl, Cywen, and bring her back. *And only just in time.* Veradis had taken command of watching the girl, given her to Bos with a stern warning to watch her closely. Even though Conall had beaten her bloody she had been more worried about her horse, and how to get that arrow out of it. So the first thing he had done upon their return was to take her to the paddocks in search of Rhin's horsemasters. He had bumped into Akar, who was overseeing the care given to the Jehar's mounts, and to Veradis' surprise Akar had said that he would help. Together they had tied the stallion to a series of posts, securing him as tightly as they could. Akar had called other Jehar to help, one of them attaching something to the soft flesh around the horse's nostrils, tightening it until the stallion's head had drooped, had seemed beyond calm, close to sleep even. Then a poultice had been placed around the wound – Akar said it would open the flesh a little and numb it – then with a sharp tug he had pulled the arrow out. The horse had jumped, eyes rolling, but it was over so quickly it settled almost immediately. Veradis had left them tending the wound, Cywen looking with interest over their shoulders despite her obvious mistrust of them all.

And now he was looking at his dead warriors, wondering what he could do to save lives in the next battle. *And there will be many more, as we walk ever deeper into this God-War.*

He went in search of Nathair, found him seated in a wide ring of warriors, hidden in shadow and watching Rhin as she rewarded her chieftains with plunder. A fire-pit had been dug; the carcass of a great boar was turning above it, fat crackling as it dripped into the flames. Veradis' gaze was drawn to Rhin where she was sitting upon an ornate chair, thick with furs, clothed in black sable, a cloak of the same material edged with gold about her shoulders, her silver hair spilling across it. A gold torc wrapped her neck, and the firelight flickering across her face cast it one moment in shadow, the other in light. Her hand was extended, draped with gold and silver that she was offering to a warrior who stood before her. It was an older man, with streaks of white in his red hair and silver torcs curled around broad arms.

'Who's that?' Veradis asked Nathair.

'That's her battlechief, Geraint.'

'You should be seated with her,' Veradis whispered to Nathair. 'You won this battle for her and, besides, you are high king.'

'Let her enjoy her moment,' Nathair said with a smile. 'She might well have won this battle without our help, even outnumbered. She's a sly one.'

'Yes,' said Veradis. He remembered her well from Aquilus' council. Clever, cunning and with a clear predilection for younger men, if the way she had looked at her first-sword had been anything to go by.

Bos pushed through the crowd, heading towards them, grasping Cywen's wrist. She had washed the blood from her face, but it was still patched with bruises.

'I hear you have taken on a new ward,' Nathair said, looking at the girl.

'Thought you'd be upset if she was found with her throat slit. I don't think that Conall has the temperament for guard duty.'

'You are right. And Calidus would most likely explode if she was killed. He is convinced the girl is important, perhaps a route to finding her brother.' Nathair's expression turned serious. 'The Black Sun. He is out there . . .' He looked out across the marshes, just a glimmer now as darkness fell, the sea beyond a murmur.

'So what now,' Veradis said.

'Tomorrow we shall meet with Rhin, make more plans and continue the serious business before us. But tonight. Tonight we shall celebrate our victory and the fact that we are still alive.' He raised a jug, poured from it and offered Veradis a cup. Veradis took a sip. *Mead*. He winced at the sweet taste of honey, but still managed a twisted grin.

Bos led Cywen over, freeing her when they reached Veradis. She scowled at the big warrior, rubbing her wrist.

'How is your horse?' Veradis asked her.

A smile touched her face, hesitant, for an instant transforming her. *There's actually a pretty girl beneath all those bruises and scowling.*

'I think he will be fine,' she said. 'Your friend, he is an amazing horseman.'

For a moment Veradis did not know what, or who, she meant,

then realized she was talking about Akar. 'The Jehar are skilled horsemen. I have never seen their like on horseback . . .' He blew out a long breath. 'I think they care more for their horses than people.'

She smiled again at that. 'I know how that feels.'

Veradis heard a blowing of horns, looked in the direction of the sound and saw men spilling from the woods, many holding torches aloft, a constellation of firelight in the growing darkness. At their front three men marched. One walked – a woodsman by the look of the long bow slung across his back. Beside him a warrior rode a fine horse, sitting tall, teeth glinting in the torchlight. Before them both stumbled another man, his hands bound behind his back.

Owain.

Veradis saw Evnis further back amongst the warriors emerging from the woods, his shieldmen riding close about him.

Owain's captors marched him up the hill and pushed him stumbling before Rhin. The rider with them raised a hand in greeting to Rhin, gave a wide smile and dismounted, handing his reins to a warrior.

Cywen was still standing beside Veradis, and he heard her hiss, saw that her eyes were fixed venomously on the warrior.

'*Morcant*, Rhin's first-sword and paid killer,' Cywen said bitterly. Veradis blinked. *Of course.*

Owain was cut and bruised, his lips and one eye swollen, but somehow he managed to stand straight.

'Welcome, cousin.' Rhin smiled. 'You have arrived just in time. We were about to eat.' She gestured to the boar turning above the fire. 'I am celebrating, you see.'

Owain stared at her, rage surfacing through the ruin of his face. 'Cambren not enough for you?' he said.

'Not when I am surrounded by realms ruled by idiots,' Rhin replied.

'You are a tyrant, a liar, a thief. I hope you rot in hell for what you have done.' He spat on the ground. Angry murmurs rippled the crowd, but Rhin merely laughed.

'A tyrant? Surely it's a little too early to tell. I have only been Queen of Narvon and Ardan for half a day.'

Owain lunged at her but Morcant clubbed him across the shoulders, sending him sprawling.

'You started the war between Brenin and me,' Owain snarled.

'Yes, I did. Which is why you accuse me of being a thief, I suspect. Stealing your realm from you. To be fair, you did have a choice in the matter. And Brenin did try to explain my part in things to you. He was always the brighter of you two. Besides, I have not stolen your realm; I have taken it from you. There is a big difference.'

'But . . .'

'Now, the real question left is what to do with you. You could serve me, you know. Be my vassal, govern part of my realm for me.'

'What?'

'I know, a shocking idea, and most likely a bad one. You see, I am not sure that I can trust you.'

Owain snorted.

'So what other options do I have? Exile. A lenient ruler, merciful even, might choose that, as you are kin.'

She looked around the crowd. 'What should I do with this vanquished king?'

'Mercy,' a voice shouted behind Veradis. It was Nathair, hands cupped to his mouth. 'Show him mercy.'

'Mercy,' Veradis called out, joining his voice to Nathair's. Soon it was a chant, hundreds strong.

'Very well,' Rhin said. 'And if I grant you mercy, will you accept it?' she said to Owain.

He stood silently, glowering at her.

'Please, merciful I may be, but patient I am not. Well, not tonight, anyway. I am too hungry, and that roasting pig smells very good.' She looked about the ring, all eyes on her.

She's enjoying this, Veradis thought.

'You killed my son,' Owain said.

'Not me personally, actually. That was him.' Rhin pointed to Evnis. 'But I did order his death.' She shrugged. 'It was war. Men die. But now the war is over, with you, at least. And you have the chance to live. Will you take it?'

'I would rather die than serve you.' Owain stared defiantly at her.

'Very well.' Rhin shrugged. 'Braith, hold him. Morcant, take his head.'

The woodsman kicked Owain behind the knees, dropping him to the ground as Morcant drew his sword. Owain struggled, spluttering mud, then the sword was whistling, chopping with a wet *thunk*. It did not cut all the way through Owain's neck, and his body jerked, spasmed, his feet kicking. Morcant wrenched his sword free and swung again, then Braith was holding Owain's head for Rhin to see. He turned slowly, showing the crowd.

'Well, that's done, then. Put his head on a spike, Morcant, but later. First come and cut some meat for me,' she said, rising and holding her hand out to her first-sword.

Veradis sighed at yet another life lost and looked down at Cywen. She was gone.

He snapped a curse at Bos, scanned the crowd.

'But I was watching the head,' Bos said.

Then Veradis saw her, a figure pushing through the crowd, moving determinedly towards Rhin. *Thought she would have been going the other way, trying to escape.* Then it hit him. *She can't seriously be thinking to kill Rhin.* He charged after her, warriors grunting as he shouldered them out of the way.

Rhin was standing by the spitted boar, Morcant about to slice the first cut of meat for her, when Cywen stepped into the ring. She started to run, reaching a hand low to the heel of her boot – no doubt a hidden weapon. Veradis gave a burst of speed after her and yelled a warning, knowing he was too late, that she would reach Rhin before he managed to stop her.

Morcant looked up, shoved the Queen away and stepped forwards, reaching for his sword.

Cywen threw her knife and barely paused as it hit Morcant in the shoulder, knocking him back into the boar, flames flaring around him. She leaped at him, heedless of the flames, her hands reaching for the knife. Veradis closed the gap; all about people were staring in frozen surprise. Warriors hastened towards Rhin.

Morcant and Cywen rolled away from the fire, flames licking about them from Morcant's clothes. She had a hand around the knife hilt, was trying to pull it out to use again. He managed to get a knee up and kicked out, catching Cywen in the gut, sending her rolling away. In a heartbeat he was on his feet, grabbing his dropped sword and raising it high. With a hiss of iron Veradis drew his own sword, sparks flying as he blocked Morcant's swing. For a heartbeat the warrior stood and stared at Veradis, then Cywen was leaping at him again as Veradis lunged for her, grabbing a handful of her tunic, and managing to block another strike from Morcant as the warrior tried to cave Cywen's skull in with the hilt of his sword. Veradis glimpsed Alcyon striding into sight, Calidus, Bos and Nathair close by. He pushed Cywen towards them just as Morcant seemed to decide that Veradis was an obstacle that needed to be removed.

Their blades clashed; Veradis retreated before a surprisingly fast combination of blows. He stepped out of range and then Rhin was moving between them, scowling at Veradis.

'What is going on here?' she demanded.

'She tried to kill you,' Morcant said, pointing at Cywen, who was being restrained in one of Alcyon's huge hands.

'I tried to kill *you*, you idiot,' Cywen yelled.

'What?'

'You murdered Ronan.' She struggled in Alcyon's grip, then slumped, angry tears staining her face. 'In the Darkwood, when you attacked Queen Alona.'

'I probably did,' Morcant said, 'though I don't know who he is.' He studied Cywen. Recognition flared in his eyes. 'But *you* I do remember. She should be executed.'

'No. She is under my protection,' Nathair said, stepping forward.

Rhin frowned, staring icily at Cywen. Then she smiled at Nathair, a sudden change to graciousness and charm. 'As you will, Nathair. She is fortunate to have your patronage. But I wonder who will protect my first-sword from *her*?' She cast a look of derision at Morcant as laughter erupted from her chieftains.

'I can look after myself,' Morcant said indignantly. He grabbed the knife hilt sticking from his shoulder and pulled it out with a grimace. 'Think I'll keep this.'

'I'll just find another one,' Cywen said.

Veradis strode over to her, furious at having been put in such a position in front of Nathair. *She does not know when to quit*. 'Bos, bind her hands. And you.' He stepped close to Cywen and pointed a finger at her. 'You *really* need to stop trying to kill people.'

She glared at him.

'Well, I'm glad that's all over with now. Good, then perhaps I can finally have something to eat?' Rhin said.

Morcant strode back to the fire-pit, drawing his knife. As he reached to make the first cut for his Queen another figure stepped into the ring.

It was Conall. 'I contest your right,' he said loudly, for all to hear.

It was written in the Lore of the Exiles that each ruler would have their champion, their first-sword. Tradition said that only they had the right to carve the first cut of meat for their king or queen. That right could be challenged, though, to be decided in the Court of Swords. The victor would be first-sword.

'Ahhh,' Rhin groaned, 'am I never going to eat tonight?'

CHAPTER FORTY-EIGHT

CORBAN

Corban had lost track of time, his world contracted to the ground before him, the burn in his lungs and legs, the shadows of his companions about him.

How long have we been running?

It was still dark; the only light was the burning torches that had been hastily fashioned from branches back in the dell where the wolven attacked them.

Dawn cannot be far off. Shapes were starting to emerge from the darkness, boulders, steep rocky cliffs to either side of the narrow path they were travelling.

In front of him Farrell stumbled, still carrying his da's body. Corban grabbed Farrell's belt, steadying him.

Heb and Brina dropped back, Heb looking at Farrell.

'You should lay him down,' Heb said.

'No,' Farrell grunted. 'I'll not leave him for his bones to be picked by scavengers.'

'He would not want you to die on his account.'

'I'll not be dying yet,' Farrell breathed, sweat dripping from his nose.

'I think—' Heb said, but Brina interrupted him.

'Less thinking, more shutting up. Leave him be.'

'She loves me really.' Heb winked at Corban.

'What you did in the dell,' Corban said to Brina and Heb. 'You saved us all. It was amazing. I never imagined what you could do.'

'Neither did we,' Heb said. 'Never done anything remotely close. Blind terror is a good motivator.'

There was a fluttering of wings above – Craf swooping down to perch on Brina's shoulder.

'*Wolven*,' the bird croaked loudly, sending a tremor of fear running through Corban.

'Where,' Brina managed to ask through her laboured breaths. '*Above.*'

Corban looked up: sheer cliffs disappeared into the darkness. *They are up there, then, hunting us. The slopes must be too high, too steep for them to attack us. Yet.*

'What shall we do?' he gasped to Camlin, who still ran rearguard behind him.

'Keep running,' the huntsman said, eyes searching upwards. A handful of stones came skittering down the cliff. Corban saw Camlin loosen an arrow from the quiver at his belt.

Dawn gradually crept over them, unveiling a grey, steep-sided land. At some point during the night Corban had noticed their path had levelled off; now it began to slope downwards and their pace picked up. Suddenly they spilt out of the path onto a hillside with pine trees covering the slopes only a few hundred paces below them. Beyond that wooded hills rolled into a green land.

'Domhain,' Halion said.

Storm growled and Craf squawked urgently from overhead. Corban looked back and up, seeing wolven high above, outlined by the sun.

One leaped down a sloping escarpment, sliding on gravel, then a pack behind – five, six – Corban could not tell how many. All that he was sure of was that they were coming fast.

'Run, to the trees,' Camlin yelled, pushing Corban on. 'Turn and face them there.'

All of them ran on, except Dath and Corban, Storm snarling beside him. Camlin drew an arrow to his cheek and let fly; seconds later Dath's bowstring thrummed. The first wolven on the slope tumbled and rolled, sending gravel cascading. It came to a stop and did not move. The other wolven surged past it, much closer now.

'Run,' Camlin yelled again as he turned and dashed towards Corban, dragging Dath with him.

Corban needed no more encouragement: he turned and ran with the rest of them, pounding down the slope. The group started to disappear into the treeline, Farrell last of all. Moments later, branches were whipping across Corban's face, bodies jostling all about. A glance back showed the wolven still powering down the escarpment.

They drew up, breathing hard.

'Can you make the fire again?' Edana asked Brina and Heb, the first spoken acknowledgement of how they had been saved.

'Yes. I think so,' Heb said. He was breathing hard, pale faced, blood congealed from a wound on his arm.

'There's no guarantee,' Brina added. 'We'll try.'

Something rustled in a bush, sending them all reaching for their weapons. A bundle of black feathers fell out of it. A bird with a dagger sticking from its wing. Craf flew down from above, head cocking to one side as he studied this new bird.

Vonn reached a hand forward to touch it.

'*Get off,*' the bird said, clear to them all. Vonn jumped back.

Craf squawked. Brina ripped off a section of her cloak and threw it over the bird. It croaked a protest as Brina bundled it up into her arms.

'Can't just leave a talking bird lying around,' she said, and with a quick movement pulled the knife from the bird's wing.

Storm looked back, growling, her hackles rising.

'They're coming!' a voice shouted from behind. Gar. He stood beside Camlin at the rear of the column, looking back, hand on the sword still sheathed across his back.

'Face them here?' Edana said to Camlin.

'Deeper into the trees, break their charge. That way.' Camlin ran, the rest of them following fast.

All other sounds were filtered, distorted through the pounding of Corban's heart. They burst into a wide glade, voices from the front of their group shouting in exclamation, those ahead of him stumbling to a halt. The bulk of Farrell moved from in front of him, giving Corban a view of what was before them.

Figures stood at the glade's far side, beneath the trees, five or six of them, maybe more. They looked like men, but were larger.

Giants.

They were wrapped in fur and leather and for a moment just stood there staring. Then Corban saw them pull axes and hammers from their backs, some of them striding forwards. One came straight at Corban.

Storm leaped at him, burying her fangs in the giant's head, her momentum carrying her body over the giant's shoulder, flipping him with her.

Corban drew his sword, eyes searching for his mam. She was to the side, close to Halion and Edana.

A giant swung his hammer at Vonn. He dived for safety but the hammer clipped his ankle, sending him careening into Brina. Farrell stepped forwards, his own hammer whistling about his head, crunching into the giant's hip.

The other giants bellowed war cries and came rushing forward. Then there was a crashing from behind Corban, the sound of bodies speeding through the undergrowth, and he remembered the wolven.

They burst into the glade, one leaping at the first form it saw, a giant. It sank its teeth into the giant's shoulder. Another skidded to a halt, colliding with a bunch of figures – Corban saw Edana spinning through the air, then he heard his mam scream. She was tumbling across the ground, entwined with the wolven.

He yelled wordlessly and ran after them.

CHAPTER FORTY-NINE

UTHAS

Uthas stared in disbelief at the people who poured out of the trees. At first he thought it was Rath, that the warrior had somehow managed to lead his band of giant-killers around them in a flanking manoeuvre, but these were on foot. And a wolven was with them, white with dark streaks across its torso, like great claw marks.

Fray and Struan were the first to move. The wolven leaped at Fray, the giant and beast tumbling to the ground. Struan waded in with his hammer, but one of the newcomers who looked like a giantling stepped forwards, complete with his own war-hammer. He ducked and swung, landing a blow on Struan's hip; there was a sound of bones snapping.

Uthas gripped his spear, unsure whether to attack or retreat, the knowledge that Rath was still behind gnawing at him. *How close?* He took a step forwards then paused as more wolven charged out of the trees, attacking indiscriminately.

If we stay here we will die; we must fight free. He strode forwards, Salach defending him on his left. Giants and men and wolven were everywhere, a heaving mass. Kai's mangled body lay on the ground, throat torn out. Nearby, Struan was surrounded, swinging his axe at half a dozen human attackers. *I must help him. I have spent so long grooming them, preparing them.* An arrow flew out of nowhere and sank into his shoulder, the impact rocking him. He looked about, saw two figures crouched amongst the trees, both with bows in their hands. He moved, feeling another arrow whistle past his face.

'It is too late; this battle is already lost,' Salach said, gripping his arm. 'You cannot save them. We must leave.'

Struan had fallen to one knee, warriors about him stabbing and slashing.

Uthas bellowed in frustration, then saw Eisa locked in combat with a wolven. He said her name and charged, Salach following, sending his axe whistling into the spine of the wolven Eisa was fighting. Uthas grabbed her arm, pulling her. Then they were running for the trees.

Something made him pause – an invisible change in the air about him, a pressure emanating from the glade behind.

The earth power. Someone uses it.

He turned and scanned the glade, his eyes drawn to two of the humans. They were standing together, a man and woman, both gripping a broken branch. As Uthas watched, he heard them speak a word in his tongue, and the branch burst into flames.

He felt the great anger stir within him, looking at these men, these upstarts, destroyers of his people, stealers of his land and the life he had lived.

And now they were thieving the giants' greatest treasure. The earth power. He had taught Rhin something of it, but she was different, was his key to the future, to changing the fate of his clan. And she had saved him. These two before him were just vermin, scavengers of a noble order laid low by time and misfortune. Unlike many of his kin he was not ruled by his emotions, was proud of his control amongst a people who were dominated by the great tides of their passion. But as he looked back he felt his walls of self-control crumbling, a rage building until he was consumed with only one thought. Kill these usurpers.

With a snarl, he strode back into the glade.

CHAPTER FIFTY

CORBAN

Corban stood over the body of his mam, too scared to check whether she was alive or dead. Storm was locked in battle with the wolven that had attacked Gwenith; Corban and Gar were searching for an opening to finish the beast. Gar darted forward, stabbing, his blade coming back dark with blood. Then Storm had the wolven by the throat and was shaking it. The other animal's legs kicked, weakened, then went limp.

Corban caught a glimpse of Halion, Marrock and Farrell circling a giant, the hulking warrior bleeding from many wounds. Vonn stood before Edana, slashing at a pair of crouched wolven.

There was a crackling sound, a wave of heat and Corban saw Heb holding a burning branch. The old man ran at the wolven stalking Vonn and Edana, brandishing the branch. They crouched low and retreated, snarling. Arrows suddenly sprouted from one.

Camlin and Dath.

A voice rang out in the glade, discordant. It took a moment for Corban to realize the words were being spoken in giantish.

'*Sglamhair, thu rach do fada, truailleadair,*' a giant yelled, taking long strides, rage pulsing from each word.

Heb turned, saw the giant coming for him, stood frozen a moment.

'*Mi riar gun ruith,*' Heb called out and raised the burning branch.

The giant barked a command and the flames snuffed out, smoke curling upwards.

No. He cannot face a spear-wielding giant with a stick. Corban thought. '*Lasair,*' he cried out as he launched into motion, fear for Heb's life overwhelming all other thoughts.

The stick in Heb's hand burst back into flames, fiercer and brighter than before. Heb looked stunned, and the giant's gaze snapped onto Corban. For a moment he faltered in his charge, the hatred in his gaze a palpable thing. Then Heb smashed the branch into the giant's face with an explosion of sparks.

The giant howled and snarled, then thrust with his spear. Heb moved, swinging the branch again. Their weapons connected at the same moment, Heb's burning branch crashing into the giant's chest, the giant's spear-blade piercing Heb's shoulder. He cried out, sinking to his knees as the giant pulled the blade free.

'No!' Corban screamed, leaping forwards.

Brina was there before him, lunging at the giant, sinking a knife into his thigh. He bellowed and hurled Brina to the ground. She screamed as the giant buried his spear in Heb's belly. Blood sprayed as he wrenched it free, Heb toppling sideways. The giant stood over Brina, spear raised high, then a bundle of feathers fell from above, squawking, claws raking at the giant's face.

Craf.

Then Corban was there, Storm a step behind him. He swung his sword, the giant stumbled back, Storm bunched to leap. Other giants appeared, one stepping before Corban, another grabbing the one that had stabbed Heb, dragging him away. At the same time there was a crashing from the far end of the glade as mounted warriors poured out of the trees.

Corban exchanged a flurry of blows with the giant before him. They parted and there was a whistling sound, an arrow skittering off the giant's chainmail coat.

Dath?

The huge warrior snarled once at Corban and then he was fleeing, following his two companions as they disappeared amongst the trees.

The riders had paused. Corban saw expressions of confusion and shock, then one spurred their mount on, sword raised, others following, spreading through the glade. Many of them chased after the fleeing giants. One speared a wolven as they galloped past.

'Storm, to me,' Corban yelled, fearing she would be attacked by these newcomers. Gar lowered his sword and ran to Gwenith's body, fingers touching her neck. Corban felt a wave of fear and nausea. *She is so pale. Elyon above, please let her live.*

Gar looked up at him. 'She still breathes.'

Corban bent and stroked her face, felt a shallow pulse. Her eyes fluttered open, then closed again. Corban gave Gar a weak smile, relief flooding him. Gar had tears in his eyes, running down his face. *He must have thought she was dead.* He felt tears of his own and brushed them away.

There was one giant remaining, fallen to his knees. Farrell, Marrock and Vonn were circling him. The riders pulled close, weapons flashing. With a roar the giant stood, lashing out, sending Farrell and Marrock and Halion flying in different directions. Farrell rolled to a rest at Corban's feet, and with a groan pushed himself up.

One of the riders spurred their horse forward, skewering the giant with a spear as they passed, then leaped from the horse's back, one hand clinging to the giant's cloak, the other pulling a knife across its throat. Blood fountained and the giant toppled to the ground, its killer rolling and rising in one graceful move, almost right in front of Corban. The warrior's helm had fallen in the roll and Corban blinked. It was a girl, red hair tied tight, wisps of it come loose.

Halion shouted and he ran towards the girl. She stared at him, body tensed, then grinned as Halion reached her. They embraced.

'Who's she?' Dath said as he emerged from the trees.

'Don't know, but I think I'm in love,' Farrell said.

Still grinning at each other, Halion and the girl parted, then Halion looked about and saw Corban and Farrell staring at him.

'Corban, this is Coralen. My sister.'

CHAPTER FIFTY-ONE

EVNIS

Evnis stared at the scene unfolding before him, with Conall stepping into the ring about the fire-pit.

When he had returned, Evnis had heard a whispered report that Conall had had some quarrel with Veradis, something to do with Cywen. What he was doing now was clear, though. *He is taking an opportunity, making his mark. What was it he said to me, back in Dun Carreg? Risk much to gain much.* Evnis smiled – if he had been Conall, in his position and with his skill, he most likely would be doing the same thing. *It is a shame to lose him, though.* For, win or lose against Morcant, Evnis would lose Conall from his service, now; either to death or to Rhin.

Conall walked towards Morcant, stopping a dozen paces from him.

'My first-sword is injured. He has a knife wound in his shoulder. I do not think it would be fair to do this now,' Rhin said.

'I have a knife wound of my own,' Conall said, holding his left arm up so that all could see the bloodstained bandage. 'And given by the same person,' he added, glancing at Cywen.

'Really?' Rhin frowned at Cywen. Rhin looked at Morcant, and Evnis saw the warrior nod. 'Very well,' Rhin said. Noise erupted as men started swapping bets on the two warriors. Evnis saw Rhin pause as she was returning to her chair, cocking her head as if listening to something. He saw her lips move, as if she were talking to someone, then people were pushing in front of him and he jostled through them to keep his view. When he could see Rhin again she was seated in her chair.

'Begin,' she said.

Both warriors held only a sword, no shield or second weapon. Evnis remembered seeing Morcant duel with Tull, and he knew that Morcant was fast, deadly, even though he had lost that duel. But he had also seen Conall spar many times, often against four or five of his own men. He had never lost.

The two men touched blades, then Conall was lunging forwards, his sword moving quickly, a combination of four, five, six strikes, all blurred into one long move. Morcant retreated, blocking with a touch, a sidestep, until his heels were almost touching the fire-pit. He sidestepped again, swung overhead, pivoted, chopped at Conall's ribs, but Conall was not there; the man was in constant motion, spinning away, striking as he moved. And he was smiling.

Morcant followed, parrying, pressing Conall, restricting his space. Evnis nodded approvingly; he had never seen anyone take the fight to Conall like that – most tried to weather the storm, defend until Conall raged himself out, but not Morcant. He blocked, struck, parried, stepped forwards, struck again, mixing stabs, slashes, lunges.

This cannot last long.

Conall was no longer smiling.

The two men moved apart, both breathing heavily. Morcant rested a hand on his thigh, leaning on his blade, sword-tip digging into the earth. Conall took a step forwards and Morcant flicked his wrist, sending earth straight at Conall's face.

Conall stepped away, the smile returning.

'I saw you fight Tull,' he said.

'Worth a try,' Morcant said, then he was moving forward, sending Conall backwards with long sweeping cuts. Conall retreated to the edge of the ring, almost leaning against the men who made it. Then he was attacking again, Morcant retreating. For a while they just stood, feet planted, trading a flurry of blows, sparks flying. Then Conall's speed increased, and Evnis could see that finally Morcant was struggling to block the torrent. Conall concentrated his attacks on Morcant's injured side, striking harder and harder, faster and faster, the blows repeating down Morcant's arm, into his wounded shoulder.

Morcant lunged inside Conall's blows and wrapped his sword arm around Conall, pulling him close, punched him in the face, then hammered his wounded arm. Conall staggered, screamed, tried to pull away, but Morcant would not let go and continued punching Conall's wound, blood spraying with each punch.

It is over, thought Evnis, surprised to feel a pang of sadness for Conall.

Then Evnis saw Conall's face twist in a snarl, and he barrelled forwards, headbutting Morcant full on the bridge of the nose. Now it was Morcant's blood that spurted, his turn to stagger backwards. Conall followed, swaying, punched his sword hilt into Morcant's shoulder. Then Morcant was on his back, Conall's sword at his throat.

'You've been here before,' Conall said through ragged breaths, then he looked to Rhin.

'Morcant has served me well, and today especially. It would be poor treatment if I were to take his life as payment. Let him live, just blood him a little.'

Conall sliced his cheek, opposite to where Tull had done the same.

'And it would seem that I have a new first-sword.' She held her hand out. Conall crossed to her and helped her rise, then they performed the ceremony, cutting their hands and mingling their blood, Conall swearing the oath of loyalty.

He is moving up in the world, then. I wonder if he realizes what he has let himself in for. Evnis smiled grimly, knowing of Rhin's appetites.

Evnis rose early, his body aching and stiff from the previous day's battle. Groaning, he pulled his boots on, splashed water in his face and left his tent to relieve himself in the fresh morning air. He nodded to Glyn, his warrior standing on watch at the tent's entrance. As he was fastening his belt, a messenger ran up to his tent.

'Queen Rhin wishes to see you,' the lad said.

Conall opened the tent flap for Evnis, beckoning him to enter.

'Risk much to gain much,' Evnis said to him as he brushed by.

'Just so,' Conall said.

'You look tired. A long night?' Evnis said.

Conall raised his eyebrows and smiled.

Rhin was seated in one of a handful of chairs around a wide table, maps and parchments strewn across it. When she saw him she rose and took both his hands in hers.

'It has been a long time, since that night in the Darkwood.'

'It has, my Queen,' Evnis said, surprised to find his voice choked with emotion. 'We are close, now, so close.'

Conall poured them some mead.

'So,' Rhin said to Evnis. 'I find myself in a wonderful position. Cambren, Narvon and Ardan are mine. And soon I will add Domhain to that list.'

'The dream has become reality,' Evnis said and they raised their cups and drank.

'Ardan I will leave to you,' Rhin said.

'Thank you, my Queen.'

'It is only what we agreed, all those years ago. I must turn my attention to Domhain, and I will need someone that I trust to over-see things here. I understand that Owain left some cleaning-up to do?'

'There are rumours of resistance in the south,' Evnis said.

'I have heard that. You will put an end to it.'

'I will.'

'I shall give you men, gold, resources. And I will leave Morcant with you. He has served me well. Even if he has been bested he still has a reputation. He slew Tull, after all, and brought me Owain.'

'As you wish,' Evnis said. *I do not like Morcant – we all need a little pride and arrogance to see us through these times, but he is too proud, too arrogant. And he had some help in bringing Owain to heel. It was Braith who found him.* 'And shall you stay a while in Ardan, before you leave for Domhain?'

'I think I must leave soon. I have received some strange news this morning – troubling. A messenger arrived from Cambren, and also I have heard from Uthas.'

Evnis remembered the Benothi giant, the comrade who had been present in the Darkwood all those years ago when Evnis had made his pact with Asroth. He remembered the giant with some fondness, because he had tried to help Fain, had told Evnis of the book beneath Dun Carreg and had urged him to take Fain to the cauldron. 'Is he well?' Evnis asked.

'No. He tried to contact me last night, but I was busy and the connection faded before it had begun. Then, this morning, I have spoken a little longer with him. He gave me much to think on.'

Evnis was silent, waiting for Rhin to continue. He knew it was better not to rush her.

Then there was a noise at the tent flap, voices. Conall went to see. 'It is Nathair, my Queen.'

'Ah, earlier than I expected. Show him in. And, please, next time announce his full title. He is a king, after all.'

Evnis smiled, seeing Conall's discomfort. *Even as first-sword there are things you will not like to do.*

The usual group of people attended Nathair: Sumur, Calidus, Veradis and Alcyon, his bulk overshadowing them all. Quickly they were all seated and sipping at their cups, except the giant.

'My thanks for your help, yesterday,' Rhin began.

'You're welcome. Though I think the result would have been the same, just a little delayed,' Nathair said. He was reclining in his chair, looking relaxed, happy even.

'Perhaps.' Rhin shrugged. 'But I shall not forget your aid. What would you ask of me? If I can give it, I will.'

'Straight to the point,' Nathair said.

'When you get to my age, you learn not to waste time. It is too precious. So, what would you ask of me?'

'Join my alliance, as my father wished. Join me and add your strength to the mustering against Asroth and his Black Sun.'

Rhin sat there, staring at Nathair. Slowly she nodded. 'I shall do that, gladly. From this moment my realm, or realms, are part of your alliance, Nathair. When the time comes I shall bring my armies to you, and we shall fight the Black Sun together.' She lifted her cup and they all drank.

'Would you ask anything else?'

'I will be travelling north. Help or advice with the journey would be gratefully received.'

'Yes. We spoke of this. To Murias, in Benoth. You seek the cauldron. It will be dangerous – the Benothi giants are no friends to men.'

Most of them.

'I am aware of that. But it is what I must do.'

'Then I will help you, grant you safe passage to the northern border, and give you scouts that know the land.'

'And what of you, my lady? Is there more aid that I could give to you?'

'I will be travelling to Domhain, to pay Eremon a visit. My goal is to unite the west.'

'I would help you in that,' Nathair said. 'I have troop ships anchored in the bay at Dun Carreg. It would be a simple thing for them to take your warband across the seas to Cambren.'

'That would be helpful,' Rhin said. 'Morcant crossed the channel on a hundred fisher-boats and lost more than a few to the sea along the way, I have heard.'

'Then it is done,' Nathair said. 'And more than that – take Veradis and his warband, a thousand men.'

Evnis saw the young warrior stare with surprise at Nathair. *He looks as if he wants to object but dare not*, Evnis thought. *Good, a soldier who takes orders without question. If only there were more blind followers such as he in our cause.*

'He is my first-sword and my battlechief, and he has proven himself many times. In Tarbesh he defeated a charge of draigs and giants, in Carnutan he defeated Mandros in battle and took his head, and in Forn he turned the battle against the Hunen. You will not regret his being in your ranks.'

Rhin studied Veradis; the young warrior quickly averted his gaze and looked into his cup.

'Can you win Domhain for me?' Rhin asked him.

'I-I would not be so bold as to make that prediction, my lady. But whatever Nathair asks of me I will do or die in the trying,' Veradis said.

'Such loyalty and passion the young have,' Rhin said, smiling drily. 'You are fortunate, Nathair.'

'A question,' Nathair said. 'It is already high summer. Even with my ships taking you there, it must take several moons of travel to reach Domhain.'

'Yes, perhaps longer, with a warband on the march.'

'So you will be undertaking a winter campaign? I hear the winters here are not as mild as those we are used to in Tenebral.'

'There will be blood spilt in the snow,' Rhin said with a shrug. 'There is a road the giants made that cuts through the mountains between Cambren and Domhain, and forges a line right to Eremon's seat, Dun Taras. As long as we have that we can wage war, no matter the weather. I have ample stores of provisions in Cambren. You may need a warmer cloak, and some woollen breeches to cover those legs of yours,' she said to Veradis, who promptly blushed.

'There is something else that we would ask of you,' another voice spoke. Calidus. 'A small thing. News.'

'News of what?' Rhin asked.

'A young man, not much more than a boy. He escaped the fall of Dun Carreg in the company of Edana and some others, we think.'

'Yes, I have had many men hunting the land for her. Who is the boy?'

'His name is Corban. He travels with a wolven. A white wolven.'

Rhin sat up straighter.

'What is it?' Nathair asked her.

'That is interesting. A messenger arrived today, bringing news from Cambren. My warriors have tracked what were thought to be Owain's spies through most of Cambren and I have had reports that each night my men have been hunted and killed, by a wolven. Stories are growing that whoever is roaming my land is in league with Asroth and becomes a wolven at night, or commands a pack of wolven, or something. At first I put it down to superstitious warriors, but . . .'

'It is him,' Calidus said.

'I am inclined to agree – it is too much of a coincidence. Edana must be fleeing to Domhain. She must have some capable people about her.'

'Indeed,' said Nathair.

'Well, then, I am glad to have helped,' Rhin replied. 'Perhaps you can travel some of the way north with me – we will take your ships together, and try hunting this lad and his wolven before our journeys force us to part. You want him, and it sounds as if he is with Edana, and I *really* want to find her.'

'Agreed,' Nathair said.

They drank some more together, toasting their past and future victories, and in time Nathair and his retinue left.

As soon as they were gone, Rhin called in a messenger boy and whispered in his ear. He ran off.

'There is something about that Nathair,' Rhin said.

'There is,' Evnis agreed. *How much does she know? We are both bound to Asroth, to bringing about the God-War, to making Asroth flesh.*

And we have both grown powerful, in our ways. But she far more than I, and she loves her newfound power – that is plain to see. Would she relinquish it, even for Asroth or his avatar?

'What do you think of Nathair?' she asked him.

Unusually blunt, thought Evnis. The question shocked him. *What should I tell her? How much of what I guess? Sometimes a direct question deserves a direct answer. Roll the dice.*

'I think he is the Black Sun. I have heard the voice.'

She regarded him thoughtfully. 'I have heard it too,' she said eventually.

'We should do all we can to help him,' Evnis said, trying to prompt her. He saw thoughts spiralling in her mind.

'He is the Black Sun, Asroth's chosen avatar to bring about the great war. He is *not* Asroth himself. Remember that, Evnis.'

'What do you mean?'

'Do not serve Nathair blindly. I don't think that Nathair realizes who his *master* is.'

I had not thought of that. 'Perhaps you are right. There is a sincerity about him . . .'

'Exactly. Be careful what you tell him. He must be steered, controlled.' She tapped long nails upon the arm of her chair, making a clicking sound. 'This boy and his wolven that Nathair searches for, I have heard more about him than I have told Nathair,' Rhin said.

Evnis just looked at her, waiting.

'I spoke with Uthas earlier; through the fire, you understand?'

'Yes.'

'He has been sneaking around Domhain, spying and killing, stirring things up for my arrival. Well, he has encountered some misfortune: most of his company has been killed, slain, in a battle only last night. The boy Calidus asked about, he was there, with his wolven.'

'Why did you not tell Nathair?' He knew the answer already. *Knowledge is power. And she does not want to relinquish any of it.*

'There is no rush,' she said with a smile.

The tent flap opened and a man walked in, tall, skin weathered, a scar running down his face from forehead to chin.

Braith.

'You sent for me, my Queen,' Braith said, sinking to a knee.

'I have a job for you. Someone to find.'

'Of course.'

'They are in the mountains between Cambren and Domhain, close to the giants' road, or were last night. I guess that they are heading into Domhain, so you will have to move carefully through enemy country. It is Edana and her helpers, amongst them a boy with a pet wolven.'

Braith frowned at her. 'I have met this boy before, at Dun Carreg when I rescued Camlin, and he fought in the Darkwood, when I had Alona. That wolven is no pet, I saw it tear my men to pieces,' Braith said.

'I want him, this Corban. Alive and in chains before me. There are other parties that are very interested in him, which means that I am interested, too. Take as many as you need, whatever supplies, all the gold necessary, but it must be done now, quickly and quietly. You must leave now.'

Braith bowed and kissed Rhin's hand, then turned to leave.

'Braith,' Rhin called as he reached the exit.

'Remember, I want the boy alive, but you can kill the rest of them, including Edana. Actually, especially Edana.'

'What about the wolven? Do you want that alive as well?'

'Of course not. Kill it.'

CHAPTER FIFTY-TWO

MAQUIN

Maquin sat with his back to the wall of Dun Kellen's stone bridge. His hands and ankles were shackled. The place where his ear had been was throbbing; a blood-stained bandage wrapped around his head stemmed the bleeding.

He was part of a group of defeated men, at least a hundred of them, the number being added to all the time. A dozen warriors – all men from the ships – stood guarding them. Further away, towards Dun Kellen, Jael's warband was busy, organizing the clearing of the town, bringing order back where chaos had ruled. The newcomers who had arrived on the black-sailed ships were busy around the river, restocking supplies, it looked like.

Heads on spikes lined the bridge; Maquin was sitting beside one. He looked up and saw a crow perched on the head, tugging a strip of flesh from it. Further along he saw Gerda's head, one eye already taken by these looters of the dead.

Orgull's head was not on a spike. Not yet. The big man had laid down his axe to save him. In a way Maquin wished Orgull had kept fighting, that they had both died in that tunnel underground. But he hadn't. As soon as Orgull's axe had touched the ground they had both been bound and taken from the fortress. He had no idea where Orgull was.

He had failed.

Jael was alive – not only that, he had won. And Maquin had been so close. He put his head in his hands.

The only hope to cling to was that Tahir had escaped with Gerda's son, or at least had not been captured yet. If they had been caught, surely their heads would be on spikes alongside Gerda's.

There was a glimmer of hope for Isiltir while Romar's son still lived and that would surely tarnish Jael's victory. That was something.

A noise caused him to lift his head. A group of riders had emerged from the town and gathered at the end of the bridge, laughing. One of them dismounted.

Jael.

He felt a shadow fall over him, refused to look up until his boot was kicked. 'Someone's angry,' Jael said, smiling. 'Ulfilas, protect me from the poison in this man's gaze.'

Maquin lowered his eyes. Jael kicked his boot again and suddenly Maquin was lunging forwards. Even with the chains it was so fast and so unexpected that he had his fingers around Jael's throat before anyone could react. As Jael's eyes bulged, Ulfilas clubbed Maquin across the head with the hilt of his sword and Maquin's legs turned to gruel. He slumped to his knees.

Jael kneed Maquin in the face. He fell backwards, the sound of his nose breaking was like a branch splitting. Blood sluiced from his nose and his head cracked against the stone wall of the bridge.

Maybe now I'll die, he thought as he lay sprawled, staring up at Jael.

'Help him up,' Jael said, brushing himself down. Ulfilas grabbed Maquin under the arm and hoisted him back to his knees.

'You've come a long way from Haldis,' Jael said. 'And survived Forn Forest. I am guessing that you are the reason that Gerda and Varick were not surprised to see me. And yet you lost. You must feel terrible.'

Maquin just looked at him, the words filtering through layers of dizziness and pain.

'And, of course, I haven't mentioned your greatest loss. Kastell.'

Maquin felt the world pull into focus, juddering; Jael's face, his mouth, his lips moving, filling the entirety of his vision.

'He died badly, you know, if you didn't see. A gut wound. He screamed, a lot. Not very brave in the end, for all his words, his giant-killing – one of the Gadrai indeed.' Jael spat on the ground, as if the words gave a bad taste.

'So you are quite the failure. You failed Kastell. You have failed Gerda. Are you the worst shieldman in all of the Banished Lands? Ulfilas, remind me never to enlist this man in my service. The day when I do that I will surely lose whatever battle I am fighting.' Laughter drifted about him, from dark places that Maquin could not see.

'I call . . .' Maquin coughed on his words, hawked and spat. 'I call you out,' he said, little more than a whisper. 'I challenge you, to the Court of Swords.'

Jael threw his head back and laughed. A deep, genuine sound. He wiped his eyes. 'I think it is a little late for that. In case you are not clear: you have already lost.' There was more laughter at that.

'I challenge you to the Court of Swords,' Maquin said again, louder. 'I do not expect you to accept. You are afraid. A coward, dung that I would scrape from my boot.'

'Be careful,' Jael said, his expression hardening, 'before your jest loses its humour.'

'A coward – as you have always been,' Maquin continued, aware now that others were listening, people moving closer to hear. 'I have watched you grow, seen you pick always on the weaker man. You are a coward, a traitor, you have betrayed your own kin. Kastell you stabbed in the back, too scared to face him. I saw.'

'I did not,' Jael roared, angry, looking about at the gathering crowd.

'And your victories – given to you like crumbs from your better's table. These men –' he looked to those on the bridge that had come from the ships – 'Nathair's men? Of course they are. There are few warriors in Isiltir who would follow you.'

Jael backhanded him across the face. He swayed but managed to remain upright.

'Put a sword in my hand. Face me, as a man. Look at me – beaten bloody – yet you are still too scared to face me.'

'Unchain him and give him a blade,' Jael snarled at Ulfilas as he stepped back and drew his sword.

Ulfilas moved hesitantly forwards and helped Maquin stand.

'Why do you follow him?' Maquin whispered. Ulfilas looked sharply at him, then looked away. He fumbled at the chains about Maquin's wrists.

'I have no key.'

'Just put a sword in my hand,' Maquin said. 'I'll still win.' He knew that he would not, had seen Jael spar many times in the weapons court at Mikil. But at least he would die that much closer to his dream, not chained to an oar, a thousand leagues from home.

'Do as he says,' Jael yelled, spittle flying.

Maquin smiled. He had witnessed Jael goading Kastell many times over the years, Jael always with that maddening smile on his lips. It was not there now. It was nice that at the end he at least had this small victory.

A crowd had pulled in about them now. Even some amongst the chained warriors along the wall were standing, trying to see the confrontation. Some called out encouragements to Maquin, or jeered at Jael.

There was a pushing and shoving further back in the crowd, men moving to let someone through. It was the leader of the ship men: Lykos, Maquin had heard him called. Behind him strode a lean warrior, his face disfigured, part of his nose missing. He led a man by a chain. Orgull.

His friend was bleeding from a hundred cuts, all small wounds, his face bruised and swollen. He shuffled behind his captor, head bowed.

'What's happening here?' Lykos asked Jael.

'I am going to teach him some truths,' Jael said, his rage adding a tremor to his voice.

'What truths?'

'That I am no coward, and that I am the better swordsman.'

'He is in chains,' Lykos said. 'And close to collapse; look at him. You will prove nothing fighting him now. And besides, he is not yours to kill. He is my captive, remember?'

'He has insulted me; I will not ignore that.'

Lykos frowned and stepped close to Maquin, studying him. 'You have the death wish upon you. You want to die – I can see it in your eyes.'

Maquin just stared back at him.

Lykos grinned. 'He is baiting you, Jael. He wishes to die and is using you.'

'Then I will grant him his wish,' Jael said, stepping forwards.

'No, you will not,' Lykos said, a harshness in his voice. 'He is mine, and I do not want you to kill him.'

'I am king here,' Jael said.

'Not yet,' Lykos replied. He stepped in close to Jael and whispered in his ear. Maquin strained to hear, but could catch nothing of it. But he did see Jael's expression change – from anger to fear. Jael stepped away.

'Have him; he is yours, a gift from me,' Jael said.

'Run away, coward,' Maquin said, seeing his opportunity slipping away.

Jael smiled at him, that familiar, maddening smile. 'But, Lykos, some advice. Kill him soon. Otherwise he is likely to bring you bad luck, as he has his previous masters.'

'I am more than his master,' Lykos said. 'I am his owner. He drew a knife from his belt and stepped close to Maquin. He grabbed a handful of Maquin's hair and cut it with his knife, then opened his palm for Maquin to see.

His warrior braid.

'You are mine, my property, a warrior no longer.'

The warrior who was leading Orgull turned and did the same, cutting Orgull's warrior braid from his beard. All along the line of captives the same thing happened.

'Now let's get these useless piles of dung onto the ships,' Lykos yelled, pushing Maquin. 'You've got a long way to row.'

Laughter ran through the ship men.

As Maquin walked away he looked back over his shoulder.

'I'll see you again,' he shouted at Jael.

'I doubt that,' Jael said. His laughter followed Maquin as he shuffled towards the black ships.

CHAPTER FIFTY-THREE

CORBAN

Corban stared at Halion and his sister Coralen. She stared back.

Before anyone had a chance to speak, a warrior rode up. He was old, his hair a mix of grey and white flowing from beneath an iron cap. Corban remembered him, from the gathering at Badun on Midwinter's Day. Brenin had invited the rulers of the west – Owain, Rhin and Eremon – to a council and to witness the day turn to night, as had been prophesied. This man had been the representative of King Eremon at that meeting. Rath. He slid from his saddle and gripped Halion by the shoulders. 'It's good to see you, little bastard.'

'And you, old man.'

Another warrior rode up, younger, a jagged scar running through the empty socket of one eye.

'Some still live,' the man said. 'They have fled into the mountains.'

'We must talk, but later,' Rath said to Halion. 'Let's see if we can run the swine down before they reach Cambren.' Rath yelled orders as he rode after the giants' trail, some men following him, others staying, moving amongst the dead. The red-haired girl, Coralen, picked up her fallen helmet and, tucking her hair back into it, mounted her horse and rode after Rath.

Corban looked about the glade, bodies twisted in death littering the ground – men, giants, wolven. Brina crouched beside Heb, holding his hand. Corban hurried to her and knelt beside her. She looked at him with bloodshot eyes. Corban wanted to say something, to comfort her, but knew that no words could take away the pain in her eyes. He put a hand over hers.

Corban remembered Heb standing before the giant, defying it.

'I heard him say something to the giant – in giantish. What did he say – at the end?'

'He said, *I will not run.*'

'He was a brave man. Good and kind,' Corban said.

'He was an old fool, and now he's dead and has left me,' Brina whispered. She bowed her head and wept. Craf fluttered down out of the branches and landed close to them. He stared at Brina and Heb, head cocked, then shuffled over to Brina and leaned his beak against her.

Gwenith was sitting up now, Gar feeding her sips of water. Corban rushed over and embraced her.

'I thought you were dead,' he said, fresh tears springing to his eyes.

'Can't get rid of me that easily.' She smiled weakly.

Edana was sitting with Marrock and Vonn, who lay with his back to a tree, white faced, clutching his broken ankle. Marrock sat with his arm across his lap, blood staining the bandages around his wrist.

Corban moved amongst them all, checking their wounds, fetching salve and bandages from Brina's seemingly endless stores. Finally he checked Storm. The wolven was covered in a mass of new wounds, claw and tooth marks all over her body. They were all superficial, nothing so deep that would not heal, if kept clean. 'My brave girl,' he whispered as he poured water over the cuts. She nuzzled him and licked his cheek.

Farrell stood over the body of his da, lying at the fringe of the glade where he had placed him.

'I'll raise a cairn over him here,' Farrell said.

'I'll help you,' Corban said.

'We all will,' said Edana.

They lay Heb and Anwarth side by side, then those that could set about gathering stones and rocks from the surrounding area.

As the last rocks were placed on the cairn a sound drew Corban's attention, a scratching, rustling sound. Storm stared with her ears pricked forward at a bundle of cloth on the ground. It was moving, feebly, something inside it.

The bird, Corban remembered. Brina had tucked it into her cloak. *It must have fallen free during the battle.* Cautiously he unwrapped the bundle and a ruffled black bird stared up at him. It flapped its wings, or tried – one of them hanging limp – and squawked, sounding to be pain.

Corban reached a hand out and the bird pecked at him, catching his finger. Blood welled and Storm growled.

The bird wriggled to its feet and shuffled away from Storm, but Dath and Farrell helped contain it.

'Craf, do you know this crow?' Farrell called.

'*Raven*,' the bird with the injured wing croaked, a correction. It sounded offended.

Craf fluttered over and for a moment the two birds regarded each other in silence, then the raven hopped over to Craf and started pecking him. Craf squawked and flapped his wings, buffeting the unsteady raven away.

'Don't do that,' Edana yelled, who had joined them. She jumped in and grabbed the raven, pinning its wings as she lifted it.

'*Get off get off get off*,' the bird screeched. Vonn started laughing.

'What, so you can attack our Craf again?' Edana said. 'No, I will not. But I will wring your scrawny neck if you keep trying to peck me.' The raven was twisting in her arms, but at Edana's words it went limp.

'That's better. It's clear that you can't go anywhere – look at your wing. And it must hurt. I would help you, but only if you behave. I'll not have you attacking me or my companions, and that includes Craf.' The bird looked at her resentfully.

'So, what will it be? Shall I tend your wing. Or do you want to try attacking us again, and I twist your neck.'

'Is she reasoning with a crow?' Dath whispered to Corban.

'It's a raven,' he said. 'And yes.'

'It's up to you,' Edana continued, and with that she put the raven back on the ground.

The raven stood still, looking up at Edana, then it hung its head.

'*Sorry*,' it muttered.

'All right then,' Edana said, and bent to look at the bird's wing.

The sound of hooves grew and riders appeared from amongst the trees: Rath and his warriors who had given chase to the surviving giants.

'Did you catch them?' Halion asked.

'No. They're well into Cambren by now. We'd have followed

further, but saw patrols of Rhin's warriors in the mountains, as well as filling the giants' road. Something's stirred them up.'

'That'd be us,' Camlin said.

'Well then, think it's time we had that talk now,' Rath said, sliding from his saddle and striding over to Halion. Rath's band followed him, and soon the two companies were standing close together, all listening to the two men speak.

Halion told Rath of the fall of Dun Carreg and their escape by sea, of their landing in Cambren and a brief outline of the flight that had led them here. Edana rose and stood beside Halion as he spoke. When Halion had finished, a silence filled the glade.

'I thought I recognized you, under all that dirt,' Rath said to Edana. 'My lady.' He dipped his head and lifted her hand to his lips.

He doesn't look used to doing things like that, Corban thought. It looked as if Edana agreed, as she had a faint smile on her lips.

'I shall escort you to Dun Taras and Eremon,' Rath said. 'You can rest easy now – you are out of danger.'

For the time being, thought Corban.

'You hear that, lads? We've a queen amongst us. Show some respect.' Rath bowed lower to Edana. His rugged band did the same, some cheering, all except the girl, Coralen. She remained upright, a frown creasing her face.

'And welcome home, Halion,' Rath said. 'Your da'll be pleased to see you.'

'Will he?'

'Well, we'll find out soon enough,' Rath said. 'I for one am.'

'And so am I.' Coralen grinned at Halion.

They gathered around Heb and Anwarth's cairn, then. Edana spoke kind words over the stones, tears running freely down her cheeks. Farrell stood beside her, head bowed.

He has just lost his da.

He remembered that pain, a distant echo of it twisting inside him, and his sympathy went out to his friend. *Are they the last to die? Are we safe now?* He wished it were true – so many had died since that night in Dun Carreg, he had lost count. And here, now, looking at Heb and Anwarth's cairn he felt . . . numb. He had liked Heb always – his stories had felt magical to Corban as far back as he could remember, but over the course of the journey he had come to care for the old man, to think of him as a mentor, and as a friend. And yet no tears came.

Am I becoming numb to all this murder and death? The thought bothered him. He remembered Dylan, his friend – murdered, his body burned – remembered the ocean of tears he had cried for him. And then the overwhelming grief at the death of his da, and so many others when Dun Carreg fell. Life was so frail, and he had not just seen men die, an impartial observer; he had taken lives himself. *More than I can remember.* That thought shocked him. *What am I becoming?* He looked about the faces of his companions, all lost in their own thoughts, Edana's voice a wordless blur now.

His eyes settled on Brina, appearing suddenly older, frailer than he had ever noticed. Devastation was scribed upon her face. Finally he felt grief stir in his gut, an empathy for this harsh, sharp-tongued old lady whom he had come to love; he felt the urge to go and stand next to her, to squeeze her hand, or something, but the silence felt almost like a physical thing, a purity to it, so he did not move. Instead a tear rolled down his cheek.

When Edana had finished speaking, Rath's men brought up their horses. Rath and two other men – one the warrior with the scar where his eye should have been, Baird, Corban heard him called – gave their mounts up for Edana, Brina and Gwenith. Craf perched on Brina's saddle, the black raven on Edana's, its wing now with a makeshift bandage about it.

Coralen turned her horse and spurred it over to Halion. 'Where's Conall? Why did he stay in Ardan? You haven't quarrelled again?'

'He fell,' Halion said.

He was a traitor; he killed Cywen, thought Corban.

A look of horror swept Coralen's face. 'I thought he was indestructible, that he would live forever.'

'I did not,' Rath said, who was nearby.

'How did he . . . ? Did he die well?' Coralen asked, a tremor in her voice.

'No', another voice said. His mam.

'Not now,' Halion said. 'Please.'

'What do you mean by that?' Coralen snapped.

'It's complicated. I'll explain another time,' Halion said.

'No. She'll explain now.' Coralen rode closer to Gwenith. 'Won't you?'

Gar stepped between them. 'Let her be, girl.'

'Don't be telling me what to do,' Coralen said. 'And who are you, anyway?'

She has her brother's temper, thought Corban, seeing the colour rise in her cheeks.

Storm growled.

Coralen glanced at Storm. 'Hal, who are these people you ride with? Bird-lovers and wolven-tamers.'

'She's not tame,' Corban said.

'She'd make a good cloak, keep me warm in the winter.'

Corban felt his own anger stir at that.

'That's enough, girl,' Rath said, riding closer.

'But—'

'Enough, Cora. Ride on.' He stared her down, waiting until the fire went out of her eyes. She yanked on her reins and rode ahead.

'You'll tell me about Conall soon,' Rath said to Halion. It was not a question.

'I will.'

'She had a good point, though. It is strange company you keep,' Rath observed, looking between Storm and the two black birds perched on saddles. 'Lad, your wolven's not going to eat any of my men, is it?'

'She, not it,' said Corban, feeling his anger still lurking, with no obvious target for it now that Coralen had ridden off. He took a long breath. 'Her name is Storm. And the answer's no, she'll not hurt any of your men, unless they try to harm us. We are her pack, you see, and she's protective.'

'I'll remember that,' Rath said.

With a click of his tongue Corban called Storm closer. *A good cloak, indeed.* He looked back at the glade, the cairn of stones in its middle, the corpses of wolven and giants scattered around. His eyes came to rest on the body of a wolven, dark furred and sharp clawed, and he remembered the night attack that he and Storm had been part of. *A good cloak.* The seeds of an idea stirred in his mind.

'Move out,' Rath called.

'Hold a moment,' Corban said, marching across the glade.

'What is it?' Camlin said to him, bloodied but still vigilant.

'Just an idea – one that I may need some help with.' Corban pulled his knife from his belt as he crouched beside the dead wolven.

CHAPTER FIFTY-FOUR

VERADIS

Veradis focused on his opponents' blades, all three of them, his body automatically moving to defend and attack. He combined a long sweep to block two different blows, pivoting suddenly and cracking his practice blade into one opponent's ribs, then striking another on the wrist, sending his weapon spinning. Then there was only Bos left and Veradis pressed forwards against the taller man, one blow turning into another – neat, economical, and deadly until Bos stumbled and fell, Veradis' blade at his throat.

'All right, you win,' Bos said good-naturedly. He held his hand out and Veradis pulled him up.

'I think you're getting faster,' Bos said, wiping sweat from his bald head. He waved a hand at the other eagle-guard that Veradis had called out to spar with, both nursing bruises on ribs or wrist.

'Feel like I need to,' Veradis said. He knew that the recent battles were won, but something about this whole situation felt unsafe to him, and a voice in the back of his mind was telling him to sharpen up, to be ready, prepared. What for, he did not know, but he had learned to listen to that voice before. Maybe it was just the politicking of the last few days, which always made him feel uncomfortable, or the sword-crossing between Conall and Morcant. Both masters with a blade – that was obvious. Things were so fluid in these lands, it was not a great stretch of the imagination that one day soon it could be him facing either one of them, or someone equally skilled in the Court of Swords. He would not be found wanting.

He was near the top of the hill they had been camped upon since the battle, two days gone now. It was early, and the smell of the sea wafted on a cold breeze, salty and sharp. There was a slight chill in the air, the first hint that summer was retreating, autumn encroaching. In the valley at the foot of the hill the only movement Veradis could see was the Jehar gathered together, going through their sword dance. It had been an impressive sight on the journey to Forn Forest, performed by a few hundred. Now over two thousand warriors stood in regimented lines, moving through the forms with precisely the same timing. It was inspiring. *I would almost like to join them.*

The valley was emptier today, a large force of Rhin's army having left the day before, tasked with keeping order in Narvon. Veradis had watched them leave, a few thousand men disappearing into the distance. Strange that out of all those warriors Braith's face stood in his memory – leaving before the main bulk of Rhin's force, almost definitely leading a scouting party ahead, a pack of hounds with him, as well as a score or so of hard-looking men.

'What's the plan?' Bos asked as he came and stood beside Veradis.

'We'll break camp today, march back to Dun Carreg, then spend a few days on a ship to Cambren, and help Queen Rhin win some more land.'

'We are getting good at that,' Bos said, 'winning land for others.'

'Aye. But it suits Nathair. Besides, we're just soldiers; we go where we're pointed.'

'That we do.'

'We'll put the lads through some moves before we leave, though. Go make sure they're on the field. I'll be along soon.'

Veradis did not want his warband to miss any training in the shield wall. After the meeting with Nathair and Rhin he was sure they would be seeing battle again soon. Veradis walked towards the ramshackle tents that had sprouted on the outskirts of the warband's camp, containing all those who went hand-in-hand with a warband on the move. Wives, lovers, children, blacksmiths, tanners, weapons-smiths, brewers, whores: all manner of trades made a living from an army. He made his way through the tents, weaving amongst the rope lines and makeshift walkways until he found what he was looking for. The heat hit him first. A tall wiry man was working a bellows, each pull causing a fire to flare and crackle. He stood and watched the man work a little while, enjoying it.

'Here you go,' the blacksmith said when he saw Veradis, throwing him a pair of boots. 'How do they suit?'

Veradis inspected one closely. Long strips of iron, thin enough to keep the weight down but thick enough to turn a blade, were sewn in a half-circle about the front of the boot's leg.

'I think that'll do the job,' Veradis said. The leg wounds on his fallen warriors had troubled him for a while, and this seemed the obvious option. 'I want two thousand pairs like it.'

The smith's eyes bulged. 'That's a lot of boots, and iron.' He was silent, working things out. 'You supply the boots, I'll come up with the iron, for the right price.'

That shouldn't be a problem. Owain's dead were all wearing good boots. 'And how long will it take you?' Veradis said. 'I need them all within a ten-night.'

Veradis made his way to Nathair's tent. They had been on the road for two days now, and Dun Carreg was a faint smudge on the horizon. He felt slow, tired, his sleep disturbed by dreams. *More accurately: dream.* Always the same one, the dead King Mandros looking at him accusingly. *Murderer*, the man called him.

It was not murder.

And always the accusations about Nathair, blaming him for Aquilus' death. He rubbed the sleep from his eyes.

Nathair's tent was situated in the shelter of a wooded cove, towards the paddocks and pen that had been erected for Nathair's draig. *Not close enough to smell it though, thank Elyon*, thought Veradis.

It was early, so he was surprised to find the tent empty, although two Jehar still stood guard outside it.

'Where is the King?' Veradis asked, but they gave no response. Veradis began to pace, thinking of where Nathair could be, when the King of Tenebral appeared, Sumur walking a few paces behind him.

'You're up early,' Veradis said as Nathair ushered him into his tent. Nathair just grunted something unintelligible.

'Something important?'

'Yes,' Nathair said.

Veradis looked at him inquiringly.

'I've just come from Rhin's tent,' Nathair said.

'It must be urgent for her to summon you so early.'

Nathair stared at Veradis. He looked embarrassed. 'I've been in her tent all night, Veradis.'

'Oh.' A silence fell between them. *That's disgusting.*

'We were toasting our alliance,' Nathair said, rubbing his temples. 'And one thing led to another. She can be very persuasive.'

'You don't need to explain to me,' Veradis said quickly.

Nathair looked up, blushing. 'I'm never drinking that mead again. I don't even like it.'

'Never mind,' Veradis said. 'As you're fond of saying, I'm sure it was for the greater good.'

Nathair laughed, a little sheepishly, Veradis thought.

'What was it you wanted to see me about?' Nathair asked.

'I wanted to talk to you about things that have been on my mind.'

'Sit, then,' Nathair said, reclining and gesturing Veradis to a chair. 'What things?'

Now that it came to it, Veradis was unsure. There were few specifics; it was more of a general feeling, a sense of foreboding that had settled upon him, ever since the battle in Forn Forest.

'I'm worried,' Veradis said.

'Go on.'

Veradis looked at Sumur, a silent shadow behind Nathair's shoulder.

'Sumur, wait for me outside.'

Sumur did not move.

'Veradis is my oldest friend. My most loyal companion. There is more chance of my mother assassinating me than of Veradis turning against me. Please – outside.'

Sumur left quietly, looking back once at Veradis.

'You can trust Sumur,' Nathair said, 'but sometimes I long for the old days, before my father . . .' he trailed off, his hand searching out the draig's tooth about his neck. Veradis instinctively touched the tooth in his own sword hilt.

'Aye,' Veradis agreed. 'Everything seemed simpler then. You, I, your warband on a noble cause.'

'It is still a noble cause, Veradis.'

'I know that, up here,' Veradis tapped his head. 'But sometimes it does not feel it.'

'Go on.'

'In Forn, things were done. By Calidus. Betrayals. What you and I would once have called dark deeds. Dishonourable.'

'You speak of Romar?'

'In part.'

'Romar was setting himself up in opposition to me. Becoming my enemy. In the coming war realms will either join me or fight me. There will be no middle ground.' He looked enquiringly at Veradis. 'Do you know what happened in the catacombs beneath Haldis?'

'Only that Romar went in and never came out again. And that Calidus and Alcyon were part of that.' *And that my friend Kastell died as a result.* He remembered Maquin's words to him – *be careful whose side you choose.*

'I see. Calidus has told me that Romar took the starstone axe, refused to give it up. He would have used it against me, and we have both heard of its power. That could not be allowed.'

Veradis sighed. *Maybe. But it still does not feel right.*

'There is more you have to say.' It was not a question.

'Jael. I do not like him. You have told me to leave the politicking to Calidus, which I am more than happy to do, believe me . . .'

'But?'

'Aye. But, his choices in allies.' He shook his head.

Nathair leaned back in his chair, nodding. Something in his face changed then – a glimmer of Veradis' friend before the weight of kingship and prophecy had fallen upon him.

'I agree with you. Have worried over these issues – and many others besides – for countless nights. But let me tell you that every single time I come back to the same point: Calidus is one of the Ben-Elim, a servant of Elyon. We both *saw him change.* I will never forget it. There are other arguments, convincing arguments – the alliance is fragile, and at present I do not hold the power to forge an empire. I hope that will change, but until it does, the future is the alliance and politics, and politics is compromise. I do not like Jael, I do not approve of some of the things that have been done to further my cause, but they have all been done for the greater good.'

The greater good – how many times have I told myself that?

Nathair paused and smiled. 'I can see from your face that you have had the same thoughts. And they would be troubling indeed, if we did not have Calidus. Remember what we saw in Telassar; remember what we witnessed. He is a servant of Elyon. It is that memory that strengthens my will, that keeps me on my course. Let it do the same for you.'

He did remember, could still feel the shock, the awe of seeing Calidus transform before his eyes from an old man into a winged warrior. 'It does,' Veradis said. 'I just . . .'

'I know. War places a burden on us all, Veradis. The lives we have taken or ordered taken in the furtherance of our cause. The choices made.'

Veradis had no words for that, his thoughts spiralling.

'Thank you, my friend,' Nathair said, leaning forward and gripping Veradis' wrist.

'For what?'

'For being honest. There is no one in all the earth that I can talk to as freely as you. Talking helps, eh? Crystallizes the problems and solutions.'

'Aye.' And it had helped, talking to Nathair. Discovering that his friend shared the same doubts and worries eased the sense of foreboding that had haunted him for so long.

'So let us continue our war, in the knowledge that our cause is just and our goal vital.'

'Aye, onwards.'

Veradis stood on a shingle ridge that overlooked the bay at Dun Carreg. The Vin Thalun transport ships were almost loaded, over three thousand warriors filling their decks. There was not room enough to take all in one crossing, so the ships would have to return for the rest of them. It would not take long – a day's journey to the shores of Cambren, a day to unload, and a day back. It would still be much quicker than walking.

The call came for him to board. Most of his men were already on the ships, only a handful standing with him. They walked down the ridge onto the beach, along a wooden pier towards a wide boarding-plank, his new boots thudding heavily. They would take some getting used to, and his men were already grumbling, but they would save lives. Beside him walked Bos, and next to him one of Evnis' warriors, a young lad, Rafe, from Dun Carreg. Calidus had asked Evnis for someone who would recognize this Corban if ever they met him. Cywen walked next to him, her hands bound, and it was obvious there was little love lost between the pair of them. But at least she hadn't tried to kill him yet. Or anyone else.

Veradis put that down to the fact that he'd offered her the now-healed horse she seemed to care so much about, in return for her good behaviour, and he had even committed to bringing it with them to Cambren. It was no great inconvenience, as she would need a mount to ride. She had actually smiled at him when he had offered it to her, and he had asked only in return that she stop trying to escape, which she had attempted four times in the first day and night after Owain's defeat. It was tiring, always keeping an eye on her, or making sure that someone with wits enough not to be fooled by her was watching her. Her fine mood had lasted until this morning, when she had discovered that Morcant was staying in Ardan as Evnis' battlechief. Now she was sullen and brooding, no doubt devising imaginative ways to carve more holes into Morcant's hide.

'It's not going to happen,' Veradis said to her as they walked up the boarding-plank. 'You should let it go.'

She knew instantly what he was talking about. 'He killed the man I was to be handbound to,' she said. 'I'll never let it go.'

Veradis believed her. *I'm glad I have not wronged her*, he thought. *I would not sleep well at night.*

They stood at the railing and looked back as the fleet slowly moved out of the bay, banks of oars sweeping into the water. Veradis could make out Rhin on the ridge he had recently been standing on. Conall stood close to her, Evnis and Morcant a little further along.

Farewell, Ardan, he thought, and deliberately turned to look ahead, through the ranks of sailors, masts and ropes to the open sea beyond the bay.

And now to Cambren; to more bloodshed in the name of righteousness, to claim my destiny as the most trusted servant of Elyon's Bright Star.

CHAPTER FIFTY-FIVE

FIDELE

Fidele followed Ektor down the staircase, torchlight shining off the balding patch on the crown of his head. He was leading her into the tower at Ripa, down to the library in the depths of the tower's foundations. It was quiet, almost stifling, the deeper they went, with only the crackle of torches and the slap of their feet on stone breaking the silence. Orcus' footfalls were heavy behind her.

Eventually Ektor stopped before a door, fumbled with some keys and ushered Fidele inside.

It was dark. As Ektor bustled around with a candle, opening lanterns and lighting more candles, Fidele made out the outline of a bed, a table, some scattered chairs.

As the candlelight filled the room, Fidele almost gasped. The first half of the room looked like a ruin, bed sheets strewn on the floor, mouldy fruit and rotting trenchers of half-eaten food. Beyond the detritus was a marvel. The library, as Ektor called it, was one great curved stone wall with a thousand alcoves carved into it, ladders leaning against it at intervals. Box-like alcoves were dug into the wall, becoming clearer as Ektor lit more lanterns. There were regimented rows of them curling around the chamber, retreating into the shadows, all with the ends of scrolls protruding from the square holes.

It was impressive indeed. She had been looking forward to this moment, ever since Lamar and Ektor had spoken of this library during their council, but a pile of endless tasks had filled her days since then, most of them concerned with the rooting-out of the Vin Thalun fighting pits. And she had stayed in Ripa far longer than she had originally intended. The truth was that she liked it here. The sea air held a freshness that Jerolin lacked, and going home meant a return to the weight of memory. She could put it off only a little longer, though.

'Come, sit here,' Ektor said, pulling out a chair and sweeping the debris on his table into a pile.

'Do you live in here?' Fidele asked, trying to keep any hint of revulsion from her voice.

'Of course,' Ektor said. He looked at her as if the question had not been a sensible one. 'Otherwise I'd spend half my life walking to and from this room.'

'Of course. So you think there are some clues here, about the God-War, and specifically about Meical?'

'I do,' Ektor said, abruptly animated. He hurried to one of the ladders and climbed, one hand holding a lantern high. 'You must remember, of course, that everything written here was done so by the Kurgan, so there will surely be a degree of bias, and therefore of in-accuracy, in all that they wrote, but nevertheless also a large portion of truth.'

'The Kurgan were the giant clan that ruled here?'

'Yes. One of the five clans that survived the Scourging,' Ektor said distractedly. 'When our ancestors, the Exiles, were washed up on these shores there were five giant clans still in power. The Kurgan here, ruling in the south, the Jotun in the north, the Benothi in the west, the Shekam in the east, and the Hunen in the central regions – where Helveth, Carnutan and Forn are situated now.'

Ektor returned with a bundle of scrolls under his arm, the first one he rolled out being a map. 'You see,' he said, pointing, 'here is Ripa; the Kurgan ruled this area.' He traced a line with a finger.

Fidele nodded, intrigued by the map, seeing Ripa, Jerolin, Forn Forest, other names she was familiar with, and many she was not.

'The Kurgan wrote much about their history, and that is mostly what fills this room, and most of that is after the Scourging, detail-ing their clan wars, day-to-day life; much of it would be quite tedious to you.'

'I can imagine. Have you read every scroll in here?'

'Yes, at least once. There are so many, though, that some I have forgotten by now. It may take some time to locate what I need. There is one scroll in particular that I remember; I thought it more philosophical than historical at the time I read it, but now . . .'

'Well, let's make a start with what you have now, shall we?'

'Yes, yes.' He flicked through his armful of scrolls, then paused at one. 'This isn't the one I was speaking of, but I'm sure . . .' He opened it, eyes flicking across the archaic script, then paused. 'Here it is. A reference to Halvor. He is the giant that you mentioned, and that Nathair spoke of when he came here; the writer of your prophecy. Listen. *We have rebuilt Balara, but Taur and Haldis are lost to us. The Hunen hold them now, and Drassil, though they will never find it, not if Halvor spoke true.* It is talking about the contestation of borders between the Kurgan and the Hunen, I think. Halvor is mentioned a few times throughout their histories, or the Voice, as they refer to him in other passages. Apparently he was counsellor to the first giant King, Skald. Somehow this Halvor survived the Scourging and ended up in Drassil, the giant city that is said to lie in the heart of Forn Forest.'

'Counsellor to the first giant king, and yet alive after the Scourging. That is a long life to live,' Fidele said. 'This is the difficulty I have,' she continued, 'discerning where truth ends and faery tale begins. I believe in much that has been spoken of – Elyon and Asroth, the God-War – I have seen too much not to believe. But some of these things – they just cannot be true, surely?'

'The giants often talk of long life,' Ektor said, a rare enthusiasm sparking in his demeanour. 'If the histories and tales are true then all that lived on this earth were immortal once – giants and mankind alike – until Elyon ripped our immortality from us as judgement for the first murder – the giant King Skald, slain by his brother, Dagda. But even then, after that, there are many references to giants especially that have lived extraordinarily long lives. Nemain is written of somewhere here.' He thumbed through scrolls, a silence stretching.

'If you remember it well enough, you don't have to find every reference,' Fidele said, growing impatient.

'All right then,' Ektor said, putting the scrolls down. 'In the later scrolls, written – from what I can deduce – just before our kin the Exiles arrived on these shores, Nemain is written of, spoken of as Queen of the Benothi, the giant clan that held sway in the west until we Exiles took it from them, though their remnants still rule in the far north-east.'

'What of it?'

'Nemain was Queen to Skald, the first King. Measures of time are a little unreliable, but by anyone's counting that was over two thousand years ago.'

'It must be a different Nemain to the one ruling today, then, surely. An honorific?'

'The giants don't do that. They would never take another's name; they think they'd be cursed.'

'But that is just impossible.'

'You would think so,' Ektor said.

'Well, then surely it is just mistakes in the scrolls,' Fidele said.

'Textual inconsistencies are remarkably rare in the giants' histories; they were quite particular.'

He paused, studying Fidele, as if considering whether she was capable of understanding.

Or worthy of hearing, she thought.

He nodded to himself and resumed talking.

'But if we are digging through the mysteries of our past, and giving weight to the argument that myths we previously considered to be faery tale, or elaboration at least, could possibly – in fact likely – be true, then we *must* consider the Seven Treasures.'

'Yes. Aquilus mentioned them to me,' Fidele said, trying to remember the specifics of their conversation. 'Some of them were weapons, yes?'

'That is correct,' Ektor said, beaming like a tutor at a favourite pupil.

'Aquilus spoke of trying to find them, to use in the God-War. He had set Meical to the task.'

'Ah, well, whether that is good or bad we have yet to discover. But the Treasures, yes. In a way, I think they were all eventually used as weapons, even if that was not the purpose they were fashioned for. They were carved from the starstone, you see; a star that fell to earth, the tales say, through Asroth's design. Each of the Treasures held different properties, or power. One of them, the cup or chalice, if you drank from it you were given unnaturally long life.'

He looked at her expectantly.

'So that would explain some giants living far longer than others, such as this Nemain,' Fidele said.

'Exactly.'

'What else did the Treasures do? What are they capable of?'

'Well, there were the axe, spear and dagger, all fashioned after the War of Treasures began – they were obviously weapons, no real powers but they'd never blunt, never break. Also there was a cauldron – to eat from it would cure ill health. The cup would lengthen your life and increase your natural state – make you stronger, faster and so on. There was also a necklace. I cannot remember what that could do, or the torc. I shall have to return to my studies.' He looked longingly over his shoulders at the rows of scrolls in their compartments.

'But not right now, Ektor,' Fidele said.

'No, no. I shall do that later.'

'Was there anything else that these Treasures could do?'

'Well actually their main design, or Asroth's main intention, was said to be that they made the veil between the Otherworld and our world . . . thin. Asroth desired to break through this veil and become flesh. Obviously it was not as simple as that – I would imagine that it would need willing parties on both sides of the veil, spells, sacrifice, other unpleasant things. That of course is when Elyon stepped in and decided enough was enough.'

'Yes, I know that tale well enough,' Fidele said with a wave of her hand.

She drew in a long, thoughtful breath. *So much to learn, so much to understand.* But somehow, deep in her bones, she knew this was important. She felt excited by this, and a little scared as well.

'You are a treasure yourself, Ektor; there is much value in what is inside your head.'

Ektor blinked at her. 'Thank you,' he said, blushing.

'Now, shall we talk about Meical, and what you think relates to him.'

'Yes, of course,' Ektor said. He went back to his bundle of scrolls, now strewn across the table. He picked one up, examined an inscription and then put it down, moving on to the next one. Fidele noticed the tip of his tongue protruding from his mouth.

'Here it is,' he said at last. 'When I first read it I paid it little mind, as it seemed a philosophical work, and my interests lean towards the histories. Also it is quite maudlin – the giants were – I imagine still are – a melancholy bunch, but who can blame them, I suppose, after the tragedies they have survived: death, humiliation, defeat, near-extinction, loss of lands, more death . . .'

'Ektor, you're rambling now. As much as I would love to stay here for the next moon, I am queen and have other tasks that I must see to. Please, back to Meical.'

'Yes. Sorry. There were some phrases in this scroll that sparked a memory, particularly when my father questioned Nathair about this Meical. So.' He spread the scroll on the table, finger tracing a line as he read. 'Here it begins: *We make war, we bleed, we gain, we build, but for what purpose? If Halvor spoke true then it is meaningless. It is all meaningless.*' He looked up at her. 'You see what I mean: melancholy.'

She nodded trying to stay patient.

'*Halvor says the end-days are coming – but what will they end? An era, a life, all life? When the white wyrms spread from their nest, and the Treasures stir from their rest, he says, but the wyrms are sleeping, dust covered, perhaps dead, and the Treasures are scattered, spread.*'

'Those words in the middle of that – wyrms' nests and the Treasures at rest – they are familiar to me. Meical spoke them, read them, at Aquilus' council.'

'Did he? Good, then we can be almost certain that this is referring directly to Halvor's writing, then. There is more here, though, I am sure – scattered amongst the melancholia.'

'*And what of the Firstborn? Where are they now? In the end-days they shall tread this earth, Halvor says, the Faithful and the Fallen, strange-eyed men clothed in flesh and bone, one Ben-Elim, the other dread Kadoshim. One Lightbearer's servant, Black Heart, Spider that spins the web, high king's counsel, one guide of the Hundred, Outcast, messenger of dread.*' He looked at her thoughtfully. 'And what to make of that,' he mused.

'It just sounds confusing to me, like one of the riddles my father used to ponder over. The Lightbearer part sounds good, though,' Fidele said, her brow furrowing.

'A riddle: yes, that is exactly what it is. A two-thousand-year-old riddle. Messenger of dread. Black Heart. Outcast. Spider that spins the web. Are any of these terms that you are familiar with?'

'Only Black Heart – that is mentioned elsewhere in the prophecy,' Fidele said.

'High king's counsel,' Ektor mused. 'Aquilus was high king, and Meical his counsellor . . .'

He was. Uneasiness gripped Fidele, another thought splintering in her mind. *And Nathair is high king now, with a counsellor of his own.* She felt abruptly anxious, a seed of fear expanding rapidly until she felt short of breath. 'I must go,' she mumbled as she rose unsteadily, feeling the weight of stone all about her, suffocating her. 'Solve these riddles for me,' she gasped, grasping a hand to her chest, and rushed for the door.

CHAPTER FIFTY-SIX

CAMLIN

Camlin walked along the giants' road, its stone slabs cutting a line through green fields. He was near the rear of their company, which had been swollen by the addition of Rath's warriors.

Hard men they were, of that he had no doubt. There was something about them that reminded him of Braith and his old company of woodsmen living off the land and their wits. But, unlike his previous band of outlaws, there was an honour in what these men did, putting their lives on the line to keep the roads safe and free from the giant spawn. Almost a ten-night they'd spent in each other's company, since the battle with the giants and wolven in the mountains. Their pace had been steady, but not fast, as most of Edana's company were on foot. Still, they were safe now, had been for a ten-night, or a measure of safety at least, as much as could be expected anywhere in these Banished Lands.

He looked up; the sky was blue, the sun warm on his face, clinging to the end of summer. It was a good day, in more ways than one, so why did he have this sensation creeping over him, a hollow uneasiness taking shape in the depths of his gut?

Perhaps it's vanity, he thought, knowing that he felt a growing sense of disappointment since they had crossed the border into Domhain, a sense of being no longer needed. He had guided this company, led them from danger to safety. And that had felt good, he could not deny it. *You are of no use to them any more. They are no different from the rest you've dipped your head to – Braith, Casalu – all out for their own gain, using you until you've nothing left to give. Just watch, you'll be forgotten about soon enough.*

He felt himself frowning. Sometimes he really didn't like the voice in his head.

Dath was walking beside him now, using his yew bow as a walking stick. Camlin noticed that the youth was watching him, following his gaze to the warriors on horseback in front of them.

'That one there's Baird, you know,' Dath said to him, nodding at the back of the one-eyed warrior. After Rath he was the most famous, or infamous, of this bunch, and even Camlin had heard many tales told about the man whilst sitting around campfires in the Darkwood. The most common one told of how Baird's hold had been raided by giants, back when he had been a lord of Domhain. His wife, bairns and shieldmen had been put to the sword, and he'd been left for dead, his hold burning around him. He had been found the next day, close to death, and taken in by a neighbour. Slowly Baird had been nursed back to health – the tales told – and as soon as he was able, he had borrowed a horse and ridden into the mist that hung over Benoth, land of the giants. No one had expected to see him again.

A ten-night later Baird had ridden out of the mist, back into Domhain. Half a dozen giant heads were tied to his saddle pommel, and he had a new scar on his face, the one that had taken his eye. Apparently he had never spoken of what had happened in the mist.

'I know,' Camlin said. 'I've heard the stories too.' He smiled at Dath's awestruck face, and felt a pang of jealousy at the same time. He'd become used to seeing that look in Dath's eyes when the lad was looking at him.

Don't be an idiot.

Baird was trying to calm his horse, which kept shying from Storm. Camlin felt a swell of protective anger. Storm had been the subject of more than a few suspicious glances over the last handful of days. Not that he could begrudge these warriors their glances. He was part of a strange bunch, warriors, wolven, a dethroned queen and two talking birds. Craf had flown off early, but the other one still had its wing bandaged, and was sitting on Edana's saddle pommel croaking quietly to Edana. After a few days of silence it had warmed to the girl, and now seemed to be in constant conversation with her. The other thing that drew the attention of their new companions was Gar. At first he had gone unnoticed, other than his unusual sword drawing a few glances. That had all changed the next morning when he had put Corban through his forms. He'd drawn a crowd then, sure enough. Gar was a mystery, his technique and skill with the blade earning him an instant respect amongst this band of warriors. *They have not heard the half of it, though. All that he said about the God-War, and Corban.* Camlin had not known what to think at that revelation and had chosen not to dwell on it. Something like that, if it was the truth, well, there'd be no keeping it hidden. If Gar was a mad man – and really that was the only other option – let him keep his hallucinations and fantasies. As long as it meant that he and Camlin fought on the same side, all was well and good. Corban had earned himself not a little respect after his training, as well; Camlin had even caught Coralen watching him with something like admiration in her eye. Not that she hadn't had her own fair share of attention from others in Camlin's company, Dath and Farrell especially. Each in turn had tried to impress her in his own clumsy way, though Farrell had been most persistent. He'd eventually come away with his ears glowing, though. The girl's tongue was as sharp as the knife she'd used to cut that giant's throat.

Camlin sniffed, catching the smell of decay seeping from the packages Corban and his friends were carrying – the skins they had carved from the dead wolven in the glade. Corban had been determined to take them, though he had been vague about the reasons. Brina rode a horse close by. She sat slumped in the saddle, like a sail with no wind in it. The life had seemed to have gone out of her with the death of old Heb. *I liked the old codger, shame he's gone.* The death of someone close always did things to a person – grief, regret, anger, all left their mark. A lesson he'd learned all too well back in his youth, when he'd watched his mam and brother butchered by raiders. With an effort he pushed the memories away.

He heard a sound behind, faint, blending with the sigh of the wind in the grass. He turned and looked back along the giants' road, seeing a dark smudge in the distance. Dath hovered with him. It was a horse and wain, gradually gaining on them; something walked alongside it – a hound?

'Dath, run ahead and let them know we've got company.'

Dath sprinted along the column, returning soon with Marrock and Rath behind him. They studied the wain, which was clearer now, seemingly driven by a solitary man. It was close to highsun when the wain caught up with them and Rath called a halt, some of the riders taking their horses down a steep embankment to a stream.

The wain's driver slowed, a wiry man with sharp eyes who was obviously wary of such a body of grim-looking warriors filling the road. His wain was piled high, a patchwork of skins tied over whatever was underneath. Not that long ago it would have been a tempting sight to Camlin and the type of men he used to mix with.

Camlin looked closer and realized he recognized this man – a trader who had passed through the Darkwood more than once. He was one of those that had come to an arrangement with Braith and paid a toll rather than be robbed and left for dead.

One of the practical ones.

The man saw something on the road that made him yank on his reins: the wolven, Camlin realized. His hound was crouching low, hackles raised. Then Corban was approaching the wain.

'Ventos, is that you?'

The trader frowned, then jumped from his seat, smiling. He snapped a command at his hound and met Corban in the road. They clasped wrists and spoke to each other like old friends, any tension that there had been draining from the air.

Corban introduced the man to them as Ventos, a trader whom he knew. Camlin kept his head down; for some reason he did not want the man to see him.

He probably won't recognize me, but just in case . . .

Camlin did not even quite understand why that would bother him, but it did. *Maybe I want no association with my past. I am a different man, now.*

They shared some bread with the trader, his hound lying beneath the wain, watching Storm suspiciously through the spokes of a wheel. Soon after, the man was back in his bench seat and urging his sturdy, thick-boned horse on.

'Remember,' Rath called out to him. 'Not a word of us to anyone. If we get to Dun Taras and anyone seems forewarned, I'll know who to come looking for.'

'No chance of that,' Ventos called back, and soon he was blurring into the horizon.

Shortly afterwards a band of riders appeared on the road ahead, coming towards them; Rath approached them and exchanged some words with them. They were only a handful, four or five, and wearing cloaks of the same woollen checks as Rath and his comrades. Camlin kept one eye on them as he sipped from his water skin, his other hand resting on the pouch where he kept his bowstrings safe from the damp. *I am a mistrustful soul*, he thought, then shrugged to himself. *Old habits die hard, and besides, it's better to be mistrustful and live a little longer, in my book.*

Rath returned to them and spoke to Edana. 'We are close to Dun Taras now; they were Eremon's men from the fortress. I've sent them on their way, though. I still have some influence here – amongst the warriors, at least.'

'My thanks,' said Halion.

'I trust your judgement, Rath. Whatever you think best,' Edana said.

Camlin had heard this situation discussed already. Rath suggested that if surprise could be engineered it would be best. That way they would stand a good chance that their first meeting with Eremon would be free of Roisin, his young wife. She had been mentioned around the campfire after their first night of travelling with Rath. Apparently she was growing in influence and ambition in Domhain, Eremon becoming more content to listen to her counsel. 'It's not the best time to have returned to us, Halion. You're da is fading and she is on the rise,' Rath had said.

'I had little choice in the matter,' Halion had replied. 'And it is Edana's safety that I'm thinking of, not my own.'

'She'll be safe enough; don't worry about that,' Rath had said.

'And so will you be, brother, or I'll have Roisin's scalp for a trophy,' Coralen had snapped. Camlin had smiled at that. *Fiery little thing.*

It had not been so much of a worry to Camlin when they had been sitting around a campfire, a ten-night away from this Roisin. Now, though, Camlin felt a creeping anxiety take root in him.

As they rode on, Edana dropped back, Marrock and Halion walking beside her.

'I wanted to talk to you,' she said, looking seriously at Camlin.

'What about, my lady?' Camlin said. *Those words still don't fit well on my tongue.*

'You have served me well, during our journey here.'

He looked up at her, not really knowing what to say. 'The way I've seen it, the task has been t'stay alive,'

'Yes, it has. But you would have had an easier time of that if you'd just walked away.'

He blinked at her. *Have I been talking in my sleep? Thinking out loud?*

'But you did not. You stayed and guided me, advised me, fought for me. Risked your life, time and again, when you need not have done so. Can I ask you: why?'

He was caught by surprise, stunned. *Same question I've been asking myself since we landed in Cambren.* 'I don't know,' he mumbled.

Marrock snorted laughter. 'You see, he is more honest than you may be prepared for.'

'Honest? I'm a thief from the Darkwood – not been called honest since, well, never.'

Marrock laughed again, Edana and Halion joining in.

I suppose I'm still here, with you all, because I want to be,' he said, only realizing at that moment that it was the truth. He looked about, at Dath and Corban and the others. 'I like being here – not here as in Domhain, but here.' He waved a hand and flushed. 'With you all.'

Edana smiled at him then, warm and genuine. 'That is what I thought,' she said. Her expression changed, became serious. 'And I want you to know this, Camlin. I may not have a kingdom, or wealth, but I am a queen, and I mean to win back what is rightfully mine. If—'

'When,' Marrock interrupted.

'*When* I do that,' Edana continued, 'I will not forget those who have helped me and, more than that, been loyal to me, through the dark times, when death looked like the only road, when winning a kingdom was the furthest thing from my thoughts.' She smiled again. 'If I ever sit a throne again, you shall have no need to return to thieving in the Darkwood, I promise you.'

He shrugged. 'We'll cross that bridge of thorns when we get to it, eh?'

'Indeed. But for now, we have moved from one danger, but only to slide into another one, I fear, one more sly and devious. An ambitious woman. We must keep our wits about us. Our eyes and ears open. And where we are going you may be more practised at doing that unnoticed. I would ask you to learn what you can of this Roisin and her followers when we reach Dun Taras. It may well save our lives.'

'I will do all that I can, my lady.'

She reached down and squeezed his shoulder. 'I do not doubt that.'

Rath called out from the front of their column. 'Dun Taras. Dun Taras is in sight.'

Edana kicked her heels against her horse and rode to the front. Halion followed as quickly as he could on foot, Marrock lingering.

Camlin looked at the warrior's arm, where a bandage covered the stump of his wrist.

'How is it?' Camlin asked him.

Marrock raised his left arm, gazing at the stump.

'It itches,' he said. 'Or at least, it feels like my fingers itch. And they're not there.'

'I've heard similar said before. Comrade of mine lost an ear, but was always trying to scratch it.'

'I'll live,' Marrock said, 'though it's hard getting used to the idea I'll never draw a bow again.' He shrugged. 'I'm alive, so I'll not complain.' He looked hard at Camlin then. 'I'm grateful to you, Camlin, for all that you've done. Edana's right: we'd not be here if not for you.'

Camlin walked along in silence as they crested a rise in the road, the grey walls of Dun Taras appearing in the distance. He did not pay too much mind to it; he was too busy smiling.

CHAPTER FIFTY-SEVEN

MAQUIN

Maquin pulled on his oar. He had lost track of time, had no idea how many nights had passed since Dun Kellen had fallen and he had been herded onto this ship. A ten-night? Twenty? It had merged into one long, hellish slog, each day the same: kicked awake at dawn, sitting and pulling on the oar, hour after hour, all marked by the constant beating of a rower's drum, the only marker of time that seeped into his awareness. He'd thought he was fit and strong, with a warrior's stamina that could last all day on the battlefield, and recently he had done just that, but nothing had prepared him for this. The muscles in his back and shoulders, neck and arms burned, felt as if they were ripping, tearing apart with each stroke of the oar. And his hands – they were bandaged now, the palms crusted with oozing blood and pus where they had blistered and burst and blistered again. His wrists were the same, the skin and flesh worn by the ill-fitting chains that bound him to the other rowers on his bench. Each day would end with the coming of night, a bowl of something closer to vomit than food, and then sleep – instant, exhausted, dreamless sleep.

He had picked up the technique of rowing well enough – he'd pulled an oar a few times with the Gadrai, along the dark tree-shrouded waters of the Rhenus. He'd done better than others, anyway. Some of them were dead now, unable to master the technique, whipped until their backs were a shredded mess; some the fever took, others just collapsed with exhaustion. Regardless, they all went the same way, tipped unceremoniously over the side and fed to the river.

Orgull was still alive, a few benches in front of him. He was not in good shape, though. The warrior with the ruined nose made a point of visiting Orgull each day, giving him a taste of a whip or cudgel. One time he clubbed Orgull unconscious, then had him dragged down the centre isle and doused with a few buckets of water, then clubbed some more. Orgull took the torture in silence, his only response being to stare at his tormentor, which seemed to incite the man to greater acts of violence. Maquin was surprised even Orgull could survive the beatings he was taking, and manage the torture of rowing every waking hour.

Part of him just wanted to lay down his oar, to tell these pirates to go to hell, and smile as they sent him across the bridge of swords; part of him would welcome that. But there was a stubbornness in him that refused to quit, that refused to admit the battle was over. And one thought above all others kept him going. Jael. Each day he remembered the smile on Jael's face as Maquin had been dragged onto the ship, remembered the man's mocking laughter drifting after him. He fantasized about killing Jael, quickly, slowly, painfully, every conceivable way, and those thoughts stoked the fire in him, kept him pulling, league after league after league.

A shadow fell across him and looking up he saw Lykos, his captor and the leader of these corsairs staring down at him, arms folded across his chest. His face was unreadable, a sharp intellect dancing in his eyes. The pirate captain regarded him a long while.

'You still live, then,' Lykos said. Maquin was unsure whether it was a statement or a question.

'Clearly,' Maquin said, focusing on his rowing.

'I mean in here,' Lykos said, tapping Maquin's chest. 'The death wish is on you, I can see it plainly, but there is more to you than that – something deeper. A will to live.'

Maquin said nothing.

'Most of your comrades with the death wish, they've gone over the side, food for fish by now. Yet you're still here.'

Maquin shrugged.

'I'm glad of that, my friend.'

'I'm not your friend,' Maquin said, unable to keep the passion from his voice. 'And why do you care?'

'No, you are right: you are not my *friend*. You are my *property*,' Lykos said, grinning, his teeth white and straight. 'And I would not say that I care. But I am interested. You may be useful to me.'

'Isn't pulling an oar for you use enough?' Maquin asked.

'I've something more entertaining in mind.'

'What?'

Lykos grinned again, clapping Maquin on the shoulder. 'We'll talk again, when we're home. If you're still alive.'

As the days merged, Maquin began to judge the passage of time by the changing of the landscape around them. The rolling hills of Dun Kellen were far behind now, the horizon opening up into a flat vista, trees disappearing, replaced by tall, thick banks of reed and dense walls of scrub, punctuated by spindly sycamore and willow. Every evening was defined by great clouds of mosquitoes, and every morning Maquin would wake with a multitude of itching bites.

One morning their fleet landed against the silt-edged riverbank and they were all herded onto the spongy ground. A level of shock seeped through Maquin's exhaustion and confusion as the corsairs began dragging their ships onto land, using thick, tar-crusted ropes. The ships came onto land surprisingly easily – they were sleek and shallow-draughted – and once out of the water the corsairs fetched the long timbers that they used as masts or kept as spares against storm damage. Maquin watched with growing understanding as the masts were placed under the prows of the boats and they were dragged further onto land, then the second mast put in place, and the third, the first one fetched from the rear and carried around to the front, beginning the process all over again. It was quite a sight, thirty ships being pulled across the land, all in a row.

Then orders were yelled and the whips started snapping, and he and his fellow captives were set to work, some put on the ropes to drag the boats across the land, others to do the running with the makeshift rollers. More than one man on that task ended up crushed under a ship's keel. They crossed countless leagues of fenland, the ground flat and treacherous. After a day of this, Maquin was praying to return to rowing; a whole different set of muscles was feeling close to failure. Also his feet were quickly soaked through, and by the second evening felt as if they had swollen to twice their normal size.

On the third day they reached another body of water, only a little wider than a stream. They followed its course and within half a day it had widened into a river. Soon after, the fleet of ships was dragged back into water, Maquin collapsing for a few instants' rest. Something bumped into him and he turned, looking up into Orgull's bruised and swollen face.

'Be strong, brother,' Orgull whispered as he brushed past, being herded back onto their ship. Maquin did not have the strength or wits to respond, then Orgull was gone, trudging up a wide plank.

It took a while to get everyone back on the ships, into their places at the benches. Maquin used the brief moments of rest to empty his boots of water, then the oar drum was beating again and Maquin was back to the rhythm of pull, lift, stretch, dip, pull, over and over.

They rowed through leagues of swamp and fen, the smell of rotting vegetation mingling with the odours of the ship – of tar and timber, but mostly sweating men. Slowly the landscape around them changed, the river broadening as they reached the edges of marshland. The land became greener and soon Maquin saw trees again. A day after that and they were entering woodland, trees growing thick and dense upon the riverbanks, branches almost blotting out the sky, reminiscent of Forn, though not so ancient, not so daunting. A tennight later the river curled out of the forest; a wooden fortress sat on a hill to the north. People watched them pass, warriors ranked upon the fortress walls arrayed in black and gold. They passed under a stone bridge that would have smashed their masts to splinters if they had been raised. Soon, the river widened into an estuary and Maquin heard the call of gulls. Now the masts were raised, great sails of cloth bound with strips of leather were unfurled and billowed as the ships met the swell of the sea. The beat of the drum increased and Maquin's ship felt as if it was cutting a line through the waves, almost flying.

That first night on the ocean Lykos and his corsairs set a fire burning in a cauldron, with metal rods resting in the flames. Lykos soon approached Maquin, who was still chained to the oar and bench. Lykos was holding a rod of iron, a swirling design at its tip glowing white hot. With one hand and a knee, Lykos pinned Maquin down and pressed the rod into Maquin's back, just behind his shoulder. There was a sizzling sound and the sudden smell of burning flesh. Maquin stifled a scream, struggling as pain lanced through him, but he was weak to the point of collapse, and Lykos had an iron strength in his frame.

'Never doubt that you are mine, old wolf,' Lykos whispered as he branded Maquin, the blood trickling hot and wet down his back. 'I have marked you now, as my slave. You belong to me. This mark is part of you now, as am I, until death.'

'Your death,' Maquin snarled, jerking violently as Lykos released the pressure from his back.

'That's the spirit,' Lykos laughed and cuffed him across the head.

The next day Maquin was shivering, his body burning. He was still led to his station at the oar, forced to row. The fever took him, giving him wild hallucinations. Gerda's head on a spike, twisting to look at him, berating him for failing her son. Kastell, his body pale, bloodless, sitting on the chair in the burial chamber beneath Haldis. *You failed me*, Kastell said to him, and Maquin wept, even as he rowed. He vomited, rowed through it, the stink of it turning his stomach, causing him to vomit once more, but he did not stop rowing. He knew if he faltered, if he stopped, he would be heaved over the ship's rail. Some days he felt close to embracing that end, felt he had not the strength to pull one more stroke, but something kept him pulling. Jael. The thought of him was a burning coal in his gut, a cleansing pain, a beacon in an otherwise dark, fog-shrouded world. Rage kept him alive through those days, when others all about him surrendered to exhaustion and hopelessness and died. It was a cold white rage, burning, holding the emptiness of submission at bay, forcing a strength into his muscle and sinew that had otherwise long since departed.

Slowly the climate changed. Maquin knew that they must be moving towards autumn, but somehow it did not get colder; the opposite – it felt warmer, the sun brighter, the sea bluer. Some days he would see dolphins swimming parallel to the ship, racing it, sea spray sparkling like gems as they arced out of the water.

Always ahead of him he saw the broad back of Orgull, the benches thinning around him as men died, but Orgull was always there.

Time passed and the heat of Maquin's anger began to dim, the flame fading; the thought of Jael seemed to lose its power, and a day came when Maquin could not even conjure up the man's face in his mind. Dispair closed in upon him; the knowledge that this was the sum of his existence, to pull an oar for the rest of his life, drained him of will and purpose. The only counter to this was that, slowly, a little each day, he felt his strength returning to him, a new power in his back and arms and grip, a physicality that he thought had deserted him. He welcomed it through the long days, nurtured it, prayed that he would have an opportunity to use it, even if only against Lykos, or any one of his captors. A last burst of defiance before the end came.

The next day, before highsun, Maquin spied a shape on the horizon – first a dark line, rapidly solidifying, growing quickly larger. Land. Rocky coves soon loomed close, waves smashing against high cliffs. The fleet followed the coastline until it reached a bay. Horn blasts echoed on the cliffs that surrounded it. Maquin's ship moored up to a long quay that stretched out into the water, the other ships in the fleet dropping anchor in deeper waters. It was not long before Maquin and the others were herded from the ship, shuffling down the gangplank and onto a beach of white sand. Maquin and Orgull sat together, no words to say to each other, or no strength to say them.

In time, Lykos' shieldman with the mangled nose, Deinon, approached and, unshackling Maquin, dragged him to Lykos. The sea shimmered turquoise behind the corsair.

Now is my chance, thought Maquin. His eyes flickered to Deinon, a thick-muscled man, each striated cord defined and shifting under his skin as he moved.

'Don't do it,' Lykos said, a hardness in his voice. 'It will be the last thing you do.'

Maquin's fingers twitched but he resisted the urge. *Small chance if I took them by surprise, none with them ready.*

'I wanted to talk to you.'

Maquin stared sullenly at the corsair.

'You are the only survivor from Dun Kellen I took for myself who has survived the voyage. True, I did not claim many – I am a generous man and shared your sword-brothers amongst my crew. But still, for you to survive the journey only to be cut down now would be a shame.'

They stared at each other a while, Lykos crossing his arms, fingers twisting the silver ring about his bicep.

'I am leaving, almost immediately, and you will be staying here,' Lykos said.

'Where is here?'

'Panos, one of the Three Islands. My home.'

'And where are you going?'

'Away. That is not your concern. But what I want to tell you is that I do not want to find you dead when I return. The death wish wars within you, I can see it still. It has not consumed you yet, but hopelessness feeds it. You feel you have nothing left, nothing to live for, yes?'

'Yes.'

'You are mistaken. Deinon here was in your position once. He earned his freedom.'

'Really?' Maquin looked Deinon up and down. 'Then why is he still here?'

'I offered him a place as my shieldman. He chose to stay. Others have not – some leave, some stay and work my crew, some are now captains of their own ships.'

'How?'

'By fighting for me.'

'I'll not be a corsair for you – robbing, burning, murdering.'

'Corsair is too good for you.' Lykos snorted. 'I am not asking anything of you,' he continued. 'I am not bargaining or negotiating. I am telling you the facts. One day soon you shall be thrown into a pit. Others will be thrown in also. Only one will come out alive.' He shrugged. 'You will be that man, or you will not. It is up to you.'

'Pit-fighting,' Maquin said, twisting his lips as if the phrase tasted sour. 'I'll not be your slave warrior, spilling others' blood to earn you gold.'

'That is up to you,' Lykos said. He turned to walk away, then paused and looked back over his shoulder. 'But I saw how you looked at Jael. A rare hatred you have there. I am giving you a chance – admittedly a very small one, but nevertheless it is a chance – to walk away from here, to find Jael and take your vengeance.'

He walked away then, called back as he left.

'All you have to do is fight – and win.'

CHAPTER FIFTY-EIGHT

CYWEN

Cywen was riding in a sprawling column. Behind her Rhin's warband stretched all the way to the sea, the slate-grey waters merging with the horizon. The ships they had arrived on were just a mass of small dots bobbing upon the white-flecked waves. A little way ahead of her Nathair rode atop his lumbering draig, its head low to the ground, tail swaying from side to side. Beyond him Rhin's warriors marched northward into undulating foothills.

Cywen leaned forward in her saddle and ran her hand down Shield's shoulder, her fingers searching out the smooth circle of scar tissue. It was all that was left of the horse's arrow wound. From his movement you would never know he had been injured at all.

Those Jehar are gifted – cursed but gifted, she thought, looking about instinctively to catch a glance of them. *Amazing riders*. She had been shocked to see that so many of them were women, and remembered them on the night Dun Carreg had fallen, how she had thrown knife after knife at them, seen the way they fought. She remembered their leader, Sumur, asking her questions about Gar. *Why is he so interested in Gar?*

Surrounding Nathair was a circle of the Jehar, all mounted, a substantial space between them and the draig. She had seen Nathair feeding it earlier, but it seemed very fond of horse, so the Jehar were wise to keep their distance.

The rest of the Jehar, and there were many of them, thousands, Cywen had noted, were riding out on the wings of this disordered column, appearing fleetingly between rolling hills and stretches of woodland. No one was likely to ambush Rhin's warband in Cambren, her own realm, but the Jehar, apparently, were not inclined to leave such things to chance.

The sound of hooves grew behind her, out of time with the rest of them – faster. It was Veradis, the giant with the black axe striding easily next to him. Veradis pulled up beside her and glanced at her wrists. They bore red marks where she had been bound, though the ropes were cut now.

'Bos, is she behaving?' he asked the warrior who rode close to Cywen, her guard since the night she had tried to kill Morcant. He was a big man, bald though young and not as dim as she had first thought.

'So far,' Bos said. 'Biding her time, maybe.' He said it with the flicker of a smile.

'Can you be trusted to not cause any trouble?' Veradis asked her.

'There's a sea between me and Morcant now,' she said, scowling. She had hated seeing him standing on the beach at Dun Carreg – her home – as she had sailed away. Just another thing to put on the long list of *wrong* in her recent past.

'I know. But now that he's not here for you to obsess over, I am thinking you might turn your attentions onto someone else.'

'Starting to regret cutting my bonds?'

'A little. Should I?'

'I hate you all,' she said with conviction, 'but there's no one here I'd pick out above the rest to try and kill.'

The giant chuckled at that, a rumbling sound, like stones rattling down a hill.

'Except perhaps Rhin,' she added. *Or Nathair. He played a part in opening Stonegate to Owain.*

'What about that lad, Rafe? I've seen the way you look at him. I think you might be tempted to try sticking a knife in him. I can't have that.'

Is it that obvious? 'It's fair to say I don't like him, but he's not worth being tied all the way to wherever we are going. Domhain, I am guessing.'

'You guess right. I think perhaps I should bind your wrists again.'

'Please, no,' Cywen said with feeling.

Veradis looked at her long and hard. 'I'm going to trust you, against my better judgement, and leave you unbound. For now.'

'My thanks. I will not cause any more trouble. Besides, if that friend of yours – Calidus?'

'Aye.'

'If he was right, then I am moving closer to my family – to Corban at least.' She chewed her lip. 'How could Calidus tell that Corban was across the water, in Cambren, just by touching Ban's old smith's apron?' *If you don't ask, you don't get.*

'I don't know,' Veradis said uncomfortably. 'He is . . . gifted.'

The giant snorted. Veradis looked at him.

'That was nothing compared to what he can do,' the giant said. 'If Calidus had a lock of hair, he could do much more.'

'Like what?' Veradis said.

The giant shook his head. 'Better that you do not know,' he muttered.

'It's all right,' Veradis warned with a smile. 'Best not let Calidus close with a knife, then, lest he take a lock of your hair.'

'He already has some of mine,' the giant said. Something crossed his face, sadness, anger? He slowed down and dropped behind Cywen and Veradis.

'What does he mean by that?' Cywen asked. Veradis didn't answer; he was looking over at the giant, a troubled expression on his face.

Slowly the warband crept through the densely green and fertile countryside of Cambren. The landscape was beautiful: sweeping hills of meadows filled with wildflowers, sparkling streams and dark, still lakes. Much of the land was covered in swathes of dense woodland, the leaves turning to red and gold as the days passed.

Cywen's guards were always close by, mainly Bos, although Veradis also spent much of his time riding alongside her. So there was never any opportunity for her to attempt an escape. Her two guards were far more vigilant than Conall had ever been. It was frustrating. When their duties took them elsewhere – such as each morning when Veradis would spar and drill his warband before the day's marching began – Cywen would be bound hand and foot and left to watch them going about their training. She had seen Veradis spar against Conall, back in Dun Carreg, but he seemed different now: faster, more aggressive. She doubted that he would draw against Conall if they faced each other again.

Part of her resentfully enjoyed the journey. It was a joy to be upon Shield's back. She could feel the power of him; he was quick to follow any command and he was a part of Corban, somehow, as Buddai was a part of her da. One night she was sitting in front of a crackling fire with Bos and a handful of eagle-guards, a thousand similar tiny beacons in the darkness clustered all around. Buddai was curled at her feet, gnawing on a bone that Bos had thrown him, when Veradis appeared out of the darkness and sat with them. Bos passed him a skin of mead.

'What news?' Bos asked.

'A band of Rhin's warriors joined us today,' Veradis said, 'come from the north. They brought a strange tale. It's probably not worth the telling – just superstitious faery tales.' He paused and drank from the skin of mead.

'Just tell us,' Bos said. 'We'll hear it anyway, soon enough.'

'True enough,' Veradis said. 'All right then, they said they had chased a small group across these very hills, thought they were spies of Owain. Said they ran with wolven, that they were attacked at night with tooth and claw.'

There was a silence then, a twig popping in the fire making Cywen jump.

'Wolven don't run with men,' someone said.

'Changelings,' another whispered.

'What happened?' Cywen said, feeling a shiver of excitement, of kindled hope.

'They caught up with them in the mountains that border Domhain,' Veradis said, waving his hand into the darkness. 'They said they'd cornered them, were leading a final attack, and then they were set upon. By more wolven; a pack of them.'

'How many of Rhin's men were tracking these people?' Bos asked.

'Fifty of Rhin's warriors, or thereabouts. Only three have returned.'

'What about the ones they were chasing? How many of them survived?' Cywen asked, trying to sound only mildly interested.

'From the sound of it no one was counting – they were too busy running.' Veradis shrugged. 'I don't believe the half of it,' he continued, 'we all know how tales grow in the telling. Perhaps there's a stone of truth at the heart of it. When we reach the mountains we'll have a look at the place where this is supposed to have happened. See what we see.'

'It's nothing to worry about, anyway,' Bos said. 'Not for us. We've faced worse than wolven. Draig-slayers and giant-killers, we are.'

'That we are,' Veradis said. His hand dropped to the hilt of his sword and absently stroked it. 'I'll drink to that.'

Cheers and laughter rang out, all of them lifting skins of mead.

Cywen had stopped listening, only one thought swirling around her mind. *Storm*, she thought. *It must have been Storm and Corban.*

Rain dripped off Cywen's nose. It had been raining since she woke, a soft, gentle drizzle that slowly seeped into everything, and now it was highsun, though it was hard to judge from the faint glow leaking through the low clouds. She was soaked through. A mist shrouded the land, reducing visibility to a score of paces all around. Veradis and the giant were on one side of her, Bos the other. She was not really paying them any attention, or the rain for that matter. She was consumed by a bubbling excitement mixed with worry, last night's conversation still fresh in her mind. *Storm, Corban, Mam, Gar, somewhere out there, and – best of all – these people, her enemy, were taking her to them. But were they still alive?*

'Why is your King so interested in Ban?' she asked suddenly.

'Eh?' said Veradis, looking at her sharply.

'Ban – Corban, my brother. Why is *he* the subject of a king's attention?'

'I am not going to discuss Nathair's thoughts with you,' Veradis said. 'He is the High King of the Banished Lands.'

'So?' Cywen said. 'He's not my King, high or otherwise, and Ban's my brother. What does he want with him?'

'Tell me about your brother,' Veradis said, and she noticed the giant walk a little closer.

'Ban? What's there to tell? He can work in the forge – our da was a blacksmith; he asks more questions than there are answers. He's annoying. He could beat even you with a sword, given half the chance.'

Bos laughed at that. *So everyone's listening now.*

'He can make a poultice and cure an illness, he is loyal to the point of stupidity, his friends love him, I love him . . .' She felt sudden hot tears blur her vision. *I've never told Ban that. Why am I telling Veradis?* She looked at the warrior beside her and felt a sudden swell of suspicion – *Is he trying to trick me? To give something away about Ban?* – but he was looking at her so openly, no deceit or cunning written upon his face. *He is not so old himself, and first-sword to a king. Such responsibility for one so young.* She felt her misgiving melt and sighed. 'He's just *Ban*. My brother.'

Veradis nodded thoughtfully.

A mounted figure suddenly appeared – Calidus. He spoke quietly to Veradis and the giant, then turned and rode away, back into the mist.

Veradis and Bos followed after him, Bos snapping a short command back to Cywen to keep up with them.

'What's going on?' Cywen asked.

He ignored her and rode after Veradis and the giant, a group of warriors peeling from the warband to join him. Cywen touched her heels to Shield and cantered after them.

Calidus stood beside Nathair on his draig with a handful of the Jehar surrounding them, and Rhin, accompanied by Conall, watching close by. They were all looking in the same direction. Then Cywen saw something out in the mist as three big figures appeared, wrapped in fur and leather. Giants. She saw some of the eagle-guard reach for their weapons.

'Hold,' Nathair snapped, raising a hand.

The giants came nearer, approaching Rhin and Nathair. Their leader held a long spear, whilst one of the two behind had an axe slung across his back. With shock Cywen realized that the third one was female, although really the only difference was that she did not have a long, drooping moustache like the other two. Cywen glanced between these newcomers and the giant with Veradis, saw that he regarded these arrivals with narrow eyes, ridges furrowing his broad forehead.

Then Rhin spoke.

'Greetings, Uthas of the Benothi; you and your kin are welcome here.'

CHAPTER FIFTY-NINE

TUKUL

Tukul the Jehar blinked as he looked up. Light was breaking through the canopy above, more than he had seen in many moons.

They were almost out of Forn.

Meical's arrival at Drassil and its resulting lurch into action had lit a spark in his slumbering heart: tension, excitement growing, the promise of resolution to a lifetime of waiting.

It felt strange, but he had grown fond of Drassil, and even of Forn Forest, and the thought of leaving, of moving into a world of open spaces and a sky that went on forever felt almost uncomfortable. He laughed at himself – this from a man who had been raised in an oasis in the desert.

He put the thoughts aside and marched on, following the tall frame of Meical, while inwardly complaining at the stiffness in his knees. *The damp. I hate the damp here. All else I can cope with, but the damp . . .*

Behind him wound the long line of his sword-brothers and sisters, walking their holy pilgrimage in the name of All-Father Elyon. His, theirs, was a life of worship, devoted to the absent god. Soon it would become a pilgrimage drenched in blood, of that he had no doubt. The culmination of generations of devotion, of discipline.

I hope you are taking note of this, All-Father. Surely you watch, even if you no longer intervene. All I have done, my whole life, has been in the hope that you watch. That you would notice me.

They had left Drassil two days after Meical's arrival and had made much quicker going of it than Meical's journey into Forn. The central task at Drassil had been preparing the old fortress for what was to come: repairing it, making it defensible. During their explorations

340

of the stronghold throughout the years tunnels had been discovered, initially bored by the roots of the giant tree, then extended by the giants. They ran for leagues upon leagues beneath the tangle of Forn, and they had made good use of one such tunnel to bring them close to the forest's edge. He looked up to the heavens again, blinded for an instant by the glow seeping through the branches high above.

The trees about them now were spread widely, great-trunked monsters that stretched their roots wide, drinking deep of the earth. Soon they came to a space where trees had been felled, the round bases of the trunks white and leaking sap. Tukul ran his fingers over one – they came away sticky.

People. Tree-fellers, loggers. We are moving into another world indeed.

They moved through a field of stumps, came upon a wide river, roughly trimmed trunks stacked along the riverbank, the odd pier that struck out into the river's black waters, but no sign of people. *Yet.*

Meical paused and waited for him.

'We are nearly there,' he said. 'We are moving into Gramm's land now. You remember him?'

'I do,' Tukul said. On their journey into Forn – *fourteen, fifteen years ago?* – Meical had led them to a hold built close to the outskirts of the forest. It had belonged to a man, Gramm. He had had a wife and two sons, youthful but old enough for some labour, and was full of boldness and dreams, his plan back then to trade timber along the river and to breed horses. By the looks of things he had made good on the timber trading, at least, and carved a life for himself out here, on the edge of the wild.

'He'd better have looked after my horses,' Tukul said.

'You'll see soon enough,' Meical said.

They marched on, and in short time Tukul heard the sound of hooves on turf. Instinctively, his hand reached for the hilt of his sword, and without looking he knew his sword-kin were doing the same, all three score and ten of them. The Hundred, they were called, though they did not number that now. But a hundred had ridden out from Telassar all those long years ago, straight-backed and zealous.

Riders appeared, at least a dozen of them, dressed for war in mail shirts, with helmets and long-hafted spears couched at their saddles, most with axes strapped to their backs.

Axes – awkward, clumsy weapons.

The riders saw Tukul and his companions and cantered towards them, one of their number peeling away and heading back the way they had come.

'They are shieldmen of Gramm's,' Meical said, 'scouting his lands.'

'They look like more than scouts to me,' Tukul said.

'Their land is bordered by Forn Forest to the east, and the Desolation to the north. Nowhere is safe in these Banished Lands, but here least of all.' Nevertheless Meical frowned as the riders approached, his own hand straying to the hilt of his sword.

As they approached, the riders gripped their spears, bringing them lower. *Not committed to the charge yet, but prepared for it.* Tukul felt a detached respect flicker to life. Their horses were bred for war, tall, big-boned yet with a rare grace to them, long, thick manes streaming, some plaited with leather.

The first rider raised his spear, and reined in his mount before Meical. He took his helmet off and hung it from his saddle, his men lining up behind him.

'Well met, Meical. Father said to look for you.'

Meical stepped forward and gripped the rider's wrist. 'And you have found me, Wulf. Well met.'

'And your companions – they have the look of those who were with you, all those years ago.'

'You have a good memory, Wulf – you were only a bairn.'

'Eleven summers – and I'll never forget the day I saw you all. The horses!'

'Are you riding my horses?' Tukul asked, stepping forward.

'Not yours exactly,' Wulf said, turning his gaze upon Tukul. 'But bred from them. My father says he had your permission.'

'Aye, that's true,' Tukul said, moving towards him, holding his hand out for Wulf's mount to smell, murmuring softly as he ran fingers down the animal's muscled chest. 'Your father has done well.'

'You are not the only one who thinks so. Our horses are sought by many, both north and south,' Wulf said, sitting straighter.

'Come,' Meical said. 'I'll be happier talking horse trade with a cup in my hand and my backside in a comfortable seat. We've walked a long way.'

'Of course,' Wulf said. 'We shall escort you home.'

With that they set off, the riders spreading around them, a protective hand.

My sword-kin need no protection, Tukul thought, but he liked the gesture. It was good manners.

'You are always ready for danger, here on the edge of the northlands,' Meical said as they walked. 'But you looked about ready to skewer us back there.'

'Aye. You will not have heard the news, I guess, coming from Forn as you have. There is war to the south. In Isiltir. War parties have been raiding from the south, sweeping further and further north – burning out holds. They won't be doing that to us.'

'War? Between whom?'

Wulf shrugged. 'We hear different things. An internal struggle for the throne. Romar is dead – in Forn, fighting the Hunen. At least, that's the tale we've heard the most. Those he left behind are fighting over his scraps.'

Meical glanced at Tukul and they shared a grim look.

So many years we've waited. Have we waited too long?

Gramm's hold was upon the crown of a low-lying hill, a tall timber wall ringing it. They approached from the south-east, walking through a series of fenced paddocks. Tukul saw a herd of horses like the ones these warriors were riding, at least a hundred strong. A thrill coursed through him at the sight and smell of them, and he shared smiles and appreciative nods with his followers. *All-Father be praised, maker of such beauty.* He wanted to stop, to watch, to ride, but knew it was not the time.

Soon.

They marched up the hill, Tukul catching a glimpse of barns and buildings clustered along the side of a wide river to the north of the hold's walls. Beyond the river stretched a wasteland, punctuated by a scattered range of mountains receding into the distance. The Desolation: a peninsula of land where the Scourging had raged hottest, so the histories read. The land was all but barren, pitted and scarred and broken from the outpouring of Elyon's wrath. Tukul paused, gazing reverently into the distance.

To see such a place, where Elyon once touched this earth.

Reluctantly he moved on and soon passed through a wide arched gateway into a busy courtyard.

Gramm had changed – he was thicker about the waist, with streaks of grey in his fair hair. His face was still open and friendly, though, something that Tukul remembered from their first meeting. Gramm greeted them, hugging Meical and Tukul, then showed them to rooms with fresh-poured steaming bowls of water.

'Wash away the dust of the road. We shall feast tonight,' he said, 'and celebrate. An auroch is being slaughtered as we speak.'

Tukul wiped grease from his chin, savouring the hot meat as he chewed. They had not starved while living in Drassil, but the journey through Forn had been long and dark, with little time for hunting and cooking. This roasted auroch tasted like the finest meal he had ever eaten.

A long hall lay at the centre of Gramm's hold, and tonight it was filled. It seemed that Gramm had done well indeed. His timber trade had made him wealthy, and he was famous for leagues round about for the quality of his horses. He had told Tukul that he had bred two lines from the horses Tukul and his warriors had left here fifteen years ago. One he'd kept pure; he said the herd numbered in its hundreds now. The other he had crossed with a hardy breed from the north, big boned and heavily muscled, bred for heavy work and lots of it. The result had been the horses Tukul had seen today, and he had to admit that he was impressed.

Gramm had been successful in other ways as well; he had introduced Tukul to more sons, daughters and grandchildren than he could possibly remember. Tukul had felt a stab of jealousy at seeing the joy that family brought this man. He had always dreamed of many sons, of laughter and the sound of running feet in his halls.

It was not to be. He sighed. He had left his only son in a strange place with a task greater than any other he could conceive. He struggled even to remember his face now. And Daria, his beloved wife, she had crossed the bridge of swords over twelve years gone. Wounded in a clash with a draig in Forn, taken by the fever a tennight later.

He lifted his cup in a silent toast. *My Daria. My son.*

All of his Jehar warriors were sitting together, taking up about half of a long table that ran down the centre of the hall. Having been so solitary, he could tell they were a little overwhelmed, to be surrounded by so many people, so much noise. While Gramm's family filled a large portion of the hall, he also had a number of other people under his roof – men and their families that worked for him, tree-felling, logging, working the barges that took timber downriver, stablehands, as well as a group of warriors, employed to protect his lands and trade. Usually they were busiest defending against raids from the north, out of the Desolation, but of late they had been busy further south, where rumour of war and raiding parties had increased the boldness of lawless men.

A handful of these warriors were gathered between Tukul's table and the rest of his Jehar. They were throwing axes at straw targets, laughing, either applauding or mocking the various attempts. Tukul was surprised to see how accurate many of them were.

'They are all handy with an axe,' Gramm said from beside him, seeing where Tukul's gaze was drawn. 'Though none can out-throw my Wulf.' He raised a cup and drank, slapping Wulf across the shoulder.

'Would you like to try?' Wulf asked.

'I like an axe well enough, when I need to cut some firewood,' replied Tukul. He heard a snort of laughter from Meical.

'An axe has more uses than that,' said Wulf stiffly. 'Especially here, where we are so close to the Desolation; there are things that come out of it that need some extra persuasion to stay dead. There's a lot more weight in an axe. If you come face to face with a war party of the Jotun you may find your sword isn't so well suited.'

'I've survived fifteen years in Forn, fought wolven, draigs, other things that don't have names, and I'm still here.' Tukul shrugged. 'But I am curious. Let me have a throw of one of these axes then.'

Wulf led him down to the gathered men, who parted to let him through.

'Here, I'll show you once,' Wulf said. 'All the weight's in the head, so you let that do the work for you.' He hefted a short-hafted axe that someone passed him, fixed his eyes on the target and threw.

The axe spun through the air, landed with a *thunk* a hair's breadth from the target's centre.

'Here,' Wulf said, passing another to Tukul.

Tukul swung the axe a couple of times, gauging its weight and balance. He took a deep breath, held it, then threw the axe.

Instinctively he knew he had thrown wrong. The axe head slammed into the target a handspan above Wulf's and bounced off, falling to the ground. Raucous laughter burst around him.

'You see the advantage of an axe,' Wulf said loudly. He was grinning. 'If you miss with the blade, you still stand a good chance of braining your enemy.' More laughter at that. Even Tukul smiled. A quick glance at his Jehar, all sitting silent and grim, told him they were not so amused.

'Another,' Tukul said, holding his hand out.

'Fair enough,' Wulf said. 'You've blackened your enemy's eye already; let's see if you can give him a matching pair.'

Tukul repeated his ritual – test the weight, fill the lungs, throw. This time he knew it was a better effort. It spun, hit with a satisfying *thunk*, the blade sinking into the straw, two fingers from Wulf's. A silence fell upon the group, then loud cheers and applause. Wulf slapped his back and Tukul grinned.

'I think I like your axes,' Tukul said to more laughter. He noticed some of his sword-kin rising and walking over – Enkara, Jalil, Hester, others behind them. *I knew they would not be able to resist.* 'Again,' he said, holding out his hand.

Just then the great doors of the hall swung open, letting a cold draught of air swirl in, making the fire flare in its pit. Figures filled the doorway, two men with spears – guards, Tukul realized – leading two others. The hall fell silent as they approached Gramm.

The two being escorted were an odd pair – a young warrior and a boy who walked beside him, not more than ten or eleven summers, Tukul guessed. The warrior rested a hand on the boy's shoulder. They were both travel stained, looked close to exhaustion, their steps unsteady. They stopped before Gramm.

'They were found on the southern border,' one of the warriors told Gramm. 'Said they've got something to say, but only to Gramm.'

'My mam said Gramm's the one I need to speak to; no one else,' the boy said, his voice reed-thin, a tremor in it.

'Is that so?' Gramm said. 'You look more in need of hot water and something in your belly than talking to me,' he added, peering at the two. 'I am Gramm, so tell me who you both are, and then let me hear what it is you have to say.'

'I am Tahir, last sword of the Gadrai,' the warrior said, standing straighter. A ripple ran through the hall at that. 'We bring news of war. Jael of Mikil has slain King Romar and claimed the throne of Isiltir.'

The boy stepped forward, pushing past Tahir's protective hand. Tukul saw the tremor in his limbs. *Fear and exhaustion combined, but he will not hide behind his protector. I like him.*

The boy raised his chin. 'I am Haelan, son of Romar and Gerda, rightful King of all Isiltir. And we have come here seeking your Sanctuary.'

CHAPTER SIXTY

CORBAN

Corban woke with a stiff back.

Strange, after my first night in a bed since . . .

He pushed the thought away, still not liking to think of his last days in Dun Carreg. Always the first memory would be of Nathair driving a sword through his da's chest. With a sigh he climbed to his feet and picked his way towards the kitchen, the stone floor cold.

They had arrived at Dun Taras yesterday. Halion, Edana and Marrock were taken almost immediately to an audience with King Eremon, while the rest of them had waited in a secluded courtyard and gardens. That had been after they had managed to get through the gates of Dun Taras, which had almost not happened. The guards had taken a very dim view of allowing a wolven to walk into the fortress. Craf flying up to the battlements and hurling insults at them hadn't helped matters much, either. But eventually Rath had over-ruled the captain. Word spread about them quickly enough; a crowd of children followed them, as well as a fair few adults, most of them pointing at Storm, not Edana.

The meeting between Edana and King Eremon had gone well, according to Halion, though Edana had not looked so convinced. They had been housed in a large stone dwelling on the outskirts of the fortress, where it was easier for Storm to stay with them. Edana had been offered chambers in the keep, but she'd chosen to stay with 'her people', as she was referring to her small band of companions.

Dawn was close, pale light leaking through a shuttered window in the kitchen. The bulk of Farrell was a dense shadow sitting near the glowing hearth. Corban pulled a chair over and joined him, warming his hands. Soon Corban heard the pad of feet and Dath came to join them. The three of them sat in silence a while, watching the embers in the fire.

'Does it get easier?' Farrell said, his voice harsh in the silence.

Corban sighed, instantly knowing what Farrell was talking about. He missed his da too. They'd all lost their fathers to battle in just a few moons.

'A little,' he said. 'At first it felt as if I had a hole inside me, an empty space that hurt more than any wound. Just to think of him would take my breath from my body.' He looked at Farrell and Dath. 'But with everything that's happened since we left Dun Carreg – the possibility of dying each and every day. It's been distracting.'

Dath snorted an agreement.

'Not that you forget,' Corban continued. 'I'll never forget.' In his mind he was suddenly back in Dun Carreg's feast-hall, smoke and screaming thick about him, watching Nathair sink his sword into his da's body. A rush of emotion swelled within him, almost a physical pain, a fist gripping and twisting his heart.

'All that talk about your da,' Dath said, looking at Farrell. 'About him being a coward.'

Farrell looked at him, eyes narrowing.

Anwarth, Farrell's da, had been shieldman to Ardan's old battle-chief. In some conflict or other Anwarth had been accused of cowardice, of playing dead while his chief had been slain. Nothing had ever been proven, but accusations like that, they never went away.

'I don't believe it,' Dath said. 'He volunteered to stay with Marrock, knowing that to stay meant to die. And I saw him in the battle. He was no coward.'

Farrell reached out and squeezed Dath's shoulder.

'Ouch,' said Dath.

'Your da was no coward, either. He tried to storm that boat all on his own.'

'He did, didn't he?' Dath said. He looked at his hands, his face crumpling. Tears spilt down his cheeks.

'He loved you, you know, Dath,' Corban whispered.

'Did he so? Why was he always hitting me, then?'

'I don't know,' Corban shrugged.

'I'd hit you if I were your da,' Farrell said.

'I'm a coward,' Dath said quietly, almost to himself.

'What?'

'Every day, every battle, I'm scared. More than that, terrified. It grips me, freezes me.'

'Fear hasn't hurt your aim much,' Farrell said.

'All men feel fear,' Corban said. 'Gar told me that. It's what you do about it – stand or run, fight or give up – that's what makes you a coward or hero. Without fear there is no courage.'

'In that case you're no coward,' Farrell said.

'Does that make me a hero?' Dath said with a weak smile.

'I'd rather my da be a coward and still be here,' Farrell said.

They sat in silence some more; Corban had no answer for that.

'Talking of Gar and heroes,' Dath said. 'What's all this about you being, you know, the *seven disgraces*, or whatever it was.'

'Seren Disglair,' Corban corrected with a grimace. Life had been too filled with danger and imminent death for him to think much on Gar's claims. Now that things had changed, though, and a measure of safety restored to them, he found his thoughts constantly return-ing to Gar's words. Both his mam and Gar were sure that something would happen, that he would change his mind.

Not likely. I don't want to be some Bright Star, fighting the Dark Sun. I've seen enough of war and death for a lifetime.

'Yes. So when did you become the saviour of the Banished Lands, then?'

'Shut up,' Corban said. 'It's not funny.'

'Gar doesn't think it's funny,' Farrell said. 'He seemed to take it seriously, and he strikes me as a serious man. Never seen him smile, even.'

'Just because he's serious, doesn't mean he's *right*,' Corban said with a frown.

'What's he on about, then?' Dath asked.

'He's just made a mistake, that's all.' Corban shrugged. 'You're best off paying him no mind.'

'There must be more to it than that,' Farrell persisted. 'Look at how he fights, his sword, those warriors back at Dun Carreg like him – the one guarding Nathair that he fought, and the others.'

Corban shifted uncomfortably. *Those are thoughts I've had myself.*

Gar is no fool, and until recently not someone I'd consider mad. 'Anyone can make a mistake,' he said. 'Let's leave it at that.'

The other two gave him sidelong glances, but they said no more about it.

'One thing that you can't just leave lying about is your stinking bag of wolven pelts,' Dath said, wrinkling his nose and pointing at a large sack.

'I know. I need to ask Halion's help in finding a good tanner.'

'What do you want them for?' Dath asked him.

'Just an idea. I'll say no more about it yet.'

Corban blocked Gar's practice sword, flicked it away, used the momentum to form his own lunge, saw Gar shift to block his blow. He pivoted on his feet, spinning, ducking Gar's weapon as it whistled over his head and swung at Gar's ankles.

Gar jumped over his practice blade, struck at Corban's head, but Corban was rolling forwards, using the force of his failed swing to carry him out of the way. He came up onto his feet, sword gripped two-handed over his head, and launched a fast combination at Gar – two chops to the head, one lunge to the heart, another short chop to the ribs, a swing and lunge at thigh and groin. All of them were blocked. He felt sweat trickling down his forehead, sensed shadows around him, still and watching, his eyes flickering to them for a heartbeat. And then somehow Gar was inside his guard, the practice blade at his throat.

'You lost focus,' Gar said as Corban stepped away. 'Until then. Good.'

Good. That was the fastest I've ever moved, the longest I've kept you from killing me. Corban smiled ruefully and wiped the sweat from his face. He glanced about, saw warriors all around the practice court watching them. That had been happening a lot since they'd arrived at Dun Taras. Rath was there, with some of his giant-killers, including the girl, Coralen. She wasn't looking at him or Gar, though. Nearby were Dath and Farrell, standing with Marrock and Camlin. The woodsman was strapping a buckler to Marrock's injured arm.

'Stop looking at girls and raise your sword,' Gar snapped at him.

'I wasn't,' Corban objected, then had no more time or breath to complain.

When they had finished sparring, Gar put Corban through the sword dance. Corban loved the routine of it; it was a time when his mind became still and calm, and he could forget for a short while the turmoil and upheaval that defined almost every other waking moment.

When he was finished and about to put his practice sword back in the basket he felt a tap on his shoulder. He turned to see Coralen standing there.

'Don't put it back,' she said and stepped back into a space on the grass. She raised her own practice sword and waited. In her other hand she had a wooden replica of a knife. *She fights like Conall, then.*

'What?' said Corban.

'Don't keep her waiting, she'll only beat you worse,' someone yelled, to a burst of laughter. Corban thought it was Baird, Rath's warrior with the scar.

'Come on, then,' Coralen said, spinning her blade in a slow arc.

Frowning, Corban stepped back onto the grass and lifted his wooden sword. *Stooping falcon*, the standard first position. In a blink Coralen was lunging forwards, her blade coming from unusual angles, moving faster than Corban had expected. Her wooden knife left a red welt across one arm. *She uses it like a wolven uses claws.* That set an idea growing. *One that I must talk to Farrell about.* Another blow slipped through his guard.

Focus, you idiot, he scolded himself. *You saw her slay a giant. She's fast, and deadly.* He stepped back, seeking time to regroup, but she did not allow it, following him, striking high and low. He managed to block it all, though clumsily, then began to fight back. They moved backwards and forwards over the grass, the clack of their blades marking a sporadic beat. Time passed, Corban losing all track, getting lost in the block and strike, his body and brain working faster together, overriding his thoughts, employing the responses that only uncounted hours of practice could instill.

Then he saw an opening, his blade sweeping forward before he'd had time to think about it, his body following, stepping close into her guard. Somehow she turned his blade and they slammed together, blade to blade, chest to chest. He could smell her breath, sweet, a hint of apple on it. He blinked, then somehow her foot was behind his ankle and he was falling, the air knocked from his lungs as he hit the ground. Her blade touched his throat and she smiled.

He frowned, remembering seeing Conall execute an almost identical move on Marrock back in Dun Carreg. 'You cheated,' he muttered.

She grabbed his wrist and helped him up. 'And you're still dead,' she grinned.

He blushed as he looked around, saw a crowd watching them, Dath and Farrell amongst them. Gar shook his head, his lips twitching in a brief smile. Halion strode over. *Come to rescue me, I hope.*

'Come on,' Halion said to him. 'We've to meet Queen Edana. Da . . . the King wants to see you.'

'Me?' said Corban. 'Why?'

'Because he's been hearing tales about the young warrior that tamed a wolven. He wants to meet you. Come on.'

'She's not tame,' Corban muttered as he left the practice court, shoving his weapon into a wicker basket.

They had been in Dun Taras over a ten-night now. Edana had been back to see Eremon five or six times since her first meeting with him, but there was still no definite answer from the King about his commitment to aiding her cause. Also the King's wife, Roisin, had been present at the meetings, and according to Halion she was more poisonous than he remembered her.

Storm uncurled herself and fell in by Corban's side as they left the weapons court and walked through the streets of Dun Taras. It wasn't so different from Dun Carreg, the streets as wide, paved with huge flagstones, the grey keep looming above everything. The rock was darker here, and there was no sound of the sea, though, no calling of gulls, no salt on the air.

'Your sister, Coralen, she doesn't fight fair,' Corban said, a throbbing in his back reminding him of their sword-crossing.

'No. She's good, though.' Halion grinned at him.

'She put me on my back easy enough. Reminded me of Conall, though with a sharper tongue.'

Halion looked sad at that. 'Aye. She spent a lot of time with Conall, growing up. He was always the one she looked up to. She's not as hard as she pretends, though.'

'I'd have to disagree. Did you see her kill that giant back in the hills?'

'I mean on the inside. She's grown up around men, been around warriors her whole life. Her mam abandoned her when she was young, and Rath took her into his hold, but that is a place for warriors, not bairns.' Halion shrugged. 'That's all she's ever known.'

Hard on the outside, soft on the inside. A list of her cutting comments came to mind. *I'm not seeing it.*

'Where's Edana?' Corban asked Halion.

'She's already with the King – and it's Queen Edana, remember. If her own people can't give her due respect, neither will the folk of Domhain.'

'Sorry,' Corban mumbled. It was not that he didn't respect Edana as his queen; of course he did; it was just that she was his friend, too. He understood Halion's logic, though.

'A word of warning, Corban. Be wary of Roisin. She is proud, cunning, jealous. Her son Lorcan is heir to the throne, and protecting his claim is her one ambition. Think before every word that you say to her. Also, because my father is old, do not think his wits have deserted him. He has a sharp mind when he is not distracted, and he still likes looking at the women.'

'He is still the same, then, as you remember him?'

'Much the same, though diminished. More cautious. This meeting with you could help – my da is a complicated man, part of him a thinker, part of him spontaneous, wild in his youth, I am told. He can be ruled by his heart, as with Roisin. He likes Edana, I can tell, partly because she is young and female, true, but he likes her spirit, I think. She is no longer the meek sheltered child that she was. And you and your wolven – there is a magic in your story, our story, the escape from Dun Carreg and through Cambren to here. It appeals to my father. That could be helpful in the end. We need his help. And if we are right, Rhin will probably be turning her covetous glance this way soon enough.'

'It doesn't sound very safe here for Edana,' Corban said.

'No. But where is safer? Ardan, where she would have been hunted by Owain, or Cambren, where Rhin rules? I trust Da where Edana is concerned. He knew Brenin and respected him. I am sure he will treat Edana well.'

'Would this Roisin do anything to Edana?'

'I'll not let her,' Halion said. 'I swore an oath, to Brenin and Edana. I could not save Brenin, but I'll die before I see any harm come to his daughter.'

Looking at Halion's expression Corban did not doubt him.

Soon they were in King Eremon's chambers, situated in the lower levels of Dun Taras' tower. Apparently he had given up his rooms at the top of the tower a long time ago, because he didn't like the long climb.

It was a large room, a fire burning in a hearth against one wall holding back the autumn chill. Eremon was sitting upon a fur-wreathed chair, his hair white, his skin waxy and loose. His eyes were still young, though, sea grey, like Halion's. They lingered upon Corban, then dropped to Storm.

'Ah, the wolven tamer, at last. Stories of you are spreading about my keep faster than the west wind,' Eremon said.

Corban walked forward and dropped to one knee, bowing his head.

'Rise,' Eremon said.

'My Queen,' Corban said to Edana as he stood, seeing her seated on a smaller chair close to the King. She gave him a warm smile. Fech the raven was perched on the arm of her chair. A jet-haired woman sat at Eremon's other side.

Roisin.

With her lips a deep red in a face as pale as alabaster she was beautiful, and Corban's eyes were drawn to her as he bowed.

'I have heard much about you and your wolven,' Eremon said. He held his hand out to Storm.

'Careful,' Roisin said.

'Hush, woman,' Eremon said irritably. 'I've two hands, and I only need one to scratch my arse with.' He looked back to Storm.

'Friend,' Corban whispered, and Storm padded forwards. She seemed bigger, now that she was indoors, tall enough to look the seated King in the eye. Her long canines glinted in the firelight. She took a long sniff of Eremon's palm, her amber eyes regarding him. Then she went to Edana and nudged the Queen's leg with her muzzle. Edana ran her fingers through the thick fur about Storm's neck. The wolven flopped down at her feet.

Eremon was watching her keenly. 'Amazing. She is quite relaxed, and knows you well, Edana.'

'Of course. We are pack,' Edana said.

'Come then, Corban,' Eremon said. 'Tell me how this came to be. I imagine it's quite the tale.'

Corban sat at Eremon's feet and recounted his tale, of finding Storm's mother in the Baglun, then saving Storm as a pup. Eremon called for a chair to be brought forward for Corban as the tale wound on to when Corban had given Storm up, after she had wounded Rafe, and how she had followed him to Narvon, how she had helped track Edana through the Darkwood, and on until they had reached the mountains between Cambren and Domhain. When he was finished Eremon sat there a while in silence.

'What a tale,' Eremon eventually said. 'How old are you?'

'Nearly seventeen summers, my lord,' Corban said.

'Nearly.' Eremon grinned. 'I remember wishing my years away. As you get older you start wishing for the opposite. Or at least for a time when you didn't have to wake to use the pot half a dozen times a night.'

Corban didn't know what to say to that. He found himself liking Eremon.

'Quite the tale,' Eremon repeated, 'at any age. Made all the more so by its truth. I don't know you, but I know Halion well enough to be an honest man, and Queen Edana of course vouches for your tale's accuracy. Remarkable.'

'I have never given any thought to it, my lord,' Corban said. 'It just happened.'

'And I bet it gets you a lot of attention from the ladies.' Eremon winked.

Corban felt himself blushing at that.

'You are very lucky, Edana, to have such devoted – and unique – protectors about you,' said Roisin, speaking for the first time. Her voice had a lilting quality, almost musical.

'Yes, I am,' Edana said. 'Corban is part of the reason that I am still alive. As is Halion. When I have regained my kingdom they shall both be rewarded for their loyalty. As will any who support me in my quest for justice.'

Eremon smiled slyly at that, but said nothing.

'You must be thirsty, Corban, after all that talking,' Roisin said, clapping her hands. Servants brought a table and filled it with cups, jugs, an assortment of foods: fruits, cold meats, cheese and dark bread.

'You are Eremon's kin, and he will do what he can to help you,' Roisin assured Edana. 'But we need to have all of the facts at our disposal first. Then we can make an informed decision of what is the best course of action for Domhain.'

'But I have told you the facts,' Edana said, an edge to her voice. *This is not the first time they have had this conversation*, Corban thought.

'Owain has invaded Ardan, my mother and father have been betrayed and murdered. And Rhin is the puppeteer behind it all. She plans to rule the west.'

'With all due respect, those are the facts as *you* know them. But one version of events is never usually the whole truth.' Roisin turned her gaze pointedly at Halion.

'I understand that,' Edana said, 'but I am worried. Not only for me, but for you also, for Domhain. While we sit idle Rhin prepares, of that I am sure. I fear that by the time you have gathered these facts that you so desire it will be too late. Rhin will be marching an army into Domhain.'

'We thank you for your concern. But you must try and see things from our perspective. While the events in Ardan are terrible, wars do happen. And at this moment no form of aggression has been made towards Domhain, by either Owain or Rhin. So whilst we can feel sympathy for your plight, there really is no action that we can take. And also you must remember that, just as you are kin to Eremon, so are Owain and Rhin.'

Edana bowed her head. 'And if the worst happens? If I am right, and Rhin is plotting to take your crown? She does not play by the rules. She will not behave politely, or respectfully, or fairly. She will use all means at her disposal to succeed in her aim, and then you will have no kingdom to pass on to your heir. I have already seen how Rhin deals with heirs – Uthan, Owain's son was assassinated by Rhin. She has tried to kill me more than once. I imagine she would wish a similar fate upon your young prince Lorcan.'

Roisin's eyes narrowed at that.

You are learning this game of politics quickly, Corban thought.

A young girl poured drinks for them. She was fair haired, older than Corban, he guessed, but not by much. Corban saw Eremon's eyes following her, his head turning as she left. Corban saw that Roisin noticed too.

'You're leering at your daughter,' Roisin hissed.

'Is she?' Eremon said, frowning. 'Pity.'

'The possibility of Rhin invading has been considered, hasn't it, my King?' Roisin said sharply.

'Eh? Yes, it has,' Eremon said distractedly. 'As you know, as soon as you arrived, scouts were sent out to Cambren and Narvon and even Ardan. I have means of gathering information, my young Queen. We shall have the facts soon.'

'But what about Rhin? What about the danger of invasion?'

'I have alerted my barons. They will be ready. If the call to war is given, my battlechief is not to be dismissed lightly. Rath is no stranger to combat. You worry too much for one so young. You are safe, now. You must learn to relax a little. And to trust me.' He reached out and patted her hand.

Frustration flickered across Edana's face, but then it was gone.

There was a knocking at the door and a guard looked in. 'A messenger, my King.'

'Send him in,' Eremon said.

A man strode in and knelt before the King.

'Rise, and tell me your news.'

The man stood, looking about the room, his eyes growing wide at the sight of Storm. 'There are many tales spreading through Domhain about a boy and his wolven. In Cambren I heard similar tales; though bloodier.'

Boy! Corban frowned.

'You have returned from Cambren, then?' Roisin asked.

'I have, my Queen. Tales are rife, and many different. The one I heard most often is that there has been a great battle in Ardan, between Owain and Rhin. They all agreed on the outcome – that Owain is dead. And there is more. There is rumour that Rhin has gathered a great warband, and that she is marching it to Domhain.'

A look of shock and dismay swept Roisin's face, quickly masked.

In a sentence her political duelling has become a reality.

CHAPTER SIXTY-ONE

MAQUIN

Maquin sat against a wall, trying to keep as much of his body in the shade as possible. The heat in this place was unrelenting, as cruel in its own way as some of the Isiltir winters he half remembered from his childhood.

He was in a courtyard full of slaves like him. Twelve nights he'd been here, if the marks he'd made on the white-clayed walls were accurate. They were starting to blur. Orgull was not here. They had been herded from the beach where he had last spoken to Lykos, up a sandy path that wound through steep cliffs, then they'd been separated into pens like cattle, ten to a pen. Maquin and his nine companions had been led away as night was falling. He had looked back once and seen Orgull watching him.

They had not walked long, passing through white-stoned ruins and wide streets until they reached this place, a complex of buildings. They had been led into this courtyard, no words from their captors, unchained and just left.

At first he and the men he had been brought here with had stayed together. They were all survivors of Dun Kellen, a bond in a strange place. One of them he remembered from the battle on the walls, though he did not know his name. A lean, wiry man with a pock-marked face. The others in this place had greeted them with silent stares. Maquin had studied them the next morning as the sun had risen, most of them sun darkened, a mixture of ages from little more than boys to old, though he guessed that he numbered amongst the oldest.

At first their captors had returned every evening. Maquin recognized some from his first night, one especially – a wide, barrel-chested man, with an abundance of rings bound into an oily black beard. They brought with them a great trough of food. Or what passed for food. It was mostly a brackish liquid, with unidentifiable items floating in it. Their captors had handed out wooden bowls, ensuring that everyone had one, and then left. Maquin had not eaten on the first day, but by the second he was famished, and knew that abstaining would only result in him losing the strength he had gained in the latter part of his journey. So he ate. It was disgusting, but he found that if he did it quickly, and when the guards first brought the food, before it had had time to ferment in this ferocious sun, then he could manage to keep it in his stomach.

The last time they had seen their captors, or anything resembling food had been five days ago, though. The first day Maquin thought it was just a mistake. By the third he knew it was intentional. Yesterday two men had fought over a rat that had scurried across the courtyard. One man had died, and the rat had escaped. They were all weak, becoming desperate now. But why were they being starved like this? Had the corsairs just decided they did not need them, and so were just going to let them starve to death? Lykos' words from the beach still rang in his head – *One day soon you shall be thrown into a pit. Others will be thrown in also. Only one will come out alive* – and as yet he had no answer to them. All that he knew was that, at this instant, he was not ready to give up and die.

And death was in the air. Already he could tell that some of those in the courtyard were succumbing, even if they did not realize it. Forty men had been in the courtyard when he was thrown in. There were thirty-eight now.

Initially there had been an unspoken organization to the courtyard. There had been an area at one end that had become the midden heap. All had used it, and although the pile was high and stinking, constantly swarming in flies, at least the rest of the courtyard was relatively clean. Now, though, people were starting to defecate where they lay. Maquin could smell it, could see urine staining the hard-packed red earth. *Death is going to start coming more quickly.*

The sound of chains rattling in the gate brought him sharply out of his thoughts.

'On your feet,' a voice shouted, the barrel-chested man.

At first no one moved, but then other men came through the

gates. They spread about the courtyard and began hitting people with clubs.

Maquin stood, feeling lightheaded. His stomach growled and he steadied himself against the wall, putting a hand to his head. His fingers brushed the lump of flesh that was left of his ear. It had healed well enough, and he could hear as well as he ever could. At first it had felt strange, as if his head was unbalanced, but he was used to it now.

With much staggering and grumbling the men in the courtyard were formed into a line and marched out.

'Where are we going?' one man called out. Maquin heard the dull crunch of a club breaking bone.

No questions, then. I do not need to ask, though. I can guess where we are going.

They marched through streets bordered by houses of sun-dried brick, roofed with reeds. Children chased along behind them, some throwing things – bits of food, stones, sticks, until they were chased away by one of the men with clubs. The children laughed as they went, and soon reformed, like a swarm of flies.

Broken walls loomed ahead of them and they passed beneath an archway carved from white stone. More Vin Thalun stood before them with short, curved swords in their hands. They were standing guard before a wide and deep stairwell, leading steeply down, beneath the ground. Silently they moved down, the walls closing in about them, the shuffle of their feet echoing, the air thankfully cool after the unbearable heat.

Soon the stairwell opened up into an underground chamber, with large iron bowls crackling with fire attached to the walls. There were crowds down here, all gathered around holes in the ground. Big holes, and lots of them, too many to count – forty? Sixty? Many of the men about them were holding torches high.

The fighting pits.

Maquin saw other men, under guard like him, being pushed to the edge of the pits and thrown in. For a moment he thought he saw Orgull amongst them. The same thing was going on all around the chamber: groups of men thrown into different holes, crowds closing about them, bags of coin waved in the air, changing hands.

The barrel-chested man who had entered the courtyard first turned and looked at them.

'You are going into those pits. You will fight and live. Or you will die. Those of you that come out alive will feast like kings tonight.' He looked at his men and nodded. Maquin smelt the acid tang of urine as someone's bladder loosened close by.

Quickly the line of captives was divided up into smaller groups and Maquin was herded to the edge of a pit. He only had a brief chance to look down before he was shoved from behind and then he was falling. He landed on something soft, or someone, heard a crack, then a scream as he was rolling off, crouching low on his haunches, unsure what to expect. He looked about wildly, fists clenched.

The pit was too deep to climb out of, roughly circular in shape. The bowls of fire from above sent light flickering into the pit, but there were areas of shadow. Instinctively, he counted those with him. Eight other men had been thrown in, all looking about, some at him, all with the same sense of panic, wildness. Then a figure was looming over the edge of the pit, the same barrel-chested man, holding a sack.

'Nine of you in there. Four knives in this bag.' He emptied it, the knives clanging as they hit the ground.

Briefly there was silence, utter stillness. Then men were bursting into motion around him. Maquin was still frozen. *I don't want to fight. To become their entertainment.* But he did not want to die, either. He stepped back into the shadows as the screaming began.

Men were wrestling, punching, gouging, scratching. One was on his knees, screaming, hands at his stomach trying to stop his guts from spilling about his fingers. Even as Maquin watched, the man toppled to his side, his screaming fading to a mewling, his feet twitching.

Maquin became aware of yelling up above him, at the pit's rim. He glanced up, not wanting to take his eyes off the men gone mad on the pit floor. Some of the Vin Thalun had seen him hiding in the shadows, were shouting and pointing. One threw a lit torch, its flame leaving a writhing trail through the air as it fell. It landed right at his feet, sparks flaring. It sputtered but kept burning, banishing the shadows that had cloaked him.

A man in the pit saw him. He was gore spattered, a knife clutched in one hand, red to the hilt. They locked eyes and then the man was charging, knife held low.

Without thinking, Maquin snatched up the flaming torch and sidestepped as the man lunged at him. He thrust the torch out, felt a lance of pain as the knife scored along his ribs, heard a sizzle, heard the man scream as he ground the torch harder into his attacker's face.

The man's arms waved and Maquin grabbed the wrist holding the knife, pulled the torch back and swung it down. Flames caught in the man's hair and he staggered back, dropping the knife. Maquin snatched it up, saw his attacker career into another pair of men locked in combat. The three of them went down.

Something slammed into Maquin's side and he fell, a weight on top of him. Foul breath washed over him and fingers reached for his throat, his eyes. There was a sharp pain in his shoulder as the man bit him. He stabbed with the knife, felt it turn against ribs, stabbed again, lower, punching into flesh. Blood gushed hot over his fist. His attacker gasped, tried to pull away, but Maquin held him, kept striking with the knife until the struggles faded, the man going limp, a dead weight upon him.

He pushed the body off and rolled to his feet, his shoulder throbbing, his ribs feeling on fire. Something warm and wet trickled down to his waist. His own blood. He did not have time to check how bad his wounds were.

There was one other man left alive in the pit. He recognized him – the pock-marked warrior from Dun Kellen. He too held a knife, blood dripping from it. Half of his face was blood spattered.

Live or die? a voice whispered in Maquin's head. *Drop the knife. You have lost all. Keep your honour and accept death.*

The memory of a face formed in his mind, a mocking smile. *Jael.* Lykos' words from the beach returned to him. *You want your revenge? Then fight for it.* Jael's face merged with the man in front of him.

I am not ready to die.

Maquin raised his knife and moved forwards. Cheering erupted from the top of the pit, but Maquin barely registered it. He slipped to the side as his opponent stabbed, swept his own knife in, raking a red line along the man's shoulder, then they were out of each other's range, crouched, circling.

Maquin lunged, grabbing for his opponent's wrist, stabbing at the same time. The man twisted, avoiding Maquin's knife, trying to tug his wrist from Maquin's grip. They staggered about the pit, pulled apart, slammed together. Maquin headbutted him in the face. Cartilage crunched, blood spurted and the man staggered, his legs wobbling. Maquin stayed close, moving with his opponent. He head-butted him again and the man dropped to the floor. Then Maquin's knife was raking across his opponent's throat. Blood spurted and Maquin stepped back, watched the man topple and die.

More cheers came from the pit's edge.

Maquin staggered back a few steps, dropped the knife and sank to the ground. He put his head in his hands and wept.

CHAPTER SIXTY-TWO

FIDELE

Fidele walked out of the shade of Ripa's hall into the sunshine. It was autumn now, but here in the south of Tenebral summer lingered. Only a chill to the sea breeze hinted at the changing seasons. She strode down the steps and through a courtyard, beneath wide wooden gates and onto the plain beyond, her shieldman Orcus at her heels. It was here that Krelis trained his warband in the shield wall.

Men were lined up on the field, gripping their great round shields, while a small clump of men yelled orders at them. Krelis stood tall amongst them. The warriors raised their shields, interlocking them so that they became a solid wall. Other men ran and battered against the shields. A horn blast and the shield wall was moving forwards, those before it falling or giving way. Some fled to the flanks of the wall, where they renewed their assault. Another horn blast rang out and the shield wall rippled as men from the back reinforced the flanks. It worked well enough, repulsing the attackers, though something about the movement looked ragged.

She approached Krelis as horns signalled the end of the session. The rows of men in the shield wall breaking up, dissolving into individual sparring sessions.

'My lady,' Krelis said as she drew near. Peritus was there, talking with a white-haired man, Alben, the sword-master of Ripa. He was old, but had a sprightly energy about him. Fidele had spoken with him and found him to be humble and intelligent. He had even made her smile, something in short supply of late. Two younger men were there. One of them had a large tooth tied by a strip of leather about his neck. A draig's tooth. She recognized him – Maris – as having served in Nathair's warband and returned with him from his campaign to Tarbesh. *These are the two Nathair sent to teach Krelis the shield wall.*

'It looks very impressive,' she said to Krelis. 'Well done,' she added to the two behind him. 'I am sure my son will be pleased with you and the work you do here.'

The two warriors bowed.

'Their hearts are not in it,' Krelis said, looking at the field of warriors. 'This is the way men should fight. Looking into each other's eyes. Skill and courage deciding the victor. It is honourable.'

Fidele sighed. 'We've been over this. It is unlikely that Asroth, the Fallen One, will be concentrating on honour upon the battlefield. The priority is to win. I do not intend to discuss it again. I came to tell you I will be travelling to the Vin Thalun shipyards today. I will leave at highsun.'

'Are you sure that's wise?' Krelis said, a frown creasing his large head.

'Yes, I am. I will have my own honour guard with me, obviously, but I thought you might wish to accompany me. To see and hear for yourself.'

'Yes. Of course. I will be ready to ride by highsun.'

The road through the forest was dappled with sunshine, but it was cooler under the swaying branches, the smell of autumn, of decay, much stronger. Peritus rode one side of Fidele, Krelis the other, but there had been little conversation since they had left Ripa. She had too many warring thoughts swirling around her mind. Foremost of those were the hints and suggestions discovered in the underground library back at Ripa, with the help of Ektor. *He is a rare find indeed, such a mind.*

Fidele had left him in his library, determined to sift through every single one of the myriad scrolls in search of the briefest mention of Halvor's writings. Just the memory of her time there unsettled her. *One Ben-Elim, one Kadoshim walking this earth. And the reference to high king's counsel.* She felt worried, scared for Nathair, had thought of writing to him, warning him. Had even reached the point of putting quill to parchment, but the words had dried up in her mind, with any warning that she would write sounding even to her like the mad ramblings of someone struggling for their sanity.

Warning him of what? A riddle in a parchment written before our kin even set foot upon these Banished Lands. It is too unclear, the riddles bewildering. Perhaps Ektor will find more, something clearer.

Her thoughts turned to Meical – *Who is he? An ally? An enemy?* Part of her could not bring herself to believe that. She had never liked him, exactly, but there had been an honesty to him, even if it had been cold, sometimes even cruel. Something clean. *And Aquilus trusted him. Could he have been so easily fooled?* The answer to that came back quick and sharp. *Of course he could be fooled. He was murdered in his own chamber by a king that he trusted.* She pushed away the pain that threatened to rise in her at that thought.

I have more pressing concerns to focus upon.

The Vin Thalun.

What was she to do with them, now that their fighting pit had been discovered? Nathair had great plans for the Vin Thalun. She knew that much relied upon them, and yet Lykos had deliberately disobeyed her – worse, lied to her. Far worse than that: some of those she had found in the pits had been her own subjects, stolen in raids. And how many were dead?

They rode out of the shadow of the forest and soon turned south, following the river on its journey to the sea. It was not long before she saw the Vin Thalun's settlement – large storehouses and barns, a ramshackle village made mostly of timber and reed; the skeletons of half-formed ships lay along a flat sandy beach, looking like a leviathans' graveyard.

Fidele had been here before, the day after they had raided the fighting pit at the ruins of Balara. They had come with carts full of the dead: Vin Thalun who had been killed during the raid and corpses that they had found in the labyrinth of fighting pits. Fidele had questioned the leaders here. They had been sullen and denied the existence of any other pits in Tenebral. Of course Fidele did not trust them, and that was why she was back.

She kicked her horse into a canter, wanting to give the Vin Thalun as little time to react as possible. Those with her kept pace, and she saw Krelis loosening his great sword in its scabbard.

'No killing, unless we are attacked,' she yelled at him.

They swept through the makeshift village and boatyards, warriors spreading out and searching the place as people poured out of buildings – men, women, children. Bony dogs chased the horses through the streets, yapping and nipping at hooves.

Fidele reined her horse in close to the beach, in the shadow of one of the ships standing upright in its timber frame. Orcus and a handful of eagle-guard stayed with her; the rest spread out to search the buildings.

A group of Vin Thalun approached them, mostly warriors by the number of rings tied in their beards. One led them, a bow-legged older man.

'What's the meaning of this?' he demanded.

'I am searching,' Fidele said.

'For what?'

'You're talking to the Queen of Tenebral,' Orcus snapped. 'Show some manners.'

'Tenebral has a king, but no queen, last time I heard,' the Vin Thalun said.

He's right, Fidele thought. 'My son is King. I am regent in his absence,' Fidele said coldly. 'The result is the same. I rule here.'

The Vin Thalun glared at them. 'Searching for what, my Queen?' he said.

'For evidence of your fighting pits.'

'There was only one, and you've destroyed it.'

'We shall see. What is your name?'

'Alazon. I am chief shipwright here.'

'Wait with us, Alazon.'

It was not long before Krelis and Peritus appeared, leading a line of ragged men. Krelis' warriors were holding back the Vin Thalun crowd that followed them. Fidele saw that the men were chained together, their clothes threadbare. Most of them were covered in wounds of some description, from clean cuts to scratches and bite marks.

'Will you insult me with an explanation?' Fidele said to Alazon.

'They are rowers. A ship came in from one of the islands last night,' Alazon said. He spoke boldly, holding Fidele's gaze, but she did not believe a word of it.

'You.' She pointed to the first in line, a young man, surely younger than her Nathair. He had a scabbed cut that ran the length of his forearm. 'How did you get that cut on your arm?'

'They are slaves – taken from foreign lands. They often come damaged,' Alazon said. He stared at the captive as he spoke.

'You have nothing to fear,' Fidele said. 'As of this moment you are all free men. We shall escort you to Ripa, feed you, and then your future is yours. So – tell me, with fear of no repercussions: how did you come by that wound?'

'In the pits,' the lad said, looking at his feet, as if a deep shame had been revealed.

'He lies,' Alazon said, stepping forwards. Krelis moved in front of him.

'Find some wains for these men, then continue your search,' Fidele said. 'And, Krelis, make sure you have searched under every rock in this rats' lair.'

She looked at the captives, and saw harrowed looks sweeping them, some silently weeping, others just utterly wretched. It turned her stomach and brought the sting of tears to her eyes. She turned away and rode onto the beach a little way, looking out to sea. Orcus followed her, staying a short distance behind. He had learned to read her moods.

Where are you, Lykos? In some distant land? Dead? I hope that you are, you swine, for if you ever return to my homeland I shall see your head struck from your body.

CHAPTER SIXTY-THREE

CORBAN

Corban walked in a grey world. The ground was mist wreathed, the sky boiling with dark cloud. In the distance there were flashes, veins of red pulsing through the iron grey, fading, then brighter, like a distant storm. He walked towards it, the world about him ethereal, shifting from fields of grey rock to green woodland to barren plains of ash.

He drew near to the clouds, saw darker specks moving in them, swirling in tight formations. They were up above now. One fell, growing rapidly larger. Distantly he heard screaming, the clash of weapons. The shape crashed into the earth before him, a cloud of ash rising about it, settling slowly, like black snowflakes. He walked closer, peering cautiously.

A figure lay upon the ground, its skin alabaster, dark veins set in marble. Great wings were spread about it, like a cape of leather. It was wounded, a deep gash across its chest. Something that was not blood wept from the wound. Close by lay a spear, its shaft broken.

Then it opened its eyes.

They were black, no iris, no pupil, just a black soulless well. Corban took a step back.

It tried to move. Pain swept its face, its mouth twisting, revealing jagged teeth, a thick tongue, all as black as its eyes. It reached out an arm, steadied itself, its eyes fixing on Corban.

'Who are you?' it said.

A sound came from above, the wind whipped to a storm. Figures were approaching, great wings of white feather speeding towards Corban. The creature before him scrabbled for its broken spear, its wings jerking feebly, then the others landed with a thunder that made the ground tremble. One stamped a foot onto the wounded creature, knocking it flat, then buried a spear in its belly, twisting as he drove it in, through the writhing, hissing form, pinning it to the ground beneath. It drew a longsword from its back and hacked the creature's head from its body.

Others of its kind gathered around Corban, dressed as warriors in mail and leather. The air moved from their gently twitching wings.

'Who are you?' they asked.

'I . . .' Corban mumbled. He did not want to say his name, something batting at his memory like a moth against a shutter. Had he been here before? In a dream? A nightmare?

Hands reached out for him and he staggered backwards.

Corban woke with a start; his mam was standing over him. She looked worried. Gar hovered in the background.

He sat up and put his head in his hands.

'What's wrong?' Gar asked him.

'A bad dream,' he mumbled.

'Probably of that Coralen kicking him in the stones again,' Dath said. 'Come on, Ban, get up. We're going to the feast-hall for a drink.'

'For a meal,' Gwenith corrected Dath.

Just then the door to their home creaked and footsteps echoed. Edana walked in, Halion and Vonn behind her. With a flap of feathers Fech flew in before the door was pushed to.

Edana sat at a long table and groaned.

'What's wrong?' Brina asked her. Craf was perched on the edge of the table, pecking at a chunk of bread that Brina was feeding him. Fech landed close by, eyeing the bread.

'Roisin,' Edana said, shaking her head.

'What's she done now?'

'She's agreed terms for committing to the battle with Rhin,' Halion said.

'Terms?' said Corban. 'Rhin's invading. There's no need for terms.'

'That's what I said,' Edana muttered.

She's a sly one,' Halion said. 'She didn't say it, of course, it came from my da's mouth; but it had her influence behind it.'

'What?' several voices asked at the same time.

'That the alternative to battle with Rhin was negotiation, and that Edana would make a good gift.'

'Your da said that?' Dath blurted.

'Not in those words, but the meaning was clear. He offered an alternative, of course. And Edana took it. She had no choice.'

'What alternative?' Brina asked.

'To agree to be handbound to Lorcan, Roisin's son, Eremon's heir. When the time comes and Rhin is defeated.'

But he's only fifteen summers, thought Corban.

A silence settled over the room, then they all began talking at once.

'You should have said no.' Vonn's voice rose through the crowd. 'Rhin will attack them and then they will have no choice but to defend themselves.'

'True enough,' said Halion. 'But by then Roisin would have handed Edana to Rhin on a plate. Rhin will hardly turn down that offer. After that Edana's head would be on a spike, whatever happens in Domhain.'

More arguments rose up, but Edana slammed a hand on the table.

'I've agreed,' she said. 'The deal is done. I'm not happy about it, but it is a sacrifice I must make. And it's a smaller one than the many we've suffered already. Besides, it could have been worse. Eremon told me he'd marry me himself if it wasn't for Roisin.'

'That's disgusting,' said Vonn.

'Roisin won't like him saying things like that,' Marrock said.

'He's said things like that all his life. It's when she thinks he'll act on it that you have to worry about Roisin. Edana's safe from her now that Lorcan benefits,' said Halion.

Corban sat in the feast-hall of Dun Taras. It was noisy, voices rising as they often did once the mead started to flow. Or the ale that he was drinking: it was dark, bitter stuff, but after a bit of getting used to it he was starting to like it. Dath at least certainly seemed to be liking it, judging by the jug in his hand and the smile on his face.

All of the company that had survived the journey from Dun Carreg were in here somewhere, most of them sitting together about a long table. Storm was curled underneath the table, though it moved every time she changed position. Corban suspected that even Craf and Fech were lurking somewhere up in the rafters of the vaulted ceiling. The rest of the room was full, pulsing with excitement and activity. Dun Taras had been like this ever since word had arrived of Owain's death and Rhin's march on Domhain, a ten-night ago. Warriors were drifting into the fortress, from ones and twos to warbands of a hundred or more. Halion said King Eremon's barons would muster far greater numbers, but would most likely join the King's warband somewhere along the journey to Domhain's border. There was only one main route into Domhain from Cambren, and that was the giants' road. All other routes were little more than trails through the mountains, and winter was coming, so they were unlikely to be used. Thus the plan was a simple one: stop Rhin at the giants' road.

Corban was not yet sure what part his group would play in the coming conflict. Halion had told him that King Eremon would be staying at Dun Taras, too old for the journey, and that Rath would be leading the warbands of Domhain against Rhin. It was likely that Edana would have little choice other than to stay with Eremon. But Corban, along with many others in their small company, wanted to fight. Rhin had taken everything from them, and they all wished to play some part in taking it back.

The doors to the feast-hall opened and a figure came in from the dark, the wind hurling a spattering of rain in after him. Ventos, the trader. Corban had seen Ventos a handful of times since he had arrived in Dun Taras, and always enjoyed talking to the man. He felt like another part of home, somehow, a reminder of happier times. And he was a great teller of tales, the places he had been.

'How long will you be staying here?' Corban asked him as he settled next to him and took a drink of ale.

'For a while.' Ventos shrugged. He looked around the overflowing feast-hall. 'Seems as if the whole of Domhain is coming to Dun Taras, so it would be stupid to walk away. It's a good place to sell.'

'Even though war is coming?'

'War's good for business. People get reminded that we're not here forever – they like to enjoy life a little more, make the most of it.'

Nearby a man leaped onto a table and started dancing a jig to the applause of his friends.

'See.'

'I just thought that this is what they are like in Domhain,' Corban said.

'Oh, they are more inclined to a song, a good tale and a drink than many places I've been,' Ventos said. 'Maybe it's the rain. It rains so much here, you have to balance it with something.'

'Where is your hound?' Corban asked.

'He's guarding my wain. It's full of goods I've collected from all over the Banished Lands. Wouldn't want them to be robbed in the night. Talar won't let anyone take what's not theirs.'

Corban nodded his agreement. It was a vicious-looking hound. *I remember that from the first time I saw him. I fell on him and he looked at me like he wanted to eat me.* 'And what of your bird? The hawk you won from the Sirak in a game of dice?'

'Ah, Kartala. She is around. She can leave me for days at a time, even moons, but she always finds me again.'

The doors opened again and in walked a large crowd. Leading them was Quinn, Eremon's first-sword. He was tall and thick muscled. Corban had seen him training in Dun Taras' Rowan Field. There seemed to be little finesse to him, but he had a strength and speed that he used to overwhelm his opponents – literally battering them to defeat. Beside him walked Lorcan, Eremon's only recognized heir, Roisin's son.

Edana's betrothed, now.

He was slim, dark haired, fine featured like his mam, though Corban could see something of Halion about him – perhaps it was his eyes, sea grey like Eremon's. Lorcan was fifteen summers, not yet sat his Long Night, but he trained in the Rowan Field and looked close enough to ready from what Corban had seen. He had expected there to be some animosity between Halion and Lorcan, but Corban had seen nothing to suggest that. If anything, the boy seemed to admire Halion, or at least his skill in the weapons court. Corban often noticed Lorcan watching Halion when he was sparring, and there was no malice that Corban could read in his face. A host of others walked in with Quinn and Lorcan. One of them pushed a hood back and Corban saw it was the serving-girl from Eremon's chambers. Maeve. She looked at him and smiled. He'd seen her a few times about Dun Taras, and this was not the first time that she had favoured him with a smile. She walked over.

'Hello,' she said. 'I heard your story – that you told to the King.'

He didn't know what to say to that, so he didn't say anything, just nodded.

'It's quite the tale. Special,' she said, bending lower. She put a hand on his and squeezed it. 'I think you must be too.'

Corban didn't know what to say to that either, so he blushed instead. Maeve smiled. She looked along their table and saw Halion.

'Brother,' she said to him.

Of course, another sister, thought Corban.

Halion dipped his head in response, then she walked away.

Corban looked up to see Dath with his mouth open, Farrell staring at him.

'Why are they all smiling at you?' Dath said.

It was true, Corban had been noticing a lot of attention of late. He put it down to Storm, remembering it was the same in Dun Carreg, at first. But it was different here – in Dun Carreg it had been children following and warriors frowning. There was still a fair share of that here in Dun Taras, but there were also a lot of smiles and waves, mostly from girls.

Corban shrugged at Dath.

'You'll need to get yourself a pet wolven,' Farrell said to Dath.

She's not a pet, thought Corban.

'Like that's going to happen. How about a crow?' Dath said. 'Brina – can I borrow Craf for a while?'

'Ha,' said Brina, who was sitting a little further along the table. 'We all know Craf scares you witless.' It was the largest number of words Corban had heard Brina put together for days, since Heb's death.

'He does not,' Dath said.

Farrell squawked in Dath's ear and he jumped, then scowled.

'There's still hope for us, Dath. Not all of the lasses smile at Corban, anyway,' Farrell said. 'Coralen doesn't.'

'Now, I am scared of her. I think she actually tried to kill you in the practice court today, Ban,' Dath said.

Each day after Corban finished his training with Gar, Coralen challenged him to a sparring match. He had stopped losing to her, though the bouts were more often closer to draws than outright victories. She was vicious, and a cheat, with more tricks in her head than Corban thought possible.

'She's a fine lass,' Farrell said. 'Formidable. I'd like to marry her.'

Dath spat out a mouthful of ale.

'I think she hates me,' Corban said. 'At least she hits me as if she does.'

'There's a knife's edge between love and hate,' Brina said. Farrell frowned.

What does she mean by that?

'Like you and Heb, then,' Dath said. His smile withered the instant the words were in the air.

Brina looked at him, pain radiating from her.

I thought she'd be angry, but she's not. She's heartbroken.

Brina stood with a scrape of chair legs and left. Dath spluttered something after her, but she ignored it.

Corban watched her for a few moments, then followed her. Storm crawled out after him, spilling drinks as she rocked the table. Last to follow was Gar.

They made their way through the rain, back to their temporary home on the outskirts of the town, a black shadow winging above them. Brina lit candles and Gar set to sparking flames in the fire-pit. As light flickered into life Corban saw a figure sitting in a chair. He jumped, but it was only Vonn.

'What are you doing, sitting here in the dark?' Brina asked him, not too kindly.

'Nothing. Thinking,' Vonn said, blinking in the sudden light.

Brina bustled about the fire that Gar had started, hanging a pot of water.

'I'm making tea. Who wants some?'

Vonn stood. 'Think I need some air.' And he left.

'Better keep an eye on him,' Brina said.

'Just what I was thinking,' said Gar. 'He is still Evnis' son.' He headed out the door after him.

'I'm here to keep an eye on you,' Corban said to Brina.

She raised an eyebrow at that.

'I'll make the tea,' Corban said.

'No. I will.' Brina collected cups, sprinkling tea leaves into them and squatting by the pot, waiting for the water to boil.

'Dath didn't mean anything by what he said.'

'I know,' Brina snapped. 'He's an idiot. He can't help that.'

She poured the hot water into two cups.

'You miss Heb.' It was more statement than question.

Brina scowled at him, a spark of anger in her eyes. She spooned some honey into Corban's tea, knowing how he liked it, and stirred ferociously. She sighed. 'Corban, I know you mean well, but I cannot talk about Heb . . .' She trailed off, blinked hard. 'It is a raw wound. You understand?'

He nodded. She passed Corban his tea, then sat beside him.

'During the battle in the glade,' Corban said, unsure if he should speak of Heb. Brina remained silent so he continued. 'The giant put Heb's burning branch out, with the earth power.'

'Aye, he did. But Heb relit the branch. Not that it did him much good.'

'No, I lit the branch.'

'Did you?' There was a hint of genuine interest in Brina's voice. 'How did that happen, then?'

'I don't know. I saw the flame go out, was terrified for Heb, and just . . . did it.'

'Well, there you are then. Sometimes it's better not to think – especially those of us that lean towards the cynical.'

'Are we going to continue, with the book? Learning?'

'I don't know, Ban. Truth be told, I don't want to do much of anything. Things were different when . . .' She trailed off again.

When Heb was here, he finished for her. Awkwardly, scared that she might shout at him, or hit him, he reached out and put a hand over hers, gently squeezed.

He felt a tremor pass through her as tears spilt down her cheeks.

They sat there like that for a long time. The only sounds were the crackle of flames in the fire-pit, the occasional slurp of tea.

CHAPTER SIXTY-FOUR

VERADIS

Veradis paused in his climb up the mountain path. He was sweating beneath his clothes, but as soon as he stopped he felt the bite of the wind. It was cold in these mountains, colder than Veradis had ever felt. He had traded his leather kilt and iron-shod sandals over a moon ago for woollen breeches and boots, and his cloak was lined with fur, but still he was cold.

'Stop shivering. Keep walking,' Alcyon said to him as the giant reached him.

That's helpful.

They were part of a scouting party sent into the mountains that separated Cambren from Domhain. The bulk of the warband was camped a few leagues east, where a road cut a deep crevice through the mountains. Scouts had confirmed that King Eremon had massed a sizeable force further along the road, where it spilt into Domhain. The battle for Domhain would most likely take place there.

The giant Uthas led their group, he was showing a handful of Rhin's scouts the route he had taken through the mountains. Veradis had asked to come along because he wanted to see the site of this battle that had become almost legend, between Rhin's warriors, those they had been tracking and a wolven pack. For some unknown reason Alcyon had decided to come too, even though it was clear to Veradis that he did not like the company of Uthas or the other two giants that had joined them.

They had stopped up ahead, Uthas and his giant companions outlined at the ravine's head. Veradis pulled his cloak tight and marched on.

Snow sprinkled a wide dell that the narrow path opened up into.

Tiered cliffs curled around it, wind-beaten trees growing on ledges. Veradis could only stare and wonder at what had occurred here.

There were bodies everywhere, or what was left of them. A mound of half-eaten corpses was piled close to the dell's entrance, arrows and broken bones evidencing the violence that had sent them across the bridge of swords. They weren't just human. Wolven scattered the ground, wide rib-cages picked clean of flesh, as well as other animal carcasses – horses, Veradis realized. Parts of the dell bore the signs of a great fire, even trees and boulders blackened and charred.

Some at least survived, were victorious even. The ones that Uthas and his band met further along the road.

Alcyon was inspecting the twisted trunk of a burned-out tree. He rubbed his fingers against the blackened bark, sniffed them, touched them to his tongue.

'What is it?' Veradis asked him.

'The fire.' Alcyon frowned. 'It was not natural.'

'You mean, sorcery?'

'Elementals.'

'But how? Who?'

Alcyon shrugged. 'Your enemies are resourceful.'

'Our enemies,' Veradis corrected.

Alcyon showed him his teeth, what passed for a humourless smile.

They searched a while longer, but the scene yielded little more information.

Veradis had brought the lad from Ardan, Rafe, thinking that he might be useful, but the bodies were too decomposed or gnawed upon to be recognizable. Uthas and his two giant companions – one with a great axe, the other female – stood to one side, watching.

'This is not where I met these people. That place is further on,' Uthas said to Veradis.

'Then lead on.'

They spent a night on the mountain; Veradis shivered through most of it. It was Hunter's Moon, the seasons passing from autumn to winter, but back in Tenebral the chill would be easily banished by a good cloak. Not here. Veradis woke with frost in his beard and a dusting of snow over the ground. Back at the main campsite it had been cold, the morning training taking place in frost-stiffened grass, but nothing like this.

Uthas grinned at him as they shared strips of salted meat and washed it down with cold water.

'This is warm,' Uthas said. 'Never come north to Murias. On a cold day your urine will be frozen before it hits the ground.' His companions chuckled at that, but Veradis didn't find it funny.

'We will enter Domhain today,' Uthas said. 'We may have to stop before we reach the site you wish to see. Eremon will have scouts up here.'

'We will see,' Veradis said.

They walked for half a day, following a winding path little more than a fox's trail. They crested a ridge, all of them hurrying across its peak so as to give no easily seen silhouette, and then stopped a little way down the other side. Hills carpeted in thick pine rolled into the distance, the hint of green land beyond them.

Domhain.

They set off along a quickly widening trail, the ground sloping ever downwards now. Veradis saw a humped mound on the path, saw it was a dead wolven, again its carcass mostly stripped. They passed into light woodland, the ground thick with pine needles, and soon came to a clearing. It was full of bodies. Veradis whispered an order and Rhin's scouts moved through the glade and then faded into the surrounding trees.

The female giant gave out a fractured wail and crouched by a corpse – a giant.

Veradis tried to make sense of it – wolven and giants ranked highest amongst the dead this time, and this time there was a cairn, so the victors had lingered to pay respect to their fallen. The wolven corpses drew his eye, though. *Something about them.* It took Veradis a few moments to realize what was different.

They've been skinned. Though I'm not surprised, a wolven pelt would be a handy thing in this cold.

'Tell me again what you saw, Uthas,' Veradis said.

'A company burst upon us – they were a mixed company – warriors, women, carrying injured.'

Those that had survived the previous battle, Veradis thought.

'And there were wolven with them?'

'Aye. One to begin with. Then others came soon after. Four, five, I am not sure.'

'The wolven fought each other,' the giant with the axe said. *Salach.*

'That is true,' Uthas said. 'I remember now. A black one fought a white one. Over there.'

They all moved to where Uthas pointed. Close by were the remains of a wolven, little flesh left on the bones, the skull picked clean. The ground was littered with torn fragments of skin, sinew. *No fur.*

'A white wolven, you say?'

'Aye.'

That must have been Corban's wolven. It was them, then, fled all this way from Ardan. So Edana was here as well. And Rauca's killer, most likely: Gar.

And Corban. The Black Sun. Cywen's brother. His thoughts turned to her. She had proved pleasant company, once she had left Ardan and stopped trying to murder people. Over the last part of their march through Cambren he had found himself seeking her out, enjoying the conversations they had. She made him laugh, even if her tongue was often as sharp as the knives she liked to use. He liked her.

He shook his head. *Concentrate on what's in front of you.*

'Let's have a look inside that cairn.'

There were two corpses inside, a warrior, sword placed across his chest, and an old man, white hair whipping across the stones. His body looked deflated, creased, like a sail with no wind in it.

'One's Anwarth, Farrell's da,' Rafe said, pointing to the warrior. 'Word was he was a coward.'

'He died fighting, not running away,' Veradis said, noting the puncture wounds in the warrior's torso.

'The other one's old Heb,' Rafe looked sad. 'He told a good story.'

'Well his story's over,' said Veradis. 'Cover him up.'

Footsteps thumped on pine needles and Rhin's scouts burst into the glade.

'Run! They saw us,' one snapped.

Veradis turned and ran, Alcyon keeping pace with him; the other giants soon drew ahead, their long loping strides eating up the ground. It felt like a longer journey, running back up the hill to the ridge they had recently passed over, the woods silent apart from their heavy breathing, the thud of feet. He heard footsteps behind, voices calling in the woods. As they broke from the woodland onto open ground and sprinted for the ridge Veradis heard men shouting behind him, the whistle of a spear cast high. He ran faster. The spear skittered off a stone a few strides away. He slid over the crest of the ridge and down the other side. They kept running, long after his lungs and legs were begging him to stop, and eventually paused when they were sure their pursuers had given up. They rested a while, then began the journey back to Cambren and Rhin's warband. Veradis was pleased; he had learned much. Much to share with Nathair.

Most importantly, that the Black Sun is probably in Domhain. And there is nowhere further west that he can run to.

The camp was a sprawling mess, spreading along the giants' road and for leagues about it, great clusters of tents and campfires huddled in the rain. The setting sun was just a faint glow beyond the mountains' rim.

At least it is warmer here, though wetter.

The journey back through the mountains had been uneventful, just cold. He was glad to be back; he singled out Nathair's tents and aimed for them. As he reached the outskirts of the camp he changed his course, weaving between tents and ropes until he reached the eagle-guard's section – a more organized area, he was pleased to note. He passed through it, staying within shadows, not wanting to be seen, until he reached the paddocks. His eyes searched, then he saw her, grooming her horse as she always did around this time. Her brindle hound lay almost invisible at her feet.

'You're back, then,' Cywen said as he approached. She smiled to see him.

'Aye.' He stood there hesitantly, returning her smile. Unsure. *Why have I searched her out.* 'He has recovered well,' he said, moving to stroke the chest of her stallion. He was a beautiful animal, proud and strong. A good warhorse.

'Yes, he has.' Pride filled Cywen's voice. 'Where have you been, then?'

'Scouting. Through the mountains.'

'I didn't know first-swords and battlechiefs went scouting. They must do things differently in Tenebral.' She smiled faintly.

'I wanted to see if there was any sign of these wolven packs. I went in search of changelings and shape-shifters.'

'Did you find any?'

'No. Dead wolven. Dead people.'

She just looked at him now, eagerly and with some fear, waiting for him to tell her more.

'There was a cairn in the mountains, two bodies in it. Rafe said it was two men named Heb and Anwarth.' He stared at her in turn now, studying her reaction.

Tears filled her eyes, a tremor in her lip.

'You knew them, then?'

She nodded, not trusting her voice. He felt the urge to wipe her tears from her face. They traced streaks through the grime on her cheeks.

'I have to go,' he said instead and walked away.

'Were there any others that Rafe recognized?' she called after him.

He paused, looking back. 'Your mam and Corban were not amongst them,' he said, then walked into the darkness.

Veradis leaned back in his chair, enjoying the heat from the fire in Nathair's tent.

'You are sure?' Nathair asked him again.

'I am sure that there were men from Ardan amongst the dead up there, in the mountains. I am sure that they came from Dun Carreg. Evnis' lad, Rafe – he didn't just recognize them. He knew their names. All of them warriors or men loyal to Brenin and his daughter, Edana.'

'I see.' Nathair looked to Calidus. 'So Edana is in Domhain, likely under Eremon's protection.'

'It would seem so,' Calidus said.

'Which means that this Corban is probably with her. He was definitely not amongst the dead?'

'Not that we saw – there were many dead, and most unrecognizable, just bones and gristle. But Edana's group appears to have won both battles; at least, enough of them survived the first battle to carry on and then kill a number of wolven and giants. And they buried their dead in a cairn, which would suggest they did better than those they were fighting. Corban's body was not there.'

'So the Black Sun is in Domhain. Possibly camped with Eremon's army on the other side of those mountains.' Nathair drank from a cup. 'It seems almost unbelievable. I have chased this Black Sun in my dreams and in my waking imaginings for so long. I am torn. I was to leave soon for Murias. I must find the cauldron. My dreams . . .' He trailed off. 'Elyon commands me. I cannot fail him. And yet the Black Sun – if we could defeat him here – kill him. The danger would be over, surely.' He looked to Calidus. 'What should I do?'

'A dilemma, indeed,' Calidus said. He was silent a while, his expression pensive, unsure. Eventually he sighed. 'My advice is that you should go to Murias. We need the cauldron. Elyon has come to you in your dreams, I know this. And he has not asked you to defeat the Black Sun. No, he has asked you to get the cauldron.'

'But why, Calidus?' Nathair shook his head. 'I don't understand. Defeating the Black Sun is the goal. That is my task.'

'Yes, ultimately. I do not know Elyon's mind, but I know that the cauldron is a weapon. Perhaps it is impossible to defeat Asroth and his Black Sun without it. Maybe that is why finding it is so important in Elyon's plans.' He shrugged. 'I don't know. But I do know that Elyon has asked you to find the cauldron and claim it. So that is what you should do.'

'To be so close to my enemy,' Nathair growled, anger sweeping his face, 'only to walk away from him.'

'You were closer still in Dun Carreg, and watched him walk away,' Calidus said quietly.

Veradis shifted uncomfortably. *He is Ben-Elim, but still, to rebuke my King.* He felt his own anger stirring.

'I have punished myself a thousand times for that,' Nathair snapped, slamming his cup on the table.

'Asroth is the enemy,' Calidus said calmly, ignoring Nathair's flash of temper. 'To defeat him and thwart his plans we must have the cauldron. We must focus on that. Of course, if your faithful first-sword has an opportunity to kill this Corban over the coming days, well then . . .' He smiled at Veradis.

Nathair drew in a deep breath and blew it out slowly. 'All right. You are my counsellor, so I should listen when you give counsel.' He smiled, the anger of moments before evaporating. 'And you are well suited for advising on this subject.'

Yes, he is, thought Veradis. *If one of Elyon's Ben-Elim cannot advise on this, then no one can.*

'Indeed,' said Calidus. He grinned. 'Commit yourself to your task, Nathair. Focus on that. It will be difficult enough. The Benothi giants will not just hand the cauldron over to you.'

'Well then, Veradis,' Nathair said. 'I shall leave you this task. Help Rhin to destroy Eremon, this King that would harbour my enemy.'

'I will do all that I can,' Veradis said. 'But I would rather be travelling north with you. I am your first-sword; I would keep you safe.' He traced the scar on his palm where he and Nathair had sworn a blood-oath. It seemed a very long time ago.

Nathair saw the movement, turned his own palm over to look at his scar. 'We are brothers, you and I. That is why I want you to stay. Rhin must be watched – I do not trust her. I would like her to see what your shield wall can do. It may temper her ambitions.'

'I will do as you ask, then join you when it is done.'

'Good. And in doing so, hunt down this Corban. Perhaps he is the Black Sun, perhaps he is not. But if you have the opportunity, kill him. Just in case.' He smiled at Veradis and raised his drink.

They all touched cups, Veradis trying to smile back at Nathair. All he could think of was Cywen's face, her tear-stained, dirty, grimy face, framed with black curls. Nathair had just ordered him to kill her brother. He felt a wave of sympathy for her.

So be it, a voice said in his head.

CHAPTER SIXTY-FIVE

CORALEN

Coralen slid and moved, spinning around Corban as he swung his practice sword at her head. *He doesn't hold back any more.* She liked that, knew that when she had first challenged him in the weapons court he had not tried his hardest, had held back because she was not a man.

A few falls on his arse had soon served to disabuse him of that notion. And now he sparred against her with the same intensity that she saw in him when he fought against Gar.

Corban's sword glanced off her shoulder, knocking her off balance.

Focus, you idiot, she scolded herself, but before she was able to she was on her back, staring up at a cold sky, Corban's sword-tip hovering against her chest.

Did he just use my move against me?

He held out a hand for her, grinning, but she slapped it away and rolled fluidly to her feet. She saw men staring, various expressions of shock and surprise on their faces. It was not often that she was knocked on her backside in the weapons court.

'Again,' she said, wiping the smile from his face.

When she left the weapons court later with Baird, they encountered her half-sister Maeve hovering near the entrance, casting cow eyes in Corban's direction, her face painted up like her mam's. Coralen glared as she walked past.

Gods, she hated Dun Taras. It was the bedrock of all of her earliest memories, of her mam and da, King Eremon, when she thought the world revolved around them both, when her mam was the most beautiful woman in the world. Or so she thought. Eremon seemed to think so as well, if only for a little while. Then the spurning had come, the constant tears and wailing from her mam as Eremon had tired and moved on to different fields to sow. At the time Coralen had felt as if her world was collapsing, imploding in upon itself, a constant of destruction and misery.

Never shall I be like my mam. Reliant on a man's good will. Giving myself up for a few smiles and some time under a dry roof. A man's play-thing to be tossed away when he gets bored. She felt herself scowling as the memories bubbled up inside her.

She saw the wolven come stalking out of the weapons court, all muscle, teeth and power. She had to admit, it was quite something, seeing a full-grown wolven prowling around the fortress. Corban and his friends followed behind. Well, at least Corban was good with a blade, she had to concede. Better than her, perhaps, if you took out the dirty moves she specialized in: a score of tricks that Conall had taught her, for when a fight got up close and personal.

Maeve dropped something on the road, a piece of linen, and Corban bent to pick it up.

Maeve said something and touched Corban's arm, smiling at him. Coralen couldn't hear the words but she saw Corban's face flush red, then saw Maeve lean forwards and kiss his cheek.

'What's wrong with you?' Baird asked her.

'What? Nothing,' Coralen snapped. 'Can we go now?'

'Of course.'

She saw Corban's friend, the big one with the hammer, staring at her. She scowled at him for good measure before she walked away.

Baird caught up with her and together they walked to the feast-hall. She was starving hungry, ready to eat her weight in food. She lost some of her appetite when she walked into the hall, though, seeing Quinn and Lorcan sitting close to the entrance.

Quinn smiled at her. She hated that. Hated the way that he looked at her: like she had seen men look at her mam, so many times.

'Come over here, lass,' Quinn called out. He patted his knee.

'If I do it'll only be to cut your stones off,' she said.

'I'll take the risk,' Quinn said, his smile growing broader.

She changed her direction but Baird held her arm.

'He's not worth it,' Baird said to her.

She paused a moment, then saw someone else whom she wanted to talk to – Halion. She strode to him instead, sitting down opposite him. He was with a warrior, the one who had lost a hand.

'Cora,' Halion said.

Baird slipped onto the bench beside her.

'I've waited long enough. Tell me about Conall,' she said to Halion.

Halion's expression grew guarded. She'd seen that face before, a thousand times, and understood that he would not be telling her much.

'There's not much to tell, Cora. There was a battle, Conall fell.' Grief travelled across his face, a ragged cloud skimming the sun on a summer's day, then it was gone, replaced with the cold face that he had taught her so well.

'There's more to it than that,' Coralen pressed. 'Were you together?'

'No, we were not.'

'Why not? You were always together. Inseparable. Had you argued?'

Halion rubbed his face. 'It was a battle, Cora. Chaos. Enemies had broken into the fortress; there were people fighting everywhere.'

'So how do you know he's dead?' Coralen said, a spark of hope flaring in her belly. She had loved Conall fiercely.

'I saw him die,' the warrior beside Halion said.

'You are?'

'Marrock. I was fighting on the walls above Dun Carreg's gates. Conall was there too.'

'What else did you see?'

The warrior's eyes flickered to Halion, something passing between them. With the palm of his remaining hand he rubbed the stump of his other wrist, capped now with leather.

'He was fighting; we all were. He fell.' Marrock shrugged.

'But he may have survived.'

'No. It's a long drop.'

Coralen leaned back, studying them both. *There's more they're not telling me. It's in their eyes.*

'You are sure? Did you see—'

'Enough,' Halion said, his voice fraying with anger. His face softened. 'Conall is gone, Cora. It is a hard fact, one I don't want to accept myself, but it's the truth. Accept it. Let him go.'

CHAPTER SIXTY-SIX

TUKUL

Tukul grinned with the joy of being on horseback again. His legs and backside ached as if he'd been kicked by an auroch, but he didn't care. The wind in his face, the rhythmic drum of hooves at a canter, the bunching and expanding of muscle, the sense of power in the horse he was riding.

It was wonderful.

They had stayed at Gramm's for two nights. The arrival of the child-king Haelan and his guardian had set a fire in Meical. They had stayed long enough for Gramm to gift them with horses and provisions and then left. Finding seventy-two horses for warriors as fussy as his Jehar was no easy task but they were wonderful animals. Gramm had given them free choice from both of his herds – the pure bloods and the cross-breeds. Many of Tukul's people had chosen the pure-bloods, he suspected out of a sense of nostalgia, a reminder of home, the white-walled city of Telassar. He had chosen one of the cross-breeds, a powerful piebald mare, because he was riding to war, and if ever he had seen horses made for war, these were it. Daria, he had called her, after his wife. She wouldn't have minded – horses were almost family to the Jehar.

There was one other gift that he had been given whilst at Gramm's, but not from Gramm. It was an axe, presented by Gramm's son, Wulf.

In memory of our axe-throwing, the young warrior had said. It was strapped tightly to Tukul's saddle now, a single-bladed weapon covered in soft leather. For nearly two moons they had been riding through the flat plains of northern Isiltir, the black columns of smoke on the horizon telling the tale of war. They had seen few people,

Meical taking them by less-travelled ways. Nevertheless, they had needed to cross rivers, and these were guarded. The bridge that crossed the Rhenus had been manned by a band of Isiltir's warriors – about a score of them. They were too few and unprepared for the Jehar, who just rode through them, thundering across the bridge like the north wind. No one had pursued them.

They had carried on southwards, for days skirting leagues of stinking marshland, then crossed another river – the Afren, Meical told him, and moved into the realm of Ardan.

That had been three nights ago. They were cantering across a rolling moorland of gorse and heather now, watched only by goats and auroch. To the north the horizon was edged with a wall of trees, dark and brooding, though insignificant compared to Forn.

'That is the Darkwood,' Meical said, following Tukul's gaze. 'It marks the northern border of Ardan. On its far side lies the realm of Narvon.'

'I know, I have studied many maps over the last few years. Soon we shall come upon the river Tarin, which will take us to Baglun Forest, Dun Carreg and the sea. And the Seren Disglair.'

'Indeed,' Meical said.

Excitement was growing in him. They would soon be there. Dun Carreg, home of the Seren Disglair. He could hardly believe these times were upon him. *And I will see one other. My son. All-Father be praised.*

When they reached the river Tarin they skirted south and followed the fringe of the Baglun Forest towards the sea, the ground carpeted in leaves of orange and gold. After another two days riding Tukul heard the call of gulls. He looked over his shoulder and saw Enkara first amongst his sword-kin. They had all heard it too. He grinned fiercely at them.

Soon they came upon a great road running across their path; it was made of cut stone, though worn and broken, with grass and weeds growing in its cracks.

'This is the giantsway,' Meical said.

Tukul stared, could see in the distance a dark smudge upon a high cliff top. Dun Carreg. A jolt of excitement passed through him.

'We cannot approach in strength – they would bar the gates at the sight of you all,' Meical grinned. A fierce excitement was scribed on his face. 'Tukul, you and I will go. The rest of you, there is a glade within this forest, further along the road. A giant-stone stands in it. Wait for us there.'

Tukul nodded his agreement to his sword-kin and they parted ways – he and Meical riding the road northwards. The road cut through a landscape of rolling moors. A low hill stood nearby, a cairn sat on its crest, outlined by the cold blue sky.

They rode on in silence, then from between the undulating moorland the road spilt onto a plain, the fortress of Dun Carreg rearing high above.

The Seren Disglair is up there.

A village nestled at the foot of the hill that the fortress was built upon, beyond it the roar of a distant sea. As they drew nearer, a group of men rode from the village: warriors carrying couched spears and swords at their hips. They wore cloaks of black and gold.

'Something is wrong,' Meical said. 'Those are not Brenin's colours.'

The riders were closer, had seen them, some pointing. Tukul counted twelve of them.

'They wear the colours of Cambren. Rhin's colours,' Meical said.

'Should we turn back?' Tukul asked.

'Too late. They would only follow. Let us see this through, find out where it leads us.'

'As you wish.' Tukul reached down and slipped the leather cover from his axe. *All-Father, may my arm be strong and my sword sharp.* He glanced at Meical, at the longsword hanging at his hip. 'When was the last time you used your sword?'

'In this world of flesh? Against the wolven that gave me these.' He ran a finger along the silver scars that raked his face. 'Do not worry, my friend. If it comes to sword-work, I think I can remember what to do.'

The warriors rode up, pulled up before them.

'What's your business here?' asked one of them, an older man, grey hair pulled back from his face.

'We are travelling to Narvon. Just looking for a place to rest the night,' Meical said, his voice warm, relaxed.

'Where are you from?' the old man asked. Men moved to their sides, curling around them.

'Carnutan. Leaving the war behind. We've been on the road since midsummer. What's the news, here?'

'You've come to the wrong place if you're running from war,' one of the other warriors spoke up, a younger one, his beard thin with youth.

'I heard Brenin was a peaceful king,' Meical said.

'Brenin's dead. Rhin rules here,' the young one said.

'What about you?' the older man said, fixing his eyes on Tukul. 'You don't look as if you're from Carnutan.'

Tukul just stared at him, not sure what to say. Diplomacy had never been his strength.

'He's got the look of one of those that came with that foreign king,' another man said.

'That's what I was thinking,' the older man said.

'There were Jehar here?' Tukul blurted.

'Jehar – that's it. And I'm thinking you know that already. Are you a deserter? Not got the stomach for war? You should be across the water with the rest of your lot, with Rhin and Nathair.'

Tukul saw Meical stiffen at that.

'He rode here from Carnutan, with me,' Meical said, hiding his shock.

The old man looked at them both. 'Think you'd both best come with me. We'll see what Evnis has to say about this.'

'Evnis?' Meical said.

'Aye. He rules here in Rhin's place. Come along now.'

Riders closed about them.

Without a word, or even a warning look to Tukul, Meical burst into motion. His sword arced into the warrior nearest him, cutting upwards into his jaw, teeth and blood exploding. The man fell backwards, gurgling. Before any could react, Meical was turning his arm, using the momentum of his first strike to form his second, looping his blade down to crack into the helm of another warrior, denting the helm, the man slumping, senseless or dead.

Tukul pulled his axe free, threw it, and was drawing his sword from its scabbard across his back as the axe buried itself in the old warrior's chest. Then the others were moving, shouting, yanking on reins, horses neighing, crushing together, weapons hissing from scabbards.

A spear-blade grazed Tukul's cheek as he swayed in his saddle, using his knees and ankles to guide his mount straight towards the man with his axe in his chest. He grabbed the shaft as the man toppled backwards, wrenching it free, used the axe to turn another spear thrust and sliced his sword through the man's throat, leaving blood arcing.

Four down, eight left. You need space, old man; don't let them crowd you. He spurred his horse on, crashing through the loose circle that was pulling tight about him, sword and axe swirling, deflecting, cutting, another warrior toppling in his wake. Then he was in open space, turf instead of horseflesh about him. He tugged on his reins, his mount turning a tight circle, and caught a glimpse of Meical with blood on his face, his horse rearing, hooves lashing out. Riders were approaching from the village, galloping: more warriors seeing the conflict, five, ten, more.

This is not looking good.

He swayed in his saddle, leaning heavily to avoid a sword cut, slashed the man's leg as he pulled back up, the muscles in his back straining, complaining, his axe-blade biting deep, turning on bone. He pulled it free, deflected a sword stabbing at his chest, heard the pounding of galloping hooves drawing closer, closer.

Meical, I must reach Meical.

Then horses were all about him. It took a moment to register who their riders were – holding their swords two-handed, carving through their enemy with great swooping blows, tracing crimson arcs through the air. His sword-kin, the Jehar. All of them.

Within heartbeats their enemy were dead or dying, the ground about them churned, slippery with blood and bodies. A riderless horse trotted away, stopped and began cropping when it found some grass.

Tukul saw Enkara. 'You were supposed to wait,' he said to her, then grinned. 'I am glad you didn't.'

She grinned back.

No more riders were issuing from the village, though many were milling about on foot, pointing. A horn blast rang out, answered from the fortress on the hill.

'Come,' Meical yelled, 'we must ride.'

They thundered back along the giantsway; Tukul's blood was racing, pounding in his ears, the joy of battle still coursing through him. *Blessed are those who stand before the darkness with a pure heart, though their swords run red. Thank you, All-Father, for the gift of combat.* Wind whipped his face and a thought seeped through the fading euphoria. *But where is the Seren Disglair?*

They sped along the giantsway, putting league after league between them and Dun Carreg. If there was any pursuit, by nightfall it would have fallen hopelessly behind. Eventually Meical called a halt and they made camp in a sheltered cove. Huge moss-covered boulders and dense stands of wind-beaten trees provided some cover from the rain that had begun to fall.

Where is the Seren Disglair? And those warriors, they spoke of the Jehar, here. How can that be? 'Where are we going?' Tukul asked Meical.

'I must find him,' Meical said. 'I have avoided the Otherworld for too long. Going back there has its dangers: Asroth tracks my steps there, and I would not lead him straight to the Bright Star. So I have trusted to King Brenin and the guardians I have set about the Seren Disglair in this world of flesh. I have been too cautious. I must go back to the Otherworld and find him there.' He spread a blanket on the ground and lay upon it.

Your ways are not our ways, Tukul quoted to himself, *but if it were up to me I would have kept a closer watch on the Bright Star.*

'Do not try to wake me,' Meical said.

Almost instantly Meical's breathing changed, deeper and slower. His eyelids twitched, his breaths slowing further, becoming shallow now, the gap between them so wide that a casual observer might think Meical was dead.

Tukul stood the first watch. When he was relieved he lay down beside Meical, who was as still as the dead. Tukul's body was stiffening now, his joints and muscles protesting at the day's events. He woke to someone touching his shoulder. Meical. Dawn's grey light outlined boulders and trees.

'I have found him,' Meical said, looking drawn, eyes dark and sunken. 'We must ride to Domhain.'

CHAPTER SIXTY-SEVEN

CYWEN

Cywen was standing with the giant, Alcyon, who had apparently taken over the duty of guarding her.

She'd been told only a short while ago that she was leaving. Bos gave her the news. Where she was going he would not, or could not, say.

She looked up at the giant, a head taller than Shield, his black axe curving over his shoulder.

'Where are we going, then?' she asked him. *Might as well try asking – someone might give me an answer.*

He just stared down at her a moment, then looked away.

Not the most talkative of travelling companions, then. He looks as miserable as I feel.

The Jehar were milling around her, climbing into saddles, harness creaking. The other three giants that had joined them recently stood close together, and near to them she saw Veradis appear, his eyes searching. They focused on her and as he marched over, her mood lightened, just a little.

'Why wasn't I told about this?' he said to Alcyon.

'What?' His voice sounded like stones grinding together.

'This.' Veradis gestured at Cywen. 'Taking her north with you.'

I'm going north, then.

'I don't know,' the giant said with a shrug.

'Why does she need to go with you?'

'Calidus wants her near to him.' Alcyon shrugged again. 'You'll have to ask him why.'

Veradis frowned, emotions sweeping his face. Anger, worry.

What are you worried about? Me? She felt pleased to see him. He had not been a bad travelling companion, in his way. Since they had camped here, at the foot of the mountains, she had seen little of him, though. 'Good day to you too,' she said.

'What? Oh, yes.' Veradis looked at her, seemed about to say something.

'What?' Cywen said.

'Nothing.' Veradis shook his head.

Instead he looked to Alcyon and stared at him.

'What's wrong?' he asked the giant.

How does he know something's wrong with the giant? His face looks like a rock.

Alcyon didn't answer, but his eyes flickered across the crowds, towards the other three giants.

'I thought you'd like travelling with others of your kind,' Veradis said.

'I am Kurgan; they are Benothi. It is an old blood-feud.' He smiled, looking for an instant more human to Cywen. 'If nothing else we giants know how to bear a grudge.'

'Look after Nathair,' Veradis said to Alcyon.

'Calidus will not let any harm come to him.'

'Aye. If it is within his power to stop it.' Veradis looked over to Nathair, sitting tall on his draig. Cywen could just make out Calidus near him.

'Yes. And his power is formidable.'

Veradis nodded, still looking troubled. 'And look after her,' he muttered.

'I will,' Alcyon said. 'And you try and look after yourself. I will not be around to keep saving your skin.'

'No. I shall do my best.' Veradis smiled now.

'You will be fighting soon – today, tomorrow. Think on that, not about us walking north. We will be at least a moon travelling through Cambren before we even reach Benoth. We will not see trouble until then.'

Just then a group of warriors rode by, wearing the black and gold of Cambren. Queen Rhin led them. Cywen saw Conall close to her, wrapped in a dark cloak.

'Is she going with you?' Veradis asked Alcyon.

'Aye, part of the way. She has some reason for returning to Dun

Vaner. She is leaving Geraint in charge of her warband, but he seems capable enough. He did well against Owain.'

'That battle ran to Rhin's plan,' Veradis said. He shrugged. 'It does not matter to me who leads the warriors of Cambren. I will lead my shield wall and fight whoever is foolish enough to stand in front of it.'

'You are fighting today?' Cywen said to Veradis.

He nodded. 'We are pushing into Domhain. I don't think that Eremon will just allow that to happen. There will be a greeting arranged for us. Maybe not today, but soon.'

'Oh.' Cywen felt a knot in her stomach. She looked back, at the broad road that cut a swathe into the rain-shrouded mountains. *Are my mam and Corban through there? Will they fight for Domhain? And Veradis . . .* She looked at the young warrior, his expression so earnest.

Horns sounded, echoing through the throng.

'Time to go,' Alcyon said. 'Stay safe, True-Heart.' Alcyon offered his arm to Veradis, who gripped the giant's forearm.

'What did you call me?' Veradis asked him.

'True-Heart. It is your name,' Alcyon said, then turned to Cywen. 'On your horse, child.'

'I'm not a child,' she grumbled as she swung onto Shield's back. She was feeling miserable again.

'Farewell,' Veradis said to her as she sat in her saddle. He reached out, his fingertips brushing the top of her hand. 'Stay safe,' he said, quietly.

Looking at him she could not find the words to answer, just stared back at him as she rode away. A strange thought struck her.

I shall miss him.

CHAPTER SIXTY-EIGHT

CORBAN

Sweat dripped from Corban's brow. The heat from the forge and the ache from swinging a hammer felt like familiar friends. They brought back a flood of memories, of working with his da in the forge back in Dun Carreg, Buddai slouched by the doorway. *Good times*.

Corban had asked Halion to find him a blacksmith who wouldn't mind him using his forge for a day or so. With war looming close, that had been harder than Corban originally thought, but Halion was well liked at the fortress, so eventually somewhere had been found. It was cutting it close, though. The muster was finished, and Eremon's warband was set to march on the morrow.

'Enough,' Farrell grunted, his tongs turning the piece of iron that Corban was hammering. It was the length of a dagger, but curved.

Corban hammered an iron pin through the wide end, punching a hole, then Farrell dipped it into a bucket of water, steam hissing. Finally he placed it beside a pile of similar pieces.

'That the last one?' Corban said, almost disappointed.

'Aye. Fifteen blades. Still some work to do, though. They all need sharpening, and then there's some leather work to be done.'

'Aye. Let's go see my mam.'

The streets of Dun Taras were packed, the population of the whole fortress seemingly determined to enjoy their last night of peace. Musicians strumming upon lyres or beating rhythms out on leather-skinned drums lined every street corner, men and women dancing jigs and singing loudly. Corban, Marrock and Camlin were winding their way towards the feast-hall through the growing crowds. Storm helped them through the throng, a pathway opening automatically wherever she padded. Once upon a time Corban would have shared the excitement – once all he wanted was to be a warrior, to fight in defence of his king and kin. He had had a taste of war now, though, and the thought of more of it filled him with dread. He was not scared, not of battle, anyway. It was more the knowledge of what came after – the loss of life, the grief and heartache. Memories of his da and Cywen flickered through his mind, and other faces: Heb, Anwarth, Mordwyr, those who had fallen on their flight to Domhain. With an effort he pushed the memories away.

'There'll be a lot o'sore heads on the morrow,' Camlin observed.

'They'll have a nice long walk to the border to work it off,' Marrock said. 'Besides, I don't blame them. Live life while you can, for who knows what the morrow will bring.'

'Didn't take you for a philosopher.' Camlin smiled.

'Events change us,' Marrock said. Corban saw him glance at his wrist.

'Aye, that they do.'

He seems to be coping better, Corban thought. The bitterness that had stained Marrock's voice every time that he spoke of his injury had faded during their time in Dun Taras. *Perhaps he has come to terms with it now.* Somehow Corban did not think that was true. *If anything, his bitterness is buried, like rocks at high tide. I still see it surface every now and then.*

The doors to the feast-hall were flung open, a wall of sound pulsing out. All manner of merriment was going on inside – dancing, wrestling, singing, dice and throw-boards, all to a tune and barrels of free-flowing ale.

'Where are they?' Corban said, almost having to shout over the noise.

'Over there.' Camlin led them to a great crush of people. Vonn and Halion greeted them.

'What's going on?' Corban asked.

'Farrell,' Halion said with a grin. 'Look.'

Farrell was sitting at a narrow table, a warrior opposite him, all thick muscle and hair. They were arm-wrestling. Both their faces were red with strain, veins bulging in arms that seemed frozen, carved from stone. As Corban watched, Farrell's opponent gave a great roar, his arm starting to move, first a tremor, and then Farrell had slammed it onto the table. The crowd erupted with cheering.

Dath appeared with a jug in each hand.

'That's the third one he's beaten.' Dath grinned, passing a jug to Corban, who took a drink and then passed it to Camlin.

'Is it a tournament, then?'

'Aye, and he's entered another sort too, by the looks of it.'

Farrell was still seated at the bench, but now sitting opposite him was Coralen. She was filling two pewter cups. Farrell took one and together they tipped the contents down their throats. Farrell screwed his eyes shut. Coralen laughed.

Corban slapped Farrell on the back.

'She thinks I can't hold a drink,' Farrell said to him.

Coralen handed Farrell another cup.

Corban looked along the bench, saw Baird slumped upon it with his head resting on the table, half a dozen empty cups beside him.

'What happened to him?' Corban asked Coralen.

'He's sleeping off round one,' Coralen said, flashing a grin. Farrell downed his drink.

Corban leaned close to Farrell's ear. 'Maybe you should concede, and stick to the arm-wrestling.'

'Thish is my chance to impresh her,' his friend replied loudly.

'Never met a lady who's impressed with vomit in her lap,' Dath said.

A warrior sat down opposite Farrell; Coralen shifted along for him. He put his arm on the table, another challenger for Farrell.

This one didn't last more than a dozen heartbeats.

'Have a drink,' Farrell said to his defeated opponent. Coralen handed out cups and they drank them down.

Someone tapped Corban on the shoulder – his mam.

'Are they done?' Corban asked her.

'Aye. My thumb feels like it's going to drop off – stitching leather is not easy, you know – but they're done.'

'Thank you, Mam.' Corban hugged her.

A commotion drew his eyes back to Farrell. A group had approached the bench, a handful of men, Quinn, the first-sword of Domhain leading it. He was a big man, broad and thick muscled, with a flat nose that spoke of the pugil ring. His build reminded

Corban of Helfach, Evnis' dead huntsman. Maeve, Halion's sister, was hanging on his arm. Quinn grabbed the warrior sitting opposite Farrell and dragged him out of the way, then sat and grinned at Farrell. He tried to wrap an arm around Coralen, but she slipped out of reach.

'Want to try my arm?' Quinn said to Farrell.

'Coursh I do,' Farrell slurred.

'Keep an eye on your friend,' Halion said in Corban's ear. 'Trouble follows Quinn.'

'I don't like him,' Corban said. 'He reminds me of Helfach.'

'I can see the likeness.' Halion snorted. 'Not a good reason to dislike someone, but this time you're right.'

'How so?'

'Let's just say I wouldn't want him guarding my back in a fight. There are rumours.'

'What rumours?'

Just then the warrior whom Quinn had dragged from his seat crashed into Quinn's back, sending him flying into Farrell. There were a few moments of chaos, fists flying and chairs turning over. Corban pushed forward to Farrell's side, then Quinn's followers were holding the warrior who had started it all upright, his hands pinned behind his back. Quinn punched him with a solid uppercut and the unconscious man was dragged from view.

'How about that arm-wrestle, now?' Quinn said as he sat back down.

Farrell wiped blood from the back of his hand, a cut during the brief skirmish, then gripped Quinn's hand.

'Begin,' Maeve declared and instantly both arms were straining. The crowd around them roared to life, shouting encouragements, making wagers, some singing. Quinn was the bigger man, his arms bulkier, slabs of meat for biceps, but Farrell's strength had been honed in the forge, like Corban's, with years of hammer-pounding packing every fibre with strength. For a long time both arms remained fixed, immovable, then, slowly, a tremor appeared in Quinn's forearm. His face was contorted with strain, jaws clenched, eyes bulging. His arm moved, just a fraction, and the crowd around them hushed, sensing the end.

Quinn's arm moved again, a downward jerk this time. He

checked it somehow, a handspan from the table, pausing the flood.

It's over, Farrell's won. Corban felt a grin slipping onto his face.

Then Farrell grunted, a shiver running through him. His head lolled and Quinn's arm slowly rose again, their fists back at midpoint. Farrell shifted, his head coming up, glaring at his arm as if it had betrayed him. Long moments passed, frozen in time, then Farrell's head dipped again, and suddenly Quinn's arm was forcing Farrell's back, ever lower. With a final roar, the strength seemed to drain from Farrell and Quinn was punching the air in victory.

Farrell just sat there, staring at his hand, clenching and unclenching his fingers.

Quinn caught hold of Coralen, who had stayed nearby. He pulled her close, kissing her hard. She struggled in his grip, stamped on his foot and elbowed him in the face.

Farrell lunged across the table, grabbing Quinn's wrist.

'Let her go,' Farrell growled.

Quinn let go of Coralen and swung a fist at Farrell, catching him high on the temple.

Corban leaped forwards, vaulting the table as Farrell sagged to the ground. He crashed into Quinn, sending him stumbling backwards.

'Stay behind me,' he said to Coralen and pushed forwards, fists raised.

Don't punch at all if you can help it, he heard his father's voice, clear as if he were standing next to him, *but if you must, punch first and punch hardest.*

Quinn swung at him and Corban ducked, still moving forwards, slammed a fist into Quinn's belly and sent a hook to his chin. The big man staggered and a straight right sent him toppling backwards.

That should do it.

Quinn climbed to his feet, blood running from his nose.

'So it's a fight you're wanting,' he said, his fists bunching. He spat blood.

Oh dear.

Then men were moving everywhere, some gathering about Quinn, others closing beside Corban – Gar, Halion, Dath, Vonn. Others. A sound rose over them all, silencing the clamour. A deep rumbling.

Storm, growling.

Corban felt her brush past him, place herself in the space between Corban and Quinn, teeth bared, slavering. Quinn took an involuntary step backwards. His hand moved to his sword hilt. There was a moment when all was still, violence hanging in the air. Then a figure stepped between them – Rath, a handful of his giant-killers with him.

'Best save it for Rhin,' he said. 'And you'd better calm that beast down.'

Corban touched Storm and she stopped growling.

Quinn wiped blood from his face, then grinned. 'These southerners are too serious; and that one can't take his drink.' He waved at Farrell, then turned and walked into the crowd.

'Well, aren't you the brave one?' a voice said. Corban turned and Maeve was there, standing uncomfortably close. 'You just put the first-sword of Domhain on his arse. Think that deserves a kiss.'

She pressed her lips to his, her arms wrapping around his waist, and for a moment the world went blank, shrinking to the taste of wine on Maeve's breath, the sensation of her lips against his. Then someone was pulling him. He spun to see Coralen glaring at him. She slapped him hard across the face.

'I'm no maiden to be saved; I can look after myself,' she spat at him.

'I know you can,' he spluttered.

'So why did you do that? Fight my fight?'

Because . . .' He shrugged. *Why did I do that?* 'The same reason they were all at *my* side.' He gestured to Gar and the others. 'We look after each other. Because you're a friend.'

That stopped her a moment, her mouth open but nothing coming out. Then her eyes slipped to Maeve.

'Enjoy your victory,' she said with a sneer and walked away.

CHAPTER SIXTY-NINE

MAQUIN

Maquin sat at a table brimming with food and drink: bowls of fruits – oranges, figs, plums – olives, meats, as well as eels and squid and anchovies, warm flatbread and jugs of watered wine to wash it all down with. Maquin had tasted wine like it when in Jerolin and hadn't liked it. Now, though, after his months of gruel whilst chained to an oar, it all tasted like a feast made for kings.

He felt sick, though, his stomach sending him pains of warning. He swiped grease from his beard and leaned back in his chair.

He was not alone at the table; at least fifty or sixty other men were also stuffing their bellies to overflowing. They were the survivors, the victors, of the fighting pits. Maquin had seen Orgull sitting further along, too far away to talk to. The big man had tried to catch his eye, but Maquin had looked away. He still felt ashamed of what he had done in the pit, what he had become, and he knew Orgull would share his disgust.

He has killed today, just as I have.

This all felt like a dream.

Men were standing in the shadows, guarding the men and women bringing the food and fresh jugs of wine. One pit slave grabbed a woman and dragged her onto his lap. He was quickly taught that he had crossed a line – his arm was held flat on the table and a finger broken.

The servants were left alone after that.

A man walked into the chamber, the barrel-chested man who had led Maquin to the pit.

'I am Herak,' the barrel-chested man said. 'I am your mother, your father, your sister and brother. I am the closest thing to family

405

you will have here.' He smiled at them all. 'And you are my children. I am going to train you, discipline you. No doubt I will have to punish you, and I hope that I will have cause to reward you.' He waved a hand at the table. 'You have done well today, and for some of you this will just be the beginning.'

'Beginning of what?' a man said, small, dark skinned.

'Of your new lives. You belong to the Vin Thalun now. As you have started, so you will continue. You will fight for us in the pits. You will kill for us and make us rich.' He nodded, grinning at that. 'And some of you will earn your freedom. Emad, step forward.' One of the guards moved closer, huge, as big as Orgull, with skin as dark as the small man who had just spoken. His beard was knotted full of rings.

'Emad came here as you did – an oar slave. He was fifteen summers then. How long ago was that, Emad?'

'Nine years,' the big man said.

'Nine years. He fought in the pits and earned his freedom. He was given a choice and chose to join my family. You could do the same – or a ship's crew, or just walk away, if that is what you wish. You will fight for your freedom, and that is what we will give you.'

'Fight who?' the small man asked.

'Whoever is in front of you.' Herak shrugged. 'I will train you now. Most of you think you know how to fight, but I promise you, you do not. Yet. Then we shall put you against the pit-fighters of the other islands – Nerin and Pelset. If you live that long, then we shall talk of what comes next. That is all. I shall see you on the morrow.'

He turned and strode from the chamber. Maquin felt his stomach lurch and only had time to lean in his chair before he vomited onto the tiled floor.

Maquin spent the night in a cell underground, part of the labyrinthine complex that formed the fighting pits. He was led out into the ruins that he had seen before, the sunshine making him blink, and given breakfast along with the men from last night's feast. He did not indulge, only chewed on some fried goat's meat and warm bread. He washed it down with water.

Herak greeted them with a score of guards. Maquin didn't like the look of the whips wound at their belts, or the wicked-looking knives that they all carried.

'This is where it begins,' Herak said. 'Follow me.' He turned and moved into a loping run, heading off up a wide paved street. Maquin and his companions milled around, looking at one another.

'You heard him,' a voice barked. Emad, the guard from last night. He cracked his whip. Maquin saw Orgull run after the disappearing Herak. He followed Orgull, others joining him. The ones who were slower felt the touch of whips as other guards lashed out.

Soon they were all running through the ruined city. The ground was littered with rocks and debris; Maquin had to concentrate on every step. More than once he heard someone cry out as they fell, and cry out again as they were whipped back onto their feet by the guards who ran with them.

Maquin's lungs were burning, his legs felt as if they were pumped full of iron, and the sun was burning hot. Sweat sheeted him, blurring his vision. He focused on every step, every breath, willing himself to carry on. He had already vomited as he ran, bile splattering his feet and legs. He became aware of someone running next to him. Orgull.

'Keep the faith, brother,' Orgull gasped over his own heaving breaths. Maquin didn't have the breath to answer, and didn't know what he would have said if he had. *What faith? Not in Elyon, the absent god. Not in justice, or right defeating wrong. Maybe in vengeance, in its power to keep my legs moving.* He pictured Jael, gritted his teeth and increased his stride.

Herak let them rest a while after the run, gave them water. It was not long before they were led into a courtyard – this one cleared of debris, the floor bearing stains that looked suspiciously like old blood. *Some marks never wash clean.* More than anything the place resembled a weapons court; wooden weapons were stacked along one wall, different areas roped off.

'First things first,' Herak said as he stepped in front of them. 'Most of you probably know your way around a sword and spear. But to use them you need space. In the pit, space is a stranger. Pit-fighting is close and personal – close as lovers.' Some of the guards chuckled. The one called Emad nodded seriously. 'For that you need to learn to use these.' Herak lifted his arms and clenched his fists.

'And this.' He slapped his forehead. 'And these,' he touched his knees and pointed to his feet.

'When you've learned how to use all of that, you'll move on to this.' He drew a knife, curved and wicked looking. 'This'll be your best friend in a pit-fight. Closer than kin. So, let's begin. You, big man. Over here.' He beckoned to Orgull.

Orgull walked over cautiously, his eyes fixed on Herak. Herak ushered him into one of the roped-off areas.

'So, try and kill me,' Herak said amicably.

Orgull frowned, then took a deep breath and swung a punch at Herak.

Herak deflected it easily, like swatting a fly. 'Try harder,' he said irritably.

Orgull snapped a combination of punches out. He was fluid, well balanced on his feet. *He's no stranger to the pugil ring.* But Herak blocked or avoided the punches with little effort, swaying this way, the palm of his hand steering Orgull's arm that way. He darted inside Orgull's guard and slapped Orgull's face, hard, then moved out of range, just as quickly.

He doesn't look as if he should be able to move that fast.

Orgull scowled and moved after Herak, throwing a flurry of punches, one of them glancing off Herak's shoulder. Herak laughed. 'Better,' he said. Then he weaved inside Orgull's guard again, slammed two solid blows into Orgull's gut and kidney, finished with an uppercut flush on Orgull's chin as he bent from the gut blows. Orgull wobbled, then dropped to his knees.

'Take a man's legs away, and he's as good as dead,' Herak said to the watching crowd. 'He is now disoriented, a little stunned, and his legs are still weak. He is ready for the kill.'

With no warning, Orgull exploded from the ground, his hands grasping Herak by the throat, fingers squeezing. They both staggered backwards, Orgull's fingers gouging into Herak's flesh. Herak started to turn purple, his eyes bulging, but to Maquin it still looked as if he was smiling. Slowly, he saw one of Herak's hands move down, past Orgull's belt. He clutched at Orgull's groin, gave a sharp twist and the strength drained from Orgull in a heartbeat. He fell back onto the ground, curled like a baby, groaning.

'When in trouble, always go for the stones,' Herak said. 'Good effort, though, big man. You're faster than I thought.' He reached down an arm and helped Orgull stand. 'Remember, there's no honour in the pit. Just living or dying. Don't ever forget that.'

They spent the rest of the day sparring like this. Herak ordered them to avoid killing each other, with the incentive that if one died during the sparring, he would kill their partner. Maquin was teamed up with the small man who had asked most of the questions the night before. His name was Javed, a warrior from the land of Tarbesh, taken during a Vin Thalun raid. He was very fast, as Maquin found out all too soon.

Time passed like this, days merging, running, training, sparring, day after day. The weather grew cooler, though never truly cold, except at night, when the sky was free of cloud and stars shone sharp as ice. Maquin felt the aches of the first weeks begin to fade, replaced by a new strength in his body that he had never experienced. Not just strength, but a speed, flexibility and stamina that he thought he'd left behind with his youth. They had been taught hand-to-hand fighting skills that Maquin had never dreamed of: combinations of fist, knee and foot, as well as headbutting and biting. *Anything goes in the pits*, Herak was fond of saying. *There are no rules.* For a ten-night Herak made them spar tied wrist-to-wrist, said it was like that in the pits, where you could not escape another's touch. It sounded more and more to Maquin as if Herak spoke from experience.

Eventually Herak issued them all with wooden replicas of his own knife, curved and thick. They were taught the different grips, how to use both hands, how to stab to kill, to maim, to weaken, where to cut to disable. How to combine the knife with fist and knee and head and foot.

Then the day came when they were brought out from their cells beneath the ground and led in the opposite direction to their training courtyard. They were led to the coast, down the path that wound down the cliffs to the beach where Maquin had arrived so long ago.

'Where are we going?' Javed called out. They had all seen the single ship in the bay.

'To the island of Nerin,' Herak said. 'Where you will either die, or make us rich.'

CHAPTER SEVENTY

CAMLIN

Camlin warmed his hands over the fire. It had stopped raining now, stabs of sunshine piercing the emptied clouds, but he was still cold and wet. He was sitting in a sprawling camp, staring at the mountains that he had struggled across not that long ago. Marrock and Dath were sat either side him. Marrock was adjusting the straps of the buckler that seemed to be a permanent fixture on his left arm now. It was a small, round piece of iron, a spike sticking a handspan from the central boss.

Gotta hand it to him – he's adaptable. If I'd have lost a hand an' couldn't draw a bow ever again I think I'd still be weeping into my cups.

Volunteering to join the warband that had marched from Dun Taras to fight Queen Rhin had seemed brave and noble at first, the right thing to do. There had been a lot of singing and drinking on the night before the warband left Dun Taras. The next morning there were a lot of sore heads, and a few bloody noses as well, but that was all part of it. Since then, though, things had gone steadily downhill. So far this war had involved a lot of walking and holding your head down in the face of wind and rain. In fact, in many ways, it was not too distant an experience to thieving in the Darkwood, but with more men and guaranteed food and drink at the end of each march. And that was nothing to be sniffed at. Still, the rain had stopped, and so had the walking, so things were looking up. On the downside, Camlin was fairly sure that a warband would be marching through the mountains in the near future, full of men with cold iron in their hands, looking to stop his heart from beating.

You can always leave.

'Shut up,' he muttered.

'What was that?' Dath said beside him.

'Nothing.'

I might moan, but I'll not be leaving this crew anytime soon. I'm not going to turn my back on the first true friends I've ever had.

They had all come in the end, every last one of those who had survived the journey from Dun Carreg. Even the crow and the raven. Somehow Edana had talked her way into coming; Halion said that King Eremon's wife had supported Edana's efforts to come – probably in the hope that Edana would meet a tragic end and remove herself from the political throw-board. She was camped elsewhere, though, close to Rath, who was Eremon's battlechief.

I suppose it is fitting. Meet Rhin here – win or lose – at least there'll be an end to it. And this is as good a chance as we're likely to get.

Eremon's warband had grown to about ten thousand strong over the journey to the mountains. Camlin had never seen so many men in his life. In fact he didn't like it; sometimes he even found himself having to stare up at the sky and take deep lungfuls of air, just to escape the sensation of being crushed.

Footsteps sounded and Corban and Farrell came and sat by the fire, Gar hovering behind them. They both had bulky sacks slung over their shoulders.

'What've you got there?' Camlin asked him.

Corban looked to the hills they were camped before, at a few riders disappearing into the wooded slopes.

'Are they scouts?' Corban asked.

'Aye. Rath will put his men in the hills, I'd imagine. Make sure that Rhin's warband doesn't try anything sneaky as they march into Domhain.'

'Do you remember what Halion said back in Cambren, about teaching our enemy to fear the night?'

'Aye. What of it.'

'I think there's more to that lesson. I'm going to go find Rath, see what he thinks of it. I thought you and Dath might want to come along.'

Camlin looked at Dath. The lad smiled at him, a nervous twitch to it. 'Something tells me we'd best string our bows, then,' Camlin said as he stood.

CHAPTER SEVENTY-ONE

VERADIS

Veradis looked out along the giants' road. He was stood part way up a ridge.

'There are a lot of them,' Bos said beside him.

'Yes.'

'What's the plan, then?'

Veradis was silent a while. His warband was camped below, spread along the giants' road that they had marched upon. Two days it had taken them since they had parted from Nathair and marched through these looming mountains. Cywen's face formed in his mind, turning back in her saddle as she rode away, staring at him with her dark eyes. He shook his head.

They were almost the rearguard, a position that he was becoming used to. Rhin's warband stretched ahead, a sprawling mass filling the giants' road and its embankments.

'Geraint will push ahead at dawn on the morrow, then we'll see what the warriors of Domhain are like.'

'So we'll be watching, from the back.'

'Most likely. These warbands we march with – they don't want us stealing their glory.'

'Against a warband of that size I think there's plenty of glory to go round,' Bos said. 'And this road is made for the shield wall. We should be in the van, not the rearguard.'

'I know. But there's nothing I can do about it. Geraint is battle-chief here, not I. We'll just have to wait and see how things go.' He looked up at the hills either side of him. Bos followed his stare.

'It's a good spot for an ambush,' Veradis observed.

'Aye. We should put some men up in those hills.'

'We don't have them to spare. I'll talk to Geraint about it. Bos, you make sure our camp is tight tonight; all are to stay on this road – no tents set close to these slopes – and double guards.' He looked up at the hills, dense with pine and scrub, black boulders of granite looking like bones of the mountains poking through the hill's green flesh here and there. There could be a thousand men up there and he would not see one.

In the distance, high above them, a sound rang out, eerie and ululating. A wolven howling. Throughout the camp heads turned, fear spreading like seeds on the wind. Veradis and Bos looked at each other.

'I think I'll go and see Geraint right now. You see to the camp.'

CHAPTER SEVENTY-TWO

CORBAN

'Did you make her do that?' Rath asked Corban.

'No. She must sense something,' Corban said.

They were all looking at Storm, the last notes of her howl fading into the dusk.

'We are hunting. She knows it,' Gar said.

'Well, it was good timing.' Rath grinned. 'I nearly soiled my breeches, so Elyon knows what they're thinking down there.'

Rhin's warband stretched out below them like a dark river. Dusk was settling, and even as Corban looked, pinpricks of light winked into life, torches and campfires being lit to guard against the dark.

Soft footfalls sounded and Corban looked up to see figures emerging from between the trees. He reached for his sword hilt but Gar put a hand on his arm. Then he saw it was Camlin, with Dath close to him, and a handful of others, Baird the giant-hunter amongst them.

'We chased off a handful of scouts,' Baird said to Rath. 'They put a few arrows in backs as they were running.' He nodded at Camlin and Dath. 'Think it's clear up here, for now. I've put a guard on the trails from the mountains.'

'Good,' Rath said. 'Corban, Farrell, empty your sacks.'

They dumped a pile of fur and iron onto the ground, then each of them dragged a fur over their shoulders and began fastening them with leather buckles.

Thank you, Mam. Corban looked up with a wolven pelt draped about him, its head pulled up like the hood of a cloak. Storm growled at him and he tutted her silent. He bent down and pulled something else from the pile, a leather gauntlet, three iron claws at the end of it. The iron claws clinked as he strapped it onto his left forearm and flexed a fist.

'We skinned the wolven that attacked us up here,' Corban said to the warriors facing him. 'There are three more skins here.'

He threw a skin and gauntlet to Coralen, who buckled it onto her left arm. She growled and slashed with the claws, some of Rath's warriors laughing.

'Now you have three claws instead of a knife,' Corban said to her. He enjoyed the fierce grin she gave him.

'I've heard that Storm and our small company have made quite a name amongst the warriors of Cambren. Apparently they are telling tales of shape-shifters, and changelings, deals with Asroth, stories that we were raised by a wolven pack, that they run with us still; all sorts of tales.'

'I've heard a little of that too,' Baird said, grinning. 'Can I have one of those,' he said.

'Help yourself,' Farrell answered.

'Thought we might help those stories along a bit,' Corban said. 'You never know, there might be fewer ready to fight in the morning than are there right now. Superstitious bunch, warriors. What do you say?'

Rath nodded approvingly.

Coralen stepped forwards. 'Let's bring their nightmares to life.'

Corban crouched stiffly behind a boulder. It was dark now; only a sliver of the moon was visible, appearing from behind ragged clouds. And it was cold. The wolven fur he wore helped to keep the cold out, though. Storm had had a good sniff of it after he'd put it on, until she was accustomed to the smell on him. He'd gone through the same process with the others who had put on the wolven furs – Baird, Farrell, Rath and Coralen. Otherwise he had visions of Storm attacking them in the confusion of battle. After that they'd made up a paste of mud and blood, smearing it over their faces in swirling patterns to hide their skin.

'You look more like a bear than a wolven,' Coralen had said to Farrell.

'Thank you,' Farrell said.

'It wasn't a compliment.'

They were spread out along the slopes above Rhin's warband now with over a score of Rath's warriors – all huntsmen used to this terrain. They waited for the signal. Corban felt his eyes drooping. He was tired, had had trouble sleeping for a while now, ever since Dun Taras. And he always woke the same: sweating, scared, a half-remembered dream fluttering in his mind. Dreams of war, but with great winged creatures fighting in the air, almost like tales of the Scourging, when the Ben-Elim and Kadoshim had fought. *Probably nightmares brought on by Gar's mad delusions.* He scowled at Gar, who was crouched beside him.

'Rub your hands together,' Gar whispered. 'When the signal comes we must be quick, and you will be stiff with cold.'

'I can't,' Corban said. 'I'll chop my arm off.' He held up the makeshift wolven claw buckled to his left arm.

'Oh yes,' Gar said. 'Remember what Rath said, Ban. In and out. You and Storm will be targets.'

'This is important, Gar,' Corban muttered.

'I know. But so are you.'

Because I'm this Seren Disglair. I can't even pronounce it, how can I be it? He glanced at Gar, wished that this talk of Elyon and Asroth had never happened. He felt that it had driven something between them. *When will he accept that it is all in his mind?*

Gar drew his sword, grabbed a handful of loose soil and rubbed it along the blade. 'Do the same. It will stop reflections – moon, stars, firelight.'

Corban nodded and copied Gar.

A noise drifted up from the valley, shouting, higher-pitched screams. Rath had said he had arranged for a feint to be led against the front ranks of Rhin's warband. That would be their signal.

That's it.

Corban shared a look with Gar and then they both slipped around the boulder they were hiding behind, half-slithering down the hillside. Storm followed silently.

Tents were set all along the giants' road; directly below Corban many were spread along the embankment and grass that led to the hill slopes. Crouched low, sword in one hand, claws in the other, Corban reached the bottom of the slope, his heart thumping in his chest, fear bubbling in his gut.

Control it, master your fear, he ordered himself.

Men were outlined against a campfire, at least a dozen of them, all standing, looking towards where the noise of battle was drifting down the valley.

Corban heard a thrum, saw one of the men before the fire stagger, an arrow shaft sticking from his shoulder.

'Foe,' Corban whispered to Storm and together they leaped forwards, slashing, stabbing, biting. Gar surged forwards to his left, his curved sword moving in swooping arcs. Men fell before them, crashing into the fire, sparks flaring, the smell of scorched hair and flesh everywhere.

Corban slashed with his claws, stabbed with his sword, Storm close by pinning someone to the ground, their terrified screams suddenly cut short. A man before him fumbled with his sword as he staggered backwards, utter terror etched on his face. Corban snarled and followed him, caught a weak sword blow between his iron claws and punched his own sword into the man's stomach, slashing him across the chest as he toppled over.

And then there were no more men standing about them.

'Come on, Ban,' Gar called to him. He was running towards an embankment that led up onto the giants' road. Warriors were milling in confusion up there, campfires blazing periodically, framing the chaos. 'They need to see you,' Gar was yelling. 'There's no point only leaving the dead behind.'

He's right, we are a fear that needs to spread like a disease. He bent low and ran up the embankment, barrelling into a warrior, knocking him to the ground, slashing at his face as the man fell. Storm and Gar burst onto the road on either side of him, Gar cutting deep into a man's chest, Storm snarling, crouched low. Corban saw a warrior turn and run at the sight of her.

All about the road men were milling, weapons drawn, looking fearfully out into the darkness. Corban saw another man near a blazing campfire stagger and fall, an arrow jutting from his chest. *Camlin or Dath.* He glanced left and right, heard pockets of shouting, the clash of weapons in both directions. Rath's plan was for each warrior wearing the wolven skin to attack at different points, and a few men about them to protect and add to the confusion. They were not supposed to stay long, just long enough to kill a few, to maim more, and let their wolven pelts be seen.

'This way,' Gar said, leading him along the road, deeper into the mountains. Corban followed, running low, slashing with his claws as he went. Storm kept pace, men running from her.

Others began to appear along the road: warriors grouped together, grim faced, weapons levelled.

'They are rallying, it's time to go,' Gar said. 'Quick.' He pointed into the night, towards the embankment. Corban ran.

He sprinted along the edge of the road, Storm bounding ahead, Gar's feet slapping behind. Corban was about to slither down the embankment when he saw a sight that pulled him up short.

A knot of combat seethed before them, the clash of iron ringing out, sparks flying. Figures were rolling on the ground, one of them fur-covered. Corban caught a flash of red hair. *Coralen*. Nearby Corban recognized one of Rath's warriors trading blows with someone, saw Rath's warrior crumple as he was stabbed with a spear in the back. Further on Corban saw a row of warriors, their shields raised. Something about it stirred a memory in him, but then Coralen was shouting, snarling, drawing his eyes.

He ran forwards, hacked at the spear still buried in his comrade's back, splitting its shaft, and slashed the warrior holding it. The man fell away screaming, clutching at his face. The two rolling on the ground came to a halt, the warrior on top of Coralen, sword arm rising. Corban leaped forwards, grabbed the man and rolled, lost his grip of his sword, just kept slashing and stabbing with the claws on his left hand, slowly realizing his enemy was limp in his arms.

Hands grabbed him, pulling him to his feet – Coralen. She returned his sword. Gar stood close by, holding back two men. Storm was ripping a hole in a warrior's belly, blood spraying. Gar's sword slashed through one man's throat, sending him reeling back; the other man fighting him drew away, one arm hanging limp.

'We must leave, *now*,' Gar said. Corban turned and began to run, then saw the wall of shields on the road again, closer now. He stopped dead, remembering where he had seen its like before.

In Dun Carreg. The feast-hall, the night his world had changed. The night his da was killed.

They were Nathair's men, eagle-guard.

He walked closer, for a moment forgetting all else, shaking off Coralen's hand as she tugged at him.

'Nathair!' he yelled, his voice cutting the night.

Gar followed him, sword held ready, eyes scanning the wall. Corban remembered the man Gar had fought. Storm padded on his other side, snarling, fangs dripping red.

'Nathair,' Corban yelled again, emotion cracking his voice. 'Come out, face me.' A memory consumed him: Nathair plunging a sword into his da's chest. His knuckles became white about his sword hilt.

A figure stepped from the wall, a warrior. Not Nathair, stern faced, fairer haired, though of a similar age.

'Nathair is not here. But I will face you, Black Sun.' He took another step closer and raised a short sword.

Black Sun? The words registered, but were stripped of meaning as Corban was gripped by a swirl of grief and anger. He made to move forwards, then Gar was before him, his curved blade raised high. The world froze.

A shout rang out and the shield wall shuddered into life, lurching forwards one step, more. A space opened behind the unsuspecting warrior who had challenged Corban, moving about him before he realized what was happening. Shields pulled tight before him with a crack of wood. Corban heard a muffled voice, shouting. The shield wall continued to move forwards.

Corban stood there in shock, glaring, almost ready to launch himself at the wall of shields, but his bubbling rage did not erase his memory of what would happen if he got too close to those shields: a host of swords darting out. He could not break through it, he knew that.

'Tell your Nathair I will kill him one day,' he yelled, then turned and slithered down the embankment, his companions following. They swept through tents, not amongst warriors now, but the people that always accompanied a warband – families and tradesmen. Corban and his companions chopped at ropes, tents collapsing, kicked pots and cook-stands into fires, spreading panic as they went, and then they broke out into the night and were scrambling up a slope back into the safety of the hills. Coralen led them, twisting around black boulders and through patches of loose soil until Corban felt the soft cushion of pine needles beneath his feet. Here they paused, all four of them catching their breath and looking back down into the valley.

Points of light drew the eye, the campfires looking like candle flames from this height, winding along the giants' road. Towards the rear of the warband flames spread as tents caught fire in the wake of Corban's passing. The sound of battle was gone now, but confusion still seemed to be spreading amongst the warband, horn blasts ringing out.

'Best get back to Rath,' Coralen breathed, her voice raw, and they moved off. Corban paused, sure he had heard the sound of something in the woods behind him, but nothing moved, so he set off again. He frowned to himself as he ran, though. It had sounded like the whine of a hound.

CHAPTER SEVENTY-THREE

VERADIS

Veradis was calm now, though it had taken until the break of day for him finally to become so. Behind him the rising sun was a pale glow on the horizon. *I have seen the Black Sun, come a hair's breadth from crossing swords with him.* And then his shield wall had closed about him, Bos standing silent, holding him in an unbreakable grip until Corban and his followers had fled.

In a way he was grateful, glad that he had been stopped from fighting. He had wanted to hate Corban, had stared at him and tried to muster some righteous anger, some hatred of Asroth and his dark ways, but all he had seen was Cywen staring back at him. Their resemblance was striking. Veradis would have known that it was Cywen's brother, even without the wolven. The same dark eyes, the high cheekbones, the scruffy hair, even the expression. Corban had been angry, and he had seen that emotion writ across Cywen's features more than once.

He felt guilty. For Nathair's sake he should have fought him.

He heard footfalls behind him, stopping a few paces away. He turned to see Bos.

The big man sank to one knee. 'I have come to speak for the eagle-guard, and myself. We disobeyed you. We are sorry, and will accept any punishment you judge fit.' He looked at the ground.

'Get up,' Veradis said.

'I have more to say.'

He sighed. 'Go on then.'

'You are our leader, have led us through many dangers. You are our lord, our general, our brother, and we love you. Any one of us would give our life for you, without thought. Last night you would have died. I, we, could not just watch . . .'

'It was the Black Sun, Bos; Asroth's champion, right there, before us. I had the chance to slay him, to end the God-War.'

'The one in the wolven pelt?'

'Aye.'

'It was not him that worried me; it was the other one, the warrior with him. He was Jehar. You are the first-sword of Tenebral, but I doubt even you could best one of them.'

'I think he was the man who killed Rauca,' Veradis said.

Bos frowned at that and seemed to think about it for a while. 'The man who killed Rauca and then ten of our eagle-brothers. On his own.' He looked at Veradis, letting his words sink in.

I would have died, most likely. He stepped forward and squeezed Bos' shoulder.

'Disobey me again and I shall dismiss you from the eagle-guard.'

Bos looked up at him and nodded.

'Now get up.'

'What happens now?' Bos asked him.

'Geraint will march soon, and there will be a battle. We shall watch and wait; be prepared to be called upon.'

'There is much talk. Many have fled,' Bos observed.

It was true, the night raid had set a fear coursing through Geraint's warband like a disease on the wind. Talk of changelings and demons prowling the night had been one thing, but corpses bearing claw marks, and witnesses testifying to seeing wolven and changelings slaying warriors with tooth and claw had led to hundreds slipping away in the darkness. Veradis had spoken to Geraint, told him it had been men in wolven fur, but he was not sure if even Geraint believed him. There were a lot of dead with their throats torn out.

'I know. But the battle will still happen. Geraint cannot just turn around and go home. Rhin scares him more than wolven in the night.'

'Sensible man.' Bos chuckled. 'But his men, they will fight with fear already planted in their guts.'

'That was the goal of last night's raid, I think.' Veradis shrugged. 'We shall see what we shall see. And we shall also keep an eye on those hills – I don't want any more surprises.'

*

Horns rang out and the warriors of Cambren began to move along the giants' road, no songs of war rising up, only the tramp of many feet. Veradis could see Geraint at the front, surrounded by a knot of his shieldmen. In the distance he saw Eremon's warband standing ready, iron glinting in the weak sunlight.

He was standing with Bos; a score of his eagle-guard were spread a little higher up the slope. They were a long way from the trees that gave cover at the hill's crown, and out of bow shot. Any attack from above would be seen early on.

The warband juddered to a halt, only a few hundred paces from Eremon's lines.

'They'll do some drinking now,' Bos said quietly.

'Aye.'

It was a hard thing, starting a war, and harder still for those in the front ranks, those who would have to put some will into their legs and go willingly to battle, and very possibly to their deaths. The first steps were always the hardest. A few mouthfuls of wine or mead often helped summon the courage that was needed and Veradis could see skins being handed about between warriors in Eremon's warband, too. *I doubt if they're full of water.* A dose of courage to face a charge.

A roar went up from Geraint's warband, rising up from the front and rippling back through its masses, like the muscular contractions of a snake in motion. The front ranks moved quicker, breaking away, running at Eremon's warband.

They too roared, clashing swords and spears on shields, then charged to meet their foe.

Veradis saw the impact of the front rows before he heard it, then there was a great crash, like thunder overhead, ringing along the ravine, echoing about the hills. The two warbands filtered into one another, a patchwork of the green of Domhain and the black and gold of Cambren. The battle descended into a thousand duels, each warrior finding a foe to fight, the one left standing moving on to the next. And so it would go, until all the enemy were dead, or one side lost heart and ran.

Bos drew in a deep breath. 'It's going to be a long day.'

CHAPTER SEVENTY-FOUR

CORBAN

Corban walked through the huge paddock that spread across the meadows behind the camp, then he saw her.

'Morning,' Coralen said as he approached.

They had only had a few hours' sleep since their return to camp after the raid, but Coralen looked fresh and alert, ready for anything. She was checking the girth on a horse, other riders nearby preparing their mounts.

'What are you doing?' Corban asked.

'Rath's sending me into the mountains. In case they try and sneak around our flanks.'

'Should be a quiet day for you, then. Don't think any of them will dare step into those woods. Not after last night. They might get eaten by a shape-shifter.'

She flashed him a smile at that, a rare sight from her. It scattered his thoughts for a moment.

'I wanted to talk to you,' he said.

'That's what I was thinking.' She looked at him appraisingly, one eyebrow raised.

'About Conall.'

'Oh.'

Corban didn't know what Halion had told her, but he didn't think it was much. After last night, the way he had seen her risk her life, he felt she deserved to know.

'He killed my sister, Cywen. And he betrayed Brenin, sided with the man who opened the gates to Owain and let the enemy into Dun Carreg.' *There, I've said it, plain as I can.* He tried to keep the anger from his voice, just tell the facts, without his own feelings creeping into it.

Emotions swept Coralen's face, one chasing the other: anger, disbelief, disappointment.

'Con did that? He's a lot of things, but – betrayal? He's always had his own code.'

Corban took a deep breath, keeping the anger at bay. 'Something happened to him. He grew jealous of Halion, who rose in Brenin's service – Halion was Brenin's first-sword for a while.'

'Was he now?' Coralen said.

'Did he not tell you?'

'He's not told anyone that,' Coralen said.

'That's the kind of man Halion is. Humble.'

Coralen nodded. 'I know. And Con didn't like it?'

'Not at all. I thought him siding with Evnis was as much to spite Halion as anything else. Just my opinion.'

They stood there in silence, Coralen fiddling with a buckle and strap in her mount's girth. After a while she looked up at him, her eyes narrowing.

'What are you waiting for? Are you wanting a kiss now? I'm not Maeve, you know.'

'What?' For a moment he was back in the feast-hall, Maeve's arms about him, his face stinging from Coralen's slap. *She's just jealous*, Maeve had said to him. Somehow he didn't believe that.

'Maeve said you were jealous,' he said, thinking Coralen would find that funny. She didn't. *She's going to kill me*, he thought and took a step back.

'Jealous!' Coralen spat the word.

'She kissed me,' he mumbled, some kind of defence. 'Just thought you should know about Conall, that's all.' *A kiss?* He found himself looking at her lips, then remembered the long list of cuts and bruises she'd given him in the weapons court. He shook his head. *What's wrong with me?*

'All right then. Thank you,' Coralen said. He nodded and walked away.

'Corban,' she called after him. He paused and looked back.

'I'm sorry about your sister.'

'So am I,' he said and left.

*

Corban wanted to cover his eyes. It was horrible. Just the noise of it was deafening. He had witnessed a battle of a similar scale once before, between Owain's warband and men of Ardan come to relieve the siege at Dun Carreg. But he had been sitting high above on the walls over Stonegate, with the battle fought on the plains far below, where warriors had looked as small as ants.

This was different.

The warbands had crashed together like two great waves, a concussive explosion of noise slapping him, a physical blow that made him stagger. From his vantage point he could see individuals, see pain etched upon faces, see limbs severed from bodies, hear the screaming, smell the sweat and blood, the urine and excrement as death claimed victim after victim. Crows circled the air, hundreds of them, and he wondered if Craf and Fech were in the carrion horde.

He was standing on a small rise at the rear of Domhain's warband, overlooking the battle. Tents were behind him, a score of healers gathered close by, bracing themselves for the coming work. Brina was amongst them, and had asked for his help. At first he had said that he would be fighting, but Rath had come and seen him soon afterwards and told him to keep out of the combat until dusk, if it went on that long. He had another plan up his sleeve.

So Corban had found Brina and told her he was able to help. It would be better than doing nothing. He was not so sure now.

Warriors started to trickle into the tents – some staggering, supported by comrades-in-arms, other carried on litters. Many were screaming, others delirious with pain. Corban spent much of his time giving men sips of usque, or poppy-milk that had been ground and mixed the night before. He had never seen so much of the pain reliever in his life, but it did not last that long. By highsun most of the jugs were empty.

'Hold him tighter,' Brina snapped at him. They were hunched over a warrior lying upon the ground, his foot and ankle a bloodied mess. He had been screaming, flailing with the pain a short while ago, but half a jug of usque had quietened him. Now he was groaning, until Brina started digging around in his wound with her knife.

'Tighter,' Brina ordered as she moved her blade around. 'No point stitching him up with all of this filth in here,' she muttered, pulling out slivers of leather and cloth, bits of the man's boot that had followed the blade that had stabbed him into his wound. 'His leg will just go green and swell, and he'll die half a ten-night later.' She stood up straight. 'It's going to have to come off.' She looked about. 'You'll need help to hold him.'

'I'll help,' a voice said behind them, a man stepping close. Ventos the trader.

Brina bustled off to get hot water and cloths, a saw.

'I didn't know you were here,' Corban said to Ventos.

'Might as well do something useful,' he said. 'The best way out of Domhain for a wain is the giants' road, and it's blocked at the moment. If I'm stuck here I might as well help in some way. And, as much as I like Eremon and Domhain, I don't feel strongly enough to draw my sword and stand out there.' He nodded towards the battlefield, where the muted roar of battle drifted on the cold wind.

Brina returned with her arms loaded. 'Hold him tight, both of you,' she said. 'It'll be hardest at first, but he won't stay conscious for long.' She looked at them both. 'Ready?'

'Aye,' they both said, although Corban wasn't.

The man screamed like Asroth was ripping his heart out, but Brina was right, he lapsed into unconsciousness soon after Brina's saw started cutting into the bone of his lower leg. Still, after Brina had sawn for a while, Corban wasn't sure which sound he hated most – the screaming or the iron grating through bone. Then came the cauterizing of the wound, the stench of burning flesh, the sewing of skin. The wrapping of bandages. By the time Brina was finished Corban's hair was plastered to his face with sweat.

'Go and rest for a while, get some air, drink some water,' Brina muttered to him and Ventos.

Corban looked about the tent they were in and made for the entrance. He passed another healer bent over an injured warrior, saw the healer cut the man's throat with a sharp little knife. It was not the first time he had seen that small mercy handed out today. He saw his mam, mopping blood from a gaping wound in someone's shoulder.

He left the cloying heat of the healers' tent and stepped into the cold air. It was late in the day now, the sun sinking into the west, sending shadows stretching east.

The battle still raged. It had moved back towards the mountains, leaving a field carpeted by the dead, startlingly still in contrast to the frenetic activity only a few hundred paces further on. The bravest crows were already swooping down. He just stood there, breathing deeply, the cold air sharp in his lungs, then turned around and stepped back into the healers' tent.

A hand tapped his back. He was emptying a bowl of blood for Brina. He turned and saw Rath, blood spattered, a cut grazing his forehead.

'Brina will see you soon,' Corban said.

'I've come to see you, Corban. Come, step outside now.'

Corban followed him out of the tent, felt a presence behind him and saw his mam had followed. Gar was leaning against a tent post.

'We're winning this battle,' Rath said. 'I think we could end it with you and your wolven's help.'

Corban looked past him, saw Rath's giant-killers lined behind him. Coralen nodded to him. She was already wearing her wolven pelt.

'What do you want me to do?' he asked Rath.

Corban buckled on the clawed gauntlet and drew his sword.

'I'm ready,' he said.

He was standing with Rath, Coralen, Farrell and Baird, all of them in their wolven skins. Storm stood beside him. At their back were the rest of Rath's giant-killers, ten men, and Corban's companions: Gar, Dath, Camlin, Marrock and Vonn. His mam was there as well, wearing a leather cuirass and clutching her spear. Knives were belted across her chest. Gar had told her she wasn't coming.

'You'll not be stopping me,' she had said, giving Gar a look that silenced any reply. She was still angry from last night, that she had not been told about the raid. She had been in a state of fear and rage combined when Corban had returned to their tents, and she had wept and scolded both Corban and Gar.

'Come on then,' Rath said, and they set off.

It was dusk. Rath's plan was to launch an attack on one of the flanks of Rhin's warband. They had already been pushed back, were tired and faltering. Seeing a pack of wolven and changelings attacking them might start a rout. That was Rath's hope.

They skirted the battle at a distance, looping out wide. The sky was purple, an orange flush on the horizon the last of the sun. Then Rath signalled and they ran at a cluster of Rhin's warriors.

They saw Storm first, her bone-white fur drawing the eye, then the rest of them, fur and blood covered. They must have been an eerie sight in the half-light of dusk. Corban saw men slapping each other and pointing, some scrabbling away, slipping and falling. One stood and stared in horror. He was the one that Storm leaped upon, her jaws latching onto his neck and shoulder, her momentum flipping him through the air and slamming him to the ground.

Corban and the others were only heartbeats behind her, carving into any who were wavering between fight and flight. Corban slashed a warrior across his gut, ripping into chainmail, and stabbed him in the throat with his sword; the warrior collapsed in a spray of arterial blood. Marrock ran past him, punching a warrior in the face with his buckler, the iron spike piercing the man's eye. He collapsed into a boneless heap.

They cut down all resistance within moments and then moved on, carving deeper into Rhin's warband. Coralen was close to Corban and he saw her raise her head and let out a keening, wordless war cry.

Corban echoed her, the rest of them following suit. They howled as they killed, and wherever they trod, men ran. First in ones and twos, but soon knots of warriors were breaking away, heading back towards the mountains. Then the trickle became a flood, and the whole of Rhin's left flank was in flight. Geraint must have realized that the day was done, for horn blasts rang out, and the centre retreated slowly, fighting as they went.

Rath ordered the signal to break from the battle, and soon the field was full of men standing, exhausted, watching their enemy flee back to the hills. A ragged cheer went up, Corban and his wolven pack howling as euphoria swept them – relief at being alive, the mad joy of victory. Then Corban heard the screaming, men dying about him on the battlefield, the stench of blood and excrement. *How can we do this to one another?* For a sickening moment he felt overwhelmed with shame. *Look what we have done.* Then his mind flew back to the Darkwood, where Queen Alona had been kidnapped and killed, a spark that had started a chain reaction of death. Started by Rhin, and still happening, even here. He felt something harden inside, a resolve to see this through. *I cannot run forever. To stop her we must fight her. And we have won. Today, at least.*

CHAPTER SEVENTY-FIVE

CORALEN

Coralen prodded her sword into the back of a prisoner, making him increase his pace.

The battle had been won, but she had not stopped to celebrate, or rest. Rath had sent her with a band of others back into the foothills to patrol for stragglers or surprise attacks.

'Just because we did it last night, doesn't mean they can't do the same to us,' the old warrior had said. Coralen didn't mind, anyway. She'd rather keep busy – less time to brood about all that Corban had told her of Conall.

Horses appeared out of the gloom as she approached their makeshift camp. She handed over the man – a blacksmith by the look of his scarred and pitted features – she had found creeping through the undergrowth to Baird. Without a word, she slipped back into the woodland, heading for the slopes that led down to the giants' road. That would be where deserters or raiders would appear, climbing up from the camps below.

She moved silently through the woodland, gliding from tree to tree, using the shadows, a lifetime's worth of training just habit now, an automatic response bypassing conscious thought, like fighting. Without realizing, she found Conall hovering in her mind's eye, the expression on his face a mixture of insolence and humour, daring the world to throw all it could at him. She felt a physical pain at the thought of him, a knife twisting in her gut. *Con, betraying Halion.* One thing she knew about Halion: he would do the right thing, or at least what he considered to be the right thing, no matter how hard it was to see it through. And he was a peacemaker. He would not have driven any dispute with Conall. No matter how she looked at it, she came back to the same conclusion. Corban had told her the truth.

And I am grateful for that. He had treated her like an equal, not a bairn, which was what Halion had done. She knew now that Halion had kept the truth from her out of an effort to spare her pain and to save Conall's name, his reputation, but she'd rather have the truth, no matter how unpleasant.

Corban. Regarding her with his dark, serious eyes. *Waiting for a kiss. Why did I ask him that? What an idiot I am.* She liked him, she was coming to realize. He was certainly good to have around in a scrap, him and his wolven and Gar. Between them they could put the fear of Asroth into most that faced them, and she respected that. But it was more than that. She liked the way he spoke to her. Open, genuine, nothing hidden.

Something caught her eye and she paused, squatting. She was close to the edge of the woodland now, where the slope suddenly dropped down to the camps far below.

Spoor, scattered about, as if it had been kicked to hide it. From a big animal, not big enough for a wolven, but not deer or anything else she would expect to see up here. She lifted it and broke some off, sniffing.

Hounds. No question. And more than one. But what are hounds doing up here, and where are they now? It was drying, but still moist at its centre. Half a day old, no more.

There was a rustling to her left. She dropped the spoor and moved closer to a tree, merging with its shadow.

A figure appeared, climbing the slope, breathing heavily. He staggered upright, looking about. A young man, fair haired, a warrior.

She stepped out of the shadows.

He stumbled back a pace, reaching for his sword hilt, then paused.

'You're only a girl,' he said.

Your first and last mistake. Do, don't think.

She exploded forwards, swatting a hand away, one hand grabbing his collar, the other pressing her knife to his gut.

'I am,' she said, 'and if you don't walk where I tell you, I'll slit you from belly to throat.'

He licked his lips. 'Think I'll choose the walking.'

CHAPTER SEVENTY-SIX

CORBAN

Corban sipped from a skin of ale, smiling at Dath and Farrell as they traded stories from the raid of the night before.

'I saw you,' Dath said to Farrell. 'You slipped as you ran up the slope, flat on your face. Have you ever seen a clumsy wolven?'

'It was steep, and the ground was loose,' Farrell said, slurring his words a little. He'd had a lot of ale. He was smiling, though – they all were, celebrations sweeping their camp.

'Good job Coralen didn't see you slip. Don't think she likes the clumsy type.' Dath grinned.

'She called me a bear,' Farrell said, frowning.

Dath and Corban laughed.

'Do you think she likes bears? I'm hoping she does.'

Their tents were set on the edge of the camp, close to the paddocks. Corban heard the creak of harness, saw the outlines of a few horsemen now. A group of figures followed them closely on foot, one falling and being dragged for a few paces before the riders stopped.

Prisoners, tied to the horses, Corban realized. As the rider turned to look at the fallen man the campfire highlighted her face. It was Coralen.

She should be celebrating with the rest of us.

'Look, there's your future wife,' Dath said to Farrell.

'I'm going to ask her if she likes bears,' Farrell said, concentrating as he stood, but still managing to look unsteady.

'Are you sure this is a good idea?' Corban asked him as they walked towards Coralen.

'Coralen,' Farrell called out.

'Too late,' said Dath.

'You should join us, for a drink. To celebrate,' Farrell said, looking up at Coralen in her saddle.

Other riders were there. Corban recognized Baird and nodded a greeting at the warrior.

'There's still a war going on and, besides, you fall over after a few drinks,' Coralen said.

Farrell blinked at that. It was obviously not the answer he'd been expecting.

'Do you like bears?' he said instead.

'What?'

'Bears. Big furry animals. Do you like them?'

'What's going on here?' Coralen said, looking at Dath and Corban. Her eyes fixed back on Farrell. 'Are you dim-witted? Or are you mocking me?'

Farrell, you need to stop, before she stabs you.

'I'm not mocking you,' Farrell said, face twisting in shock. 'I would never mock you.'

Please stop.

'I love you.'

Oh no.

Dath laughed and staggered.

'You're drunk,' Coralen said.

'A little,' Farrell muttered.

'You must scare these lads,' a voice said behind Coralen, 'if they need a drink to muster the courage to talk to you.' It was Baird, grinning from ear to ear.

'Shut up,' Coralen said over her shoulder.

'I don't need a drink to find my courage,' Farrell said, scowling at Baird. He looked back to Coralen. 'You haven't answered my question. Do you like bears?'

'What? Yes, I suppose. If they're not trying to eat me. I've heard they make a good meal, and a good bearskin will always keep you warm.'

'I think he'd like to keep you warm,' Baird said, nodding at Farrell.

'You see,' said Farrell to Corban and Dath. 'She does like bears.' He grinned.

'Well, if we've exhausted your conversation, perhaps we can get on,' Coralen said. 'We're in the middle of something.'

'Who are they?' Dath said, pointing to the line of figures bound behind Coralen and her companions.

'The enemy,' Coralen said. 'Found most of them up in the hills. Might be deserters, might be spies.'

Corban stared at them, a huddled mass in the darkness, fire-light from the camp flickering across shapes and faces. There were warriors amongst them, but also women, even children.

'I think the raid the other night sent a lot of them running to the hills,' Baird said. 'And for all the ones we've caught, there'll be a score more still out there.'

Corban frowned, staring hard. There was something familiar about one of the figures. Standing hunched over, head down, but still . . .

He stepped forwards.

'Careful,' Baird said. 'They've been checked for weapons, but you never know.'

Corban ignored him, shouldering his way through the huddle of figures if they didn't move quickly enough.

'You,' he said. 'Look at me.'

The figure ignored him.

'Look at me,' Corban said, then drew his sword, a slow rasp.

A face appeared, fair haired, dirt stained and gaunt, but still one Corban would never forget.

It was Rafe.

CHAPTER SEVENTY-SEVEN

LYKOS

Lykos leaped from the boat into the foaming surf and waded to shore. He stood upon a long strip of beach, a wide river flowing out into the sea behind him. On the horizon he could see a dark strip of forest.

Tenebral, it is good to see you again.

He had been away from here far too long. This place was too important to his plans.

Can a god read my mind? Even a fallen one? I hope not, even though he can speak into it.

His hand reached inside his cloak, fingertips touching his gift from Calidus.

Calidus had given it to him at Dun Carreg. 'Help Jael take the realm of Isiltir for his own, then you must return to Tenebral. Fidele cannot be left unwatched. She is changeable, and Tenebral is important. She will need to be steered. Use diplomacy if you can, but if all else fails, use this.' Calidus had given him a box, in it something wrapped in linen, no bigger than his thumb.

It had been good to return to the Three Islands, to Panos, Nerin and Pelset, and see that old oaths were renewed, but he had taken too long in his visiting, he knew. It was the eve of winter now. He should have been back sooner.

On the beach still reared the bones of ships, hulls half-fitted with long strakes of oak supported by timber scaffolding.

He frowned. *They should be finished, ready for the ocean.*

He looked about, saw Alazon the old shipwright striding towards him with his rolling gait. He didn't look happy. Behind him, at the beach's edge, stood a knot of warriors. Men of Tenebral, dressed in leather kilts and black cuirasses embossed with a white eagle. They started making their way towards him.

Something's wrong. Deinon and his other shieldmen splashed ashore behind him. He heard Deinon draw his sword.

'Put it away,' Lykos said.

Alazon drew close. 'They have found the fighting pits, have slain men, taken prisoners, freed our slaves,' Alazon blurted. That was all he had a chance to say before the warriors of Tenebral reached them.

'Lykos of the Vin Thalun,' one of them said.

'Aye, you know I am.'

'You will come with us. The Lady Fidele orders your presence.'

'Of course. I'd like that.' He grinned. 'We've got a lot to talk about.'

CHAPTER SEVENTY EIGHT

CORBAN

Rafe lunged at him, but, surprised as Corban was, he managed to step to the side and club Rafe with the pommel of his sword.

Dath and Farrell dragged Rafe to his feet.

'What's going on?' Baird said as he rode close.

'We know him,' Corban said. 'From home.'

It felt strange to say those words, to hear them spoken aloud.

'Not a friend?' Baird said.

'No.' Corban remembered the night Dun Carreg had fallen, how Rafe and his da, Helfach, had attacked him, separated him from his own da as he fought Nathair's eagle-guard.

'Your wolven killed my da,' Rafe said.

'She did,' Corban said. 'And I am glad.'

'Let's kill him,' Dath said.

'No.' Corban said it, but it was echoed by Farrell. 'We'll take him to Halion and Edana. I think they'll have much to talk to him about.'

Edana's tent was simply furnished – a table, a few chairs, a curtain to separate her sleeping area. She just stared at Rafe as Corban led him before her, his hands still bound. Halion stood to one side of her, Marrock and Vonn to the other. Fech sat on the back of a chair, his head cocked to one side.

Dath and Farrell filed silently in. They had not told anyone else, just marched straight to Edana's tent. Corban heard the tent flap rustle, saw Coralen slip inside.

Rafe looked nervous, his eyes darting from one person to the next.

'How is it that you are here?' Edana said to him coldly.

Rafe looked at the ground.

'Answer your Queen,' Vonn said.

Rafe's head snapped up at Vonn's voice. 'She's not my Queen. Evnis rules in Ardan now. That's right, Evnis – your da. It was him that told me to come,' he said, staring hard at Vonn. 'He'll be pleased to know you're alive – he tore Dun Carreg apart looking for you. And he'll be angry as hell to know you're fighting against Rhin, and him.'

'My father is a traitor and a murderer,' Vonn said. 'He is *dead* to me.' Vonn's face turned a darker shade.

Rafe shrugged. 'Have it your way.'

How does he really feel about his da? Can he just cut him off, be his enemy? I don't think I could ever have done that to my da, but then, my da wasn't Evnis.

'You haven't answered the question,' Corban said. 'Why did Evnis send you here?'

'I suppose because they were hunting you, and Evnis wanted someone with them who would recognize you. All of you, but Corban most of all.'

Evnis. Corban felt a pulse of anger at the name. 'They?' Edana asked.

'Nathair. Rhin.'

What do Nathair and Rhin want with me?

Edana took a deep breath and sipped from a cup. Corban didn't think it was water. This ghost from the past was unsettling her, too.

'Tell me of what has happened in Ardan, since . . .' she trailed off.

'Since you turned traitor and helped Owain take Dun Carreg,' Marrock said, his voice cold as frost-touched iron.

'Why should I?' Rafe said.

'Because we'll kill you if you don't,' Marrock said. 'Painfully.' Corban believed him.

It seemed that Rafe did, too, because he began to talk.

Corban stood in shock as he listened to the tale of Owain's defeat and Rhin's victory. He had known, of course, that Rhin had conquered Owain and ruled Ardan, because it was Rhin's warband they were fighting now. But to hear it told, to hear the details, it brought it home, somehow: the depth of scheming and planning, the cold malice that had fed Rhin's ambitions.

'And you'll all taste soon enough what Rhin is like in war,' Rafe said. 'You won't be sitting around a campfire singing, then.'

'If you believe that, why were you running?' Edana said. 'You were caught in the hills, trying to get back to Cambren.'

Rafe shrugged. 'That raid of yours, the other night, it reminded me of how my da died.' He looked to Corban. 'Didn't like that much. Just wanted to get away.'

'If Rhin is so cunning in battle, why has she not been victorious today?' Marrock said.

'Because she's not here. Her battlechief's leading. She's off in Cambren somewhere, with Nathair. A fortress – Dun Van something.'

'Dun Vaner, her capital.'

'That's right. I imagine she and Conall will be back soon enough. She wouldn't want to miss the fall of Domhain.'

'Conall?' Halion and Coralen said together.

'That's right. Conall's her first-sword now. He challenged and beat Morcant the night of the battle with Owain. I imagine he'll be pleased to see you.'

'Conall's dead,' Halion said, the colour draining from his face. 'He fell.' He looked to Marrock. 'You said he fell, from Stonegate with Cywen.'

'They did. I saw it clearly,' Marrock said.

'Aye, they did fall; I saw their bruises,' Rafe said. He looked around at the group, a vicious smile creeping across his face at their stunned expressions. 'Did you not know? Conall and Cywen are *alive.*'

Corban just stared at Rafe. *Cywen's alive.* The words rang around his head, echoing, growing louder, filling his senses. He felt unsteady and reached out a hand, supporting himself on a tent pole.

'Cywen's alive.' His voice, strangely detached.

'She was, the last I saw her, half a ten-night gone.'

'What do you mean? You're lying. Dun Carreg is moons from here.'

'She's not in Dun Carreg, is she? She's the other side of those mountains, going north with Nathair and Rhin.'

'And Conall's with them?' Halion spoke now, looking much like Corban felt.

'Why?' Corban said. 'Why would Cywen be Nathair and Rhin's prisoner? She's of no consequence to them.'

'I don't know.' Rafe shrugged.

Corban grabbed Rafe and spun him round, slammed his back against a tent pole. 'You're lying.'

'I'm not,' Rafe said, his smirk gone, fear in his eyes. 'Why would I lie?'

'As a last spite from you, when you can do nothing else.'

'I swear, she's alive, and Conall. Ask anyone.'

'I will,' Edana said. 'And if you are lying I shall let Corban feed you to Storm.'

Corban walked through the camp, avoiding the celebrations.

Coralen had questioned a handful of prisoners: a mixture of people, some warriors, others tradesmen, smiths, tanners, a few women. All had given similar information, that a girl, a captive, had travelled from Ardan with Rhin's warband. Each description sounded like Cywen, dark haired, fiery, though none had known her name. It was easier still with Conall – all had known his name, told of how he had bested Morcant.

Corban felt sick. Cywen was alive, and he had left her, run away. Abandoned her. How must she have felt. Tears stung his eyes. Then he smiled. *Cywen's alive.*

He reached their part of the camp, saw some of his friends around the fire – Brina with Craf perched on her knee, Camlin and Ventos sharing a skin. Then he spotted who he was looking for. His mam, sat with Gar. They were talking quietly, smiling. He stood in the shadows and watched them, not wanting to break this moment. Then his mam looked up and saw him. Her smile withered as he stepped out of the darkness and she saw his expression.

'What's wrong?' she asked him.

'It cannot be. Tell me again.'

'Mam, I've told you twice already.'

'My poor Cywen – alone through all of this.' She started to sob, trying not to. Gar squeezed her shoulder and she turned and pummelled his chest. 'You said you'd go back, that you'd go back and get her!'

Gar let her. 'But she was dead,' he said.

'I'm going to go and find her,' Corban said. 'Bring her back.'

'Ban, you can't,' Gar said.

'Yes, he can,' Gwenith said, standing and putting her arm around Corban's shoulder. 'We can. I'm going with him.'

Gar sighed, holding back his objections as he looked from one to the other.

'I'll go and pack,' he said.

Corban stepped into Edana's tent. Rafe was gone now; only Marrock, Vonn and Halion remained with Edana.

'Quite a night,' Edana said to him with a sorrowful smile.

'Yes. I have come to ask you something.'

Edana studied him. 'You mean to go after her.'

'I wish to.' Corban nodded. 'But I have sworn an oath to protect you. I did not take that oath lightly . . .'

'I know you didn't,' Edana said, 'and you have already fulfilled it a hundred times over. But Cywen is alive, and your heart breaks for her. I can see it in your eyes.'

She stepped around the table and took his hand. 'Go. I give you permission.'

'But the battle, the war . . .'

'Is almost won,' Edana said. 'You saw today – did more than see, you played a great part. The spirit of Rhin's warband is broken, nearly half of their warriors dead. Tomorrow we will end this.'

'You don't mind?'

'No, I don't mind. I will worry for you, but you must go. Cywen is part of us, is she not? She is like family to me. As are you. Go and get her, Corban. And hurry back.'

'Thank you,' he said, his voice cracking.

'I wish I could come with you, that we all could go. I know we were running for our lives, but there was something about our journey, living day to day. Here it is just politicking: I have to be so careful of every word I say.' She sighed. 'Now, let's see what I can do to help you.'

It was still dark as Corban climbed into a saddle. He should have been tired, exhausted, but an energy coursed through him, giving him strength. His mam and Gar sat on horses beside him, and Coralen just in front.

Edana had taken Corban to Rath, and he had provided horses and provisions, and also Coralen as a guide to lead them north. She had not complained about the task, though she had been quiet, none of her sharp comments forthcoming. She looked thoughtful. *Perhaps it is the possibility of seeing Conall.*

'Ready?' she asked them.

'Corban nodded.

'Best get on, then.'

They set off at a slow walk as the edge of dawn was turning the land a uniform grey.

'Wait,' a voice called and Corban turned to see Edana appear, figures behind her. Some led horses. Dath and Farrell, Brina riding at their head. A squawk drifted down from above.

'You'll only go and get yourself killed without us,' Brina said. 'Well, without me.'

'Thought you might need some protecting,' Farrell said, looking at Coralen. She rolled her eyes.

'It's not right,' Dath said to Corban, 'you going off into the wild without us.'

'I won't say I'm not glad, but what about Edana?' Corban said.

'I am quite safe here,' Edana said. 'I have Halion and Marrock, Camlin and Vonn.'

Camlin stepped over to Corban and offered his arm. Corban gripped it.

'Look after yourself,' Camlin said. 'I would come, but I cannot leave Edana. I'll look forward to seeing Cywen, though, when you bring her back. Always knew how to get herself into a scrape, that girl.'

'She does.' Corban grinned.

'And you,' Camlin said, pointing to Dath. 'Keep your bowstrings dry and your head down. I'll see you after.'

Dath nodded, looking as if he wanted to say something, but just swallowed instead.

'Any more?' Coralen asked. 'Shall we invite Rath's warband, see who volunteers?'

'I like her,' Brina whispered to Corban.

'No? Good then.' Coralen kicked her mount on.

CHAPTER SEVENTY-NINE

VERADIS

Veradis stared out of the shield wall.

'Are you ready?' he said to Bos and the other men pressed close about him.

'Aye,' Bos said.

'Then let's get on with it.' He lifted a hand and a horn rang out from the rear. His shield wall began to march along the road, the rhythmic thumping of a thousand men's boots. Behind them followed Geraint's warband, or what was left of it, sprawled across the road and down the embankments either side, spilling into the green meadows about them, like the wings of a great bird.

The sun rose higher and figures materialized ahead, still a long way off, a great horde filling the giants' road and the meadows flanking it. Thousands, iron glinting in the rising sun, grim-faced men, confident with yesterday's victory fresh upon them.

Veradis had watched the battle the day before with growing horror as Geraint's warband was slowly beaten into submission through the long day of bloodshed. So many lives, so many brave men slaughtered.

The survivors had limped back along the giants' road and into the shadow of the hills. The healers' tents had been full, the cries of dying men filling the night. Veradis had gone in search of Geraint and found him having a bandage wrapped around his arm. He was covered in blood and looked close to exhaustion. He looked away when he saw Veradis.

'You fought with honour today,' Veradis said. 'But you were outnumbered.' It was a lie, but Geraint was a prideful man.

'Numbers had nothing to do with it,' Geraint muttered.

'No. You lost today because your enemy had sown seeds of fear in the hearts of your men, and they used that.'

'Tomorrow's another day,' Geraint said.

'It is, but it will end the same, if not worse, if you plan just to march out again, as you did today.'

'What else can I do? I cannot retreat – Rhin would have my stones on a platter. And they are in no hurry to attack us – I have to take the battle to them.'

'Let me lead the van. My shield wall, it will win the day for you.'

'You have fewer than a thousand men – they have nearly ten thousand.'

'I know. If you protect my flanks, stop them from getting behind us, then we will cut the heart from Domhain's warband and give you a victory.'

Veradis was close enough to see the faces of his enemy now. Wariness, suspicion as they watched the shield wall march closer. He raised an arm, a horn blew, and the wall pulled to a halt, with rows of warriors from the back of his shield wall moving quickly down the embankments to either side of the road, reforming quickly. Now three shieldwalls stood arrayed before the warband of Domhain, each forty men wide, seven rows deep. Shields came together with a concussive *crack*. Geraint's men hovered at their rear.

A warrior stepped out of the milling front ranks of Domhain's warband. He banged his sword on his shield, others copying, the sound rippling through the warband, growing in volume. Then with a wide-mouthed scream he charged, his comrades following close behind him.

'Ready now,' Veradis said to those around him. He drew his short sword, looking out through a gap in the shields. Three hundred paces away. Two hundred paces. One hundred paces now, warriors screaming, weapons raised. He widened his stance, lowered his shoulder, bracing for the impact. Then it came, a bone-numbing crash into his shield, shivering through his body, a myriad of successive blows as body after body piled into a claustrophobic crush on the far side of his shield.

The shield wall weathered the impact; the weight upon it grew and Veradis grunted with the strain. The noise was deafening, all along the shield wall, and further off as well, a distant roar as

Geraint's warband entered the battle. Then the stabbing began. He plunged his sword through the small gap between shields, felt it punching through leather into flesh, felt blood wash over his hand. He stabbed again and again, the same happening all along the line. Battle-cries turned to screams. Fingers grabbed at the rim of his shield and he chopped at them. Swords and spears slid beneath his shield, stabbed at his legs. They were turned by the strips of iron on his boots. Hands clutched underneath and he severed them with his short sword, or stamped on them. Blows rained on his shield, the wood creaking, but he just kept on stabbing. Bodies began to pile along the line.

The weight on Veradis' shield lessened. *It is coming.* He kept stabbing, sweat stinging his eyes. He heard Bos grunt in pain but could not look. Two hands grabbed the top of his shield and yanked it down, almost tearing it from his grip. A red-haired warrior stared at him, fumbling with a longsword in the crush of men. Veradis stabbed out, his short sword biting into flesh just below the man's jaw line. He staggered backwards, blood jetting from the wound, bubbling crimson from his mouth; the press of warriors behind him kept him upright until the strength went from his legs and he sagged slowly to the ground. Veradis brought his shield back up.

He yelled over his shoulder, heard the cry ripple back through the rows behind him, then horn blasts rang out. He took a step forwards, the whole front row moving with him, shoving forwards. Another horn blast, another step. He slipped in a pool of blood, stumbled over a body, but the men behind and beside him kept him upright. Then more death-dealing, his sword snaking out. Another horn blast, another step, the weight on their shields lessening each time, then they were moving forwards steadily, no pause between steps, just a steady, grinding momentum as they carved their way through Domhain's warriors.

Occasionally he would feel a ripple pass through the shield wall as a man was pulled out of formation and killed, his position being taken by the man behind. Veradis' arm grew numb, his grip slipping, and he called out another order, the message moving back until horn blasts sounded. A space opened behind him; every other man in the front row stepped back, replaced smoothly by the man behind. Veradis moved back through the shield wall until he took his position in the last row, still lending his weight to the march, but having a chance to rest his burning lungs and aching muscles. Soon the horn sounded again and the other half of the original front row filtered back through the ranks, others moving forwards. Veradis saw Bos fall in beside him. His head was bleeding, his iron cap missing.

'I'm too tall for this shield wall,' Bos muttered, wiping blood from his eyes.

'Maybe you need a bigger shield,' Veradis said, taking a swig from his skin of water, then passing it to his friend.

The sun was warm, the only way of reckoning the time. *Halfway to highsun*. The roar of battle sounded. Through the shields Veradis caught glimpses of warriors locked in combat, blood on the grass, faces snarling, cursing, bodies still, twisted unnaturally. Thuds and blows crashed against their flank, but never in a concerted attack. *Geraint is keeping them off us.*

Slowly they moved forwards, as the sun rose and then fell, until Veradis found himself back in the front row again. He hefted his shield and gritted his teeth, began stabbing into the constant press of men beyond the wall of wood and iron.

Is Corban out there, or has he been slain already, one of the anonymous many who have been killed and trampled like so much meat on the butcher's table? The thought didn't bring him joy. He wanted to see this Corban again, to talk to him, work out for himself if he was really who Calidus claimed he was. How could the Black Sun be a mere boy? It just didn't make sense.

And he wanted to see Cywen again. He found that he missed her, missed her voice, her smile, her sharp words.

A thud on his shield dragged him from his thoughts. A crack had appeared, the wood beginning to splinter. He pressed his shoulder tighter to it, stabbed high and low.

Then the weight pressing against him was diminishing. He heard horns blowing wildly, heard shouting, running. He risked a glance through the gaps in the wall and saw that the line had broken and the warriors of Domhain were in full retreat, here and there Geraint's men pressing after them, though he no longer had the numbers to finish the retreating men decisively. Already Veradis saw him pulling his warriors back, not allowing them to become too stretched over the land.

Good decision.

Nearby a low hill reared up, tattered tents and abandoned wains all that was left of the enemy's camp. In the distance Veradis saw riders on the giants' road rallying the fleeing warriors, pulling them into a semblance of order. Veradis watched them for a while, wondering if they would regroup and return to the battle, but they dwindled into the distance.

'The day is won, then,' Bos said as he came to stand beside Veradis.

'It looks that way.'

'What now.'

'A good meal. Then on to Dun Taras.'

CHAPTER EIGHTY

MAQUIN

Maquin stood and stretched. Twelve days of rowing had set his back and shoulders to aching. Not like before, though. The training that he had been put through during his stay on the island of Panos had had some benefits, at least.

He looked up at the slopes of Nerin. They were anchored in a sheltered bay, with a beach angling up into rocky slopes. On the skyline ruins reflected the glow of the sinking sun.

'Get a move on,' Emad barked, cracking his whip.

They all filed off the ship. At the crest of the hill a town appeared, similar to the one on Panos: houses built of baked clay bricks and reed roofs, hordes of children and skinny dogs rushing to greet them.

'These Vin Thalun have too much time on their hands,' Javed said beside him, 'if they have all this time to be making children.'

Maquin laughed. He had grown to like the little man, who came from Tarbesh, a land far to the east that Maquin had vaguely heard of. A place of sun and desert, mostly like these islands, although even here winter was making itself known. Maquin tried not to get too friendly, though. He had lost too many who were close to him, and he never forgot what it was that they were being trained to become. Killers. He was a warrior already, no stranger to death, to combat, but this was different. Then he had fought for a cause, or so it seemed. Now the only cause was life over death.

No, there is more than that. There is freedom, and then Jael.

But nevertheless, if he were to fight for that cause, the possibility that he would see Jael again and attempt his vengeance, then he had to embrace the fact that he would have to kill in the pit, and soon.

I've taken that ship already. Better just get used to it. And that was why he kept his distance from Javed, from any attempts at friendship that came his way. He did not know who would be thrown into the pit with him. Who he would be forced to slay or be slain by.

They were herded through bustling streets, an abundance of smells doing battle as they passed through a great market, a variety of meats cooking on spits – including big lizards – as well as mountains of figs and dates, mushrooms and onions, olives and melons, oranges and peppers.

People stopped and stared as they passed by, some even daring to prod shoulders and chests, testing muscle.

Wondering who will survive the pits, who to bet on? We are an investment to them, as well as an entertainment.

They left the market and streets behind and walked out onto a wide plain with a slope rising higher in front of them, a great mountain in the distance, its top jagged like a broken tooth. Night fell and still they walked, eventually seeing torches ahead. Maquin caught a glimpse of a cavernous opening in the ground, then they were being led down, through open gates and into tunnels – giant-craft again, tall and wide. Eventually they were ushered into a circular room with alcoves dug into the rock all the way round, cots with straw mattresses in them. A long table stood in the middle of the room with food and jugs laid out, a good meal, though nothing as lavish as on the night of the first pit-fight.

Their guards unchained them and locked them in.

Before much food could be consumed the barred gates opened and Herak strode in, a handful of guards behind him, big Emad one of them.

'You'll fight on the morrow,' Herak said. Maquin and the rest of them gathered in a half-circle before him.

'Not like before. You'll be in a big pit, big as the chamber on Panos that had all the other pits in it. You'll fight the recruits of Nerin, this island, and of Pelset, the third island east of here. The men you'll be up against, they'll have come through their first pit-fight, just like you, and been trained on their island, just like you have by me. All of you, against all of them. The fight won't stop until only one side remains. That means one of you might survive, or fifty, or none.' He shrugged.

'How will we know who's who?' Javed asked.

'By these.' Herak held up a big iron ring. You'll all have one around your necks. The men of Nerin, around a wrist, the men of Pelset, around their ankle. Line up.'

Maquin rolled his shoulders after the ring was clamped shut; a thickset smith twisted the iron pin that bound it. It felt like his warrior torc, which had been taken from him by Lykos after the battle of Dun Kellen.

Herak was standing beside the smith. 'That'll be cut from you on the morrow, from your dead body or your living one.' He slapped Maquin's shoulder. 'I think you'll be one of the living. Lykos told me about you, old wolf.'

Maquin didn't say anything. He went and sat on a cot, sipping a cup of water, watching. Herak spoke with every man, relaxed, friendly even, like a comrade-in-arms.

I hate him. He builds them up, grooms them, us, for his own purposes.

When they were all done, fifty-six men bound with iron, Herak stood before them again.

'There is food here for you. If you survive the morrow, it means you have become a champion of Panos, and that you have defeated Nerin and Pelset. That will make me very happy.' He grinned at them. 'I hope I will be rewarding you. Enjoy your meal.' He walked from the room and looked back as the iron gates were locked. 'It may be your last.'

It was dark when Maquin woke, but then he realized he was under-ground and most of the torches had burned out in the night. He lay there, listening to other men sleeping, snoring. Eventually he sat up; there was enough light from beyond the barred gates to pick his way to the table and pour himself a cup of water.

Soft footfalls sounded behind him and Orgull loomed close. Maquin passed him a cup. The moons of rowing and training had taken their toll on him, too, his body lean and striated, his face look-ing stretched, his bald head skull-like.

'We could work together, today,' Orgull said quietly, little more than a breath. 'We are still sword-brothers.'

Maquin wasn't sure if Orgull was making a statement or asking a question. He nodded, though. Working together made sense, was practical, and that was what his life had been distilled down to. The practicalities of staying alive.

'Good, then,' Orgull said and slipped back into the shadows.

The roar of the crowd was deafening.

They were standing behind an iron-barred gate, looking out into a great ring, rough stone walls rising two or three times the height of a man, then tiered rows spreading above them, climbing higher. The tiers were full of people, shouting, laughing, drinking, betting. Sunlight poured in from above, making Maquin blink, though in truth it was weak, holding little warmth.

Herak appeared, flanked by Emad and another guard, holding a great iron key.

'There will be weapons in there – be quick, get them first. Kill or be killed.' He put the key in the lock, then waited.

A hush fell in the great pit, heartbeats marking time. Then a gong rang out, booming off the stone walls. Herak turned the key, the gate swung open, and the men rushed through.

Maquin was carried along in the crush of it, spilling out onto the hard-packed earth.

He stepped to the side, moving out of the momentum, saw doors opening across the ring, men pouring from them like water through sluice-gates. Littered on the ground were piles of weapons – knives, butcher's cleavers, hatchets, small bucklers, other wicked pieces of iron that Maquin did not recognize. Before he had a chance to think about it, he was running for the nearest pile, elbowing someone in the face, rolling and grabbing.

He came to his feet with a thick-bladed knife in his hand, end tapered to a sharp point. A man was lunging at him, a ring of iron about one wrist, swinging something sharp at his face. He ducked, stepped in close, punched the man in the gut, his knife sinking deep, three, four times, then shoved the man away, saw him slump to the floor, clutching at the wounds in his belly, his entrails glistening like slimy rope between his fingers.

It was chaos, everywhere men grappling, stabbing, yelling, screaming. The stink of blood and death was already overwhelming, worse than his memories of Dun Kellen. He looked for Orgull but could not see him. Two men rolled before him, gouging and stabbing. One rose from the embrace, one remained motionless on the ground. Maquin was close, could just step forward and finish the man rising.

Kill or be killed.

But he hovered, knife half-raised. *I don't want to do this.*

Then the opportunity was gone, the man up and ready, a cleaver in his hands, his eyes flickering to Maquin's knife. He sidestepped, then moved in, one hand grabbing for Maquin's wrist, the cleaver rising in his other, swinging at Maquin's head.

Maquin stabbed at the hand grabbing for him, felt the knife bite, then grate on iron, a ring about the man's wrist. He kicked out, connected with a knee, throwing his attacker's balance off, the cleaver whistling past his ear. He stepped in, tried to stab low, but his enemy twisted, Maquin's knife scoring a graze along his back instead. They grappled, the cleaver ricocheting off the iron ring about Maquin's neck, leaving a gash on his jaw line. Maquin managed to grab the man's wrist, stepped in close and headbutted him, sank his knife into his chest as he staggered back. The cleaver dropped to the ground and Maquin picked it up.

Kill or be killed. He felt a berserker rage bubbling up inside – rage at what he was being made to do, rage at what he was becoming. Suddenly he was back in the catacombs beneath Haldis, watching Jael stab Kastell. Tears blurred his eyes. He shook his head angrily. Jael's face hovered in his mind, smiling, mocking. He looked about again, at the death all around.

There is only one way out. Fight for me. Lykos' words. With a snarl, he hefted his two weapons and stepped into the battle.

He moved through the throng, staying light on his feet, cutting hamstrings, muscle, maiming, killing, always moving, imagining it was Jael that he cut, stabbed, killed. He kept searching, looking for Orgull. Somehow it was important that he find him, fight with him. He had said he would; could he not even fulfil that promise?

Then he saw him, a hatchet in Orgull's hand dripping red as he faced two men with iron around their ankles. Orgull was cut, bleeding from thigh and shoulder. Maquin moved forwards, threading through the combat as quickly as he could, deflecting a knife here, a punch, a kick there. Two men stumbled into him, arms flailing. One lashed out with a knife, scoring a red gash across Maquin's chest. He chopped and stabbed as he spun away from them.

By the time he had reached Orgull one of his attackers was on his knees, clinging to Orgull's leg as blood pulsed from a wound in his back. The other was dancing around to Orgull's left, where his arm was cut, blood soaked. Orgull staggered and the man tensed, ready to strike, then Maquin was burying his knife low into the man's back, the cleaver thumping into his shoulder. He collapsed.

Maquin shared a look with Orgull and then he slipped to Orgull's left, covering his back, became the big man's shield, as they were used to doing. They stood and traded blows with anyone who fell within their range, then slowly pushed through the madness, men stumbling to get out of their way. Orgull picked up a buckler and slipped it onto his arm, Maquin fighting with knife and cleaver.

A knot of bodies went down before them, men stabbing and wrestling. Maquin grabbed one and yanked him back, out of the way of a swinging blade. The man twisted in Maquin's grip, then relaxed. It was Javed, one half of his face matted with blood, his eye swollen shut. He fell in beside them and they slipped into a loose half-circle.

Maquin's chest burned where he had been slashed; sweat ran into his wounds, stinging like a thousand bites. His knee throbbed where he had rolled badly, muscles in his back spasming, a hundred other pains crying out for attention. The pumping of his blood seemed to drown it all out, dulling it. He was consumed with intoxication, everything broken down to moments, the angle of a strike, the flexing of muscle and tendon, speed, body and mind working together. And he still lived. He grinned and looked about the great pit.

The ground was littered with the dead or dying, crawling, twitching. Knots still fought, here and there, mostly in ones and twos.

Orgull banged his hatchet on his buckler, started yelling.

'Iron throats, iron throats, to us. Iron throats.'

Maquin looked at him. *Strength in numbers.* He took up the cry, Javed following.

There were not many left. One iron collar was cut down as he stared at the three men, but others broke away from their combats, joining Orgull and Maquin and Javed. Almost instantly there were eight of them grouped together. Then twelve. The men left with iron about wrist or ankle looked on wildly, then set to attacking each other. None would risk assaulting twelve men.

'What now?' one of the iron collars said.

'Wait for them to come to us,' another said.

Kill or be killed.

Maquin gave a yell and ran at the last few men scattered around them. Orgull hesitated briefly, then followed, as Maquin knew he would. The others were close behind Orgull. Together they killed every other surviving man left in the pit.

CHAPTER EIGHTY-ONE

CORBAN

Corban looked back along the range of hills. It was late in the day, and they had travelled leagues already, but he could still see the battleground in the distance, a dark shadow on the green plains. Birds circled the air above it in a dark swarm.

I hope that Edana and the others are safe.

'Come on,' Coralen called from the front of their small column. 'Keep up.'

'*Keep up, keep up,*' Craf squawked from Brina's saddle. He had been much more vocal since being separated from Fech.

Corban kicked his horse on. Guilt gnawed at him for leaving Edana and his friends, but a fierce joy filled him every time he thought of Cywen. He had felt so overwhelmed by the losses of friends, the death of his da and him supposedly being a god's avatar that at times he'd felt like a small twig tossed and turned by great waves. Now for the first time he felt that he was actually doing something. Taking control. He did not care for the politics of the west, who ruled where. For him the last year had been all about their survival. Survival of his loved ones – his family and friends. And Cywen was part of that. *At least, she will be.*

Storm appeared out of the darkness, stepping into the firelight of their camp. She was carrying a young buck between her jaws. She dropped her kill at Corban's feet and he rested a hand on it, accepting her gift. He and the others then set to skinning and cooking it.

'She's quite useful,' Coralen said, using her knife to strip the last piece of meat from a bone.

'Changed your mind about turning her into a cloak, then?' Dath said cheerfully.

Corban put a hand protectively on Storm's shoulder. She was spread beside him, cracking bones for marrow.

'All the while she brings me dinner,' Coralen said. 'Besides, I have a wolven cloak already.' She patted the saddlebag she was sitting upon.

Corban had kept his wolven pelt too, as well as the gauntlet and claws. He looked at Coralen, their small fire highlighting the lines of her hair and face. *You must find this hard, leaving Rath and your people behind. But can I trust you?*

'Are you leading us in the hope of seeing Conall?' he asked her.

'Conall?' She regarded him for what seemed a long while. 'He's my brother. When I heard he was dead, it was like a punch in the belly. And now I know he's alive, somewhere on the other side of those mountains. But what's happened between him and Halion . . .' She shook her head. 'They were always so close. You need that, growing up the way we did. Someone to rely on. To turn to.' She looked up and Corban saw tears glistening in her eyes. He was surprised at the number of words coming out of her mouth. Usually she just gave out sharp-edged dour remarks.

Her eyes focused on Corban. 'Why are you asking me this?'

Then her eyes narrowed suspiciously.

'Oh I see it: you don't *trust* me. Think I might betray you to your enemies for the sake of Conall. Well, feel free to find another guide, and I'll ride back to Rath and *my* people.' She almost spat the last words, then stood up and walked away, slung her saddlebag down beyond the reach of firelight.

'Very tactful,' Brina whispered to him.

'I trust you,' Farrell called out after her.

'Shut up, oaf,' Coralen's voice drifted back.

The next day dawned cold, with frost stiffening the grass. They broke their fast with cold meat and watered-down ale, then set off again. Coralen was silent the entire time; Corban decided it was prudent to do the same.

A while after highsun Coralen stopped. They were winding their way through the foothills that skirted the mountains, and were high up a slope. Domhain was spread to the west like a great tapestry.

'What is it?' Gar asked Coralen.

'I think someone is following us,' she said, staring back into the distance.

They all stared.

'I see it,' said Dath. He'd always had sharp eyes.

'You're looking in the wrong direction,' Coralen said. 'Over there.'

'Oh,' said Dath. 'But I thought I saw . . .'

'What?' Coralen said, following his stare. Corban looked too, but could only see rolling hills and patches of woodland.

'Nothing,' Dath said, abashed.

Coralen pointed.

'Ah. Yes.' Dath stared hard. 'I can see something.'

'How many?' Gar asked.

'Hard to tell. Only one, that I can see. Could be more.' He squinted. 'Maybe two.'

'I'll send Craf,' Brina said, and the bird flapped into the air.

They carried on for a good while, keeping to the trail that Coralen had been leading them on.

Shadows were lengthening, darkness sinking into the hills like deep pools amongst rocks, when Craf returned. The bird was squawking, an edge of terror to the sound. He swooped out of the grey sky, hurtling straight for Brina. '*Help help help help,*' Craf croaked as he all but crashed into Brina, trying to flap his way into the inner recesses of her cloak. '*Eat me,*' Craf screeched, his head poking out of Brina's cloak, looking up at the sky.

They all looked up. For a fleeting moment Corban thought he saw a dark smudge, then it was gone. 'What about those following us?' Coralen asked Craf.

'*Man, hound, follow,*' Craf said.

'Thank you,' Coralen said.

'*Welcome,*' Craf muttered.

Corban blinked. He'd never heard Craf be polite before.

'We'd best get off the trail and see who it is that's behind us,' Coralen said.

Corban took his place on a shelf of rock above the path; Storm and his mam crouched nearby. Dath was on the other side of the trail, on a ridge amongst trees and scrub, his bow strung. The rest of them were spread either side, hidden behind rock or tree. It felt like a long time before Corban heard the sound of hooves.

Eventually a figure appeared in the gloom, emerging from the shadows. A man on horseback, a tall hound padding beside him. Then Corban recognized him and leaped forward, yelling, 'Don't shoot him,' to Dath.

The man reined in, his hound growling. He aimed a clipped command at the hound. 'Hello, Corban,' he said.

'Ventos.'

CHAPTER EIGHTY-TWO

FIDELE

Fidele stood on the battlements of Jerolin. It was cold, snow from the mountains carpeting much of the slopes and plains to the north. The lake glistened beneath a pale sun. Looking east, she saw at last the sight she had been waiting for. Riders, eagle-guard cantering past the stockaded walls of the lake town and onto the road that wound up to Jerolin. As they drew closer she saw that they circled another figure.

Lykos. She felt a flare of anger, saw in her mind the faces of those she had rescued from his fighting pit, as well as a pile of the dead.

Her eyes drifted to the lake, settling again on the ships that had arrived yesterday, half a dozen at least, rowing out of a river into the lake's waters. Vin Thalun ships.

Lykos is not stupid enough to attack me, surely. To attack Jerolin. A good portion of Tenebral's warriors may be on the other side of the Banished Lands, but there are still enough here to defend Jerolin. He must know that. Still, she wondered why a few hundred of his warriors were now anchored only half a league away.

She turned and strode down a stairwell, Orcus behind her, and made her way to her chambers in Jerolin's black tower.

Does Lykos bring news of Nathair? She felt a weightlessness in her belly at that thought. *My brave son. Elyon above, let him be well and safe, if safe is still possible in this dark world. And what of the war – the God-War? I have arrested the only man that may actually have knowledge of developments in the Banished Lands.*

In silence Fidele climbed the spiral stair of Jerolin's tower, where two eagle-guard stood outside the doors of her chamber. Once inside, Orcus poured her a cup of wine and assumed his position behind her chair. It was not long before there was a knock at the door and Lykos was admitted.

He strode in confidently, his gait rolling as if he still walked a ship's deck. An easy smile stretched across his face.

'Please, sit,' Fidele said politely.

He poured himself a cup of wine and took a long draught.

'I hate riding,' he said as he wiped wine from his beard.

'I am sorry for that, but it was important that I saw you.'

He leaned back in his chair and smiled at her. 'You are as beautiful as ever.'

She blinked at that. She had seen the way he looked at her but he had never been so bold as to comment on the thoughts behind his eyes. *Something was different . . .*

'You have done a terrible thing,' she said.

He laughed at that, a short bark. 'I have done many terrible things, my lady. To which one do you refer?'

'I refer to the fighting pit at Balara. Don't play games, Lykos. I am sure that you know why I have brought you here.'

He leaned forward, serious now. 'Yes, I am aware.'

'You have committed murder. That poor boy, Jace. His body was dragged up from the lakebed by fishermen. And all those others at Balara, forced to fight for your entertainment. And you have disobeyed and lied to me. I cannot and *will not* let these things go unpunished.'

'I see. Well, before this conversation takes us into unpleasant waters, let me give you my news. Your son was well, the last time I saw him.'

'Where?' she asked, for a moment her other priorities swept aside.

'Ardan. Dun Carreg. He was mired deeply in the politics of the west, strengthening the alliance.'

'Has he found Meical? I know that he was keen to track down my husband's counsellor.'

I pray he hasn't found him. Not before I tell him of what Ektor and I have discovered.

'Meical has been seen in Dun Carreg, but he left long before Nathair arrived.'

Good.

'And Nathair, he was well?'

'Yes, although he was troubled, concerned. For you. He thinks perhaps he has placed too much responsibility upon your shoulders, too soon after the death of your husband.'

What? Am I really hearing this? Lykos is lying.

'He regrets his decision making you regent in his absence, thinks you do not have the strength that is required in these difficult times.' Lykos reached inside his weather-stained cloak and pulled out a crumpled scroll. 'He proposes that I take over the regency, for the time being.'

She snatched the scroll and tore it open. It was as Lykos said, written in her son's hand. *This cannot be. Something is wrong; he would not do this.* She looked over the scroll at Lykos. He was studying her intently.

She ripped up the scroll and tossed its pieces to the ground.

'I will *never* allow you to rule Tenebral,' she said.

Lykos sighed, long and deep. 'I was afraid you would say that.'

He burst explosively from his chair, launching across the table, and Fidele instinctively flinched backwards. She was not his target, though.

Orcus had his sword drawn by the time Lykos reached him, but Lykos was inside his guard, something in his hand. He punched hard upwards, under Orcus' chin. Blood erupted from Orcus' mouth. Lykos held him close, then lowered him to the ground, where he twitched a few times, then was still.

Fidele stood, opening her mouth to scream.

'Don't do that,' Lykos said, turning to face her. He reached into his cloak and pulled something out, something small. 'Don't make a sound,' he said.

Fidele felt a hand clamp around her throat, fingers squeezing. She tried to scream but nothing came out. She reached to her throat to pull away the choking grip, but nothing was there, only her own flesh.

'Amazing,' Lykos said, holding the thing in his hand up. It looked like a lump of clay, a few hairs sticking from it. 'Come back here.'

She felt her feet moving, tried to stop them, but could not, just walked, haltingly at first, back towards Lykos. She saw blood pooling behind him, almost black, spreading like spilt ink.

'Stop.'

She stopped.

'Lift your right hand.'

She lifted it.

Lykos laughed. 'This is wonderful. Calidus, I owe you greatly.' His brow furrowed in thought. 'Tell me that we shall rule Tenebral together. And be polite.'

Never. I will see you dead . . .

'We shall govern Tenebral together, my lord.' She could not believe the words were her own, the voice her own. She formed a sentence in her mind, mostly curses. 'Your will shall guide me.' She wailed inside.

What? She stared at the lump that Lykos held in his hand. This close she could see that the hairs in it were black. Lines were scrawled across the clay. *Runes?*

'Yes,' he said, following her eyes. 'It is a lock of your hair.' He looked behind him, at Orcus sprawled on the stone floor. 'We'll arrange for my men to clean this up; don't want rumours spreading through your eagle-guard. I shall leave shortly and send Deinon and a few others up here. Later today you shall announce that I am forgiven all previous misunderstandings and that the people of Tenebral are about to enter a new age of kinship with the Vin Thalun.'

'I shall do as you say, my lord.'

He grinned, then looked at her, up and down.

'Perhaps we should seal this new beginning while we are alone.' He reached out, ran a hand up her thigh, over her hip and onto her waist.

Get off. Don't touch me. She spasmed inside, willed her limbs to move, to kick, to shove, her voice to cry out. Nothing happened.

'Lie back on the table,' he commanded.

In her mind she screamed.

CHAPTER EIGHTY-THREE

CORBAN

'What are you doing here?' Corban said to the trader.

'Why are you following us?' Coralen asked as she moved from behind a boulder.

'Yes, why are you following us?' Gar strode close to him. Ventos' hound growled. Storm jumped from the rock shelf; her hackles were raised and she matched snarl for snarl.

This could turn bloody. 'Ventos, tell your hound; Storm will not tolerate a challenge from him.'

'Talar, down,' Ventos snapped. The hound crouched lower and stopped growling.

'Easy, everyone,' Ventos said. 'I am no danger to you.'

'An explanation, please,' Gwenith said.

'I wish to get out of Domhain, and I saw you all leave, saw you heading towards the mountains.' He shrugged.

'Why not just use the giants' road? And what about your goods, your wain at Dun Taras?' Corban asked.

'You don't know, do you? Domhain's warband has been routed; it is fleeing to Dun Taras. Rhin controls the giants' road, and that's the only way in or out of Domhain that a wain can travel.' He shrugged, a guilty expression crossing his face. 'I'm cutting my losses. If I get out of Domhain with my life I'll count myself lucky. I just want to get away, and I thought, you know, safety in numbers.'

'Rath's warband is routed?' Coralen gasped. 'That's not possible.'

'That's what I thought,' Ventos said. 'But it happened. It wasn't the warband from Cambren that turned it. It was the warriors of Tenebral. They made a wall of shields, just walked up the giants' road and killed every man that threw himself against their shields.'

He shook his head, passing a hand across his brow. 'It was terrible to see.'

Coralen leaned against a tree, the colour draining from her face.

'We'll make camp here,' Brina said, 'and you can tell us properly.'

As they ate a broth made from the leftovers of Storm's kill, Ventos told them in detail all that he had seen. It was a grim tale. When he had finished, a silence settled over the travellers.

That is no way to fight, thought Corban. *There's no honour in it.*

'Does Rath still live?' Coralen asked.

'I don't know. I think so. At least, someone was still in control and organized the retreat. It wasn't just a flood down the giants' road. Not when I left, anyway. It was still daylight when I set off – I wanted to pick up your trail before it was too dark to find it.'

'What of Edana?' Corban asked the question that was on all their minds.

'Again, I did not see. But she would have had good warning of the retreat, and she would not have been in the fighting to begin with. I would imagine she is one of those more likely to have been on the road back to Dun Taras.'

'You must have ridden hard to catch up with us,' Gar said.

'I did. I rode like the wind, once I found your trail. Nothing like the thought of an angry warband behind you to put some fire beneath your feet.'

'Did anyone see you, follow you?' Gar asked.

'No. Or not that I saw. You can never be sure, but . . .'

'Up before dawn,' Coralen said. 'We'll travel hard.' Then she stood and walked to where the horses were hobbled. After a while Corban followed her.

'You could tell us the way, and go back,' he said to her back as she checked her horse's feet.

'You'd never find it,' she said. 'You'll end up dead and frozen for foxes to nibble at.'

'But Rath, your kin.'

'Don't you think I know?' she snapped, turning a glare on him. 'I said I'd show you the way, and that's what I'll do. That's what Rath would say to me. He'd skin me if I just left you here. Anyway, this newfound care for my well-being – is it genuine, or just an excuse to get rid of the guide that you don't trust?' She started pulling out knots from her horse's mane.

'I'm sorry about that, last night. I do trust you. I just thought how I would feel, if it were my brother or sister.' He shrugged to her back. She didn't say anything so he just walked away.

For another eight nights they rode steadily north, Coralen pushing them hard. The path wound out of the foothills and into the mountains, passing through sweeping woods of pine until they climbed beyond the treeline and into the mountains themselves. Here the paths were icy, the slopes dusted with snow. They camped on a grassy slope near a dark still pool. Corban sat first watch of the night, sitting with his back to a boulder and his cloak pulled tight.

They would be crossing into Cambren soon, another one or two days' travel through the mountains. Then they would be in Rhin's realm, voluntarily walking back into the danger they had spent so long escaping. *But this time we will be chasing, not running.*

When his watch was up he passed guard over to Ventos, then tried to get comfortable on the ground, hard and cold as iron.

His thoughts swirled, thinking of Edana and Halion, Marrock and Camlin and Vonn, praying silently that they were still alive, had made it back to Dun Taras. And then Cywen. How alone she must feel with only her enemies surrounding her. He felt a wave of anger at the people and events that had treated them so cruelly. Rhin. Nathair: the man who had slain his da – plunged a sword into his chest. His thoughts had strayed to that image many times since he had fled Dun Carreg, always accompanied by a measure of pain. Here, though, alone in the dark, suddenly the anguish threatened to drown him, pain as deep and dark as the lake they were camped beside. He turned over and squeezed his eyes shut.

He woke with a start, the memory of strange dreams hovering, of wings and warriors and battle, but even as he tried to cling to it, it faded. There was a noise: a rustle up above, a whisper on the wind, then he heard soft footfalls, moving away. He sat up.

Ventos was gone.

He saw him disappearing along a path, his hound padding alongside him. Quietly Corban rose. He looked about for Storm, but she was nowhere to be seen. Probably off hunting. He crept after Ventos.

He followed the path, taking it slowly. A half-moon gave some light, though frequently clouds scudded across it. The path wound upwards, the ground slippery with frost. He reached a bend and paused, then peered around it.

The path opened into a wider space, boulders littering it. A hawk sat on the rock.

Kartala, the bird that Ventos won from the Sirak.

Ventos was writing, then rolling something up, tying it to the hawk's leg.

A growl sounded in the darkness.

Corban reached for his sword, then remembered he'd taken it off. He had a knife at his belt, though, and gripped its hilt.

'Who's there?' Ventos said. 'Come out now, where I can see you. Or I'll set my hound on you.'

Corban stepped away from the shelf. 'What are you doing?' he said. 'Who are you writing to?'

Ventos stared at him, none of the open friendliness Corban was used to showing now. He looked cold, calculating, weighing up the situation. 'Someone who's interested in you.' He drew a knife of his own.

He's made his decision, then. If I shout, will anyone hear me? How far have I walked?

The hound Talar stepped out of the shadows. He was still snarling. Saliva dripped from his teeth.

There was the sound of movement above, the rattle of stones falling down the rock face. A blur of white fur hurtled out of the darkness and crashed into the hound. Storm. The two animals rolled towards the edge of the path, the hound yelping. Ventos ran at them, knife raised, and Corban hurled himself at Ventos. They went down in a bundle of limbs, Ventos gasping sharply, stiffening, arching his back, then flopping limp.

Corban struggled free, saw that his knife was buried in Ventos' torso, beneath his ribs, a dark stain spreading about the blade.

Ventos put a hand to the knife hilt and groaned.

Snarling behind him. Corban turned to see Storm kick with her back legs, hurling the hound through the air. It crunched to the ground, skidded, rose unsteadily, dark gashes down its shoulder, blood dripping from its belly. Storm braced and leaped, crashing into the hound again and in a scrabble of earth and stone they both disappeared over the edge of the path. There was the sound of scratching, claws on rock, then a silence, followed by a splash.

'Storm!' yelled Corban, running to the path's edge.

He couldn't see anything, just the glimmer of water here and there, a fast-flowing stream by the sound of it.

'Storm,' he shouted again, thought he saw a flash of something white moving fast – in the stream's grip. There was no way down so he turned, began running along the bank's edge, following what he thought, hoped, had been Storm carried in the flow of the stream. He left Ventos lying in a pool of his own blood, didn't even know if the man was alive or dead.

He ran in the dark, tripped and fell, pushed himself back up, feeling panic growing in his gut, a pressure building.

He heard something – the scuff of feet? He looked about wildly – had he been heard from the camp, missed? Then he heard a sniffing, the whine of dogs, more than one, and figures were appearing out of the darkness. Two, three, more movement at the edge of his vision. A man strode towards him, tall, a scar running down his face. Memories flared, of the Darkwood.

Braith.

Then hands were grabbing him.

Corban felt a sharp pain in his ribs. He jerked his hands, but they were bound tight and there was a cloth over his head.

'I'm going to take your hood off now. Make a sound and it'll be the last thing you do. Feel that?' Whoever it was poked him harder with the blade in his ribs.

'Yes,' he said inside the sack.

The sack was pulled off and Corban blinked in the light. It was early, the sun weak and pale, but it still made his eyes water.

He had been walking half the night, it seemed, or stumbling, hands before and behind pulling, dragging, steering him onwards.

Braith stood before him, leaner than Corban remembered him, deep lines in his face, around his mouth and eyes, almost matching the silver of his long scar. Around them men were sitting, drinking from water skins, chewing on biscuit or strips of meat. A few hounds sat close to Braith's feet.

'I know you,' Corban said, his voice a croak.

'And I you. You've grown up a bit since the well at Dun Carreg.'

'Last time I saw you, you were running away,' Corban said. 'In the Darkwood.'

'Oh aye,' Braith said. 'Are you sure you want to be reminding me of that? Angering me, right now?'

Corban shrugged. He felt angry himself, more than anything else right now. His journey through the night had been filled with other things – panic, worry, fear. For Storm, for the people he'd left behind.

'Was it you that shot Queen Alona in the back?' He took a deep breath, hearing Gar's voice in his mind. *Control your emotions. Use them; don't let them use you. That's a quick way to getting killed. Could he rouse Braith enough to get him to make a mistake?*

Braith stepped closer, twisted his knife a little. 'That's enough, now. Think I'll put that sack back on your head.'

'Camlin told me about you,' Corban said.

'Did he now? How is Cam?'

'He's well. A good man.'

'Good? He was a thief and murderer, last time I saw him. And a turncoat.'

'He chose to do the right thing. He still does, unlike you,' Corban said.

'Right has a habit of changing, depending on who's paying your wages,' Braith said with a frown. 'Eat this. You'll need your strength.' He put a biscuit in Corban's bound hands.

'Where are you taking me?' Corban said.

'Someone wants to see you,' Braith said.

'The same that Ventos spoke of.'

'Ventos? The man you left for dead. No, I believe he worked for another.'

'And you work for Rhin, unless you've changed masters since the Darkwood.'

Braith just smiled at him. A humourless thing.

Cywen is Rhin's prisoner. Maybe we'll end up in a cell together. He thought of his mam and Gar, all the others, waking to find him gone.

'They'll find you, and when they do, they'll kill you,' Corban said, loud, for the others to hear.

'I don't think so. We've a good start on them, and I know these mountains well. Grew up in them as a bairn. Think I know a few paths that your pretty guide doesn't.'

'That doesn't matter,' Corban said. 'Storm will find me, and lead the others.'

'She's dead, lad. We saw her fall. There's no way she's coming out of that water. Too cold, too fast. Lots of sharp rocks.'

'No.' Corban refused to think on that.

'I'll leave the bag off, see if you can behave.'

You need me to go faster, you mean.

Braith organized his men, a dozen that Corban could see, though then some others joined them from further down the trail – scouts, he supposed. Braith prodded Corban and they set off. Just then a sound rang out, distant but clear. It echoed against the cliffs, long and mournful. A wolven's howl.

Muttering spread amongst the men, and Corban saw Braith scowling, looking back over his shoulder.

Corban smiled. 'Dead, is she?'

CHAPTER EIGHTY-FOUR

CYWEN

Cywen looked forward into the distance. A snow-capped mountain loomed on the horizon, dominating the range they had been following steadily north. Lower down its slopes she could just make out the walls of Dun Vaner, where torchlight flickered from battlements and windows, little more than pinpricks in the distance. Queen Rhin's stronghold and, originally, the seat of power of the Benothi giants. She could not help but look at the slopes and plains before her, imagining what it had been like for her ancestors to battle the gathered strength of the Benothi here. And her ancestors had won, Cambros striking down Ruad, the giant king. A memory sprang to life in her mind, of old Heb telling the tale of that battle to a crowd gathered on the meadows below Dun Carreg, on the day Marrock had been handbound. She could see herself, sitting on the grass with her mam and da, Corban and Gar, all of them entranced by Heb's story. And now Heb was dead, so Veradis had said. From nowhere she felt emotion swell in her chest, her vision blurring with tears.

'Time to stop, child,' Alcyon said from beside her. He'd appointed himself her guardian. *I preferred Veradis. At least I could have a conversation with him.* It had been over a ten-night since they had left Veradis at the giants' road, and she had spoken only a few sentences since then, to the reluctant giant or the Jehar Akar.

She climbed from Shield's back and led him to the makeshift paddocks that the Jehar built every night, unbuckled his girth and took his saddle and rug from his back, then rubbed him down and checked his hooves, all the while under the watchful eye of the giant. When she was finished he led her to the edge of the camp, looking for a spot to make their camp. They passed the draig paddock, where Cywen glimpsed Nathair climbing from the back of his long-tailed mount. Soon after, she heard the bellows of an auroch as the draig ripped into it. The same happened every night, Nathair leading an auroch into the draig paddock for it to hunt and eat. By morning there would be little left but patches of fur and some bone.

Alcyon found a spot to his liking, beneath a copse of withered hawthorns. He set about making a fire, hanging a pot over it and boiling up some water. This had been their routine every night, Alcyon reluctant to share a place round a fire with any others.

That suited her just fine. They sat in silence, Cywen stroking Buddai.

'Here,' Alcyon said, handing her a bowl of porridge. She let it warm her hands first, then blew on it as she spooned some into her mouth.

'Of all the things the tale-tellers say about you giants, they never mention how good your porridge is,' she said.

Footsteps thudded and she looked up to see the other three giants walking by. Alcyon's dark eyes tracked them.

'Why don't you like them?' Cywen asked.

'They should be with their clan, not here.'

'But you're here.'

'They have a choice. I do not.'

'What does that mean?'

'Nothing.' He shrugged. 'Also, I am Kurgan. They are Benothi. We are different clans. There is blood-feud between us. Between every clan.'

'Wasn't that from before the Scourging, though?' Cywen's grasp of history was a little vague.

'And after,' the giant said. 'The clans have warred since they were formed – since the War of Treasures. And they did not stop until your kin were washed up on these shores and began the Giant-Wars.'

She listened avidly. Alcyon usually kept his peace, no matter how many questions Cywen asked him.

'So you are Kurgin?'

'Kurgan.'

'Where are your kin, then?'

'A long way from here, child. They live in Arcona, the sea of grass, far to the east.'

'How have you come to be so far from home?'

A look swept his face – sorrow, regret, shifting to misery, all in a heartbeat – replaced by something cold. 'That is not your concern, child.'

'Just trying to learn something about my captors,' she muttered.

He looked at her a while, then, just as she thought the silence was permanent, he spoke again. 'I am Calidus' servant. I do his bidding, that is all. His business is here, with Nathair, with Rhin, so I am here also.' He looked into his bowl and slurped from it. He didn't use a spoon.

'Calidus,' Cywen said. 'His business is with Nathair, and Rhin. And Corban, my brother. That's why I'm here, isn't it. Something to do with Corban.'

'Aye,' the giant rumbled.

'What is it? How can Corban be of any interest to Calidus, to kings and queens?'

Alcyon just looked at her over the giant axe resting across his knees.

They reached Dun Vaner by highsun the next day and stayed one night in its cold and damp halls. The fortress was almost deserted; most of Rhin's warriors had joined the warband attacking Domhain, with only a small garrison left to man the stronghold.

Early the next day they set out, Nathair and the three Benothi giants leading as Rhin bid them farewell beneath the stone archway of Dun Vaner. Cywen rode Shield towards the rear of the column, Buddai beside her, Alcyon's strides keeping easy pace with the horse. As they left the mountain slopes and the ground levelled out, Buddai stopped, frozen to the spot, looking back. He whined.

'What is it?' Cywen said to him. The hound just stared into the distance, ears pricked, head cocked.

Alcyon paused, listening. Then she heard it too, faint as a sigh, floating on the wind from the mountains. A wolven howling.

CHAPTER EIGHTY-FIVE

CAMLIN

The walls of Dun Taras appeared through a dense curtain of sleet. Camlin rode in the van, close to Edana and her other shieldmen, Halion, Marrock and Vonn.

It had been a hard and slow march back from the mountains, a wall of sleet and snow bringing death quickly to those too weak to keep up.

Rhin's warband had not pursued at any great pace but Rath's scouts reported that they were coming, marching steadily behind them.

They're happy to herd us into Dun Taras and watch us starve to death.

Camlin could still not believe how decisively the battle had been lost. He had never seen anything like the wall of shields that had marched out of the foothills and along the giants' road, never seen death dealt out so efficiently and clinically. Something about it had felt so wrong: it took the heart from the battle – no deeds of valour, no great displays of skill or strength that won the day – just a cold, soulless distribution of death. It had scared him. He remembered seeing something similar back in the feast-hall at Dun Carreg, forming up to protect Nathair as all hell had broken loose. But it had been on a much smaller scale, and he had been close enough that he had been able to find a few gaps with his arrows. This time, though, three blocks of warriors, each two or three hundred men strong, shields and swords bristling. It would take a lot more than a few arrows to crack that nut.

Horns rang out as they rode through the streets beyond the fortress' walls, then they were passing beneath a stone archway, grim-faced warriors upon the battlements. Rath headed straight for the keep and an audience with Eremon. He beckoned for Edana to go with him, so her four shieldmen followed dutifully behind.

Eremon was looking even older. Up close he could see every line and crease, his skin sagging, waxy. *He looks like a candle burned too long.* Beside him sat his pale-faced and dark-haired queen. Roisin. Camlin disliked her greatly, mostly based upon the grief she had rained down on Halion. This was a woman who was prepared to kill to see her plans made real.

There was a fluttering sound and a bird appeared at the window, peering through a flapping shutter – Fech. When he saw Edana he hopped through the gap, shook himself and started running his beak through his feathers.

The King listened solemnly to Rath and Edana recount the battle at the border.

'How can we defeat them?' he asked as Rath fell silent.

'I don't know,' Rath said. 'I have never seen its like before. We threw ourselves against it for a long day and could not stop it. I could not say if we even slew one man. A warband of giants would be easier to defeat.' He hung his head.

Eremon looked from Rath to Edana.

'There must be a way, my King,' Edana said. 'And your strong walls and harsh winter will help us, I am sure.'

'Aye, true enough,' Eremon mused, rubbing his wispy chin.

'Is that all you have to offer?' Roisin said. 'After you bring Rhin's warband howling into Domhain, snapping at your heels, slaughtering our warriors. And you say rock and rain will save us?'

Edana coloured, looking speechless.

'That is not true,' Halion said, stepping forward. 'Rhin was always coming, whether Edana was here or not.'

Roisin turned her look on Halion. 'That is something we shall never know, now. You play on your father's good nature.'

Halion stared at Roisin, but said nothing in response. A silence settled over the room, then Rath spoke.

'Edana and her followers have fought in the battle,' Rath said. 'Risked their lives in the defence of Domhain. That counts for something.'

'In defence of their own plans, more like,' Roisin said.

'Enough,' snapped Eremon, looking more irritated than angry.

Edana took a step forwards. 'I did not force Rhin to invade Narvon, or Ardan. Did not steer her into killing Owain, or my own mother and father. Rhin has her own plans, and to her I am only one minor inconvenience amongst many. As are *you*. It is your throne she has her eye on now, the reason she is here. She wishes to rule the west – perhaps the whole of the Banished Lands for all I know. Her ambitions reach far higher than hunting down the last heir to a kingdom that barely exists any more.' She spoke clearly, her eyes on Roisin the whole time.

Well done, girl, thought Camlin. *Give the snake a little venom back.*

Eremon patted a chair beside him and clapped his hands. 'Come and sit, Edana. Drink some ale with me. You must be tired, but I would hear more from you before you retire.' Servants appeared, carrying food and drink. Camlin and the others were ushered away, leaving Edana with Eremon and Roisin.

'Let's get a drink,' Halion said, blowing out a long breath.

'I don't like her,' Vonn said, taking a sip from his cup.

They were sitting in a corner of the feast-hall, the four of them, huddled in conversation.

'There's not much to like,' Marrock agreed.

'There's plenty to like, until she opens her mouth,' Camlin said.

'Poor Edana.' Vonn shook his head. 'She has had enough to deal with, without vipers like that.'

'Roisin must have been raging inside,' Halion said. 'Usually she pours honey from her lips. All that she says is thought through, has a purpose.'

'Something is disrupting her composure, then?' Marrock said.

'Perhaps that's to do with a foreign warband marching up the giants' road,' Camlin pointed out. 'Don't read me wrong – she strikes me as an evil bitch, sure enough. But she's also a mother, and I get the feeling she loves her son to death and beyond. Might be that the thought of Rhin putting his head on a spear is upsetting her a little.'

Halion nodded thoughtfully.

'For an ex-thief and murderer you talk a lot of sense sometimes,' Marrock said.

'You get a lot of time to think, living in the Darkwood. All that waiting around for people to rob.'

'What's going to happen, now?' Vonn asked. He was looking at Halion.

'I don't know,' Halion said. 'Like Edana said, I suppose. Hide behind these walls, let them and winter put Rhin off. Then try and think of a way to beat that wall of shields by spring.'

'I know how to do it,' Camlin said calmly.

'How?' They all looked at him.

'Don't go getting excited. It can't be done here – or out there, anyway, in all those open meadows. That's the perfect terrain for them. We need to fight them in the woods, where they can't form their wall. Either that or sit on the top of a hill and roll a few score boulders at them. They might not want to stand so close together, then.'

Halion nodded. 'You know what – you might just have something there. I'm going to find Rath.'

Marrock clapped Camlin on the shoulder. 'You are a good man to have around, you know.'

Just then the doors opened and in walked Roisin. Her son Lorcan walked beside her, Quinn the first-sword behind him, with a few others. Roisin saw Halion and strode to him.

'What are your schemes here?' she hissed, leaning close to Halion.

'There is no scheme,' Halion said. 'Open your eyes, Roisin. Edana and I, we are swept on the wave of someone else's plans. Rhin is the great manipulator in all of this. You may have met your match at last.'

'I don't trust you, Halion the bastard. Using a young girl to worm your way into Eremon's court? It will not work.'

Halion jerked away from her. 'Your paranoia grows, Roisin. I thought it had peaked when it led you to murder my mam.'

'You accuse me?'

'I don't need to. Those who matter know it was you.' He took another step back, took a deep breath. 'I did not come back to Domhain to settle past wrongs. That is done. There is a shared enemy to fight. I am not here to contest Lorcan's right to the throne, but there is a warband out there that will. Think on that, Roisin; think on who your true enemy is here.'

With that he strode away, past Lorcan and Quinn and through the feast-hall doors. Roisin watched him leave with narrowed eyes. Camlin suspected this would not be the end of it.

CHAPTER EIGHTY-SIX

MAQUIN

Maquin ate his food slowly.

All about him men ate and drank to excess, laughed and sang. He was sitting in a room that looked out over the cliffs of Nerin onto the Tethys Sea. It was sunset; the sun's last rays were turning the sea to molten gold.

Amongst the men he was sat with were the survivors of the pit. Ten men. There had been twelve, but two of them had become fevered through the night and Herak's men had hauled them away, to healers, supposedly.

Unlikely. It is strange how men will believe what they want to believe, cling to it, even when the truth is there to see.

His fellow pit-fighters were not the only men sitting at the table. Herak was there, as well as some of his guards – ones that had worked with Maquin and the others, helped to train them. They all ate and drank with vigour, smiling and laughing as if they were friends, equals, not masters and slaves. Guards still lined the walls though, standing in the shadows.

It made Maquin feel sick.

He had come to terms, finally, with what he was doing, what he had become. He didn't like himself for it, but the face of Jael drove him, made his decisions possible. And when it had come down to it, when given the choice of life or death, he had chosen life, or at least the right to fight death's efforts to claim him.

I want to live.

But that did not mean he would be grateful to his captors, or that he would welcome their company and eat with them as if they were brothers. Looking about, though, no one else seemed to share his feelings. Except Orgull. He was sat at the far end, looking much as Maquin felt. Repulsed.

He sipped a cup of wine.

Herak banged his cup on the table and slowly a silence fell.

'You are champions now,' Herak began. 'Champions of the pit, champions of Panos. You will fight again, but not like that; not amongst so many. That is for the new arrivals, the initiates.'

'When will we fight?' a voice called out. *Javed. Always the question-asker.*

'Not for a while.' Herak shrugged. 'You'll have long enough to enjoy this victory.'

'Who will we fight?' Orgull.

'Whoever is put in front of you,' Herak said, all friendliness erased from his voice.

The days passed. They were moved from rooms below ground to ground level, a measure of weak sun and fresh air helping to revive Maquin and his companions. To make them feel human again. The ten of them lived in the same room. Their training with Herak continued – most of it focused on close-quarter combat, knife work and weaponless battle. They were treated better now, fed well, spoken to, given rewards. Those who excelled in the day's training were given special meals or an extra drink. Occasionally a woman.

Maquin abstained from all of the rewards offered to him. He wasn't a *pet*.

Javed laughed at him. 'Live, man; enjoy what you can. Life will not treat you better because you say no.'

Maquin just smiled and shook his head at the little warrior. *I will not be bought, purchased, manipulated like some half-witted fool. I do what they want because I have no choice. I will not play their games. They are my enemy.* The only other man who refused as he did was Orgull. They spoke little, but Maquin often caught Orgull watching him. They were sword-brothers, a bond forged in the Gadrai and tempered in the catacombs of Haldis. Nothing could change that. Maquin did not want friendships, though, had no desire for anything that could distract him from his course. *I should have hunted Jael down as soon as I was out of the tunnels beneath Haldis.*

Should have. Forget that. There is only now, and what happens next.

Often during training Maquin would see groups of men, shackled hand and foot, led past them, towards the entrance to the underground chambers. They all had a look about them that he knew too well. Half starved, desperate, but still a glimmer of hope in most eyes. They were the latest captives brought in from various ships, more fodder for the fighting pits. Not yet gone through the horror and torture of that first push into darkness.

It was evening, almost a moon since the last pit-fight. Maquin sat on his cot, knees drawn up, dipping dark bread into a spicy soup. Their chambers reminded Maquin of the great stables at Mikil. Each room a stable, sharing a communal yard that was fenced in with iron bars. Beyond those bars was their training ground, further off a town. People would often come to look at them through the bars, even to speak sometimes; they were mostly children, play-acting champions of the pits. Some of the ten liked it, would go and talk and laugh with the visitors. Maquin didn't. Whenever he saw movement at the bars he would retreat inside his cell, into the shadows.

There was a rattling at the gates and Maquin rose to see who was coming in, soup and bread still in his hand.

It was Herak, flanked by two guards.

'Wanted to tell you, it's your last night on the island,' he said. 'You'll all be getting something to remember Nerin by soon. Food, wine, women.'

A cheer went up from most of the men.

'Where are we going?' *Javed, of course.*

Herak smiled viciously. 'Tenebral.'

CHAPTER EIGHTY-SEVEN

CORBAN

Corban stumbled again; hands reached out to steady him.

'Keep moving,' a voice growled close to his ear.

Corban was exhausted. They had been walking a day and a night since he had heard the wolven howl in the distance. He was sure it was Storm, although other wolven prowled these mountains.

Do I just want to believe so hard that I will not accept anything else? No. It was her.

There was little hope of him making an escape. Corban had counted fifteen grim-faced men in Braith's employ, though there were never more than twelve about him at any one time – the others scouting ahead or behind. There was also a brace of hounds – two tall, rangy things, skinny with matted hair. They loped ahead, close to one of Braith's men, himself tall and long-limbed, beard and hair a tangled mess.

Whether they thought Storm was behind them or not, they kept a fast pace, determined to outpace her and any of his companions who might be following behind. *Mam'll skin me, getting caught like this. All the worry I'm giving her.*

It was still dark and bitterly cold. As a jagged horizon began to edge in grey Corban realized it was snowing, the flakes looking like slow-falling leaves. They were moving out of the narrow ravines that had marked their passage through the mountains, onto wider paths, ever downwards now.

We must be almost through, nearly into Cambren by now.

Braith was up ahead. Corban saw him send a man back along the path they had travelled. Corban had noticed him doing that through-out their journey, rotating the scouts to front and rear. Soon whoever had been on rearguard would join them. Braith broke up a biscuit and threw it to the hounds. They snapped at each other over the crumbs.

The snow fell more heavily now, a cold wind sending it swirling about them, thickening beneath Corban's boots, muting sound. Corban was bustled to the centre of the group. Each breath and the pounding of his blood seemed to grow in volume, filling his head.

After a while Corban realized that the rearguard had not joined them. Braith must have noticed too, for he was looking over his shoulder. They were moving through pine trees now, the branches dipping with the weight of snow, an eerie world of white stillness. A tension seemed to have crept amongst them; Corban could see it in the set of shoulders and faces, the twitching glances all about. The way their pace had increased.

A shadow flitted across Corban's path, merging with the shadows of tree and branch. He looked up, saw a black shape moving above the treetops, flitting in and out of view. He gave a cold smile.

One of the hounds up ahead stopped and turned, ears twitching. Heads peered back, searching through the trees, through the curtain of snow. Then Corban saw her, an off-white blur, bounding out from between the trees, mouth open, teeth bared.

Storm.

Behind her other forms, wolven in shape, more upright. Corban blinked. One was carrying a war-hammer.

Farrell and Coralen in their wolven pelts.

Storm hit the first of Braith's men, the two of them ploughing through the snow, a great fountain of blood exploding as they rolled. They came to a rest, Storm standing, her jaws dripping red. The man did not move.

Braith yelled orders, reached for Corban and started dragging him on. The hounds ran back, throwing themselves at Storm. A few men hung back; the rest ran on.

He heard snarling and shouting behind, the yelp of a dog, then the clash of weapons – Farrell and Coralen.

'No!' Corban yelled, lurching to the side, his feet clumsy in the snow, his bound hands not helping his balance, then he was tumbling to the ground, his face hitting snow and pine needles.

Get up,' Braith snarled, looming over him. He pulled Corban up, punched him in the gut, backhanded him across the face, then held a knife to Corban's throat.

'I'll bleed you here an' now if you try that again,' Braith hissed. 'Rhin'd like you alive, but dead's better'n nothing at all. You understand me?'

Corban nodded, feeling the knife burn at his throat. A hot trickle of blood ran down his neck.

'Get moving, then,' Braith said. He looped some rope around Corban's bonds, and pulled him on.

Corban staggered forwards, risking a glance back. Shapes moved amongst the trees, iron sparking as weapons clashed. A hound screamed in agony. One figure moved fast and smooth, more a swirling snow wraith than a man: Gar. Corban knew him by the way he fought, the way he killed. Arcs of blood glistened about him, scarlet pearls against the snow.

'On.' Braith's boot crashed into his back and Corban was moving forward, half-running, staggering through the trees. An arrow whistled close by, hit one of Corban's captors.

Dath.

The trees thinned and then they were on a bare slope, the snow ankle-deep, blanketing the ground. Corban caught a glimpse of grey walls and dark towers further below them, cloaked by the snow.

Dun Vaner.

Braith shouted orders and more men dropped back, drawing weapons as Corban and Braith ran past them. There was yelling and screaming behind, iron on iron.

I will not run to Rhin, to my own captivity, torture and death, Corban decided. He threw himself to the right, legs first, and kicked at Braith's ankles. The man went down in a tumbling roll, his knife flying from his hands. Corban clumsily climbed back to his feet and ran after the still-rolling form of Braith, kicked him in the chest as he came to a stop. Braith grabbed at Corban's boot and the two of them fell together.

Corban rose to his knees, punched two-handed at Braith, caught him on the shoulder, sent him rolling backwards, Corban's momentum carrying him further. Braith grabbed Corban's hair, yanked hard, his other hand reaching for Corban's throat, squeezing. Corban felt his veins bulging, heard his blood pounding like hooves; black spots edged his vision. He bucked in Braith's grip, brought a knee up into Braith's gut. The grip around his throat disappeared and Corban rolled away, lurched to his feet, took staggering steps back up the slope, towards his friends.

They were all there, merged with the treeline, fighting Braith's men. He saw Storm crouched, a man and hound circling her. Coralen was swirling gracefully around a warrior, slicing his hamstrings with her wolven claws. Then he saw his mam, spear in hand, blocking a flurry of sword blows. Gar stepped in and took the man's head from his shoulders.

He forced his feet to move, labouring back up the slope, his lungs burning. The sound of pounding, like hooves, grew louder and louder. Someone yelled behind him – Braith – and he looked back. He realized it wasn't his blood pounding in his head, it was riders, emerging through the snow, warriors with long spears, surging up behind him.

Braith pointed at him and he turned and ran, making a last effort to reach his friends and the trees.

Something heavy crashed into his back and he was sprawling forwards, a face full of snow.

He tried to rise, then hands were grabbing him, lifting him, and he was slung across a saddle; a blow crunched into his head making the world spin. He was moving, bouncing across the saddle, the shudder of hooves on snow passing through his body. Somewhere behind him a voice screamed, high and clear. His mam. She was calling his name. He tried to look up but something clumped him across the head again and all the strength flowed from his body. The sound of combat faded behind him, then he heard hooves clattering on stone and he was riding under an archway, huge gates closing behind him.

CHAPTER EIGHTY-EIGHT

TUKUL

Tukul pulled his cloak tighter and scowled at the mountains. They were half veiled by heavy falling snow. It had started with dawn, and kept falling all day long.

I hate snow. Cold, rain, sun, I can cope with, but not snow. He looked up to the heavens. *Forgive me, Elyon, it is part of your creation, but* . . .

Telassar had been warm, always, even in winter. Even in Drassil when it had snowed they had been protected from the bulk of it by the dense treetop canopy. Some flakes would make it through the lattice of branches, but not enough. *Not like this.* He looked down and saw his horse's hooves disappearing into the snow, past its fetlocks.

He rode beside Meical, his Jehar warriors riding in column behind.

They had travelled over a hundred leagues since Dun Carreg, had passed through Ardan and Narvon, then crossed rolling hills into Cambren. Here the going had been slower as Meical had taken them along less-frequented paths, through uninhabited lands, avoiding towns, villages and holds, though always heading for Domhain.

Once they had ridden into a band of warriors, scouts of Queen Rhin, riding back to Narvon. Meical had stayed their sword hands, suggesting that talking was attempted as a first resort in an effort to glean some information.

It had turned out to be simple enough. The warriors had taken one look at Tukul and his Jehar warriors and decided that they were part of a larger force that apparently rode with Rhin's warband, in service to Nathair, King of Tenebral. Meical and Tukul had managed to keep their surprise hidden, and the warriors had ridden on.

'The Jehar ride with Nathair,' Tukul had hissed to Meical, once they were alone. 'How can that be?'

'I should have watched Nathair,' Meical said, shaking his head. 'And he was right under my nose, all the time I was with Aquilus. It makes sense; Nathair spent time in Tarbesh.'

'It must be Sumur,' Tukul said. 'Sumur must be leading the Jehar. He was always in opposition to me. I should have killed him when I had the chance.'

'What's done is done,' Meical said. 'At least we have had warning.'

They had also discovered that Rhin's warband was set to invade Domhain and was somewhere ahead. They had continued onwards and eventually they had come to a point where they could see the giants' road leading into the mountains: the pass through to Domhain. It was filled with warriors. The warriors choked the path through the mountains, a constant line of wains going along the road, taking supplies towards Domhain. There was no way through.

They had discussed their options and decided to move northwards, to find a safe spot and then let Meical search for Corban.

'I have spent two score years laying plans, finding people that I trust, preparing for these days,' Meical said. 'And yet now I feel like a chicken chopped for the table.' He gave Tukul a rueful smile.

'Asroth has been making plans, too,' Tukul said.

'Aye, he has. I have been too cautious.' He shook his head.

'But we stand on the side of right, and the battle is far from done,' Tukul said. *I will not consider defeat. I have not waited all my life just to lose at the end.*

'Aye. And we are close now, my friend. I have found the Seren Disglair's shadow in the Otherworld and tracked him through it. He is close. I will sleep now and travel the dream road. I will not lose him again.'

Tukul still found it strange how Meical could fall into a sleep so deep that he could not be woken, in which he almost appeared to be dead, and from which he would wake, looking as if he had fought with death himself, and say that the Seren Disglair was in Domhain, or in Dun Taras, or to the east, or north-east.

He is not of this world. What do I expect?

This time Meical had said that the Seren Disglair was still in Domhain, but travelling north, on the far side of the mountains.

That had been a ten-night gone. They had travelled north,

searching for a path to cross into Domhain. Meical said he knew of one, but that they would have to tread carefully.

'We are close to Dun Vaner,' Meical said to him, leaning in his saddle. Tukul just grunted, trusting Meical's judgement. How Meical could tell where they were in this whitewashed world he did not know, but briefly he caught a glimpse through the swirling snow of dark walls in the distance, high on a slope a cluster of towers and pinpricks of light. The day was turning to grey, the obscured sun retreating behind the mountains. They found a place to make camp, taking some shelter beneath a stand of birch and hawthorn in a cup-shaped dell.

'I will search for him again tonight,' Meical said as they sat huddled close together around a small fire. Soon Meical lay down and Tukul saw the familiar signs of his breathing slowing, becoming shallower.

Find him, Tukul thought. *Find the Seren Disglair, and with him my son.*

CHAPTER EIGHTY-NINE

CORBAN

Corban was hauled by two warriors through high-vaulted corridors, mostly empty, though in some alcoves fire-pits burned and warriors stood close to the flames to warm themselves. There was a feeling of emptiness here, and decay. Footsteps echoed behind him, following him. Braith.

Eventually he was dragged into a small chamber with weak light filtering in through slits in shuttered windows. One torch burned in a sconce, sending shadows dancing. Corban was slammed against a wall and his hands shackled to an iron ring above him, his ankles below.

Braith sat at a table, poured himself a cup of something dark and drank thirstily.

He leaned back, studying Corban. 'What does Rhin want with you?' he said at last.

'Huh,' Corban muttered. He still felt sick, and Braith's words seemed as if they were reaching him through water, or the snow-storm that had raged outside. Distant and muted.

Braith repeated his question.

I don't know, thought Corban. He looked up to the shuttered window opposite, thinking of his mam and friends out on the hill-side. Were they still fighting? Had they escaped? Stray flakes of snow drifted through the gap in the shutters and floated lazily down.

Someone came in, a woman, carrying a platter full of food – bread, fruits, cheese, cold meats. Corban heard his stomach growl as he watched Braith tear into it.

'Here,' Braith said, walking over and holding out a chunk of bread. 'I should let you starve, after what your wolven and friends did to my men back there, but I think Rhin's going to want to talk with you; so passing out is to be avoided.'

Corban chewed a mouthful. The bread was still warm. It tasted delicious. Braith gave him a sip of his drink – watered ale.

'My thanks,' Corban said when he had swallowed and was sure that the food and drink was not going to come straight back up.

Braith sat down and finished his food.

'Did they get away?' Corban asked, his voice a croak.

'I don't know,' Braith said. 'Only two of my men still live, and one of those was the man I sent ahead to tell Rhin we were close. The riders wouldn't have followed your friends if they ran, not into those trees and possible ambush.' He rubbed his eyes.

A silence fell on the room.

A muffled sound came from the far wall. Corban saw the outline of a door appear, and what he thought was undressed stone swung open. Two figures emerged from the darkness. Corban recognized both of them.

Rhin, Queen of Cambren. *Of Narvon and Ardan, too, now.* She was old, appeared much older than the last time he had seen her, in Badun at the Midwinter gathering, when Tull had fought her champion, Morcant.

Morcant was no longer her champion, though; he knew that and he saw Conall walk into the room behind her.

The warrior didn't say anything, but their eyes locked for a long moment. Conall was the first to look away. Corban wasn't sure what he saw there: pride, definitely, but there was more, a flicker in his glance, an unwillingness to hold Corban's gaze. Was that shame? Corban remembered when Conall had first come to Dun Carreg, riding up the giantsway with Halion. He had seemed happy then by comparison, carefree.

'Well done, Braith,' Rhin said. The woodsman dropped to one knee before her and kissed her hand.

'You've done well,' she said, motioning for him to stand. 'Even if half my riders are now lying dead on the slopes of Vaner.'

'Are they caught?' Braith asked. 'His companions?'

'No. I have riders out searching, but I don't have enough men here to do the job properly. Most of them are busy conquering Domhain.'

'I can take a party out. I know the land well hereabouts.'

'Perhaps.' Rhin nodded. 'If Edana is out there it would be a shame to let her get away.'

She thinks I travelled with Edana.

'So, you are Corban,' Rhin said, turning to him. It was not a question. 'I do remember you from Badun. At least, I remember seeing the boy who had tamed a wolven.'

She's not tame, Corban thought.

'I should have given you more attention then but I was preoccupied. I hear she's grown, your wolven, and is happily tearing people apart in my woodlands.'

She's not dead, then. Corban felt a flutter of relief in his belly. He opened his mouth and asked the question that had been hovering there.

'Where's Cywen?'

'Cywen?' Rhin said.

Corban felt his spirits sink. Rhin didn't know who he meant.

Conall whispered something in her ear.

'Oh, your sister. She's well on her way to Murias. You'll not find her here,' Rhin said. 'Is that what you thought? Were you coming here to get her, when Braith found you wandering around my mountains? How terribly noble of you.' She stepped closer to him, ran a pointed fingernail along his jaw line, down his neck, across his chest. He pulled away, tried to kick out but the iron collars about his ankles held him.

Murias.

'Admirable qualities,' she murmured, close enough that he could smell her breath, a hint of honey on it. *Mead?*

'What do you want with me?'

'I'm not sure,' Rhin said. 'Yet. There are certain parties that are extremely interested in you, though, and that has piqued my interest. Tell me of yourself, Corban of Dun Carreg. Of your kin, your friends. I would know *everything* about you.'

Corban woke to a throbbing pain in his wrists.

Where am I?

His eyes fluttered open and he saw a pot sitting over a small fire, could hear water bubbling within it.

Rhin.

Pains started registering, first his wrists, where the shackles had borne his slumped weight, then his ribs and kidneys, where Conall had beaten him.

'You should have told her what you know,' Braith advised. 'She'll get what she wants out of you anyway, so you might as well save yourself some pain.'

'Where is she?' Corban asked. He took his weight on his legs, removing the pressure from his wrists. He felt blood trickling down his forearms.

'Don't worry, she'll be back soon enough.'

A noise seeped into his consciousness, a creaking, tapping sound. He looked up at the shuttered window, high on the opposite wall. Light still streamed through, the occasional snowflake. Then a shadow crossed the gap between the shutters, something beyond blocking the light. He heard the tapping again, followed by a squawk.

Craf?

Just then the secret door opened and Rhin walked back in, shadowed by Conall. She marched to the pot and threw something in. A herbal smell wafted out, and an acrid steam rose.

'Hold the pot close to him,' she ordered Conall and Braith. They carried it by an iron spit and held it close. He tried to kick at it but his shackles stopped him. The steam floated about his face, curling into his mouth, his nose, stinging his eyes. He clamped his mouth shut and held his breath.

'He's stubborn,' Rhin said, a smile twitching her lips.

Corban's lungs started to burn, the beating of his heart growing louder in his head. Eventually he took a breath, throwing his head around, trying to disperse the steam. It didn't work. He had a bitter taste at the back of his throat, closely followed by a sense of warmth radiating from his chest, seeping through his body. He felt more relaxed than he could remember.

'There we are,' Rhin said. 'Take the pot away. Corban, look at me.'

He felt his head swing up and stared at her.

'Good boy,' Rhin said. 'Now, tell me. Where is Edana?'

He clamped his mouth shut, resolving to tell her nothing. He had taken Conall's beating before, concentrating as Gar had taught him in the sword dance, clearing his mind. He would take it again, and tell Rhin nothing.

'In Domhain, with Rath's warband,' he heard a voice say. His own. Rhin chuckled.

She asked him question after question, and each time he heard his own voice respond, like a betrayer wrapped within his own body. She went through his family, asked about his friends. He heard himself speak of Gar, tell of his curved sword, his skill in combat, of Dath and Farrell, finally of Coralen.

Rhin paused from her questioning, just studied him long moments. 'All very nice, but what makes you so interesting to Nathair. Why are you considered so special?' she mused.

'Gar says I'm the Seren Disglair,' he heard himself say.

Rhin grabbed his chin, her grip surprisingly strong, and looked into his eyes, studying him. 'Repeat that,' she ordered.

He did.

Her eyes grew wide and she released him. 'Can it be?' she murmured, excited. She looked scared as well.

She paced the room, looking in heavy thought. 'There is only one way to know for certain,' she said to herself. She ordered the pot hung over the fire again and left the room. By the time the water was bubbling she was back. She threw something else in, the steam turned black and smelled of sweet rot.

'Hold the pot close to him,' she said, dragging a chair over to Corban. 'Make sure that we both receive the fumes.' She drew a knife from her belt and cut Corban, a red line on his arm. Then she licked his blood, smeared it over her lips and whispered words unrecognizable to him.

'We shall both sleep – see that nothing wakes us.'

Then the pot was boiling, steam hissing from it, swirling about them both. Again Corban tried to hold his breath, to turn away, but he could not avoid the steam as it snaked its way inside him. Then his vision was dimming, darkness closing in.

Corban looked around. A world of grey surrounded him, the ground, coated in mist, the sky, thick iron-coloured cloud.

I have been here before. In my dreams. He felt a shiver of fear as the memory of those dreams flooded his mind: a kaleidoscope of images, mist-shrouded landscapes, fierce-eyed warriors.

Something tugged at his arm, a scarlet cord. Someone held it, a woman, fierce and beautiful, black hair cascading like a dark river about her shoulders. She smiled at him and he recognized the twist of her lips.

Rhin.

'This way,' she said, tugging at the cord again. He went after her, the mist parting around their feet. He tried to resist, but found that he couldn't.

They followed a river, its waters black, its course straight. Occasionally something moved in it, broad and sinuous, intimating a great mass hidden beneath the surface.

In the distance a shape appeared, materializing out of the mist. A mountain, casting a long shadow. Something was hidden in the darkness: the outline of a great building built into its embrace.

Corban looked up. In the sky shapes swirled, winged shapes. Some were faint in the clouds, others lower, closer. They circled down, pale-skinned warriors with shields, spears and swords in their hands, wings looking like leather or stretched skin. *I know them. In my dreams they have chased me, fought over me. I am in the Otherworld.* Fear threatened to overwhelm him. The ground shuddered as they landed, then they fell in silently about Corban and his companion, escorting them on.

They reached the building in the shadow of the mountain. It was a huge dome, with an arched doorway before them. They walked through a long tunnel; Corban gazed about in wonder, his hand touching a column that the doorway was attached to. It seemed to pulse, almost as if it were living, breathing. He lifted his fingers away, shaking off a mucus-like fluid. The whole building was carved from the same material. The walls were thin – the diffuse glow of light passed through them – with thick curving columns bracing the tunnel like huge, membranous ribs. The columns throbbed, as if blood were passing through them.

They stepped out of the tunnel; a domed roof made from the same material arched high above. A wide space opened before them, punctuated by great pillars rising high to the roof. About them were more of the winged creatures. They fell silent as Corban and his captor passed by, a pathway opening amongst them.

They came to a set of wide steps that stretched across the entire room. They climbed them; with each step a mounting dread grew in Corban.

At the top he stopped, Rhin walking forwards a few paces. She knelt before a throne and the creature seated upon it, then abased herself, arms outstretched, palms flat on the ground. Corban just stared. The throne looked to be carved from the same fabric as the rest of the building, its legs and back looking like the looping coils of a great snake, like the white wyrm Corban had seen in the tunnels beneath Dun Carreg. He did not want to look at the creature sat upon this throne – everything in him trying to look away, to turn and run – but fear held him tight. Against his will his eyes rose.

Upon the chair sat a great winged man. He wore a coat of mail, black and oily. His skin was pale, like all the others of his kind, flaking like the scales of a snake. Dark veins mapped his alabaster flesh. A sword lay across his lap, the hint of smoke rising from its blade. All this Corban saw in a glance, his gaze drawn to the man's face. It was as pale as milk, all sharp bones and chiselled angles, coldly handsome. Silver hair was pulled tight into a warrior braid that curled across one shoulder. But it was the eyes that drew and held Corban – black as a forest pool at midnight, no iris, no pupil, just a pulsing malice. Something lurked beneath those eyes, something feral, a barely contained rage.

He regarded the woman and Corban with those black eyes. Corban felt a cold fist clench deep in his belly.

'On your knees,' a voice said from behind him, and a blow hit the back of his legs. He dropped to the ground.

'What have you brought me, faithful servant?' the creature on the chair asked.

'A great prize, my lord,' the lady said. She kept her eyes down. 'I believe I have found the enemy's avatar. The Seren Disglair.'

The creature leaned forward, eyes boring into Corban. He took a deep sniff, a black tongue flickering from his mouth, tasting the air.

'Yes. I recognize his stink.' He laughed. 'Rhin, your reward will be great indeed for this.'

'Who are you? What are you?' Corban asked, the words coming

out as a whisper. Deep down he knew, a name surfacing like a fist from water.

'We have met before. Do you not recognize me?' the creature asked. It rose and stepped from the throne, sinuous and graceful, the ground rippling with each step. With the wave of a hand its shape changed, shimmering and blurring. Then a man was standing before Corban, the wings replaced by a travel-stained cloak. Old, handsome, a neat beard and lines of laughter about his eyes. Yellow eyes.

Corban did remember him. 'I saw you, at the oathstone in the Baglun.'

'Yes. I offered you my friendship once. My patronage. The chance to side with me. That chance has passed now. I have found another.'

'I don't understand.'

'Yes, you do. You just do not want to. You humans are all the same. Willing to live a lie, any lie, as long as it is prettier than the truth. It's one of the few things that I love about your race.' He held his sword loosely in one hand.

'Who are you?' Corban repeated, more a last denial than a question.

'I am Asroth, Lightbearer, Fallen One, Death of Nations,' the man said. 'Death of *you*.'

He reached out and laid a broken-nailed hand upon Rhin. A shiver ran through her body.

'Stand,' he said to her. 'You must go back to your world of flesh, and slay him. Cut his heart from his body. I shall keep his spirit here, and talk a while until you do the deed.'

'As you command, my lord,' Rhin said.

A noise filled the dome, a long, eerie note, a horn blast.

'To arms,' a voice rang out as the horn faded. There was a great cracking sound, as of a thousand whips struck at the same time, the wings of all the creatures in the hall spreading. *The Kadoshim*, thought Corban. *The host of angels that fell with Asroth.*

A noise sounded above, high on the dome, a concussive boom, and a hole appeared, shards of whatever the building was made of exploding inwards. Figures poured through the hole, warriors with great white wings. One threw a spear and it pierced the ground between Corban and this creature that named himself Asroth. It stood quivering.

The man before Corban blurred again, his shape changing, cloak spreading, transforming into wings.

'You dare to come here,' he snarled, pointing his black sword upwards, then with a scream of rage launched himself at the invading warriors. The sound of it hurt Corban's ears.

Battle erupted all around as the new winged arrivals fell howling down upon Asroth's host. They were clearly outnumbered, but surprise and the advantage of height helped to drive them through the first waves that rose to meet them. Before Corban had time to move, a handful of them were alighting about him, forming a ring of shield, spear and sword.

He felt something tugging on his arm, turned to see Rhin trying to drag him back down the stairs by the red cord that was still attached to him. One of the warriors about him saw and struck the cord with a sword. There was a cracking noise and the cord detonated in a spray of blood. Rhin fell backwards, toppling down the stairs, disappearing amidst the conflict. Corban dragged in a juddering breath, felt new energy fill him. Before, he had felt terrified, frozen by that fear, but now the urge to fight rose up in him, coiling in his limbs. He saw a spear fallen on the ground, the white wings of its owner twitching as it lay there, a deep hole in its chest, something dark and slimy oozing from the wound.

He grabbed the spear. It was lighter than he expected, the shaft smooth and warm. Air beat down upon him and he looked up, saw one of Asroth's Kadoshim above him, wings beating hard. It reached out to pluck him from his circle of protectors. Corban stabbed up with the spear, pierced the outstretched hand, the blade carrying on, raking a line across the creature's ribs. It screeched at him and pumped its wings, rising quickly. Corban yanked the spear free, something wet splattering his face.

Screams and battle-cries filled the room, echoing about the dome, so loud that Corban wanted just to curl up on the floor and cover his ears. Everywhere was furious battle. More of the white-winged warriors were streaming through the hole high above.

They are the Ben-Elim, the angels of Elyon. Am I dreaming all of this?

For a dream it seemed real enough – he could touch, hear and smell the violence surrounding him. Figures filled the air, striking at one another, grappling, spinning, many falling to crash into the ground. The circle around him was hard pressed, blades clashing, limbs being severed, dark ichor that seemed to pass for blood spraying in great fountains.

Then a shadow was looming above, the air beating him down. Corban looked up and saw white wings, a flash of pale skin and dark hair, then he was being hoisted upwards, so fast that he felt as if he'd left his guts on the ground. Other warriors swooped in close, forming a wedge that flew straight up, to the now clear hole in the dome's ceiling.

Bodies crashed against them. Corban caught a flash of leathery wings, heard screeching and hissing. One of the Ben-Elim close to Corban dropped away, a sword-point erupting through his chest, but they flew on, higher and higher, until with a roaring in Corban's ears they burst through the hole in the rooftop and into the sky above.

The white wings pumped, driving them away, higher, until Corban could almost touch the clouds. A handful of Ben-Elim flew about them, and further back Corban saw the dome, shrinking now. He could just make out white-winged figures emerging from the dome's peak, mixed with others. The Ben-Elim were retreating, pursued by their ancient enemy.

Corban looked at the warrior who was carrying him. He was dark haired and pale skinned as all the rest, with a tracery of veins visible beneath his skin, high, sharp cheekbones, the hint of faded claw marks running down one side of his face. His eyes were dark, though not black like the Kadoshim; there was a purple tinge to them. Something about him stirred a memory, too faint to remember. 'Who are you?' Corban asked.

The warrior regarded him for long moments. 'A friend in a dark place,' he said.

CHAPTER NINETY

CORALEN

Coralen glared through swirling snow at the walls of Dun Vaner.

After the desperate chase yesterday, the fight in the woods and slopes, coming so close to reaching Corban, only to see him carried away through the fortress gates, she felt drained. Exhausted.

And angry.

She had not wanted to run, so close were they to rescuing Corban. Most of the enemy were down, bleeding into the snow, when the riders appeared, a relief force hurrying from Dun Vaner. It would have been foolishness and fatal to stand and face them in the open. So they had run when the riders came at them, scattering into the woodland. Storm had killed one horse and rider, Dath picked off a couple with his bow, Gar another, and she had leaped onto one more, dragging him from his saddle and opening his throat with her wolven claws. She was wearing them still, blood crusting about the iron blades.

Why am I here? She had volunteered to guide them north as soon as Rath had told her of Corban's plan to go after his sister. *Why?* Even now she felt herself avoiding that question. Others were moving about her, Gwenith and Brina whispering together, Farrell and Dath talking quietly. Gar stood beside her, staring at the walls. She could feel the worry leaking from him, through the cracks in his cold face. Storm was pacing amongst them, like a wounded bear, restless, crouched, the occasional growl rumbling deep from her belly. Coralen empathized with her – she felt frustrated, scared, angry. There was something about this group of people, similar to the camaraderie she had felt amongst Rath and his giant-killers, but more, somehow. Something deeper. She just knew that each and

every one of them would die for the other, and Corban was somehow at the centre of that. She felt his absence keenly, as she knew
they all did. And he was gone, inside those thick walls, perhaps even
already dead. She felt a wave of feeling, white-hot rage, and she
clenched a fist, her wolven claws chinking.

It had all happened so fast, waking to find Corban gone, then
hearing Storm howling, all of them running from the camp to find
the wolven dripping wet, standing over Ventos' corpse. They had
searched the area and Coralen had found the tracks of those who
had taken Corban. The rest had been one long run, blood in the
snow at the end of it.

And what now?

Something fluttered above her; a dark smudge emerged from the
swirling whiteness. Craf, the healer's crow.

It landed on a tree branch and began hopping about.

'*Cor-ban,*' it squawked. '*Found him, found him, found him.*'

'Where? How is he?' Gwenith blurted.

'*Alive,*' the crow said. '*Craf take you.*'

'How are we going to get over those walls?' Farrell said.

'This might help,' Dath said, lifting a long rope that was tied to
the saddle of a horse they'd found wandering the wooded slopes.

Gar smiled, a grim flash of his teeth.

CHAPTER NINETY-ONE

TUKUL

Tukul was dozing when Meical awoke. It was still dark about him, though a grey light framed the slopes above their dell. The brunt of the snowstorm seemed to have blown over. Orange flames from the fire sent shadows dancing around the bowl they were camped in.

He heard Meical gasp, saw him lurch up onto an elbow. The fire-light washed across his face, highlighting the sharp angles, making the lines around his eyes and mouth deep crags of shadow. For the first time Tukul thought he looked old.

Tukul sat up, blinking. 'What is it?'

Meical leaped to his feet. 'I know where he is. Corban. We must leave now; it may already be too late.'

'What do you mean? Where is he?' Tukul asked as he climbed to his feet, signalling for his Jehar to move about him.

'He is in there,' said Meical, pointing to the dark blur of walls and towers nestling amongst the white slopes of the mountain. 'Dun Vaner. Rhin has him. And she knows who he is. He will not be draw-ing breath for much longer. If he still does.'

The camp moved into action, silent and efficient.

By the time the sun had fully crested the horizon they were riding across a featureless white plain, approaching the slope and road that led to the gates of Dun Vaner.

'Those walls are thick, and the gates are shut,' Tukul observed.

'Yes,' Meical said. His earlier sense of franticness had receded, although Tukul could sense it, lurking beneath a veneer of calm.

'So how are we going to get in there?'

'We know that the Jehar ride with Nathair, and that they came north with Rhin. The men who are standing on that wall will know that, too.'

Tukul thought about that. 'So they will think we are their allies.'

'Exactly. To be safer still, as I stand out a little from the rest of you, I am now your prisoner, sent back to Rhin for questioning.'

'But what if Nathair and Sumur are in there?'

'They are not. They are heading north, and I have a good idea why, but we shall think on that after.'

'Excellent. So that's getting in. What then?'

'Let's cross that bridge when we get to it.'

'With our swords in our hands?'

'If needs be.'

'Best you try and look as if you're a prisoner, then,' Tukul said.

Meical clasped his hands behind his back, underneath his cloak, as if they were bound. Tukul and a few of his warriors moved around Meical, giving the appearance of guarding him. They rode up the road that led to Dun Vaner's gates, identifiable only because the snow lay more flat and even across it.

'Remember,' Meical said as they drew closer. 'The Seren Disglair is in there. He is a captive and will soon be killed. We cannot fail in this.'

Tukul felt a shiver at those words, knew that it was passing back through the column of his sword-kin.

This is it. The moment I've waited for. All-Father, I will not fail you.

The world was quiet and still, a beautiful white as far as he could see. Even the clouds up above him seemed to glow.

A perfect moment. He drew a deep breath, as he did before he began the sword dance, then he rode ahead of the column, looking up at the walls above the stronghold's gates. Heads peered over.

'Name your business,' a voice called down to him.

'I bring a gift from King Nathair – a spy found on the road north. He thought your Queen was better equipped to extract some truth from him.' He turned and beckoned for Meical to be brought forward. Enkara led Meical's horse, a few others riding close about him.

A silence lengthened. Tukul saw more heads peering over the battlements, heard muted words.

'Open your gates,' he yelled. 'It is cold down here.'

There was still no answer.

'Would you have me ride back to Nathair to tell him we crossed fifty leagues only to be turned away at his ally's gates?'

There was another silence. Tukul felt his pulse beating faster, had to concentrate to control it as the huge gates creaked open.

He rode in calmly, nodding to the guards who stood by the gates. *Four of them.* A courtyard lay beyond the gates. More warriors were milling about, performing various tasks – sweeping drifts of snow from the flagstones, piling it in deep banks with shovels, breaking ice in water buckets. *A dozen.* As Tukul rode deeper he glanced back, and up, scanning the battlements. *Another eight, maybe ten.* A great keep loomed straight ahead, doors of oak closed against the cold. Other buildings spread about the courtyard, a handful of doors. Shadows moved inside. *Maybe barracks. More warriors*, Tukul thought. *There could be anywhere between one and two hundred inside.*

They dismounted on the far side of the courtyard; doors opened to a huge stableblock from which issued a dozen stable boys. Tukul and his warriors were led into a feast-hall by two of the guards who had stood at the gates.

The feast-hall was almost empty; a score or so of men sat close to the firepit, breaking their fast, a few others scattered about the room.

'Your men can eat and drink here,' one of the guards said. 'Word has been sent to Queen Rhin. Bring your prisoner and we'll take you to the dungeons.'

'Where is everyone?' Tukul asked as they walked through the hall. At a nod, five of his warriors followed with Meical, the rest spreading through the feast-hall, pouring drinks, taking food.

'Most are down south, fighting in Domhain.'

'Of course,' Tukul said. He drew his sword, heard his warriors do the same behind him, all about the hall.

The guards both reached for their blades. Tukul let them draw before he killed the first one.

Let him cross the bridge of swords with his sword in his hand.

The man tried to block, but even fifty-eight years and the freezing cold snow of Cambren could not slow Tukul that much. They did not even touch blades.

The other guard opened his mouth to yell, at the same time stepping away and raising his sword.

'Don't kill him,' Meical snapped.

In a heartbeat Tukul's sword-point was at the guard's throat.

'Your choice,' Tukul said. 'Make a noise: die now. Stay silent: live a little longer.'

The guard's eyes darted about the room. Tukul didn't need to look: he knew all of Rhin's warriors in the room were dead.

The guard dropped his sword.

'Take us to the dungeon,' Meical said.

Tukul left a score of his Jehar in the feast-hall to guard against any newcomers, and the rest followed Tukul. As they left the hall Tukul looked back, saw the main doors open and a handful of guards walk in. His warriors fell on them, but some of the enemy stumbled back into the courtyard. Instants later he heard the blaring of horns.

'Faster,' he said to the guard leading the way.

'How many warriors are here?' Meical asked the guard. He didn't answer, but then he felt Meical's sword-point at his back.

'Three, four hundred. Enough.'

He's lying, thought Tukul. *And even if he's telling the truth, we are Jehar.*

The sound of combat drifted behind them. They strode through empty corridors, down a long staircase, the steps wide and worn, then into another corridor. Tukul barked an order and some of his warriors peeled away from the back, groups of five positioning themselves at each new doorway. Soon fifty warriors became thirty.

'We're going to need a way out,' he said to Meical.

Horn blasts echoed through the stronghold – the call to arms. Tukul heard the slap of running feet.

Guards appeared at the far end of the corridor, more than Tukul could see to count – at least a score, more coming behind them. The first ones paused for a heartbeat, then ran at him. He drew his sword, heard the familiar sound behind him as Meical and the others followed suit.

The corridor was wide, built by giants. Three men could stand abreast and still swing a sword. Tukul cracked their guide on the head with his sword pommel, saw him slump unconscious, then stepped into summer storm from the sword dance, his left hand forwards, blade arched over his right shoulder. He felt Meical and Enkara move to either side of him.

Let my heart be true and my sword be sharp.

Then he stepped into battle.

It was like coming home. He swayed and spun, ducked and lunged, and then his whole world was filled with blood, with the sounds of men dying. Most didn't have a chance to make a sound, others just a surprised grunt or yelp, in an instant moving from life to death, to empty husks of meat and bone.

The battle swirled past him, the two groups filtering into each other. He carved a red path through all that stood before him. He turned an overhead blow and followed through with a short horizontal slash, saw the man stumble and fall, his blood draining from his throat and his life from his eyes.

Then it was over.

Meical and Enkara still stood either side of him; both were covered with blood. None of it seemed to be their own. The corridor was littered with the dead. At a swift glance he did not think any of his sword-kin had fallen. Then a sound drifted into the corridor. The clash of iron. Yelling, but it came from ahead, not behind.

Tukul and Meical shared a glance and moved on, their pace fast but not reckless. The sounds of combat ahead grew. They turned a corridor, followed the sound down a staircase, then Tukul pulled up short.

Before him he saw the backs of at least a dozen of Rhin's warriors. Tukul heard the clash of weapons, shouting, a scream. Something was holding the warriors here. He glimpsed a form at the far end, a movement, the trail of a sword, a body moving fast, gracefully. Meical moved past him, sword high, and launched himself into the enemy. Tukul followed, chopping a head from its body with his first blow.

Panic ripped through Rhin's men as they tried to turn and face this new enemy. In moments twelve men fell, bleeding out their lives into the cold stone.

Just one man had been holding the corridor against them. He fought still, against the last of Rhin's warriors. He parried a frantic lunge, spun on his heel, reversed his sword and drove it into his opponent's belly. They stood there briefly, close as lovers, then the victor pulled his sword clear and turned to face Tukul.

He was clothed in leather and fur and wool, a long, curved sword held loosely. But Tukul's eyes were drawn to the warrior's face. Weathered skin, dark, earnest eyes, a ridged nose.

Garisan. My son.

Tukul saw recognition dawn in Gar's face, first a question in the eyes, then a twitch of the mouth. A hesitant smile.

Without a word Tukul strode forward and wrapped his son in his arms.

CHAPTER NINETY-TWO

CORBAN

Corban opened his eyes. He was hanging suspended, his arms stretched above him.

'He's waking up,' a voice said.

He lifted his head, the effort launching a pain in the back of his head, a white-hot needle twisting inside his skull. He groaned and saw Conall and Braith staring at him.

A figure sat slumped in a chair close by. Rhin. Her head was resting on her chest, her breathing deep and slow.

Rhin. He closed his eyes, trying to contain the stabbing pain in his head. *The Otherworld.* Had it been a dream? Then it all came back, a flood, a kaleidoscope of fractured images – a domed building, a host of winged creatures, battle.

Asroth. Asroth had spoken to him, and to Rhin. *Slay him,* Asroth had told Rhin. *Cut his heart from his body.*

Fear rippled through him. His head snapped up and he pulled himself upright, ignoring the pain in wrists and head. Rhin still slept. Braith and Conall were moving closer, expressions of concern on their faces. Braith knelt beside Rhin and touched his fingers to her wrist.

Don't wake her. The thought filled Corban like a silent scream.

'I'd not do that if I were you,' Conall said. 'She said not to wake her, and I've seen what happens to those that disobey her.'

'So have I.' Braith pulled his hand away.

Corban breathed a sigh of relief. *Rhin, stay sleeping,* he willed. *How am I going to get out of these shackles?*

'What happened?' Braith said to Corban. 'Why are you awake and she is not?'

Then a noise rang out, distant but clear. Horns sounding the alarm.

Conall went to the door and looked out, then he closed the door. There were more horn blasts, louder, spreading through the fortress. 'I don't like the sound of that,' Conall muttered, pacing now.

'Me neither,' Braith said.

Rhin whispered something, little more than an exhalation.

No.

'Kill . . .' she said; more sounds followed, but they were incomprehensible.

'Water, please,' Corban said.

Braith leaned closer to Rhin, trying to make out her whisperings.

Corban rattled his chains. 'Please, a drink.'

'Shut up,' Braith snapped. Conall brought him a skin of water and held it to Corban's lips. It was warm, but tasted wonderful and soothing to him.

Corban's mind was racing. He had to get out of his shackles before Rhin woke, but how? They were locked wrist and ankle, and he did not even know who had a key. He felt panic bubbling up like high tide in the rock pools of home.

Rhin's eyelids fluttered and she moved in her chair.

'My lady,' Braith said, seizing her hand. 'You must wake.'

The sound of booted feet running echoed from beyond the door, men shouting. A muffled scream. The sounds of battle rang clearer and Conall stuck his head out of the doorway, looking down the corridor.

'What's happening?' Braith called.

'There are wolven in the corridor,' Conall said. 'One of them is hitting people with a hammer.'

Farrell.

'It's the boy's companions,' Braith said. 'They're coming for him.'

'They're tearing strips out of a dozen men out there,' Conall said. He took a last look down the corridor and slammed the door shut, throwing an iron bolt across it.

'We need to get Rhin out of here,' Conall said, striding to the far wall. He reached into an alcove and then Corban heard a hiss, saw the outline of the secret door appear. It swung open.

There was a clash of weapons beyond the door Conall had just locked, a scream, something sliding down the door. Blood seeped beneath it, a dark pool spreading into the room. 'That'd be our guardsman,' Braith said. A great blow struck the door, dust exploding from the frame. The iron bolt and hinges creaked.

'Bring Rhin,' Conall snapped at Braith. He drew his sword and knife.

Braith scooped Rhin into his arms. Her eyes opened then, and she looked around.

'The boy . . .' she said.

Braith strode to the secret doorway and Rhin began to struggle in his arms.

'We are under attack, my lady,' Braith said. 'I am taking you to safety.'

'The boy,' Rhin snapped, still groggy. 'Kill him.'

Another blow slammed into the door; one of the hinges tore from the wall.

Braith and Conall shared a look, then Braith carried Rhin into the darkness beyond the hidden door, and Conall walked towards Corban.

Corban threw himself about, slamming against the wall, tearing away from it, the chains rattling. Nothing happened, though.

'Sorry, lad. No hard feelings,' Conall said as he raised his knife. He hesitated. 'Your sister's not going to thank me for this.'

I'm going to die.

Another blow hit the door and it crashed into the room, a cloud of dust filling the doorway, billowing out. A figure burst through, a dark-furred wolven standing on two feet, wielding a huge warhammer, other blurred forms behind.

Farrell.

He saw Conall and with a burst of speed Farrell threw himself across the room, hammer raised high. Conall just had time to duck. The hammer crashed into the wall behind Conall, close to Corban's head, chips of rock flying.

Conall stabbed with his knife, but the blade turned on Farrell's coat of mail. There was a brief flurry as the two traded blows, Farrell gripping his hammer like a staff, striking with both ends. They grappled together, then abruptly Farrell was on his back, Conall's sword hovering over him, his knife at Corban's throat.

'Con, no!' A scream.

Conall froze, eyes drawn to the voice.

It was Coralen, standing in her wolven pelt, streaks of blood and grime coating her.

'Cora?' A whisper from Conall.

'Don't do it, Con.'

Time stood still – a heartbeat that felt like a year to Corban.

'*Please*,' Coralen said.

A look of pain swept Conall's face. He lowered his weapon and ran for the hidden door. Briefly he paused at its entrance, standing half in light, half in darkness, and looked back.

'Con, wait.'

He melted into the darkness.

Coralen ran to the doorway and shouted after him. Only her echoes answered her. Then she turned and stared at Corban and Farrell. Corban saw tears like pale claw marks streaking her face. She crossed the room, stepped over Farrell and hugged Corban tight, burying her face in the arch of his neck and shoulder. He felt sobs shaking her.

Farrell shifted on the ground and Coralen stepped away, eyes downcast. Then Corban's mam was there, clutching her spear. She filled Coralen's place, squeezing him tight, stroking his face. Farrell climbed to his feet, a frown on his face.

'The keys?' his mam asked as she let go of him and began searching for a way to set him free.

'I don't know.' Corban said.

Coralen was back at the smashed doorway, her hands at the belt of the dead guardsman.

'Keys,' she said, taking a bundle from his belt and jangling them.

They tried them, and the third key clicked in the lock, the shackles about his wrists opening. He slumped down and Farrell caught him. Another click and his feet were free.

'Where are the others?' Corban asked.

'Brina and Dath are guarding the rope we climbed in on. Storm's with them,' his mam said. 'Gar. We need to get back to him – we were chased. He dropped back.' The fear in her eyes said more than her words.

'To Gar, then,' Corban said.

'No need,' a voice said from the doorway.

Gar stood there, a mass of shapes filling the corridor behind. There was something strange about him, then Corban realized what it was.

He's smiling.

A man stood beside him, of similar build, holding a sword the same as Gar's. The similarities did not end there. They shared the same nose, the same serious gaze, this man's dark hair streaked with grey at the temples.

'This is my father, Tukul, lord of the Jehar,' Gar said.

They all stared at him. Tukul crossed the room to Corban and dropped to one knee, taking Corban's hand in his.

'I pledge my sword, my heart, my strength to you,' he said.

Corban gaped, too dumbfounded for words. Then another figure stepped past Gar into the room. He was taller, with black hair pulled tight from fine, chiselled features. Silver scars layered his face.

'I *know* you,' Corban said. 'Who are you?'

'A friend in a dark place,' the man said, and smiled.

CHAPTER NINETY-THREE

LYKOS

Lykos stood on the battlements of Jerolin, looking out over the lake, which glistened under a wan winter sun.

The lake bristled with ships. His ships. They were full of warriors, their families, slaves for rowing, merchants and traders from the Three Islands, all gathering to him.

Over two thousand warriors. They had arrived slowly, over a matter of moons, so as not to arouse suspicion or panic. And during the same time he had ordered Fidele to send off the bulk of the eagle-guard that had been stationed at Jerolin to various distant locations in Tenebral, where they could be of little threat to his plans. Now only a few hundred remained here at Tenebral's capital, so his Vin Thalun warriors outnumbered them almost ten to one. And that was not all that he had brought to Tenebral.

Housed on the ships in the lake were his pit-fighters, as well. On the plain between the fortress and the lake a wooden construct was taking shape, circular tiers rising high, supported by huge timber beams. *A new type of fighting pit.* He smiled to himself.

Finally, after so many years, it is happening. He turned to look over the dark stone buildings of Jerolin, the sharp spike of the tower overshadowing them all.

This is all mine now, he thought. *Jerolin is the heart of Tenebral, and it belongs to me. By proxy.* His fingers dipped inside his cloak, seeking the effigy of Fidele. He felt a moment of fear, a weightlessness in his gut as his fingers searched. Then he felt it, smooth clay and brittle hair. *Such power. With Fidele a puppet in my hand I rule Jerolin, and with it, all of Tenebral.*

Riders appeared on the road to the north, eight or ten of them.

Lykos watched them draw closer, until he could see the white eagles embossed on their cuirasses and shields.

Peritus has returned, then. And the first thing he will do is seek an audience with Fidele.

A chill wind blew out of the north along with them. He shivered and pulled his cloak tighter. *It is warmer on the Islands. But I have Fidele to keep me warm here.*

He felt a stirring in his blood, just at the thought of her. He closed his eyes and drew in a long breath, could still smell her, a residue on his beard of rose petals and sweat. With the thought of her fresh in his mind he turned and made his way towards Jerolin's tower.

People looked away as he passed them, none brave enough or stupid enough to give him the black looks he had once become accustomed to. At first, when Fidele had announced him forgiven of his crimes and welcomed into the heart of Jerolin he had still received those looks, but as the days had passed and with them demonstration after demonstration that he could do as he wished without consequence the angry glares had turned away. Initially a horde of people complaining too loudly had been dragged to the dungeons, and that no doubt had helped to silence the complainers, but Lykos could still sense the animosity. These people were not cowed, yet. A stronger lesson was needed.

He passed a roped-off courtyard with bloodstains still on the flagstones. He had already begun the pit-fighting, on a small scale. A few contests in makeshift rings in the lakeside town at first, then moving to the stronghold. There had been an outcry, of course. Petitions had been sent to Fidele by the wainload, but, under his control she had just ignored them. And people had come, had watched, had bet silver and gold. A trickle at first, furtive looking, trying to stand in the shadows, but more had turned up with each bout. Soon he would spread the entertainment throughout Tenebral, but not until the arena on the plain had been finished. *We will need more slaves soon, else we'll run out of fighters.*

The spoils of war would supply that need soon enough.

He found Fidele in her chambers high in Jerolin's tower. She stared at him with such a look of hatred and contempt that he smiled – he had seen that look before, on the recently conquered, warriors he had made his slaves. In time the look would pass, would merge into other things. First would come despair, then acceptance, then servitude. He reached a hand into his cloak and her expression changed, became fearful. That made him smile as well.

'Speak your mind,' he said.

She opened her mouth, not trusting her voice. 'My son will kill you for this,' she breathed, beginning little above a whisper. She looked surprised that her thoughts had aligned with her words.

'I don't think he will,' Lykos said. *Soon enough he will have more on his mind than the governance of Tenebral.*

'Then *I* will kill you,' she said, her voice rising, her back straightening, as if control of her vocal cords gave her actual strength.

'Enough,' Lykos commanded. *Or your guards will hear.*

A struggle took place within the confines of her face and behind her eyes. She was clinging to her freedom of speech, refusing to let it go. Her mouth opened, lips twisting, but nothing came out. A few more moments passed as Lykos watched, entertained. Then her shoulders slumped, her body sagging.

'You will have a visitor soon,' he began . . .

There was a knock on the door.

'Enter,' Fidele called.

She was sat in a high-backed chair, wrapped in a cloak of darkest sable contrasting with her milky skin, her lips a deep red.

I shall have her when this is done, thought Lykos. He was standing further back, half in shadow. Deinon stood the other side of Fidele's chair. Other Vin Thalun were hidden about the dark edges of the room.

Two men walked into the chamber: Peritus, the old battlechief, and Armatus, his childhood friend and also first-sword of the dead king, Aquilus. They were both older men, the wrong side of forty, Lykos guessed. Both had deep lines in their faces and more grey than black in their hair. They both had a reputation with their blades, though, and Lykos was not one to underestimate an enemy.

'My lady,' Peritus said, bowing to Fidele. Then he saw Lykos. A look passed between him and Armatus.

'Welcome back to Jerolin,' Fidele said to them both. There was little warmth in her voice. 'How are things in the north?'

'Quiet,' Peritus said. 'The giants' raids have all but stopped. It was good to be home. I have returned early, though, because I am hearing strange things. About Jerolin.' He paused, looking uncomfortable.

'What things?' Fidele said.

'Where is Orcus?' Armatus asked. His eyes had seen Deinon standing in the shadows.

'I gave Orcus a leave of absence. There was illness in his family.'

He does not believe her, Lykos thought, watching Armatus.

'What strange things do you speak of, Peritus?' Fidele continued.

'May we speak alone?' Peritus asked, eyes flickering to Lykos.

'No, we may not,' Fidele said. 'My son, your King, trusts Lykos, and so do I.'

'You had a different opinion the last time that I saw you.'

'Opinions change.'

'But, the fighting pits. The dead, the boy dragged up from the lake – Jace. They were facts, not opinions. Lykos and his kind are murderers. You *know* this.'

Fidele stared at Peritus. Muscles in her face twitched. She opened her mouth but only a breath hissed out.

Lykos squeezed the effigy concealed in his hand and Fidele groaned.

'Are you well, my lady?' Peritus said to her, stepping forwards.

'Stay where you are,' Lykos said, moving out of the shadows.

Peritus froze, but Armatus moved forwards now. 'The last time I was in Jerolin, the Vin Thalun didn't give orders to the battlechief of Tenebral,' he said.

'Things have changed,' Lykos replied. He smiled at the two men.

'How so?' Peritus said. There was an edge in his voice now, one that Lykos recognized. Of violence restrained.

'Because I have willed it,' Fidele said, breaking a taut silence. 'We must move forwards, not backwards, and grudges and outdated rules cannot hold us back. The alliance with the Vin Thalun is vital to our cause. Lykos has given us great aid.'

'Outdated rules?' Peritus breathed. 'Since when has the punishment of murder become an outdated rule?'

'I have decided to forgive and move on,' Fidele said. Her tone was angry now. Only Lykos knew that that anger was not roused by Peritus' questions.

'Fidele,' Peritus said, 'you are not in your right mind. How can you say such things? You saw the pit at Balara – the dead heaped in piles.'

'Enough,' Lykos barked. He was losing patience with this now. 'Tell him all of it,' he said to Fidele.

'To honour this new beginning, games are to be held. A celebration. I have commissioned an arena to be built. Tenebral shall watch our enemies fight to the death.'

'Pit-fighting, in Jerolin,' Peritus hissed. 'You are out of your mind, or under a spell.'

Fidele's body jerked at that, her eyes screwing shut.

'What is *wrong* with you?'

Strong-minded bitch, thought Lykos. *How can she fight this?* He gripped the effigy tighter, and willed her to obey.

'Nothing,' Fidele said with a shudder.

'Something ails you,' Peritus said. He looked at Armatus, something passing between them. 'You are not in your right mind, not able to rule, at present.'

In a blur of motion, faster than anything Lykos had anticipated, Armatus had drawn his sword and was holding it levelled at Lykos' chest.

'As battlechief of Tenebral I claim the regency while you recover,' Peritus said. He was watching Deinon, who had taken a stride closer, his sword half-drawn, but had frozen now.

Fidele's gaze drifted over Peritus' shoulder, just a flicker of her eyes.

Peritus whirled, drawing his own blade; the Vin Thalun who had stood hidden in the shadows fell on him. Peritus managed to stab one in the shoulder, but there were six Vin Thalun, four of them pit-trained. Within moments Peritus was on his knees, half stunned. He was dragged to his feet and a blade held across his throat.

'Put your sword down,' Lykos said to Armatus.

The warrior had hesitated, just for a heartbeat, and that was all it had taken for Peritus to be overwhelmed. Lykos had not moved.

'Put it down,' he repeated.

'Kill him,' Peritus slurred. Blood ran down his face from a blow to the head.

The dilemma warred across Armatus' features. Lykos saw the

decision in the man's eyes before it reached his limbs. He lowered his sword.

Immediately Deinon surged forwards, holding his own blade at Armatus' chest.

'Weak fool,' Lykos said. He stepped forwards and punched Armatus in the throat, the old warrior dropping to one knee, gasping for breath.

'He should have killed me,' Lykos said conversationally to Peritus. 'My Queen,' he said to Fidele. 'If I am not mistaken, I think we have just witnessed an act of treason. What is the punishment for such a crime in Tenebral?'

Fidele struggled, paused and then answered through clenched teeth. 'Execution.'

CHAPTER NINETY-FOUR

CORBAN

Corban ran through the corridors of Dun Vaner, past a trail of the dead. He hurt in a dozen places – his wrists, ankles, ribs, jaw, too many pains to recognize – but it felt so good to be free, to be reunited with his mam and friends. And more. He had been certain his death was at hand, bound, with a knife at his throat and no way to fight it off. To be saved from that, to still live and draw breath. He felt euphoric. He felt reborn.

And so much had happened. Not least Gar's father joining them. Even as they ran through the halls and stairwells, more of these strange warriors were joining them. The Jehar. Four at the entrance to the first stairwell, corpses piled about them, then another three, then five, another two, until Corban felt as if he was part of a small warband rather than an escaping prisoner.

The sound of combat drifted from ahead, growing louder. Then they were in a feast-hall, a pitched battle raging through it.

There were at least a hundred warriors in the room, most of them Rhin's men. Amongst them swirled the dark shapes of Jehar warriors, fast, graceful and deadly, leaving only the dead or dying in their wake. Force of numbers threatened to overwhelm them, though. Corban could see a pile of corpses in a half-circle about the doorway, but the battle had been pushed back from there, with more of Rhin's men crowding the entrance.

All about Corban warriors surged forwards, Tukul and Meical at their head. They crashed into the battle, an unstoppable force. Gar hesitated, lingering close to Corban, his familiar position. His mam, Farrell and Coralen did the same, pulling close about him, an unbidden, instinctive reaction in them.

In moments the battle was all but done in the hall. Meical, Tukul and forty or so Jehar warriors at his back turned the conflict in heartbeats. The remnants of Rhin's warriors fled through the doors, the Jehar following them, their battle spilling out into the courtyard.

Corban and the others followed.

All was chaos out here. Fresh snow had fallen, coating the flagstones, more was swirling down. As Corban looked, he saw Tukul storming into a knot of warriors. A severed arm spun through the air, jetting a trail of blood, startlingly red on the fresh snow.

Gar was dancing on his toes, desperate to join the battle, then the battle joined them, a handful of men rushing them.

Gar took the first one's head; the warrior's body ran on a few paces before the legs gave way. Another fell with one of Gwenith's knives in his chest, then Farrell and Coralen were wading in. Corban hefted the sword which had been returned to him by Gar in the dungeon and joined the fray.

He blocked a wild swing, twisted his wrist and stabbed the man through the throat, blood spraying his face as he ripped his blade free. He moved forwards, ducked another slash, chopped three, four blows in retaliation, the fifth breaking through a weakening defence, crashing into an iron helm, denting it, the warrior staggering. Corban kicked the dazed man's legs away and stabbed down hard as he stepped over him. He found a release in this battle: a simplicity that focused his mind, feeling both a sense of calm and a wild joy, barely contained. He concentrated on each breath, the shift of weight on his feet, his balance, the flow of muscle in hip and back, shoulder and arm, and faceless warriors fell like wheat as he cut through their ranks.

Then there was no one left before him. He looked about, slashed the shoulder of a man who was attacking Coralen. She finished him with her wolven claws. His mam was retreating before a sustained assault, turning a blade with her spear shaft. Corban and Gar saw at the same time. The man fell with two swords piercing him.

There was a clatter of hooves from the stableblock, shouting and yelling, and horses exploded from the stable's gates. Rhin was at their head, Braith and Conall close behind, a dozen other warriors following. They rode hard across the courtyard, trampling friend and enemy alike.

Coralen ran forwards, calling Conall's name. He must have heard, even over the din of battle, for at the open gateway he reined in and looked back. He saw Coralen, just stared for a heartbeat, then kicked his horse on.

Coralen ran after him, Corban and his companions following her. They stopped in the archway of the gates, watching as Rhin and her shieldmen galloped down the snow-covered slopes of Dun Vaner.

A rider stiffened in his saddle, a black arrow sprouting from his back. He toppled from his mount and was dragged through the snow.

A streak of movement caught Corban's eye, a blur moving after the galloping shapes, speeding across the snow much faster than the labouring horses.

Storm.

Silent as smoke, she caught up with the escaping riders and launched herself into the air. With a crunch that Corban felt as well as heard, the last horse and rider tumbled to the ground, an explosion of snow concealing them all. As it cleared, Corban saw a man rise from the ground and begin running. The horse didn't move. Storm shook herself and leaped after the man, crashing into his back, jaws sinking into his head. She gave a savage wrench of her neck and there was a spray of blood.

'Storm,' Corban called.

She looked up at the sound, ears twitching, saw him and ran at them. She skidded before Corban, jumped on him, her hot breath washing his face, rough tongue scratching his skin. He staggered under her weight, hugged her tight, burying his face in her bloodied fur.

He realized a silence had fallen and he pulled away from Storm, turned and looked into the courtyard.

The battle was done, all of Rhin's remaining warriors dead. A few score of these strange Jehar warriors stood staring at him, the place eerily silent and still, the only movement the gently falling snow. Tukul stepped forward, drew his sword and pointed it at the sky. 'The Seren Disglair.'

With a cry, the other warriors did the same, then together they all dropped to one knee and bowed their heads before him.

They searched the fortress and found it to be deserted. Only a small company had been garrisoned there; the bulk of Rhin's warriors and their kin were on the move in the south, invading Domhain. Tukul patrolled the entire stronghold personally, and only then did he declare it safe. They collected their dead – eight Jehar warriors – and made a pyre in the courtyard, Tukul singing a solemn lament as the fires burned. Snow was falling heavier again, and the light was already failing, so they barred the gates and made camp in the feast-hall that night with Jehar patrolling the walls.

'Ventos,' Corban said to himself, thinking of how he had ended up in this place. 'Where is Ventos?' He was exhausted now, sitting close to the fire-pit and chewing on a leg of mutton, one of many discovered in a huge cold-room.

'Dead,' Dath said. 'We found him with your knife in his belly. You should have seen your mam – she would have liked to bring him back to life, just so she could kill him again.'

He smiled at that. It saddened him, thinking of Ventos. He had liked the man, had thought him a friend. But he had betrayed him.

'How did you get in?'

'We climbed the wall to the north,' said Dath. 'It's a sheer drop, but they weren't very vigilant. I guess they didn't have enough men here to man every wall, and they weren't exactly expecting an attack. Brina tied a loop in some rope and Craf flew it up to the battlements and dropped it over something solid.'

'But how did you find me? How did you know where to look?'

'Craf again,' said Dath. 'He looked in every hole in this fortress until he found you. He's handy to have around, that bird, even if his eating habits would make the dead vomit up their last meal.'

'He is indeed,' Corban agreed. He tore off a strip of meat and threw it to Craf, who was perched contentedly on the back of Brina's chair. He caught the meat in the air and gulped it down.

Brina had hugged Corban tight when she had seen him, then berated him sharply for having let himself be captured. Corban had not minded, though. He had felt a swell of emotion at seeing the old woman, at seeing all of his friends. And what they had done for him.

He felt it again now, looking about the room at them – his mam sitting quiet beside Brina, Gar talking to Tukul – his da, Corban could still not get over that – Dath and Farrell sitting either side of him, Coralen, further apart, brooding, silently scouring crusted blood from her wolven claws.

Such friends. Following me through the mountains, attacking Braith. Storming a fortress. Rhin's fortress. Just looking at them, he felt a pressure building in his chest. *This world may be full of greed and tragedy and darkness, but I am fortunate beyond measure to have such people about me.*

His eyes drifted deeper around the room, at the scores of Jehar warriors. Most were quietly going about small tasks – repairing torn leather with thread and needle, replacing rings in a chainmail shirt, using a whetstone to work out a notch in a blade, cleaning and binding a wound.

Every now and then he would feel eyes upon him, would catch some of the Jehar looking at him, just staring. It made him feel uncomfortable. There was something in their eyes, almost adoration.

Then he saw Meical. He was sitting in the shadows beyond the firelight, long legs stretched out before him, his face a dark pool, but something told Corban he was staring straight back at him.

He remembered his dream – *not a dream, something more, something real* – and Meical's part in it. He was the Ben-Elim who had saved him, who had carried him from Asroth's palace.

They had hardly talked in the dungeon, Corban struggling to take in what he was seeing, but they would have to, soon. He knew that.

He looked away from the shadows, his gaze settling upon his mam. She was watching him, too. She rose and sat beside him.

'So,' she said.

'Thank you, Mam.'

'What for?'

'For coming to get me.'

She hugged him fiercely.

'I knew him. He was in Dun Carreg, briefly. But I recognize him from my dreams,' Corban said, looking back to Meical.

'I saw, in the dungeon. So, do you believe, now?'

He was dimly aware that Dath and Farrell were leaning forward, listening intently.

'I . . . my dreams, Mam. They weren't dreams, really, I was somewhere else. In the Otherworld.'

'Yes. You've been having them for years. They stopped for a while.'

'Rhin was in the last one. She took me to Asroth.'

His mam tensed, her hand squeezing his leg.

'I was terrified. Asroth, he wants to kill me – you were right.'

'So you do believe, then?'

He had not wanted to think about this, to face it. All the while he was busy it was just a shadow hovering somewhere behind him, but now he could no longer avoid this subject. He had walked in the Otherworld, come face to face with Asroth and his Kadoshim, and with the Ben-Elim. How could he deny the truth of it? Clearly it was no lie, so either he was mad, as he had thought Gar was, for a while, or it was the truth. There was no longer any option for an alternative explanation. He sighed.

'How could I not, now? I'm sorry for not trusting you.'

She smiled. 'I have found it hard to believe, myself, at times.'

'I don't want to believe it, though. I'd rather not think about it. And when I do think about it I end up with a lot of questions,' Corban said.

'Of course you do.'

A voice rang out, then. Corban looked up and saw that Meical was standing close to the fire-pit, almost before him.

'What would you do from here?' Meical said, looking straight at him.

'You're asking me?' Corban said.

'Everyone in this room is here because of you, Corban. You are the Seren Disglair, the Bright Star.'

Corban cringed inwardly at that. He caught a glimpse of Dath and Farrell staring at him – Dath wide eyed, Farrell nodding thoughtfully. Coralen regarded him with a raised eyebrow.

'We will follow your lead,' Meical continued. 'I will offer you my counsel, and you can do with it what you will. For myself, I would advise that we should go to Drassil, deep within Forn Forest.'

'Why?' Corban asked. He heard Brina chuckle.

'Because Halvor's prophecy says that is where you will go, where the resistance against Asroth and his Black Sun will gather.'

Who is Halvor? What prophecy? A hundred other questions lined up in his mind, fighting to be asked first.

I'm going to Murias to get my sister,' he said instead.

'Murias. Where Nathair is going?' Meical said.

'That's right. My sister Cywen is his prisoner.'

'She is his prisoner to lure you to him, surely you must know that?'

'I was starting to guess as much,' Corban said. 'But it makes no difference. I cannot abandon her.'

'No, we cannot,' his mam echoed.

Meical just looked at him for a long drawn-out moment. Corban returned his gaze.

'All right then,' Meical said. 'We shall go to Murias.'

'You don't have to come,' Corban said. He did not want the lives of so many on his conscience.

'It is our choice,' Meical said. 'And as you feel about your sister, so we feel about you.'

Corban thought about that, thought about standing before Asroth and seeing a band of the Ben-Elim brave the hosts of Kadoshim to save him. He nodded.

'And Sumur is with Nathair,' Tukul said from the fireside. 'I would like to see him. We have things to discuss.'

I can imagine what they are.

'What is at Murias?' Corban asked.

'Giants,' Coralen said.

'She's right,' Meical said. 'The Benothi giants. And one of the Seven Treasures. The cauldron.'

The Seven Treasures? Now those were tales I used to love hearing old Heb tell.

'The cauldron?'

'Aye,' Meical said with a sigh. 'Asroth used it before, in the War of Treasures. It was made for good but, like most things, can be put to a different use depending on the hand that holds it. It has the potential to be a powerful weapon.'

'What did Asroth want it for?' asked Corban.

'To slaughter every living soul that Elyon has created.'

'That doesn't sound good,' whispered Dath to Farrell.

'Well it obviously didn't work, did it?' Farrell whispered back. 'Else none of us would be here.'

'That is because Elyon unleashed his Scourging,' Meical said.

'That was bad enough, and Elyon is unlikely to intervene this time.'

'So we need to stop Nathair getting to this cauldron, then,' said Farrell.

'Perhaps. I do not know if we can. It is protected, though. There are some of the Benothi that live still who saw the destruction wrought by the War of Treasures. Nemain, the Benothi Queen, was there. She saw. She will not willingly allow the cauldron to be used to wage war again.'

'But Nathair has the Jehar with him. If any are capable of taking it, it is them,' said Tukul.

'Aye. So, to Murias it is,' said Meical. 'North of here, a hundred leagues through Cambren and then into Benoth.'

'It will be hard going, fighting all the way through Cambren,' said Coralen. 'The bulk of Rhin's warriors may be to the south invading Domhain, but that does not mean the entire north is empty of enemies. And the best roads are littered with settlements – they will not look on you kindly. You may be forced to travel leagues out of your way, through difficult terrain. You would be better off travelling back into Domhain and then heading north on a clear path. You may even catch them.'

'I do not know the way through Domhain,' Meical said.

'I do,' said Coralen. 'I've lived half my life patrolling the borderlands, I know every path and fox's trail for a hundred leagues, and I've been in sight of Murias before. I'll take you.'

Meical looked between Corban and Tukul.

'Thank you,' said Corban. She nodded at him, as if something long considered had just been decided, then leaned back on her bench and crossed her arms.

'So then, we should gather supplies for a mountain crossing,' said Meical. 'We'll leave at dawn.'

They settled down for sleep soon after, the fire-pit still crackling. Storm stretched close to Corban. The murmur of Gar and Tukul's voices blended as they talked into the night.

Corban's mind was whirling, but he was exhausted and sleep rose up like a tide to wash over him. Strangely, after all that had happened to him today, the most prominent thought in his mind as he drifted off wasn't that he had come face to face with Asroth, or seen one of the Ben-Elim walk into his dungeon, or seen Rhin evicted from her own stronghold. It was the embrace that Coralen had given him whilst he was hanging from his shackles. He could still feel her hair in his face, smell her skin, feel the beating of her heart and the heave of her suppressed sobs against his manacled body.

CHAPTER NINETY-FIVE

VERADIS

Veradis gazed at the mist-shrouded walls of Dun Taras. He had looked at the same walls every day for more than a moon now, through snow, rain and winter sun.

His and Geraint's warbands ringed the fortress, allowing no passage in or out.

'They must be hungry by now,' Bos said beside him.

'I would think so.'

Geraint had wanted to assault the walls as soon as they had reached Dun Taras, not far behind the last stragglers of Domhain's fleeing warband. Veradis had refused to commit his men, not wanting to throw lives away for uncertain gain. He had counselled patience, to lay siege to the fortress, despite how he hated the thought of waiting here through the heart of winter.

'We have the upper hand now,' Veradis had said when Geraint asked him to join in the assault. 'They are beaten, disheartened. If you assault the walls you will lose hundreds, and in likelihood fail, at least at first. Why lose good men and boost your enemy's morale when we can just sit here, eat good food and watch them starve?'

Geraint had gone ahead without him, taking a day to build ladders and battering rams. Over a thousand men had died in the assault; they gained the walls once, but were beaten back. Geraint did not attack again.

So they had set up camp, encircled the fortress and waited. Midwinter's Day came and went. The days started to grow longer. Veradis hated it; the inactivity frustrated him. Each day he set his men to training – first the shield wall, then individual sparring. And he had been meeting with weapon-smiths, the battle at Domhain's border having planted the seeds of ideas in his mind. And always in his mind the same recurrent thoughts crept to the surface. *Nathair. Where is he? Has he reached Murias? Is the cauldron his? Is Cywen safe?*

'How much longer of this?' Bos asked him.

'Depends what they choose to do. They could surrender. Or they could decide they've had enough of not eating and march out and take us on.' Veradis shrugged. 'What would you do?'

Bos scowled. 'I don't like being hungry – makes me mad. I'd probably come looking for someone to kill.'

Veradis smiled at that. He could almost picture it.

'Also, much rests on their king. This Eremon, he's old, and not so well liked as he could be by his people, I've heard. Makes me think he's more likely to order an attack sooner than later, before his people decide they've had enough of him.'

'So why haven't they come looking for a fight already?' Bos mused.

'My guess is us,' Veradis said. 'The shield wall. They know what we can do now, and this ground is perfect for us. Would you march out to face us again?'

'Probably not. At least, not without an idea of how to win.'

'Exactly. So they sit behind their walls, and starve.'

The sound of riders drew their attention, from behind, along the giants' road. Veradis saw a small group, perhaps fifty, moving at a canter. Rhin's banner rippled above them, a broken branch.

Veradis was ushered into a tent; furs were scattered liberally, a fire burning brightly in an iron basket. Rhin sat close to it, warming her hands. She looked older, somehow, or perhaps just exhausted. Blue veins traced a map beneath her papery skin. She looked up at Veradis as he entered and ushered him to a seat.

Something is wrong.

Geraint was already there, sitting and sipping from a cup. Conall stood behind Rhin, a bearskin cloak draped over his shoulders.

'Where is Nathair?' Veradis said. 'My lady,' he added as he remembered who he was talking to.

'Nathair is on his way to Murias. Or was when I left him at Dun Vaner.'

'He was well?'

'Yes, yes.'

Veradis breathed out a sigh and felt a measure of tension melt away.

'May I ask, what troubles you, my lady?' he said.

'Is it that obvious?' She frowned.

Veradis shrugged.

'At Dun Vaner I had a prisoner brought to me, caught as he was crossing the mountains into Cambren. It was this Corban, the one that your King seeks.'

'What was he doing there?'

'He was chasing after his sister. Somehow he knew she was with Nathair.'

Cywen. Unbidden, her face flashed into his mind. She was always tear-stained in his memory, always so sad.

'What did you do with him? Nathair will be grateful for your help.'

'I don't think so,' Rhin said with a twist of her lips. 'He was rescued. I only just escaped with my life.'

'How? What happened?'

A look crossed her face, harrowed, scared even. 'That doesn't matter now. I have sent a large force north to deal with them.' Her eyes became unfocused, then she shivered and sat straighter. 'There is nothing more to be done about that now. Let us get on with the business of conquering Domhain. So . . .' She smiled at him, something of her usual spark returning. 'Geraint tells me you broke the back of Domhain's warband and sent them scurrying back here.'

He didn't answer that, just took a sip from the drink in front of him.

'I shall have to think of a way to reward you.' Rhin's smile deepened.

Dear Elyon in heaven, no.

'So now we have all the rats in this trap, how are we going to finish them?' Rhin said. 'Eremon is the key, I think. I am told he is generally kept in hand by his wife, Roisin, and she is less popular amongst the people than Eremon. Perhaps it is time to go and talk to them, see if a few moons of empty bellies have made them more receptive to negotiation.'

'What have you in mind?' Veradis asked.

'Him,' she said, pointing a bony finger at Conall. 'He is Eremon's bastard – the blood of a king flows in his veins. Why not make him a king – one who will bend the knee to me, of course, High Queen of the West. He is young, handsome, strong, full of . . . *vigour*.' She paused, a sly smile twitching her lips. 'Eremon is in the twilight of his reign and his heir is only a boy – fourteen, fifteen summers?'

'He will be fifteen now,' Conall said.

'I think our offer will be quite tempting to those inside the walls of Dun Taras. Not to Roisin or her brat, of course, but to most of the rest. Especially if food is part of the bargain. And peace, of course.'

Never underestimate this one. Her mind's as sharp as any of us in this tent, probably sharper.

CHAPTER NINETY-SIX

MAQUIN

Vin Thalun warriors walked before Maquin, the crowds parting around them. Dimly he was aware of them, of the iron-grey clouds overhead, the cold air snatching at his skin. It all merged, a semiconscious blur as his eyes focused on the space opening before him, a ring of turf churned to mud, tiered rows rising about it, crammed with shouting people. At the ring's centre stood a tall post, iron chains hanging from it. Beside it was a basket with weapons poking from it: a spear, a sword, maybe more.

He saw a huddle of men emerge from the far side, herded by Vin Thalun behind them.

Maquin sprinted for the basket.

There were three at least, maybe more. They saw Maquin charging towards them; he registered the confusion in their eyes before they realized he was heading for the basket of weapons, not them. One started running for it, others behind him were slower.

Maquin reached the basket first. He grabbed the spear and hurled it into the baying crowd; before its flight was completed he was reaching back into the basket, pulling out the remaining sword and knife. Then he stepped past it to meet his attackers.

The first one saw he was too late and tried to slow, twisting away, his feet slithering on the muddy ground. Maquin's sword caught him in the head as he dropped, just above the ear. The blade stuck, the weight of the lifeless body dragging it out of Maquin's hands. He stepped over the twitching corpse, switching the knife from left hand to right.

There were three more. They spread about him cautiously. Maquin could see the raw rope wounds on their wrists – his own had healed to silver scars – recent captives, then, not long come to the Vin Thalun fighting pits.

He surged at the central man, not wanting to give the group a chance to circle him. He ducked swooping arms, a blow glanced off his shoulder; he collided with his opponent, his momentum burying his knife to the hilt in the man's belly. He ripped up, at the same time spun away, turning to face the sound of approaching feet.

This one was almost upon him. He saw a blur of movement, dropped to his knees, a hooked punch whistling over his head. Then he rolled forwards, slashed with his knife as he passed the man. He felt it bite, came out of his roll on the balls of his feet and stood.

A thin line scored the man's calf, blood sheeting down. Maquin advanced, the man retreating, hands held high, backing past the man whom Maquin had just gutted, lying in a pool of glistening entrails. Behind him Maquin saw another figure, stooping over the corpse that had a sword lodged in its skull.

The man before him lunged forwards, perhaps seeing Maquin's distraction. One hand clamped around Maquin's wrist, pinning the knife, the other reached for his throat.

Maquin pulled backwards, using the weight of his enemy's desperate rush to send them both crashing to the ground. The man flew over Maquin's head, helped along by his boot. With a twist of his body Maquin was rising, surging forwards. He punched his knife into the man's chest as he slipped in the churned ground.

The last survivor was still tugging at the sword stuck in the dead man's skull as Maquin approached him.

He was young, surely not much past his Long Night, downy wisps on his chin where a beard should be. He tugged harder as Maquin drew closer, putting a foot on the dead man's face.

A spear thudded into the ground close to the lad's feet, laughter rippling the pit. It was the spear Maquin had hurled away. The lad gave up his tugging at the sword and desperately grabbed the spear shaft, pointing it at Maquin. It shook.

Maquin refused to care, just kept advancing. The lad lunged and Maquin twisted, the spear-blade scoring a thin line along his upper chest and shoulder. Then with one hand he gripped the spear shaft and he powered forwards. The lad pulled on the spear, then collapsed with Maquin's knife in his eye.

Maquin watched the boy drop to the ground, his eyes drawn to him, a collapsed heap, limbs twisted. Whatever the spark of life was, it was instantly snuffed out; now he was just an empty bag of meat and bones.

What have I become?

He sat on a bench beside Javed, the small pit-fighter from Tarbesh. They were grouped with a handful of other pit-fighters – the elite, as Herak had started calling them – looking through iron bars into the ring where Maquin had just fought. He wiped something from his face, mud or blood, he did not know.

He looked through the broad timber struts at the plain and fortress of Jerolin on its hill. *I have been here before. The council of King Aquilus. It didn't look like this then.* He had been here a while now; after the sea journey it was another ten-night of hard rowing up a river before they had reached Jerolin's lake. They had not been the first ship to arrive, nor the last. A small fleet of Vin Thalun war-galleys now spread across the horizon and their warriors were thick around the fortress and town.

He did not know what Lykos' plans were, but they clearly involved Jerolin and probably all of Tenebral.

Not that I care, he told himself. *My task is to kill any put before me. Earn my freedom. Find Jael and kill him.*

How Lykos had managed it, though, this shift in relations and power in Tenebral – that did intrigue him, no matter how hard he tried not to think on it. *The Vin Thalun were not so popular the last time I was here. And now they all but rule the place.*

At first the anger and resentment had been clear. Almost as soon as Maquin had arrived, he and his fellow slaves had been ushered into fighting pits, little more than makeshift rings bound with rope. First in the lake town, with mostly Vin Thalun as spectators, some others huddled together, watching from the anonymous shadows, then soon after moving to the fortress, fighting in courtyards. Soon the crowds had grown and become louder, braver. Life had become almost a mirror image of that back on the Island of Nerin, where they were trained each day, then put on display in open cages, like prize cattle. Many from the town and fortress came and now people were travelling to visit this new arena. Looking about, Maquin saw all manner of people: fishermen, traders, trappers, warriors, women, even children.

Is the human heart so fickle? So ready to embrace such evil? He snorted at himself. *Listen to me. I am the heart of this wickedness, its root.*

The crowds hushed as the next entertainment entered the ring. Lykos led the way.

No, he is the root of all this. I am just a foot soldier in it all. A willing participant.

Behind Lykos walked a woman, Fidele, the dead king's widow, mother of Nathair. Perhaps she was in league with Lykos; Nathair certainly had taken the Vin Thalun into his confidence. Something about her, though, told Maquin that wasn't the case – the stoop of her shoulders, the way her gaze swept the crowd, something in it speaking of desperation and a fierce anger.

But she must be in league with him. Why welcome the Vin Thalun to your realm, allow them to do this, if you did not want to?

It was not as if she did not have the means to keep him out. Maquin had seen eagle-guard about the place, dressed in their black and silver, although there had been fewer of them about of late. Behind Lykos and Fidele two men walked, hands in chains, a handful of Vin Thalun about them. Maquin saw Deinon, Lykos' shieldman, amongst them.

Last of all, following this group, walked Orgull, standing a head taller than anyone else. Beside him was another pit-fighter, shorter, leaner, still with a warrior's confidence and grace. Pallas, Maquin had heard him called. He was pit-fighter who had survived countless contests, was close to earning his freedom, or so Javed had said. Orgull was to fight him, the last bout of this day's contests.

The two men in chains were shackled to the post at the centre of the ring, the Vin Thalun guards drifting to the edges. Orgull and Pallas stood close by, patiently waiting.

Fidele raised her head, turning in a circle to take in the crowd. A hush fell.

'These men are traitors. They tried to assassinate me and take the crown of Tenebral. The punishment for treason is death.'

Shouting rippled through the crowd, insults were hurled, as well as food. Amongst the baying for their blood Maquin heard some shouting for the men to be released, heard words such as *injustice.*

They are well known, then, these two. And liked by more than a few.
Fidele held up a hand.

'First we shall witness a display of skill at arms. The victor shall have the honour of carrying out the death sentence on these two traitors.'

Lykos led her from the ring and they walked up through the tiered benches of the arena to a viewing platform, where they sat.

The crowd became silent and still as Orgull and Pallas walked to the centre of the ring. Some Vin Thalun warriors entered the ring, carrying a table between them. Upon it were weapons. They put the table down between Orgull and Pallas and left.

There were three weapons: two short curved swords and one war-axe. A big one.

I recognize that axe.

Pallas took the two swords and Orgull took the axe.

It is his axe, from the tombs in Haldis. Deinon must have kept it.

Pallas sliced the air with his two swords, muscles rolling like rope.

'I've not seen swords like that before,' Maquin said.

'He is from my country – Tarbesh. It is our weapon.'

'Not very good for stabbing,' Maquin observed.

'Better for slashing, especially from horseback,' Javed said.

'Good thing he's not on a horse, then.'

Maquin felt a knot of tension settle in his gut, like a sinking stone. He was surprised at himself, thought he had killed off any sentimentality or concern for others. He realized he did not want to see Orgull die – the last of his Gadrai brothers, his last link to honour and his world before slavery. Instinctively he shifted on his bench, looked about, but there was no way down to the ring from here. Iron bars caged him in.

Even after all this time, some bonds must run deep. Orgull gave a great two-handed swing of his axe, the air whistling as it swept around him. Whistles and cheers drifted from the crowd.

Without any announcement or warning, the contest began, Pallas lunging across the table with one of his swords. Orgull had been ready and just stepped away, the sword slicing thin air. Orgull moved around the table, holding his axe two-handed across his chest, like a staff. Then they were at each other. The sound of iron on iron rang out as Pallas' swords slashed at Orgull, clashing on the axe as it blocked and struck. The two men were a blur, Maquin straining to follow as they swirled about each other, in and out, slash, block, strike, lunge, and then drifting apart.

Pallas crowded Orgull, knowing the big man needed space to use the axe well, and for frozen heartbeats Maquin could not see how his friend could survive the snake-quick strikes of the smaller man. Without realizing it he was standing, holding the bars that caged him.

Then Pallas was reeling back, blood running down his forehead where Orgull had caught him with the iron-bossed butt of the axe.

Orgull was not unharmed, though. Blood ran in a dozen places, tracing a web of injury across his body. Nevertheless he followed Pallas, swinging his axe now in great looping strokes.

Pallas ducked one slash, rolled from another and turned a third with his two swords crossed above him. Orgull kicked him as he tried to spin away, knocking the man off balance; at the same time the axe swung around, catching Pallas a glancing blow across the shoulder. Blood spurted. One sword went spinning away, Pallas' arm hanging limp, and then the axe took his head from his shoulders.

There was a breathless silence, then the crowd erupted, Maquin yelling as loudly as any one of them.

Orgull turned and without any preamble walked to the two men shackled to the post. He raised his axe and swung, sparks flying. The man dropped to his knees, his chains sundered. Before there was any reaction, Orgull did the same for the second man, chopping his chains with the axe-blade.

Maquin gazed open-mouthed.

Then men were jumping from the crowd, cloaked men drawing weapons, grabbing the two men in the ring, hustling them to the far exit. Orgull strode with them. A group of Vin Thalun appeared before them and Orgull swung his axe, blood spurting across the benches. Vin Thalun poured from the sides, some leaping across rows of benches, trying to get into the ring. Lykos was screaming commands, his voice merging with the cacophony of the crowd.

Orgull and the others were at the exit now, the harsh ring of iron punctuating the bass roar of the crowd. Their way looked clear.

Fly, my sword-brother. Maquin smiled.

Then the Vin Thalun closed in, like iron filings to a lodestone.

535

All became chaos, the crowd's roaring deafening, benches torn up, ripped from their fixings and hurled into the ring, more and more bodies piling into the battle that was raging near the arena's far exit. Maquin shook the bars of their cage, Javed joined him, but there wasn't even the slightest give in them.

He saw Orgull's bald head in the crowd, looking as if he was acting as a rearguard now, his back to the exit, facing into the arena. Every time he swung his axe blood followed, limbs and heads spinning. A few others stood alongside him, holding back the tide of Vin Thalun, but it was not long before the numbers were overwhelming and the corsairs flowed over them like a great wave.

It took some time to restore order, the crowds dispersed by Vin Thalun with clubs and swords and spears. The dead in the ring were dragged into two heaps; Vin Thalun and the others. The pile of Vin Thalun was much bigger.

Maquin watched with a sense of dread, waiting to see Orgull's corpse dragged to the pile of the dead. Eventually he did see Orgull, but he was carried away from the others and laid out on the ground. Another was put beside him, one of the two prisoners who had been chained to the post.

Lykos appeared then. He marched up to them, without a word drawing his sword and hacking at the neck of the man beside Orgull. It took three blows to sever his head. He raised his arm to do the same to Orgull, then Deinon was there, speaking quickly. Lykos listened, then he lowered his sword and wiped it clean on the dead man's body. Two men came forward and carried Orgull from the ring, his boots dragging in the mud.

CHAPTER NINETY-SEVEN

CYWEN

Cywen dipped her head against the wind. It carried with it an edge of ice that set her skin prickling. Over the last few days they had travelled through a mountain pass, tall peaks so high they blotted the sky, and now they were moving into a rolling featureless moorland with patches of heather peeking through the snow. A hundred glittering streams dissected the land.

As always, Alcyon accompanied her. Not far ahead Nathair rode his draig, Calidus and Sumur riding with him. The Jehar warriors stretched in a wide column behind, trailing into the mountain pass. The sound of wolven howling floated on the wind, a noise Cywen had become accustomed to. The further north they travelled, so the wolven population seemed to grow, although she never saw one. Obviously two thousand Jehar were too big a meal for even a wolven pack to chew on.

Buddai padded the other side of her, nose low to the ground. The wolven didn't seem to bother him, either. At least, not since the first time they had heard them, howling like a mournful farewell the day she had left Dun Vaner. Buddai had been restless all that day, often pausing to look back at the mountains. For long heartbeats Cywen had harboured the hope that it had been Storm, come with her kin to rescue her.

Idiot, she scolded herself. *No one's going to rescue me, except me. I should have gone south with Pendathran when I had the chance.*

No point fretting over that, now. She would just have to bide her time and wait for an opportunity.

I wish I had my knives.

*

They camped in a dip in the land that night. It did little to ease the constant cut of the wind; icy fingers crept through layers of fur and leather. Cywen shivered and tried to shuffle closer to Alcyon's small fire. She had already finished the porridge he had made, its warm glow spreading through her like a hot coal thawing the frost. But that small heat had long since evaporated.

'I can't feel my toes,' she said.

'Try wiggling them,' Alcyon said. He was full of helpful advice like that.

A figure came striding out of the darkness, a great hawk perched on his arm. Calidus. He saw them and came over.

Calidus gave the bird a piece of meat from a pouch at his belt, then raised his arm. With a flap of its wings the bird flew away, the sound of its passing little more than a whisper in the night.

Calidus held a thin strip of parchment in his hand.

'This is the last night that we can risk a fire,' he said as he held the parchment over the flames, reading silently.

Wonderful, thought Cywen. *I'm going to freeze to death*.

'What news?' Alcyon said.

'There you are,' a voice called out. It was Nathair, with Sumur and the giant, Uthas, behind him.

'I'll tell you after,' Calidus said quietly.

Nathair, Sumur and Uthas joined them about the fire.

Cywen drew back from the flames, shuffling into the shadows so that she wouldn't be forced to talk to them. Alcyon had changed, sitting straighter, a stiffness in his shoulders that spoke of his discomfort.

'I must leave soon,' Uthas said. 'Murias is little more than a tennight away for you, at your pace.'

'All is set. You know what to do?' Calidus said.

'Of course. The gates of Murias will be open to you. I can do little more than that. You will have to defeat the Benothi that stand against you.' He looked at Calidus. 'And you will honour our agreement. You will spare the Benothi that stand with me. They shall not be harmed.'

'Of course,' Calidus said. 'You have given great aid. It will not be forgotten, and it will be rewarded.'

'Good.' Uthas bowed his head.

'Can you do this, Uthas? Can you see it through?'

'Yes. I will open the gates to you and I will split the Benothi defence. That is all I can do. Nemain and those loyal to her you will have to deal with yourself. I will not shed their blood. And the brood of wyrms. I cannot raise my hand against them.'

Calidus reached across the fire and gripped Uthas' forearm, his own engulfed by the giant's.

'In the morning, then.'

'Yes, in the morning,' Nathair echoed. 'And may Elyon watch over you. May he watch over us all.'

'The absent god,' snorted Uthas, then he rose and walked into the night.

Cywen had been captivated as she had watched the exchange, hardly daring to breathe. *They must have forgotten I'm here*, she thought. Now as Uthas walked away she saw a frown crease Sumur's face. He stared after the giant long after he had been claimed by the darkness.

'Do you think he will see it through?' Nathair asked Calidus.

'I do. But if he does not, we will still complete our task. We have two thousand Jehar warriors. We have Alcyon and the starstone axe. We have you, the Bright Star of Elyon.'

'And we have you, my friend,' Nathair said, reaching out to grip Calidus' arm. 'One of the Ben-Elim, standing by my side.' He closed his eyes and breathed out a long sigh. 'It has been so long, since my dreams began, since I heard Elyon's voice, since I first heard of the cauldron. And now we are so close. I almost cannot believe it.'

'The end of this quest is close, my King. You have made this happen. The All-Father will be proud.'

Nathair smiled at him. Then he and Sumur stood and walked way.

Calidus watched them leave. Alcyon sat gazing into the fire, Cywen trying to remain still, keep her breathing slow, pretending to sleep.

'It would appear that our gambit has worked. The bait is drawing our fly,' Calidus said, breaking the silence. He screwed up the parchment that he still held in his fist and dropped it into the fire. Cywen watched it curl and then ignite into flame.

Alcyon nodded. Briefly his eyes flickered to Cywen.

'They are two days behind us, maybe less. I think you should take some men with you and meet them.'

'How many are there?'

'Ventos says six, and the boy's wolven.'

He's talking about Corban and Storm.

'Take a score of Jehar with you. That should be more than enough.'

Alcyon nodded, a rippling of his bulk. 'Where?'

'Not out here, in the open moors. We'll carry on along the road to Murias. There's some woodland about a day's journey ahead. The road to Murias passes straight through it, so they'll be on it, or close to it, depending on how careful they're being. Wait for them there.'

'Do you want him alive?'

'No,' Calidus said. 'Kill them all.' With that he rose. 'Hurry to me once the deed is done. I would like news of his death before we reach Murias. I'll keep a watch over our bait once you're gone.' He stood and disappeared into the night.

'You can breathe louder now, child,' Alcyon said. 'And come back to the fire, before you freeze.'

'What did he mean by that?' she said as she moved closer, panic loosening her tongue. 'He was talking about Corban, wasn't he? About my brother.'

Alcyon said nothing, but would not meet her gaze.

'He told you to kill him.' Fear was twisting its way through her now, her voice rising. 'You've used me as bait, haven't you, to lure him after you? Damn you; damn Calidus; damn you all.'

'That is already beyond doubt,' Alcyon said quietly. It did not help to calm Cywen.

'You'll find Corban's not so easy to kill,' Cywen hissed at him. 'More likely he'll be the one killing you.'

Alcyon just looked across the flames at her with pity.

CHAPTER NINETY-EIGHT

CAMLIN

Camlin stood on the walls of Dun Taras, watching the riders approach along the giants' road. Mist swirled about their horses' legs, as high as their knees, giving them a ghostly quality, as if they were floating, not walking. A banner was held above them, the broken branch of Cambren. At its top a strip of white cloth was tied, declaring their intention to talk rather than to fight.

Horns had blown from the camp surrounding the fortress, announcing the advance, and the sounds had been taken up in Dun Taras, ringing all the way to the keep.

Will Eremon come?

He felt a presence at his shoulder: Halion, Marrock, Vonn and Edana stood beside him. Countless others were streaming up the stairwell to see what the horns portended. Everyone looked gaunt and listless, more than one appearing surly, even angry, a black mood enfolding the fortress like a sullen cloud.

Three moons of not eating will do that to a person.

People were dying. Of starvation, of the fever that swept the stronghold, a score of other diseases winnowing away the weak. Every day wains were pulled through the streets, clearing the dead.

A procession appeared in the street below, warriors forcing a path for it: a grand carriage pulled by two glossy black stallions. Eremon and Roisin sat within. The carriage halted by a stairwell close to the gates and Eremon and Roisin disembarked, warriors escorting them up the stairwell to the walls.

A figure with blonde hair squirmed its way between Camlin and Halion – Halion's half-sister, Maeve, the one who was sweet on Corban.

Camlin looked back to the giants' road, saw that the party was close to the gates now. A woman rode near the front, a black cloak of sleek fur about her. Silver hair fell about her shoulders, shining like liquid starlight.

'Rhin,' Edana hissed from beside him.

Warriors were about her, most in the colours of Cambren. One close to her wore the black and silver of Tenebral, his hair close cropped like all of their warriors. Another sat on his horse with the hood of a cloak pulled up over his head, his face in shadow.

Rhin reined her horse in and gazed up at the wall above Dun Taras' gates.

'Eremon, are you there?' she called out, 'or are your legs too frail for the stairs? Come, speak to your kinswoman. We have not talked in an age.'

'I am here,' Eremon called back, stepping closer to the wall's edge. His voice was loud and deep, belying his age. 'Though I don't think you'll have much to say worth listening to.'

'Time will be the judge of that,' Rhin said. 'You look tired, kinsman. Age knocking at your door?'

'I'm not the only one getting older,' Eremon called back. 'Your face looks like my arse – saggy and creased.'

Good, thought Camlin as laughter rippled along the wall. *He still has his wits, at least.*

Rhin scowled at that, but before she could respond a screaming burst from the road behind Camlin. He turned to see a crowd surging around Eremon and Roisin's carriage, pulling at the horses. One of them was neighing wildly, rearing and lashing out with hooves. The other was stumbling as blood gushed from a wound in its neck. Warriors rushed to protect the animals from the hungry mob.

'Trouble in your streets?' Rhin called as the noise quietened, warriors restoring a frayed order.

'Only of your doing,' Eremon replied.

'I can fix that.'

'Aye, you can. By leaving my country. Go back to Cambren. We've already bested your warriors in combat. Save yourself a long hard wait through the cold and go home.'

'Bested my men in battle? If that were the case, why did your warband run all the long way from the border to here? And why do they hide inside your walls?'

'It was not your warband that won any victory. It was your allies from Tenebral who turned the battle. Tell them to stand down and the men of Domhain will finish the lesson they began teaching your men of Cambren.'

Camlin could see the effect of Eremon's words in those about Rhin, her shieldmen scowling. Ragged cheers spread along the wall, some even drifting up from the streets behind.

'I'm not here to talk about the past; it's the future that needs our attention, before any more of your people starve to death. This can all stop, today. Now.'

A silence fell upon those on the walls. Even Camlin felt drawn to listen, despite knowing that what Rhin said was unlikely to be anything good.

'Step down, Eremon. You are an old man, in the twilight of your life. I will give you your life, to enjoy how you see fit. Just renounce your throne, and your heir—'

'No,' a shout rose up, fraying at the edges. Roisin.

'Ah, your wife is there, too. Or should I call her your mistress? I have heard that it is she who rules Domhain, not you, Eremon. Should I be talking to her, or you?'

'Be silent,' Eremon hissed to Roisin.

'I rule Domhain; no one else,' Eremon said louder.

'Then rule now, do what is best for your people. Step down. You cannot win. Domhain will be mine. You will be conquered. Both roads lead to that point, but one is littered with your people dead – through starvation and battle – the other can be reached peacefully. No more death. Just hand over your crown.'

'I do not think the people of Domhain would like you for their mistress,' Eremon called back.

'They do not have to have me; only the regent I leave in my place. One of your own, a man of Domhain, a warrior, with the blood of kings flowing in his veins. Your blood, in fact.'

With that she beckoned the hooded man forward and pulled back his hood.

Camlin blinked, recognizing the face but not being able to place it in this context. Then he heard someone close by whisper the name.

'Conall.'

It was Maeve who spoke it first, taken up by a hundred others, a thousand, rippling along the wall like a wind soughing through long grass. Halion just stared, his face hard and cold.

'So you have something to think on,' Rhin said. 'I'll be back at highsun on the morrow to hear your answer.'

Camlin sat at the table in their kitchen, wrapping sinew about iron arrowheads, tying them to a bundle of arrow shafts he had cut and left in a local smokehouse to dry out. He'd already fletched them. He finished the one he was working on, placed it in a pile, then took another unfinished shaft.

He had spent the rest of his day here, after Rhin's speech. The five of them, six if you included the bird, Fech, had hurried back to their rooms through streets thick with unrest. Conall's unveiling had had an effect similar to a boot kicking an ants' nest. Everywhere there seemed to be activity, people standing in groups, talking, arguing, where only the day before the streets had been deserted.

'We should have expected it,' Edana said. 'Rafe told us that he lived, and that he was Rhin's first-sword.'

'It is a clever move,' Marrock said. 'It gives people a way out of starving without losing any honour. And Roisin is hated, which makes matters worse.'

'Halion, are you well?' Edana asked.

Halion was sitting with his head in his hands. When he looked up his cheeks were stained with tears. 'He's my brother. Once things seemed so simple, just the two of us against the world.' He took a shuddering breath and sat straighter.

Camlin felt a stab of sympathy for the man. *How old is he? Not yet thirty summers, I'd guess, yet he is forced to be older, more like Conall's da than his brother. Responsibility has been the force that guides his every choice.*

'There was always something dark in Conall's heart,' Halion continued. 'A bitter seed. Evnis and Rhin have cultivated it, and now I do not know who he is. Rule Domhain! He should have laughed at the thought, and refused it. Who has he *become*?'

'The enemy,' Vonn said clearly. 'That is what he has become. He stands with the woman who plotted the fall of Brenin, of Alona, and

Edana. Not just their fall, but their deaths. She would see Edana dead still. Sharing the same blood sometimes is not enough.'

They all looked at Vonn then; he rarely spoke, and never about his da, Evnis. Even though he had not used his name, they all knew it was him that Vonn was speaking of.

Fech fluttered nearer to Edana at Vonn's words, as if his closeness would somehow protect her.

'What will Eremon do now?' Vonn asked.

'I don't know,' Halion said. 'If it were me, and I was sure of my people's loyalty, I would wait longer – hope that they would resort to an attack while we are still safely behind these walls. But I don't think that Rhin is that stupid. Geraint maybe, but not Rhin. She will be happy to wait until we've all died of starvation and there's nothing left but the bones of the dead.'

'And I do not think the loyalty of your da's people can be guaranteed,' Edana said.

'No. So he must do something. And soon. Perhaps muster an attack.'

'It would need to be something clever to beat that wall of shields,' Marrock said, 'otherwise it would just be warriors marching to a certain death.'

'What's your advice, Fech?' Edana asked the raven. She had taken to talking to the bird more and more as if it were a human, and what was more, a wise one. Camlin wasn't wholly comfortable with that.

'*Kill Rhin*,' the bird squawked. '*Sever the head, the body wriggles and dies.*' He snapped his beak as if to emphasize his point.

'Aye, good advice,' Marrock said. 'It's just the how that is a problem.'

'I am sorry,' Halion said. 'For bringing you here. I should have listened to you, Marrock. We should have gone to Dun Crin.'

They all looked at him in silence, none knowing what to say.

'Do not blame yourself for this,' Marrock said. 'All along you've done what you thought was right. I cannot fault you for that. And who is to say that things would have fared any better at Dun Crin? For all we know, our heads could be on spikes by now. We live. We have one another, oaths and friendship that bind us.' He held Halion's gaze until the warrior nodded at him.

There was a knocking at the door, a warrior from the keep. 'Eremon wants to see you,' he said. 'All of you.'

Almost silently they passed through the streets, the only movement a rat in the gutters. That surprised Camlin: there had been a distinct drop in the number of animals wandering Dun Taras' streets – even down to dogs and rats. *Disappearing into people's bellies.*

Camlin heard a sound in the distance, faint but growing. The roar of a crowd. An orange glow floated like a nimbus in the sky, highlighting buildings in the direction the noise came from, and the sudden smell of burning wood hit his nose and throat. There was a sense of tension amongst them, like a rope pulled taut, close to tearing. They picked up their pace and soon were walking into the keep. Warriors stood vigilantly beneath flickering torches. The group was eventually ushered into Eremon's chambers.

The King and Roisin were there, along with Rath. His wounds had almost healed, though Camlin saw a stiffness in his movements. A pair of serving-girls hovered, refilling Eremon's cup as he drained it. One of them was Maeve.

'Thank you for coming,' Eremon said. His eyes were sunk to dark hollows. He held out a hand to Edana and she stepped forwards and took it.

'You must leave, tonight,' Eremon said. 'I have sent messengers ahead. A ship will be waiting for you on the coast. Baird will take you.'

'What?' Edana said.

'I shall muster my warband on the morrow and order them to give Rhin battle,' Eremon said. 'The sensible choice is to stay behind these walls until they try and climb them, but I think my people would have opened the gates to Rhin before then. We are likely to lose,' Eremon said. 'We have no answer to their wall of shields.'

'We will stay and fight,' Edana said.

'No. I am not asking you to leave, I am telling you, as one of my last acts as King of Domhain.' He patted her hand. 'You are young, but with a wise head on your shoulders, Edana. You are the best hope for all those who would stand against Rhin. You must not throw your life away.'

'But where will I go?'

'My ship will take you to wherever you wish to go. My advice would be to sail back to Ardan, to the south-west and the swamps of Dun Crin. I have had word that a resistance to Rhin grows there even now. Go back to your people, and lead them.'

A frown wrinkled Edana's brow as she considered his words.

'I will do as you say,' she said. She leaned forward and kissed Eremon's cheek. 'I thank you for all that you have done for me. You may yet win the day. Your warriors are brave, and Rath is no fool.'

'If Rhin's host fought like honourable men we would have won already,' Baird muttered.

'Do not think me so selflessly kind,' Eremon said. 'I have one thing to ask you, in return for safe passage on my ship. Take our son, Lorcan.' His eyes flickered to Roisin. 'I know that you have agreed to be handbound to him, but if Domhain falls and I die then it is your choice whether you honour that agreement or not. Either way, take him to safety with you.' He smiled at her then. 'And for myself, I hope that you and Lorcan do marry. You've good hips on you – there'll be plenty of fine children, I'm sure.'

This man would have been good drinking company, thought Camlin.

'I'll go, as you ask,' Edana said, blushing. 'But why do you not come as well? We could all leave, now.'

Camlin watched them all carefully, saw the redness around Roisin's eyes, the way Eremon's gaze dropped to the floor.

They have already discussed this, Camlin thought. *Disagreed about this.*

'I cannot run,' Eremon said. 'My people may be in the process of choosing another over me, but they have not done so yet. I cannot just abandon them.'

'But if you stay and give battle, many will die. If you run, you will be saving lives,' Edana said. 'Bring your loyal shieldmen, let them live to fight another day.'

'I cannot slink away like a kicked hound,' Eremon snapped. 'I will not do that.'

This honour thing, Camlin thought. *It has its downside. I'd not think twice about running away.* He looked at Edana. *Or maybe I would.*

A silence settled on the room. Maeve stepped forward with a jug and refilled Eremon's cup. Camlin saw her hand was shaking. She spilt some ale, then dropped the jug. It smashed on the stone floor, shards exploding.

For an instant all eyes were on the jug. Then Camlin saw Maeve move, a glint of metal in her hand. She lunged forwards and drove a knife into Eremon's throat, blood gushing in a steady pulse.

Everyone moved at once: Maeve diving across Eremon's kicking legs towards Edana; Rath, Baird and Halion surging towards Maeve; Roisin rising from her chair.

Edana lifted her arms, an instinctive reaction, but Maeve was not aiming at her. They collided but Maeve was rushing with her knife at Roisin, scoring a gash across her ribs. Then Rath had Maeve about the waist, was hauling her away. The knife clattered to the ground as he twisted her wrist.

Eremon was white, his skin almost translucent. Life flickered in his eyes and then vanished. Roisin screamed and fell across his body, hugging him and keening. Eremon's head flopped.

'Why?' Rath said, clutching Maeve tight.

'Because he would let so many die. Because he was old and close to death, anyway. Because I hate Roisin and her spawn. Because I want Conall to be king.' She glared at him unflinchingly.

Rath drew his own knife and plunged it into her chest, then embraced her as her life fluttered away. He lowered her gently to the ground. Tears filled his eyes as he turned back to them.

Roisin stood slowly and stepped away from Eremon, blood staining her gown.

'I think this changes things,' she said.

'This way,' Baird said, leading his horse through a hole in the stable wall that hadn't been there short moments ago.

Those giants were a mistrustful lot, Camlin thought, remembering the tunnels beneath Dun Carreg, *always with their bolt holes*.

They were in the stableblock of Dun Taras, Edana and her shield-men alongside Roisin, Lorcan, Quinn and about two score shieldmen whom Rath had gathered, their loyalty beyond doubt.

'It's the only way out of here,' Roisin had said of the tunnel that they were now descending – a shallow path sloping down into dark-ness, tall and wide enough for men and horses alike. Hooves thudded, muffled with cloth for when they reached the open road.

The tunnel stretched for a league or so before it spilt back above ground, taking them beyond the ring of Rhin's warriors, they hoped.

Rath had refused to leave, saying that his presence in the fortress would mask Eremon's death and buy them vital time in making their escape. There had been no changing his mind. Halion had hugged the old warrior tight.

They walked a long while in the dark, following a flickering light ahead, then Camlin emerged into the night. It was still dark, the sky perforated by a thousand stars.

Edana walked just in front of Camlin, Fech perched on her saddle. Camlin saw her hold out an arm for the bird and it hopped onto it and rubbed its beak against her face.

'I would ask a great favour of you,' Edana said to the bird. 'Find Corban for me, and tell him of what has happened. Tell him that I am sailing to Dun Crin. And that I hope to see him again.'

The raven protested at first, but Edana asked again, and with a flapping of wings the bird lifted into the air and faded into the night.

Edana looked back and saw Camlin watching her. Tears glistened in her eyes. 'Looks like we're running away again, Camlin.'

'Like old times,' he said, and with a smile tried to give her some courage that he didn't feel.

CHAPTER NINETY-NINE

CORBAN

They made camp beside a fast-flowing stream, the water clear and icy cold, seventy-one people strong, plus Storm and Craf. They had passed through the mountains back into Domhain, and then Coralen had led them north, their pace fast and ground-eating. Over a moon had passed since they had left Dun Vaner, the weather changing, snow turning to sleet turning to rain. It was still cold here in the north, but each day there was a growing hint of spring in the air. Corban could smell it. New life, rebirth.

It will be my nameday soon. It's been almost a year since we sailed away from Dun Carreg.

Coralen had said that they would soon be crossing the northern border of Domhain into Benoth. From there it would be less than a ten-night until they reached Murias.

And Cywen.

He had had a lot of time to think. The reality of his time in the Otherworld had not faded. And even if it had, he had a physical reminder riding close to him every day.

Meical.

The man had seemed cold and aloof at first, unapproachable, but as the days of the journey had passed, conversation had begun to flow between them. It was mostly Corban asking questions and Meical answering. Corban had for the most part asked about Nathair and the political circumstances of the Banished Lands, of kings and queens, of where they would stand in the scheme of things. Meical seemed to know everyone, or if not know them, at least know of them. For the most part Corban steered away from anything that navigated close to what he thought of as spiritual – the Otherworld,

Asroth, Elyon, the Ben-Elim and Kadoshim – even though he had a thousand questions bubbling away in his mind. But once he started asking them, he knew he would have to acknowledge the truth of it. It was one thing to acknowledge it to himself, or to his mam. It was another thing entirely to admit it to this band of fanatics who would willingly cut someone's head from their body at his mere suggestion. Besides, once he admitted it to Meical and the Jehar, the consequences of that were staggering. *Where to go from there?*

No, he could not walk down that path yet. It scared him, like standing on the edge of a cliff and looking down, waves of giddiness sweeping up, consuming him. He had decided to focus on the task at hand. To find Cywen and take her from Nathair. That was task enough. If they lived through that, then there would be plenty of time to consider the bigger questions.

Just the thought of seeing Cywen again sent a swell of emotion coursing through him – hope, worry, fear. *Elyon in heaven, let us save her.* He smiled to himself as he realized what he was doing. *Strange how we pray in these times. Even to an absent god. A shred of hope is better than no hope at all, I suppose.*

Corban saw Coralen a little way off, standing on a ridge of rock, looking at the horizon.

'What are you looking at?' Corban said as he drew near.

'Benoth,' Coralen said. She pointed. 'Between those peaks is a wide vale – and on its far side is Benoth. Murias will not be much further, if we do not run into a band of the Benothi patrolling their borders.'

'Is that likely?'

'Perhaps.' Coralen shrugged. 'You never know with the Benothi. They can stay locked in their halls for years, and then they will raid a dozen times over a few moons.'

She was wearing her wolven pelt. Corban had taken to wearing his too; it was warmer than his cloak. They both stood gazing at the gap between the mountains, the sky a deep blue. Stars winked into life.

'I wanted to thank you,' Corban said into the silence.

An in-drawn breath. 'For what?'

'For everything. For guiding us. For risking your life at Dun Vaner. For coming to save me. For leading us north. For what you're about to do, taking us to Murias. We wouldn't be here, if not for you.' There was more that he wanted to say, more that he'd thought about, every day, but he couldn't find the words.

'It must have been hard for you, seeing Conall like that,' he eventually managed.

'It was,' she said. The silence lengthened and he thought she would say no more about it. Then she spoke. 'Con was always my favourite. I shouldn't say that. Halion was always kind, thoughtful, always looked out for me; but Con was so much *fun*. He was always exciting to be around. Maybe not good, but exciting . . .'

Corban could understand that. Conall had the ability to make you hate him and love him, sometimes at the same time. 'I thought you would have gone south, when Conall fled with Rhin. They probably went to Domhain. To join her warband.'

'They probably did,' Coralen breathed.

'I thought that's where you'd want to be,' he said.

She turned to look at him then, her gaze straight and firm. She had green eyes.

He thought she was about to say something, then he heard footsteps behind him, and voices.

Dath and Farrell joined them.

'Those Jehar, I don't like them,' Dath said.

'They saved our lives,' Corban said.

'I like them,' Coralen said.

'Didn't think you'd like meeting women tougher than you,' Dath said.

'I admire them,' Coralen replied.

'Well, so do I, but they still scare me, and . . .'

'Everything scares you,' said Farrell.

'And Gar's one of them,' Corban pointed out.

'Aye, but he's one of us, as well.'

'And he doesn't look at you as if you're made of gold, like the rest of them do,' Farrell said to Corban.

He couldn't deny that, and the fact of it made him uncomfortable, every day.

'No, they don't,' he said weakly.

'You know they do,' Dath said, smiling now. 'They think you're this Seven Disgraces.'

'Seren Disglair,' Corban corrected automatically.

'Maybe you are made of gold. Is there any gold under all that fur?' Dath said, pulling at Corban's wolven pelt.

'Get off.' He slapped at Dath's hand.

The next thing he knew, Farrell was grabbing him, Dath trying to lift his shirt. The three of them fell wrestling to the ground.

'Idiots,' Coralen snorted and Corban glimpsed her heels walking away.

Corban woke before dawn, Gar prodding him awake. He didn't protest, was used to it by now. Besides, these days he was far from alone in training. All of the Jehar were up, some already sparring.

The first morning after the rescue at Dun Vaner had been strange. Corban had felt like a stage performer, every single one of the Jehar gathering to watch him train with Gar. He had even felt tension radiating from Gar.

The faces of the Jehar had been unreadable, but after an unsteady start Corban had forgotten they were there, losing himself in the sword dance. Afterwards Tukul had patted Gar on the shoulder and whispered a few words in his son's ear. Whatever those words were they made Gar stand straighter, his face glowing with pride.

It was still strange, seeing Gar with his people. In many ways he was just like them – the composure, the cold face, even the way he walked, all grace and coiled strength. But after travelling with them a while Corban began to see differences. There was an openness about Gar, a softening, like a sheathed sword. And Gar smiled more. Corban thought he'd never say that about the stablemaster. The only Jehar who smiled as much or more than Gar was Tukul. Corban liked him – a fiery man, he guessed, despite the veneer of control. A man of great warmth and great anger. He reminded him of his own da, Thannon, somehow. And Tukul and Gar clearly adored each other. Corban had felt a surge of jealousy, seeing them laughing and talking together. He wished he still had his da to talk to.

The Jehar were not the only ones up. Brina was doing something with a pot over the fire. Closer by he saw his mam and Coralen going through some moves with one of the Jehar – a woman named Enkara. She was blocking his mam's and Coralen's strikes, turning each block into a smooth attack, all in slow motion.

Then Corban had no more time to watch; Gar was prodding him, stepping into stooping falcon, ready to begin.

They set off soon after the sun had risen, a column riding steadily towards the gap in the mountains. Corban rode beside his mam.

'Cywen's through there, Mam,' he said.

'We've come so far, eh?'

'That we have.'

'And we are only here because of you.'

'That's not true, Mam. You would have set off straight after Cywen the moment you found out she was still alive.'

'Me? Yes, probably. But no one else. And I don't think I would have made it this far without them, do you?'

'I wouldn't have got very far, either. Without all of you I'd still be in a cell in Dun Vaner.' *Or lying in a grave, my heart cut from my body.*

She smiled at him then. 'You're growing into a good man, Ban, with a good head on your shoulders. A man who I'm willing to trust, son or not. I'd follow you, put my faith in you, and I'm not alone. I just have to look at everyone – they love you, Corban, would follow you anywhere.'

'I think your judgement's biased, Mam. You are my mam, after all.'

'Well, there is that,' she said, and laughed. The sound of it made him smile; it was warm and genuine.

'But still . . .' Her expression changed then, moving from playful to clouded faster than a storm sweeping in from the sea. 'I wish your da was here to see you. He'd be so proud of you, Ban. I think his heart would just about melt.'

He felt a pressure in his chest, the flush of tears rising to his eyes. *Strange how a memory can do that to you*, he thought, *catch you unawares, like one of Gar's blows.*

'I wish he was here, too,' Corban said, emotion catching his voice. He smiled at his mam and she smiled back. 'At least we'll have Cywen back soon.' *Or die in the trying.*

MAQUIN

Maquin spent a ten-night after the conflict in the arena languishing in the pit-fighters' quarters, a stone block of a building close to the stables in Jerolin. He and the other pit-fighters – five of them remaining of the ten who had survived that day on the Island of Nerin – had been left alone. Usually Herak or some of his other more trusted guards would see them through a daily training session, but not since Orgull's shocking turn. Food and drink came at regular intervals, but that was all.

Maquin felt as if he was going mad, the sheer boredom gnawing at him. He had no idea if Orgull was still alive, though that was unlikely. It was clear to Maquin that Deinon had stayed Lykos' hand that day in the arena, saving Orgull's life.

Not out of kindness, though. Not a chance of that. Probably so they could hang Orgull up somewhere and make him scream at their leisure.

He was sitting on a stone bench when he heard the keys rattling in the main door. Light shafted in as the door opened, Herak's unmistakable shape standing outlined in the entrance.

'On your feet, fighters,' he called.

They gathered quickly – Maquin, Javed and the few others who had survived this far. They all had the same look of bottled energy mixed with despair.

A dangerous combination.

'Follow,' Herak ordered and turned on his heel.

Maquin blinked as he stepped into the daylight, even though it was weak, filtered through slate-grey clouds overhead. He noticed guards closing behind them as they all left their prison. Emad, the tall guard from Pelset, was one of them.

Herak led them through wide streets. Maquin saw Vin Thalun warriors on every corner, the occasional man in the black and silver of Tenebral. Then they were walking into the keep, through a feast-hall, up a winding staircase. At the top Herak nodded to guardsmen and a door was opened; all of them were ushered into a large chamber. Maquin pulled up short.

Orgull was hanging from shackles on the wall. He was naked apart from a stained loincloth, his body a tapestry of pain. One side of his face was fire scarred, blistered and weeping, his eye a ruin of twisted skin and flesh. His torso and legs were criss-crossed with cuts and weals, a combination of whip and blade. Someone had taken their time on him. Mercifully he was unconscious, his head hanging limp, chest rhythmically rising and falling.

Maquin looked away, feeling his stomach buck. Then he looked back, ashamed of himself. This was his sword-brother, the closest thing to a friend that he had left. As if feeling his eyes, Orgull stirred. A groan, then a shifting of his weight, taking the strain on his wrists bound above his head, a ripple in his thighs, a tension in his neck.

Sleep longer, brother.

'Welcome,' a voice said, drawing his attention.

It was Lykos, leaning casually against a desk. Five chests were placed on the ground before him. Deinon hovered in the shadows.

'My apologies for neglecting you all, the past ten-night,' Lykos said. 'There have been distractions.'

'What distractions?' Javed asked.

One day your questions are going to get you a knife in the belly, Maquin thought.

'That's none of your concern,' Lykos said. 'They're dealt with now, anyway. What does concern you is what I have to say.' He paused, one hand reaching inside the recesses of his cloak. Maquin saw the outline of his hand close about something. Lykos didn't seem to be aware that he was doing anything; something about the whole gesture seemed habitual.

'You've done well,' Lykos continued. 'More than well, living this long, surviving the pits. You're close to earning your freedom, all of you. See these chests.' Lykos walked to each one, kicking them open. They were stuffed to brimming with gold coins. 'Each one is what we've earned from you. You've made us rich.'

He walked back to the desk and poured himself a cup of wine, taking a long drink.

Freedom. The word hit Maquin like a blow, making his dizzy. Jael's face floated into his mind, sneering at him, as always.

'One more fight you all have. Win and you've earned your freedom. Win and I'll give you a pouch of gold each from these chests. And I'll make you an offer to think on, too. I want you to join me – join my crew. Sail with me. Swear a blood-oath to me. What you see in these chests is nothing to what's in my future. Those who stay close to me are going to be rich men, and I don't mean just gold: land, men, women, respect.'

'One more fight,' Maquin said.

'Aye, that's right. So let's not get ahead of ourselves, eh?'

'When?' asked Javed.

'A ten-night, maybe a little longer. You'll go back to your training from the morrow.'

'Who are we fighting?' Maquin asked.

'Whoever I put in front of you,' Lykos said. 'Just remember: obey me and you may end up with this.' He nudged one of the open chests with a toe. 'Cross me and you'll likely end up like him.' He pointed at Orgull. 'That's all I have to say.'

Herak opened the door and waved them out. Maquin looked back as he reached the door. Orgull was looking at him with his one good eye. His lips moved, only a sigh coming out.

'Get on,' Herak ordered, pushing Maquin into the corridor. The door slammed shut.

Maquin lay back on his cot, hands laced behind his head, staring at the ceiling. He wanted to sleep, but every time he closed his eyes he saw Orgull's ruined face. Saw his lips moving, a silent plea. He hadn't heard the words, but he was sure what Orgull had mouthed to him across the room.

Kill me.

VERADIS

Veradis stood beside Rhin and Conall. Behind them stood the combined warbands of Cambren and Tenebral, waiting. Amongst them were also two dozen wains, on open display and filled to overflowing with bread.

Smoke billowed from a dozen points within the walls of Dun Taras. Throughout the night rioting had been heard, even the clash of arms close to the gate, so a watch had been set, warriors put on alert to storm the gates at the first hint of them opening.

'It will not be long,' Rhin said to Veradis. 'Conall was the nudge that they needed.'

I think she's right. Shrewd and sharp; a good ally, a fearful enemy.

The sounds grew as the day lengthened, the roar of rioting drifting closer, then ebbing away. Eventually, around highsun, the noise reached a crescendo, the screams of pitched battle drifting over the walls. Then a shiver ran through the gates and they swung open.

A roar went up from the warriors behind Veradis.

'Slowly,' Rhin called. 'We are their deliverers, not their conquerors.'

Riders pulled in close about Rhin and then she moved off, entering through Dun Taras' gates to shouting and cheering. The wains followed in a line behind; Conall and a handful of other warriors leaned to grab loaves of bread and throw them into the crowd.

Veradis marched behind the wains, three hundred of his men massed behind him. All of them were alert, tense. Behind them came more of Rhin's warband, spreading into the crowds, searching the side streets, up stairwells and onto the walls. The wains stopped at points along the way, quickly emptying to pushing and shoving crowds, then reversed slowly out of the fortress to be refilled. The crowds thinned about Rhin and Veradis as they pushed deeper into Dun Taras, aiming for the keep.

We are being greeted with open arms right now, but I don't think all feel the same way in this fortress.

As if Veradis' thoughts willed them out of the shadows, a band of warriors appeared from a side street and hurled themselves at Rhin's shieldmen. There was a brief clash, a few of Rhin's men were dragged from saddles, but the attackers were quickly repulsed. Veradis and his men drew closer together, not yet a shield wall, but ready.

Then they were at the keep.

There was a stillness, an emptiness that set Veradis' skin prickling. That moment when the wind dies, just before a storm breaks.

'Be ready,' he said to Bos.

Rhin stopped in the courtyard, her men fanning out before her. The keep doors were shut, but when warriors pushed on them they swung open freely. A score of Rhin's men entered, more, then like a wave. Then there was a concussive bang, air blasting from the open doors, followed by an explosion of heat and flames. A handful of men staggered out, human torches, the stench of seared flesh filling the courtyard. Veradis felt his stomach lurch.

'No one's going in that way for a while,' Bos said beside him.

Geraint appeared with more men in his wake. He sent scouts around the keep, searching out other entrances. They soon returned with more reports of ambushes and traps, barricaded corridors, more fires. Conall forged ahead anyway, leading a few score warriors into one of the entrances. Veradis settled his men in the courtyard. While he was proud to be involved in any battle, to represent Nathair and honour the alliance, he was not about to lead his men into a potential fiery death. So he waited.

The fires in the keep's feast-hall guttered out a little before sunset. Other reports came back that pitched fighting was occurring as Geraint's men moved deeper into the building.

'Time to go in,' Veradis said and marched into the keep, shield held high, his short sword drawn, his men following suit.

In the feast-hall timbers still smoked, amongst them the blackened remains of Rhin's warriors. Veradis found an arched doorway and led his men out of the hall into a wide, high corridor. Archways branched off it, entrances to other corridors, the sounds of battle drifting out to them. Veradis kept going. Every closed doorway was tried, opened, rooms searched. Nothing. As they progressed deeper into the keep a thought hit him.

This corridor isn't barricaded or defended because of the fire in the feast-hall. That was barrier enough. But whoever set it must have known it would burn out, eventually. Then he understood.

These are not the efforts of a last defence; they're delaying tactics.

They came to the end of the corridor, a broad stairway before them leading up and down, one last wooden door beside it.

'Check inside, Bos. Then we'll split the men – half up, half down, though I'm starting to think there's no one here to find. I think old King Eremon has flown this coop.'

Bos turned the iron ring, pushed the door open and stepped inside. There was a brief pause, then a wet *thunk*, a grunt and Veradis saw Bos drop to the floor.

No.

Time slowed. He saw a blade stab down into Bos' back, between shoulder blade and neck, saw Bos' leg twitching. Veradis heard himself shouting, felt himself slamming into the door, hurling it open as he leaped over Bos' prostrate form and knocked Bos' attacker stumbling back into the room. A pool of blood was growing around his friend's head and shoulders.

Veradis lifted his shield high, felt an impact and swerved away from the door, instinctively making room for his men, knowing they would be following close behind him.

A warrior swung at his head with a sword. Veradis took the blow on his shield, flung the blade wide, slashed once across the man's gut, his sword turning on chainmail, then stabbed high, catching the man in the throat, sending him tumbling backwards in a spray of blood.

It was a large chamber, with only a few men standing at its far end – ten, maybe twelve. One was an old man, his shoulder bandaged, holding a longsword in one hand, a knife in the other. He limped as he stepped forwards. Between him and Veradis the room was littered with furniture – tables, overturned chairs, huge chests.

'No room for your wall of shields in here,' the old warrior said. 'Let's see if you can fight like *real* warriors.'

'Brave words, for so few of you,' Veradis said.

'I am Rath, and these are the Degad, my giant-killers. We've fought a lot worse than you.'

Over a score of his eagle-guard were already in the room. Soon they would be as squashed as the warriors that ended piled against his shield wall. He yelled an order, making them wait, his eyes drawn to the still form of Bos lying on the ground.

'We've slain giants of our own,' Veradis said and moved forward.

Warriors surged past Rath, howling, swords raised high. They met his eagle-guard with a savage crash.

A great longsword split Veradis' shield. The blade stuck a handspan from his wrist; he threw the shield and stabbed the swordsman in the belly, shouldering past him as he sank to the floor, switching his short sword to his left hand and drawing his longsword at his hip. He lost himself in each moment, revelling in it, in finding a man to look in the eye, knowing that within heartbeats one of them would be the victor, the other dead. He had not fought like this for so long; there was a beauty in it, somehow, a passion that was missing from the cold ferocity of the shield wall. All about him was a chaos of movement, men yelling and screaming, swords grating and sparking, blood making the floor run slick.

Then there were only a handful of men before him, four of them, backed about a closed door. One of them was the old man, Rath, both knife and sword running red. He was breathing hard, but smiling. He knew his end was close, and had made his peace with it. Veradis looked back, saw the room littered with the dead and dying, the vast majority his eagle-guard.

A voice rang out from the back of the room.

'Where are they?' it called.

Veradis saw his eagle-guard part for Conall. He too carried a sword and knife in his hands, both blades red with blood. Other warriors followed him – Rhin's men.

'Where are they, Uncle?' Conall said as he stood before the old man.

'You'll have to earn that knowledge,' Rath said.

'Drop your weapons, Uncle. You can't win.'

'Sometimes it's not about the winning, Con. It's about how you lose.'

'It's always about the winning,' Conall said.

'That's always been your mistake,' the old man said, shaking his head sadly.

'Last chance,' Conall said. 'Give the old man and his brat up. Be my battlechief.'

'He was my brother, Con; your da. How can you be doing this?'

'Was?' Conall frowned, then he was moving, almost too fast for Veradis to follow. There was a flurry of ringing clashes, sparks, both men chest to chest, ridged veins mapping their arms as they strained against each other. Then Rath had a foot behind Conall's leg, was pushing him back. Conall stumbled, somehow regained his balance, used his momentum to slip out of range as Rath's knife whistled where his throat had been.

Rath taught him, Veradis realized, and instantly it was obvious, from the preference of sword and knife to the way they held their balance, the angles of their attacks, the way they were in constant motion, defence flowing into attack after attack. Conall's knife snaked forwards, Rath blocked, at the same time both swords whistling through the air, clashing. Rath ducked and spun in close, stabbed. There was a thud, a grunt, then the two men parted. Conall only held his sword now.

His knife hilt stood from Rath's chest.

There was a silent moment as the two men regarded one another, then, with a rattling sigh, Rath sank to the ground.

The other defenders at the doorway leaped forwards then, but Veradis' eagle-guard and Conall's warriors intercepted them before they could reach Conall. There was a flurry of hard combat, and then these last defenders were overwhelmed and cut down.

Conall opened the door they had been guarding and walked into an adjoining room. Veradis followed him, saw the warrior staring at a bed. A smell hit Veradis' throat, sweet and rotten. Decay.

King Eremon lay upon the bed, hands crossed over his chest. He was dead and, from the smell, had been for a while. Conall walked up to the bed, staring at his father – no expression in his eyes.

'It looks as if Domhain is now yours,' Veradis said.

'Not until I have Lorcan's dead body before me.' Slowly the chamber was cleared, the injured tended to, the dead moved. Veradis felt a knot of grief swelling in his chest, but breathed deep and buried it, at least for a little longer.

Later, he told himself.

The heavy tramp of many feet sounded in the corridor and Rhin entered the room, her shieldmen about her. Another was with them, a young man, dirty and bruised. Veradis realized it was Rafe, the lad they had brought from Ardan to help them in the hunt for Corban.

Rhin gave Eremon's corpse a disdainful glance, then approached Conall.

'We have some information,' she said, beckoning for Rafe to be brought forward.

'I've been housed with other prisoners, in a building block close to the stables,' Rafe said. 'Last night, late, I heard some noise, looked out through a gap in the shutter. I saw Edana go into the stables. Halion was with her,' his eyes flickered to Conall, 'and a lot of others – warriors, another woman – dark hair, a young lad with her—'

'Roisin and Lorcan,' Conall breathed. 'It must be. Which way did they go?'

'I don't know. They never came out,' Rafe said.

Veradis took Bos' body out of the fortress, laid it in a wain along with their other fallen brothers. A cairn was built over them out on the plain. The eagle-guard gathered in a half-circle about the cairn as Veradis spoke of their sword-brothers, stories about their individual honour and courage, valour and loyalty. He drew his sword and saluted the dead, his brothers-in-arms. And his friend. Behind him his warriors did the same, the sound like a wave breaking. His thoughts spiralled about Bos, a fragmented patchwork of memories – recalling the day they'd met on the weapons court in Jerolin, Bos alongside Rauca, Bos' great appetite, his easy-going nature, his loyalty as a friend. Both of them were dead now, first Rauca and now Bos, gone from this earth. Both in aid of Nathair's cause. He felt tears fill his eyes and looked away, to the walls of Dun Taras.

After Rafe's revelation, Rhin and Conall had ordered the stable-block to be searched. It was not long before a hidden tunnel was discovered, a secret exit crafted by the giants. Conall had set off in pursuit, a hundred or so warriors trailing him, and Veradis searched the plains beyond Dun Taras now, looking for a glimpse of Conall's passing, but he could only see an empty landscape rolling into the horizon.

We are strangers in a strange land, he thought. *Shedding our blood, spending our lives, for what?* He looked at his palm, saw the white scar of his blood-oath to Nathair. *That is what for. For an oath given, a cause worth fighting for, a cause worth dying for.* He looked to the north, his thoughts filled with Nathair. Then another face crept into his mind, drawing into sharp focus.

Cywen.

UTHAS

Uthas strode through the dark corridors and cavernous chambers of Murias, shadow-filled places with flickering blue torchlight and the constant drip of water. Salach and Eisa walked at his heels. They passed a fire-pit with giants gathered about it. One called to him and he paused, raising his hand in greeting. It was Balur One-Eye, his white hair gleaming and his tale of thorns covering both of his arms in a dark spiral.

How many lives has he snuffed out?

'Ethlinn said you would return soon,' the ancient warrior said.

'She was right,' Uthas said. *What else has she said of me? Dreamed of me?*

Balor looked at Salach and Eisa. 'I remember more of you leaving.'

'Aye. It has not been a smooth journey.'

'I have earned my first thorns, One-Eye,' Eisa said, lifting her arm to show Balur.

I must watch her. They worship Balur, as if he were some god.

'Good,' Balur said. 'The first of many.'

'That is my wish,' Eisa replied.

'Ethlinn, how is she?' Uthas asked.

'She dreams more now than she wakes.' Balur rubbed his good eye.

He worries over her like a first-time mother. She is his weakness.

'She says that battle is close; that the Black Sun comes for the cauldron.'

'Best keep your axe sharp, then,' Uthas said as he walked away.

'I always do,' Balur called after him.

Uthas made his way deeper into the stronghold's belly, passing more of his kin gathered in huddles about fires. Occasionally he would catch an eye, give a nod of greeting. There were enough amongst them who had committed to him, would stand with him when the time came. Not a majority, but enough. Eventually he paused at an arched doorway. Two warriors stood before it. They nodded and allowed him to pass; Salach and Eisa waited there.

The chamber was enormous, even by giant standards, the vaulted ceiling cloaked in darkness. Torches radiating their cold blue fire lined the walls, and numerous wyrms slithered around the floor, passing from light to shadow.

The cauldron stood at the centre of the chamber, a fat bloated deity of pitted iron. A light-sucking entity that, to Uthas, looked almost as if it was breathing, a shimmering about its edges, a blurring of its hard lines.

Before it stood Morc, keeper of the wyrms, his beloved reptiles surrounding him, last and most deadly guardians of the cauldron.

Morc had raised this brood of wyrms, once they had hatched, only two years or so ago. He had fed them, cared for them, and they seemed to have some measure of affection for him, as they slithered about him, great milky grey creatures of muscle and teeth. One even reared up, its head as large as Morc's upper torso, and rubbed its scaly jaw across his chest. He patted its head.

'Didn't know you were back,' Morc said. 'Welcome home.'

Home. 'Thank you,' Uthas said. He'd always liked Morc. He was not the brightest of his kin, but there was a sincerity to him that was endearing.

'Do you need to be in here?' Morc asked. 'Only, it's feeding time.' He nodded to a wain sitting in the chamber, upon it a huge cage full of hogs. At least a score of them, fat hairy things with tiny eyes. They were squealing, eyeing suspiciously the wyrms that were coiling around the wain.

'No. I'm just . . .' *What? Why am I drawn to this thing?*

'Well, it's still here,' Morc said, looking over his shoulder at the cauldron.

'So I see. I'll be going then. It's good to see you, Morc.'

'Going – yes, good idea. It's going to get messy in here.'

*

Uthas stood on a balcony high in one of the towers of Murias, gazing out over the land of Benoth. A featureless moorland rolled into the distance, here and there lumps of dark granite poking through the earth.

Nathair is out there. And Calidus. He shivered. *How many nights before you reach these walls? Eight? Ten?*

'Are you rested?' a voice asked from behind him.

He turned to see Nemain, Queen of the Benothi, once wife to Skald, the first king, and the first slain, first casualty in the War of Treasures. Over two thousand years had passed, yet she still wore the grief of it in her eyes, the twist of her mouth, the set of her shoulders. Dark hair framed a face of sharp angles and deep shadows. All giants were pale, but her skin appeared paper thin, almost translucent. *The weight of years hangs heavy upon her.* Despite that, strength radiated from her still, tempered with the weariness in her grey eyes. It was more than just the physical contours of her musculature. *She is formidable yet.*

At the sound of her voice ravens burst to life from their roosts in the cliff face about the balcony, a swirling, raucous host. For a moment they flew so densely about her that she was hidden from sight, covered by a diaphanous, black-winged cloak, then they cleared and spread apart, some returning to their nests, others floating on the updraughts. Nemain smiled at them.

She actually likes them. He remembered throwing his knife at Fech, putting it through the bird's body. It had been satisfying.

'You have had a hard journey,' Nemain said as she walked closer. Sreng, her shield-maiden was a shadow behind her.

'Aye. Five of the kin slain.'

'The south is a dangerous place now.'

'That it is.'

'And what news?'

'There is much,' Uthas said. 'Most of it confirming what we suspected, or had heard whispered. Rhin is spreading across the west, already Ardan and Narvon have fallen to her. She was invading Domhain as I began my journey home. Eremon did not march with his warband to meet her, but Rath rides at the warband's head – he is Eremon's battlechief once more.'

'Perhaps they will all kill each other. Even if only Rath were to fall, some good at least would come from this.'

'Aye. We can hope.'

'Yes, we can. And what of the Black Sun – Ethlinn's dreaming, she says he is coming. Have you seen anything? Divined any sign?'

He shook his head. 'Nothing.'

She moved closer to him then, gazing into his eyes, so close that their bodies almost touched. She lifted a hand and cupped his cheek. He returned her gaze for as long as he could bear, then he glanced away.

What does she see? The desires of my heart?

'You saw the walls of Dun Taras. I can see the memory of it weighing heavy upon you.'

'I did. It has been so long, but I remembered . . .' His words faltered.

'Memory is a double-edged sword, Uthas. It can keep you strong through dark times, but it can also cripple you, keep you locked in a moment that no longer exists.' The focus of her eyes shifted, glazing as she remembered events from long ago.

You speak so true, my Queen. Your memories are shackles about you, stopping you from using the Treasures, snaring you in a web of fear. Not I. I will do what must be done.

She dropped her hand from his face and stepped away.

'Recover your strength and we shall talk again soon. Ethlinn says the time of testing is almost upon us. We must be ready.'

It is already upon us.

'Aye, we must.'

She left him then, her shield-maiden Sreng following. Soon after the door had closed behind them a figure stepped from a shadowed alcove. Salach.

'Does she suspect?' the giant asked.

Uthas drew in a shuddering breath. 'No. I don't think so.' He shrugged. 'The die is cast now. There is no going back.'

TUKUL

Tukul felt the blow ripple through his arms, from wrist to shoulders, then dissolve into his chest and back. He spun on his heel, surging around his opponent, using the momentum for a backswing that would kill if it connected with flesh.

It didn't; the blow was deflected, the power leaking from it as Tukul was momentarily forced off balance.

'Well done,' Tukul said, and patted Gar on the shoulder. *My son.* Gar all but glowed at his father's praise.

'That's enough for an old man,' Tukul said, unbinding the cloth and lambswool from his blade, used both to protect it during sparring and to mute the noise. He smiled to himself.

I am happy, he realized. The journey northwards had been one of quiet camaraderie, spent in the company of his son, his sword-kin about him, and the Seren Disglair riding at their head. *I am reunited with my son. My beloved son, who has surpassed all of the hopes and dreams I have nurtured about him for so many years. He is capable, measured, strong, compassionate. Different from us other Jehar who have been hidden away from the world. More open, a mixture of proud and humble.*

And I am in the company of the Seren Disglair, finally doing, after all these years of waiting. Setting about the serious business of defeating the Black Sun. He smiled at the clouds above him. *It is good to be alive.*

They were in a dip in the land, a meagre shelter from the wind that seemed to blow permanently across this barren moorland. All about them sparring partners separated, moving into the tasks of breaking camp. Gar's eyes flickered between two people, Tukul following his son's gaze.

Corban and Gwenith. And you love them both. That was easy to understand, having lived seventeen years around them, Corban the centre of his world. *But Gwenith . . .* Tukul frowned at that. *The Seren Disglair's mother.* Tukul had waited for the Seren Disglair all his life; in his mind he was more than human, and so his mother was special too. But to see them, human, flesh and blood. It felt strange. *And Gar is somewhere between elder brother and father to Corban. And I have seen how his eyes follow Gwenith . . .* He shrugged, a fatalism that he had long ago embraced. *It is as it is.*

Brina the old healer was hovering close as the sparring ended, a book cradled in one arm. She beckoned to Corban and the young man followed her. *What does she want with him?* His inquisitive nature won out and he followed them, checking on his horse which was paddocked nearby.

He went through the ritual of inspecting hooves, checking for stones, testing the buckles and tightness of the harness. All was ready; they were just waiting for Coralen to return. She'd left with the first sight of the sun, scouting ahead as she had each day since they'd passed into Benoth, the giant realm. She had taken the wolven with her, and Tukul had sent Enkara as an added surety.

He heard Brina and Corban talking, then Corban speak words in the first-tongue. There was a long pause, Corban standing perfectly still, braced, then his shoulders slumped.

Meical appeared and sat upon a boulder close to Corban.

'You are learning the earth power,' Meical said.

'Aye. Brina has been teaching me.'

'And how does it go?' Meical asked.

Corban shrugged. 'I just tried to summon mist. Nothing happened.'

'With the earth power there is no trying, only doing. Faith is the key.'

'Aye, well, I'm sure that's easy for you to say, seeing as you've a personal acquaintance with the All-Father. Me, it's proving to be a bit more difficult.'

Meical laughed, something that Tukul rarely heard. 'That's fair enough, I suppose.'

'I've been thinking, about this Seren Disglair business,' Corban said, turning to regard Meical.

'Aye. Go on.'

This sounds like progress.

Tukul had spent much of his time observing Corban since their meeting at Dun Vaner. There was much to like, a respectful, inquisitive lad beneath the solemn layers that experience and tragedy had accumulated. And strength, not just physical. Back at Dun Vaner he had stood up to Meical, refused to go to Drassil in favour of seeking his sister. As much as that was troublesome, not sticking to the plan, Tukul liked Corban for it. It took courage to stand up to one of the Ben-Elim. One thing that Tukul had noticed, though, was that when the questions came from Corban, which they frequently did once he'd started talking, he never asked about who he was, or about Elyon and Asroth. All of his questions were to do with kings and queens, politics, the strategies of war. *All good questions, to my mind.* But there was always an underlying avoidance of all things spiritual. This was the first time Tukul had heard him broach the subject.

'Last time, when Asroth crossed the boundaries between the Otherworld and here, Elyon intervened. He stopped Asroth. Yes?' Corban asked.

'Aye. The Scourging. Much was destroyed.'

'Yes, but Asroth was defeated. Will Elyon not just do that again? It seems to me the obvious thing to do, and would avoid all the war and slaughter that is certainly coming.'

'That would be the best and surest way to defeat Asroth,' Meical said, his expression becoming sad. 'But Elyon is absent. Gone. After the Scourging his grief was immense, indescribable. He took himself into mourning, to a place of solitude that we cannot find. So he is not here to intervene. That is why he is sometimes called the absent god. It has been my prayer for uncounted years that he return to us.'

'Oh.' Corban became silent, clearly pondering that information. 'I have heard you call me the Seren Disglair, but what does that mean. What am I supposed to do?'

'There was a prophecy written down by Halvor, a giant from the time soon after the Scourging, when the world was broken and battered, healing. The prophecy speaks of Asroth and his Kadoshim returning, of the Seven Treasures coming to light again and of two champions, avatars of Elyon and Asroth. The Bright Star and the Black Sun. The Banished Lands will be divided between these two, so the prophecy says, and they shall go to war.' Meical shrugged. 'It should not be so hard to believe, any more. War is already spreading through the land.'

'That it is,' Corban said quietly.

He does not look happy about that thought.

Hooves drummed, Coralen and Enkara riding over a crest in the surrounding moorland, Storm loping silently beside them. They reined in hard before Corban and Meical.

'Someone is out there,' Coralen said, gesturing behind her.

'Who?' Meical asked.

'I don't know, but Storm did not like the smell of them. There is woodland further along the road to Murias. They were taking care not to be seen.'

'Did they see you?' Tukul asked.

'I don't think so,' Coralen said. 'Storm scented them first, so we dismounted and crept closer.'

'We took great care,' Enkara added.

'How many?' Corban asked.

'I saw at least a dozen moving in the trees, but there could be more.' She shrugged.

'Can we go around them?'

'We could, but it would take us leagues out of our way, and they would most likely still see us; there is little shelter on the surrounding moorland.'

'That would only matter if they are waiting for us,' Corban said. 'Brina, would Craf take a closer look for us?'

'He will if he wants any supper,' Brina said.

Tukul approached the trees, a small wooded dip in the land. He tightened the hood of his cloak, a bearskin taken from Dun Vaner, masking his face. His sword and axe were strapped on either side of his saddle, within easy reach. Overhead the sky was grey, clouds low and heavy.

Highsun, already.

Craf had returned with the information that a score of men and at least one giant were hidden in these woods, off the road, no fires.

He rode amongst the first trees; the light dimmed instantly, shadows encroaching all around. *It is nothing compared to Forn.* He stared straight ahead; half a dozen of his sword-kin were about him, as well as Dath and Farrell.

They rode in silence for a while, only the sound of hooves echoing on the road, the creak and sigh of branches around them. Then Tukul thought he saw movement, just a shifting of shadows. He resisted the urge to touch his sword hilt.

Undergrowth crackled as the woods burst to life, figures leaping out at them, ten, fifteen, more. In a blur, Tukul had drawn his sword and thrown his axe, heard the satisfying crunch of it cleaving flesh and bone. He smiled, then froze as he saw his attackers clearly.

They were Jehar.

He stood tall in his saddle, shrugging his cloak away, revealing his coat of mail and dark robes.

'Hold,' he bellowed, the power of his voice freezing everyone.

A score of the Jehar stood about him, swords raised in various stages of attack. They stared at him and his companions as if they were ghosts.

They are Sumur's; there is no other explanation. I do not want to slay these, my sword-kin.

'Brothers, sisters, you have been deceived,' he cried out. 'Put down your swords; there should be no bloodshed between us.'

For a moment indecision hung in the air, everyone still, staring at him. Then another figure burst from the shadows, this one huge and broad, muscled like a bull.

A giant.

He charged straight for Dath and Farrell, a black-bladed axe raised high.

Dath drew and shot an arrow, the shaft skittering off the giant's coat of mail, then the giant was on them, roaring as it swung its axe.

Dath yanked on his reins; his horse danced away and Farrell kicked his own mount on, barging into the giant, knocking him to one knee. He stood quickly, swinging his axe overhead at Farrell. One of Tukul's Jehar spurred in between them, raising his sword to deflect the axe. The weapons met in an explosion of sparks, the axe-blade shearing through the Jehar's sword, carrying on to slice into the warrior's head, carving through into his chest, blood and gore spraying.

The act was like a spark being lit. The other Jehar who had frozen at Tukul's words sprang to life, leaping forward with a roar. Tukul parried a sword swing and countered, saw his attacker stagger. Then other figures were bursting from both sides of the trees, Storm leading the charge, leaping upon a Jehar warrior, blood spraying as they tumbled across the ground. Meical appeared, Corban and Coralen in their wolven cloaks and claws, Gar close by, more of Tukul's Jehar. The battle was short and furious, the surrounded Jehar fighting with the skill and ferocity he would expect, but they had no chance, outnumbered and surprised.

The giant burst for freedom, smashing through the chaos of fighting bodies with two of his Jehar guarding his escape, holding off any pursuers for a handful of moments. By the time they were dead the giant was gone.

FIDELE

Fidele sat at her desk with a quill hovering in her hand. Her other hand held a sheaf of parchment flat. She was sweating.

Just write it. Lykos controls me by some spell. The words my mouth speaks cannot be trusted. Kill Lykos.

That is what she wanted to write, what she was willing with all of her mind and strength for her hand to write, but it refused, as if it were a separate, sentient entity. It hovered over the parchment, a tremor of will setting droplets of ink splattering across the parchment. With a strangled yell she flung the quill away and collapsed on the desk, breathing hard.

Lykos. She could feel him, even now. A caress in her mind, a presence, like a watcher in the shadows, a maggot crawling across her skin. It made her feel sick. For a moment she could feel his hands on her, smell his sour breath, a wave of revulsion spasming through her body.

She sat up. Parchments were spread across her desk, the one before her empty, others full of her flowing writing. Most of them were orders pertaining to the movement of troops, her eagle-guard, her protectors, and she was ordering them to details in the far corners of Tenebral. Scattering any of those loyal to her away from her reach. Another wave of frustration welled up inside her.

She stood and walked to a window, gazing out over the lake and plain. Winter was on the retreat, a hint of spring coming. Her eyes were drawn to the arena that sat between Jerolin and the lake town, a malignant growth in her once-perfect view, a symbol of what was happening to Tenebral.

And how the people of Tenebral had taken to it – to pit-fighting, a fight to the death as entertainment. She would never have believed that they would scream so loudly for the sight of blood, like a pack of frenzied hounds.

Have I been so naive? Does such a darkness beat in every heart?

With a startling clarity she remembered the contest she had witnessed, the man with the axe against a warrior wielding two swords, behind them Peritus and Armatus chained to a post. Her heart had leaped as she'd seen her two old friends set free, other warriors rushing into the ring, pulling them to safety. Then the Vin Thalun had fallen upon them, the ensuing chaos ending in Armatus having his head hacked from his body by Lykos.

Peritus, at least, had escaped. Lykos had been in a rage for days after, sending warriors to scour the countryside, but Peritus had disappeared. Her guess was that he had gone home, to his village in the northern mountains. The Vin Thalun would never find him there.

Their ships studded the lake, more arriving almost every day. She didn't know how many Vin Thalun sailed the Tethys Sea, but surely every last one of them had swarmed to Jerolin. Lykos and his kind were like one of those parasites that attached themselves to a host, laying eggs in its body and eating it from the inside out.

That was how she felt, consumed from the inside out, her whole world spiralling into an ocean of permanent despair. As she looked out of the window the urge to just step out took hold of her, to step into nothing, to just fall and fall and fall. But even that was beyond her, she knew. She'd already tried to take her life. Anything to be free of the hold on her, but Lykos' will was a compulsion in her mind, a cage that she could not escape.

Lykos strolled in, the sight of him making a fist of fear clench in her gut. He looked her up and down as he approached, his eyes lingering.

'I have some good news for you,' he said, running a finger down her cheek. 'Your time of mourning Aquilus is passed.'

I will never stop mourning Aquilus.

'Surprisingly, at this stage in your life, you have found love again. You thank Elyon for this rare blessing.'

Dear All-Father, no, let this be a dream, a nightmare. Let me wake from it.

'We will be wed in a ten-night. There will be much celebrating in Tenebral at your newfound happiness. Games will honour the occasion. The fighting pit will run red.' He grinned. 'You may smile.'

She felt her muscles twitch, her lips moving involuntarily. She fought it, of course.

'Not your most beautiful look,' Lykos commented, frowning at the expression on her face.

Nathair – where are you? Please come home and end this nightmare. Not for the first time she marvelled at Lykos' sheer audacity – that he would do the things he was doing in light of Nathair's return.

'What's going on behind those eyes?' Lykos said. 'Speak freely.'

'Nathair,' she said. 'How can you do these things, knowing that he will return one day?'

Lykos laughed. 'Kingship changes people, my lady. Responsibility, pressure, it does things to a man. And Nathair will soon have far more on his mind than who his mother shares a bed with. I don't think you'll recognize your son when he returns.'

CYWEN

Cywen stamped her feet and blew on her hands. It was cold and damp, her breath fogging before her. A heavy mist cloaked the ground. She crouched and scratched Buddai behind an ear; the hound leaned against her, nearly pushing her over.

'Mount up,' Calidus said as he rode out of the mist.

She was close to the head of the column, the smell of Nathair's draig strong in the air.

It had been half a ten-night since Alcyon had left the column, staying in the woods they had passed through. Calidus had been poor company since then, refusing to answer a single question she put to him. That didn't stop her trying, though.

'Alcyon is waiting for my brother, isn't he?' she asked the silver-haired man, not for the first time.

He turned his yellow eyes upon her, the first reaction she had achieved. 'Today is a momentous day,' he said quietly, though she felt scared, suddenly, a threat in his voice. 'You are a curiosity to me now, nothing more. I do not need you. If you distract me again I will put a knife through your eye, and enjoy watching you die.' He held her gaze. 'Do we understand one another?'

'I . . .' She nodded, all her anger and defiance draining away.

A shout went up from the back of the column. Calidus pulled on his horse's reins, turning to look back. A figure loomed out of the mist, tall and wide.

Alcyon.

He approached Calidus with his head bowed. As he drew closer Cywen saw that he looked exhausted, his usual pallor deathly white now, cuts upon his arms, matted blood in his hair. He came and stood before Calidus, dropped to his knees.

'I have failed you,' the giant grated. 'My life is forfeit.'

'It's forfeit when I have no more use for you,' Calidus snapped. 'Get up and follow me.'

Calidus ordered a warrior close by to watch Cywen, and then he rode a distance away with Alcyon in tow. Cywen strained to hear them, but only caught a few disjointed words as they returned to her. 'Half a day behind, maybe more,' was all she heard Alcyon say.

'We'd better get this done, then,' Calidus said and cantered to the head of the column.

'I told you,' Cywen said to Alcyon.

'What?' the giant growled.

'That Corban would be the one doing the killing.'

Alcyon glowered at her. 'Mount up,' he ordered.

As she climbed onto Shield's back the giant reached out, his long arms encompassing her. Before she realized what he was doing she had a rope knotted about her waist, the other end tied to Alcyon's belt.

'What's that for?' she said.

'There'll be fighting today, and I won't be able to spend it all watching you. Can't have you running off in the confusion.'

'Fighting today?'

'Aye.'

'Can I have my knives back?'

'No.'

'Why not – I might need to defend myself.'

Alcyon smiled at her. 'I can see why Veradis likes you,' he said. 'You've got spirit.'

Veradis? That stilled her tongue.

'Put your knives out of your head; there's not a chance in Asroth's Otherworld that I'll be putting a blade in your hand. I might like you, but I don't trust you. And don't worry; if you need defending, I'll be the one to do it.'

She couldn't think of an answer to that, so she just scowled at him instead.

All about her the Jehar were already mounted, waiting. Horses whickered, harness creaked, chainmail jangled, then a horn call rose up somewhere ahead, eerie and muted in the morning mist. The host set off, two thousand warriors riding to battle.

'The fighting will be at Murias, then?'

'No more questions,' Alcyon said. Something in his tone warned her not to press him.

'I'm glad,' she said to him.

He raised an eyebrow. 'Glad?'

'That you're still alive. That my brother didn't kill you.'

'Come, faster,' he ordered, opening his stride, moving past rows of the Jehar, heading for the head of the column. Shield slowed as they neared Nathair astride his draig, but Cywen encouraged him forward and they fell in beside Nathair and his bodyguards.

By mid-morning the mist had mostly burned away, revealing hills and vales of sweeping moorland, much the same as they had been journeying across for days. Up ahead a lone mountain loomed, dark cliffs soaring into the clouds.

'Murias,' Calidus declared.

It was not until the sun was hovering over the horizon that they had ridden close enough for Cywen to make out towers and walls, though the place did not look like any of the giant strongholds she had seen before. The towers looked as if they had grown out of the mountain, as if the rock had been melted and reformed by crude hands. Something organic, rather than built.

The ground started rising, sloping up to meet the mountains. Cywen saw a wide road, cutting a line into long shadows cast by the mountain, leading to a huge arched gateway of carved stone. The gates were closed.

'Not planning a stealthy attack, then?' Cywen said to Alycon.

Nathair overheard her. 'I am the Bright Star, the Seren Disglair,' he said from his draig's back. 'It feels as if I've been waiting for this moment all my life; I'll not lessen it by sneaking up like a thief in the night. This is my destiny.' He looked at her and smiled.

Have it your way. Though I'm wondering how you think you're going to get in there. Just walk up and knock on their gates?

In the distance a sound drifted on the air, a wolven howling, as if heralding the coming of night. Buddai whined, and Shield slowed, his head pulling around.

'Walk on,' Cywen ordered, digging her heels into Shield's sides. Buddai was standing stock still, his head cocked to one side. Then he bolted away, back the way they had come, quickly disappearing into the gloom. Cywen called him, reining Shield in.

'We can't stop,' Alcyon said, tugging on the rope about her waist.

'But Buddai . . .'

'He doesn't like the look of Murias,' Alcyon said. 'Sensible animal. He'll be out here when we're done, waiting for you.'

'But . . .'

'Keep moving.' It was Calidus who spoke now. After a last look back Cywen urged Shield onwards.

CORALEN

'Murias,' Coralen said, pointing into the distance. A tall peak reared before them, the first mountain of a range that faded into the distance.

They had ridden hard since the ambush in the woods, two nights gone. At first she'd thought they would catch the giant, but he had not stopped running for two days and nights solid, each morning the gap between them widening a little.

It had been a shock, seeing the other Jehar in the woods, a lesson of what awaited them once they caught up with Nathair and his warband. Tukul had been grim faced ever since, something unspoken passing between them all.

Blood was going to be shed.

But I knew that, anyway.

She saw Corban gazing at Nathair's host, a dark line winding its way towards the mountains. They were standing beneath a handful of wind-blasted trees, gnarled and twisted branches grasping at the sky. Everyone had taken the opportunity to dismount and stretch their legs, drink some water, chew on some meat, tend their horses.

'Nathair,' she heard Corban whisper.

'He's there,' Meical said, standing close beside them.

'He killed my da. Put a sword in his chest; right here.' Corban tapped a finger against his leather jerkin.

Meical gave him a searching look. 'This is about rescue, not revenge,' he said. 'Or is it?'

She saw Corban close his eyes, screwing them shut. After a while he blew out a long breath.

'Cywen is what matters here,' he said.

'Good. There are too many of them for us to take on. Another time. Of course, if there is an opportunity to take Nathair's head from his shoulders . . .'

'And Sumur's,' added Tukul.

Storm was standing nearby, sniffing the air. Suddenly she lifted her head and howled. Dath jumped. Coralen froze, half expecting to see the line of Nathair's warband stop and look at them.

'Is she trying to tell everyone within a day's travel where we are?' Tukul said.

'I don't know why she did that.' Corban frowned.

'If we ride hard we'll catch them by nightfall,' Tukul said.

'And then what?' Dath this time.

'We find Cywen and get her out of there.' Gwenith's lips twitched into a half-smile as she said Cywen's name.

Coralen looked back to Nathair's warband crawling like ants towards the mountains. Sheer cliffs rose into the sky before them, peaks wreathed in cloud.

I don't like this. Murias' walls are thick, its gates strong. How are they planning on getting in there?

Craf started squawking, hopping about on Brina's saddle. The bird was looking up at the sky. A black dot was circling above them, spiralling downwards. They all watched the dot grow into a bird, big and black.

'It's Fech,' Brina said.

The raven seemed to study them, eyes scanning the crowd of seventy or so people, then it saw Corban and sailed down to him, alighting on a branch close by.

'*Corban*,' it said, then began preening its feathers.

'Fech, is that you?' Brina said. Craf cawed.

'*Fech, yes*,' the bird said. '*Message from Edana, for Corban.*'

'What is it?' Corban asked.

'*Eremon is dead. Domhain fallen. Edana sails for Dun Crin.*'

The blood in Coralen's veins turned to ice. 'What?' she hissed. She felt dizzy, unsteady on her feet.

'Edana and the others, are they all alive?' Corban asked.

'*When I left them*,' Fech croaked.

'You are sure about Eremon?' Coralen said.

'*Yes. Saw him die. Girl killed him. Maeve.*'

Maeve. My half-sister, murderer of my da. It was all coming too quickly, the bird's words taking on a dreamlike quality, like some herald from the Otherworld.

'Is there anything else? Any more you can tell us?' Meical asked.

'*Rhin there. Made Conall ruler of Domhain.*'

With a groan Coralen turned and walked deeper into the stand of trees.

MAQUIN

Maquin sat in a chamber, staring at his hands. He had been waiting all day; they all had, the last of his comrades, Herak's elite, their final contest upon them. In the distance he heard the roar of the crowd, knew that blood was being spilt in the arena.

Whose blood, though?

He hoped that Javed survived, for what it was worth. He had avoided making friends amongst these pit-fighters, knew when he made his decision in the pit on Nerin to live and fight that there was no room for friendship in his life any longer. There was only Jael. That was the focus, the goal, the justification for all that he had done. For all that he would do.

But Javed was hard not to like, with his easy smile and open nature. Perhaps he would survive, earn Lykos' chest of gold and his freedom. He hoped so.

He continued to stare at his hands.

A killer's hands. A murderer's hands. I have become all that I hated, and if that takes me to Jael and his death, then I shall be content.

He raised a hand to scratch an itch in his ear, only to touch a stub of flesh, all that remained of his ear since Deinon cut a slice out of it. *Strange how something that isn't there can itch.*

A key rattled in the door of his chamber – rooms that lined the courtyard of Jerolin. The guard Emad walked in, two other Vin Thalun with him.

'You're up, old wolf,' Emad said.

Maquin stood and walked to the door, stepping out into the sunlight.

Petals littered the courtyard as he walked through it and out of the gates, drifting about his feet. Crowds had been celebrating earlier, lining the streets as Lykos and Fidele had passed through on their way to the arena. Tonight they would be handbound, the culmination of a day of celebrations.

How has Lykos managed that? He did not know Fidele, had only seen her on a few occasions, most of them back in the life-before, as he thought of it, when he had been here for Aquilus' council. But even then she had not seemed even remotely suited to the likes of Lykos.

The sound of the crowds grew louder as he approached the arena. Vin Thalun were everywhere, spread about the meadow, ringing the outside of the arena, lining all the entrances.

He ignored them as he was led into a tunnel, more guards closing about him, shouldering a way through the crowds.

Then he was there, stepping out into the ring, the ground a churned quagmire of mud. Off to his left a patch of blood and gore marked the end-place of the last contest.

He was the first to arrive, no one else in here yet. He moved forwards and saw a sack in the middle of the ring. Two knives were in it, curved and thick bladed, tapering to wicked points. He took them out, twirled them in his hands, did a slow turn of the arena.

All around the crowd were shouting, cheering. He had built a reputation now. Close to the ringside in a boxed tier sat Lykos and Fidele. Lykos looked relaxed, enjoying himself, a cup of something in one hand. The other was inside his cloak, and something about his posture told Maquin he was gripping something, as he had before.

What is it?

Fidele was sitting beside him, a fixed expression on her face, part smile, part grimace. She looked as if her countenance had been frozen in place.

A sound drew his attention, snapping his head around. The gateway to the far tunnel had opened. His eyes focused on the dark entrance: a handful of figures stepping out into the daylight; Vin Thalun guards and the man he would fight.

His eyes narrowed as he saw his final opponent. It was Orgull.

CORBAN

Corban found Coralen alone amidst the trees, strapping on her wolven claws with sharp, jerking movements. Tears stained her cheeks.

She heard his footsteps and looked up.

'What do you want?'

'I am sorry,' he said.

'You? You've nothing to be sorry for,' Coralen said. 'What have you done?'

'I mean, I wish I could help, and I'm sorry that I can't. I'm sorry that I can't make you feel better, that I can't take your pain away.'

'No one can,' she snapped. 'Don't concern yourself.'

'But he was your da.'

'Yes, he was my da,' she murmured, sorrow coating each word. 'Not that he ever acted like it.' Her eyes were unfocused now, seeing something other than Corban and the trees about them. With a shiver she came back. 'You should go now.'

'Come with me. You're amongst friends now.'

'I'll be along after.' She wiped the tears from her cheeks. Corban understood her meaning – she did not want anyone to see the evidence of her grief. She held her emotions hidden deep and secure, a wall of her own making. He turned to go.

'Corban,' she said, the word stopping him dead. He stood, waiting.

'You asked me before, why I have come on this journey.'

'I did.'

He turned to face her then, and for a long, timeless moment they just looked at one another. She smiled, a vulnerable, tenuous twist of her lips. 'The reason—'

Then horns blew in the distance, harsh and long. They kept ringing.

'That sounds serious.' Coralen strode past him, back to the others, no sign of the previous moment's fragility left about her.

All were mounted when they returned, waiting for him. The horn blasts were still ringing, whether from Nathair's host or from the walls of Murias he could not tell. It did not matter – the purpose was clear. Battle was about to begin. He climbed into his saddle and looked to his mam.

'Cywen,' he said, and they set off.

They rode across the heather-clad moor, the sun melting into the horizon. Fech flew above, quickly outpacing them, blending with the darkness that was Murias. No one spoke, all eyes on the dark slopes ahead. Then Corban saw something, a movement in the heather. Something coming towards them, fast.

It was a hound, running hard.

Have we been spotted by Nathair's scouts?

Before he could say anything, Storm was outpacing him, moving from her ground-eating lope into a run. Corban scanned the shadows for scouts. He had no doubt that Storm would deal with the hound.

Then wolven and hound were clashing together, bodies intertwining, rolling, Storm's bone-white fur contrasting with the hound's darkness. They separated, came together again. Corban squinted.

Something's wrong.

There was no snarling or growling, no teeth baring, no blood. Then Storm was rolling on her back, the hound bouncing around her in great excited leaps.

Then he realized.

'It's *Buddai*.'

Together he and his mam slid from their saddles and ran to the wolven and hound. Buddai was jumping around Storm like a pup, licking her face, nipping at her ears as Storm rolled on her back, paws swatting at the hound. Buddai saw Corban and Gwenith, paused long enough to take a great sniff, then he was leaping on them, bowling them over, snuffling and licking at their faces.

Corban looked up and saw seventy faces staring back at him, the Jehar all wearing the same mildly confused expressions. All except Gar, who was grinning at them.

'Wolven, crows, ravens, hounds,' Tukul said. 'What will it be next?'

'Cywen is there, Ban,' his mam said. 'There's no doubting it now.'

'I know. Let's go and get her.'

With that they mounted back up and headed for Murias. A noise rose up before them, drifting from the mountain stronghold, sounding like a great wind. It was followed by distant screams.

UTHAS

Uthas stood beside Nemain, looking out from a balcony on the host approaching Murias. Ravens soared on updraughts above them, looking like black leaves in a whirlwind. Behind him Sreng and Salach stood, shield-warriors, both dressed for war. Uthas could see Nathair now, riding his draig at the head of the column, Calidus and Alcyon close to him.

The road to Murias was wide, gently twisting through a landscape of granite boulders and rocky scree. The balcony that Uthas and Nemain were standing upon looked out from a curve in the cliff face, giving them a view of the approach to Murias as well as the stronghold's gates themselves. They reared the height of ten giants, wider than twenty, and were fashioned from the rock of the mountain, like everything else in Murias, the last great feat of the stone-masters. And they were barred, of course.

Nathair's approach had not come as a surprise. Ethlinn the Dreamer had woken a day ago, sweating and disoriented, and declared the coming of the Black Sun and his Black Heart. So they were ready, or as ready as they could be. The cauldron was surrounded by its protectors, the brood of wyrms restless and hungry – Morc had not fed them since Ethlinn's words, and the entire strength of the Benothi stood armed, most of them the other side of the barred gates. Five hundred Benothi warriors gathered together had been a sight to see. It reminded him of better times, of the host that had faced Eremon's ancestors on the plains around Dun Taras. There had been more of the Benothi then, but the outcome had still been dire. Sometimes it seemed that since the Sundering life had been one long spiral into despair.

He sighed, feeling the old melancholy sweep through him, a sense of fatalism, of destiny coiling tight about him, like the death grip of a wyrm.

A raised voice pulled Uthas from his reverie. It was Nathair. He had reached the gates of Murias.

'I am Nathair ben Aquilus, the Bright Star foretold, and I have come for the cauldron,' Nathair declared, his voice echoing about the cliffs. 'There is no need for blood to be spilt. Just open the gates, accept the inevitable. Join with me in the coming war; let us stand united against Asroth and his Black Sun.'

The echoes of his voice faded. Nemain stared down at him.

'Am I hearing correctly?' she said. 'Did he just call himself the Bright Star, avatar of Elyon?'

'He did,' Uthas confirmed.

'Is he mad, or deluded?' she said.

Uthas shrugged. 'Perhaps both.'

'Open your gates to me,' Nathair yelled, his voice strong with the conviction of his cause.

Nemain closed her eyes, breath whispering across her lips. Then her eyes snapped open.

'There he is,' she pointed. 'Black Heart.'

One of the figures close to Nathair was suddenly defined, a dark nimbus around him, as if he were standing before a doorway leading into darkness. The shadows of wings flared around him.

Calidus.

'I see you, Black Heart,' Nemain called down, her voice raw with the anger of ages. 'You will not gain the cauldron so easily. We are not bairns to be tricked.'

Calidus stared back, saying nothing.

'I do not understand you,' Nathair shouted. 'I am no black heart. I stand against Asroth and his darkness.'

'You will not pass through the gates of Murias by honeyed words and lies,' Nemain called out. 'You ride with the Black Heart at your side – that is all I need to know.'

Nathair looked about him, frowning as he stared at Calidus.

'She lies to you, Nathair,' Calidus proclaimed, his voice ringing against the walls. 'She serves Asroth, and would hold the cauldron for him.'

'He does not know,' Nemain whispered. She shook her head, pity sweeping the contours of her face. Then she raised her arms and began to speak.

The ravens were abruptly thick in the air, more joining them, swirling in a tight vortex, hundreds, thousands of them, more appearing all the time, bursting from cliff nests, flocking from the skies. She swept her arms forward, pointing at Nathair and Calidus, and the ravens flew at them, a gigantic spear of beak and feather and claw.

Calidus lifted one hand and the air shimmered. The ravens hit it, the first of them exploding into chunks, those behind spreading out about something almost invisible, a shield of air curving around Calidus and Nathair, protecting them and the warriors immediately behind. The birds swept about it, ploughing into the warriors behind. Screams rose up as these men were engulfed by the dark flock of ravens, horses rearing, warriors drawing swords and slashing the air.

They cannot reach Calidus or Nathair, but even so these birds will turn the battle. The Jehar cannot fall. Their numbers are needed if the cauldron is to be taken.

Uthas looked from Nemain to the birds, still more of them gathering and flying at the host before the gates. The air was thick with them, swirling all about the Jehar, blood and feathers exploding in a hundred different places as the Jehar tried to cut the ravens from the sky. Uthas saw horses and warriors collapsed on the roadside, torn bloody by the remorseless tide of beak and talon.

Now. I must do something, now.

He looked to Nemain, all her will focused on the scene before her. Beads of sweat stood on her brow, dripped down her face.

His hand drifted to his knife hilt, but still he hesitated. Nemain had been queen for close to three thousand years; how could he strike her down?

She stands in my way. In the way of my kin. She will see us all in our graves. Kill her.

He squeezed his eyes shut, feeling as if his whole life, two thousand years, had come down to this one moment.

I cannot kill her. I will talk to her, convince her.

'Nemain . . .'

She didn't hear him, her focus entirely upon the host at her gates. He said her name again, louder, and her gaze flickered towards him.

Then there was a fluttering sound from above. A raven drifted down, wings stretched to slow its descent. It landed on her shoulder and put its beak to her ear.

Is that Fech? It can't be . . .

Nemain's eyes snapped onto him, her mouth opening.

'Sreng,' she called.

Uthas stepped forwards, drawing his knife.

'*Greim*,' Nemain said, and Uthas felt the air grow thick about him, congealing like spilt blood. Around his limbs, his chest and hips, his face, slowing him, binding him. He tried to push through it, to force his knife into her flesh, but he moved as if through sand. Behind him he heard the clash of weapons, dim and muted – *Sreng and Salach*. He came to a halt, his fist quivering as he tried to move it, the invisible pressure constricting about him, a fist around his throat.

'*Fuasgail*,' he whispered with the last breath in his lungs. There was a moment when his life hung in the balance, a pressure growing in his head, a burning in his lungs, then the grip about him evaporated. He staggered forwards and lunged at Nemain, the clash of weapons behind him suddenly loud, deafening. Nemain grabbed his wrist and twisted, her other hand reaching for his throat. Her strength took him by surprise and he staggered backwards, managed to grasp her arm before her fingers fastened about his neck. Locked together, they reeled about the balcony, knocking chairs over, crashing into a table.

'Traitor,' she hissed at him, a depth of pain in her eyes that caused him to falter. The sound of combat stopped.

Either Salach has killed Sreng, or she has slain him. He waited for Sreng's axe to fall, but instead Nemain jerked before him, was thrown into his arms. They stood like that, gazing into each other's eyes, then blood gushed from Nemain's mouth. She flew across the room as Salach wrenched his axe from her back, her body draping over the balcony.

Uthas stared at her, at the great wound in her back, blood and bone mixed.

What have I done?

He stumbled over to her, lifted her legs and threw her from the balcony, an instinctive reaction to his shame, a childish denial. She toppled over the balcony's edge, tumbling over and over as she sped to the ground. He leaned over, watching her fall.

'Uthas, we must be quick now.' Salach's voice, as if from a great distance. He tore his eyes from the ruin of Nemain, spread across the mountainside, his gaze brushing across Nathair's host. They were recovering now, the ravens dispersing about them, melting into the sky, purposeless and confused.

Without a word he turned and strode from the room.

The kin parted around him as he made his way through the great chamber before Murias' gates. Whispers followed him, murmurs. He ignored them all, his eyes touching on the faithful, those he had turned to his cause over the ages. Silently they gathered behind him, until he led a party of forty, fifty strong.

No one hindered him, or questioned him.

They think I follow Nemain's orders. Perhaps that I am come to speak to them, to offer words of encouragement, of honour and courage.

In the end he reached the gates and stood to one side, turning to face the crowd – the gathered mass of the Benothi giants.

'Where is Nemain?' a voice cried. It was old One-Eye, stepping out before the others. His white hair was tied back in a thick braid, his arms bare, displaying his tale of thorns, a war-hammer in his hands.

'She is dead,' Uthas cried.

A ripple went through the crowd, mutterings of discontent.

'We stand on the edge now,' he called out. 'What happens next will determine the fate of the Benothi. Annihilation or rebirth. Join me; join us.' He swept his hand at the giants with him, standing in a line before the gates.

'And if we do not join you?' One-Eye again.

'Then you shall be buried and forgotten with the rest of the dead,' Uthas cried, at the same time signalling to his followers.

As one they shouldered the oak timbers that barred the gateway, letting them fall to the ground with a crash. The gates swung open, a widening shaft of twilight cutting into the chamber. Uthas looked out, saw Nathair on his draig, the Jehar massed behind him.

The draig roared and charged forwards.

CYWEN

Cywen guided Shield after Alcyon, trying to avoid the surrounding battle, looking for any opportunity to make her escape. Alcyon had hung back after Nathair had charged through the gates of Murias, letting the Jehar stream past them. Cywen had the impression that Alcyon would like nothing more than to take his axe to the Benothi giants of Murias, but he had been ordered to watch her and keep her safe, and charging into battle would not be the best way of accomplishing that task. Plus fighting giants was not so easy with someone tied to your belt.

Cywen had only just recovered from the horror of the raven attack. Although she had been close enough to Calidus to be protected by his shield she had still seen the full effect of the attack on the warriors behind her. There had been so many of the ravens, a torrent of talons and beaks, too many to defend against. She saw Jehar cut ten, twenty, thirty from the air, even as they were being clawed and gouged by a hundred others. And the poor horses. Hundreds had been left dead or dying on the slope before the gates.

And then, as suddenly as it had started, it had ended, the birds wheeling away in confusion.

It had seemed that only heartbeats had passed before the gates of Murias swung open. The roar of Nathair's draig had set the ground trembling, and then all had been a chaos of movement: horses galloping, men drawing swords, Alcyon tugging her forwards.

They were standing now just within the gates, on the edge of a huge chamber, the roof cloaked in darkness, too high for torch-light to reach. It was deafening, a thousand noises mixing: screams of the dying, enraged battle-cries, horses neighing, the draig's basal roaring, the ring of iron on iron, the crunch of war-hammers pulping flesh and breaking bone.

Cywen saw Nathair on the back of his draig, swinging his sword, Calidus one side of him, Sumur the other, the three of them a spear-tip carving its way deeper into the chamber.

'I cannot just stand here,' Alcyon said. 'Stay close to me.' He hefted his black axe. 'But not too close.'

With that he was moving forwards, striding through the wake of Nathair's passing. The giants had lost their height advantage with all of the Jehar fighting from the backs of their horses; the chamber was so huge that it easily accommodated them all.

Alcyon swung at a giant that had one hand wrapped in a horse's bridle, the other pulling a hammer back ready to crush the animal's skull. Alcyon's axe sheared through the giant's arm, the backswing chopping into his back. The giant collapsed in an eruption of blood, then Alcyon was stepping over him, past a dead horse, its rider crushed beneath it, looking for his next opponent.

Two giants stumbled close to them, grappling one another. Cywen yanked on Shield's reins and the horse reared, lashing out with his hooves. The giants were knocked off their feet, rolling amongst the fallen.

They were close to Nathair now. Cywen saw him swinging his sword at a white-haired giant wielding a war-hammer. A handful of the Benothi stood about him, guarding the entrance to a corridor.

The giant blocked Nathair's sword blow, swung his hammer at Nathair, but the King of Tenebral swayed back in his saddle, the hammer whistling past. The draig reared then and swatted at the giant, sending him and the few gathered about him hurtling through the air like so many twigs. Cywen saw the white-haired giant crash into a wall and slide down it, dead or unconscious.

Then Uthas was there, standing beside Nathair, yelling something over the din of battle.

Nathair gave a great shout as he pointed his sword at the corridor. Uthas strode into it, another giant at his shoulder, carrying an axe. Nathair's draig powered after them, hundreds of the Jehar following in its wake.

Calidus looked back and saw Alcyon.

'Stay close,' he ordered, then rode into the corridor.

Alcyon glanced at Cywen, checked the knot of the rope that bound her to him and then strode into the corridor. Battle still raged in the hall behind them, though the way ahead sounded to be clear, only the sound of hooves on stone echoing back along the passageway.

It felt like a long time that they sped into the bowels of Murias, sporadically the corridors opening out into high-vaulted chambers. Intermittently the sound of battle rang out, as Nathair and his guard encountered another group of the fortress' defenders. These clashes were always savage but short, Nathair, his draig and the Jehar an inexorable wave pushing forwards. Alcyon increased his speed, Cywen kicking Shield to keep pace, and they gained on Nathair. Then they turned a corner and were before an arched doorway. The entire host rippled to a halt.

'We are here,' Uthas said. 'The cauldron lies in there.'

A silence fell over them, just the deep rumble of the draig's breathing filling the corridor.

Nathair lifted his reins, about to urge the draig on.

'Wait,' Uthas said. 'It is not undefended.'

'I will slay a nation of giants to get to the cauldron,' he snarled.

'There are more than giants in there.'

'I have come too far. Nothing will keep me from my destiny now.' Nathair snapped a command to his draig and the beast scuttled forwards. It reared up, slamming both of its clawed front feet into the doors. They crashed open, tearing from their hinges and toppling into the chamber beyond.

Without a backward look Nathair entered the chamber.

MAQUIN

Maquin stared across the space of the arena at Orgull. His old Gadrai sword-brother walked straight-backed, though slowly, and favouring one leg.

How is it possible? Maquin thought. *He should be dead, or crippled.* His mind raced back to when he'd seen him last in Lykos' chamber – Orgull hanging from the wall, chained, beaten, broken, his face a bloody ruin. *How has he recovered so much? It is not possible.* He took an involuntary step forwards.

The guards about Orgull fell away. Emad appeared from behind him carrying Orgull's giant axe, the one he had taken from the tomb beneath Haldis.

Orgull should not be able to lift it, let alone wield it.

Orgull took the axe, holding it two-handed across his chest, and paced forward.

The volume of the crowd rose. Close by, Maquin heard cage bars rattling; he looked and saw a line of pit-fighters in a viewing cage. Javed amongst them. He looked back to Orgull.

They were only a dozen paces apart when they both stopped. Close up, Orgull was not as recovered as Maquin had thought. The left side of his face was a mass of puckered skin, burned and raw. One eye was gone, just a fold of wax-like flesh covering the place where it should have been. Teeth were missing, his body was scarred. He was standing straight, gripping his axe, but Maquin could see that took considerable effort. Sweat beaded Orgull's face, and his limbs were trembling.

Even his voice was different, hissing through missing teeth and cracked lips. Almost nothing was left of the man from the time-before.

'It's good to see you, brother,' Orgull said.

'Orgull, what is this madness?'

'They want you to kill me – me, the one who rose against them, slain by my former Gadrai brother. They've given me seed of the poppy, for the pain. My strength isn't what it was, though.'

'Why are you doing this?'

'Because death will be a sweet release. Every man has a limit, Maquin, and they have found mine.' A tremor rippled through his voice. 'And because I wanted to see you again. Talk to you.'

The cheering of the crowd grew louder, and Maquin looked to see Lykos entering the ring, flanked by Deinon and a handful of shieldmen. He was striding towards them.

'Whatever you want to say, you'd best say it quick,' Maquin hissed.

'Kill me now; release me from this hell. Earn your freedom from slavery. I know you will seek out Jael, and I wish you well. If you succeed, though, do one thing for me.'

'What?'

'Find Meical, the man I told you about. Tell him I stayed true, to the end.'

Lykos was upon them then, arms raised, turning to take in the crowd.

He has become a showman. He knows how to manipulate and control people – that is for sure.

Maquin thought briefly about killing Lykos, after all the bastard had done to him, the hellish nightmare of the journey from Dun Kellen, branding him, taking his warrior braid, forcing him on this road to murder. The torture and breaking of his Gadrai brother. His grip tightened on his knives. Then he saw the guards – Deinon, Herak, Emad, a few others behind, all watching him, all tense, ready to move, as if they could read his mind.

I would not get close.

And then the moment had passed.

Even as Lykos finished his turn, one of his hands was creeping inside his cloak, searching for something.

Is it a knife? Is he so certain of being attacked at any moment?

'This is the final contest of the day, on this most happy of days,' Lykos yelled, the crowd quietening to a murmur. 'Two sword-sworn brothers to compete. One the betrayer and renegade, against the old wolf, the fighter who has kept his honour, fought his way through all put before him. One will live, one will die; there is no other way out of the pit.'

Lykos has a strange idea of what honour is.

'Begin,' he called.

Orgull moved on him, jabbing with the butt-end of his axe. Maquin easily slipped out of its way, instinctively raising his two knives. He almost lunged into attack, so ingrained was his training; when he realized what he was doing he pulled back.

Orgull jabbed again, then with gritted teeth swung the axe in a two-handed blow. Maquin ducked, the blade whistling over his head. The crowd yelled their approval. Maquin danced back again. Behind him someone booed.

'What are you doing?' Orgull hissed. 'We have to make this convincing for them.' He rushed forward then, his axe swinging in looping arcs over his head, only Maquin seeing the spasm of pain that twisted his face.

Maquin retreated, using his knives to strike glancing blows on the axe haft, turning it as Vandil, their Gadrai captain, had taught them to turn a giant's blows – not taking the brunt of them, but striking at angles, turning weapons, using their own momentum, changing angles with a twist of the wrist, a sliding blade.

The crowd burst into life, cheering as Orgull surged on, continuing his flurry of blows unrelentingly.

Just kill him, Maquin thought, shifting his weight, avoiding another axe swing, seeing an opening to drive a knife between Orgull's ribs. *It would be so easy. He wants me to do it; it would be a mercy killing. And then I will be free. Free to hunt down Jael, to take my revenge, to leave all this life behind.*

He looked at Orgull's face; the physical effort was putting deep lines in his skin. Spittle hung in long strings from his lips. *What have they done to you?* Memories rushed through him, snatched images: Orgull riding patrol along the banks of the Rhenus, fighting Hunen giants before the walls of Haldis, dragging him into safety in the tomb where Kastell died, sitting around a fire telling the tale of his youth.

My friend. My last friend. How can I put a knife in your flesh, watch your life spill on the mud? But kill you I must, it is my only way out of here. An anger filled him then, churning inside, focusing sharply on Lykos. *You have done this to us. Taken everything away, even our humanity. Made us animals. For what? Entertainment?*

For Jael – that is why I have done this, become what I have become. For a chance to see Jael again. I must see this through, else all I've done, the lives I've taken, would be for nothing.

He grimaced, knowing what he must do, the finality of it settling upon him like a heavy cloak. *I must kill you, sword-brother.*

Orgull was tiring now, his mouth hanging open as he fought for the breath to drive his body; Maquin could see him withering, the signs of it in the wildness of the big man's swings, the control fading with each move, each contraction of muscle, the fibres pushed beyond the point of obedience to the will. In short moments the facade would be undone. If Maquin was going to do this, he would have to do it now.

He snarled, more at himself and what he had become than for any other reason, ducked a high blow, shuffled back, swayed to the right, then pushed forwards, dropping into a roll, slashing a knife across Orgull's leg as he rolled past him.

He heard the grunt and the impact of Orgull's fall before he had finished his roll.

He stood and turned slowly, saw Orgull lying face down in the mud, his axe slipped from his grasp, hands reaching blindly for it. There was a gash in one of his legs, blood pumping from the wound, and Maquin felt a stab of guilt at inflicting more pain on this man. His sword-brother, his captain, his friend.

I will make it quick.

The crowd roared as Maquin bore down on Orgull, at the last instant the big man flipping over onto his back to look into Maquin's face. That made him pause, just for a heartbeat as they locked eyes, sharing that comradeship that can only be crafted from fighting side by side, from saving each other's lives, from sharing the same cause.

Orgull smiled at him, just a twitch of his scarred lips, and nodded. *I am ready*, the smile said, and *thank you.*

Maquin raised a knife, paused as he looked down at Orgull.

Kill him. Else all you've sacrificed is for nothing.

The moment stretched, utter silence in the arena. With a snarl Maquin stood straight and dropped his knives.

'I'll not be killing you, my brother. Not this day; not ever.'

CORBAN

The land around Corban changed from rolling heather to rocky scree. They had talked long and hard about plans of approach, how exactly they were going to take Cywen from among close to two thousand Jehar.

'She is bait to trap you, so she will be kept close to Nathair,' Meical had said. 'So all we need to do is find Nathair.'

'That looks like a big fortress,' Corban had commented.

'Nathair is here for the cauldron. Find the cauldron and we find Nathair. Find Nathair and we find Cywen. How we shall then take her from him is another matter.'

In the end the plan was a simple one. They would abandon stealth for speed. A battle would be going on, between the giants of Murias and Nathair and his Jehar. It would be chaotic. This was their best and only opportunity. They were riding quickly at a ground-eating canter, the cliffs of Murias looming high above now, night upon them. The moon was a pale glow behind streaks of cloud. Corban glanced to either side, saw Gar and his mam, Tukul and Meical, Dath, Brina, Farrell and Coralen; Storm and Buddai loped in the shadows. Behind them spread three score Jehar warriors. His kin, his friends, others, all come to this place because of him. Their lives, their deaths – all his responsibility because of his decision.

Focus, now, as Gar's taught me a thousand times. There is only now, this moment, and the one that follows . . .

Then he was passing the first bodies, horses and men fallen together, their flesh torn in strips, raked down to their bones. They slowed to a trot, picking their way through the human and equine detritus. Black feathers sprinkled it all, sticking to blood, floating on the breeze.

They moved past the concentration of bodies, the open gates looming closer. Corban saw movement to the left of the gates, amongst the rocks. It was a big black raven on a granite boulder, hunched by a corpse and pecking at itself, muttering.

'Fech, is that you?'

'*Yes, I am Fech. Fech Fech Fech. I am a selfish, disloyal bird. Selfish, selfish.*' The raven resumed pecking himself. Corban saw blood welling through his charcoal feathers.

'Stop that,' Brina snapped as she slid from her horse and picked her way through rocks to the raven. Craf fluttered out of the sky and alighted on a boulder close by.

Tukul and the Jehar fanned out before them, protecting against any attack.

'Don't do that to yourself,' Brina said, grasping the raven.

'*Deserve it, deserve it, deserve it,*' the bird muttered.

If it is possible for a bird's voice to express an emotion then I am hearing abject misery, thought Corban.

Meical followed Brina and stared at the body on the ground. From its size it was clearly a giant, probably female from the long black hair, though otherwise it was hard to tell. It was lying with limbs splayed at unnatural angles, most of its features a pulped ruin.

'Is that Nemain?' Meical said.

'*Yes,*' wailed the bird. '*Nemain, Nemain, Nemain.*'

Meical looked up. Corban followed his eyes and saw a balcony high above, the curved shadow of a doorway or window behind it.

'Nemain would not just fall,' Meical said. 'And someone opened the gates of Murias.'

'*Uthas,*' Fech spat. '*Uthas killed her. Uthas the betrayer. Peck his eyes out and eat them. Should have returned sooner. Sooner, sooner.*' He tried to peck himself again, but Brina gripped his beak. Craf flew over, landing on the same boulder as Fech. He peered at the raven, then shuffled closer and began running his beak through Fech's ruffled feathers.

Is Craf grooming him? Is he being nice?

'Will you help us?' Corban said.

'*How?*' Fech asked when Brina let go, cocking his head to one side.

'We need to find the cauldron,' he said. 'Take us to it.'

'*Cauldron is bad,*' Fech said. '*Why go there?*'

'Because that is where Nathair will be, and he has my sister. We have come to save her.'

'*I know,*' Fech muttered. '*Save Cywen. Fech remembers.*'

'Yes, that's right. Will you help us?'

'*Help me kill Uthas.*'

'He will probably be with Nathair,' Meical said.

'*Nathair's at cauldron,*' Fech croaked. '*I take you to cauldron, you find sister, we kill Uthas.*'

'Agreed,' said Corban. He didn't want to become embroiled in hunting and killing anyone right now, but if it meant finding Cywen quickly, then it was worth doing.

'*Come,*' Fech squawked and flapped into the air, flying towards the open gates of Murias.

They followed Fech through the open gateway. A wall of sound hit them. Battle was raging, though mostly at the far end of a cavernous chamber. Clearly many had fallen. Closer to them, bodies littered the floor, men and giants and horses, all bleeding into the dark stone. Corban saw Gar and Tukul tense as they saw Jehar locked in battle with giants.

'*Too many. Can't go that way,*' squawked Fech as he flew back from the far end of the hall. '*Follow me, come, come,*' and he winged away towards the edges of the room. He took them to a wide stairwell that spiralled up. No one made a move towards them; if any saw Corban and his followers they were too busy to do anything about it. In seconds they were all dismounted and running up the stairs, trying to keep up with the bird. Corban drew his sword and flexed the wolven claws strapped to his other arm.

Cywen, we are coming.

CAMLIN

Camlin reined in his horse.

'There it is,' Roisin cried, pointing.

The sail of a ship had come into view, poking above a ridge in the road. The sea churned behind it, an undulating blanket melting into the horizon. Camlin was glad to see it; a ten-night of hard riding south-west to the coast had set muscles aching that he didn't know he had. Their column set off again, fifty or so riders. Camlin hung back a little, saw Edana's fair hair up ahead, flanked by Marrock and Vonn. *Though this is no end. Just the beginning of the next race. At least it will give us some breathing space, though.* He glanced over his shoulder, looking for the tell-tale signs of their pursuers.

For three days now he had glimpsed riders following them, a cloud of dust marking them that suggested many more than their fifty horses. Now though, green hills behind hid anyone from view, and the clouds were low and thick, masking any dust trail.

They're back there somewhere, but we just need long enough to jump onto a ship and row away. He dipped his body low against his horse's neck and willed it to gallop faster.

He had told Marrock and Halion of the pursuit, and they had in turn told Edana and Roisin, the word spreading through the warriors. A bleakness had settled over them that night, the knowledge of pursuit suggesting that Dun Taras had fallen. Baird had picked a fight with one of Quinn's men, knocking the man cold for little more than a lingering glance. Halion had had to step in before Baird had taken on a dozen others. Quinn had challenged Baird, of course, but Halion had forbidden it, saying they were all on the same side, and to save their anger for the enemy, if they ever caught up. Camlin suspected that Quinn had not really meant the challenge, anyway; he had backed down too easily, although he had glowered at Halion's back afterwards. Camlin had not liked that. He'd heard the man was proud and arrogant, and nothing he'd witnessed during their journey had dissuaded him of the notion. Besides that, anyone with the title of first-sword didn't take well to being told what to do by another warrior.

Later that night Camlin had watched Quinn as he'd cleaned and sharpened his blades – a longsword and two knives laid out before him. At the end he had poured a dark liquid over them, working it into the iron.

'What's that?' Camlin had asked.

'Just an extra bite,' Quinn had said. 'Something to slow a man down a little.' He'd smiled.

Camlin hadn't liked that either. A memory rose in his mind of the night Farrell had arm-wrestled Quinn in the feast-hall, a cut on the back of Farrell's hand. 'Best be careful not to cut yourself by accident, then,' he'd said.

'I never cut anyone by accident.'

'Doesn't look exactly honourable,' Vonn said, who had been sitting close by, silent as usual.

'Honourable's for bairns' bedtime tales,' Quinn said. 'Me, I'm all for winning and living.'

'My da used to say something similar,' Vonn said. 'I used to think he was wrong. That people were honourable, that good should stand against wrong.'

'And you're right to think so,' Marrock had said.

'Am I? I'm not so sure any more.'

They powered over a ridge and the ocean opened up before them, the trail they were following winding down a lush green slope. They were upon the crest of a hill, beneath them a sharp rocky drop leading to a quay that jutted out into the water, a larger ship moored to it.

Our ship. Our safety.

The road they were on wound down the slope, curling away from the quay and then looping back, turning to sand as it spilt onto a narrow strip of beach. A few huts were scattered about, nets hanging along the beach, ridges in the sand where fisher-boats had been beached. They rode onto the beach, sand and surf spraying, and after a last gallop were finally at the quay, a milling chaos of people dismounting, pulling provisions from saddles, climbing narrow wooden stairs to reach the quay.

Camlin shouldered a bag, mostly full of arrows, his bow gripped in his other hand, and then he was running along the quay, past Halion, who stood rearguard by the stairs, sword in hand, eyes fixed on the approach to the beach. Half a dozen warriors stood with him, the rest hastening to the ship. Waves churned beneath the timber boards as Camlin ran fast, the waiting vessel further along than he'd realized, fifty, sixty paces.

Roisin had already boarded, holding her hands out for Lorcan. Edana was aboard, Vonn and Marrock beside her. Marrock saw Camlin and waved him on. Quinn stood close to Lorcan on the quay, waiting his turn to climb aboard. Other warriors were milling about, only a few being able to board at a time. To Camlin's eye there was no way they were all going to fit on this ship; there were just too many of them.

Then a cry was rising up behind them, a warning.

Camlin looked back and saw a row of dark silhouettes lining the slope above the quay, more and more swelling the line as every moment passed. One of them kicked his horse closer, moving to the edge of the slope, stones skittering down to rattle on the quay.

Conall.

'Give the boy up,' he yelled.

'Never,' screeched Roisin.

'Give up the boy and Eremon's bitch, and I will grant you pardon. More – I'll reward you. I'm regent of Domhain now, and I have power and riches to spare. You'll not have this chance again. Join me now, or I'm coming down there to kill every last one of you.'

A buzz of muttering spread through the warriors massed on the quay. That bothered Camlin – if he could work out that the ship was too small to take them all, then so could others. Men faced with being left behind and dying made rash choices. Roisin screamed for Lorcan to board the ship. Camlin took a few steps away from the crowd, back towards the beach. He saw a figure climb the stairs on the quay and step into Conall's view.

Halion.

Conall saw him. The colour drained from his face.

'I thought you were dead, Con,' Halion called up to him.

'Me? I'm hard to kill, you should know that.'

'What are you doing, Con?' Halion said.

'What we should have done together, years ago. I'm righting the wrongs of our father, and of that murdering bitch.' He jabbed a finger towards Roisin. 'The question is what are you doing, Hal? Protecting her and her spawn, when our mam died because of them, and we've lived a life on the run longer than I can remember because of them. Join me; together we can have our vengeance and rule Domhain into the bargain.' He grinned. 'A good day's work, if you ask me.' He held a hand out to his brother, his eyes pleading.

Camlin froze, waiting on Halion's answer. It felt as if everyone was doing the same; even the wind and waves were momentarily calm.

'I swore an oath to Brenin. I'll not be breaking it, Con. Not for you, not for anyone. But you don't have to do this. Just let us go. We'll sail away, never to trouble you again. For Elyon's sake, man, they're women and children.'

'That's not going to happen, Hal. You're either with me or against me.'

'Then I'm against you,' Halion said and raised his sword.

Conall snarled and yanked on his reins. He rode away, following the trail towards the entrance to the beach, his warband moving behind him.

Shouts and screams rang out behind Camlin, close to the ship. He turned to see Quinn surrounded by a knot of warriors pushing back along the quay, towards the beach. Quinn was carrying Lorcan over his shoulder, the lad flopping senseless. Roisin was screaming, trying to climb from the ship, hands pulling her back. Weapons were drawn, clashing. Camlin saw Baird chop one man down, then set upon another. He glimpsed Marrock leaping from the ship's rails back onto the quay. Quinn was running now, away from the main huddle of bodies, four or five warriors with him, another score at least forming a crude barrier holding Marrock, Baird and his men at bay.

Camlin reached for an arrow, nocked it, let fly; one of the warriors with Quinn staggered and fell, rolling off the quay into the churning sea. He fired again, another man dropping to the ground.

Then Halion and the men with him were mixed with them, iron sparking. Quinn dropped Lorcan, drawing both sword and knife. Camlin saw him open a wound on a warrior's bicep. Their weapons clashed again in a long flurry of blows, then the man was staggering away, legs unsteady, as if he were drunk.

Poison on Quinn's blade.

Quinn stepped after him and with a slash of his sword opened the man's guts.

Camlin shouldered his bow and ran, drawing his sword.

In slow motion he saw Halion step in front of Quinn. Camlin opened his mouth to scream, to warn Halion of the poisoned blades, but then they were at each other, the harsh ring of iron drowning out all other sound. There was a succession of blows, Halion shuffling forwards, then Quinn's knife was spinning through the air, landing with a *thunk* in the wooden boards, just a few handspans from Lorcan's prostrate body.

Camlin was closer now, twenty paces, fifteen. He hurdled over Lorcan, part of him noticing that the lad was still breathing. Ten paces. He saw Halion duck a sword swing, step in close and smash his sword hilt into Quinn's mouth, blood and teeth spraying. Quinn staggered back, arms flailing, then the tip of Halion's sword exploded through his back, blood showering Camlin as he reached them.

Halion ripped his blade free and Quinn sank to his knees, then toppled forwards onto his face.

Relief swept Camlin and he called to Halion. 'Come on, time to leave.'

Then he saw the red gash across Halion's shoulder.

CYWEN

Cywen dismounted from Shield and was almost dragged into the chamber behind Alcyon.

At first she could not understand what was going on; images were swarming her in a fragmented rush. The chamber was vast, at its centre a stepped dais – a cauldron hulking upon it. It seemed to pulse, somehow, a black halo radiating from it. And all around were giants, horses, men, all clashing, with blood streaming in great crimson arcs. But there was more, something else, another presence in the room. Huge coils rippled around the floor, grey skinned like a corpse, but scaled. Then Cywen saw one rear up, a massive flat-snouted face, small eyes, a flickering tongue. Teeth – huge, long, curved.

Wyrms.

Even as Cywen stared with a mixture of fascination and revulsion, the serpent lunged forwards, its jaws simply engulfing a warrior's head and shoulders, with a contraction of its coiled muscles tearing him from his saddle and slamming him to the ground. Then in great muscular ripples it started to swallow him. She felt her stomach lurch and vomited.

The wyrms were everywhere, quartering the floor with their undulating movements. She saw three of them attacking Nathair's draig – one the draig had managed to pin down with a taloned claw and was biting great chunks out of the snake's head and torso. Two others were striking at it, though, one's teeth fastened at the top of the draig's rear leg, the other twisting about a foreleg, great loops of its body swirling under the draig's neck, trying to get purchase. Nathair was hacking at that one with his longsword, cutting red gouges into its flesh. Somehow it managed to loop its tail around the draig's neck, and with one fluid move contracted, pulling the neck and foreleg sharply together. The draig roared and toppled over, Nathair's arms flailing.

The serpent's head reared up now, pulling back to strike, then Calidus was there, his sword slashing in great two-handed blows. The snake's head flopped, almost severed, only a fragment of flesh connecting it to its body. With a crash it fell to the ground, its grip about the draig loosening. The draig scrambled back up, turning to grip the body of the wyrm still latched to its back leg. The draig's jaws dragged it from the ground and Nathair chopped into it, Calidus joining him, and together in a flurry of blows they cut the wyrm in two. The draig moved on, the decapitated wyrm's teeth still sunk into its hindquarters, its neck dragging on the ground, leaving a red trail.

Cywen watched transfixed. Then she was hurtling through the air as Alcyon barrelled forwards, ducking under a snake's striking head. He managed to regain his balance, swinging his axe to chop into the snake's skull. Its body rippled in a death spasm and it collapsed. Alcyon wrenched his axe free.

Cywen staggered to her feet, only to see a blur of movement; instinctively she ducked, a wyrm's jaws snapping shut where her head had just been. Its body slithered forwards, colliding with her, hurling her through the air, only for the rope about her to pull tight and stop her flight dead. She dropped to the ground with a thud, felt the snake's torso brush against her, one great coil looping about her, pinning her arms to her side. Then it squeezed. She heard her bones creaking, felt every last drop of air expelled from her lungs in one great rush as the beast heaved her upright. She saw its long curved fangs, smaller teeth rowed inside its mouth as its jaws opened wide. There was a wild neighing behind her and a horse's hooves were lashing over her head, slamming into the snake's head.

The snake shook its head, like a man in the pugil ring recovering from a heavy blow, then fixed its eyes on Shield, who was standing beside Cywen, nostrils flaring.

Get out, Shield, run; run away, as fast and far as you can. Black dots were floating in her vision. She saw the snake's head pull back for another strike, this time angled at Shield; then its head exploded, an axe chopping into it. Blood, brains and bone splattered her, the coils about her collapsing heavily to the floor. She fell to her knees, dragging in heaving gulps of air, her throat burning like she was breathing in fire.

Alcyon lifted her up, frowning as he checked her over.

'Can you speak?' he asked her.

'Cut this blasted rope,' she croaked, her throat raw.

He grinned at her. 'You're fine.' He patted her shoulder with a big hand, nearly knocking her over again. 'You have a good horse there.'

The battle in the chamber was moving away, Nathair and the Jehar pushing steadily towards the dais where a handful of giants had gathered, intertwined with hissing serpents – a last stand. Cywen was shocked to see the giants and wyrms side by side; there was something about the way they were grouped together, bodies touching, weapons and teeth bristling outwards, as if they were allies, brothers-in-arms. What was so important about that cauldron that they were all willing to die protecting it?

With a roar that made the ground tremble the draig surged up the steps of the dais, sending one giant hurtling through the air, its claws raking a serpent's torso while its jaws clamped on another giant. Nathair slashed either side at wyrm and giant. Calidus and Sumur rode behind him, swords swinging in bloody arcs, hundreds of Jehar following their lead. Giants and wyrms surged forwards to meet them, bodies slamming into horses and riders, axes and hammers swinging in this last great defence of their guarded treasure.

Uthas was there, Salach his shieldman close by, attacking the last protectors of the cauldron. A giant saw Uthas. An expression of utter rage swept its face and it threw itself at Uthas, both of them falling to the ground, rolling down the steps, the other giant wrapping fingers around Uthas' throat.

They tumbled across the floor, grappling, then Salach was above them, his axe hovering. He hesitated in striking – the two giants were too closely locked – so he reversed his axe and struck down sharply; Uthas' attacker went limp. Uthas climbed to his feet, Salach helping him, his victim lay motionless on the ground.

'I am sorry, Morc,' Cywen heard Uthas say.

She suddenly realized that silence had fallen on the chamber. The battle was over.

The Jehar moved amongst the fallen, here and there stilling the twitching of a wyrm's tail or holding the hand of a wounded comrade or ending their pain with a sharp blade, speeding them on their journey across the bridge of swords. Nathair had dismounted from his draig and was now standing before the cauldron. It stood almost as tall as him, a squat, malignant presence. Nathair stared at it with a look of ecstasy upon his face. Calidus moved up beside him, reaching out a hand towards the cauldron. There was something hesitant in the gesture. As his fingertips touched the black metal a spasm passed through him. He stayed like that for a while, head bowed, hand pressed against the cauldron's belly. Then he turned, a sudden energy filling him.

'We will not delay. We will perform the ceremony now.'

'Is that wise? We are not secure here,' Nathair said.

'The cauldron is a weapon. Let us use it. We can open a gateway to the Otherworld right now.'

'Not alone. The other Treasures are needed for that to be possible,' said Uthas.

'We have the starstone axe,' Calidus said, pointing at Alcyon. 'The gateway will be narrow, but it will be enough.'

'A gateway for the Ben-Elim?' Nathair asked. He looked unsure, suddenly.

'Yes, the Ben-Elim. With a host of angels at your back the Dark Sun will soon be crushed. Victory will be certain.'

Nathair stared at him; a silence lengthened, then he gave a curt nod.

'Good. I need blood, from a heart that still beats.' Calidus' gaze swept the room.

Alcyon moved slightly, stepping in between Calidus and Cywen. She saw the giant's hand reach to his belt and draw a knife from its sheath, cutting the rope that bound them together. For a moment their eyes locked.

Someone groaned, the giant who had fought Uthas. He moved.

'He'll do,' Calidus said. 'Uthas, bring him to me.'

'Not him,' Uthas said.

'I need a sacrifice, now. It could be you, or your shieldman.' Calidus took a step towards Uthas, who stood frozen for a moment, then Cywen saw something crumble within him.

Uthas and Salach lifted the semi-conscious giant and carried him up the steps.

Cywen peered around the bulk of Alcyon, her curiosity getting the better of her.

Calidus slit the giant's throat.

'What are you doing?' Nathair cried.

'Throw him in,' Calidus ordered, ignoring Nathair. Uthas and Salach heaved the giant's body into the cauldron, blood pumping from its throat.

Calidus' voice rang out, loud and harsh.

'Fuil de beatha gen oscail an bealach, dorcha aingeal eiri feoil.'

Silence fell, heavier than the mountain about them. Calidus' voice rose again, more fiercely.

Cywen felt a vibration, a deep base hum, in her feet, spreading through her body. The pressure grew in her ears; she found it hard to draw breath, as though the air was being sucked from the room, and the cauldron blurred, the air around it growing dark, as if it were leaking night.

'Gather before the first born,' Calidus cried out, his voice almost shrill against the deep rumble that pulsed through the chamber. 'Welcome them to this world of flesh.' He gestured for the Jehar to step forwards, and uncertainly they approached the dais, hundreds of them, their numbers greatly reduced from the host of two thousand that had ridden through the gates of Murias.

Sumur stood with them, facing the cauldron, a look of rapt wonder on his face.

A darkness formed at the rim of the cauldron, overflowing as if a black liquid were boiling within. It streamed into the air, a dark roiling cloud, expanding before their eyes, churning, a lighting storm within it.

'Bow before the Ben-Elim,' Calidus said. Sumur fell to his knees, followed by the rest of the Jehar.

A shaft of darkness from the cloud lanced out, piercing Sumur's chest. His arms spread wide, his body convulsing. Other shafts, hundreds of them, simultaneously impaled the remaining Jehar, until every single one of them writhed transfixed upon a spear of darkness. They started to scream.

Cywen was terrified; a wave of crippling, all-consuming terror numbed her mind and filled her veins with ice. Beside her Shield whinnied and stamped the ground, his ears flat to his skull.

Cywen saw a flicker of movement, up and to her left. She blinked.

Is that a bird? A black smudge fluttered high in the chamber, on the edge of shadow. No – two black smudges. They circled, then plummeted straight down, swooping upon Uthas, their talons outstretched.

Their attack took Uthas by surprise. One crashed into his face, talons raking, the other gripped his back and pecked at his head. Uthas flailed wildly with his arms, a scream of shock and pain bursting from his lips. The birds rose higher, out of range, hovering, looking for an opportunity to plunge down again. Then Cywen heard it, a croaking torrent of speech flowing from one of them.

'*Betrayer,*' it squawked, time and time again.

MAQUIN

Maquin dropped his weapons to the ground. A hush fell upon the crowd, then they were yelling, hissing and booing. Maquin sat in the mud beside Orgull.

'I'm sorry,' he said. 'I cannot do it.'

Then Vin Thalun were running across the arena, big Emad ahead of them all, reaching him first.

'Get up, finish him,' the guard ordered.

Maquin just glared at him.

Emad aimed a kick at him; Maquin rolled to the side, came up on his feet, ducked a hook aimed at his jaw, slapped another kick away.

'Finish him,' Emad yelled. The crowd were roaring now, the sound deafening. Maquin's eyes flickered left and right, saw more Vin Thalun bearing down on him. A blow struck his chest – Emad, seeing his distraction. He collapsed to the ground, fighting for breath. Emad stood over him and drew a knife from his belt.

'Last chance,' the guard said. 'You live or die in the pit; you know that.'

'Go eat shit,' Maquin said.

Then Emad exploded.

A great tear in his flesh opened up from his shoulder to his belly, blood and bone showering Maquin. An axe-blade ripped clear of the wound as Emad collapsed. Orgull stood framed behind him.

He reached out a hand and Maquin took it, snatching up Emad's knife as he rose. Guards were descending on them now, more pouring from the tiers. Maquin glimpsed Lykos, his face contorted with rage.

'This end will do me just fine,' Maquin said, grinning at Orgull.

'Let's see how many we can take across the bridge with us.' He hefted his axe.

They stood back to back, braced for the rush. Maquin caught a man's wrist and punched his knife through leather into flesh, stabbed again, then threw the dying man backwards, tearing a sword from his weakened grip and snarling as another Vin Thalun filled his vision. He felt Orgull moving behind him, felt the whistle of the axe, heard the meaty sound of its blade cleaving muscle and bone, a scream cut short.

Then time fell into dissected moments – blocking a sword blow, stabbing, muscles stretching, hot breath in his face. He expected every next instant to be his last.

A sound filtered through his consciousness: a murmur, vast, surrounding him, like the sea when he had been a slave oarsman. Then louder as the crowd started shouting, not their usual cries for blood, but panicked, discordant, and behind it horn blasts, frantic, not celebratory. Then the clash of iron.

Fighting. They are fighting.

Abruptly there were no more Vin Thalun rushing at him. He saw his attackers running towards the arena's edge. Even as he watched, a section of bench crashed into the pit, smashing two Vin Thalun to the ground. Everywhere he looked was chaos, upheaval. In the stands men were fighting, all the way up to the tiered heights. Lower down, men in dark cloaks with white eagles on their breastplates were leaping the barriers, engaging the Vin Thalun warriors in battle.

Eagle-guard – some, at least.

But the Vin Thalun were not unprepared this time. Everywhere Maquin looked he saw more of the corsair warriors appearing, throwing off cloaks, pouring from the tunnels that led into the arena.

'This way,' a voice said in his ear – Orgull, tugging him. He followed the big man, saw he was limping, one arm pulled tight to his waist, as if staunching a wound. He was covered in blood, some of it his own.

They reached the cages where the pit-fighters were watching and Orgull raised his axe and swung it, the blade biting into a thick chain, sparks flying as it severed. The barred door swung open, Javed appeared in the doorway.

'My chest of gold,' Javed said.

'Better to take freedom than have it thrown to you as a scrap by your master,' Maquin said. He put an arm under Orgull and helped him stand.

Javed grinned and stepped out of the cage. A handful of others followed him.

Maquin scanned the crowd. Everywhere people were fighting. He glimpsed Lykos and Fidele, a huddle of men about them, trying to carve a way through the crowds to an exit.

'Won't get a chance like this again,' Maquin said and headed after them, breaking into a run.

As he powered through the crowd he hamstrung one Vin Thalun, hacked another's head, knifed one in the belly, shouldered others flying, then he was scrambling amongst the benches, almost upon Lykos' shieldmen.

Herak saw him first and turned, fluidly drawing a long curved knife. Maquin was trying to slow his momentum, skidding on the mud. He twisted his body, feet sliding forwards, torso dipping backwards. Herak's knife whistled through space, scoring a red line across the top of Maquin's chest.

They collided, Maquin's feet ploughing into Herak's, their bodies coming together, crashing to the ground in a grappling roll. Maquin's sword spun from his grip. He headbutted Herak, felt cartilage break, felt a knee crunching into his gut. Dimly above them Maquin was aware of the other pit-fighters appearing, slipping into combat with Lykos' shieldmen.

Pain focused him back onto Herak; the man was biting into his shoulder. With a curse, Maquin rammed his shoulder forward, forcing it into Herak's mouth, pushing his jaws apart. There was a momentary loosening of Herak's grip as the man gagged. Maquin twisted his torso and flipped over, spinning Herak, grabbed a handful of his hair and dragged his knife across the man's throat.

He rose fluidly, saw Javed kick a Vin Thalun's legs out from under him and stab him. Orgull was labouring against another. In a bound Maquin was at his side, punching his knife into the Vin Thalun's back. Orgull nodded a breathless thanks.

Maquin turned to see Lykos looming in his vision, Deinon at his side. He glimpsed Fidele behind, sat meekly, her hands folded across her lap. Then Lykos was at him. Their weapons clashed, Maquin's knife against Lykos' short sword, trading a flurry of blows. Maquin staggered back. There was a concentrated fury in Lykos' assault that was hard to contain. Lykos was still clutching something in his other hand. Deinon swept past him, Maquin knowing instinctively that he was headed for Orgull.

He launched into an attack of his own, the resentment and pain of the last few months focusing on the man in front of him. Lykos' advance was halted – he was shuffling back. Maquin stepped away, risked a glance to Orgull, saw his friend stumble over a bench and topple backwards, Deinon following. Javed appeared from nowhere, throwing himself at Deinon, the two of them tumbling into the benches.

Then Maquin was ducking, slashing, blocking as Lykos was at him again. The corsair King was quick, moving fluidly from one attack to another. Pain seared along one of Maquin's thighs, then across the opposite shoulder as Lykos managed to get past his defence.

I'd rather fight a giant than someone this fast. Mustn't give him space, or I'm a dead man. Maquin barrelled forwards, crashing through Lykos' guard, slashed, scoring a gash across Lykos' ribs, crouched and smashed a fist into the man's knee, rocking him, then stabbed at Lykos' throat.

The Vin Thalun wobbled, just managing to turn Maquin's blade as Maquin grabbed his sword wrist. Lykos gripped his forearm, whatever he'd been clinging to in his other hand fell to the floor and Maquin felt it crunch underfoot.

Just heartbeats later Fidele rushed at them, a look of utter hatred contorting her face.

Maquin flinched, thinking she was attacking him, but she crashed into Lykos, screaming incoherently at the Vin Thalun.

Thought this was her wedding day.

The three of them fell to the ground, weapons spinning away, Fidele's fingers tearing at Lykos' face, ripping bloody streaks across his cheeks.

'You control me no longer,' she spat at him.

Not a happy marriage, then.

Maquin scrabbled for a weapon, just as Fidele snatched his knife and plunged it into Lykos' back, below the ribs. Lykos was only wearing a silk shirt – *this is his wedding day* – and the knife sank to the hilt into his flesh. He screamed, an animal cry of pain, and sank to one knee.

Maquin shoved Fidele behind him, saw Lykos struggling to rise, Deinon standing over a motionless Javed while Orgull started to drag himself upright from behind a bench. Deinon stepped over Javed's body and sank his sword into Orgull's chest.

Maquin screamed a wordless howl, launching himself through the air and colliding with Deinon, his sword puncturing the Vin Thalun's back, its tip bursting out of the killer's chest. His friend was still breathing, his chest rising in short, ragged bursts. Blood and froth bubbled at his mouth. Maquin cradled his head.

'I'm sorry, my brother. I'm sorry, I was too slow.' Maquin's vision blurred, tears streaming down his cheeks, dripping from his nose.

Orgull's eyes fixed on him. His mouth moved but only a bubbling hiss came out. He reached for Maquin's hand and squeezed it, then gave out a long, fading breath.

Time dissolved for Maquin, becoming an arbitrary thing, moments or days passing – he did not know. He felt a hand on his shoulder pulling the world back into focus. Fidele.

The battle still raged around them, though it had moved further away. Lykos was nowhere to be seen, only a bloody handprint on the ground. Vin Thalun were everywhere, though, fighting the crowd, as well as warriors in the black and white of the eagle-guard here and there.

'Where is he?' Fidele gasped. Terror and loathing swept her face. 'He still lives,' she said.

'Aye, maybe.' She did not look as if she wanted to be found by Lykos. 'Best get you out of here,' Maquin said. He pulled on Orgull's axe and placed it on his friend's chest, fixing it in his grip.

'Take that across the bridge of swords with you. And walk tall, brother. You've earned it.'

Then he was leading Fidele by the hand, being swept by the crowd as they flowed towards the exits, out into the meadow. Once there, Maquin saw the extent of the uprising that was taking place. Nowhere was safe, battle spreading across the field. More Vin Thalun were pouring from the gates of Jerolin, others from the lake town, still more boats rowing towards shore from the ships on the lake. Maquin paused and sucked in a great lungful of air.

Free air. I am free, a slave no longer. The thought made him dizzy. He grinned fiercely, then turned and led Fidele away, the two of them heading towards the trees that bordered the meadow.

CAMLIN

Camlin stared at Halion, then at the red gash across his shoulder. A handful of warriors stood with them, men Rath had entrusted to escort Roisin and Lorcan.

Quinn's blade was poisoned. I saw what it did to the man he fought. At the very least it's going to put him on his back, and soon. At worst it may kill him.

'Get back to the ship,' Camlin said. They looked along the quay. Lorcan was sprawled unconscious where Quinn had dropped him; beyond the lad the last of Quinn's men were still fighting, separating Camlin from his comrades. He glimpsed Baird and Marrock. He heard his friend call his name.

The drumming of hooves grew. Conall and his men were reaching the beach, galloping hard, sand spraying.

'You go, Cam, get Lorcan back to the ship, take a few from here to finish Quinn's men. The rest of us will stay and hold Con a while, give you a chance to get away.' Halion looked at the men with him, each one nodding.

'Don't think I'll be leaving you in a fix like this,' Camlin said, reaching into his quiver and grabbing a fistful of arrows. One by one he stabbed them into the soft timber of the quay.

A tremor shook Halion and he swayed, resting his sword-point against the floor, leaning on it.

'Quinn's blade was poisoned; it may just have been a drug, a sedative that may pass. If not . . .' Camlin shrugged. 'Either way you're no good here – go back to the ship.'

'I'll not run from Conall. He'll never let me forget it.' Halion attempted a smile.

Camlin just stared at him.

'I need to look him in the eye,' Halion said. 'He's my brother, and there's good in him yet.'

'If there is he's buried it good 'n' deep.'

'I have to try.'

Camlin shrugged. 'You won't have long to wait.'

Conall was only a few hundred paces away now, galloping along the beach, at least a hundred warriors trailing behind him. Halion shuffled closer to the stairs that led down from the quay to the beach, the warriors with him spreading in a half-circle.

Only ten or twelve steps, but it's a good place to hold them, anyway. Camlin plucked an arrow from the timber, nocked it and drew it back to his ear.

Chop off the head, kill the body. He aimed for Conall's chest, held his breath and released.

Conall's horse dipped down a ridge in the sand, the arrow flying high, taking someone behind in the throat. The warrior was hurled backwards over his saddle in a spray of blood.

Damn.

Conall was less than two hundred paces away now, the sound of his approach drowning out the sea and sounds of battle along the quay. Camlin reached for another arrow, went through the same automatic ritual, centring the arrowhead on Conall's chest again, holding his breath, releasing.

This time Conall rode up a sandbank, the arrow sinking with a wet slap into his horse's chest. It screamed, reared and toppled backwards in an explosion of sand.

Hope it crushed him. Camlin reached for another arrow, drew it back, held his breath, released. This time it punched through a warrior's cuirass and flung him from his saddle. Then warriors were at the quay, yanking on reins, jumping from saddles, drawing swords, running at the steps. The first one climbing up got Halion's sword in the neck, a blow that almost severed the man's head. Halion put a boot on the man's shoulder and pushed, sending him flying back into those below.

Camlin fired an arrow into the milling warriors, drew and fired again.

It's like fish in a barrel.

Out of the corner of his eye he saw Halion sway, men either side of him reaching out to steady him.

He glanced back towards the ship, saw Marrock frantically fighting, trying to cut through the warriors that barred the way.

More men were climbing the stairs now, trying by force of numbers to push through. There was a lot of sword swinging and screaming, men or parts of men falling back into the crowd gathering at the bottom of the steps. Others were spreading either side, jumping to hang on the timber and pull themselves up. Halion's men chopped at fingers, stamped on hands.

Halion stabbed a man through the chest. The dead man toppled backwards, Halion pulling on his sword. For a moment his strength seemed to leave him and he stumbled, then fell off the quay. Some of his comrades leaped after him, hacking wildly. Camlin drew and fired, drew and fired, the consistency of his shots forcing warriors to retreat. Then he saw Halion, standing, swinging his sword in two-handed blows, a few men about him, fanning out from the steps. Others jumped down from the quay, until a group of five or six stood about Halion. Their attackers hung back, gathering their courage for a final rush, then Conall forced his way through them.

Third time lucky, thought Camlin, nocking another arrow and taking aim.

I've got you now.

A force slammed into Camlin's left shoulder, spinning him, sending his arrow skittering away. He staggered, almost fell, looked at his shoulder.

An arrow shaft protruded from it. As if brought on by the sight of it, pain suddenly bloomed, radiating outwards in great waves. He looked up, working out the direction of the arrow's flight. Up the slope before the quay, onto the hill. A figure stood at its top, part sliding down the slope, a bow in one hand.

Braith.

'Good t'see you, Cam, you traitorous runt.'

'Always knew you couldn't shoot an arrow worth a damn,' Camlin shouted.

'Be fair now – I'm sliding down a mountain.'

Camlin lifted an arrow and tried to draw his bow but pain spiked in his shoulder, black dots dancing before his eyes. He dropped his bow and drew his sword instead. Dimly he was aware of combat below him, on the sand. He shot a quick glance, saw Conall trading blows with one of Halion's men, Halion himself standing before the steps, hacking someone down.

Braith was halfway down now. Camlin was already moving forwards; he knew better than to let Braith get his balance, the best swordsman he'd seen in the Darkwood in a score of years, the man who'd bested Rhagor, battlechief of Ardan.

And now I'm crossing swords with him, and me with an arrow in my shoulder. Not the best odds.

Their swords met in a harsh percussion of blows, Braith pressing forwards, an overwhelming force, six blows, ten, twelve, his attack not faltering. Camlin retreated, pain shooting in spasms from his injured shoulder as he twisted and turned, using everything he knew to keep himself alive a few heartbeats longer. He tried to push forwards, get inside Braith's guard, but Braith just smiled at him – that knowing smile – stepped in to meet him and grabbed the arrow shaft in Camlin's shoulder, twisting it.

Camlin screamed, almost fainted, lost the grip on his sword and heard it clatter to the ground. Braith gave him a scornful shove, sending him stumbling backwards. A handspan from him was Lorcan, Roisin's lad. He groaned and stirred, his eyelids fluttering. Something else was between them, a knife, stuck in the timber.

Quinn's knife. Poisoned.

'Get up, Cam. At least die on your feet, not grovelling on your arse.'

With an act of will more than muscle Camlin lunged for the knife, grabbed its hilt, wrenched it from the timber and threw it at Braith, aimed straight at his heart.

The woodsman was quick, his sword moving on a reflex. Camlin heard the sound of metal connecting, the knife deflected.

It's over. He closed his eyes a moment, tried to struggle to his feet, but only got one knee under him.

Braith strode towards him, then Camlin saw the knife hilt sticking from the woodsman's shoulder.

'Take more'n that t'stop me,' Braith said. He gripped the knife and pulled it out, threw it into the sea, then levelled his sword at Camlin.

'Any last words?' Braith said.

'Rot in hell.'

'Told you to stick with me, didn't I, Cam?'

'You did. Told me a lot of other things, too, most of 'em lies.'

Braith paused, a ripple passing through his body.

It's affecting him already, quicker than Halion – because the wound was so deep? Halion's wound was only a scratch. Camlin climbed to his feet and took a step backwards.

'Not feeling so good?' he asked Braith.

'What?' Braith blinked and shook his head, his eyes becoming unfocused.

Camlin darted forwards, stooping to pick up his sword. Braith lunged at him, the blow going wide. Camlin struck at Braith then, but the woodsman seemed to rally, his eyes sharpening, and they traded blows, Camlin steadily retreating towards the steps. Even poisoned, Braith was a better swordsman than he was. They slammed in close, Braith scoring a gash along Camlin's ribs that burned like a line of fire. Camlin managed to punch Braith in the gut and step away, then Braith swayed again, his sword-point wavering. Camlin smashed his own sword down, knocking Braith's blade from his grip. The woodsman just stared at him, confused. Camlin swung hard, with all his strength, his blade biting into Braith's neck. There was a spray of blood and Braith toppled backwards, off the quay into the lapping waves below.

For a moment Camlin just stood there, not quite believing he was still alive. *Halion.*

He turned to see Halion on his knees, leaning on his sword.

How is he still conscious?

He was circled by a ring of the dead, beyond them a crowd of warriors. Conall stood before them.

'Give it up, Hal. You've lost.'

With an effort that set his limbs quivering, Halion climbed to his feet. Camlin could hear his laboured breathing.

'Come back to me, Con. Be the man you were – my brother. Not this oathbreaker, obsessed with what? Yourself? Revenge?'

Conall sneered. 'I was pathetic – your puppet. No longer. I've risen far without your help. Evnis was right: it was you who has always kept me down. Now get out of my way. I'm wanting a chat with young Lorcan.'

'Con, listen to yourself. I know you – you're better than this. Please . . .'

Conall hesitated, staring at Halion, a softness creeping into his eyes. He blinked, then a cold expression passed across his face. He took a step forwards and Halion raised his sword, the tip hovering in front of Conall's chest. Conall laughed.

'If you'll not see reason, Con, I'll have to stop you another way.'

'Don't be a fool, Hal. Look at you, you can hardly stand.'

'I'd rather stand and die than see you become the thing we've both hated.'

'Careful what you wish for, brother.'

Halion swung his blade; Conall, parrying, swept it away and down, Halion's sword-point digging into the sand. Halion staggered forwards a pace, then punched Conall in the face.

The warrior stumbled back, wiped blood from his mouth.

'I'll not warn you again, Hal. Get out of my way.'

Footsteps drummed behind Camlin, a handful of warriors running along the quay, Marrock at their head. *Quinn's men are all dead, then.*

Conall saw them too.

Halion staggered back against the steps, one hand reaching out to grip them, holding him upright.

'You'll not be climbing these stairs while I draw breath,' Halion said. 'I swore an oath.'

'This is madness. Out of my *way*.' Conall strode forwards and Halion swung his blade again. Conall blocked and lunged, punching his sword hilt into Halion's face.

Conall froze, looked shocked, surprised at what he had done.

Halion slumped to the ground, motionless before the steps.

'Get him out of my way,' Conall said.

Warriors rushed forwards and dragged Halion's body away, laying him out in the sand. Conall climbed the steps, others following.

'Help me.' Camlin heard a voice – Lorcan, trying to stand.

Camlin retrieved his bow and put an arm under Lorcan, helped him upright and together they staggered along the quay. Men reached them – Marrock and Baird.

'Halion?' Marrock hissed.

'Back there. Conall has him.' He saw the look in Marrock's eye. 'It's too late – there's no saving him. Too many of Conall's men.'

'Drop the boy,' a voice cried – Conall, powering along the quay.

'Get him out of here,' Marrock snarled, shoving Camlin into Baird's arms.

The scar-faced warrior grabbed Camlin and Lorcan and half dragged them back along the quay.

Boots thudded behind, warriors sprinting after them. Camlin heard the clash of weapons as he reached the ship; the boarding ramp was already pulled up. Baird hoisted the still-groggy Lorcan onto his shoulder and jumped across, then Camlin was being heaved over, Vonn grasping his arm and pulling him aboard.

A deep voice was shouting orders, poles pushing the ship away from the quay, oars splashing into the water and pulling.

'Halion? Where is Halion?' It was Edana, holding his face in her hands, almost yelling.

'Conall has him,' Camlin breathed.

Horror swept Edana's face. 'And Marrock? Where is Marrock?'

Camlin didn't answer, just stared back down the quay as the ship moved away. A crush of men was gathered a way back, shouts drifting across to the ship. A man screamed and toppled into the water.

Marrock held them off. Gave us time.

Then Conall was marching clear, dragging a man with him: Marrock, battered and bleeding.

'Give me Lorcan,' Conall yelled across the waves.

'Never,' Roisin screeched at him.

Conall pulled Marrock close, putting a knife blade to his throat.

'Edana, is that you, with your pretty fair hair? Bring me Lorcan. I'll trade you.'

Edana did not answer, but Camlin saw her eyes darting about the ship, weighing the odds.

Only me 'n' Vonn with you for sure, probably Baird and a few others loyal to Eremon. The rest by far are Roisin's men. Nearly two score of them. He saw by Edana's face that she'd come to the same conclusion.

'Last chance,' Conall yelled, his voice fainter. 'Marrock's your only kin. And I like him. Don't make me kill him.'

'Camlin, put an arrow in Conall's eye,' Edana hissed fiercely.

Camlin looked at the arrow shaft sprouting from his shoulder.

'I've a hole in my shoulder, can't draw a bow worth a damn.' He grimaced. *I'm sorry, Marrock. You've been a good friend to me. The first.* He glared balefully at Conall.

'This is on your head,' Conall cried. He drew his knife across Marrock's throat and let him topple into the waves.

Edana screamed.

CORBAN

Corban ran through the corridors of Murias, Fech and Craf flutter-ing ahead, staying just within sight.

They had encountered no one, the halls seemingly abandoned. *Everyone that lives in this place is fighting for it now.*

The stairwell they were climbing spilt out into a chamber, a single fire-pit flickering near its centre. Fech led them unerringly towards an archway on the far side. They were almost there when shouting broke out from behind. Corban spun around, saw giants appearing from another opening – a dozen, perhaps more. At their head stood a white-haired giant, blood caking his face. He held a war-hammer, the entirety of his muscled arms a swirl of tattooed thorns. He saw Corban and his companions and bellowed a battle-cry, his comrades echoing him. They began running towards them.

The Jehar drew their swords, Tukul taking the lead, moving to meet the attack, holding his sword in one hand, axe in the other.

Brina stepped into Corban's vision, holding a sword in her hand, long and thin.

Where did she get that?

Corban heard her muttering, the words sounding strange and guttural, then the blade of her sword burst into flame. She winked at Corban.

The giants eyed her warily.

Then Meical was in front of him, standing between the two groups.

'I know you, Balur One-Eye,' Meical said.

Balur One-Eye. Even I have heard of him, thought Corban.

'Balur One-Eye,' Dath whispered. 'He's ancient. Even older than Brina.'

'I heard that,' Brina snapped.

The giant's strides faltered as he stared at Meical. He took another few hesitant steps.

'That was a long time ago,' the giant said.

'It was. The time of fire and water.'

'Aye. And why are you here now? Fighting alongside the Dark Sun. Have you Fallen?'

'No. I made my choice. The Dark Sun has a captive, someone dear to us. Dear to the Bright Star.' Meical pointed at Corban.

I wish he wouldn't do that.

Balur and the other giants peered at him.

'He has my sister. I mean to take her back,' Corban heard himself say.

'We are not your enemy,' Meical said.

'*Hurry, hurry, hurry,*' Fech squawked. Balur stared at the bird.

'Fech?' He shook his head.

'He is taking us to the cauldron. That is where Nathair will be, the Black Sun,' Meical said.

'And these others?' Balur asked, looking suspiciously at the Jehar. 'We have just fought their kin in the great hall.'

'It's complicated,' Tukul said, 'and time does not allow its full telling. The short version is that the ones you have fought have been deceived.'

'Join us,' Meical said. 'If we wanted you dead we would be killing you now.'

The giants bristled at that.

True, but not very tactful.

Slowly Balur nodded. 'We shall join you. But you go first.' He smiled.

'Agreed. Lead on, Fech.'

Then they were running through corridors again. Slowly Corban became aware of a sound, a deep humming, more a feeling than a sound, vibrating up through his feet, out of the rock walls about him. It grew until it was all he could hear, filling his senses.

'*We are here,*' Fech said.

The doorway was wide, like everything in this underground stronghold, room for a score of them to stand across.

It took a few heartbeats for his eyes to adjust, the light in the room lurching from shades of darkness to bursts of incandescent light, leaving after-images seared into his mind. Slowly the scene before him coalesced into a wholeness. First he saw the bodies. They were everywhere, men, horses, giants – *wyrms*. Most of them had been hacked to pieces.

In the centre of the room stood a cauldron. It was elevated, sitting high upon a dais. Above it hovered a black roiling cloud, bolts of darkness radiating from it, joined to people, hundreds of people, kneeling on the ground before the cauldron.

The Jehar.

They didn't appear to be enjoying the sensation. Most were writhing, groaning, arms outstretched. And it looked as if something was pulsing through the dark columns, like when a snake swallows an egg, but faster, moving from the cloud into the bodies of the Jehar.

'No,' Meical hissed.

Corban hardly heard. Upon the dais he saw two men, one old, silver-haired, a look of rapt awe upon his face. The other he recognized. Nathair, the slayer of his da. He was staring at the cauldron, something close to shock on his face. Corban closed his eyes, for an instant was back in the feast-hall of Dun Carreg watching Nathair stab his da through the heart.

I told him I will kill him.

He scanned the room. Then he saw her. *Cywen.* She was standing to the left, between Corban and the kneeling Jehar. Next to her a horse stood, pawing the ground.

Shield. It is Shield.

He forgot about Nathair, the sight of his sister filling him with hope, and a great fear. *So close, we have come so close. Dear All-Father, do not let us fail now.*

He felt a hand grip his arm, squeezing. His mam. She was grinning, tears streaming down her cheeks.

'What do we do?' Corban whispered to Meical.

Then there was squawking, yelling, shouting; a giant that Corban hadn't noticed was waving his arms in the air as Fech and Craf attacked him.

'Uthas,' Balur growled from behind him.

Without thinking, Corban ran into the chamber, veering left, heading straight for Cywen.

He heard footsteps next to him, glanced to see his mam, her face determined, gripping her spear in one hand, a knife in the other. Storm and Buddai flanked them, overtaking, bounding low and silent towards Cywen. Somehow he knew that behind him others were following.

Someone passed him, taking great bounding strides – Balur, fixed on Uthas.

The giant in front of Cywen turned then. He saw them all pouring into the chamber, his eyes widening, and lifted an axe before him, its blades a black metal that seemed to shimmer and pulse, like the cauldron.

'Balur – he has the starstone axe,' Meical called from behind him. The giant shifted his course slightly, barrelling straight at the axe-wielder. Other giants were close behind him.

The one with the axe bellowed, shoving Cywen to one side and swinging his axe above his head. Cywen flew through the air, hit the ground and rolled, coming up to stare back at the giant. She hadn't seen Corban or her mam. Shield had, though. The stallion clattered over to Corban, swung his head into him and almost knocked him from his feet.

'It's good to see you too,' Corban said, patting his neck.

'Get the axe,' Meical was yelling. 'It will break the spell.'

One of Balur's kin reached the axe-wielding giant – a female. She lifted a war-hammer to block the axe as it came swinging towards her head. Sparks exploded as the dark blade sliced through the thick handle, carrying on to crunch into the giant's face and upper chest. She collapsed in a boneless heap, the axe-wielder ripping his weapon free, turning to face the next attacker.

It was Balur.

He ducked the axe, blades hissing over his head, slammed his hammer into the giant's gut, doubling him over, then swung the hammer-head up, catching his foe full in the face. The blow lifted him from the ground, hurled him backwards, where he crashed to the ground and slid into the corpse of a wyrm. He did not move.

Balur rushed after him and grabbed the black axe, looking back to Meical.

'Get it out of here, as far away as you can. That will break the spell.'

Balur didn't need telling twice. He ran for the doorway, disappearing amongst those coming the other way.

Cywen jumped up and ran. Away from Corban, back towards the giant that had thrown her. She crouched down beside his still form, a hand reaching out to probe his neck.

She's checking for a pulse.

Then Buddai and Storm reached her. Corban saw her throw her arms around Buddai, then tense as she saw Storm, her first reaction to leap backwards. Then she must have realized. She tentatively reached out to Storm, the wolven sniffing her hand, pushing close to lick her face and rub against her, knocking her over. Cywen leaped to her feet, looked around, and saw him and his mam.

CYWEN

I must be dreaming.

Figures were pouring into the chamber, swift and silent, any sound of their movement masked by the throbbing hum emanating from the cauldron. At their head were a man and woman. She stared at them, knowing them instantly, despite the changes. Older, leaner, a grimness about them, in their eyes. And a joy as well.

Mam. Corban.

She felt her heart lurch, as if a fist had grabbed and twisted it.

Then she was running to them and they were together, the three of them, hugging, crying, no words, just a deep heart-swelling euphoria.

Her mam was holding her face, kissing her. 'I'm sorry,' she was saying, over and over again.

'You left me,' Cywen said, remembering in a flood how she'd woken up in Dun Carreg, finding herself alone and abandoned, and all she had been through since then. A swell of fresh emotion welled up in her. 'You left me,' she repeated.

'We thought you were dead; we were told you were dead,' her mam said. Corban just looked at her with his sad, tear-filled eyes.

'Why are you here?' Cywen asked then.

'For you, Cy. We came to get you,' Corban said.

She felt hot tears flood her eyes again at that and she hugged them both, so tight, squeezing as if she'd never let them go.

'No!' a voice screamed, shrill above the deep reverberations.

Cywen looked up and saw Calidus close to the cauldron. His eyes were wide, rage twisting his features.

Something was changing in the room; the throbbing hum was

dying. The black lances of non-light were shrinking, folding back upon themselves towards the cloud above the cauldron. The cloud boiled, expanding then contracting, streaks of lightning sparking inside it. Then with an ear-splitting crack it burst apart, shreds of dark vapour exploding outwards, slamming those about it onto their backs. The constant droning hum was gone, replaced with a sudden silence, leaving an emptiness falling in its place. The sense of fear that she had felt earlier returned.

Something bad is about to happen.

'We need to get out of here,' Cywen said.

CHAPTER ONE HUNDRED AND NINETEEN

CORBAN

Corban gazed at Cywen's face a moment longer, saw emotions sweeping her like ragged clouds across the moon.

We've done it. We've found you. It did not feel quite real.

Now we just have to get out of here. He looked away, saw that his friends and companions had formed a loose line before them. Gar was closest, Dath and Farrell and Coralen beside him.

Gar turned to Cywen and gently cupped her cheek, his smile gentle, surrounded by the dead.

'Time to get you out of here,' he said.

'That's the best idea I've heard all day,' Dath hissed.

'Am I dreaming?' Cywen said through a grin, tears staining her cheeks.

A noise from deeper in the chamber drew all their eyes.

'It might be too late for leaving,' Farrell said.

Figures were rising, pulling themselves upright: the Jehar, those closest to the cauldron first. There was something different about them. Though they stood the same height and build there was a presence about them, as if their frames were filled with a new power, greater than the eye could comprehend.

One turned to face Corban and he heard Gar whisper a name.

'Sumur.'

The man stretched, a ripple that flowed from head to foot, like a cat. Something was wrong with his face. It was moving, as if insects were crawling under his skin, or fingers were clawing for escape. He gripped his clothing with both hands – a leather cuirass of boiled leather, beneath it a coat of mail, and tore it off as easily as Corban would tear a loaf of bread.

Others were rising about him, performing similar rituals.

The one called Sumur smiled as his hands travelled his body, fingers stroking, probing, the skin pale, translucent, dark veins threading it, pulsing. Then Corban saw his eyes: they were black, no iris, no pupil. Sumur threw his head back and howled.

The whole room filled with the sound as others joined him. Hundreds of them. Corban put his hands over his ears, trying to keep the sound out; it felt like a vapour, filling his senses, creeping into every part of him, drowning him in anguish.

Others were rising now, the Jehar on the outskirts of the room. They looked different to the first – ordinary, appearing dazed, wearing expressions of confusion. One close by looked at Gar and frowned.

'Garisan?' he said.

Gar stared at him.

'Akar?'

The Jehar drew his sword and took a step towards Gar. 'I'm guessing you still follow your mad fool of a father.'

'Who's the mad fool? Look who *you've* followed.'

Akar paused and glanced towards the cauldron, saw his sword-brothers and sisters transformed. Colour drained from his face.

'You've become the servants of the Black Sun.'

'No, it cannot be . . .'

'Out of here, now,' a voice shouted. Meical. He was standing, sword in hand, staring at the thing that had once been Sumur. About the creature more of its kind turned to face Meical.

Then they began to run. They moved awkwardly at first, lurching across the floor, quickly becoming smoother, like newborn animals, the process condensed into a few heartbeats.

Other Jehar were in their way. The first one that Sumur met was sent spinning through the air. At the second one Sumur slowed for an instant, lifting the man from the ground with a strength that did not seem even closely approximate to a man's capabilities. With a savage wrench, a cracking and tearing sound, Sumur tore the man in two. Blood and gore drenched him and he hurled the two parts of the man in separate directions.

'They are demon possessed!' Meical yelled. 'The Kadoshim are amongst you.'

639

That seemed to break the spell that Sumur's grisly act had cast. All about, the untainted Jehar drew their swords, joined by Tukul and his company, uniting to face this new enemy.

Corban saw Tukul grin.

This is a fight they've waited for all their lives.

The two sides met, a thunderclap of sound, the Kadoshim powerhouses of destruction, the Jehar swirling about them in their skilful dance of death. Corban saw Tukul chop into ribs with his axe, in the same breath drive his sword into the creature's chest, straight through its heart. It sagged a moment, shuddered, then backhanded Tukul, sending him spinning through the air. Corban stared open mouthed as the creature pulled the sword from its chest and tossed it away.

They cannot die.

A roar filled the room, echoing, and Corban saw a draig from faery tales stamping into the fray.

We cannot win this battle. We must get out.

He spun to look at his mam and Cywen, his friends about them.

'Out,' he said.

Then something crashed into them, sending them flying in different directions.

Corban rolled, staggered back to his feet. One of the Kadoshim had fallen into them, surrounded by a handful of Jehar, chopping, slicing, stabbing, then spinning away. It had a dozen wounds, all leaking blood, though even that was different. It was dark and thick, as if part congealed. And it was angry: enraged, lashing out, trying to catch the swift forms about it. Lifting its head, it bellowed, flailing its arms, a fist striking one of the Jehar, hurling him from his feet.

An arrow sank into its chest, making it stagger.

Dath. He was standing a dozen paces behind Corban, drawing another arrow to his ear, letting fly. It hit the possessed Jehar in the throat. It grabbed the shaft and tore it out.

Corban saw Farrell and Coralen attack it, Farrell smashing his hammer into its knee, Coralen darting in and sinking her wolven claws into its back. It just seemed to make it more angry, a white foam frothing from its jaws. Then Gar was there, his sword a blur, beside him Akar, the two of them working together now.

Corban snatched his sword from the ground, flexed his wolven claws and ran at the beast. As he did, he saw a flash of white to his side, Storm loping in close, then bounding away. With a burst of speed she hurled herself at the Kadoshim, slammed into his chest, jaws clamping around his head, teeth sinking deep. They both crashed to the ground. The creature writhed, great muscular spasms, Storm refusing to let go. Its hands sank into her fur, deeper, spots of blood welling about each finger. She whined, but still she would not let go.

Buddai appeared, bit into the creature's knee, shaking it.

Corban saw the creature's muscles standing taught, veins rigid. He screamed, remembering the man torn in two, and hurled himself forward, slashing wildly, hacking into its belly, its thigh.

Storm's body spasmed and she shook her head, violently. There was a popping sound, then a wet ripping and she staggered away, spitting the beast's head from her jaws.

Its body convulsed violently, feet kicking, arms flailing, blood leaking like oil from its neck. It stiffened, a black vapour boiling out from it, issuing from every pore, converging above the spasming body. It took shape, human-like, but with great leathery wings upon its back, glowing amber eyes like hot coals sweeping them. The mist figure screeched, a frustrated rage, then evaporated, melting into the air. The body on the ground collapsed, abruptly limp.

'So that's how you kill them,' said Farrell.

'Their heads,' Gar yelled. 'Take their heads.' The cry went up about them, spreading through the chamber.

'Ban, with me,' Gar said to him, then turned to Cywen and Gwenith, standing close together again. He pushed them towards the exit, calling to Farrell, Dath and Coralen. They all ran, Storm limping after them, Buddai beside her. Corban saw more of the mist figures appearing about the room, swirling in the air – only a few, here and there.

The Jehar are taking their heads. The shapes screeched their fury as they evaporated, banished back to the Otherworld after only brief moments in the world of flesh.

Corban and his companions wove through the battle, calling to comrades as they passed them, gathering them, rushing towards the archway and safety. He saw Brina, still wielding her flaming sword, stabbing it into the arm of a Kadoshim that was busily pulling the limbs from a Jehar warrior. Flames rushed from the blade, engulfing the Kadoshim. It dropped the remains of the warrior in its arms and stumbled away, shrieking, a torch of flesh.

The clash of arms grew in pitch behind him. He risked a glance back and saw a man appear from the crowd – tall and silver haired, a red sword in his hand. Shadows danced behind him, a dark cloak that floated like wings. His eyes fixed on Corban. One of the Jehar swirled in front of him, sword chopping downwards. With an effortless shrug the old man blocked the blow, his sword blurring in fluid movement and then the Jehar was falling away, blood spurting from his throat. The old man stalked forwards, straight towards Corban.

Run. I must run. But something held Corban in place, kept him from fleeing. Instead, he found himself turning, lifting his sword, flexing his wolven claws, shifting his balance to face this man.

Other Jehar attacked the old man, all sent reeling away, blood spurting.

Corban moved forwards, raising his sword. It felt as if time had slowed around him. One of the Kadoshim came roaring at him and he swerved out of its path, swung his sword two-handed and saw its head fly spinning through the air. The creature's body stumbled on, then crumpled to the floor, mist congealing into a winged form above it, quickly melting into ragged tatters.

Then they were standing before each other. The old man regarded him with amber eyes.

'Bright Star,' the man said, lifting his sword and dipping his head; a recognition.

'Who are you?' Corban said.

'Your death.'

Corban heard voices behind him, calling his name, then his blade was moving, blocking a blow that moved faster than he thought possible. He pushed his enemy's sword high, over his head, and stepped in fast, raking his wolven claws across the old man's belly. They sparked on chainmail, breaking links but nothing else. The old man smiled at him. Then Corban was retreating, their swords clashing, incandescent arcs tracing the flow of exchanges, a discordant melody of violence.

Corban stumbled and the man was on him, pushing his guard away, a hand gripping Corban by the throat, pulling him close.

'I knew you would come,' the man said. 'You pathetic creatures, risking all for love.'

Corban heaved a knee into the man's groin and his grip loosened. Corban staggered back, stumbling and falling onto his back. The old man followed, but something slammed into his shoulder, making him stagger back a pace. An arrow.

Dath.

Then Gar was leaping over Corban, standing before him, sword raised. The old man snarled at him, an annoyance, and launched into a blistering combination of blows, the arrow in his shoulder seeming to have little effect on him. Gar swerved to the left, trying to lead the old man away from Corban. He blocked a dozen blows, then stepped into an attack of his own; Corban heard their blades clash, six, seven times, more. When they separated, the old man was bleeding from a thin cut along his forehead; blood dripped from Gar's elbow.

The old man touched a hand to his wound, then licked his fingertips. With shocking speed he powered forwards. Gar took an overhead blow on his blade, his legs spread, braced against the force of the attack. For heartbeats both stood there, the old man looking as if he was trying to grind Gar into the ground, Gar standing like an oak in a storm. Then Farrell suddenly appeared, ploughing into them. They went down in a mass, rolling together. The old man rose first, Gar spinning free. Farrell clambered to one knee and the old man struck out, punching him in the chest, sending him crashing to the floor. Gar rushed in, but the old man kicked out, a boot connecting full with Gar's gut, hurling him away. The old man's eyes swung back to Corban.

Corban realized he was still on the ground. He staggered to his feet as the old man strode towards him. Their swords clashed, a brief flurry, then Corban was tripping over a body, dropping to one knee. The old man snarled, a victory grin, raising his sword. Abruptly he stopped, frowning, gazing at his chest. A knife hilt protruded from it. There was another impact and he reeled back a step, another knife hilt poking from his shoulder.

Mam.

She ran past Corban, spear levelled at the old man. Cywen and Coralen appeared either side of Corban, hooking arms under him and hoisting him to his feet.

'Very touching,' Corban heard the old man say.

Gwenith stood before him, her spear raised. She thrust with all her strength as the old man surged forwards, but he slashed once, splintering the spear shaft, then again, Corban hearing the sound of iron impacting on flesh, a solid blow. He stared at his mam, saw her sway, then she collapsed in front of him.

He screamed, yanking his arms free from Cywen and Coralen, but before he could charge at the old man another figure was there, Meical.

'Calidus,' Meical said.

'Meddler,' the old man responded, his lips twisted in sneer or snarl. They set at each other then, a concussive power in their blows that Corban had never witnessed before.

'Get Corban out of here,' Meical yelled just before he and his enemy disappeared amongst the crowd.

Corban scrambled over to his mam, Cywen at his shoulder, and together they lifted her. She cried out, eyes fluttering, spots of blood on her lips. And she was pale, deathly pale. A bloody wound stretched from shoulder to chest, chips of white bone amongst the bubbling blood.

'Mam,' Corban breathed, the word a sob.

Cywen was crying beside him.

Corban stroked his mam's face, tried to wipe the blood from her lips, but more kept appearing.

Her eyes were open, looking at them both. 'My darlings,' she whispered with her last breath.

Corban howled, a raw, feral thing as grief erupted inside him, an unending torrent. Dimly he was aware of Cywen sobbing beside him, gripping his mam's hand, as if she were trying to squeeze life back into her.

'Don't leave me; please Mam, please Mam,' he heard her saying, over and over.

He wrapped an arm around her and she hugged him back.

'Quickly,' a voice yelled, the sound of hooves suddenly loud. Corban felt hands tugging at him – Brina – saw Cywen hoisted by Farrell across Shield, Coralen sitting in his saddle, and then spurring away.

Gar bent down and lifted Gwenith in his arms, cradling her to his chest, tears streaming down his face. Then they were running towards the exit again, a crowd gathering about them. At the doorway Corban paused and looked back.

Battle was still raging between the Kadoshim and Jehar; many of the untainted warriors were forming a rearguard now, beginning a retreat. The cauldron was still visible upon its dais, a figure sitting on the steps close to it. Nathair. He was just watching the battle before him, a look of shock upon his face. Then others were pushing towards the exit, a knot of Jehar warriors sweeping him through the doors and away.

CORBAN

Everything passed in a blur to Corban as they hurtled through the shadowed corridors of Murias, the sounds of violence fading behind, people all around, the clatter of hooves ahead. Time drifted from its moorings, losing its meaning. Then Corban was in the chamber before Murias' great gates, the dead everywhere. The giant with the white hair was there – Balur – a handful of his kin with him, including a pale giantess who stared at him intensely, a cluster of giant bairns about her. They had gathered horses for them, found them wandering out on the slopes. Corban felt hands upon him, helping him into a saddle, thrusting reins into his hands. He was dimly aware of more people pouring into the chamber – he saw Tukul and Meical, more of the Jehar.

Then they were outside. It was close to highsun, the air fresh and clean after the stifling damp of the underground caverns.

Corban rode from Murias, a small host about him, thundering down the slope and onto purple moorland, scattered giants running amongst them. Two birds flew low in the air above.

For the moment they did not know where they were going, just away, spurring their horses to a gallop, the wind whipping Corban's face. Beside him rode Gar, his mam's body slumped upon the warrior's saddle. At a glance it seemed that she was siting up, leaning into Gar, asleep. The man was still weeping. Cywen rode close by, still sitting behind Coralen on Shield's back, her arms wrapped around Coralen's waist. Their gazes met, a grief shared.

Meical drew ahead and veered left, guiding them towards a line of hills that rolled eastwards. Corban looked down and saw Storm loping beside him, Buddai keeping pace. He bent forward over his mount's neck and gave himself to the rhythm of the gallop.

The sun was dipping towards the horizon, sending shadows lancing ahead of them when they stopped. They had reached the foothills that Meical had led them towards and travelled a league or so into their embrace. Corban could still see Murias behind him, a dark spike on the horizon. Birds swirled above it, a black halo.

Tukul organized the making of camp, setting guards who fanned out from their small host, others constructing a makeshift paddock beside a fast-flowing stream, while some set to digging a fire-pit. Corban looked about and saw they numbered in the hundreds: the Jehar who had travelled with him from Dun Vaner, plus the ones who had escaped the cauldron's grip – at least another two hundred warriors, probably more. And giants – over a dozen were gathered about Balur, who was holding the black axe he had taken in combat, showing it to his kin. The giantess looked along with the rest, as did the giant bairns, as many at least as the adults. Corban shook his head.

Gar slipped from his saddle, cradling Gwenith's body. He carried her to the stream's bank and laid her gently upon the grass. Corban followed and stood over his mam. Her eyes were closed, her skin pale, translucent as wax. Her wound ran from shoulder to chest, blood crusted black about it. Corban felt a presence at his shoulder, knew it was Cywen. The three of them stood in silence, gazing down at Gwenith. Storm sniffed her hand, let out a high-pitched whine and Buddai curled at her feet. Then Cywen scrambled down to the stream, soaked the hem of her cloak in the icy water and came back to dab her mam's face, washing the blood from her lips. Corban and Gar did the same, the three of them silently washing Gwenith, preparing her for burial. When she was wrapped in Corban's cloak they began to pull stones from the stream, piling them about Gwenith's body, building a cairn over her.

Time drifted, Corban slowly becoming aware that others were moving around him, helping to gather stones – first his friends, Dath, Coralen, Farrell, Brina, then others, Tukul and Meical amongst them. Last of all Balur joined them. He pulled a boulder the size of a child from the stream bed, and they set it at the head of Gwenith's cairn. When they were done, the host stood about the grave, heads bowed. There was a flapping in Corban's ear and Craf alighted on his shoulder, the crow's claws pinching.

'*Sad*,' the bird croaked.

'Yes,' Corban whispered. A tear rolled down his cheek, and he heard Cywen sniff beside him.

A silence fell, the sound of the stream and wind amongst the heather framing the moment.

A voice broke the silence – old and harsh against the quiet. Brina. Alone she sang the opening lines of the lament. Gar was the first to add his voice, others joining until the hills rang. Even Balur and the giants sang.

They are not just singing for my mam; they all mourn those they have lost.

Memories bubbled up inside Corban of his mam, a thousand tender moments, sealed with her dying words, blood spattering her lips. *My darlings*, she had said. Grief welled sudden and powerful, consuming him, blotting out everything but his mam's face. He felt an impact on his knees, realized dimly that he'd fallen, hands about him steadying, comforting. He let out a great sob, his body racked by it, tremors coursing through him, all the pain and torment that he had endured since the night of his da's death surging up in one overwhelming moment.

He did not know how long he stayed there, kneeling in the dirt before his mam's cairn. Eventually he looked up, swiping tears from his eyes. A few were still gathered about him – Cywen and Gar, their eyes red and raw. His friends, Dath and Farrell, Coralen regarding him with a rare compassion. He rose slowly and looked back across the leagues they had ridden, saw the last rays of the setting sun shining off the cliffs and towers of Murias, the image fracturing in his tear-filled eyes.

He thought of the cauldron, the black cloud rising from it, the tainted Jehar ripping men limb from limb, Nathair sitting on the dais steps, and finally the old man that he had fought, who had killed his mam. *Calidus, Meical had called him.* One thought circled in his head like the black birds swirling about the mountain peaks.

They must be stopped.

Acknowledgements

Writing *Valor* has been a great experience. As with *Malice* it has had quite a few helping hands along the way.

First of all a huge thank you to my wife, Caroline, and children, both for their support and for putting up with me whilst my head has been off in the Banished Lands.

Thanks must go to my agent, John Jarrold, for his belief and guidance. A consummate professional and also a top bloke who does a wonderful Michael Cain impersonation. Also my bloodthirsty editor at Tor UK, Julie Crisp, for her astounding ability to whip my efforts into shape, as well as a strong dose of belief in *The Faithful and the Fallen*. And thanks to my copy-editor, Jessica Cuthbert-Smith, a lady with an amazing eye for detail, as well as all the wonderful crew at Team Tor UK.

Thanks also to those who have taken the time to read *Valor* – not a small book – and thus sacrificing a considerable chunk of their precious time. Mark Roberson, Rhiannon Ivens, Sadak Miah – you are now forgiven for not reading *Malice* for such a long time – and Edward and William Gwynne, whom I would like to thank for their extra dedication, involving re-enacting most of the battle scenes from the book. Plasters were occasionally required.

extras

orbit

meet the author

Pan Macmillan.jpg

JOHN GWYNNE studied and lectured at Brighton University. He's been in a rock 'n' roll band, playing the double bass, traveled the USA, and lived in Canada for a time. He is married with four children and lives in Eastbourne, running a small family business rejuvenating vintage furniture. *Malice* was his debut novel.

introducing

If you enjoyed
VALOR,
look out for

THE BLACK PRISM

Lightbringer: Book 1

by Brent Weeks

*Gavin Guile is the Prism, the most powerful man in the world.
He is high priest and emperor, a man whose power, wit,
and charm are all that preserves a tenuous peace. But Prisms
never last, and Guile knows exactly how long he has left to live:
five years to achieve five impossible goals.*

*But when Guile discovers he has a son, born in a far kingdom
after the war that put him in power, he must decide how much
he's willing to pay to protect a secret that could tear his world apart.*

CHAPTER 1

Kip crawled toward the battlefield in the darkness, the mist pressing down, blotting out sound, scattering starlight. Though the adults shunned it and the children were forbidden to come here, he'd played on the open field a hundred times—during the day. Tonight, his purpose was grimmer.

Reaching the top of the hill, Kip stood and hiked up his pants.

The river behind him was hissing, or maybe that was the warriors beneath its surface, dead these sixteen years. He squared his shoulders, ignoring his imagination. The mists made him seem suspended, outside of time. But even if there was no evidence of it, the sun was coming. By the time it did, he had to get to the far side of the battlefield. Farther than he'd ever gone searching.

Even Ramir wouldn't come out here at night. Everyone knew Sundered Rock was haunted. But Ram didn't have to feed his family; *his* mother didn't smoke her wages.

Gripping his little belt knife tightly, Kip started walking. It wasn't just the unquiet dead that might pull him down to the evernight. A pack of giant javelinas had been seen roaming the night, tusks cruel, hooves sharp. They were good eating if you had a matchlock, iron nerves, and good aim, but since the Prisms' War had wiped out all the town's men, there weren't many people who braved death for a little bacon. Rekton was already a shell of what it had once been. The *alcaldesa* wasn't eager for any of her townspeople to throw their lives away. Besides, Kip didn't have a matchlock.

Nor were javelinas the only creatures that roamed the night. A mountain lion or a golden bear would also probably enjoy a well-marbled Kip.

A low howl cut the mist and the darkness hundreds of paces deeper into the battlefield. Kip froze. Oh, there were wolves too. How'd he forget wolves?

Another wolf answered, farther out. A haunting sound, the very voice of the wilderness. You couldn't help but freeze when you heard it. It was the kind of beauty that made you shit your pants.

Wetting his lips, Kip got moving. He had the distinct sensation of being followed. Stalked. He looked over his shoulder. There was nothing there. Of course. His mother always said he had too much imagination. Just walk, Kip. Places to be. Animals are more scared of you and all that. Besides, that was one of the tricks about a howl, it always sounded much closer than it really was. Those wolves were probably leagues away.

Before the Prisms' War, this had been excellent farmland. Right next to the Umber River, suitable for figs, grapes, pears, dewberries, asparagus—*everything* grew here. And it had been sixteen years since the final battle—a year before Kip was even born. But the plain was still torn and scarred. A few burnt timbers of old homes and barns poked out of the dirt. Deep furrows and craters remained from cannon shells. Filled now with swirling mist, those craters looked like lakes, tunnels, traps. Bottomless. Unfathomable.

Most of the magic used in the battle had dissolved sooner or later in the years of sun exposure, but here and there broken green luxin spears still glittered. Shards of solid yellow underfoot would cut through the toughest shoe leather.

Scavengers had long since taken all the valuable arms, mail, and luxin from the battlefield, but as the seasons passed and rains fell, more mysteries surfaced each year. That was what Kip was hoping for—and what he was seeking was most visible in the first rays of dawn.

The wolves stopped howling. Nothing was worse than hearing that chilling sound, but at least with the sound he knew where they were. Now...Kip swallowed on the hard knot in his throat.

As he walked in the valley of the shadow of two great unnatural hills—the remnant of two of the great funeral pyres where tens of thousands had burned—Kip saw something in the mist. His heart leapt into his throat. The curve of a mail cowl. A glint of eyes searching the darkness.

Then it was swallowed up in the roiling mists.

A ghost. Dear Orholam. Some spirit keeping watch at its grave.

Look on the bright side. Maybe wolves are scared of ghosts.

Kip realized he'd stopped walking, peering into the darkness. Move, fathead.

He moved, keeping low. He might be big, but he prided himself on being light on his feet. He tore his eyes away from the hill—still no sign of the ghost or man or whatever it was. He had that feeling again that he was being stalked. He looked back. Nothing.

A quick click, like someone dropping a small stone. And

something at the corner of his eye. Kip shot a look up the hill. A click, a spark, the striking of flint against steel.

The mists illuminated for that briefest moment, Kip saw few details. Not a ghost—a soldier striking a flint, trying to light a slow-match. It caught fire, casting a red glow on the soldier's face, making his eyes seem to glow. He affixed the slow-match to the match-holder of his matchlock and spun, looking for targets in the darkness.

His night vision must have been ruined by staring at the brief flame on his match, now a smoldering red ember, because his eyes passed right over Kip.

The soldier turned again, sharply, paranoid. "The hell am I supposed to see out here, anyway? Swivin' wolves."

Very, very carefully, Kip started walking away. He had to get deeper into the mist and darkness before the soldier's night vision recovered, but if he made noise, the man might fire blindly. Kip walked on his toes, silently, his back itching, sure that a lead ball was going to tear through him at any moment.

But he made it. A hundred paces, more, and no one yelled. No shot cracked the night. Farther. Two hundred paces more, and he saw light off to his left, a campfire. It had burned so low it was barely more than coals now. Kip tried not to look directly at it to save his vision. There was no tent, no bedrolls nearby, just the fire.

Kip tried Master Danavis's trick for seeing in darkness. He let his focus relax and tried to view things from the periphery of his vision. Nothing but an irregularity, perhaps. He moved closer.

Two men lay on the cold ground. One was a soldier. Kip had seen his mother unconscious plenty of times; he knew instantly this man wasn't passed out. He was sprawled unnaturally, there were no blankets, and his mouth hung open, slack-jawed, eyes staring unblinking at the night. Next to the dead soldier lay another man, bound in chains but alive. He lay on his side, hands manacled behind his back, a black bag over his head and cinched tight around his neck.

The prisoner was alive, trembling. No, weeping. Kip looked around; there was no one else in sight.

"Why don't you just finish it, damn you?" the prisoner said.

Kip froze. He thought he'd approached silently.

"Coward," the prisoner said. "Just following your orders, I suppose? Orholam will smite you for what you're about to do to that little town."

Kip had no idea what the man was talking about.

Apparently his silence spoke for him.

"You're not one of them." A note of hope entered the prisoner's voice. "Please, help me!"

Kip stepped forward. The man was suffering. Then he stopped. Looked at the dead soldier. The front of the soldier's shirt was soaked with blood. Had this prisoner killed him? How?

"Please, leave me chained if you must. But please, I don't want to die in darkness."

Kip stayed back, though it felt cruel. "You killed him?"

"I'm supposed to be executed at first light. I got away. He chased me down and got the bag over my head before he died. If dawn's close, his replacement is coming anytime now."

Kip still wasn't putting it together. No one in Rekton trusted the soldiers who came through, and the alcaldesa had told the town's young people to give any soldiers a wide berth for a while—apparently the new satrap Garadul had declared himself free of the Chromeria's control. Now he was King Garadul, he said, but he wanted the usual levies from the town's young people. The alcaldesa had told his representative that if he wasn't the satrap anymore, he didn't have the right to raise levies. King or satrap, Garadul couldn't be happy with that, but Rekton was too small to bother with. Still, it would be wise to avoid his soldiers until this all blew over.

On the other hand, just because Rekton wasn't getting along with the satrap right now didn't make this man Kip's friend.

"So you *are* a criminal?" Kip asked.

"Of six shades to Sun Day," the man said. The hope leaked out of his voice. "Look, boy—you are a child, aren't you? You sound like one. I'm going to die today. I can't get away. Truth to tell, I don't want to. I've run enough. This time, I fight."

"I don't understand."

"You will. Take off my hood."

Though some vague doubt nagged Kip, he untied the half-knot around the man's neck and pulled off the hood.

At first, Kip had no idea what the prisoner was talking about. The man sat up, arms still bound behind his back. He was perhaps thirty years old, Tyrean like Kip but with a lighter complexion, his hair wavy rather than kinky, his limbs thin and muscular. Then Kip saw his eyes.

Men and women who could harness light and make luxin—drafters—always had unusual eyes. A little residue of whatever color they drafted ended up in their eyes. Over the course of their life, it would stain the entire iris red, or blue, or whatever their color was. The prisoner was a green drafter—or had been. Instead of the green being bound in a halo within the iris, it was shattered like crockery smashed to the floor. Little green fragments glowed even in the whites of his eyes. Kip gasped and shrank back.

"Please!" the man said. "Please, the madness isn't on me. I won't hurt you."

"You're a color wight."

"And now you know why I ran away from the Chromeria," the man said.

Because the Chromeria put down color wights like a farmer put down a beloved, rabid dog.

Kip was on the verge of bolting, but the man wasn't making any threatening moves. And besides, it was still dark. Even color wights needed light to draft. The mist did seem lighter, though, gray beginning to touch the horizon. It was crazy to talk to a madman, but maybe it wasn't too crazy. At least until dawn.

The color wight was looking at Kip oddly. "Blue eyes." He laughed.

Kip scowled. He hated his blue eyes. It was one thing when a foreigner like Master Danavis had blue eyes. They looked fine on him. Kip looked freakish.

"What's your name?" the color wight asked.

Kip swallowed, thinking he should probably run away.

"Oh, for Orholam's sake, you think I'm going to hex you with your name? How ignorant is this backwater? That isn't how chromaturgy works—"

"Kip."

The color wight grinned. "Kip. Well, Kip, have you ever wondered why you were stuck in such a small life? Have you ever gotten the feeling, Kip, that you're special?"

Kip said nothing. Yes, and yes.

"Do you know *why* you feel destined for something greater?"

"Why?" Kip asked, quiet, hopeful.

"Because you're an arrogant little shit." The color wight laughed.

Kip shouldn't have been taken off guard. His mother had said worse. Still, it took him a moment. A small failure. "Burn in hell, coward," he said. "You're not even good at running away. Caught by ironfoot soldiers."

The color wight laughed louder. "Oh, they didn't *catch* me. They recruited me."

Who would recruit madmen to join them? "They didn't know you were a—"

"Oh, they knew."

Dread like a weight dropped into Kip's stomach. "You said something about my town. Before. What are they planning to do?"

"You know, Orholam's got a sense of humor. Never realized that till now. Orphan, aren't you?"

"No. I've got a mother," Kip said. He instantly regretted giving the color wight even that much.

"Would you believe me if I told you there's a prophecy about you?"

"It wasn't funny the first time," Kip said. "What's going to happen to my town?" Dawn was coming, and Kip wasn't going to stick around. Not only would the guard's replacement come then, but Kip had no idea what the wight would do once he had light.

"You know," the wight said, "you're the reason I'm here. Not here here. Not like 'Why do I exist?' Not in Tyrea. In chains, I mean."

"What?" Kip asked.

"There's power in madness, Kip. Of course..." He trailed off, laughed at a private thought. Recovered. "Look, that soldier has a key in his breast pocket. I couldn't get it out, not with—" He shook his hands, bound and manacled behind his back.

"And I would help you why?" Kip asked.

"For a few straight answers before dawn."

Crazy, and cunning. *Perfect.* "Give me one first," Kip said.

"Shoot."

"What's the plan for Rekton?"

"Fire."

"What?" Kip asked.

"Sorry, you said one answer."

"That was no answer!"

"They're going to wipe out your village. Make an example so no one else defies King Garadul. Other villages defied the king too, of course. His rebellion against the Chromeria isn't popular everywhere. For every town burning to take vengeance on the Prism, there's another that wants nothing to do with war. Your village was chosen specially. Anyway, I had a little spasm of conscience and objected. Words were exchanged. I punched my superior. Not totally my fault. They know us greens don't do rules and hierarchy. Especially not once we've broken the halo." The color wight shrugged. "There, straight. I think that deserves the key, don't you?"

It was too much information to soak up at once—broken the halo?—but it *was* a straight answer. Kip walked over to the dead man. His skin was pallid in the rising light. Pull it together, Kip. Ask whatever you need to ask.

Kip could tell that dawn was coming. Eerie shapes were emerging from the night. The great twin looming masses of Sundered Rock itself were visible mostly as a place where stars were blotted out of the sky.

What do I need to ask?

He was hesitating, not wanting to touch the dead man. He

knelt. "Why my town?" He poked through the dead man's pocket, careful not to touch skin. It was there, two keys.

"They think you have something that belongs to the king. I don't know what. I only picked up that much by eavesdropping."

"What would Rekton have that the king wants?" Kip asked.

"Not Rekton you. You you."

It took Kip a second. He touched his own chest. "Me? Me personally? I don't even own anything!"

The color wight gave a crazy grin, but Kip thought it was a pretense. "Tragic mistake, then. Their mistake, your tragedy."

"What, you think I'm lying?!" Kip asked. "You think I'd be out here scavenging luxin if I had any other choice?"

"I don't really care one way or the other. You going to bring that key over here, or do I need to ask real nice?"

It was a mistake to bring the keys over. Kip knew it. The color wight wasn't stable. He was dangerous. He'd admitted as much. But he had kept his word. How could Kip do less?

Kip unlocked the man's manacles, and then the padlock on the chains. He backed away carefully, as one would from a wild animal. The color wight pretended not to notice, simply rubbing his arms and stretching back and forth. He moved over to the guard and poked through his pockets again. His hand emerged with a pair of green spectacles with one cracked lens.

"You could come with me," Kip said. "If what you said is true—"

"How close do you think I'd get to your town before someone came running with a musket? Besides, once the sun comes up... I'm ready for it to be done." The color wight took a deep breath, staring at the horizon. "Tell me, Kip, if you've done bad things your whole life, but you die doing something good, do you think that makes up for all the bad?"

"No," Kip said, honestly, before he could stop himself.

"Me neither."

"But it's better than nothing," Kip said. "Orholam is merciful."

"Wonder if you'll say that after they're done with your village."

There were other questions Kip wanted to ask, but everything had happened in such a rush that he couldn't put his thoughts together.

In the rising light Kip saw what had been hidden in the fog and the darkness. Hundreds of tents were laid out in military precision. Soldiers. Lots of soldiers. And even as Kip stood, not two hundred paces from the nearest tent, the plain began winking. Glimmers sparkled as broken luxin gleamed, like stars scattered on the ground, answering their brethren in the sky.

It was what Kip had come for. Usually when a drafter released luxin, it simply dissolved, no matter what color it was. But in battle, there had been so much chaos, so many drafters, some sealed magic had been buried and protected from the sunlight that would break it down. The recent rain had uncovered more.

But Kip's eyes were pulled from the winking luxin by four soldiers and a man with a stark red cloak and red spectacles walking toward them from the camp.

"My name is Gaspar, by the by. Gaspar Elos." The color wight didn't look at Kip.

"What?"

"I'm not just some drafter. My father loved me. I had plans. A girl. A life."

"I don't—"

"You will." The color wight put the green spectacles on; they fit perfectly, tight to his face, lenses sweeping to either side so that wherever he looked, he would be looking through a green filter. "Now get out of here."

As the sun touched the horizon, Gaspar sighed. It was as if Kip had ceased to exist. It was like watching his mother take that first deep breath of haze. Between the sparkling spars of darker green, the whites of Gaspar's eyes swirled like droplets of green blood hitting water, first dispersing, then staining the whole. The emerald green of luxin ballooned through his eyes, thickened until it was solid, and then spread. Through his cheeks, up to his hairline, then down his neck, standing out starkly when it finally filled his lighter fingernails as if they'd been painted in radiant jade.

Gaspar started laughing. It was a low, unreasoning cackle, unrelenting. Mad. Not a pretense this time.

Kip ran.

He reached the funerary hill where the sentry had been, taking care to stay on the far side from the army. He had to get to Master Danavis. Master Danavis always knew what to do.

There was no sentry on the hill now. Kip turned around in time to see Gaspar change, transform. Green luxin spilled out of his hands onto his body, covering every part of him like a shell, like an enormous suit of armor. Kip couldn't see the soldiers or the red drafter approaching Gaspar, but he did see a fireball the size of his head streak toward the color wight, hit his chest, and burst apart, throwing flames everywhere.

Gaspar rammed through it, flaming red luxin sticking to his green armor. He was magnificent, terrible, powerful. He ran toward the soldiers, screaming defiance, and disappeared from Kip's view.

Kip fled, the vermilion sun setting fire to the mists.

introducing

If you enjoyed
VALOR,
look out for

PROMISE OF BLOOD

Book One of the Powder Mage Trilogy

by Brian McClellan

It's a bloody business overthrowing a king...

Field Marshal Tamas's coup against his king sent corrupt aristocrats to the guillotine and brought bread to the starving. But it also provoked war with the Nine Nations, internal attacks by royalist fanatics, and the greedy to scramble for money and power by Tamas's supposed allies: the Church, workers unions, and mercenary forces.

It's up to a few...

Stretched to his limit, Tamas is relying heavily on his few remaining powder mages, including the embittered Taniel, a brilliant marksman who also happens to be his estranged son, and Adamat, a retired police inspector whose loyalty is being tested by blackmail.

But when gods are involved...

Now, as attacks batter them from within and without, the credulous are whispering about omens of death and destruction. Just old peasant legends about the gods waking to walk the earth. No modern educated man believes that sort of thing. But they should...

CHAPTER 1

Adamat wore his coat tight, top buttons fastened against a wet night air that seemed to want to drown him. He tugged at his sleeves, trying to coax more length, and picked at the front of the jacket where it was too close by far around the waist. It'd been half a decade since he'd even seen this jacket, but when summons came from the king at this hour, there was no time to get his good one from the tailor. Yet this summer coat provided no defense against the chill snaking through the carriage window.

The morning was not far off but dawn would have a hard time scattering the fog. Adamat could feel it. It was humid even for early spring in Adopest, and chillier than Novi's frozen toes. The soothsayers in Noman's Alley said it was a bad omen. Yet who listened to soothsayers these days? Adamat reasoned it would give him a cold and wondered why he had been summoned out on a pit-made night like this.

The carriage approached the front gate of Skyline and moved on without a stop. Adamat clutched at his pantlegs and peered out the window. The guards were not at their posts. Odder still, as they continued along the wide path amid the fountains, there were no lights. Skyline had so many lanterns, it could be seen all the way from the city even on the cloudiest night. Tonight the gardens were dark.

Adamat was fine with this. Manhouch used enough of their taxes for his personal amusement. Adamat stared out into the gardens at the black maws where the hedge mazes began and imagined shapes flitting back and forth in the lawn. What was...ah, just a sculpture. Adamat sat back, took a deep breath. He could hear his heart beating, thumping, frightened, his stomach tightening. Perhaps they *should* light the garden lanterns...

A little part of him, the part that had once been a police inspector, prowling nights such as these for the thieves and pickpockets in dark alleys, laughed out from inside. *Still your heart, old man*, he said to himself. *You were once the eyes staring back from the darkness.*

extras

The carriage jerked to a stop. Adamat waited for the coachman to open the door. He might have waited all night. The driver rapped on the roof. "You're here," a gruff voice said.

Rude.

Adamat stepped from the coach, just having time to snatch his hat and cane before the driver flicked the reins and was off, clattering into the night. Adamat uttered a quiet curse after the man and turned around, looking up at Skyline.

The nobility called Skyline Palace "the Jewel of Adro." It rested on a high hill east of Adopest so that the sun rose above it every morning. One particularly bold newspaper had compared it to a starving pauper wearing a diamond ring. It was an apt comparison in these lean times. A king's pride doesn't fill the people's bellies.

He was at the main entrance. By day, it was a grand avenue of marbled walks and fountains, all leading to a pair of giant, silver-plated doors, themselves dwarfed by the sheer façade of the biggest single building in Adro. Adamat listened for the soft footfalls of patrolling Hielmen. It was said the king's personal guard were everywhere in these gardens, watching every secluded corner, muskets always loaded, bayonets fixed, their gray-and-white sashes somber among the green-and-gold splendor. But there were no footfalls, nor were the fountains running. He'd heard once that the fountains only stopped for the death of the king. Surely he'd not have been summoned here if Manhouch were dead. He smoothed the front of his jacket. Here, next to the building, a few of the lanterns were lit.

A figure emerged from the darkness. Adamat tightened his grip on his cane, ready to draw the hidden sword inside at a moment's notice.

It was a man in uniform, but little could be discerned in such ill light. He held a rifle or a musket, trained loosely on Adamat, and wore a flat-topped forage cap with a stiff visor. Only one thing could be certain…he was not a Hielman. Their tall, plumed hats were easy to recognize, and they never went without them.

"You're alone?" a voice asked.

"Yes," Adamat said. He held up both hands and turned around.

"All right. Come on."

The soldier edged forward and yanked on one of the mighty silver doors. It rolled outward slowly, ponderously, despite the man putting his weight into it. Adamat moved closer and examined the soldier's jacket. It was dark blue with silver braiding. Adran military. In theory, the military reported to the king. In practice, one man held their leash: Field Marshal Tamas.

"Step back, friend," the soldier said. There was a note of impatience in his voice, some unseen stress—but that could have been the weight of the door. Adamat did as he was told, only coming forward again to slip through the entrance when the soldier gestured.

"Go ahead," the soldier directed. "Take a right at the diadem and head through the Diamond Hall. Keep walking until you find yourself in the Answering Room." The door inched shut behind him and closed with a muffled thump.

Adamat was alone in the palace vestibule. Adran military, he mused. Why would a soldier be here, on the grounds, without any sign of the Hielmen? The most frightening answer sprang to mind first. A power struggle. Had the military been called in to deal with a rebellion? There were a number of powerful factions within Adro: the Wings of Adom mercenaries, the royal cabal, the Mountainwatch, and the great noble families. Any one of them could have been giving Manhouch trouble. None of it made sense, though. If there had been a power struggle, the palace grounds would be a battlefield, or destroyed outright by the royal cabal.

Adamat passed the diadem—a giant facsimile of the Adran crown—and noted it was in as bad taste as rumor had it. He entered the Diamond Hall, where the walls and floor were of scarlet, accented in gold leaf, and thousands of tiny gems, which gave the room its name, glittered from the ceiling in the light of a single lit candelabra. The tiny flames of the candelabra flickered as if in the wind, and the room was cold.

Adamat's sense of unease deepened as he neared the far end of the gallery. Not a sign of life, and the only sound came from his own echoing footfalls on the marble floor. A window had been shattered, explaining the chill. The result of one of the king's famous temper tantrums? Or something else? He could hear his heart beating in his ears. There. Behind a curtain, a pair of boots? Adamat passed his hand before his eyes. A trick of the light. He stepped over to reassure himself and pulled back the curtain.

A body lay in the shadows. Adamat bent over it, touched the skin. It was warm, but the man was most certainly dead. He wore gray pants with a white stripe down the side and a matching jacket. A tall hat with a white plume lay on the floor some ways away. A Hielman. The shadows played on a young, clean-shaven face, peaceful except for a single hole in the side of his skull and the dark, wet stain on the floor.

He'd been right. A struggle of some kind. Had the Hielmen rebelled, and the military been brought in to deal with them? Again, it didn't make any sense. The Hielmen were fanatically loyal to the king, and any matters within Skyline Palace would have been dealt with by the royal cabal.

Adamat cursed silently. Every question compounded itself. He suspected he'd find some answers soon enough.

Adamat left the body behind the curtain. He lifted his cane and twisted, bared a few inches of steel, and approached a tall doorway flanked by two hooded, scepter-wielding sculptures. He paused between the ancient statues and took a deep breath, letting his eyes wander over a set of arcane script scrawled into the portal. He entered.

The Answering Room made the Hall of Diamonds look small. A pair of staircases, one to either side of him and each as wide across as three coaches, led to a high gallery that ran the length of the room on both sides. Few outside the king and his cabal of Privileged sorcerers ever entered this room.

In the center of the room was a single chair, on a dais a handbreadth off the floor, facing a collection of knee pillows, where the cabal acknowledged their liege. The room was well lit, though from no discernible source of light.

A man sat on the stairs to Adamat's right. He was older than Adamat, just into his sixtieth year with silver hair and a neatly trimmed mustache that still retained a hint of black. He had a strong but not overly large jaw and his cheekbones were well defined. His skin was darkened by the sun, and there were deep lines at the corners of his mouth and eyes. He wore a dark-blue soldier's uniform with a silver representation of a powder keg pinned above the heart and nine gold service stripes sewn on the right breast, one for every five years in the Adran military. His uniform lacked an officer's epaulettes, but the weary experience in the man's brown eyes left no question that he'd led armies on the battlefield. There was a single pistol, hammer cocked, on the stair next to him. He leaned on a sheathed small sword and watched as a stream of blood slowly trickled down each step, a dark line on the yellow-and-white marble.

"Field Marshal Tamas," Adamat said. He sheathed his cane sword and twisted until it clicked shut.

The man looked up. "I don't believe we've ever met."

"We have," Adamat said. "Fourteen years ago. A charity ball thrown by Lord Aumen."

"I have a terrible time with faces," the field marshal said. "I apologize."

Adamat couldn't take his eyes off the rivulet of blood. "Sir. I was summoned here. I wasn't told by whom, or for what reason."

"Yes," Tamas said. "I summoned you. On the recommendation of one of my Marked. Cenka. He said you served together on the police force in the twelfth district."

Adamat pictured Cenka in his mind. He was a short man with an unruly beard and a penchant for wines and fine food. He'd seen him last seven years ago. "I didn't know he was a powder mage."

"We try to find anyone with an affinity for it as soon as possible," Tamas said, "but Cenka was a late bloomer. In any case"—he waved a hand—"we've come upon a problem."

Adamat blinked. "You... want my help?"

The field marshal raised an eyebrow. "Is that such an unusual request? You were once a fine police investigator, a good servant of Adro, and Cenka tells me that you have a perfect memory."

"Still, sir."

"Eh?"

"I'm still an investigator. Not with the police, sir, but I still take jobs."

"Excellent. Then it's not so odd for me to seek your services?"

"Well, no," Adamat said, "but sir, this is Skyline Palace. There's a dead Hielman in the Diamond Hall and…" He pointed at the stream of blood on the stairs. "Where's the king?"

Tamas tilted his head to the side. "He's locked himself in the chapel."

"You've staged a coup," Adamat said. He caught a glimpse of movement with the corner of his eye, saw a soldier appear at the top of the stairs. The man was a Deliv, a dark-skinned northerner. He wore the same uniform as Tamas, with eight golden stripes on the right breast. The left breast of his uniform displayed a silver powder keg, the sign of a Marked. Another powder mage.

"We have a lot of bodies to move," the Deliv said.

Tamas gave his subordinate a glance. "I know, Sabon."

"Who's this?" Sabon asked.

"The inspector that Cenka requested."

"I don't like him being here," Sabon said. "It could compromise everything."

"Cenka trusted him."

"You've staged a coup," Adamat said again with certainty.

"I'll help with the bodies in a moment," Tamas said. "I'm old, I need some rest now and then." The Deliv gave a sharp nod and disappeared.

"Sir!" Adamat said. "What have you done?" He tightened his grip on his cane sword.

Tamas pursed his lips. "Some say the Adran royal cabal had the most powerful Privileged sorcerers in all the Nine Nations, second only to Kez," he said quietly. "Yet I've just slaughtered every one of them. Do you think I'd have trouble with an old inspector and his cane sword?"